Joseph Livesey

The Life and Teachings of Joseph Livesey

Joseph Livesey

The Life and Teachings of Joseph Livesey

ISBN/EAN: 9783337427733

Printed in Europe, USA, Canada, Australia, Japan

Cover: Foto ©Raphael Reischuk / pixelio.de

More available books at **www.hansebooks.com**

THE
LIFE AND TEACHINGS
OF
JOSEPH LIVESEY
COMPRISING HIS
AUTOBIOGRAPHY

WITH

AN INTRODUCTORY REVIEW
OF HIS LABOURS AS REFORMER AND TEACHER
BY JOHN PEARCE

AND

AN APPENDIX
CONTAINING
PRESS AND PULPIT NOTICES OF MR. LIVESEY'S
WRITINGS AND LIFE, ETC.

Mr. Livesey was a man of great merit; he had a great sense of justice, and his life was one dignified by constant labours in the wide field of mercy and benevolence.—*John Bright.*

LONDON:
NATIONAL TEMPERANCE LEAGUE'S DEPÔT, 337, STRAND; AND
JOHN HEYWOOD, 11, PATERNOSTER BUILDINGS.
MANCHESTER: JOHN HEYWOOD, DEANSGATE.
PRESTON: LIVESEY'S TEMPERANCE TRACT DEPÔT,
51, TITHEBARN STREET.

PREFACE.

THE circumstances under which Mr. Livesey's "Autobiography" has been previously published, are narrated by his son in the Explanatory Note which occupies page 2 of the second part of this book. I have little to add to that explanation, beyond stating, that in the work now issued the "Autobiography" has been reprinted without alteration from the stereotype plates. By adopting this course, the volume can be published at a lower price than would have been otherwise possible; and Mr. Livesey's own regard for cheap literature has thus been honoured.

Of the "Autobiography" itself it is needless to remark that its author's desire was to encourage the most humble and lowly in efforts of self-improvement; and to stimulate readers, of whatever rank in life, to labour for the material, moral, and spiritual advancement of their less favoured brethren. The *Preston Herald* has remarked of the "Autobiography," "that it is a little disappointing, chiefly because the writer has not done justice to himself,"—a defect so rare in this class of literature that its discovery is quite refreshing. We may be thankful, however, to have got so much from a man of Mr. Livesey's type. But perhaps the work would have been ampler and more finished had it been written at a time when its author could command more leisure. The "Autobiography" was undertaken in 1868, during the second year of the publication of his *Staunch Teetotaler*, a monthly magazine, the contents of which were almost entirely supplied by his own pen. In addition to Mr. Livesey's labours in editing, publishing, and circulating that admirable little periodical, he was, at the same period, giving considerable time and attention to the affairs of the Preston Bank. At the end of the year, too, he had to relinquish the magazine owing to the total failure of Mrs. Livesey's health, so that the "Autobiography" may be said to have been produced under distressing and disadvantageous circumstances.

My own connexion with the present work may be briefly stated. About two years before Mr. Livesey's death, feeling that the Temperance movement would be greatly promoted by a closer adherence to his plans, I contemplated issuing a little work directing attention to this point. The late Mr. T. B. Smithies warmly approved th_ idea, and promised his co-operation in its publication. A few weeks before his death, Mr. Smithies, whose health appeared greatly to improve, wrote me that if the amendment continued he hoped to be soon well enough to confer with me personally upon "how best to extend a knowledge of Good Joseph Livesey" and his methods.   When Mr. Livesey passed away, the idea being still in my mind, I announced a Biography of him.   Subsequently, however, his son William suggested that I should contribute an Introductory Review of Joseph Livesey as Reformer and Teacher to a new edition of the "Autobiography," and I acceded to the proposal.   We also agreed that the publication of a selection from the press notices and pulpit references to Mr. Livesey would add to the value of the volume.

The publication in part of so many sketches of Mr. Livesey somewhat increased the difficulties of my task, and I had to decide whether I should add one more to the numerous reviews of his career based on the "Autobiography," or whether I should endeavour to interpret the man from his writings.   I adopted the latter course as being the most likely to add to the value of the book, and have endeavoured throughout, as much as possible, to stand aside myself, and allow Mr. Livesey to speak for himself.   If a justification is required for the numerous and extensive quotations I have made from Mr. Livesey's writings, it is supplied by Jean Paul Richter.   "Printing ink now," he remarks, "is like sympathetic ink, it becomes as quickly invisible as visible; wherefore it is good to repeat old thoughts in the newest books, because the old works in which they stand are not read."   And there is a very exceptional and weighty reason for doing so in this instance, since the works of Mr. Livesey, from which I have principally drawn, are exceedingly scarce; they are not even to be found in the library of the British Museum.   A few words of explanation have here and there been introduced into the text of the citations, but such interpolations will always be found inclosed within brackets, thus: [ ].

Mr. Livesey's writings prior to 1832 have been largely quoted from, which in a measure may have done him an injustice.   But this course has been followed with the view of informing the world that the founder of the only efficient system of Temperance reform had previously been a close student of such topics as practical religion, and moral, social, and political reform; while for years, as a practical philanthropist, he had been devotedly labouring to extend human happiness.   The plan also shows how greatly he was in advance of his time.

Of course, many of the practices which Mr. Livesey assailed fifty-three years ago have in the interval either been greatly modified or altogether swept away; and the same may be said of several of the evils he attacked during his lengthened career; for the last half century has been one of unexampled progress.   Old ideas have given place to newer ones; religious liberty has extended; political rights have been conceded; moral and social reforms have been vigorously prosecuted, the result being that the material and spiritual condition of the people has been measurably improved.   And Mr. Livesey, as reformer and teacher, did all that one man could do to bring about these salutary changes.

It is not expected that any single reader will endorse *all* Mr. Livesey's sentiments; he was too thorough a reformer for that to be at all likely.   But "as face answereth to face in a glass," so every sincere soul will recognise in him an honest teacher and a brave man.

Reformers of every type may learn something from Mr. Livesey; Temperance reformers may learn much. Of the latter he claims a hearing ; may he be listened to with becoming respect and reverence, and may his words become an inspiration, especially to the young. Upon the legislative phase of the movement he differed from a considerable section of the Temperance party ; but he chiefly failed in agreement with them respecting the means of reaching the end which all desire. They expect to attain that end by a 'short cut' ; he objected to their methods cn the principle that what promises to be a 'short cut' often turns out to be the longest way round.

There could be no fitter memorial of Joseph Livesey than the good which would result from an extensive emulation of his useful career. The reader is strongly urged to give his principles, plans, and methods the consideration they deserve ; and, by imitating and obeying the Great Exemplar so faithfully followed by Mr. Livesey, to labour for the promotion of the cause of universal good among men, and (as far as human effort can promote such an end) the glory of God.

Of the portraits of Mr. Livesey inserted in this volume, it may be well to explain that the steel engraving facing title page is from a photograph taken in 1862; the photograph which faces the "Autobiography" was taken when Mr. Livesey was in his 88th year; while the lithographed one is from a photograph taken late in life.

I have to thank Mr. William Livesey for his hearty co-operation in this work, especially for his assistance in arranging the Appendix; but it is only just to that gentleman to say that he is in no way, even by suggestion, responsible for the line I have taken in the Introductory Chapters.

According to announcement the present volume should have appeared several months ago; but the delay has arisen from circumstances beyond control, the chief cause being the partial breakdown of the writer's health during the progress of the work.

LONDON, *October* 27, 1885.

THE DOCTOR'S ADVICE.

The following words are said to have found a place for many years in a doctor's surgery :—

> Brandy, beer, and betting,
> Domestic care and fretting,
> Will kill the strongest man alive ;
> But water, air, and diet,
> Domestic peace and quiet,
> Will make the weakest man to thrive.

"Childe Harold's Pilgrimage" are pertinent here :

> The thorns which I have reap'd are of the tree
> I planted—they have torn me and I bleed ;
> I should have known what fruit would
> Spring from such a seed.

Among the objects in which "Proud" Preston takes justifiable pride is a very uninteresting looking cottage, one of a row of cottages equally uninspiring, in the suburb of Walton-le-Dale. It is the birthplace of Joseph Livesey, the father of teetotalism. Next Saturday a memorial tablet, which has been placed upon the wall, is to be unveiled by Mrs. Lewis, of Blackburn, whose temperance mission worthily carries on Livesey's great work. The cottage has been acquired by Mr. W. E. Moss, a lifelong worker in the cause, who has arranged that it will ultimately become the property of the British Temperance League.

PART FIRST

JOSEPH LIVESEY
AS REFORMER AND TEACHER.

Mr. John Ruskin, himself a teacher and reformer of the highest type, declares:

"The more I think of it I find this conclusion more impressed upon me—that the greatest thing a human soul ever does in this world is to *see* something, and tell what it *saw* in a plain way. Hundreds of people can talk for one who can think; but thousands can think for one who can see. To see clearly is poetry, prophecy, and religion—all in one."

If Mr. Ruskin is correct in his estimate, Mr. Livesey has most assuredly rendered to his fellows the greatest and best services possible to man; for he saw and that clearly, and what he saw he described in a way so plain that it was impossible to misunderstand him. He did exactly what Mr. Ruskin calls "the greatest thing a human soul ever does in this world," and in many ways the world at large, not merely his fellow-townsmen and personal friends, is all the better for it. The right that he saw he adopted, imitated, and laboured to extend; the wrong, he shunned, avoided, and endeavoured to extinguish.

Mr. Livesey has been many times compared to Franklin, and not without good reason. They had many characteristics in common; but some writers have contended that Mr. Livesey lacked the philosophical element which distinguished Franklin in such a marked degree. I would suggest, however, that both Livesey and Franklin were philosophers, but that the philosophical faculty assumed a different form of manifestation in each. It is evident that Mr. Livesey had a deep insight into character; an extensive knowledge of mankind; a wide acquaintance with the sources and springs of human action; and a comprehensive idea of man as a material and spiritual being, and of his relationship with the Supreme. Livesey's mind was spiritual, Franklin's materialistic. Livesey's speculations took

what a scarecrow, the Church would be if it were not for Mammon—for the root of
all evil. Another prop this to the old crazy building, and still its walls are out of
the perpendicular."

CHURCH REFORM.

In Mr. Livesey's view, the Church was out of perpendicular quite as much as
its walls, and hence his idea of Church reform was of much wider significance than
its mere disestablishment.   His attitude as a political dissenter is referred to in the
chapter on politics, where an account will also be found of his resistance of Easter
Dues, etc.*   On this more comprehensive Church Reform he says :

" Complaints are perpetually being made against the Established Church : they
are reiterated in every company you meet with, and almost in every paper you read.
But what is the extent to which any of these parties would apply a remedy ?   Do
they want that form of Christianity which would condemn the excesses of the rich,
reprove and correct the vices of the poor, and penetrate, by its invincible power,
every movement in society, and every lurking-place of sin ?   No ; they want a few
verbal alterations in the liturgy—the purification of a court called Ecclesiastical,—
that every clergyman should live in his parish, and that some of them should have
more, and others not so much, of the money paid for religion.   Supposing these
changes were effected, what would it do towards accomplishing that which is the
real end of every religious institution—the effectual diffusion of knowledge and piety
among all classes, and the plain and affectionate teaching of every man, woman, and
child, in the kingdom ?   For abstruse sermons we want plain, practical teaching ;
for the prayer of words we want the simple and fervent aspirations of the heart ;
instead of consecrated ground, and church hours, we want that night and day and
' every house ' instruction which at first raised the dead to life by thousands ;
instead of those who only save souls for hire, we want those who are looking
for an eternal crown ; instead of a Church created and regulated by Act of Parliament, propped up by an arm of flesh, and whose bond of union is its wealth and its
honours, we look for a Church professing few ostensible features, scarcely known to
the worldling, but regulated and governed by the will of Christ ; the greatness of
which is best known by the exemplary lives of its members, and their activity in
doing good to others. The fact is, instead of religion in the church and chapel only,
we ought to meet with it in every cottage, in men's transactions with each other, and
in all the social relationships of life ; and any *Church Reform*, which does not contemplate these as its objects, is unworthy of the name."†

RELIGIOUS TEACHER AND INVESTIGATOR.

On page 41 of the "Autobiography," reference is made to a " Weekly meeting for
religious investigation," started by Mr. Livesey in connexion with the Free Sunday
and Evening schools, conducted by him at his own personal cost, and began soon
after his marriage. The rules of the meeting are there partly reprinted. The
placard announcing the establishment of these meetings is dated May 12th, 1825,
and its preamble, which is omitted in the " Autobiography," is suggestive, and
evidently reflects Mr. Livesey's mind.   It recites that—

" Though the free, impartial, and dispassionate examination of every religious
principle is constantly inculcated, yet, through the prevailing sectarian spirit, the
influence of the world, and the authority of men and names, it still remains little
more than a theory.   To promote its *practical* adoption, and to assist in the
discovery of Truth —to encourage the free exercise of private judgment, and to
lead the mind to regard *evidence alone* as the basis of conviction—it is proposed
to establish in Preston a Weekly Meeting, to be called The Meeting for Religious
Investigation."

* See Chap. iv. p. liv.   † *Moral Reformer*, vol. i. (1831), pp. 218, 219.

To those favoured scholars and attendants Mr. Livesey taught the pure doctrines of primitive Christianity,* and the influence of his teachiugs were subsequently manifested in the self-sacrificing, unselfish, and devoted labours of the early Preston Temperance advocates, several of whom had been attendants at his school. Mr. Edward Grubb, in his speech at the funeral of his early teacher and friend, made reference to these religious teachings, and spoke of Mr. Livesey's remarkable power in " unfolding the mysteries and wonders of the Word of God." This power or faculty will be best understood if we allow Mr. Livesey, through the the following extracts from his religious writings, to speak for himself.

FALSE VIEWS AND OUTSIDE RELIGION.

The early pamphlets of Mr. Livesey, are deeply embued with a reverential spirit; and his first periodical—*The Moral Reformer* (1831-3)—is pervaded by the same influence. Although naturally of a kindly and charitable disposition, like Ebenezer Elliot he could

> ——————hate arrogance and selfishness,
> Come where they may, and most beneath the roof
> Sacred to public worship.

Looking around on society, what did Mr. Livesey see? Not virtue, but wealth in the ascendant. Pride, arrogance, injustice, and oppression making their way to the prejudice of vast masses of the people, and the Church dumb. Commenting upon some of the changes which the extension of manufactures and commerce had effected upon the surroundings of the working people, Mr. Livesey remarks:

"Besides, the extremes to which these changes have led contribute much to the same end. Instead of a happy medium, as the general lot, we have constantly before our eyes *overgrown riches and extreme poverty.* . . . Some of the rich, voluptuous, oppressive, and austere, pride themselves upon their wealth and honours, despise the poor, and treat them with contempt. The poor envy the rich, revenge their injuries, and rejoice at the downfall of their oppressors."†

False views and objects in life prevailed even in religious circles, and he says:

"The possession of wealth is looked upon as the great desideratum of life. Virtue, usefulness, and intelligence, have been treated as minor acquirements; wealth has been the road to the possession of power, and the object of the people's

---

* Eventually, and before it was used for Temperance Meetings, Mr. Livesey took the disused Cockpit, which belonged to Earl Derby, for religious services. In his *Moral Reformer* for April, 1832, appears the following paragraph, of great interest in this counexion:—

LECTURES.—On Wednesday, Thursday, and Friday, commencing March 7th, I delivered three Lectures in the Cockpit, to crowded audiences, on the Moral Condition of the People; on the Fast Day [March 21st, the day before the Preston Temperance Society was formed] two Discourses on Intemperance and Covetousness; and on Sunday evening last I commenced a short course on Theological Subjects, which will be continued weekly. My great object in doing this is not to raise a controversy, but to give a candid statement of my opinions, to soften down the asperity of doctrinal fastidiousness, and to promote above every other object the religion of the *heart and life*. I understand it has frequently been objected that I belong to *no party*; this has been no source of satisfaction to myself: *hirelingism* existing in almost every party, has been the chief cause of this, and any other cause, arising from peculiarity of sentiment, I shall endeavour to make clear in the course of these Lectures. My rule of judging of character is the one laid down by Christ Himself. "By their FRUITS" (not by their views, their professions, or their feelings) "ye shall know them." A corrupt tree cannot bring forth good fruit, neither can a good tree bring forth evil fruit. Grapes spring not from thorns, nor figs from thistles; every tree, therefore, is known by its fruits. Though I join not in the forms of worship, I embrace in the arms of charity all who, believing that Jesus is the Christ, endeavour, so far as they know, to keep His commandments.

† *Moral Reformer*, vol. i. (1831), p. 9.

blind idolatry. Though immoral in practice, puerile in intellect, and a mere blank as to usefulness in society, a man with a large property is sure to be honoured by the world, and flattered with the most fulsome praise. How many crimes are condemned in the poor which are excused in the rich ! It is the want [absence] of equal justice, equal faithfulness to the rich and poor; it is the want of awarding praise to merit only, and not where its greatest recommendation is the elevation of its possessor; it is, in fact, that false and erroneous estimate of riches which has taken hold of the public mind, that leads so many people to be anxious to enjoy wealth. But do riches make their possessors happy? Scripture, experience, and facts, all answer—No."*

A religion of externals had no attractions for him, and that was the kind generally paraded, and of which he writes :

" I observe that at present religion is nearly all *outside* work, a system of *automatonism* which unites, both in teacher and people, a *form* of godliness with a love of the world. Power may invent and paronize forms and ceremonies, and fill the country with the externals of devotion ; wealth may give them an imposing and deceitful appearance, whilst the essence of religion, piety and devotedness to God, charity and benevolence to man, and strict attention to all the duties of life, are rarely to be found. And while religion is made the *medium of wealth* to the clergy, these effects are sure to follow. Corruption acts reciprocally ; the Church and the world keep each other in countenance ; the moral hemisphere is terribly overclouded, and until Heaven be pleased to develop the genius of a purer age, men will continue to love darkness rather than light, because their deeds are evil."†

In his view this declension was caused by corrupt influences. He says :

" If the Christianity of the New Testament claims our confidence on account of the spirituality of the means by which it was established, the adoption of opposite means now is calculated to persuade us that the cause, though the same in name, is materially different. It is in the nature of all institutions, connected with human agency, to decay ; and the lapse of eighteen centuries has produced such changes here as few persons are sufficiently unprejudiced to concede. Poverty, persecution, and reproach, have been succeeded by prosperity, wealth, and honours ; labour and self-denial have been changed for ease and luxurious indulgence ; personal piety, for ritual services, and uniform obedience, for the religion of times and places ; candour and sincerity, for imposture, fraud, and hypocrisy ; universal love, for avarice and selfishness ; and sensual gratification and present enjoyment, for that lively hope of a better world which supported the first Christians."‡

THE CHRISTIANITY OF CHRIST.

That the Christianity of Christ is very different from the Christianity of the Churches becomes obvious when the nature and character of the former is contrasted with that of the latter. Christ's own precepts and teachings have caused no controversies or bitterness amongst Christians ; have originated no conflicting sects. They are so plain, that the wayfaring man, though a fool, cannot err regarding them. Joseph Livesey taught and exemplified, as far as he could, the precepts and morals of his Master. His ideas of primitive Christianity are expressed as follows :

" Power, wealth, and fashion have moulded religion after their own likeness, and are now propagating a spurious article under a genuine name. As real Christianity was always repulsive to these agencies, nothing but a deep corruption in its vital parts could have enlisted them into its service. 'My kingdom,' said the Saviour, 'is not of this world'; and hence no worldly means were ever admitted as its auxiliaries, either to defend or to extend it. The great object being to produce con-

---

* *Moral Reformer*, vol. i. (1831), pp. 232, 233.   † *Ibid.*, vol. i. (1831) pp. 175, 176.
‡ *Ibid.*, vol. i. (1831), p. 164.

viction in the *mind*, and *allegiance* in the *heart*, the means of worldly influence were useless; the interests of this kingdom require not, they admit not, the assistants which belong to an earthly hierarchy. . . . Poverty, and a humble station in life, was the voluntary choice of Jesus Himself, and He selected for His assistants men of the same condition. He disdained the appearance of earthly authority, and at the risk of His life taught a doctrine which was universally hated by men in power. . . . If His religion had consisted of a priestly order, with costly robes, a pompous ritual service, performed in splendid temples made with hands—such as is now palmed upon us for Christianity—money would certainly have been (as it is now) the one thing needful. If it had consisted in uniting nations together, in conformity to articles of faith and worship, and claiming a domineering ascendency in society, earthly power would have been indispensable. But, aiming only to affect the mind by heavenly principles, and to change the conduct by Divine influences, and seeking no ostensible greatness beyond the personal conviction and reformation of mankind, not Cæsar himself could facilitate its progress."[*]

And again on the same subject:

"'I am not of this world,' says Christ. In the establishment of the Kingdom of Heaven, He had no recourse to means which human policy now employs. He borrowed nothing from the Jewish ritual, or from the heathen temples, to work upon the senses of the people. He sought not the aid of wealth or worldly respect-ability; poor in His parentage, lowly in His habits, to accomplish the object of His mission, He chose the illiterate fishermen of Galilee. He was obnoxious to the rulers of the state, and never courted their favour to serve His cause. They could have rendered Him no assistance; the wealth of the Indies could not have advanced His cause a single step. His kingdom was not of *this world*, for there was nothing worldly in all He attempted to accomplish. His system of religion wanted neither wealth to set it up nor power to defend it. But coming into a world which was corrupt in its principles and wicked in its practices, He began His ministry by calling upon men to 'repent'; and though He agitated all the cities of Judea, His sole object seemed to be to reach the *minds* of men, to touch their *hearts*, to change their dispositions, to lead them to worship God in *spirit* and in *truth*, to love one another, and to do good unto all mankind: and if I understand the Scriptures aright, this was the grand object of His life, ministry, death, resurrection, and ascension into heaven. As it respects the visible establishment of His kingdom, to acquire that we may easily perceive the inutility of riches or power: these may build temples, clothe priests with sacerdotal attire, raise them in the ranks of society, support an expensive ceremonial service, and purchase the 'pomps and vanities' of the world, but can never exalt that kingdom which has its seat in the hearts of men. Few besides the *sincere* became His followers (there was no motive to induce others), and those of a contrary character soon discovered their error, and walked no more with Him. *Real Christianity* offers no temptation to the hypocrite; it is in its corruptions that such have found ample field for their impositions. Poor by choice, He became a companion of the poor; He sought not the favour of the great, but testified of them that their deeds were evil. Unlike those who since have called themselves His ministers, He chose reproach rather than worldly honour, and the extremes of poverty rather than the wealth of an earthly kingdom. How opposed through the whole tenour of His life, to those corruptions which form the ostensible character of modern Christianity!"[†]

PRACTICAL RELIGION.

The following description of Practical Religion, taken in connexion with his unceasing labours for his fellows, evidences the sterling piety of its writer. Theodore Parker has reminded us that "to love the unlovely, to sympathize with the contrary minded, to give to the uncharitable, to be just to men who make iniquity a profession, to repay their sleepless hate with never-ceasing love,—that is

---

[*] *Moral Reformer*, vol. i. (1831), p. 163.   [†] *Ibid.*, vol. ii. (1832), p. 49.

the triumph of affection, the heroic degree of love." And to that degree had Mr. Livesey attained, not merely in word but by deed.

"The best part of religion," he says, "as far as I understand it, is to do good to all men, to instruct the ignorant, to comfort the disconsolate, to defend the oppressed, and to relieve the poor. There is no human being so miserable as to be beyond our notice and regard. It is not our province to judge and condemn, but to save. Our duty is to raise men from a state of misery to that of happiness and comfort; and the further any individual is from this, the more anxious we should be to assist him. . . . We should despise none, however poor, however debased; we should pity all, and share the burden of those who are heavy laden. If men do wrong, God will judge them, for He alone knows the extent of their guilt and the measure of their iniquity; and we should try to imitate His mercy, who is not willing that any should perish, but that all should come to repentance. . . . Why should we respect the man clothed in costly array more than the poor clothed in rags? [Ah, why indeed! the latter is often the *better* man of the two.] The same hand made them both. Why should we shun the wicked man, or threaten to chastise him? He is an object of pity; his wickedness is perhaps owing to the usages of society to which we ourselves have given countenance, or to the want of a faithful friend to admonish him. The more desperate his case, the more anxious we should be for his welfare. Even if he be our personal enemy, we should not injure him, but do him good, and thus lead him to repentance. However unpopular this may be, I take it to be true practical religion. It is what we should esteem and admire, and practice, and the more because it is uncommon." *

CHRISTIAN DUTY AND THE GOLDEN RULE.

Regarding Christian Duty, he observes:

"What do I do more than others? Let every reader ask himself, as *in the presence of God*, this question in reference to all matters of duty. Let this question be put *closely*, *frequently*, and *universally*, both in reference to our *secret* and our *public* deportment. 'What do I more than others' in forgiving injuries, loving my enemies, doing good to those that hate me; in avoiding all excesses in eating, drinking, or putting on of apparel; in speaking the truth and acting uprightly; in defaming no man's character, and defending the innocent and oppressed; in instructing the ignorant; visiting the fatherless and the widow; and bringing the stranger to my home; in not being soon angry, but being patient, gentle and meek; in not practising extortion, avoiding covetousness, and not laying up for myself treasures upon earth; in instructing my children and teaching them to love one another? I merely mention these applications as specimens, trusting that every sincere follower of Jesus will carry forward the inquiry as to every other duty." †

Circumspectness is again and again enforced by Mr. Livesey. In trade, in commerce, in manufactures, in politics, and, indeed, in all relationships with our fellow-men he would apply the principles of the "golden rule." The sins of the tongue he repeatedly warns against, and he especially reprobates the unchristian practice indulged in by so many professing Christians, of speaking evil of others. "The practice of this vice," he says, in opening an article on the subject, "even amongst those who profess to be strictly religious, has become so prevalent that it calls for special notice." Kindly and affectionately does he caution against this habit. He suggests:

"In reference to private character, it will generally be found advisable, if we can say nothing *good*, to say nothing that is *bad*. Whisperings and backbitings are the bane of society; and how keenly must a person feel when he hears that he has been charged and condemned without a hearing; that his faults and his sentence

* *The Struggle*, No. 34 (1842), p. 3.   † *Livesey's Moral Reformer*, 1838-9, p. 209.

are circulated in society, with a certainty of great exaggeration; and, perhaps, by persons from whom he expected better things."[*]

CHRISTIAN CHARITY,

in its practical bearings, he describes as follows :—

"Christian Charity is not a cool, formal feeling, for we are to love one another with '*pure hearts fervently*,' not transient; we must 'let brotherly love *continue*,' not disguised; it is to be 'unfeigned,' 'without dissimulation,' 'not in *word* and in *tongue*, but in *deed* and *truth*.' It is a 'love that worketh *no ill* to our neighbours,' and is therefore inconsistent with the practices of 'speaking evil one of another,' injuring one another in reputation or circumstances; rendering evil for evil, or railing for railing; or evading the wants and necessities of others, when we have it in our power to relieve them. I mention these evils in particular, because although the form and faith of religion may have been reformed, its unobtrusive, unfashionable, self-denying, charitable characteristics are too little regarded. How endearing the exhortations: 'Little children, love one another;' 'A new commandment I give unto you, that ye love one another. by this shall all men know that you are My disciples, if ye have love one for another.' "[†]

THE RICH AND POOR.

All classes in turn were addressed by Mr. Livesey, and their duties to their fellow-creatures in other spheres of life faithfully pointed out to them. He was no flatterer, but an outspoken, honest teacher, whose only object was the promotion of honesty and integrity, and the extension of human happiness. In addressing the rich, he says :

"Without sober reflection you know nothing of yourselves; you pass through the world as if in a trance, and at the end of a short-lived existence, wonder what you have been doing. Let not, I beseech you, the sound of empty names, the dazzle of a splendid equipage, or the flattery of false friends, deceive you. Try, for a moment, to forget everything *artificial*. Children of the dust, creatures of a day, your best estate is altogether vanity. . . .

"In society there are many members, but only one body, and, in a certain sense, you are more dependent upon the labouring poor than they are upon you; even the king himself, we are told, is served from the field. Never conceive, therefore, that *your* interest is separate from *theirs*; that your property can be safe, eventually, if theirs is not respected; or, that in any crisis, a neglect of the common interests of society, will bring with it a respect for yours. Where there is no higher feeling, the best policy of the rich is always to behave well to the poor, and to take their part against every oppressor."[‡]

While he never failed to remind the poor of their duties, and to urge them to self-help and self-improvement, he made allowances for the difficulties which beset them, and over which they had no control. Hence their absence from places of worship was not regarded by him as conclusive evidence of their irreligion. Mr. Livesey did not regard the reward awaiting the faithful poor in the next life as a reason for not doing justice to them in this. He rather took an opposite view of the matter, and strove heartily to ameliorate the physical and material condition of his less fortunate fellow-creatures. Of the resignation and patience of the poor in their affliction, he says :

"There are among the poorest of the people those who, sometimes from choice, —but oftener from poverty, and their inability to get clothing, or to leave home—seldom go to any place of worship. By the world, and by some strict professors, they

---

[*] *Moral Reformer*, vol. i (1831), p. 303.
[†] *Livesey's Moral Reformer*, 1833-9, p. 214.   [‡] *Moral Reformer*, vol. i. (1831), pp. 227-228.

are not deemed religious persons. God only knoweth their hearts. But amongst
these, so far as I may be allowed to speak, I have seen those evidences which fill me
with hope that many of them will be favoured to sit down with Abraham, Isaac, and
Jacob in the kingdom of heaven. I have observed their resignation and patience
in affliction; their contentment in poverty; their confidence in Providence; their
compunction for their sins, and their faith in the Divine promises; their gratitude
for mercies received; their consistent deportment; and their readiness to share their
morsel at any time with their suffering neighbours. To some, even these evidences
may not be satisfactory, but I confess I always behold them with admiration; and
when I read the Saviour's notice of the poor widow, whose mite was declared more
than the abundance of the rich—of Lazarus, whose sores were licked by the dogs,
and who craved in vain for the rich man's crumbs, being carried by angels into
Abraham's bosom—I feel justified in hoping that many who are now extremely poor
will at one day appear among the rich in faith, and heirs of the kingdom."*

CHRISTIAN SOCIALISM, AS TAUGHT IN THE NEW TESTAMENT,

—a subject which has recently occupied the attention of the Congregational Union,
and which is still before that body,—had in Mr. Livesey an advocate whose long
life was in strict accord with the requirements of that system. His Christianity was
not one of mere word, but of deed. While he never approved of the system of
Socialism advocated by Robert Owen as a whole, he admitted that in part Owen's
ideas were good and worthy of adoption. Owen's system was too materialistic for
him; it was defective chiefly in not taking into account the spiritual nature and
needs of man. Referring to persons who were favourably impressed with Socialism,
but who were unable to adopt Owen's system, Mr. Livesey says:

"To such persons a system of *Christian Socialism,* I think, would be highly
acceptable; and in searching for such a system, the New Testament lends us ample
assistance. And it has this great advantage, that it calls upon no man to abandon
his home or his connexions; it does not pronounce the external arrangement of
society to have been always in error; it does not leave us ignorant of our God and
Father, nor in darkness as to futurity. The Socialism of pure Christianity is the
most lovely in the world, and exactly suited by the Father of us all to the exigencies
and wants of the human family. It is that which our nature seems to crave for,
and in which our social desires would find substantial peace. And had not this
been changed by the authority of priests and councils into a mass of barbarous
ceremonies, and had not selfishness been nursed even in the lap of religion, we
might have been saved the attempt which is now being made to sap the truth of
Christianity altogether. . . .
"Primitive socialism was, moreover, much promoted by the mutual visits which
they paid to each other. It is said 'they brake bread from house to house, and ate
their meat with gladness and singleness of heart.' Christians ought to love one
another with pure hearts fervently, and instead of merely going to the same chapel
and scarcely ever recognizing each other, their social kindness should be such as to
lead them frequently into each other's company. In this there should be no preference given to rank or wealth, but love one to another, as members of the same
body, should be the only incentives. If there be any partiality manifested, it should
be in the rich inviting the poor more frequently than any other class. In Jerusalem, at the commencement of Christianity, this socialism led many even to part
with their possessions and goods, and to have all things in common. And although,
as is clear from Acts v. 4, this was a voluntary service, yet I can easily imagine
times and circumstances of great trial and conflict, where it would be desirable,
and attended with great advantages to Christians, even literally to imitate this
splendid example of disinterestedness and love. In fact, the precepts of the New
Testament all recognize this Christian socialism. 'Bear ye one another's burdens,
and thus fulfil the law of Christ.' 'Rejoice with them that rejoice, and weep with

* *Moral Reformer,* vol. i. (1831), pp. 213, 214.

them that weep.' 'Wherefore, comfort one another, and edify one another as also ye do.' 'Let every man look not on his own things, but every man on the things of others.' 'Be ye kind, tender-hearted, forgiving one another, even as God for Christ's sake hath forgiven you.' These and many other exhortations imply the existence of a Christian socialism, to which we are strangers at the present day. If we were more frequently together, and enjoyed more of each other's company and conversation, and were we less sordid and selfish in our feelings, we should be much more happy; there would be less jealousy and evil-speaking, and the 'hatred, malice, and all uncharitableness,' so often exhibited in the demeanour of those who bear the name of Christians, would at least be suppressed, and in many instances changed into forbearance and love; and for mere bodily service in rituals of religion, there would be substituted that charity which is the bond of perfection.

"'Behold how these Christians love one another!' was the remark passed upon the primitive Church. 'Love is of God, and he that dwelleth in love dwelleth in God, and God in him.' In the midst of all the conflicting notions as to creeds and ceremonies, those shall be my brethren who most resemble Christ in their gentleness, kindness, and sincere attachment one to another.

"Pity is it that unsettled mortals, seeking for rest and peace, should not be able to discover a system of TRUE SOCIALISM, without searching for it in the sable shades of unbelief." *

DUTIES AND METHODS OF MINISTERS.

Mr Livesey was faithful in his expostulations with the clergy and ministers regarding the very perfunctory way in which they discharged their duties. Had they all been faithful watchmen—delivered from the fear of man, and devoted to the well-being of the human family—he considered that many of the evils which afflict society would be either greatly mitigated or entirely abolished. This idea largely pervades his address to the clergy of all denominations on Temperance, which was written in London in 1837, at the instance of a friend,—by whom it was forwarded to all clergymen and ministers in the metropolis,—as will be seen from the following extract:

"Permit me further to remark, that if the people are corrupt, you should be 'the salt of the earth;' if in a state of gross darkness, you should be the light of the world; and it is to you we always look to remedy the moral disorders of society. In the public mind you are sure to be held blameable for the continuance of immorality and crime, while you never made a suitable effort to correct it. If a fire were raging in the Strand, and remained unchecked all the day, what should we say of the conduct of the firemen? If the streets be incommoded with dirt, on whom do we lay the blame but on the scavengers. If the street lamps should cease to give light, so as to endanger the lives of the passengers, the inquiry would be, What are the gas-men about? And when we see intemperance and every other vice raging in the streets, apparently unchecked, we are apt to exclaim, 'Where are the ministers? What are they doing? Are there none that will come out and stay this mighty evil?' Doubtless you have many engagements of which I know nothing; but I entreat you to spare a little time for this important work. If those who work six days in the week can do this, I hope you will manifest the utmost willingness to join them. Your office is one of labour and not ease; and hence the ministers of the gospel are compared to 'soldiers, shepherds, labourers, and husbandmen.' I know it is congenial to the flesh to sit in our carpeted parlours and indulge in literary pursuits; but it is more consonant with the spirit of Jesus to be found in the cellars and garrets of the poor, instructing the ignorant, and trying to save souls."†

In one of his note-books occurs the following memorandum (headed "Reflections

* *Livesey's Moral Reformer*, 1838-9, p. 154.   † *Ibid.*, 1838-9, p. 29.

in a chapel, 1831 "), which suggestively indicates his view of the shortcomings of many preachers, and of the inadequacy of their teaching:

"How many preachers are unfit to be teachers!
How few of the poor working people attend!
How seldom the duties of man to man are plainly explained and urged!
How much of what is prayed for and sung is never felt!"

And in the same note-book appears a further reference to the same subject:

"Their aim is not to persuade people to goodness—to honesty, charity, love, patience, piety—but first to overwhelm with the terrors of hell for their sins, and secondly to get the feeling of liberty and a sense of 'pardoning love'—a state of feeling brought on by violent prayer and strong mental or emotional excitement."

He had a very poor opinion of sermonizing generally, as may be gathered from the following:

"No plan ever tended more to pervert the true meaning of the Scriptures, to keep the people in ignorance, or to encourage the teachers in idleness. It is without analogy in the whole course of communicating knowledge, upon any subject whatever. It is condemned by every page of the Evangelists and the Acts of the Apostles. Paul never taught by sermons, nor do I think he was capable of such a drivelling method. Though we hear of 'Christ's *Sermon* on the Mount,' yet, if we examine this discourse, it was anything but a sermon. Rational teaching consists in ascertaining what the people are ignorant of, and, with plainness and sincerity, communicating such information as they need, without any circuitous route of imparting knowledge; and not in taking a detached sentence, or part of a sentence, and dividing and subdividing, till the words are exhausted, a great part of which are frequently strained beyond the real meaning and design of the writer. Indeed, the whole is looked upon rather as an effort of *ability* than as intended to convey seasonable advice. It is the man's *delivery* that is admired, and it is for this he is paid."*

Mr. Livesey's gentle and generous disposition, however, inclined him to regard men as better than their creed. He speaks out in condemnation of abuses, because truth obliges him to do so, but he is always ready to make all possible allowances, and in the brief preface to his little pamphlet on "Confirmation" he says, "It is a consolation to believe that, in many cases, the people are better than their systems;" and in a generous article on "The Brighter Side," he expresses his admiration of the self-denying labours of many ministers and clergymen, remarking:

"I leave out, of course, those who enter the office for a piece of bread, or those who convert it into a sinecure; but I include many, notwithstanding, who are receiving emoluments upon principles which it would be hard to justify from Scripture; for, in many cases, their friends, and not they, are to be blamed for this. They are irreproachable in character, exemplary at home and in the world, give good instruction, and, according to their means, are ready to join and follow, though seldom to lead, in any good work."†

In the same article Mr. Livesey speaks highly of lay preachers as "workmen of the right sort," and "generally faithful and especially attentive to that class, the poor, whence spring most of the real disciples of Christ." But the preacher most after his heart is the one that best answers to the following description:

"Give to me the man whose heart is warm; whose soul is pure; whose motives have never been corrupted by the love of lucre; whose ardour was never damped with the chilling blasts of academic learning; who, ignorant of the petty arts of

---

* *Moral Reformer,* vol. i. (1831), pp. 170, 171. † *Ibid.,* vol. i. (1831), p. 211.

embellishing truth, and regardless of his own ease, or gain, studies the condition of man, beholds his misery and his woe, and makes every sacrifice for his welfare; rustic in his habits, and clad in his own apparel, visits every abode of vice and wickedness; and whether to two or three, or to hundreds or thousands, unceasingly devotes his time and his strength in promoting the happiness and salvation of mankind."*

It would be erroneous to suppose that Mr. Livesey discouraged attendance at public worship. All outward religious exercises were regarded by him simply as *means* to an *end*, and valuable in as far as the *end* was promoted or gained. In his own case he found that constant attendance was not as helpful as visiting the poor and " doing good " to the unfortunate, and he chose the latter form of worship.

" Church-going," he reiterates, " is but a *means* to an *end,* and without this is kept in view, we are apt to think that the mere act of *attending* and *joining* in the service is the most material part of our duty. We ought every day to live ' soberly, righteously, and godly in this present world ; ' and just so far as our *meeting together* promotes *these ends*, it is useful ; but without this it were dangerous to consider that we had done any part of our duty by merely attending a place of worship."†

HOW TO DEAL WITH SCEPTICS.

In reply to a correspondent who had charged him with " conniving at the sins of the poor," and of teaching sentiments approved by infidels, Mr. Livesey says of the latter class :

" I have never pandered to their vices; I hope their consciences have often smarted beneath my remarks; but as *politicians* they are wise enough to know that the Church of Christ was never intended to be a *political instrument*, wherewith to scourge the country; and, evidently desirous to rid the country of this *political Church*, is it to be wondered at that whilst many pass over the inculcation of personal morality and religion, they would hail the appearance of so powerful an auxiliary as the *Moral Reformer ?* . . . Instead of despising or persecuting the infidel, I would *reason* with him ; and my hope of success would be in stripping Christianity of all the follies and absurdities with which it has been clothed by *hireling* priests, and presenting it to his understanding in that truly innocent, lovely, and Divine character which it originally sustained."‡

In dealing with sceptics, Mr. Livesey pursued a very different course to that adopted by the orthodox. He would not invoke the law to silence the most heterodox teacher. " Does truth," he asks, " require to be defended by a spirit of persecution, or is its defence so difficult as to exasperate its paid advocates, who are as a thousand to one against their opponents ? " Mr. Livesey was led into making these remarks by the treatment an atheistic lecturer received at the hands of the clergy. He appears to have believed, with Lord Bacon, that " God never wrought a miracle to refute atheism, because His ordinary works refute it ; " for his own method of dealing with sceptical persons is based on a similar idea :

" I claim," he says, " no extensive acquaintance with the controversy betwixt theists and atheists ; but by one very simple step I have attempted, and in which I think I have succeeded to some extent in convincing numbers of the important truth of the existence of Deity. I agreed with the proprietor of an anatomical figure of the human frame to exhibit it daily at the Temperance Hall at a penny each, and to give a lucid description of the different functions of its various parts. Nearly four thousand persons attended in the course of four weeks, and few indeed

---

* *Moral Reformer*, vol. i. (1831), p. 172.   † *Livesey's Moral Reformer*, 1838-9, p. 133.
‡ *Moral Reformer*, vol. i. (1831), p. 352.

who saw the wonderful mechanism and beautiful structure of the human form, with their extraordinary adaptations to all man's wants and to external nature, went away without some thought of nature's God. I don't know an easier, shorter, more impressive, or more important mode of teaching the existence and natural attributes of Deity than to place palpably before the eyes of man every internal part of the machinery of one of His noblest works. For eight nights I gave brief lectures in connection with this figure, in which I drew the attention of the people to themselves and from themselves to Him in whom they live, and move, and have their being. Here was an evidence worth a thousand metaphysical arguments; here were impressions produced which subtle and abstract reasoning can never overcome. With God's wonderful works before us, every teacher should try to fix the attention of the thoughtless and wavering upon them." *

BIBLE REVISION.

As early as 1832, Joseph Livesey contended for a revised version of the Scriptures, and most of the defects he then pointed out in the Authorized Version have been remedied in the new one just issued (May, 1885). To advocate such a reform fifty-three years ago amongst the common people, whose religion was tinctured more or less with a species of bibliolatry, was taking the surest course to be dubbed " infidel " or " atheist," both by the clericals and their followers; but Mr. Livesey dared, in the interests of truth, to plead for an improved translation; and failing that, he would accept, as an instalment, a revision such as we now have. Here again he is quite half a century in advance of his time. In an article especially devoted to the subject, he says:

"I am much mistaken if the crude notions and general ignorance of the plain and obvious meaning of many parts of Scripture, among religious people themselves, do not arise from the *form* in which these writings are published. Everything that tends to obscurity ought to be removed, and everything that can render the meaning and design of the writers clearer ought to be adopted. The Authorized Version would be considered excellent at the time it was made, but the lapse of two hundred years makes great changes; and is there any reason why we should not in this affair, as in every other, avail ourselves of the improvements and discoveries of the last centuries? . . . It often seems to me that something in the character of a *pious fraud* is practised upon this subject. When the Bible is spoken of in general, our divines represent the whole as 'truth without any mixture of error,' and speak as if even verbal infallibility belonged to it; but at other times we find them taking the greatest liberties, and not only changing words, but altering the construction of sentences. If the Scriptures be our best guide, I conceive it to be the duty of the clergy to present them in the plainest and most correct form that can possibly be adopted. And while improvements are constantly encouraged in the language and form of all other works, why not give the Scriptures in the very best form of which the English language is capable? But if an entire new translation, in the present state of religious feeling, be an attempt too great to succeed, might not a version be published, embodying several material improvements, yet retaining as the basis the authorized version?

It is remarkable that the principal changes suggested by Mr. Livesey have been attempted or effected in the Revised Version. They were as follows:

"(1) Rendering the language *grammatical*, according to the generally received standard.
"(2) In adopting the usual points and marks, and applying them to the same purpose as they are in other books. . . . The quotation marks are *entirely* omitted, for want of which the reader is sometimes led to suppose that he is reading the writer's own remarks, when he is, in fact, reading a quotation. . . . The

* *Livesey's Progressionist* (1852), pp. 14, 15.

points are injudiciously placed, and vary in different editions. . . . A London edition of 1819 has seven periods in the Lord's prayer, whilst that of 1822 has only two; and to show that this is not the result of any designed change, the Oxford of the later date of 1824 has adopted the former. In a school which I superintended where the boys read in classes, not by verses but sentences, we found much difficulty, owing to this irregularity. Unless we could succeed in getting a sufficient number of copies of the same edition, the boys could not read together.*

"(3) In the abandonment of the form of the present divisions. The divisions of chapters and verses have no connection with the original form of these books, and yet, absurd as they are, they are retained because the whim of a certain individual happened to place them there. For purposes of reference, divisions like these might be useful, but instead of being forced into the subject and the sentences, it would be quite sufficient to print them in the margin. We have no mangled book like the Bible, for even the historical and the epistolary parts are cut into small portions, and printed as if they were distinct aphorisms. How absurd to destroy the arguments of an Apostle, the force of which is often intended to appear at a distant part of a letter, by reducing them into shreds of three or four lines each.

"(4) References and running titles. It may be useful to admit of references where another passage is plainly alluded to, but where this is not the case, and where other passages are marked merely for the purpose of *illustration*, it is quite evident that they will be selected according to the creed of the person who compiles it. . . . This may not be sufficiently clear to those who have not examined these references; but let such examine them, and also the lists of *contents* and the *running titles* which appear on every page, and they will perceive, especially in the New Testament, that descriptions are given in which all parties do not agree. These parts at least are 'apocryphal.'"†

METHODS IN ACCORDANCE WITH PRIMITIVE CHRISTIANITY.

Naturally Mr. Livesey would be asked, "What do you propose as a substitute for the methods you dissent from as being anti-Christian?" He fully answers such an inquiry, and unfolds a legitimate plan of action, which will well repay the attentive study of all persons desirous of spiritually enlightening the masses. He says:

"'What plan would you then suggest,' it will be asked, 'in order to conform to the primitive standard?' I answer, let the simple plan mentioned in the New Testament be adopted. It is not necessary, and far from being proper, in my opinion, that buildings should be shut up all the week which might be used for a variety of useful purposes. The foolish and superstitious notion of one place being holier than another should long since have been exploded. There is no more holiness in a church or a chapel than there is in a garret or a barn, and every room in which Christians meet on the Lord's day might be turned to some useful purpose as a school, a lecture room, or a workshop. Secondly, it is not too much to expect, when persons are freed from ecclesiastical exactions, that individuals would frequently be found able and willing to provide a place and *give* the use of it for Sundays; but should this not be be case, let a place be rent'd. And instead of having *one* fine building in a respectable neighbourhood, it would be better to have several places in poor neighbourhoods, which would correspond with the 'upper rooms' named in Scripture, and which ought to be used for schools or other useful purposes. And if the meetings were conducted with more simplicity and less affectation, without any pew rents or collections, there would be a great increase of that class which constantly followed Jesus—I mean *the poor*. Such places should invariably be *rented;* and supposing that in some cases no place could be met with, there would not be much difficulty in occasionally inducing persons of property to build, upon an assurance that rent would be paid. Any plan, in fact, is to be preferred to the 'Church property' plan.* To show that all anticipated difficulties could be met, I may mention, that though the Temperance

* This incidental reference sheds light upon the advanced methods Mr. Livesey adopted in teaching the school adverted to on pages xxxvi. 41, etc.

† *Moral Reformer,* vol. ii. (1832) pp. 242-5.

societies, with about two exceptions in the kingdom, have no property of their own, I believe there is scarcely a town or a village where the friends do not manage to hold their meetings. Happily they have not as yet much "property" to contend about, and I have no hesitation in giving it as my opinion, taking a *full view of the matter*, that their usefulness is likely to diminish as they become anxious to possess it. And why should not this plan be acted upon in reference to religion? There would then not only be nothing for the members of a congregation to contend for, but their resources would be available for better purposes, and piety and goodness would then visit the houses of our populous towns, instead of being almost confined, as at present, to consecrated buildings. As to *endowments*, the bare mention of them cannot fail to arouse in the minds of those who have observed their tendency, a thorough conviction of their decidedly pernicious influence upon the interests of religion. The benevolent work of instructing the ignorant, should in all cases, be done *gratuitously*. 'Freely ye have received, *freely* GIVE;' and should any Christian teacher be required to labour, in the primitive import of the term, by travelling about, if he be *deserving*, he will get his ' hire ' from the spontaneous feelings of his Christian brethren, without either pew rents, endowments, or any kind of tax whatsoever."†

THEORY AND PRACTICE.

The following striking illustration of Mr. Livesey's method of reducing his theories to practice was published at the time of his death by the *Preston Chronicle:*

" In connexion with Mr. Livesey's early preaching we give an incident, because it is illustrative of one of the special features of his character :—Long ago, the land upon which St. James's Church is erected, with the streets on east and west sides of it, was a grass-grown field, and on the west side were a number of small gardens, which were cultivated by tradesmen of the town, for in those days they did not live on the high pressure plans of the present day, and they found time to enjoy the beauties of nature, and luxuriate amidst her choicest floral gifts. Amongst others who had one of the numerous garden allotments was the deceased. One Sunday evening, nearly 60 years ago, Mr. Livesey was walking in his garden, with some of his children, when a messenger came running across the field; he came from Vauxhall Road Chapel, and rushing into the garden, out of breath, exclaimed—' Oh, Mr. Livesey, they are waiting for you.' ' *Who ?* ' replied he. And the rejoinder to this was, ' The people assembled in the chapel. You promised the minister to preach when he went away.' ' Yes, I did,' said he, " but he was to tell me when I was required, and I have had no intimation whatever that he had gone away ; but if the people are waiting, I must go.' He hastened across the field, with the messenger, and, on entering the chapel, the latter was conducting him to the foot of the stairs leading to the pulpit, but Mr. Livesey stopped short, and went into a large square singing pew, under and immediately in front of the pulpit. The messenger fetched down the Bible, and cushion on which it rested, with the couple of tassels which it was the fashion in those days to attach to it, so that they hung down in front of the pulpit. The messenger adjusted the cushion and the Bible on the desk, in the singing pew when, Mr. Livesey, taking a look at the tasselled cushion, removed it, and, placing it on the seat he was about to occupy, sat down upon it, then commenced the service, and preached a sermon fully the usual length."

The practical application of Mr. Livesey's religious principles—viz., his benevolence to the poor, and his labours in various ways to elevate and improve mankind—will form the subjects of succeeding chapters.

* "Church property," says Mr. Livesey in the same article, "has been the prize for which religious zealots have been constantly fighting. The religious feuds of Ireland, and the divisions in England, spring from this source. Strip religion of her earthly property, and you give a fatal stroke to sectarianism, break at once the springs of hypocrisy, and present the lovely guest in her spiritual and legitimate attractions."

† *Livesey's Moral Reformer*, 1838-9, pp. 213-4.

CHAPTER II.

SERVICES TO THE POOR: CHARITY AND BENEVOLENCE.

I have known men and women in the very worst circumstances, to whom heroism seemed a heritage, and to be noble a natural way of living.—GERALD MASSEY.

When thou seest misery in thy brother's face, let him see mercy in thine eye; the more the oil of mercy is poured out in thy pity, the more the oil in thy cruise shall be increased.—QUARLES.

If a man be enkindled to a generous mind, this is the best kind of nobility.—PLATO.

God is pleased with no music below so much as the thanksgiving of relieved widows and supported orphans; of rejoicing, comforted, and thankful persons.—JEREMY TAYLOR.

The sublime pleasure of generosity stimulates its own exercise, and at last shuns even gratitude itself, that it may be more entirely pure.—J. TUCKERMAN, D.D.

If you would secure the state from within as well as from without, you must better the condition of the poor.—SOUTHEY.

Society ought to be troubled, to be shaken, yea, convulsed, until its solemn debt to the poor is paid.—CHANNING.

THE reader of Mr. Livesey's "Autobiography" will find that work abounding in references to the poor, and in evidences of its author's tender solicitude for their well-being, of his delight in their company, and his perfect freedom and homeliness with them. In early life he became familiar with their sufferings; indeed, he was bred amongst them, and the iron of poverty had entered into his own soul. His own grandfather, to whose care his early years were confided, had, from no fault of his own, gradually descended from a position of comfort to one of hardship, if not of privation; and Joseph Livesey in after years, when he had become the prosperous tradesman, never forgot these early experiences. They made him strong as the friend of the poor, and strong too as a reformer of their grievances. In dealing with matters affecting them, he exhibited all the tenderness of a woman towards the unfortunate and suffering, but in his proceedings with their oppressors he displayed the courage of the lion !

As a friend of the poor, he took a leading part in most of the public efforts made in Preston for their benefit. This was notably the case during the cotton famine. Some of the plans he resorted to for the relief of misery are mentioned in the " Autobiography," but he was always busy with some project for lessening suffering. He never allowed even ill-health to interfere with this work. The writer of a biographical sketch of Mr. Livesey in the *Temperance Spectator*, for April, 1860, says : " Nothing will sooner stir up the old man's heart, and send him hobbling through the streets (for he has been a martyr to rheumatism), on a work of mercy, than the report of an accident to some decent, but poor man, or the distress of some honest, but afflicted family."* Mr. Livesey was sometimes led by his intense sympathy with the poor into unwittingly committing an injustice on another

* *The Temperance Spectator*, vol. ii. (1860), p. 52.

class ; but wherever it was made clear to him that he had erred in this way, he readily acknowledged his mistake.   His action in getting the market tolls abolished, in the interests of the poorer stall-keepers, may be mentioned as an illustration of this.*

VIEWS ON THE POOR LAW.

In his discussion with Mr. Acland, his speeches against the Poor Law were inspired by his sympathetic feeling for the poor. Upon the Poor Law question indeed his views were very much in accordance with those of Col. T. P. Thompson, who, in 1834, had said in the *Westminster Review* that " The whole system of Poor Rate economizing, if not combined with taking off the restrictions, which create the poor [and changing their circumstances], is only improving the machinery for making the poor die quietly, and with the least disturbance to those who live sumptuously by grinding them down." Mr. Livesey championed the cause of the weak against the new legislation, and for twenty years successfully resisted its application to his native town.   He used less violent language than the Rev. Joseph Rayner Stephens, but he was equally emphatic in his opposition to the "Bastile system." If all classes were alive to their duties, Mr. Livesey contended, the deserving poor might be relieved by voluntary charity ; and this without branding them with the unchristian stigma of pauperism, or separating the members of a family from each other.   National efforts should be directed, he argued, to the removal of the causes of pauperism, rather than to its relief, and on this he says :

" In these [remedial] arrangements we ought to encourage, above all others, those measures which are calculated, not merely to *relieve* the poor, but to *reinstate* them in that condition in society which would abolish *pauperism*, and enable every sober, industrious man to obtain for himself and family an honest competency."†

But Mr. Livesey's public efforts to serve the poor were as nothing beside his private benefactions.   Charles Lamb somewhere says (or uses words to the same effect) : " The greatest pleasure I know, is to do a good action by stealth, and to have it found out by accident." But Mr. Livesey improved upon that—it would have destroyed the pleasure to him for the deed to have been discovered at all It has been remarked that the extent of his benefactions was probably not known beyond the circle of his own family.   It is likelier, however, that his services to his fellows were unknown to any other human being than himself ; for he carried into effect the noble sentiment of Marcus Antoninus : " Let the man who has done a beneficent action, not look for applause, but repeat it the first opportunity, as the vine again yields its fruit at the proper season.   Men ought to bestow their benefactions unobserved, and be almost unconscious themselves of their good deeds."

HOW THE PEOPLE LIVE.

It is a noticeable feature in Mr. Livesey's life, that from a very early period in his career he made common cause with the poor. By visiting them in their wretched dwellings—not only in his native town, Preston, but in Manchester, Liverpool, London, Dublin, and almost every town resorted to for business purposes—he acquired

---

* See " Autobiography," p. 29.   † *Moral Reformer*, vol. i. (1831), p. 11.

by personal investigation a thorough acquaintance with their wrongs and sufferings, their weaknesses and vices, and also their virtues and patience. When business took him from home, he appears to have spent his evenings and leisure time in exploring the very lowest haunts of human wretchedness. Who can tell the extent of his ministrations to the poor, the dispirited, and the wretched on these occasions? Like Goldsmith's Pastor—

To relieve the wretched was his pride,

and he seems to have found his chief delight in this work of beneficence. His plans were novel and ingenious, and eminently calculated to achieve the end he had in view. Visiting a town or city as a stranger, he would fix on an idler of the working class, and say to him, " My man, do you want to earn half a crown easily ? " —an inquiry which generally brought an affirmative answer. " Then," he would continue, " take me into the worst, the very *lowest*, streets, alleys, and courts in the town." Accompanied by his guide, he would visit the people in their wretched and unhealthy habitations, converse with them, gain their confidence, and tender them advice best adapted to their condition. In this way he won their confidence, became the trusted depository of their thoughts and feelings, hopes and fears; and learned their ideas concerning other classes in the State. He never betrayed the trust they reposed in him : but the sufferings these visitations disclosed, inspired him in his subsequent efforts as moral, social, political, and temperance reformer. Throughout his public career, Mr. Livesey was influential and powerful as a reformer, because his suggestions were framed to meet a social condition of which he had personal knowledge, and respecting which he had not to rely upon second-hand information.

Speaking of the course usually followed by visitors to cities and towns, he says : " You are never directed to the poorest parts of a place, but always to the squares, and crescents, and where there are fine buildings ; " a method sufficient, perhaps, for the mere pleasure-seeker, but calculated to give a very erroneous idea of the true condition of the people. Topographical literature has been largely written from the same partial point of view, and Mr. Livesey felt that this was no small evil, since, by misleading, it caused the rich and better classes to rest in a fool's paradise. Hence, in 1831, when Baines's History of Lancashire was announced, he pointed out a method of increasing its value and usefulness:

" I would suggest," he says, " to Mr. Baines, the able editor of the intended ' History of the County Palatine of Lancaster,' to include in his ' plan ' a description of the *residences, employment*, and *manner of living* of the great mass of the people—the poor ; and especially the poor weavers. As he intends to visit every parish, to form correct materials for his work, let him not overlook those number-less streets in every large town in Lancashire, where the sickening sight of poverty and misery has long been manifest. In works of this sort, we have generally descriptions of all the public buildings, public offices, corporate arrangements, and everything connected with wealth and splendour, whilst that which is of infinitely more importance to be known—*the condition of the working class*,—is overlooked as a matter not worth recording." *

* Moral Reformer, vol. i. (1631), p. 22.

THE WRONGS OF HONEST CITIZENS.

Before the Poor Law of 1834, he had made himself familiar with the condition of the poor in Preston by a systematic visitation of them in their wretched homes. Writing in 1831, upon the distress then existing in Preston, he says of the poor-weaver-class, working for a miserable pittance, or out of work altogether :

"A man in this situation is the most pitiable object in creation. His residence partakes more of a prison than a home; often it is a dark and noisome cellar. He has nothing to call furniture; his bed, because concealed, is often in the most wretched condition, and fit for no human being—to say nothing of one who is fatigued with excessive labour—to lie upon. Five or six persons sometimes lie upon the same bed, and, though they add their personal clothing, are unable to defend themselves from the cold. They get little refreshment, and rise to perform their arduous labour with bodies and spirits alike depressed. It has fallen to my lot to visit many of the worst cases in Preston, and it is impossible to describe the feelings I experienced, or to convey the reflections which arose in my mind on viewing their condition. I would give anything, if I could carry these cases, as they are, into the presence of kings, and nobles,* and the great men of the land, who loll at their ease, who are surrounded with splendour, and who are indulged with all the luxuries of sense."†

Tracing these evils to their causes, and finding that the poor were largely the victims of vicious legislation, greed, selfishness, and culpable neglect, it is not surprising that he occasionally refers in strong language to their oppressors. After laying bare (in the article already quoted from) their wrongs and sufferings, he proceeds :

"Who, it may be asked, are the persons of whom I have given this description? Are they aliens from the commonwealth of England? Are they of the negro tribes, of whose slavery we have heard so much? Or are they so weak in intellect as to have no consciousness of their wrongs? What have they done? Are they the idle, the profligate, the pests of society, *who live upon the labour of others?* Have they any claim upon British soil, or have they contributed anything to the wealth of the country? Have they the feelings of men, or do they deserve the regards of the humane, or the sympathies of Christians? In a word, I reply, they are the *best* men among us;—best for labour, for subordination, for piety; and yet (Heaven forgive this nation!) they have been treated like slaves." ‡

THE BITTER CRY OF WOE.

The Rev. Charles Garrett, in his funeral sermon on Mr. Livesey, says, "With a Church of Joseph Liveseys, the 'Bitter Cry' question would be settled;" yes, probably, but since the Church as at present constituted could not grow Joseph Liveseys, such a body is impossible. There was very little in common with Joseph Livesey and the spirit, aims, or methods of the Christianity of the nineteenth century—the Christianity of the Churches. "Then," you ask, "was he not a Christian?" Yea! most assuredly—a primitive Christian, with whom the teachings and life of Christ

---

* In recent years the pen of the most realistic journalist of the times—Mr. George R. Sims—has startled the nation with pictures of similar suffering existing in our midst, and the people have been visited in their own wretched homes by Sir Charles Dilke, as President of the Local Government Board, by Mr. George Russell, M.P., his able colleague, and by the Prince of Wales as a member of the Royal Commission for Housing the Poor. That Royalty and statesmanship have at last been brought into personal contact with the deplorable evils so clearly portrayed by Mr. Livesey upwards of half a century ago, is one of the most hopeful and encouraging signs of the times.

† *Moral Reformer*, vol. i. (1831), p. 36.   ‡ *Ibid.*, vol. i. (1831), p. 37.

were a matter of higher import than any doctrinal creed or ecclesiastical formulas imposed by the Church.

The " Bitter Cry " agitation has directed attention to the social evils which Mr. Livesey so ardently desired to remove from our midst. It is noteworthy that such of the remedial measures now proposed as are likely to be efficient are in accordance with his suggestions. The people must be visited in their own homes, and those homes must be made fit habitations for human beings. But the very term " Bitter Cry," which has been used with such startling effect in making known the sufferings of the people, was employed in the same connexion by Mr. Livesey as long ago as in 1831. In the *Moral Reformer* for May of that year, he has an article upon " Real Relief for the Sufferings of the Poor," in which ne asks the question, " Shall the BITTER CRY of woe never cease ? "

At various times spasmodic efforts to influence the masses have been made by the Church. The evil is too deep, however, to be eradicated by " mission hal services," even when free teas and soup kitchens are superadded. About the time Mr. Livesey was calling attention to the question in his *Moral Reformer*, there was an awakening in London regarding it. In July, 1831, commenting upon a statement made in a speech at a meeting of one of the societies in London, that " 70,000 persons in the metropolis rose every morning who had no resource for the coming day,"—and the proposal then made " to form a *new set* of ministers to carry the gospel into the shades of vice, wretchedness, and misery, where the *regular* preacher, owing to the nature of *his* labour, could not be expected to penetrate,"— Mr. Livesey says :

" Here the ' whole truth ' is out, and clearly confirms what I have constantly maintained :—that the present race of ministers is entirely different from the primitive ones—that the nature of their employment is totally different—that they are incapable of answering the end for which Christian ministers were appointed—and, that a ' new set ' is indispensable. . . . The ' set ' now proposed may be ' new ' in the eyes of our metropolitan divines, but, in reality, they are no other, in character, than the very men we read of in the New Testament. From the *nature of their labour*, the *regular* ministers cannot be expected to penetrate *the abodes of vice and misery !* Bless me ! who could think of such a degradation ! . . . No, no ; we must have a ' new set.' I subscribe heartily to the proposal, and if any of them should take an excursion to this part, most gladly will I furnish them with meat and lodgings, and go with them myself to the worst places in the neighbourhood. They need not be discouraged ; beside the example of the apostles, they have the sanction of Him who, by His intense anxiety to seek out and save the lost, obtained the appellation of being a friend of *publicans and sinners*."[*]

Referring, in a subsequent article, to this " new set " of ministers, Mr. Livesey gives advice which may be studied with advantage by the " new set " of to-day, who are entering upon a similar work in connexion with the " Bitter Cry " movement. He says :

" Let this new set care nothing about the worldly appendages of fine buildings and pulpits, music and pew-rents, gowns and bands, and all the pride and foppery of Antichrist : but, plain and simple, let them go *among the people*, and enjoin upon every soul ' repentance towards God, and faith towards our Lord Jesus Christ.' Let their object be, not the competition of parties, not the praise of men, not the profit of gospel lucre, but the glory of God, and the salvation of souls."[†]

[*] *Moral Reformer*, vol. i. (1831), pp. 215, 216.   [†] *Ibid.*, vol. i. (1831), p. 364.

HOUSE-FARMING, MIDDLE-MEN, AND CELLAR DWELLINGS.

Nearly all the evils disclosed by the recent Royal Commission, and by other present-day inquirers into the condition of the poor, were discussed and exposed by Mr. Livesey. For instance, in company with Mr. John Finch, in 1833, he visited some of the worst districts in Liverpool. They found a deplorable amount of overcrowding, as may be gathered from the following extract from Mr. Finch's report in the *Moral Reformer.* The irrepressible " middle man " also turns up.

" In all the houses we visited, with few exceptions, each room, from eight to eleven feet square, is inhabited by one, sometimes two families, in which they eat, drink, wash, cook, and sleep. . . . The rent paid for these wretched hovels, scarcely fit for pigs to live in, is from 1*s.* 6*d.* to 8*s.* per week. The landlord, not willing to be troubled with collecting the rents,* lets the house to one person, who collects from the rest; thus for a house worth not more than £12 per annum, between £40 and £50 is paid to the middle man by the sub-tenants, and thus, after the labouring classes have supported every other class in society, every six or seven families have to give one-fourth at least of their earnings to support another idler from among themselves." †

It was found that cellars were largely used as dwellings in Liverpool; but two years before, in his *Moral Reformer,* Mr. Livesey had drawn attention to this evil, and the pernicious consequences arising to health therefrom. He then invoked the remedial aid of the law. " I wish," he says, " to see an Act of Parliament, strictly to prohibit the use of cellars as places for human dwellings." ‡

GENUINE CHRISTIAN BENEVOLENCE.

Christian benevolence, with Mr. Livesey, meant something widely different from giving a few halfpence and crusts to importunate beggars; to subscribing to charities, hospitals, and similar institutions; to figuring in lists of contributors to widely advertised schemes of benevolence. All this he regarded as a poor substitute for personal exertion ; he believed in tracing misery to its source, and rendering really efficient aid to those who needed it. Hence, when treating on the subject, he invites his readers to make themselves personally acquainted with the distressed classes. After enumerating the usual channels of benevolence, which only afford means of delegating acts of charity, he says :

" I would direct your attention to benevolence in a humbler sphere, which, requiring much self-denial, is most apt to be neglected : it is to a general concern for the welfare of the poor ; *to visiting, feeding, clothing, and relieving the destitute,* and to *personal exertions* among them to *promote their happiness.*" §

The visitation of the poor was advocated by Mr. Livesey as a means of improving the visitor quite as much as the visited. The benefits, like all true benefactions, would be reciprocal. " No man," says he in the same article, " can visit the poor without being better for it; he learns humility, gratitude, and submission, and his benevolent zeal receives a fresh impulse." In one of his notebooks the following discriminating remarks about the poor are pencilled. They

---

* When will landlords learn that " property has its duties as well as its rights? "

† *Moral Reformer,* vol. iii. (1833), p. 48. ‡ *Ibid.,* vol. i. (1831), p. 116.

§ *Ibid.,* vol. i. (1831), p. 366.

are touching in their tenderness, and convey a lesson which deserves to be engraven on the memory of all visitors. Truly the man who wrote them *was a friend* to his needy brethren!

"How apt we are to forget the real condition of the poor. If food be cheap, and times are good, we jump to the conclusion that all are well off; and never think of investigating the matter in detail. I was convinced of the truth of this by numerous cases which turned up in connexion with our charity trip. The only sure way of judging of the condition of the poor, is by visiting and investigation. Consider for instance the following cases: An old woman receiving 1*s.* or 1*s.* 6*d.* per week; men, feeble and infirm; persons in whose families sickness is constant. These must all be in states of great discomfort and suffering, and good times are an evil to them because they dry up many of the fountains of charity, from which at other times they would get relief. Until there is more fraternal affection, and more humanity, there will always be a number of suffering poor."

The talk about the recklessness and improvidence of the poor,—their habits of unthrift and intemperance, so common now—was equally prevalent at this period of Mr. Livesey's active labours. Regarding those who accused the poor of being the authors of their own distresses, he remarks:

"Let the calumniators of the poor visit their cottages, inspect their beds, their furniture, their living; inquire into their earnings, especially those of the weavers and labourers; mark their time lost through waiting for employment; sickness and misfortunes to which a family is liable; and calculate the cost of rent, fire, furniture, food, clothing, etc., if honestly paid for; and I am quite certain, if they are candid, they will cease to rail against them." *

HOLIDAYS, AND THE DUTIES OF THE RICH TOWARDS THE POOR.

As a means of alleviating the condition of the people and rendering their lives more enjoyable, Mr. Livesey advocated holidays and periods of relaxation from unremitting toil. The bow always bent loses its power. Besides, Mr. Livesey hoped by these means to bring the rich and poor into closer contact. In 1831, he warmly urged the establishment of several public holidays during the year. These he would have quite apart from "holy days," and some of them, he suggested, might be fixed to celebrate national, and some local, events of importance and interest. With Ebenezer Elliott he would say:

> Oh blessed! when some holiday
> Brings townsmen to the moor,
> And, in the sunbeams, brighten up
> The sad looks of the poor.
> The bee puts on its richest gold,
> As if that worker knew—
> How hardly (and for little) they
> Their sunless task pursue.

He suggested that all classes of people should fraternize together on such occasions.

"How pleasant," he says, "to see rich and poor mingling together, exhibiting the sympathies of humanity, and striving to strengthen the social bond! So important is it to give a proper direction to all the movements of society, that nothing should be overlooked which can be made to contribute to the well-being and happiness of man." †

* *Livesey's Moral Reformer,* 1838-9, p. 3.   † *Moral Reformer,* vol. i. (1831), p. 51.

In " Hints to the Rich on Christmas Visiting," Mr. Livesey comments severely, but not too severely, upon the fashionable system of Christmas festivities and visiting, contending that the " consistent celebration of the birth of Jesus ought to recognise the great object of His coming into the world." He calls to remembrance the command of Christ to invite as guests " the poor, the maimed, the lame, and the blind," and he seriously asks his rich reader,—

" How often have you complied with this injunction? Strange as it may sound to fashionable ears, it is in perfect accordance with all the precepts of Jesus, and with His own example. When he saw the multitude who had come from a distance without victuals, *He had compassion on them*, and supplied them with food in the desert. And you may also be reminded, that in directing the observance of His disciples, it was not the *reward of men*, but of *their Father* who is in heaven, that he requested them to seek. Now, my friends, bring this subject home to yourselves; calculate how many parties you have held, how many feasts you have celebrated, and let conscience for once tell the truth, as to the *number of times* you have complied with your Saviour's words, ' Call the poor, the maimed, the lame, and the blind.' The poor, you learn, are not merely to be fed with the crumbs which fall from the rich man's table, but are to be made welcome guests, and treated as liberally as if they were your ' brethren and kindred and friends.' Never mind the carpets and the chairs; if not so fine in outward attire, with these poor you will have hearts equally as *honest* as when the presence of Lord John and Lady Jane graced your table." *

He continually pleads with the rich and well-to-do classes to display sympathy and discharge their duties to the poor. Here is an instance:

" If anything will open our hearts, and induce us to give alms, surely it is the aged widow of threescore and ten, as with careworn cheek and feeble gait she makes her humble curtsey at our door. Bereft of the partner of her cares, and even of the children of her hope, she wanders to seek the sympathy of unknown friends. How glad such are to be spoken kindly to, to be encouraged on their way, and to receive, even in small gifts, marks of attention and respect. Let children honour the aged, and let the benevolent show them peculiar respect. What an interesting employment it would be for young ladies to visit their aged sisters, to get them warm and comfortable clothing, to see that they have suitable food, and to free them from care and anxiety." †

POSTHUMOUS LIBERALITY NOT CHRISTIAN CHARITY.

Doing good by proxy, and dispensing charity by delegation, Mr. Livesey detested. He was equally severe upon that very common form of Christian liberality, the posthumous. He says:

" We brought *nothing* into this world, and it is certain we can carry *nothing* out; so that however we hug the idol of our wealth, however regular our devotions at this altar, we are compelled at last to leave it all. What the feelings of the miser are, when assured that he must die and leave his all, it is difficult to describe. He makes his will, and he who was always *too poor* to give when solicited, and too *selfish* to seek out cases of distress when he had an opportunity, is now dictating to his attorney to convey the several sums composing his property to some individuals who need it not, and to others who are likely to spend it in profligacy and excess. He leaves the world, after toiling and scraping for threescore years, never tasting that greatest of all pleasures, the pleasure of doing good. He parts with his money at last, because he is compelled to do so. That which, if distributed by the owner with discretion, would have done immense good, either passes into other hands like his own, or probably to those who, having never laboured for it, will

---

* *Livesey's Moral Reformer*, 1838-9, p. 25.   † *The Struggle*, No. 89, p. 3.

squander it away upon their lusts. A great deal is said about " faith," but while men are intent only upon laying up treasures upon earth, do they seem to have any faith in the promises of Him who said, 'I will never leave thee nor forsake thee'? That God who feeds the fowls, and clothes the fields with grass, it is said, ' will much more clothe you, oh ye of *little faith!*' If my observations be correct, many who assume a religious garb are too often the most covetous. They are delivered from the sensual and expensive vices which others indulge in; and being often favoured with advantageous opportunities in business, they begin to save money, and are consequently overcome by the love of it." *

Mr. Livesey's ideas regarding the poor were eminently humane and Christian. His deeds were in harmony with his teachings; and if a recital of some of the methods he adopted and suggested for relieving the distressed, leads only a few persons to emulate his example, nothing but good can result.

Reader! if you admire Mr. Livesey's practical philanthropy, go and do likewise.

* *Livesey's Moral Reformer*, 1838-9, p. 198.

CHAPTER III.

EDUCATION, HOUSEHOLD MANAGEMENT, AND THRIFT.

> The friend of man, the friend of truth,
> The friend of age and guide of youth;
> Few hearts like his, with virtue warm'd,
> Few heads with knowledge so informed:
> If there's another world, he lives in bliss;
> If there is none, he made the best of this.—Burns.

> The reforming of Education is one of the greatest and noblest designs that can be thought of.—Milton.

> Much forethought and discretion is necessary in the education of children. Let them be conducted into the best course of life, and habit will render it pleasant.—Pythagoras.

> Of all the men we meet with, nine parts in ten are what they are, good or evil, useful or not, by their education.—Locke.

> He who would bless his fellows must not ask
> Sublime occasions for that gentle task.—Wade Robinson.

With Mr. Livesey the question of education was of all others the most important: but with him education implied something more than the acquisition of the rudiments of knowledge, or even academic attainments. It was limited to no mere book learning, but embraced all those influences which affect the development of the physical, intellectual, moral, and spiritual natures of man. Above all, it included "That mental, moral, and physical training of youth, which is calculated to lead to the performance of those duties on which their personal and social happiness depends." * And the comprehensive meaning which he attached to the word Education may be further gathered from the following:

"Educate! Educate! cry all the journalists of the day, who seem disposed to attribute all the evils complained of to the want of education. Now to this I have no objection, provided by Education be meant the training of *all* the faculties of youth, and applying all the motives which sound religion affords."†

Education, from this point of view, therefore, begins in infancy and ends only with life. True, the absence of ordinary educational advantages in his own case, led him to offer facilities to lads suffering a similar privation; and his night and Sunday-schools were amongst his earliest efforts of systematic benevolence.

MR. LIVESEY'S FREE SUNDAY AND NIGHT SCHOOLS.

In Chapter viii. of his "Autobiography," he tells us a little, but only a little, about this important work. It is worthy of note that this first attempt of himself and young wife—who appears to have co-operated with him in all his public labours —was made very shortly after their marriage, and at a time when in a worldly sense he was anything but prosperous. The school books in common use at the time

* *Moral Reformer*, vol. i. (1831), p. 65. † *Livesey's Moral Reformer*, 1838-9, p. 20.

were found by Mr. Livesey to be ill adapted for the purposes they were intended, and he compiled a "First Book," which he tells us "had some merit." It was designed to help beginners, and proved to be very useful. It would be interesting to examine this First Book in these School Board days, but all inquiries for a copy of it have hitherto been fruitless; it is hoped, however, that one may yet be found. A stray leaf from a small memorandum book, evidently written about the time the Sunday school was started, contains entries which indicate some of Mr. Livesey's methods, and illustrate the care he exercised in adapting the means he employed to the end he had in view.

"A leaf in every teacher's book to mark where the scholars should commence.
Get sheets for teaching first class easy words, instead of books.
Sing some good and useful piece at the commencement, and exhibit something interesting at the close.
Everything that affords useful information to be sought after.
Make the head class easier, and advance a number in order to increase it.
The lowest class to be taught writing and reading in the other room.
Every new scholar to be seated in a certain place, previous to his going into any class."

The youths and young men who came under Mr. Livesey's guidance and care, in connexion with his free schools and Sunday meetings for religious investigation, drank in not only instruction, but the spirit of their teacher and friend, and in many cases their lives were largely influenced for good by his teachings and example. Some of the most conspicuous of the famous and heroic band of Preston Temperance advocates of the first period, were trained and fitted for their work in his Sunday-school, or in the Academy which he subsequently established in connexion with the Temperance Society at the Cock-pit. These young men were his disciples; they were animated by the same spirit which led him to his persistent labours for others. Under his guidance they were—

taught to prize,
Above all grandeur, a pure life uncrossed
By cares in which simplicity is lost.*

EARLY DIFFICULTIES MADE CONTRIBUTORY TO PROGRESS.

Mr. Livesey regarded his own early struggles as having exerted a valuable influence on his character, and he never lost a fit opportunity of urging others who had been similarly circumstanced, to rise superior to their surroundings. He takes this line in a very suggestive and well-reasoned address to the working classes, published in the *Moral Reformer* of July, 1831. In that address he refers to his early struggles, and to the influences which moulded his own character. The following extract furnishes points and reflections which we do not get in the "Autobiography;" and the citation is also noteworthy as containing an indication of the writer's consciousness of his own originality and power. He says:

"Free from the curses of wealth, if you can also escape the privations of poverty, your state is by far the best; and your minds are left much more free for reflection and meditation, than those who are exposed to the peculiar temptations of poverty or riches. To these advantages I am much indebted myself. Left an orphan at the age of seven, I was obliged to labour for my bread, and for about nine years I toiled at the loom in a dark cellar. With about as much education as

* Wordsworth.

is attained in our national schools, and without the means of purchasing books, in a literary sense I laboured under many disadvantages. But I thought the more; my mind was always at liberty: whilst my hands and my feet were driving on at full speed, I could summon the world before me, and criticise its character and pretensions. So busy and active was my youthful mind, that in the absence of every other object of attraction, I would sometimes engage to ascertain whether there were more males or females passed my window in an hour. It is from these circumstances, principally, instead of being the slave of education and custom, I lay claim to some degree of originality of thought; having never submitted to the trammels of authority, I have always ventured to think for myself, and to shape my course by the convictions of my own mind. It is from hence I learned the important duty of caring for, and sympathising with the poor, and of anxiously supporting any plan calculated to better their condition. To that very spot, and to these circumstances, under the direction of kind Providence, I attribute the commencement of a course of self-examination, which I shall never regret. Here I had an opportunity of viewing the world, before I was much entangled in its snares. On the weaver's breast-beam I learned the English grammar; and having never had an instructor, if you meet with anything which is more than commonplace in any of my productions, attribute it principally to that practice which I am now so anxious to enjoin upon you. I remember with greater pride my early studies and my midnight toils in the cellar at Walton, than I should any honour that the greatest monarch could have conferred upon me. It is generally acknowledged that wealth and ease are unfavourable to mental improvement; and I can say to you from experience, in this respect, that your employments afford opportunities for thinking, which you can never sufficiently prize. All businesses which consist in a repetition of the same operations are favourable to study, and I doubt not among these are many men of bright genius, correct discernment, enlarged minds, and ennobled feelings, and who are better qualified for useful situations, than those whom fortune and caprice have forced upon us."[*]

HOME TRAINING, RELIGIOUS INSTRUCTION, AND CHOICE OF SCHOOLMASTER.

In an able and exhaustive article upon Education, Mr. Livesey unfolds a plan for the education of children, admirably designed to effect the greatest good. He holds that education of some kind begins as soon as a child is capable of imitation: and hence the importance of every act witnessed by a child being one which he may safely and profitably imitate. And all that is most vital in the education of a child rests with the parents, and cannot be delegated by them to others.

"I know," he says, "that by far the greatest number of parents have neither time nor ability to superintend the literary part of their children's education. In such cases, reading, writing, accounts, etc., may be safely entrusted to others, who are properly qualified; but the moral, social, and religious instruction of children, ought to proceed from their parents, and cannot be expected to take root without a father's teaching, a mother's care, and the good example of both."[†]

Justice, sincerity, truthfulness, kindness, compassion, benevolence, order and cleanliness are principles which should be inculcated early, both by precept and by example; but

"Amidst all these," says he, "you must make the teaching of *religion and piety* pre-eminent. As soon as a child has any idea of *existence*, it should be informed of the Being of God; that He made us and everything we see, and that it is our duty to honour and serve Him. . . . Creation is a grand seminary for pious instruction to children; the green lawn, the flowery garden, the corn-fields, the warbling brook, the shady wood, the collected vapours, the ethereal blue, the heavenly

---

[*] *Moral Reformer*, vol. i. (1831), pp. 199-200.   [†] *Ibid.*, vol. i. (1831), p. 67.

bodies, the beasts of the field, the little songster upon the twig, and the busy bee,—are all objects to which the parent can point; which while they proclaim a 'Hand Divine,' tend to enlighten and purify and please the youthful mind."[*]

While (as the above quotation shows) he would never overlook religious instruction, he affirms that "The Bible was never intended for a school book," and adds, "in its *present form* it is very unsuitable for this purpose."[†]   According to Mr. Livesey, visiting the poor should form part of the education of the children of the rich.   He carried out this method in his own family; his children accompanied him in his visitations of his poor neighbours; and his boys made memoranda of the cases visited, several examples of which Mr. Livesey gives in a note to the article under consideration.[‡]   He would have due provision made for play and recreation; would introduce object teaching where practicable, and make a school as much as possible "a miniature community."   Respecting the caution to be exercised in choosing a schoolmaster, Mr. Livesey offers the following judicious advice:

"Never place your children under the care of a person whose *moral character* is not perfectly satisfactory.   The natural dispositions of a master (or mistress) are also deserving of notice: a man who is kind and affable, is to be preferred to one who is proud and austere.   Before you make any engagement, *visit the school yourselves*, and mark the order and arrangements, and the abilities of the master. This is a little unpleasant, but it is a necessary step.   If you find a dirty school, blotted books, and no order—if you see the children noisy and turbulent; if quietness cannot be commanded without threats; if the reading, writing, etc., are not satisfactory—you will know how to act.   Comparison affords the best criterion; and if you visit several schools, you will find no difficulty in coming to a satisfactory decision."[§]

A VISIT TO A PRESTON SCHOOL.

Mr. Livesey not only carried out this plan in his own family, but he appears to have been in the habit of looking up schools in the interests of the public.   In one of his rough note books is pencilled the following account of a visit he paid to a Preston school.   It is undated, and the schoolmaster referred to has most likely gone over to the majority.   If he has not, it is hoped that the influence of modern sanitation has so improved both master and scholars that they will not now be recognised:

"Went into a school at Preston (M. B.).   Before entering heard a terrible noise; knocked, a dirty boy came to the door, followed by a flock more.   Master not in, and the room emitted a most offensive smell.   'Why don't you open the windows?'   Boys mounted the desks and opened the four windows.   'When were you washed?'   'Sunday' (this was Wednesday).   It seems they wash once a week, and then merely hands and face!   How is it possible children can be healthy in such circumstances?   The master came in shortly after—one of those easy souls whose gait and manner say, 'Come day, go day, God send Sunday'—but withal a good natured fellow, and to whom a good washing would have been as salutary as to the boys."

When the parent has done his best for his children his labour is often partially neutralized, if not altogether destroyed, by outside influences, especially by those of a vicious kind, which the child meets with at school.   Mr. Livesey was not insensible to this, and he says:

---

[*] *Moral Reformer*, vol. i. (1831), pp. 73, 74.   [†] *Ibid.*, vol. i. (1831), p. 81.
[‡] *Ibid.*, vol. i. (1831), pp. 70-71.   [§] *Ibid.*, vol. i. (1831), p. 78.

"It is here the anxious parent is often foiled in his attempts to train up his children in the way they should go. He gives them good instruction; he shows them a good example in his own conduct; but most of this is lost at *school.* Here they receive impressions from a mixed number of boys (often including some of bad character), obliterating every virtuous principle, and forming a character rude, vulgar, and ungovernable. *School contamination*, of all others, should be carefully guarded against." *

A NOVEL CO-OPERATIVE SCHOOL.

To meet this serious difficulty he makes a very practical suggestion—in fact he would solve it by applying the principle of co-operation. He says:

"For those who cannot afford to employ a teacher in their own family, the most feasible plan which has presented itself to my mind, is a joint stock school, where the parents would have the sole control, and where none would be admitted but by mutual consent. For instance, let ten persons who are acquainted with each other, and whose families are, to a great extent, a guarantee for the conduct of the children, unite and establish a school for themselves, and employ a teacher on their own account. The expense would not greatly exceed the charges of the present schools, and the advantages would be manifold. Suppose the number of scholars be limited to twenty-five boys, and the expense of fitting up, maps, instruments, etc., £50, every parent would have to advance £2 in stock for every boy. This would be an investment which could be transferred to others upon the changes in the children which would occasionally occur. The power of admission being solely with the parents, all those likely to injure the school by a bad example could be kept out. The most approved plans of instruction might be adopted, and any changes made which appeared likely to advance the progress of the children. Besides a fixed superintendent, many other teachers and friends might be engaged, to attend occasionally to give instructions or deliver lectures on useful subjects. Rational amusements might be introduced. Attached to the school-room, should be a play-ground and a garden, in which the children would enjoy themselves, might take exercise, and be sometimes usefully employed. Indeed, as there is no object in promoting which parents are more willing to expend a little money, I feel convinced that, upon joint stock principle, an immense advance might be gained in the business of education, and that without any great increase in the expense. It appears to me that, at present, a great portion of the children's time is lost; their rising talents are not suitably brought out; and the school, with its appendages, instead of being an object of delight, is the most unwelcome place the children are compelled to visit. Some children attend school for a great number of years, and, after all, are ignorant upon almost every subject of importance. For private teachers to innovate, to any great extent, in their plans of instruction, would, in their own opinion, be attended with so much risk, that we need not expect them to make the attempt. I cannot see the least risk; but a prospect of the most satisfactory results, in a number of parents, anxious to give their children the benefits of a good education, uniting and establishing a school for themselves." †

And when everything possible has been done, when the best methods and appliances have been adopted, and the ablest and most reliable masters secured. Mr. Livesey well remarks upon the training of children that—

"The whole may be summed up in three particulars—judicious and affectionate teaching and admonition—the prevention of every bad association—and a standing good example of your own." ‡

LECTURES AS MODES OF POPULAR INSTRUCTION.

Mr. Livesey was always desirous of extending to his poorer neighbours advantages of every kind. The admission charge to hear high-class lectures was generally

* *Livesey's Moral Reformer*, 1838-9, p. 76.   † *Ibid.*, 1838-9, p. 134.
‡ *Moral Reformer*, vol. i. (1831), p. 205.

prohibitive to all but well-to-do people. He regretted this, and whenever he happened to enjoy an intellectual treat of this kind his pleasure was marred by the fact that the working people were not there to share it with him. He sagaciously asks, "Why should a popular man content himself with lecturing to a select company of a hundred, while with the same voice he could instruct ten times that number? Is this indicative of an anxiety to diffuse knowledge?" When Mr. James Silk Buckingham lectured in the Preston Theatre on the East India question, Mr. Livesey saw with regret that the masses were excluded from hearing that radical reformer.

"Noticing the gallery nearly empty," he says, "I stated to him my regret that the working people should be deprived of hearing a course of lectures so interesting and instructive. 'What shall I give you for the gallery,' said I, 'during the remaining evenings of your course, for the liberty of admitting them on such terms as I may think proper?' 'Take the gallery,' was his reply, 'manage it as you please, and whatever may be the proceeds I shall be satisfied.' I proceeded to make up a number of packets containing twelve tickets each, nearly the whole of which were sold to the mill-owners and manufacturers of the town, who gave them away to the people in their employ; and the proceeds of these, about £6, I presented to Mr. Buckingham. Though this was not a large sum, yet it was double the amount the gallery would have made on his terms." *

Next to Franklin, perhaps, comes Livesey, as an effective teacher of domestic management, thrift, and industry. His own home was a well ordered household. Izaak Walton, in concluding his famous life of George Herbert, says: "There is a debt justly due to the memory of Mr. Herbert's virtuous wife"; and Mrs. Livesey, who efficiently aided her husband in his domestic and private concerns, and also in his public labours, has claims to grateful remembrance that cannot be passed over. It has been truly said that a wife can either make or break a man. Mr. Livesey was especially fortunate in his choice of a partner. It may be said of him, as of the husband in Milton's "Sampson"—

> Favour'd of heaven who finds
> One virtuous rarely found,
> That in domestic good combines :
> Happy that house! his way to peace is smooth.

And not only is his way to peace smooth, but his way to usefulness, and all that constitutes true progress. In the third chapter of the "Autobiography," Mr. Livesey pays a well-merited tribute to his wife. Her character may be said to be focussed in the brief and positive injunction she enjoined upon him when about to begin his "Life"—"See thou sayest nothing about *me*."† Fit wife for such a husband! She had only done her simple *duty* as a woman, wife, mother, and practical Christian; and why need the world know anything about her?

Without such a wife, however, Mr. Livesey could never have led the useful life he did. We see her first as the clean, tidy, thrifty housewife—making the weaver's cottage a veritable paradise—attending to her household duties, and winding the bobbins for her husband and relatives. Shortly after her marriage, she devotes her leisure time on Sundays to teaching lads in the school above mentioned, and a little later she is busy in her husband's cheese business, attending to the retail

---

* *Livesey's Moral Reformer*, 1838-9, p. 51.   † *Autobiography*, p. 17.

department. And when the business extended, and Mr. Livesey, as was often the case, was unable to attend to it from ill health, she, with her boys (the eldest of whom, then only a lad, but doing more than a man's work), kept the concern going, without in the least degree neglecting her domestic duties. Then when the Temperance Movement was launched, it was her energy, tact, devotion, and administrative ability which made the early Preston Tea Meetings so famous. Her best personal service to Temperance undoubtedly consisted in her efficient management of the first Temperance Hotel in Preston, which for cleanliness, order, convenience, and home-comforts—combined with economical charges—was a model, which might yet be extensively copied to the advantage of the cause of sobriety. Taking her altogether, but especially with reference to the hearty co-operation and sustained assistance she rendered her husband in his beneficent aims, we may, without exaggeration, say of Mrs. Livesey, " Many daughters have done virtuously, but thou excellest them all."

CHILDHOOD'S HAPPY DAYS.

It will not be out of place to refer here to Mr. Livesey's well-known love for children. On page 57 of the " Autobiography " will be found references to his own family, and a perfectly charming picture of little Frank. In an article on Domestic Happiness, Mr. Livesey thus touchingly refers to the children of a well-conducted home :

"I must notice the children—the dear children. First, the lovely babe hanging at the breast—see a mother's embrace, and listen to a mother's blessing. Next the prattling child of three years old tells its pretty tales, and commands, by its infant eloquence, a seat upon its father's knee : the older boys and girls, all in their proper places, acting as they are told, speaking or keeping silence as decorum seems fit. Each one, as sharer in the happiness of the family, seems delighted to promote its increase. Though not without the thoughtlessness of childhood, nor the failings of humanity, they have no pleasure in displeasing their parents, and no enjoyments without their smile. They are managed not by physical authority, but by the inculcation of good principles, and by an attempt to convince them that their duty and their interest are inseparably connected. They are watched according to their several dispositions and the temptations to which they are exposed, and are guarded from evil by all that parental anxiety can devise. The elder are taught to consider themselves as examples to the younger, and the younger are enjoined to submit to the elder. Every reasonable indulgence is allowed, and nothing enforced that would alienate their affections from their parents or their home."[*]

The following citation affords us a glimpse of how he carried out these ideas in his own household :

"He has not the genuine feelings of a father who would consider it beneath him to play familiarly with his children. How pleased are my little folks when I run with them round the garden, affect to put them into the lock-up, or sit calling out words for them to spell, and exhibit the meanings in their own actions. Parents should always try to secure the affections of their offspring, and this is the best guarantee for consistent and sincere obedience. 'Father,' said little Frank, one night, 'I will do whatever *you* tell me to do.' I remember a woman, who was frequently crossed by her husband, observe, 'I would do anything for a *good* word!' and I believe this will be found to hold good in reference to children.

[*] *Moral Reformer*, vol. i. (1831), pp. 323, 324.

Going up the street, a man and his wife were talking to a lad twelve years of age. Among the rest, I heard one of them call him a ' blockhead.' If he be one, a very unlikely mode, thought I, of making him anything better. Children should not be compelled to do their duty by a STERN voice, by THREATS, or MENACE, but, if possible, by deference to the authority and respect for the wishes of their parents. They should never be punished for accidents. A little pleasantry and excitement should always be connected with their instruction; they are not likely to obey willingly what they hear with pain." *

THRIFT, ORDER, AND METHOD.

In the " Friendly Address to the Poorer Classes," issued in 1825, Mr. Livesey gives most excellent advice upon economy, cleanliness, industry, honesty, etc. He wrote extensively and well upon thrift, years before Smiles made the subject his own. Mr. Livesey's pamphlets and articles contain the best possible advice upon the expenditure of money on food and other household requisites. When dealing with such topics as punctuality, method, and order in business; domestic management, or household economy, Livesey greatly reminds one of Franklin. Both were eminently practical. Discoursing upon " The Disappointments and Troubles of Life," Mr. Livesey makes the following useful suggestion :

"Let a man in business, or a person with a large family, mark down for a single week, or a single day, the causes of all the disappointments, troubles, cares, and anxieties which occur, and he will find, upon a careful investigation, especially if he include those which are imaginary (and they are not a few), that my estimate of three parts out of four being brought on by ourselves, is not much above the mark." †

The following, taken from the same article, may be profitably studied by most persons in business, and many housewives :

" ' John, where is the address of that gentleman in the South who ordered the £5 worth of rods?' 'I don't know, sir; I have sought and sought again for it, but cannot find it.' The paper was lost through negligence, and of course the £5 order was lost also. 'Nelly, fetch the scissors,' says the mistress. Nelly runs downstairs, but soon returns, stating that the servant could not find them; that some of the lads had them yesterday, and they had not been seen since. 'It is always alike; I wonder what in the world you have done with them,' was the reply of the angry dame. The fact is, *no proper place* had ever been fixed for the scissors, and therefore no wonder they should want seeking. The apprentices were snuffing the candles with their fingers, and when asked the reason, replied, ' We have no snuffers; master bought a new pair only on Saturday night, but they are lost.' *No place* fixed for the snuffers either. For a month the stair-case door would not shut without being pushed to with violence, thus disturbing the whole family. The simple remedy was a single drop of oil to make the latch glide over the catch, which had become rusty. Perhaps a dozen locks have had to be picked in the course of the year, through the keys being lost or mislaid for want of a three-halfpenny ring to place them on. The servants had frequently four several breakfasts to cook, through some lying too long in bed, and others not minding the time. Peter was nearly blinded with his eyes full of soap for want of a towel, the servant having neglected to provide one." ‡

How many homes, especially amongst the working classes, are made miserable by the careless, thoughtless, and the unthrifty conduct of well-meaning wives! It is the *little things* done or neglected which govern the happiness of the home. A

---

* *Livesey's Moral Reformer*, 1838-9, p. 195.   † *Ibid.*, 1838-9, p. 35.
‡ *Ibid.*, 1838-9, p. 36.

careless wife, and an untidy and uncomfortable house, drive the husband to the drinkshop, and ruin the children by initiating them into the same pernicious habits. It is thus that evils are perpetuated from one generation to another. These little evils are admirably dealt with by Mr. Livesey in the following extracts from his

"MRS. MEANWELL'S LECTURES ON LITTLE THINGS":

"My female friends! I pretend to no oratory, though I belong to the sex who are said to be favoured with the gift of tongues. My coming here to-night is simply to draw your attention to a few practical remarks on matters bearing closely upon the peace and comfort of families. I leave the weightier matters to the Lords of the creation; and as it is often insinuated that we have but *little minds*, I intend to confine my address this evening to *little things*—things of course too insignificant for some minds to notice. I begin with remarking that if you who keep servants do not wish to have your carving knives spoiled with cutting up wood in the morning to light the fires, you should always provide a chip basket well supplied with kindling materials; and if they are at all damp put them in the oven over night. Never allow them to carry burning coals from the kitchen to kindle the parlour fire with, or your paper and furniture will be spoiled. The mistress should often look through the pantry to see that no cold mutton is moulded, no crusts of bread scattered abroad, no unsalted meat beginning to give out an unpleasant odour. She should see that the cinders are not thrown unriddled into the dust hole, or burnt in the afternoon, to get rid of them, when not needed. She should raise her eyes to the ceiling to observe that no spider's webs are fixed in the corners, and down again to prevent a collection of dirt under the rugs for want of shaking. The best way of scolding Nancy for getting up late in the morning is to rise early yourself. Never forget to supply the bed-room water bottle with fresh water every day. Always have your pins, needles, and thread in fixed places, so that you could lay your hands upon them in the dark. A little twine and waste paper for packages, and cards for directing parcels or trunks should always be ready. Let there be no bawling out, 'Where is the hat brush?' or, 'Where is my umbrella?' these should have a proper place and always be in their place. Get a few labels printed with your name and address on; and attach one of them inside every hat, overcoat, and umbrella. A file for your bills will prevent your losing them, and if you are economical enough to live under rather than over your means, you will pay them promptly. Paste all your receipts in a book made on purpose out of a number of old newspapers. Such papers as the *Family Herald* and the *Progressionist* are worth buying, but never begin to read them till you have put a stitch in to prevent the leaves being lost or scattered about the room. Take away old weekly newspapers as soon as the week is over, and put them in your collection of waste paper. Make a memorandum of every book you lend or borrow; and never be so thoughtless as to keep other people's books longer than you can help. I should be ashamed for a little boy to be knocking at my door with, 'If you please my mamma has sent me for the umbrella you borrowed last week but one.' Have a corner in some part of the house called the 'giving store'; there put all the papers and periodicals which you don't care to bind up, also your cast-off shoes, boots, and wearing apparel; and if you do your duty you will always find persons who will be glad even of these articles; charitable people never sell old clothes. There is nothing looks worse in a house than fly marks on a chimney glass; a sash cord broken; breakfast things on the table when preparations are making for dinner; a kitchen floor whitened with plaster of Paris, mottled with dirty foot marks; a sink stone crowded with glasses, pots, pans, tins, sand dish, soap box, dirty knives, forks, and spoons, cabbage leaves, coffee grounds, and potato peelings; or bleached window blinds turned grey again, hanging after the fashion of an inclined plane of six in twenty. Pictures may hang one five inches lower than another, and in other respects disproportioned, but visitors, though they may not speak, will scarcely omit observing these discrepancies.

"Now in giving you these admonitions (said Mrs. Meanwell), by way of making them more interesting, I will treat you to a few instances of not over good management by Betty Thoughtless, which you will do well to avoid. She lived in the country in a nice sort of a cot, if she had only had thought enough to keep it in good order. The first time I called upon her she was very much excited. Neglecting from day to day to order coals, she had borrowed from her neighbour; and upon paying her back, Betty was charged with seven coalboxes-full, while she maintained she had only had six. One dark night a conveyance came rattling to the gate; she lit the candle, put it into the lantern, but as she had neglected getting one of the glasses repaired, which the baby had broken, the candle went out. She tried again by covering the lantern with her apron, but as there was a large hole in it, the wind took advantage, and out the candle blew a second time. Betty's husband was a careful man, and though his wife was not extravagant, he wished her to keep a 'housekeeper's register'; that is, to put down in separate items their whole expenditure weekly. He said by this, as they had a family coming up, they would be able to see if their expenses upon any article were too large, and could abridge accordingly. But though he urged it upon Betty several times, and twice bought a shilling book for the purpose and commenced the entries, yet his wife excused herself, saying, 'she had really so many things to attend to she could not be bothered with bookkeeping'; besides, 'it was of no use, she could not be more careful than she was, and it looked so to be expected to put down every penny.' I often visited Betty, and talked with her; she was not very sharp, yet upon the whole there are many worse wives. She meant well, but had not been trained to think or do things orderly. For instance, if the candlestick shoot was broken it would remain so, and then there was a difficulty in lifting up the candle without waste. If the candle was too small for the stick, she would wrap a piece of newspaper round to make it steady, and just as her husband was perhaps reading some interesting passage, the paper would take fire, and an alarm ensued how to disengage it; of course a waste of tallow and a pair of dirty fingers were the consequence. Betty was a very sober woman; indeed she was a teetotaler, which reconciled her husband to many of her little infirmities; but she was fond of nettle beer which a country woman hawked about, assuring her customers that it was capital for the blood. John wondered how it was that nearly all the forks were gone out of shape, and had blamed the children (as those who cannot defend themselves generally come in for the blame), but upon close inquiry it turned out that these nettle beer bottles were corked very closely to prevent the spirit flying out, and as there were no other means of opening the bottles, his ready-witted wife had made the forks into a corkscrew. She had a great fault of giving the young child spoons and shells from the mantel-piece to play with; the former were beaten square, and the latter were knocked to pieces. Betty had never learnt the art of fire making; she seemed to think that the more coals she put on the sooner it would blaze up. Instead of laying all the fuel as loose as possible, with an opening in the centre to secure a draught, she always heaped up the centre higher than any other part. 'Plague on this fire, it will never burn,' she was saying, after having wasted half an hour one morning. Her husband, expecting the breakfast on the table, stepped in, and though he was generally good-tempered, he got into a passion, saying, 'I think some people will never learn sense; why what is it but the air that makes the fire to burn, and you have excluded it entirely; how can it burn?' The fact is, Betty had opened a newspaper and had fixed it at the front of the grate, which just filled the square of the fire-place. She innocently replied that, 'she had been told that this would do when nothing else would'; being ignorant that those who use this dangerous expedient always make a hole in the centre of the paper in order to secure a current and send a strong draught through the grate." *

Not only in his books and publications, but in leaflets and "Letter Linings"— small handbills just large enough to go into an envelope which he adopted at the time the penny post first came in—did Mr. Livesey advocate method, order, and system in domestic management. The contents of one of these "Linings" is here reprinted as a fitting summary of his teachings on the subject. It would be difficult to crowd more good advice into the same space, and perhaps impossible

---

* *Livesey's Progressionist,* 1852, p. 5.

to express it so forcibly and yet so kindly. It is questionable whether Franklin ever excelled it. The same matter was also printed on a large sheet, with an ornamental border, to be put up in the houses of the poor, and the kitchens of the better classes.

THE FAMILY MONITOR.

1. Remember and adore your Creator and Benefactor; be grateful to Him for His favours, and constantly endeavour to keep all His commands.

2. Choose your cottage in a clean, airy situation; free from damp, and as far removed as possible from bad examples.

3. Keep your walls clean, the timber painted, your beds, clothing, and persons as clean as possible.

4. Attend to the timely repairing of your furniture, your domestic utensils, and especially your clothing.

5. Put every article in its right place; call everything by its proper name; do every duty at its appointed time; and put every utensil to its own use.

6. Watch against a dependent disposition; support yourselves by your own industry; if possible, never get into debt or rely upon the charity of others.

7. Manage your affairs with care and economy; pay attention to the price, weight, measure, and quality of every article you buy.

8. Do not become weekly customers for your provisions, coals, or clothing; but secure to yourselves the advantages of buying with ready money.

9. Beware of the ruinous practice of pledging your goods, clothing, or bedding.

10. Let the husband love his wife, and provide well for her; and the wife respect and obey her husband.

11. Let the parents teach and train their children in everything which is good; and the children love one another, and obey their parents.

12. Let honesty, kindness, generosity, order, peace, and piety, be conspicuous in all your family arrangements.

CHAPTER IV.

POLITICS: THE CONSCIENTIOUS RADICAL.

> What is bad government, thou slave,
>   Whom robbers represent?
> What is bad government, thou knave,
>   Who lov'st bad government?
> It is the deadly *Will*, that takes
>   What labour ought to keep;
> It is the deadly *Power*, that makes
>   Bread *dear*, and labour *cheap.*—EBENEZER ELLIOTT.

We have the labour of Hercules in hand to abate the power of the aristocracy and their allies, the snobs of the towns.—COBDEN.

The sole object of Government ought to be the greatest happiness of the greatest possible number of the community."—BENTHAM.

ALTHOUGH Mr. Livesey was pre-eminently a moral reformer, and mainly directed his efforts to the improvement of the individual, he rendered, in his time, great services to the cause of political progress. He may be said to have brought a new element into politics, for while he strenuously fought the people's battles as a Radical, he disdained to resort to unfair or unworthy means. He would rather lose a fight honestly than win it by subterfuge or fraud. Hence in his native town to this day his political opponents speak of him as "Honest Joe Livesey," and the leading Conservative paper of the district affirms that " he well deserved the epithet." In Chapter X. of the "Autobiography" he gives some interesting reminiscences of his connexion with political contests at Preston, and expresses his disgust at the corrupt practices which too ʼoften prevail at both parliamentary and municipal elections.

During his early years he had keenly suffered, with his fellows, from the results of bad legislation—from the operation of laws enacted for the advantage of the few to the injury of the many. He saw thousands of weavers and other artisans and craftsmen struggling for a bare sustenance, the victims of monopoly and injustice; and, while he did not believe all the evils of life could be removed by improved legislation, he felt that considerable amelioration could be effected by such means. Bad laws could be repealed; irresponsible legislative power could be limited, if not put an end to; monopolies could be withdrawn, and equal political rights accorded to all good citizens. Mr. Livesey heartily set himself to work to promote these objects. He was a thorough radical, and when the late Joseph Sturge headed a movement for extending the suffrage to every adult male inhabitant, of sane mind and unstained by crime, Mr. Livesey was one of the first to declare in its favour, and in No. 10 of the *Struggle* he expresses the delight it will afford him to promote the reform throughout the country.

Instead of all classes sharing in the common benefits, as should be the case in a prosperous country, the rich were becoming richer, and the poor poorer. This unsatisfactory state of things is accounted for by Mr. Livesey as follows (the italics are his):

"Why these wide extremes—that, while numbers have been getting immensely rich, the *working people* have been reduced to the lowest state of poverty? *The laws by which wealth has been distributed are defective, and have constantly operated in favour of a* FEW, *to the ruin of the* MANY; *and the religious obligations of justice and humanity have been lost amidst the pride and avarice of the age.*"*

REASON, NOT FORCE, TO BE RELIED UPON.

While he spake out boldly, and with no "bated breath," against the political wrongs of his fellow-countrymen, he deprecated all violent measures, and exerted his influence against anything like an appeal to force. In an article upon Loyalty, in the *Moral Reformer*, Oct., 1831, Mr. Livesey utters the following wise caution:

"Do I, therefore, advocate bad government? No. But in applying a remedy let not the turbulent passions, but the *reason* of mankind, suggest the safest course. Let patience and pure patriotism, and not the vicious desire of plunder and the lust of revenge, lead the way. Let a nation, justly discontented, demonstrate its wishes by a strong and successive display of moral power; let everything be tried before physical force is appealed to. Revolutions may sometimes be attended with beneficial effects, but it is a question, balancing the evil against the good, whether, in most instances, by patience and perseverance in milder measures, greater good would not have accrued. The train of evils attendant upon a national convulsion are truly appalling; it is like reducing creation to chaos; and happy is it for those countries whose stability is secured by the honesty of their government, and whose liberty is achieved by the bloodless conquests of 'the march of mind.'"†

These words of caution were written at a time when the Tory party were using every means to prevent the passing of the Reform Bill, and when their conduct had so exasperated the unenfranchised "serfs," that very unpleasant results were apprehended. Mr. Livesey regarded the conduct of that party as amounting to disloyalty, as will be seen by the following:

"The Tory party is comprised of those who have been wont to bask in the sunshine of corruption, and whose measures have been gradually reducing the country to slavery and pauperism. The opposition of this party is sordid and selfish, arising from chagrin at the loss of the power of perpetuating a system, which, while it worked well for *them*, had well-nigh convulsed the nation. This is the cause of their disloyalty; they see in the measures now pursued by the present government, the loss of those opportunities by which their wealth has been accumulated, and their influence and arbitrary power maintained."‡

THE HOUSE OF LORDS—DANGERS OF RICH LEGISLATORS.

In the *Moral Reformer* for April, 1831, Mr. Livesey playfully alludes to the sudden conversion of opponents of parliamentary reform to that cause. "How strangely," he says, "have the enemies of reform turned round and become its supporters! And when the whole matter is impartially reviewed, it shows at once how few support or oppose a measure from personal conviction."§ Have we not seen in recent times the same tactics from the same party, which, after all, afford but another illustration of the truth that history repeats itself?

The action of the House of Lords in refusing to pass the Bill received Mr.

* *Moral Reformer*, vol. i. (1831), p. 45.   † *Ibid.*, vol. i. (1831), p. 292.
‡ *Ibid.*, vol. i. (1831), p. 293.   § *Ibid.*, vol. i. (1831), p. 119.

Livesey's well-merited condemnation. He was an out-and-out opponent of the system of hereditary legislation, and again and again pointed out how futile it was to expect from such an irresponsible body anything like honest or just legislation. The chief object of this exceptional class is to promote their own interests, and how they do that Mr. Livesey caustically indicates:

" There are many ways by which rich men increase, or retain their riches, at the expense of the poor, especially by enacting laws in their own favour. Such is the present corn-law ; such are the laws which compel the poor to assist in maintaining the poor ; such is our general system of taxation, which, instead of fixing upon the property of the great, enhances the price of almost every article of the poor man's consumption. . . . Rich legislators, uncontrolled by the popular voice, will legislate *for the rich*, and no bounds can be set to the ambition of some who have it in their power to serve themselves at the expense of the public."*

And again he remarks:

" The Lords are not of the people, though they live by them ; and how can we expect that the Peers will ever undertake to defend the cause of popular rights ? " †

POPULAR EXPECTATIONS SHOULD NOT BE UNDULY RAISED.

Mr. Livesey's mind was singularly clear and unbiassed. He rarely if ever took a narrow or partial view of a subject before him. And unlike nine-tenths of the writers and speakers upon political subjects, he never unduly raised the expectations of the people respecting the results of a proposed enactment. Leaders of both political parties invariably err in attributing the evils of society to enactments which they oppose, and in predicting benefits (almost millennial) from their own proposals. As a politician, Mr. Livesey was too philosophical to do this, and as a sincere friend of the people he was too honest to so mislead them ; and hence he warns his readers against expecting too much from the reformed parliament:

" But let no man delude himself by expecting too much. Many are so deceived as to refer *all* the evil in society to bad government, and hence are led to expect a thorough remedy from the same quarter. Composed of the best elements, no government is competent to the task ; and it would be much better if, instead of regarding the folks at London as the source of all evil, every man were to look occasionally to himself, and at the circle of his own influence. Besides, the legislature has to spring from the people, and while we find so little honesty, disinterestedness, and public spirit amongst the ruled, how can we expect these qualities in a superlative degree among the rulers ! . . . One single step in morals, affecting the whole people, would surpass a hundred new laws. . . . Make the people *better*, and the increase of legal enactments will no longer be required. But till such a change does take place, how can we expect perfect rulers ?"‡

CORRUPT PRACTICES AND THE ELECTORS' RESPONSIBILITY.

He makes a very accurate forecast of what might really be expected from the reformed parliament of 1832, unless undue influences and corrupt practices at elections were put an end to. He predicted that otherwise the "high expectation of the nation" would be disappointed.

" Members of Parliament," he says, " have to be sent by their constituents ;

* *Moral Reformer*, vol. i. (1831), pp. 235-236.   † *Ibid.*, vol. i. (1831), p. 358.
‡ *Ibid.*, vol. i. (1831), pp. 297-298.

and if the new race of electors, in returning members, pursue the abominable example of the old, what better shall we be? Instead of regarding an election as a set battle betwixt two parties, in which every base and corrupt practice is resorted to, instead of supporting and electing the man who spends the most money in bribery and drunkenness, be he ever such a dotard ; the electors in every place, to whom so important a trust is confided, ought to seek out persons who are qualified by their knowledge, talents, and tried integrity, to return them free of all expense. The man who buys his return can never be trusted ; instead of having to pay, he ought rather to be paid for his services, and he would be more likely to serve the people with a single eye to their interests. If, in choosing representatives, the people were as judicious as they are in choosing servants for themselves, we should have a really *reformed* House of Commons ; but if the electors act upon the old system, depend upon it, though we shall have a change of men, many of them will inherit the dispositions and follow in the footsteps of their unworthy predecessors."*

In an article upon Reform at Elections, Mr. Livesey unsparingly exposes and condemns the corruptions associated with Parliamentary elections before the passing of the Reform Act of 1832, and which unfortunately have been partially continued to the present time. He has the following wise and weighty words on the exercise of the franchise :

" Now when we consider that this is nothing less than the performing of an act, by which our lives and property and liberty may be considerably affected ; that it is to choose members of that legislature which is to make those laws on which, in a great measure, depends the happiness or misery of millions of the human family ;—it strikes me as being one of the most important duties of life, and ought to be performed with judgment, deliberation, seriousness, sobriety, and sincerity, and with no other view than the public good."†

ADVICE TO THE NEWLY ENFRANCHISED.

The following advice is well worth the attention of the recently enfranchised, and indeed of the electors of Great Britain and Ireland generally. If observed and carried out, the whole prospects of the nation, material, moral, and spiritual would be immeasurably improved.

" Think for yourselves, deliberate maturely, try to exercise an impartial judgment, and let truth be the object of your pursuit. Regard no man as a leader, however orthodox his opinions, unless he has *proved* himself a man of *sterling integrity.*"‡

The responsibility of the elector, as a man and a citizen, is further enforced by Mr. Livesey :

" Above all," he says, " let us try to govern and reform *ourselves*. If every man would reform *one*, 'political corruptions would soon vanish. And as there cannot be good government (properly speaking), nor a happy nation, till we have *good people*, the best policy is first to reform the mass out of which the selection is to be taken. How can we preach reform to others, unless we first reform ourselves ? and how can we consistently reproach others for neglect of duty, of which we ourselves are the most striking examples ?" §

Thirteen years later (in 1844), in reverting to the same subject in No. 140 of the *Struggle* :

" I wish," he says, " we could teach the electors to be honest. This is all that is wanting to cure the political evils under which we labour ; and, indeed, all that is wanting to secure to the people the rights for which they have long contended.

* *Moral Reformer*, vol. i. (1831), p. 120.　　† *Ibid.*, vol. i. (1831), p. 27.
‡ *Ibid.*, vol. i. (1831), p. 299.　　§ *Ibid.*, vol. i. (1831), p. 301.

If the electors, instead of selling themselves for meat, drink, or money—instead of voting to obtain or to retain employment—to gain this man's custom or to avoid losing that—would honestly support the best candidates, all the measures calculated to benefit the country would soon be carried. We should, therefore, constantly strive, before the election arrives, to bring men's minds up to this point of independency. An election, instead of being looked upon as a season for party fights and beastly gratification, should be regarded as an important moment, when the destinies of the country are placed in the hands of the electors, and when all that is good and sacred should be called forth to enable them to do their duty."

CANDIDATES' BLAND AND WINNING WAYS.

The arts resorted to by candidates for parliamentary honours to win the electors are painted in vivid colours by Mr. Livesey in an address to electors (*Struggle*, No. 49).   He says:

"I wish I could induce you to feel more *the importance of your station*. Others see it. They address you as 'gentlemen,' as 'brave and independent electors.' They court your company; they visit your houses; they run after you into any dirty street; they shake you by the hand; they fawn upon and flatter you; they smile and talk to your wives, and pat your children on the head; they invite you to supper; nay, they even *open their purses*, and you have only to say what you wish, and it is at your service. I mention this merely to convince you of your importance. You should know that the lives and liberty of the people are in your hand. Whilst others are courting you for their *own* ends, let me beg that you place *your country's prosperity* before you, as *your only object*."

DISAFFECTED RADICALS, TRADING POLITICIANS, AND INSINCERE AGITATORS.

Of disaffected Radicals, a class which will always exist, and which readily becomes the tool of designing traders in politics—those self-constituted friends of the masses whose activity is measured by their pay, and who are always ready to sell their clients, to either Tory or Whig—Mr. Livesey says:—

"There are some [Radicals] whose disaffection is purely the offspring of vicious feelings and profligate habits, and these, alas! too often assume the character of leaders; but *poverty*, in most instances, is the reason of the opposition which government receives from this class. But here I beg distinctly to say that, at *present*, it is poverty accompanied by *deception*, arising from the want of the means of obtaining correct information. . . . Exasperated by the pressure of their circumstances, and unable, therefore, to take a deliberate and comprehensive view of political changes, they suffer themselves to be misled by their own feelings or by designing persons. Inattentive to the tremendous task of changing the current of national policy, unless they feel the benefit *immediately*, they raise a disaffected clamour, and by thus weakening the hands of a reforming government increase the delay of those very measures in which their own amelioration is involved. I sincerely sympathise with them in their sufferings, and am looking with intense anxiety to those measures which I know will afford them relief, particularly the abolition of the corn tax, and all the taxes which press upon the industry and the articles of consumption of the working class."*

The following is a fair and honest way to treat extremists and agitators who would beguile the people into courses they are not prepared to follow themselves.

"INCAUTIOUS ADVICE.—I constantly receive papers both in prose and poetry urging the people onward to '*demand their rights*.'† Now this all sounds well on paper; but I should like to know what it means; it is not right to deceive the people or lead them into error, by loose and inflammatory generalities. Is it

---

*. *Moral Reformer*, vol. i. (1831), p. 294.
† These papers emanated from the physical-force Chartists.

meant that they are to organize and fight? If so, I ask the writers, are *they* prepared to come and *take the lead*? Don't urge the people to what you will not face yourselves. If this is not the meaning, why adopt language calculated to deceive? Rather entreat them to join in some legal, tangible movement, which has already done good, and which promises to be still more useful." [*]

FACTORY ACTS, FREE LABOUR, EMIGRATION, AND MALTHUSIANISM.

Mr. Livesey differed from many of his political colleagues upon the question of legislative interference with factory labour, and gave the movement led by Oastler his hearty support. In his *Moral Reformer* he says:

"I deprecate confined, monotonous labour for children, and never think but with horror of the number of children, of eight, nine, or ten years of age, who are turned out these cold dreary mornings, half-naked and half-fed, to be confined in a polluted atmosphere, till seven or eight in the evening." [†]

But although he supported that movement, he disagreed with Trades' unions and combinations of workpeople calculated to interfere with the freedom of labour. Whether his views upon this question were modified or changed in later years does not appear; but his attitude at that time is explicitly stated in the annexed extract from "an Address to Working Men" (*Livesey's Moral Reformer*, March 31st, 1838).

"*Let industry be free*," he pleads, "let no man encroach upon the liberty of his fellow-workmen, by interfering with his right to enter into any employment he pleases, and at such wages as he may think proper to accept. And instead of keeping up the value of labour, by unions and combinations, or instead of foolishly expecting Government to fix a rate of wages, let us, by all the means in our power, endeavour to increase the supply of employment, so that every labourer may obtain an equitable and a remunerative price for his work. Instead of petitioning Parliament to fix a minimum of wages, which, were it attempted, would certainly be evaded, I would prefer petitioning all the *English* and *Irish absentees* to come home, and engaging the capital enterprise, and sobriety of the country, to find work for every unemployed man in the kingdom." [‡]

Emigration he regarded as a temporary expedient rendered necessary by bad legislation and defective social arrangements. He would rather provide for the emigration of the drone than of the working bee. He says:

"As to emigration, ought we, I ask, tacitly to approve of such a system of national mismanagement, as to render it imperative upon the poor man to transport himself, because of his poverty? If he has not a comfortable home, let us try to make him one, but let him not be banished from the place of his birth. His labour is the price of his citizenship, and he is the last man to whom it should be said 'you had better be gone, we can do better without you.'" [§]

For the cold, heartless system of Malthus, Mr. Livesey had the most intense disgust. The evils sought to be remedied by limiting the population, he would deal with in a very different fashion. The corrupters of society, the vicious, and the profligate—these he would call to account. Of Malthusians he says:

"These reasoners condemn the working man, because, in conformity to all that is honourable among men, and acceptable to God, though the greatest producer of wealth, he presumes to marry and have children. If a curse is to rest upon the

[*] *The Struggle*, (1842) No. 22, p. 4.   [†] *Vol. i.* (1831), p. 73.
[‡] *Livesey's Moral Reformer*, p. 98.   [§] *Moral Reformer* (1831), vol. i. p. 39.

poor man who, amid his cares and toils, takes a lovely companion to cheer the rugged path of life, whom God favours with a numerous offspring, for whose support he labours with hard industry,—what shall we say of thousands, who corrupt society by their licentiousness, produce nothing to add to the general stock, but, individually, destroy as much as would support fifty poor families." *

But, while holding these views, Mr. Livesey strongly opposed the premature and improvident marriages common among young factory hands, artizans and labourers; unions which are a source of unhappiness to the parties themselves, the occasion of burden to the community, and a means of race deterioration.

SMALL AGRICULTURAL HOLDINGS AND ALLOTMENTS.

Mr. Livesey was especially severe upon the Enclosure Acts, passed by the landlords with the object of appropriating to themselves the uncultivated land of the country. He might, perhaps, be inclined to be lenient towards the man who stole "a goose from off a common"; but it was quite another matter for him to forgive the crime committed against the poor by him who stole "the common from the goose."

Just now attention is being invited to a scheme for the promotion of allotments and small holdings amongst agricultural labourers. It is proposed to buy land in large quantities and divide it up into small lots, and either to let or sell it to persons who will undertake its cultivation. As several large landowners have approved the scheme, it is most likely to be practically tested. At the time Feargus O'Connor's land scheme was under consideration, Mr. Livesey evidently examined the question very carefully, and while he was favourable to all cottagers having gardens wherever practicable, he came to the conclusion that the small holding system was a very fallacious means of improving the condition of the agricultural labourer. In an article in No. 151 of the *Struggle* (1844), he discusses the subject, and his words deserve to be well pondered. By the term allotment, Mr. Livesey meant a small holding, cultivated as a partial means of livelihood. He says:

"The least consideration will show that the allotment system, if extensively carried out, would stagnate labour exactly on those spots where that is least wanted, because it is alone where there is a redundant population that its need is apparent. The consequence of such an inducement to a further accumulation of labourers in such districts could only be, to reduce still further the rate of wages. . . . As there would be no more land to till, with an increasing number of labourers, and as at present there is not employment sufficient for all ; the mere fact of sub-dividing large fields into small allotments, would only have the effect of increasing that want of regular employment, in the proportion that the allotments were general or large ; and it is only in proportion as they are so, that they could promote the object in view. In proportion, therefore, as you apply the cure, you increase the evil, while you create a tie to the spot, which must effectually prevent that voluntary circulation of labour which is the only true cure for a redundant population."

WHERE THE SHOE REALLY PINCHED—THE INCIDENCE OF TAXATION.

Mr. Livesey saw clearly where the shoe pinched the masses, and he as clearly described what he saw. The temporising expedients suggested for improving the condition of the people by those who were relentlessly heaping taxes upon the wage-earning class, never found in him an advocate. He steadily directed attention to the

* *Moral Reformer*, vol. i. (1831), p. 41.

inequitable system of taxation devised by rich legislators. Writing in 1831, he says:

"Taxes should always press easily upon the necessaries of life, and upon those home manufactured articles, in which the principal expense of production is labour . . . The assessed taxes are not only vexatious, but operate against employment in various ways. *Property* and not *poverty*, in my opinion, ought to bear taxes. . . . I maintain that *property*, in whatsoever shape it exists, and *not labour*, should be taxed. . . . The monopolies which are kept up in the country, to enrich a few at the expense of the many—such as the game monopoly, the church patronage monopoly, the corporation monopoly, and, above all, the East India monopoly, ought, for the sake of the country, to be dealt with as they deserve." *

In his *Struggle* (1841-6) he constantly reverted to this important question, and in No. 67 of that valuable and widely circulated periodical, he presents the monstrous fraud perpetrated by rich legislators on the poor, in the following striking and conclusive manner. It should not be forgotten that the injustice is still maintained, and has yet to be overthrown ; a work which will probably occupy the early attention of a reformed House of Commons. Mr. Livesey says :

" If ever you hear a man boast a deal about his honesty, you may almost safely put him down as a rogue. It is the same with the landowners. All their talk about special burdens seems but a covering for the burdens they have taken from themselves and placed upon other people's shoulders. . . . I may state that the land, with all its pretended burdens, has increased in value at least fivefold in a century and a half. In 1692, the value of land rental was £6,500,000 ; in 1771, it was estimated by Arthur Young at £16,000,000. In 1815, it was ascertained by the property tax returns to be £34,330,462, exclusive of mines, minerals, and fisheries. This increase has not been owing to the exertions of the landowners themselves, but to the increase of trade and population. But while the value of land has been increasing, and the taxes have also increased, instead of land bearing its share, other classes have been taxed.

" Although land has generally been considered in all countries as the fairest object of taxation, as it undoubtedly is, yet in England it pays less in proportion to other interests, than in any other country. To this, the following statement will speak :—

Comparative State Taxation of England and other Countries.

Taxes upon land in England	... ...	£1,531,215
Taxes upon land in Prussia	... ...	3,992,500
Taxes upon land in Austria	... ...	8,700,000
Taxes upon land in France	... ...	23,186,760
Taxes on the people in England ...	...	£50,695,044 !!
Taxes on the people in Prussia	... ...	3,761,500
Taxes on the people in Austria	... ...	7,700,000
Taxes on the people in France	... ...	17,533,240

" Agriculturists should never refer to the Land Tax. It does them no credit. It is not much ; but when inquired into, it proves that instead of being called a burden, it ought to be placed among exemptions. In 1796, when the whole revenue was short of £5,000,000, the land was valued, and a tax of 4s. in the pound imposed, which then made £1,800,000 ; and though the land has continued to rise rapidly in rental, yet the *old valuation* has still been retained to the present time ; and now, [1843], when the revenue exceeds £52,000,000, the sum derived from this source is but £1,500,000 ! "

RELIGIOUS LIBERTY AND DISESTABLISHMENT.

Mr. Livesey was a strenuous and consistent dissenter. He opposed all compulsory demands for religious purposes, and resisted Church Rates and Easter Dues

* *Moral Reformer*, vol. i. (1831), p. 46.

as scrupulously as a Quaker. He submitted again and again to be despoiled of his goods rather than pay these unrighteous demands. *The Preston Chronicle*, for March 25th, 1826, contains a letter of Mr. Livesey's, addressed to the Vicar, upon Easter Dues and Mortuary Extortions. . The writer points out the popish origin of the latter charge, and appeals to the Vicar, in the interests of Christianity, " to forego these petty claims, and, rather than summons and go to law with your brethren, to be henceforth found healing the wounds which your severity has inflicted." An appeal which was evidently disregarded, for I write with a summons, dated June 26th of that year, before me ; in which Joseph Livesey, cheesefactor, is declared to be indebted, to the Rev. Roger Carus Wilson, in the sum of sixpence halfpenny. Which amount, with costs, etc. increasing it several hundred per cent., of course the said Joseph Livesey had to pay.

On page 52 of his " Autobiography," Mr. Livesey refers to his resistance of Easter Dues on several occasions. Finally, he tells us, " he was let alone." The last occasion on which he was troubled, appears to have been in 1843. In No. 85 of the *Struggle* he announces that the vicar of Preston, by his agents, had entered his premises and shouldered eighty-seven pounds of cheese, because he had resisted a claim of one shilling and three pence. On refusal to pay, ten shillings costs were immediately added to the original sum, and in about a fortnight, says Mr. Livesey, " this holy claim from our popular Church had increased 2,400 per cent !" In the course of the biting article referred to Mr. Livesey says :

" I freely forgive the vicar, and the cheese I resign, after many others, as a memento of spiritual wickedness in high places. This occasion has afforded me an opportunity of expressing my protest against clerical oppression, and this to me is far more valuable than eighty-seven pounds of cheese. When I consider that what was originally a *freewill* offering, is now converted into a *demand*—that the services with which it was associated are abandoned, and yet the payment retained ; when I see the poor widow in the *cellar* met by the spiritual tax gatherer for an amount equal to the lady who rides in her carriage ; when I see such paltry sums insisted upon, as would be scouted if practised by any individual except a clergyman ; when I see religion prostrated at the footstool of mammon ;—against such enormities I can never cease to raise my humble voice ; and I truly rejoice that in this case I am the *sufferer* and not the man who makes others suffer."

Years before we had a Disestablishment Society, Mr. Livesey was at work promoting the separation of Church and State. In his eyes the Church was not merely a negative evil, it was a positive one. In the Preface to Vol. I. of the *Moral Reformer*, dated Dec. 1st, 1831, he takes the following unmistakable ground :

" In tracing the immediate and distant causes of the evils which afflict this country, I could not pass over the Established Church ; and without a single ill-feeling towards any of its members, I have not attempted to disguise my conviction, that it is one of the greatest obstacles to the peace, unanimity, and happiness of the people."

And he remained to the end of his career a consistent friend of the freedom of religion from state patronage and control, advocating disestablishment in his magazines and papers, and promoting the movement in all suitable ways. Various interests are linked together in supporting a State Church, and others besides the clergy have a vested interest in its continuance. This Mr. Livesey saw, and in commenting upon the fraternal spirit which exists between members of the three professions—the Church, the law, and physic—he says:

> "It is the neglect of the religious tutor that sends so many to the attorney and not a few in addition to the care of the physician. If a minister loved his people, and was loved by them, dwelling in their midst supported by their liberality, and always sowing the seeds of peace and unity, and teaching them industry, temperance, and every Christian virtue, the people would seldom want the physician, and much seldomer the lawyer. It is clearly in the power of the parsons (if they were of the right sort) materially to injure the other professions, and therefore the gentlemen interested ought never to pray for Church Reform."[*]

IRELAND, HER WRONGS AND THEIR REMEDIES.

In 1829 Mr. Livesey visited Ireland with a view of becoming personally acquainted with the condition of things in that unfortunate country. He spent a fortnight in Dublin and neighbourhood, and was agreeably surprised to find the Irish very different from what they had been represented to him. *Generosity* he found to be their leading virtue, and *lying* their chief vice. The hotels of Dublin struck him as being much more comfortable than those of England. The car drivers appeared to be a dirty set, and Mr. Livesey was highly amused with many incidents he met with regarding them. "I saw O'Connell," he says, "riding from the Exchange one day under the guidance of a hearty fellow of this stamp, whose whip consisted of a piece of old rope with a bushy end, tied on to a rude hedge-stake." But Mr. Livesey did not go on a pleasure trip, and he tells us something about the Irish worth knowing. He says:

> "The prejudice with which I set out from home was, that I was going amongst a people next akin to barbarians, amongst whom *life* itself was constantly in jeopardy; and I was cautioned by my friends, above everything not to be out at night, lest I should be murdered. But on this point I confess I was much mistaken, and from the moment I set my foot on Irish ground I saw my delusion. And though Dublin and the neighbourhood may not afford a fair specimen of the character of the people in some parts of the country, I am still inclined to attribute most of the cruelties committed to the unjust provocation of their enemies. Though cruel in revenge, the Irish are certainly not forward to *give* offence. No kinder people exist if kindness is shown to them, and yet none more determined to resent an injury and to resist the authority of the oppressor; and this accounts for the excesses which sometimes take place in reference to the collection of tithes and other impositions. But it is to the English newspapers, principally, that we are indebted for the impressions we have received of the character of the Irish nation. In them we have regularly an article headed 'Ireland'; and every instance of outrage, collected from the Irish papers, with the exaggerated comments of the editors, is carefully detailed; and thus published together, and sent forth without a single redeeming statement, a decidedly false impression is produced upon the minds of the English. Indeed, so magnifying are the powers of the 'broad-sheet,' that events which have scarcely a reality in the minds of competent judges are not unfrequently ushered forth as of awful importance. If the enormities committed in this country were carefully reported and placed in one focus under the head of 'England,' in my opinion Ireland would lose nothing by the comparison."

In spite of the country's great natural advantages, Mr. Livesey found on every hand evidences of decay and ruin. Yet he could not but think, with a poet of the people, that—

> ————a merry world it might be, opulent for all and aye,
> With its lands that ask for labour, and its wealth that wastes away.[†]

----

[*] *Moral Reformer* (1832), vol. ii. p. 22.   [†] Gerald Massey.

And regarding remedies for Irish wrongs and weaknesses, he makes the following suggestions, which might be considered with advantage by the statesman of to-day to whom the political regeneration of the " Green Isle " is still an unsolved problem:

" Instead of *providing* for poverty, why not try rather to *prevent* it? Instead of providing *conveniences* for this demon of wretchedness, let us do what we can to expel him. Remove every just cause of discontent, restore quietness to the country, and *make it a safe abode for capital;* this, connected with moral culture, will do much towards ameliorating the condition of the people. Let government grants, and the proceeds of all property under its control, be spent upon enclosing and improving the land, which will not only find employment in the first place, but continue every year to be a constant source of labour. When I think of the universal cry for *labour;* of the millions of acres which might be cultivated or planted ; and at the same time of the millions of money sunk in raising massive buildings in every part of Great Britain and Ireland, which stand there yielding scarcely any *employment* to the labourers of the country, I feel indignant at the gross misapplication of the nation's wealth. It is *employment* that is wanted; create this extensively, and pauperism hides its face. As to the questions of the *church* and *tithes,* a wise, honest, and strong government would decide the matter shortly.

" Let each religious party, it would say, enjoy its privileges uninterrupted, let it be equally protected and eligible to the honours and emoluments of the state ; but as to *property,* which has been so long a source of contention, animosity, and even bloodshed, and which is always found inimical to the interests of true religion, we, as the rightful trustees, take it under our own care, and will apply it *to the support of the poor,* to the furnishing of employment to all who are able to work, or to any other national purpose which the fairly elected representatives of the nation may appoint.

" It is bread, not *bishops;* employment, not charity ; kindness, not coercion, that Ireland needs ; she must be ruled, not by the iron hand of despotism, but by the gentle laws of reason and persuasion ; and to effect her real advancement, party spirit must subside and national and moral principles be more widely diffused among all classes."*

MR. JOHN BRIGHT.

While as a politician, Mr. Livesey believed in measures rather than in men, with the farmer in " Festus " he thought—

Some little may depend upon the men,

and when Mr. Bright was elected as Member for Durham, in a few words he portrayed the leading characteristics of that eminent statesman, whose parliamentary career, extending over forty years, has amply justified the forecast:

" Any town in the kingdom," says Mr. Livesey, " would feel honoured by having such a man to represent its interests in Parliament. The election of this gentleman is a valuable testimony in favour of commercial freedom, and an appropriate mark of respect for his indefatigable labour to promote it. There are few John Brights ; few so honest, so eloquent, so devoted to the people's cause. Such, where they are found, are the men that ought to be placed in power to legislate for the people." †

THE STRANGERS' GALLERY.

The strangers' gallery is not the place for a reformer. It is slow and tedious, and is apt to give an earnest man a very poor opinion of the Legislature. Mr. Livesey found it so in July, 1842, when he visited it. He says:

" I was in the House of Commons on the Friday evening when Mr. Cobden

* *Moral Reformer,* vol. ii. (1831), pp. 69, 70, and 81.   † *The Struggle,* No. 85 p. 3.

delivered his admirable speech on Mr. Wallace's motion for inquiring into the distress of the country. There are several things that astonish a stranger when he attends the House of Commons. He finds himself pent up in a cock-loft, called a gallery, which holds about eighty persons, removed so far from the speakers that he frequently cannot hear so as to understand a single sentence. He is also astonished at the disorder and levity of the honourable and right honourable gentlemen who are privileged with seats in this House. A very few manage the business, and others come in and go out, and beguile the time as best they can. Such was the buzz in the House, that it was difficult to hear gentlemen of only ordinary standing, but when Mr. Cobden spoke there was profound silence. He is a clear, powerful, energetic speaker; understands his subject well, and feels the responsibility of his situation. He delights his friends, and makes his opponents tremble."

The exhibition was not one, however, which he cared for, and he remarks:

" Few who spend a whole evening in the House of Commons will be anxious to sacrifice a second night. Pledged by interest to support themselves and the interests of land, the great body of the members consider the discussion relating to manufactures as a great annoyance. But while we blame the House, can we avoid blaming those who sent them ? " *

Among the specific legislative reforms advocated by Mr. Livesey, which space will only permit a mere mention of, were—the total repeal of all taxes on knowledge, the election of magistrates by the people, the abolition of negro slavery in our colonies, such a revision of the criminal law as would bring it into accordance with humane and benevolent principles, the reduction of the national expenditure, and the removal of imposts on all commodities of consumption. His services to his country as Corn Law repealer were, however, of such an exceptional character that they are reserved for the next chapter.

* The Struggle, No. 30, p. 2.

CHAPTER V.

THE CORN LAW REPEALER.

The Corn Law is an extension of the pension list to the whole of the landed aristocracy of Great Britain.—*The Times.*

A far better case could be made out for a bounty to increase the importation of corn, than for a duty to restrain it.—J. DEACON HUME.

What the landlords really say (by maintaining the Corn Law) is, "Let *us* rob you all, and then you shall rob one another." This is the bargain they offer. . . . Two points are their laws and their gospel: one, that they will not pay taxes and other people shall; the other, that fortunes shall be made for them at the expense of other people.—COL. P. T. THOMPSON.

Each successive Corn Law has in fact been a new and cruel deception to the unhappy farmer; yet to each has he looked with renewed confidence for his salvation. . . . The first evil which the Corn Laws have inflicted on the farmer has been—*they have induced him to contract to pay rents which—except in years of scarcity—the price of wheat will not enable him to pay;* the second great mischief which they inflict upon him is, *that they spoil his market by impoverishing his customers;* the third, that *they depress prices just when his stock of corn is largest, and when he is most anxious to realize, and raise them when he has none to sell.*—W. R. GREG.

IF the Free Trade question is to be understood in its most important bearings, it will be necessary to keep in view the circumstances under which the Corn Law was enacted in 1815. The European wars in which we were engaged for so many years had artificially enhanced the price of agricultural produce, of course to the detriment of the people. War taxes were imposed, not on property, but—as Mr. Livesey would have said—on poverty. Indeed, the owners of land not only escaped additional taxation, they really profited by circumstances which were disastrous to all other classes. This is a matter of fact and not of opinion, and Southey, Tory though he was, admits its truth. He says:

"Heavy as the taxes were during the war, the rents of land were raised in more than an adequate proportion; a disposition too generally prevailed to exact from the tenant the largest possible sum."[*]

Mr. Livesey furnishes a striking illustration of the way this policy affected the farmer, in the following painful case of individual hardship. He relates:

"A decent-looking old man, 73 years of age, called to show me a letter he had received from his parish, in answer to an application for relief. He said that he had been a farmer eighteen years; that since he failed he had struggled hard to get a living by selling eggs, etc., but found he could no longer support himself. He had brought up fourteen children. The farm he had lived upon, previous to his taking it, let for either £80 or £90 a year. He took it at £105, for seven years. At the end of that term, he took it again for a similar term, at £120. During these two 'tacks' he did very well. Then came high prices during the war. He took a third seven years' lease, at £240 a year. He remained only four years, and was then sold up. The farm is now let for £160, and the only consolation offered the man, in his old age, is an order of admission into the Union Workhouse!"[†]

[*] "Essays, Moral and Political" (London, 1832), vol. i. p. 310. [†] *The Struggle*, No. 3.

HOW THE CORN LAW WAS ENACTED.

A legislature mainly composed of men, who on the one hand had availed themselves of a national calamity to increase their rent roll; while on the other they had so manipulated the incidence of taxation as to relieve their own class of the cost of wars which had greatly benefited them, might naturally be expected to attempt by legislation the maintenance of war-prices. And this they did by enacting the Corn Law.

Mr. Livesey was not in the habit of using strong language, but it is noticeable that in his "Autobiography" he speaks of the "cursed Corn Law." The indecent haste with which the Bill was hurried through both Houses of Parliament, deprecated by Mr. Livesey, was censured in other and very different quarters. Southey, who cannot be charged with pandering to the people, may be again quoted on this point. He took an equally strong view of the proceeding, and regarded the question as a speculative one, "to be considered at leisure, and dispassionately investigated in indifferent [*i.e.*, calm] times"; instead of which he complains that "it was brought forward as a practical question of immediate vital importance, and debated with all the blind vehemence of private interest and popular prejudice." *

MR. LIVESEY AN EARLY REPEALER.

Mr. Livesey was an active and persistent advocate of the repeal of the Corn Law several years before the League existed. In his "Autobiography" he devotes Chapter IV. to the question, and on page 21 he quotes from his *Moral Reformer* for March, 1831, a startling paragraph on "Weavers' Wages and Corn Laws." In the following issue of his magazine occurs an article upon "The Question of Questions for Politicians," in which he pleads, as was ever his wont, for the oppressed, the down-trodden, and the poor,—to whose cause, he says, government "*has never yet done justice.*" Regarding the franchise question as good as settled, he urges the people to be true to themselves, and to—

"**Fix** upon *the abolition of the Corn Laws*, as the rallying point, and never be driven from it until they get cheap bread. . . . *The removal of all oppressive burdens from the land, and the repeal of the Corn Laws, is your only hope,* and for these you ought to cry with all your remaining strength. Patriots of England! merge all your differences into sympathy and love for your suffering countrymen, and be determined *to discuss no other subject*, to make every other political question subordinate, and to give government no rest, till JUSTICE be done to the industrious tribes of Britain." †

In both the first and second series of the *Moral Reformer* Mr. Livesey kept the topic well before his readers, and by occasional addresses he further agitated the question. He advocated the repeal of the Corn Laws and the destruction of monopolies, on the broad ground of political justice. When the Anti-Corn-Law League was started, he joined it, and for some years acted as Honorary Secretary to the Preston Branch of the League. He threw his whole energies into the movement, rendering it services which cannot be over-estimated.

* "Essays, Moral and Political," vol. i. (London, 1832), p. 309.
† *Moral Reformer*, vol. i. (1831), p. 110.

A WEEKLY ILLUSTRATED NEWSPAPER FOR A HALFPENNY.

Mr. Livesey's inventive genius led him to adopt several novel methods of agitation. Feeling that the Press might be made to render more efficient services than it had yet done, in December, 1841, he devised and started a small illustrated weekly paper—*The Struggle*—consisting of four pages about the size of *Punch*, published at one halfpenny. On the first page of the first number appears the following introductory notice:

The character of this paper is indicated by its title—*The Struggle*. Good and evil, truth and error, are constantly struggling against each other. The struggle is now betwixt *Free Trade* and *Monopoly*; and I feel anxious to render my feeble aid in assisting to overthrow the monstrous power of monopoly. Though this Paper will at present *struggle* for *Cheap Bread*, it may occasionally step aside to contend with other evils. It has no connexion with any association, and no person is responsible for its contents but myself.—J. Livesey.

Like all Mr. Livesey's papers and publications *The Struggle* was independent, and entirely free from the control of any organization. It was designed to instruct and interest the people in the question, and it admirably effected that object. Its illustrations, roughly executed, were often spirited, and they always conveyed a truth, or gave point and emphasis to some phase of the agitation. Each issue of *The Struggle* was numbered but not dated; and as each paper was complete in itself, and contained brief articles and pointed paragraphs illustrative of the pernicious results of monopoly and the sufferings imposed on the people by the Corn Laws, the publication could be effectively distributed long after its date of issue. To persons taking quantities it was supplied at 2*s*. 6*d*. per hundred. The weight of *The Struggle* permitted its being enclosed in an ordinary letter; and readers were urged to forward it in that way to the next friend they wrote to. By this plan it reached the remotest country regions.

At the time Mr. Livesey commenced *The Struggle*, the League's only organ was the *Anti-Bread-Tax Circular*, a small fortnightly publication; and nearly two years elapsed before its weekly newspaper, *The League*, published at 3*d*., was started. According to Mr. Prentice, the sale circulation of *The League* was about 5,000.*

In the 53rd number of *The Struggle*, Mr. Livesey reminds his readers that the paper had been in existence a year, and tells them that "nearly five hundred thousand impressions have been issued," that he has had, from various sources, evidences of its usefulness; and that it had taken its stand in the "aggressive ranks *of bread reformers*." He also announces his determination to continue the holy warfare:

"With no pretensions to literary attainments," he says, "I shall go on in my plain way, sternly defending the truths of *free commerce*, and endeavouring to expose, one by one, all the objections and fallacies which are promulgated to obstruct its course."

* Mr. Prentice says: "It was resolved to expend £10,000 a year in distributing amongst 10,000 subscribers of one pound and upwards to the fund, a full-sized weekly newspaper, to be called *The League*, instead of a small fortnightly publication called *The Anti-Bread-Tax Circular*. . . . The first number . . . appeared on Saturday, September 30th, 1843." By January, 1845, the number of copies sent weekly to subscribers was 15,000. (History of the Anti-Corn-Law League, vol. ii. pp. 117-231.)

At the end of another year Mr. Livesey made a similar declaration, as may be
seen from the fac-simile reproduction of the first page of No. 105, here inserted.

THE STRUGGLE.

This number of *The Struggle* commences the third
year of its publication. It was not expected, at its
commencement, to remain in the field so long. But,
sustained by public approval, it has continued weekly
defending and illustrating the principles of free trade,
and assailing the strongholds of monopoly. The circulation of *eleven hundred thousand* copies of the *Struggle*
has contributed some little to the "Great Fact" which
is now astounding the nation. It commences a new
year with no diminished ardour; and the *Struggler*
never intends to lay down his weapons, in one shape or
another, until he see the monster Monopoly prostrate
on the field.

J. LIVESEY.

No. 105.

During its second year's existence, the circulation of *The Struggle* had increased
by one hundred thousand. Altogether there were two hundred and thirty-five

numbers of this little journal issued, and the maximum circulation attained was fifteen thousand. Taking twelve thousand as the average circulation throughout the period of its existence, which would be a very fair estimate, the aggregate number of copies of the paper issued would amount to TWO MILLIONS EIGHT HUNDRED AND TWENTY THOUSAND!

Those who are conversant with popular movements will know what a drag a weekly organ is upon the funds, and the value of Mr. Livesey's work will be better realized when it is understood that for four and a half years he sustained the most popular journal the Free Trade movement ever had. The first page of No. 105 has been selected for reproduction, chiefly on account of the character of the engraving, which was more adapted for reduction than the majority of the illustrations. It will give the reader a better idea of the appearance of the paper, than he could gather from any verbal description.

THE TERRIBLE PRIVATIONS OF " PROTECTION " TIMES.

The advocates of Fair Trade—a euphonious term for the re-imposition of a bread tax—have very little conception of the condition of the people under the *régime* of protection. Indeed, it is impossible at this time to fully realize their sad state. Privation and suffering were stamped upon their forms and faces; nor did the children escape. Ebenezer Elliott, in describing a gala-day and procession at Preston, says :

> The day was fair, the cannon roar'd,
>   Cold blew the bracing north,
> And Preston Mills, by thousands, poured
>   Their little captives forth.
>
> All in their best they paced the street,
>   All glad that they were free;
> And sung a song with voices sweet, as
>   They sung of liberty !
>
> But from their lips the rose had fled,
>   Like " death-in-life " they smiled ;
> And still, as each passed by, I said,
>   Alas ! is that a child ?

Mr. Livesey, in his *Struggle*, constantly reverted to this sad side of the question. In No. 2 occurs the following paragraph indicative of the straits into which people were brought about the end of 1841 :

"A poor woman came to visit her relations in Preston. She went to nine houses, and none of them could afford her a meal's meat; the last place she called at was in Albert Street, where the man pawned his shirt for 6*d*., with which four pennyworth of bread, one pennyworth of butter, and one pennyworth of tea were purchased for the party."

The cut which occupies the front page of No. 61, represents a poor family consisting of father, mother, and four children, about to sit down to dinner. Sit down, however, is hardly the term, since the room contains but one chair, and that is occupied by the father. The woman is in the act of emptying potatoes from a saucepan into a dish; there is nothing else on the table but salt, but the children look delighted. The mother cautions them not to " be greedy," and says that they " seem to *rejoice* as much in their potatoes as if they had tasted nothing all day." One child exclaims, " Ay, mam, pratoes are good— I wish we had always plenty of them." The father remarks, " Poor things, it is a hard case that we who *work most* should be *worst fed.*" The working classes, among whom *The Struggle* extensively circulated, could understand this kind of thing, and even those who could not read were instructed by the illustrations. The Pro-Corn-Law party brought every kind of influence to bear upon working people, especially upon agricultural labourers, to keep them in ignorance of the real merits of the question. The people were continually told that in no other country was there so much happiness as in England. Mr. Livesey's way of treating these would-be instructors illustrates his method of—

CALLING A SPADE A SPADE.

"A Thumper.—An ordinary lie, even in the mouth of a Duke, is unworthy of notice; but the following ought to be duly recorded; it may yet be of use: ' I have passed my life in foreign countries, in different parts of the world, and *this* is the only country I have ever been in, in which the *poor man*, if only sober and industrious, *is quite certain of acquiring a competency.*' Sound faith, it is said, will always produce corresponding works. And hence the Duke's declaration accounts for his liberal conduct to the sufferers at Paisley." *

Lord Ashley (afterwards Shaftesbury) came in for a considerable share of banter. In one of the illustrations (*The Struggle*, 161) his lordship is represented as administering a bath to a hungry man with a view to strengthening his *appetite*, and the poor fellow exclaims, "God bless me, my lord, that's just what I complain of: I have got the *appetite;* what I want is the food." Other aristocratic friends of the people—notably the Duke of Norfolk—prescribed "curry powder" as diet for the starving masses, and these and all similar nostrum-mongers were dealt with as they deserved to be by Mr. Livesey.

HOW LANDLORDS MIGHT EDUCATE THEMSELVES.

In No. 102 of *The Struggle*, Mr. Livesey suggests to landlords and legislators desirous of being enlightened, the following plan of education on the question:

"You talk a great deal about the harvest being ' sufficient ' or ' insufficient ' for our wants; and calculate how many quarters of foreign grain may be needed to get us the year over. Now I fear you know nothing of the extent of want and scant which exists among the poor. But in order to come to a clear understanding, I propose that you *board* yourselves for one month at the tables of your agricultural labourers. Just try it; it is worth while; for the experience you would get would qualify you for legislating far more than going to an agricultural dinner, or riding after the hounds."

His pointed and pithy articles, of which the following is an illustration, appealed at once to the working-class reader.

" WHAT DOES THE CORN LAW DO?

" *What does the Corn Law do for the agricultural labourer?* It increases the price of his food, but by impoverishing the farmer, prevents him receiving wages sufficient to purchase it with.

" *What does the Corn Law do for the farmer?* It compels him to pay a high rent, and high taxes; it makes his own living dear; enhances the price of every article he has to buy; and, by injuring trade, keeps all the farmers on the sod, bidding over one another's heads for farms.

" *What does the Corn Law do for the landlord?* It enables him to get high rents; furnishes him with the means of living luxuriously without improving his land. He receives by the operation of the law, what he ought to secure by the merit of his exertions." †

* *The Struggle*, No. 3.   † *Ibid.*, No. 133.

As did this on wages:

"The defenders of the Corn Law, instead of answering the arguments urged for repeal, proceed to talk about cheap food reducing wages.   They also rail against machinery, though they are doing all they can to advise farmers to adopt machinery. . . . Every relaxation in the price of bread, I find to be a benefit to the manufacturing operative, and to have a tendency to add to his wages. That which is saved in food is spent in clothing, bedding, furniture, etc., which give employment to our artisans. The total repeal of the Corn Laws would bring an increased demand for labour, by lessening the necessity for labour, and this must necessarily exercise an influence in favour of wages. . . . None but those who wish to live by taxing bread, or those whose judgments are sadly warped by prejudice, would try to persuade the people that cheap bread would reduce wages." *

And also the following:

"People talk as if some great convulsion would happen to the *land* if the Corn Law was repealed. The land, happy in its resources, would be entirely unconscious of the change. Cows would give quite as much milk; the same quantity of potatoes would come off an acre; and the corn fields would not yield one ear less than at present. There would be no difference; green fields would still be green; and English hens would not lay one egg less if French eggs came in duty free. There would be this advantage, that as horse keep and man keep would be much cheaper, the land would be cultivated at less expense. There would also be a difference in the *division* of the proceeds. After the labour and the farmer's profit upon capital were paid for, there would be a smaller balance in the shape of *rent*." †

In No. 5 of *The Struggle*, Mr. Livesey thus points out the persons really interested in maintaining the Corn Law monopoly:

"*Who are interested?* There are but three classes of persons who are to any extent interested in retaining the present Corn Laws:—the landowners, for the sake of keeping up their rents—the rich clergy, for the sake of reaping more from tithes and tithe-compositions—and the corn jobbers, who raise prices to get in foreign grain, and then depress them to put the money into their own pockets. Perhaps it is not generally known that the amount which is paid to our rectors, in lieu of every tenth sheaf, is calculated by the price of corn for the previous seven years. These gentlemen don't believe that riches are any hindrance to heaven, and therefore they support the Corn Laws."

MR. LIVESEY AMONGST THE FARMERS.

Mr. Livesey's business took him much among farmers, and hence he knew their circumstances, and how greatly they suffered from the operation of laws which had been ostensibly enacted for their benefit. He did much to enlighten them upon the true bearing of the case. The interests of the farmers did not lie in the direction of monopoly, and he lost no opportunity of pointing this out to those he came in contact with. But while Mr. Livesey contended that the agriculturist would be benefited by the repeal of the Corn Laws, he always maintained, both as a matter of justice and necessity, that "rents must come down." The condition of the farmer as a whole has improved since the repeal, although the general prosperity of the nation has enabled the landowners to continue to exact rents fixed in the old war times, and in many cases to increase them. The present depression of agriculture, consequent upon a succession of bad seasons, is telling upon the farmer, and will probably lead to a radical change in the tenure of land. Landlords are clinging with tenacity to their high rents,

* *The Struggle*, No. 93.   † *Ibid.*, No. 5.

f

or they are averting the difficulty by resorting to the same expedient they had recourse to during the terrible agricultural distress which existed before the Corn Laws were repealed—that of returning a percentage to the tenant—a system which one of the early Corn Law publications thus well described :

"In this dilemma," says the writer, "we have had weekly announcements in the papers of the generosity of Lord A. or the munificence of Lord B. in returning 5, 10, or 20 per cent., at the rent audits of their tenantry ; in plain English, surrendering their claims to arrears they could never get, and which in most cases they should never have attempted to exact. Liberality is a gem that ought to shine in the lease, and not in the landlord's judgment. By this act of apparent generosity, the tenant is placed under a perpetual obligation to his landlord, and is thereby deprived of that independence of speech and action in political affairs which is enjoyed by the humblest mechanic ; a position very unfavourable to the tenant, and which the landlord knows too well how to turn to account when fitting occasions offer." *

The landowners of to-day would do well to listen to, and act upon, the advice tendered to their class nearly two centuries ago by that quaint enthusiast, and persistent health reformer, Thomas Tryon.

"Art thou a man of an estate ?" he asks, "remember then that thou art God's steward, therefore do good to the needy, and let thy farms such a pennyworth that thy tenants may comfortably pay their rents with cheerfulness of heart." †

In an "Address to Farmers," in No. 73 of *The Struggle*, Mr. Livesey says :

"I was struck with this remark of a farmer yesterday, ' There was most money made before there was any Corn Law.' And I am frequently asked by them, whether the Corn Law is likely to be taken off. The fact is, farmers know well that from 1815 till now, seasons of depression have been constantly recurring, and although a few may have made money, vast numbers have yearly sunk into the ranks of paupers. . . . During the war, land acquired an unnatural value, and instead of allowing it to find its level with the return of peace, which would have been attended with fresh adjustments of the farmer's rent, the lords of the soil passed the corn bill to prevent these ; and thus *they kept up rents*, and yet the value of produce has kept dwindling down."

Undoubtedly the whole Corn Law question was really one of rent, as Mr. Livesey well states in No. 147 of *The Struggle :*

"Disguise it as we may, cover the truth as we like, by putting forward the claims of the hunger-bitten labourers and rent-ruined farmers of the soil ; these startling prohibitions, these impious interferences betwixt heaven's supply and the people's wants—proceed from nothing but the demon RENT."

RENT TO BE PAID IN PRODUCE.

One suggestion made by Mr. Livesey would, if adopted, go a long way towards settling the rent question. It was that the rent of farms should be paid in corn. He put the case in this way :

"The landlord allows the farmer the use of a piece of land, upon which the latter exclusively lays out his money and employs labour. He is ready to say, ' The land is *mine*, and I ought to have a *consideration* for allowing you to use it ' ; to which the farmer answers, ' What so *reasonable* as a sum *proportioned to the selling*

* "Dialogues on the Corn Laws," p. 7.   † "Wisdom' Dicta'es," London, 1698, p. 30.

value of the produce?' Why should he have a *fixed* sum of *money*, when the produce will not sell for a *fixed* price? If the *price* and amount of *produce* were to regulate the rent, the risk would fall upon the individual best able to bear it. . . . Under *long leases* and *corn rents*, the land would recover itself, the trade of farming become profitable and adopted by persons of capital. Land would doubtless be much improved by this regulation, and made to yield much more food than at present, consequently it would be a great national advantage." *

Amongst the reforms calculated to bring relief to the agriculturist, and which were justly his due, Mr. Livesey advocated—concurrently with the repeal of the Corn Laws—fixity of tenure, compensation for unexhausted improvements, the abolition of the Game Laws, and the transference of the burden of taxation from the tenant to the owner of the soil. The hardships imposed upon farmers by the tenant-at-will system are pictorially illustrated in No. 135 of *The Struggle* by two small wood-cuts. The first represents a farmer burying a purse in one of his fields, towards whom his landlord is seen approaching in the distance. This picture is labelled RIGHT, and has the following explanation: "When the farmer lays his hard-earned sovereigns out on a piece of land in draining, he may be said to bury a purse in the ground, as shown above." In the second scene the landlord is depicted in the act of appropriating the purse, and the poor farmer occupying the background is holding up his hands in amazement. The cut is called WRONG, and is explained by the following sentence. "When the landlord raises the rent in consequence of such improvements, his conduct may be described as digging out the said sovereigns." Then follows THE MORAL:

"Is it right for parties to reap when they have not sown? Is it right for farmers to be called upon to improve other persons' land without any security for a return? Landlords should either advance the money expended on their own land, or they should give a guarantee to the farmers that they shall receive their own back again."

THE WRETCHED PLIGHT OF FARMERS UNDER THE CORN LAW.

In No. 70 of *The Struggle*, Mr. Livesey presents a sad picture of the condition of farmers under protection. It is valuable, because based on personal knowledge.

"Something should be done," he says, "to lay before the public the real condition of farmers. I have latterly been making inquiries, and I can truly say that their privations and embarrassments exceed all belief. In fact, the public have no idea of the condition of this class of the community. The landlords hush up the matter; and if spoken to, their general answer is, 'Wait a little, and things will be better.' Farmers are naturally diffident; they seldom appear before the public, either as writers or speakers; and few, if any, in Lancashire, with whom I am acquainted, dare make themselves obnoxious by attempting to inform the public as to the deplorable state of the farming business. To enter into all the details of the labours, losses, manner of living, treatment by their landlords, and their utter dependency, would astonish the country. Rest, enjoyment, independency, good living, mental improvement, profit upon capital, advancement in the world, are all things quite out of the question,—*how they can scrape the rent together*, and meet the steward at the rent day, is their whole concern. We have had the statistics of the towns and of various trades; let those of the farming business be collected, and if evidence be wanting, it will easily be supplied to prove the farmers have been among the greatest sufferers by the Corn Laws."

In a speech at Lancaster, chiefly addressed to farmers, which occupies the whole of No. 92 of *The Struggle*, Mr. Cobden spoke of the difficulties which were

* *The Struggle*, No. 58, p. 3.

steadily increasing amongst the cultivators of the soil. In illustrating the stagnation in trade, and its effects upon employment, he made the following reference to Mr. Livesey. Depicting a farmer anxious to place a son in mercantile life, he said :

" You come into town, and you go, perhaps, to my friend Livesey here, who is a notorious man, and ask him, ' Can you take my son into your warehouse to sell cheese ? ' ' Why,' says Livesey, ' don't you read my *Struggle ?* I have been telling you for the last four or five years that the Corn Laws have ruined trade, and that I cannot find work for my own sons and servants.' "

Mr. Livesey advised agriculturists to take the remedy into their own hands, by returning practical farmers—real working ones—to the House of Commons. He pointed out the futility of their longer relying on the promises of legislators belonging to the landlord class.* In No. 183 of *The Struggle* appears an illustration representing the first tenant-farmer shaking hands with Mr. Speaker. Consternation is depicted on the faces of the aristocratic members present, and printed beneath the cut appears the following :

"THE FIRST TENANT-FARMER IN THE HOUSE OF COMMONS.

"All classes of men have had their representatives in the House of Commons except tenant-farmers. The first real *bona-fide* farmer who shakes hands with the Speaker of the House of Commons will portend a great revolution. Never since the House of Commons was established, has a tenant-farmer been seen in that House, where landlords, however, have undertaken, with much suspicious zeal, to represent his interests. Is there not something suspicious in the fact that, loud as the landlords have been in professions of zeal for agriculture, they have never permitted a real agriculturist—one who has made his living by farming—to show

* In connexion with this part of Mr. Livesey's labours for securing free trade, an interesting incident may be related, which occurred in 1844 at an election for the Northern Division of Lancashire. In September of that year the father of the present Earl of Derby was elevated to the peerage by the death of the grandfather of the present Earl, which caused a vacancy in the representation of that Division of the County. The Tory and pro-Corn-Law candidate was Mr. John Talbot Clifton, of Lytham Hall; and while there was no intention on the part of the Anti-Corn-Law League to go to the poll with an Anti-Corn-Law candidate, it was thought free-trade principles ought to be advocated on the hustings on the day of nomination, and Mr. Livesey was the man selected to do battle for untaxed bread on that occasion. The nomination took place at Lancaster on Sept. 20th, 1844, and the arrangement made was that Mr. Livesey should propose Sir Thomas Potter as a candidate. In doing so, he delivered a long and powerful speech, in which he mainly addressed the Fylde farmers, amongst whom he had travelled so long in his business of cheese merchant. From his intercourse amongst them, then extending over twenty years, he had acquired an exact knowledge of their position. His telling remarks caused considerable irritation amongst the landowners present, who frequently interrupted him in his address. In the course of his speech he alluded to the impious character of the Corn Laws, and seeing several clergymen amongst the supporters of the pro-Corn-Law candidate, he expressed his surprise that the reverend gentlemen who prayed for ' Cheapness and Plenty' should be electioneering for ' Dearness and Scarcity.' This reference roused a perfect storm, and on Mr. Clifton returning thanks for his election, he said: " When Mr. Livesey next takes a motto from the Prayer-Book, I hope you will in my name beg him to give it more correctly. He tells you there is the expression of ' Cheapness and Plenty'; now, no such expression is to be found in the Prayer-Book,—it is ' Peace and Plenty.' "—Mr. Livesey: " No ; it is ' Cheapness and Plenty.' "—Mr. Clifton : " No, no."—Mr. Livesey : " I pledge my word there are the words ' Cheapness and Plenty' in the Prayer-Book."—Mr. Clifton: " And I pledge my word there are not." The paper from which the above remarks are taken reports that a voice greeted the closing words of Mr. Clifton with—" A pretty fellow to support the Church, and have not learnt your Prayer-Book!" On the day following appeared the Preston newspaper, which was then published and edited by Mr. Livesey, and the editorial article, after noticing the above incident, gives at full length the prayer to which Mr. Livesey referred, and in which the words ' Cheapness and Plenty' appear. (It is the prayer headed "In the Time of Dearth and Famine.") Mr. Clifton and his clerical supporters, when this exposure of their ignorance was widely circulated through the county, must have felt how seriously they had committed themselves. It should be explained, that so soon as Sir Thomas Potter was nominated, his name was withdrawn; the nomination having been made solely to enable Mr. Livesey to expose the hollowness of the landowner's pretensions in supporting the continuance of the Corn Laws.

his face in that House. In the next election a tenant-farmer will assuredly be proposed for a county. On that occasion, if the farmers, be they Whig or Tory, permit
one of their order to be rejected as representative of their own interests, then
will they deserve to be trampled under the hoofs of landlords, land-agents, and
those odious creatures—toadying country attorneys—for another half-century."

MR. LIVESEY ON SIR R. PEEL.

It may be mentioned as an illustration of Mr. Livesey's political sagacity
and foresight, that he repeatedly expressed the opinion that Sir Robert Peel
would ultimately effect the repeal. Nevertheless he did not spare the premier;
but addressed the most searching appeals to him, placing his great responsibilities
in the strongest possible light. When in July, 1842, a deputation of Anti-Corn-
Law delegates waited upon Sir Robert Peel, Mr. Livesey was one of them; and
in No. 30 of *The Struggle*, he gives his impressions of the interview:

"My impression was, that the deputation was exceedingly unwelcome, and
that the only happy moment Sir Robert felt was that when he made his exit. Sir
Robert entered the room with little ceremony, made a gentle move, and fixed himself against the corner of a sofa. He stood all the time, and almost as motionless
as a statue. . . . Ten deputies addressed the premier; the audience was most
solemn; the scene most affecting; the prime minister of England standing to
listen to the deputed cries and wailings and sufferings of millions of his fellow-
subjects! repeated with a faithfulness, a fervour, and an awful solemnity, such as
I never witnessed before. He was told honestly the real condition of the nation,
and the inevitable consequences if relief was not afforded. Many an eye was
flooded with tears, especially when Alderman Brooks affectingly related the privations of the poor. The repeal of the Corn Laws and freedom of trade were
strongly recommended as the true remedies; and that if something be not done,
the deputies stated to him plainly, a convulsion was sure to take place."

Mr. Livesey expresses his astonishment at the off-hand way in which Sir
Robert dismissed the deputation by promising to bring the subject under the notice
of his colleagues; and he was much pained by the remark of the premier, that he
had "heard the deputation with great patience." When, however, the obnoxious
laws were repealed, Mr. Livesey heartily concurred in the sentiments regarding Sir
Robert, expressed by his friend and Temperance colleague Henry Anderton:

He welded brains of adverse sorts,
And solder'd all their quarrels;
Till by their aid—corn fill'd our ports,
In French and Yankee barrels;
And while this gallant game he play'd,
State quack and swindler rumpling,
He opened Britain's doors of trade,
And doubled Britain's dumpling.

THE MANUFACTURERS AND THE REPEAL MOVEMENT.

It has now become customary to reflect upon the Anti-Corn-Law agitation as a
class movement in the interests of the manufacturers. It may be true that many
of the largest subscribers to the funds of the League had an eye to the improvement of their own branches of industry, and that their subscriptions were in a
sense only a trade investment. But the movement as a whole was very much
more than this. It was for instance of far wider significance to Richard Cobden
and John Bright, who were animated by the motives of a broad and general

philanthropy. Those who took a narrower view of the crusade, helped it forward
by their means and influence, but Cobden himself afterwards lamented "how few
of those who fought for the repeal of the Corn Law really understood the full
meaning of Free Trade principles." * Mr. Livesey belonged to the few who did
understand their meaning, and his labours were rendered all the more valuable and
effective by the fact that they sprang from the highest philanthropic and religious
motives. He did not, however, condemn the manufacturers, or discourage their
proffered assistance, but says of them:

"I am neither the advocate nor apologist of the masters, and no one laments
more than I do, the pride and oppression of some of the cotton aristocracy; but
one thing I am confident of, that whether the men respect their masters or not, it
is their duty, for *their own sake*, to stand by their trade, and to fight against those
laws by which its very existence is at present threatened, and by which they are
all likely to be entirely ruined. Let me repeat, that the greatest practical *advantages, resulting from a Free Trade, would be divided* amongst the working people."†

An examination of *The Struggle* shows that Mr. Livesey's advocacy of Free
Trade principles was based on the highest grounds. And in the Declaration of
Principles, published in the first number of his *Preston Guardian* (Feb. 10th, 1844),
the question is approached from a religious standpoint:

"We consider human life a Divine gift, and as such it should be held sacred
from all inroads of human cruelty and cupidity; and we would regard its gradual
destruction or embarrassment, by means of laws which create starvation, as an
infringement of the natural rights of man, and an offence quite as heinous in the
sight of Heaven as a direct attack upon it by physical violence. These are the
highest and most cogent considerations that can be urged in support of man's
right to an adequate supply of food, and they are considerations which have the
immediate sanction of Almighty Wisdom."

Holding these views, it is not surprising that Mr. Livesey was severe upon the
clergy, who used their influence to obstruct the reform. He satirized them both
with pen and pencil; and in No. 70 of *The Struggle* the fact is recorded that
"Seven bishops—Rt. Rev. Fathers in God—opposed Lord Monteagle's motion on
the Corn Laws."

In addition to the services rendered the Anti-Corn-Law movement through
The Struggle and the *Preston Guardian*—a paper devoted to Free Trade and
liberal and progressive objects, which rapidly achieved success—he also promoted
the cause by the issue of small handbills or tracts of a striking and pithy character, and the publication of Illustrated Free Trade Sheet Almanacs, which were
very extensively circulated.

In promoting petitions to Parliament, Mr. Livesey may be said to have done
the work of an organization. In No. 7 of *The Struggle*, he announces:

"We will now employ persons to write as many Petitions as there are *families*
in Preston; and every householder is invited to call for a copy, and forward it
to his representative, signed by himself and all his domestics. Let the table
of the House of Commons groan beneath *five millions of Petitions*."

A year later, in No. 59 of *The Struggle*, Mr. Livesey gives the petition of his
own family (which he reproduces on page 23 of the "Autobiography"), and in
an article urging the general adoption of family petitions, he says: "I have now

* "Morley's Life of Cobden," People's Ed., p. 68.   † *The Struggle*, No. 3.

three or four of my boys writing family petitions for those who are either not able or have not time to write for themselves."

MR. JOHN MORLEY'S ESTIMATE OF "THE STRUGGLE."

Mr. John Morley, M.P., in his "Life of Cobden," has the following discriminating acknowledgment of Mr. Livesey's Anti-Corn-Law labours :

"A volunteer in Preston this winter (1841) began to issue, on his own account, a quaint little sheet of four quarto pages, called *The Struggle*, and sold for a halfpenny. It had no connexion with any association, and nobody was responsible for its contents but the man who wrote, printed, and sold it. In two years eleven hundred thousand copies had been circulated. *The Struggle* is the very model for a plain man who wishes to affect the opinion of the humbler class, without the wasteful and, for the most part, ineffectual machinery of a great society. It contains in number after number the whole arguments of the matter in the pithiest form, and in language as direct, if not as pure, as Cobbett's. Sometimes the number consists simply of some more than usually graphic speech by Cobden or by Fox. There are racy dialogues, in which the landlord always gets the worst of it ; and terse allegories, in which the Duke of Buckingham or the Duke of Richmond figures as inauspiciously as Bunyan's Mr. Badman. The Bible is ransacked for appropriate texts, from the simple clause in the Lord's Prayer about our daily bread, down to Solomon's saying : 'He that withholdeth the corn, the people shall curse him ; but blessings shall be upon the head of him that selleth it.' On the front page of each number was a woodcut, as rude as a schoolboy's drawing, but full of spirit and cleverness, whether satirizing the Government, or contrasting swollen landlords with famine-stricken operatives, or painting some homely idyll of the industrious poor, to point the greatest of political morals, that 'domestic comfort is the object of all reforms.' " *

THE INSTITUTIONAL *v.* THE ORGANIZATIONAL MAN.

If a person of to-day desires information respecting the great Anti-Corn-Law struggle, he will most likely be directed to Mr. Archibald Prentice's "History of the Anti-Corn-Law League." In that work he will find much valuable material— but it is simply a history of the League as an organization, and not of the still wider Free Trade sentiment and movement which permeated the masses, and of which the League was only one form of expression. We will suppose that the investigator had heard that Mr. Livesey had rendered important services to the Repeal movement, and that being desirous of verifying this, he consults Mr. Prentice's volumes. He will be astonished, however, to find that Mr. Livesey's name is nowhere mentioned throughout that work ; and unless he has learned to distinguish between the institutional reformer and the organizational worker, he will be at a loss to account for the omission. Perhaps no other incident could more strikingly illustrate Mr. Livesey's leading characteristic than this does. He was not an organizational man, but something rarer ; indeed, he was an excellent representative of the type of man which makes organizations possible. We may, and probably shall, get histories of Temperance Leagues and Alliances, done from an official point of view, in which no mention is made of Mr. Livesey or his Temperance work, or of some other independent labourers ; they may be very good books in their way, but they will not be histories of Temperance. The *idea* must precede the *movement*—must ever be kept in due prominence—or the organization will grow

* "Life of Cobden " (People's Edition), p. 29.

to be regarded as of the first importance, and the principles it is founded to teach and extend of secondary moment.

And Mr. Livesey's services to the Anti-Corn-Law movement were also fully understood and thoroughly appreciated by those who were the best judges of their value. Speaking at a meeting held in the Theatre, Preston, on March 7th, 1844, Mr. Cobden said :

"We are much indebted to one gentleman in particular in this borough, for having disseminated information in a most useful form. I allude to my friend Mr. Livesey. I don't hesitate to say, after the name of Cobbett—I might almost have added Franklin—I know of no writer who has had the happy art of putting questions of a difficult and complex character in a more simple and lucid form than my friend Mr. Livesey; and I make no hesitation in speaking thus of his work— *The Struggle.*" *

Mr. Bright held Mr. Livesey's work in equal esteem, as may be seen from the following letter:

"Mr. Livesey was one of our firmest friends in the great conflict on the Corn Law question. His paper, *The Struggle,* was of great use, and I have often regretted that I do not possess a copy of it; for it told the story of the cruelty and wickedness of the Corn Law in pictures and language that could not be misunderstood. Mr. Livesey was a man of great merit—he had a great sense of justice, and his life was one dignified by constant labours in the wide field of mercy and benevolence.

"You will have abundant material for a volume from which much useful instruction may be gained. It will, I cannot doubt, strengthen the desire for good in all who read it." †

* *Preston Guardian,* March 9th, 1844.

† Letter from Rt. Hon. John Bright, M.P., to Mr. John Pearce, dated November 11th, 1884.

CHAPTER VI.

TEMPERANCE: PIONEER AND FOUNDER.

It is made abundantly clear in the foregoing chapters that Mr. Livesey was an active participator in all the stirring reforms of his time. Indeed his labours in various fields of philanthropic effort were so extensive, that had he never been identified with the Temperance movement, it might still have been said of him that his long life was devoted to the service of humanity. Of a certainty no view of Mr. Livesey could be more erroneous than the one which obtains in some quarters respecting him—that he was a man of one idea. His active labours, however, in the promotion of Temperance—extending as they did over a period of fifty-four years—were of a character which fully entitle him to be regarded as the Father and Founder of the Total Abstinence movement.

Mr. Livesey's claims to pre-eminence amongst his fellow-labourers, as the founder of the Preston Temperance movement, are not weakened, but rather strengthened, by the fact that he never urged them himself. So long as a system equal to the cure and prevention of drunkenness was successfully set in motion, he cared little who was the first to originate it. Hence, when others claimed the honour, he was silent, content no doubt to let his teachings and labours speak for themselves. One thing about Mr. Livesey is especially noticeable—that he was extremely modest and diffident in speaking of himself. When, in 1867, the Rev. Charles Garrett urged him to give, in the *Staunch Teetotaler*, a minute account of the origin of teetotalism, Mr. Livesey hesitated. "I felt," he said, "that having been so closely mixed up with every step at the commencement, that I should seem as if writing too much about myself." And if his own reputation had alone been concerned in the matter, most likely his native modesty would have restrained him from penning the articles which were subsequently expanded into the "Reminiscences of Early Teetotalism," * an invaluable contribution to Temperance history, in which the labours of all the pioneer reformers are most generously acknowledged.

* "Reminiscences of Early Teetotalism," by J. Livesey. London: Nat. Temp. League.

The reader will find from the "Autobiography" that Mr. Livesey is satisfied with speaking of himself as "one of the founders" of teetotalism as an aggressive system of Temperance reform; and those who have access to his works and publications will be quite familiar with this phrase. Other persons, however, with far less claim to the distinction, have announced themselves as the founders of the teetotal system. This was particularly the case with the late James Teare,* who, in 1846, claimed to have been the first of the Preston band to teach total abstinence.

* I have no desire to lessen in any degree the legitimate reputation of James Teare, whose pioneer services to the movement—despite his brusque and dogmatic manner—were of a very substantial kind; but if history is to be impartial, the truth must be told. His claims to regard and affectionate remembrance as a Temperance reformer rest securely enough upon accomplished work, and it is a pity he was not content to leave them there, rather than attempt to place them on a sandy foundation. During the first few years of Mr. Teare's missionary career, he warmly acknowledged the value of Mr. Livesey's services, as may be seen from the letters addressed to that gentleman, published in the *Preston Advocate*; and when he had occasion to speak of the commencement of the Preston movement it was his habit to mention Mr. Livesey as the leader. For instance, on January 24th, 1837, Mr. Teare, addressing a meeting in the City of London Tavern, referred to the Preston work as follows: "Mr. Livesey, myself, and a few others, went to work singlehanded. . . . And what has been our success? We have now 300,000 teetotalers in the kingdom" (*Temperance Intelligencer*, London, 1837, p. 90).

In 1846 Mr. Teare's claims were made for the first time in a pamphlet, entitled "The Origin and Success of the Advocacy of Total Abstinence" (London: Charles Gilpin); in which he claims to have been the first person in Preston to advocate total abstinence, and that on June 18th, 1832. In 1861 a new edition of the pamphlet, enlarged and extended, was issued (London: Job Caudwell), in which Mr. Teare is more emphatic in pressing his claims. The pamphlet extends to 37 pages, and Mr. Livesey's name appears for the first time on the 19th page. No credit whatever is given to Mr. Livesey as having been one of the founders even of the Preston Temperance Society, nor is it any where hinted that he had a hand in establishing the movement in Preston. But he is credited with having spoken at a meeting in the Cockpit in July, 1832, Mr. Teare remarking: "This was, we believe, Mr. Livesey's maiden speech at public Temperance meetings." Mr. G. Toulmin, J.P., of the *Preston Guardian*, however, distinctly remembers both Mr. Livesey and Mr. Swindlehurst advocating abstinence from fermented as well as distilled liquors, at a meeting in Lawson-street Chapel, on April 27th, 1832. On July 5th, 1882, in presiding over a meeting in connexion with the British League Conference, held in the Skating Rink, Preston, Mr. Toulmin said: "Mr. Livesey delivered at that meeting the first speech which indicated his opinion that the pledge was not sufficiently broad to secure the object of doing away with drunkenness, inasmuch as it permitted the use of malt liquor, with which the bulk of the people in this district went to excess. He showed that the intoxicating principle, alcohol, was the same in each. *After this*, the most earnest friends of the cause began to advocate a discontinuance of the use of *all* intoxicating drinks, which ultimately led to the adoption of total abstinence" (*British Temperance Advocate*, Aug., 1882, p. 19). In 1864, Mr. Toulmin had said of the same speech, "The novelty of Mr. Livesey's ideas made a great impression upon my mind, and is the reason why I recollect that speech better than any other Temperance address I ever heard" (Refutation of James Teare, Preston, 1864, p. 12). But Mr. Livesey spoke at several meetings prior to July,—indeed he lectured on Temperance in the Cock-pit on the day before the Temperance Society was established (see note to page xv.). In 1864, Mr. Teare contributed several letters to the *Alliance News*, in which he went still further in magnifying his own claims and diminishing those of all others. Referring to his speech on 18th of June, 1832, he says: "I am sure no one in Preston advocated total abstinence *before that time*, nor for three *months after*,"—and he further declares that up to that time "neither T. Swindlehurst nor J. Livesey had ever made a speech at any public Temperance meeting in Preston." But unfortunately for Mr. Teare's theory, it is on record that both the gentlemen named had addressed meetings on the subject nearly two months before the notorious 18th of June.

It is difficult to understand how Mr. Teare could have deluded himself, or how he hoped to delude others, into believing these allegations. In fact his action in this matter is as inexplicable as his conduct in desiring appeals for pecuniary help for himself to be made a few months before his decease, on the pretext that he was a needy man, while in reality he was in very comfortable circumstances, and able to bequeath about £5,000 to his relatives. Dr. F. R. Lees, in the biography prefixed to "Bacchus Dethroned" (p. ix.), has the following reference to this incident: "Among other illusions, he (Mr. Teare) thought he was exposed to poverty; and currency was given by some undiscerning friends to his fancy, and several subscriptions were obtained. . . In fact . . . he had a *passion for little economies*, which is apt to run into meanness—and the illusion of poverty is a righteous retribution and nemesis upon the sin." Mr. Teare's claims were examined and disposed of, in 1864, in a pamphlet issued by Messrs. James Stephenson, Joseph Dearden, and George Toulmin (Preston: *Guardian* office), and so far as they relate to Mr. Livesey they are abundantly answered by the quotations given in this chapter from the first and second volumes of the *Moral Reformer*. The most charitable view of Mr. Teare's proceedings would suppose that he had either never read the volumes mentioned, or that having read them, he had completely forgotten their contents. The persons, however, most to blame were those who, for organizational purposes, flattered his vanity, and encouraged him in his pretensions.

In later years Mr. Teare carried his pretensions still further, venturing not only to assert what he himself had done, but going so far even as to say what other people had not done.   The most painful feature in Mr. Teare's so-called "History" is the laboured but evident attempt to ignore Mr. Livesey's early Temperance work, to dwarf his labours, and disparage his teachings; indeed, this appears to have been the principal object of the effort.

Mr. Teare's chief contentions were, that, excepting himself, no one in Preston had advocated abstinence from fermented liquors prior to June 18th, 1832, and that no one else advocated it for at least three months afterwards; while Mr. Livesey's services to the movement through the Press, are stated to have begun in July, 1833, when, according to Mr. Teare, "a part of the *Moral Reformer*" was "devoted to the advocacy of the Temperance cause."   While it is painful to have to point out the serious inaccuracies of Mr. Teare, it is necessary to do so, not so much as an act of justice to Mr. Livesey, as a corrective of the many misstatements which have obtained currency,* and which, uncontradicted, would continue to corrupt the history of the Temperance Movement.

Some persons may incline to the view that these disputed matters are of small importance;† but, in the interests of truth and justice, and for the credit of history, it will be well to clear them up, as far as a reference to printed documents will allow, and this can best be done by tracing Mr. Livesey's Temperance ideas and teachings as they are developed in his own publications.   His claims to precedence in point of time are of a very substantial character.   If he were not the first Prestonian to move in the matter of Temperance, his published teachings, and the part he took in the formation of the Society in that town, give him a juster title to be considered the founder of the movement, than can be urged for any other claimant who has yet appeared.   In fact Mr. Livesey always had strong leanings towards Temperance.   For instance, while yet a lad, we find him openly protesting against spirit drinking, etc., at an ordination dinner;‡ and in his first pamphlet, "A Friendly Address to the Working Classes,"§ the second edition of which, dated 1826, is before me, over two pages are devoted to Admonitions against Drunkenness, in which drinking at alehouses is condemned, and drunkards are urged, "with a full dependence on Divine strength" to overcome their habit, however inveterate.   About this time, too, he issued "The Besetting Sin," a small pamphlet

---

* The claims of some other alleged 'founders' are noticed in chapter viii.

† It can never be inopportune to correct error.   In this case it is an urgent duty to do so, as, for want of a better knowledge of the facts, both speakers and writers on Temperance are continually misleading the public.   As a late instance of this may be cited an article in the *National Temperance Advocate* (American), for August, 1885, on "The Genesis of Total Abstinence in England," in which the writer, Mr. Paul Bramwell, follows Mr. Teare's version of the origin of teetotalism.

‡ See "Autobiography," p. 11.   On page 103 of the *Moral Reformer* for 1832, in a note, Mr. Livesey gives the following account of this incident: "I recollect attending an ordination service at Accrington, where the ministers and rich friends were invited to a sumptuous dinner, after which pipes, tobacco, and spirits were used pretty freely.   Though I and a few other poor fellows had walked fourteen miles to attend the service, there was no dinner for us, excepting *their leavings* at a shilling each.'   In the course of a discussion which was going on, I took occasion to remind the ministers that if they were to follow the example of the Apostles, such services ought to be connected with 'fasting and prayer.'   Their best argument in reply was a hearty laugh."   By a singular coincidence the attention of Dr. Lyman Beecher was directed to the Temperance question by the too free drinking he witnessed at an ordination dinner in 1811, which happened within a year of this circumstance.

§ Preston: L. Clarke, 143, Church Street.

entirely devoted to the drink question; but, unfortunately, as was the case with his " First Book," no copy of it appears to have been preserved.

From the beginning of 1831, when he commenced the publication of his unique magazine, the *Moral Reformer*, he may be said to have embarked upon a crusade against intoxicating liquors which only ended with his life.   In the very first article in the first number of that periodical, when dealing with the 'Immorality and Irreligion of the Age,' he pointedly refers to the drink question, and inquires " How many precious evenings are spent in a course of intemperance, which leads to nothing less than ruin of both body and soul?"*   In the same issue, upwards of two pages of fact, information, and appeal, are given under the distinctive heading 'Intemperance.'   Amongst the topics treated are 'Dram-drinking,' 'Sale-Drinking,' 'Consumption of Spirits,' and the new 'Beer Bill,' while a long extract is given from Professor Edgar's Introduction to Beecher's Sermons.   His attitude at this time (really about the close of 1830, as the magazine would have been printed some time in December) towards malt liquors may be gathered from the following extract from the paragraph on the Beer Bill; and it should be remembered that the Temperance societies of the day were directed against the use of distilled spirits only,—wine and malt liquors being regarded as harmless drinks.†   But Mr. Livesey always was in advance of these societies.   He says:

"However they may applaud this measure in London, in the country—in Lancashire in particular—I shall be supported when I say it is considered a great curse.   This is the declared sentiment from the magistrate on the bench to the wife of the humblest weaver.   Cheap ale is a temptation which few labouring men can resist, and when taken at the public-house, where company and everything is enticing, seldom leads to anything less than intoxication."‡

In the March number, Mr. Livesey describes a visit to Manchester on a Saturday—the previous New Year's Day—and comments upon the number of persons he saw drunk in the streets, the victims of " cheap ale and cheap spirits."§   In the evening, he counted the persons who entered a public-house, described by him as " one of these hells," and found that 162 persons (two-thirds of whom were women, many being young girls) entered that single house in half an hour,—between five minutes past, and thirty-five minutes past, six o'clock! ||

In the April number, Mr. Livesey reverts to the Beer Bill question, and, as the following extract shows, he regarded beer and poison as synonymous terms:

It [the Beer Act] has been a fatal measure to the morals of the people.   To argue in favour of *free trade* in the article of intoxicating liquors is as absurd as to require the druggist to leave the vessel containing poison without a label, or the toy-shops to sell loaded pistols for boys' playthings.   To tax these liquors is a duty of police; it is a protection from the common foe of man; and a certain good to many distressed families." ¶

* *Moral Reformer*, vol. i. (1831), p. 6.

† And hence, the general meaning of the phrase 'total abstinence,' now implying abstinence from intoxicating liquors of *all* kinds, not that 'abstinence' ever meant *partial* abstinence; although in America, even the words " abstinence from all that intoxicates," were sometimes used to denote abstinence from ardent spirits only.

‡ *Moral Reformer*, vol. i. (1831), p. 26.   § *Ibid.*, vol. i. (1831), p. 85.

|| While these pages are going through the Press, Mr. George Calvert, and the Help-Myself-Society, are taking a public-house census in London on the very plan adopted by Mr. Livesey on this occasion.

¶ *Moral Reformer*, vol. i. (1831), p. 117.

The May number of the *Moral Reformer* opens with an article upon the "Morals and Behaviour of the People," in which Mr. Livesey again returns to the drink question.

The leading article in the July number (1831), is entitled "An Address to the Working Classes," on the means of promoting their own happiness, and it is especially noteworthy, from a Temperance standpoint, as containing the first avowal made by Mr. Livesey of his adoption of the principle of abstinence from all alcoholics. The declaration will be found on pages 63 and 100 of the "Autobiography." It is, however, of such importance—especially when read with the general remarks upon the drinking system which precede it—that no apology is offered for enabling the reader to peruse the whole paragraph in this connexion. After dealing with other obvious causes of discomfort to the class he is addressing, Mr. Livesey says :

" I have reserved, as the last subject of admonition, my remarks upon that all-ruinous, poverty producing, health and life destroying practice of *frequenting the public-house*. This is the bane of Britain's greatness; an universal curse to high and low. When genuine hospitality is on the wane, houses for the accommodation of strangers are necessary ; and, in mercantile districts, places of public accommodation, indispensable ; but, in either case, to be obliged to guzzle drink, in order to remunerate the owner, is a monstrous regulation. But for persons who are under no tie, voluntarily to go and spend their evenings, and sometimes even whole days, at public-houses, in drinking and bawling, to the manifold injury of themselves and families, is such a piece of consummate folly and wickedness as can arise only from deep depravity, and confirmed habits of vice. To visit these places, on many occasions, would lead one to think that men had succeeded in persuading themselves that there is neither God nor future state. Through the week, many of you have no opportunities of going to the ale-house (though the dram shops are frequently visited, more particularly by the women), but on the Saturday evenings, and on Sundays, you sometimes go to shameful extremes. Instead of going home, and taking charge of your families, and assisting your wives in laying out your wages to the best advantage, you go and get drunk on the Saturday night, repeat it again on Sunday, and on Monday morning, in place of an invigorated body and cheerful spirits, you feel a depression and languor, the sure effects of your previous excess. You spend your money, you lose your time, you distress your families, your morals are corrupted, and you corrupt others, and all for the delusive, momentary excitement which the liquor imparts ; the forerunner of disease, and the cause of premature death. Those of you to whom these remarks apply, are, in general, aware of the justness of this representation ; for amongst all the hard drinkers with whom I have conversed, I do not recollect one who ever seriously justified the practice, or ventured to recommend it to others. Once formed, it is an inveterate habit ; and the man who said to his friends, ' If the pit of hell yawned on the one hand, and a bottle of brandy stood on the other, and if I was sure I should be pushed in if I took one glass more, I could not refrain,' forms a melancholy specimen of a confirmed drunkard. What then would you have us to do? Leave off public-house company altogether ; *this is the only sure course*, for if you trust yourselves into these places, you are sure to be overcome. I am decidedly opposed even to moderate drinking in *any place*, but if you think (as I know you do) that a pint of ale is useful, *take it at home* by all means. Nothing but a deep conviction of the horrible consequences of public-house drinking, and an anxious wish for your welfare, could induce me to speak so as to prejudice the interests of any class of men. The trade of some of these houses is founded principally upon the *vices* of the people, and the more sensual, more depraved, more extravagant men are, the more this trade prospers. Can any man, therefore, feeling for the morals of his country, support and connive at such a system as this? If any of your employers are in the habit of paying your wages at the public-houses, represent the evil of it to them, and a single request from you, I am sure, would induce them to change their plan. In many of your societies you have a bad rule, which obliges your members, at your several meetings, to spend so much ' for the good of the house.' I am in possession of several facts relative to this, which would convince any one, that, whilst you are doing good in one way, you are doing much evil in another. If you could agree to pay the landlord so much for the use of the room, the weight of my objection would be removed, for it is against the *obligation* for the persons present, be they few or many, to *consume a certain quantity* of liquor to remunerate the landlord, that I solemnly protest. While drinking continues, poverty and vice will prevail; and until this is abandoned, no regulations, no efforts, no authority under heaven, can raise the condition of the working classes. It is worse than a plague or a pestilence, and the man is no friend to his country that does not lift up his voice and proclaim his example against it. So shocked have I been with the effects of intemperance and so convinced of the evil tendency of *moderate* drinking, that since the commencement of 1831, I have never tasted ale, wine, or ardent spirits.[*] I know others who are pursuing the same resolution, and whose only regret is, that they did not adopt this course twenty years since." [†]

The same number of the *Moral Reformer* contains a paragraph on the Jerry shop evil; and three closely printed pages of medical testimonies against spirit drinking, in one of which occurs the following declaration (the italics are Mr. Livesey's): "He is happy who considers *water the best drink, and salt the best sauce.*" [‡]

Nearly two pages of the August number (1831) are occupied with a criticism of the Beer Bill question. Referring to the views of a journalist who had spoken of the measure as one of relief to the poor, Mr. Livesey says :

"Surely the writers who volunteer such statements must think that the labouring class have everything but ' cheap ale,' and that nothing was wanting to perfect their bliss but this. *Let any man examine the dwellings, the furniture, the bedding, the clothing, and the food of the poor ; and he will be satisfied of the folly of talking about the Beer Bill as ' a legislative boon to the poor.'* " §

The foe of monopoly, he regarded the Beer Act as a useful measure, so far as it had struck a blow at the old public-house system, which he did not wish to revert to. As a free trader Mr. Livesey at this time was rather inclined to favour the remission of the malt duty. || He viewed the matter as a politician, and not as a Temperance reformer, exactly as we find Mr. James Silk Buckingham, M.P., regarded it two years later. Mr. Buckingham, in a letter to Mr. Livesey (who had evidently written him a note of friendly remonstrance), says : "I voted for a repeal of the malt tax on the ground that no taxes should be levied on any commodity whatever."[¶] Mr. Buckingham subsequently viewed the matter from a Temperance standpoint, and became as strong an anti-repealer as was Mr. Livesey. In the article under notice Mr. Livesey makes a proposal somewhat similar to the scheme advocated by the late Canon Kingsley, under which the license fee would be increased, the public-houses reduced in number, and the owners of the houses shut up compensated out of the fund raised by the issue of licences.

In the October number (1831) Mr. Livesey reprints a letter by Sir Astley Cooper, on spirit drinking, and Dr. Rush's well-known ' Remedies for Drunkenness '

---

[*] If this is not advocating total abstinence, it would be difficult to say what would be ; and this was written and published a year before Mr. Teare's notorious 18th of June speech.

[†] *Moral Reformer,* vol. i. (1831), pp. 205-7.   [‡] *Ibid.,* vol. i. (1831), p. 221.

[§] *Ibid.,* vol. i. (1831), p. 248.

[||] At a later period Mr. Livesey became one of the strongest opponents of the Repeal of the Malt Tax ; and in his writings against its repeal he repeatedly told the farmers what they have since fully found out, that no benefit could possibly accrue to them from its remission.

[¶] *The Preston Temperance Advocate,* vol. i. (1834), p. 36.

occupy over two pages. In an article on 'Domestic Happiness' in the November issue, Mr. Livesey says:

"*Excesses* of all sorts must be avoided, and above every other, that of *social drinking*, whether at home or at public-houses, must be *detested, as the sure road to poverty, misery, infamy, and everlasting ruin.*" *

In the same number appears a letter signed 'A Member of a Temperance Society,' in which the writer suggests that those societies (especially in country places where the mass of drunkards are produced by excess in ale drinking) "would be rendered more efficient by extending the pledge to that liquid." We now find the *Moral Reformer* becoming a recognised organ for the discussion of Temperance.

The December number contains a long letter from Mr. Ellerby, of Manchester, on Temperance Societies; and, after reviewing his first year's labours in the preface to the volume (dated December 1st, 1831), Mr. Livesey bears the following striking and emphatic testimony to the beneficial results of his first year's experience of abstinence from *all* intoxicants:

"I am often asked how I find time for all my work; and my answer is, the time which others spend at the pot-house, or in visiting and attending parties, I spend in active pursuits; and *never taking any liquor at home or elsewhere,* my head is seldom out of order; I lose no time in the evenings in extinguishing my reason, or in the mornings in trying to regain it; and thanks to a kind Providence, *my health was never better for many years than it is at this day.*"

It should be remembered that up to this time we have no Temperance Society in Preston, but there are now indications that the teachings of Mr. Livesey are taking effect. In some published accounts of the origin of the Preston Society reference is made to the way of the Society having been prepared by the circulation of tracts by Mr. Swindlehurst, and Mr. Smith (a chandler). Such may have been, and most likely was, the case. But there were no tracts in existence which took higher ground than that taken by Mr. Livesey in the *Moral Reformer;* and therefore their distributors cannot be credited with circulating more advanced teachings; and it is difficult to see how any extent of tract distribution could have equalled in effect Mr. Livesey's systematic, persistent, and sustained advocacy of Temperance throughout the entire year of 1831 in the pages of the *Moral Reformer.* There is evidence, however, that Mr. Livesey, not content with efforts for the extension of Temperance made in his own periodical, was also a tract distributor at a very early period. Mr. Henry Bradley, the first Temperance Secretary in Preston, in a letter in *The Youthful Teetotaler* for February, 1836, states that:

"Before any Temperance Society was formed in Preston, my excellent friend, Mr. Joseph Livesey, gave me a number of Temperance tracts. I read and thought upon the subject. Being a teacher of a Sunday School [Mr. Livesey's, see chaps. i. and iii., and "Autobiography," p. 41]. The teachers of that school formed a Society. Rules and regulations were drawn up, and on the 1st of January, 1832, our Society commenced." †

* *Moral Reformer*, vol. i. (1831), p. 329.

† *The Youthful Teetotaler.* Preston: J. Walker (1836), p. 12.—This little halfpenny monthly was very creditably edited by Mr. J. Brodbelt, who, at the time referred to by Mr. Bradley, was a teacher in Mr. Livesey's school. Influenced by Mr. Livesey's example, Mr. Brodbelt, and others connected with the school, had already become abstainers; and prior to the formation of the Temperance Society, he urged the adoption of a total abstinence pledge as its basis, but was over-ruled. Sentiments so advanced on the part of a disciple evidence pretty clearly the

Mr. Livesey in his " Reminiscences " makes the following reference to this first Society, which unmistakably connects his influence with its formation : " At that time," he says, " I kept an adult Sunday School, and the fruit of my example was that on Jan. 1st, 1832, the young men in this school formed themselves into a Temperance Society."* James Teare, who refers to this school, and remarks upon the Society started in connexion therewith, omits all mention to Mr. Livesey's name !

In the *Moral Reformer* for January, 1832, Mr. Livesey reports (Dec. 23rd, 1831) that he has just returned from Manchester, where he had attended the Anniversary of the Temperance Society. He was also present at another Temperance meeting held in Angel Meadow, a low part of that town, where he was " much pleased to see the spirit, and to hear the sensible and hearty declarations, of the disciples of Temperance." Regarding the results of the agitation at that early period as affecting social drinking, Mr. Livesey says:

" Many tables within the limited circle of my own acquaintance, which used to flash in the evenings with the decanters, are relieved from the disgrace of presenting *poison* to their guests ; and with reflecting people it begins to appear clear that the apothecary's shop is the only appropriate place for ardent spirits."†

In the same issue will be found an appeal to drunkards (in a New Year's address); and paragraphs upon ' Cholera and Drink,' ' Drink and Accidents,' and Gin Drinking at Sales.' In the February number the Temperance question is discussed in paragraphs headed as follows: ' The House of Reform,' ' Truck Bill,' ' Paying on the Premises,' and ' Cure for a Drunken Wife.' Mr. Livesey also makes the following announcement, which is an additional proof, if any were needed, of his connexion with the formation of the Society :

" Some preliminaries, I understand, have been entered into for establishing a Temperance Society in Preston. Its object is so praiseworthy, that I hope it will meet with the encouragement and countenance of all who are concerned for the happiness and well-being of society." ‡

In the March *Reformer*, in course of the able and sagacious article on Ireland, elsewhere referred to,§ Mr. Livesey remarks that " the vice of drunkenness, ten times worse in its effects than *cholera morbus*, prevails extensively." And regarding the excessive taxation paid by the Irish on intoxicants, he says :

" As all other taxes have distinct appellations, by way of pre-eminence I think this ought to be called ' *the devil's tax* !' Fallow is the ground, indeed, in Ireland, which the Temperance principle is now attempting to break up ; may its redeeming energy soon be visible in those streets and lanes and corners where I have seen numbers, especially women, disgustingly drunk ! " ‖

character of the master's teachings. Mr. Brodbelt, who was one of the seven who signed the famous pledge on Sept. 1st, 1832, subsequently became a clergyman. This first Preston Temperance Society was absorbed in the famous Preston Society, to which it contributed a strong contingent, including some of its most efficient working members. And it did very good preliminary service, and was instrumental in bringing Rev. John Jackson to Preston, who addressed two public meetings on the subject, held under the auspices of Mr. Livesey's disciples, and chiefly at his expense. *The Youthful Teetotaler* was the first juvenile Temperance periodical issued in Great Britain ; and to Mr. Brodbelt is unquestionably due the credit of having been the first Prestonian to draw up and urge the adoption of a pledge against the use of *all* intoxicants.

* " Reminiscences of Early Teetotalism," p. 4.
† *Moral Reformer*, vol. ii. (1832), p. 25. ‡ *Moral Reformer*, vol. ii. (1832), p. 58.
§ Chap. iv. p. lvi. ‖ *Ibid.*, vol. ii. (1832), p. 77.

Commenting, in the same issue, upon the national Fast Day appointed for the 21st of March in consequence of the cholera outbreak, Mr. Livesey refers to the very inadequate means for effecting a reformation of life amongst the people, indicated in the circular issued by the bishop of his diocese; and gives a suggested proclamation to the people of a very much more searching and practical character. The following paragraph is extracted as having a direct reference to the question of Temperance:

"To the SPIRIT MERCHANTS, PUBLICANS, and LANDLORDS, we especially address ourselves. The licences granted for inns, and for the manufacture and vending of ardent spirits, have opened the way for that awful prevalency of intoxication which is now, justly, a subject of great alarm. You are the agents of all this; vice and depravity are propagated by the agency of the spirit vendor. And many of the arrangements of the public-houses are positively so many parts of an apparatus for ' killing and slaying ' the people. Spare your victims we entreat you; cease to destroy men's reason, to ruin their health, to impoverish their condition, to distress their families, and to consign them to the grave amid the dreadful forebodings of a wicked life. Drunkenness is the curse of the land, and if we cannot effect a reform by persuasion, rather than incur the displeasure of the Almighty, we shall use the powers we possess for suppressing it as much as possible.

"Given at our court, etc., etc.

"GOD SAVE THE KING AND THE NATION." *

Several paragraphs also appear bearing on the subject, and the following information regarding the coming Temperance Society is given: "A provisional committee has been formed, and the following is the fundamental principle upon which it is agreed to base the Society." Then follows the form of pledge given by Mr. Dearden on page 100, which was the only pledge recognised by the Society during its first year's operations. This pledge, which was based upon the declaration of the Blackburn Society †—the most advanced at that time published —bears evidence of Mr. Livesey's hand.‡ It was altogether in advance of the declaration of the British and Foreign Temperance (Anti-Spirit) Society, and was

* *Moral Reformer*, vol. ii. (1832), pp. 89–90.

† *The Temperance Society Record* (Glasgow), vol. ii. (1831), p. 126.

‡ Just a word upon the Preston Pledges. In the note to page lxxix. reference is made to the pledge of the first Preston Society. Mr. Livesey's known practice of total abstinence would naturally incline the young men of his school to favour a total abstinence pledge, which indeed was drawn up by Mr. Brodbelt at the close of 1831. Mr. Livesey enforced abstinence by precept and example, and the careful reader of my 1st chapter on his religious views will understand how unwilling he would be unnecessarily to impose pledges or creeds upon others. Hence his extreme diffidence in this matter. He taught teetotalism, and in the pledge of March, 1832, provision is made for the total abstainer, and it went about as far in that direction as the persons about to be associated together were prepared to go. But a few months' experience taught them that something more definite was needed. What the *practice* before the *abstinence pledge* was, Mr. Livesey shows in an article on ' The Temperance Cause in Preston,' in the *Moral Reformer* for July, 1832. Referring to backsliders, he says: "In every case it has been the ' first glass ' to which they could trace their fall, ... but the result has generally been, that seeing the danger, they have now resolved *never to taste either ale or spirits* " (p. 210). This article, according to the usage of magazine publishing, would be in type before Mr. Teare's 18th of June! On page 64 of the " Autobiography " Mr. Livesey, whose mind the reader will perceive was actively engaged on the subject, gives the following account of the private pledge signed by John King and himself: "I, with many others, felt that there was no safety for our members without this, and we were determined to bring about the change. One Thursday (Aug. 23, 1832), John King was passing my shop in Church street, and I invited him in, and after discussing this question, upon which we were both agreed, I asked him if he would sign a pledge of *total* abstinence, to which he consented. I then went to the desk and wrote one out (the precise words of which I don't remember). He came up to the desk, and I said, ' Thee sign it first.' He did so, and I signed after him." Excepting as a step in advance, very little importance attaches to this incident. The pledge of August 23rd has been much talked about, and indeed more has been made of it than the circumstance warrants. As a matter of fact, no third person is reported ever to have seen it, and no one knows what its exact terms were. However, Mr. Livesey immediately summoned a meeting for the following Saturday evening, September 1st, to consider the subject, and the result is given by Mr. Dearden on pages 102 and 109.

also an improvement upon the Blackburn pledge, which did not contain the famous clause directed against 'giving and offering' drink to others. And while it did not bind all who signed it to abstain from fermented liquor, it condemns the use of every kind of intoxicant. Entire abstinence, which had been practised at that time by Mr. Livesey for over a year, was left an open question,—a matter of conscience for each member; and doubtless this step was fully as advanced a one as was possible at the time of the inception of the Society; but, as was soon made evident, it was only a step. It was, however, the boldest advance in the right direction which had then been taken and announced to the world.

The Preston Society was formed on Thursday, March 22nd, 1832, and the reader will find by turning back to page xv., that on the previous day Mr. Livesey had lectured in the Cock-pit on the subject of Intemperance. There appears to be no report of his Lecture, but by a strange coincidence the April number of his *Moral Reformer* opens with a paper on 'Intemperance,' occupying sixteen pages, and discussing the subject thoroughly, if not exhaustively. This article was written —and indeed it must have been in type—before the Preston Society was formed, and it is extremely probable that its substance was delivered by Mr. Livesey as his Cock-pit lecture.

By examining this article and comparing it with other productions of the time on the question, it will be found to be perhaps the most complete, philosophical, useful, and practical treatise which had then appeared. Mr. Livesey traces the causes, immediate and remote, of drinking; presents the universality of the habit; points out the disastrous results arising therefrom to individuals and the community; and indicates the remedies calculated to be effective. Indeed, but for the single exception in favour of the medical use of alcohol, the teaching of this article is quite abreast of the popular teetotalism of to-day. Its spirit, tone, earnestness, and calm persuasiveness admirably fitted it to direct the attention of the thoughtful to the question, and this is most likely what its writer aimed at. Certainly no production better calculated to prepare the way for active Temperance effort could be designed. The entire article is worthy of being reprinted, and its circulation amongst persons not at present interested in Temperance could only be productive of benefit. What Mr. Livesey's sentiments were *before* the Preston Society was started, may be gathered from the following extract:

" The people have, in the first place, *to be convinced of their errors*. Under an impression that there is something *good*, in the use of ardent spirits, they are given to children as soon as they are born, and continued through every period of life. Now if persons were convinced of the true nature of alcohol (or spirit), that it imparts no nutriment to the body; that in proportion as it stimulates the system, it wastes the vital energy; that its true use is as a medicine, and its proper place the apothecary shop; and that the opinion of its *doing a healthy person good* is a monstrous delusion; one great step, at least with the reflecting part of mankind, would be gained. In the second place, they have to be persuaded *to break off an inveterate habit*. This is a hard task. There are many who are convinced of the folly and sinfulness of hard drinking, but they appear to be unable to resist. There can be no cure for such but a STRONG RESOLUTION to abstain ENTIRELY; for to expect such persons to descend from excess, step by step, to the mark of moderation is to expect an impossibility. With these individuals it must be a desperate effort—ALL or NOTHING are the terms. But, in the next place, I observe that our greatest hope ought to be, to *prevent these* habits from being formed. However desirable it may.

be to reclaim drunkards, it is far more practicable to prevent the sober part of the population from becoming such. If there were none to fill up the vacant places of those whom hard drinking carries away daily, the vice would soon disappear, but whilst their ranks are readily replenished with the youth of both sexes, the evil will remain. With the same anxiety that we would prevent the careless and the decrepit from falling into the fire, ought we to use every possible means to PREVENT every sober person from becoming intemperate. To accomplish these three points, all hands must be set to work. Like as in the case of an invasion, interests, prejudices, and parties must be forgotten, and every hand and every eye directed to the common enemy." *

Mr. Livesey defends the pledge; points out the dangers of moderation, and calls attention to the fact that the abstinence idea is not new, instancing the case of the Rechabites who, he says, "so long since as the days of Jeremiah, never even tasted *wine*." Regarding Temperance Societies (and his words should be pondered by those who flippantly charge the early teetotalers with putting Temperance in the place of religion) † he says:

"Willing to encourage every plan calculated to arrest the progress of this vice, I heartily wish these societies every success; though I affirm again, that *if the ministers of religion had done their duty*, we should not now have been in a condition to require exertion of so unusual a character." ‡

Upon coffee houses as counter attractions to the public-house, Mr. Livesey remarks:

"What appears to be most wanting to perfect the character of a Temperance Society, are 'Temperance Houses,' or Coffee rooms as they are called in Scotland. If suitable places were fitted up, where persons could spend a social hour in the evening, or where they could transact business; where travellers could be accommodated without being under any inducement to take intoxicating liquor, and where such an article was not sold,—a great advantage would be gained to the cause of Temperance. Such places, including a reading room, and conveniences for eating, I have no doubt would answer well, and would be a speculation attended with profit. No Temperance Society, in my opinion, is complete without them." §

This truly admirable pre-Society paper is closed by Mr. Livesey in these words, which will be heartily reciprocated by all lovers of their kind:

"Hail! enviable period! when enlightened reason shall guide the actions of man; when demoralizing example shall blush to show its face; when corrupting and debasing mankind [by the licensed traffic] shall cease to be a profession; and when the men and women of every rank, in the hope of a better world, shall rally around the standard of TEMPERANCE and PEACE." ||

Mr. Livesey's teachings on Temperance have now been traced down to the period of the formation of the Preston Temperance Society, and his growth and development on the subject may be gathered from the extracts given. ¶ The prevailing idea that the Preston movement was originated and established by illiterate working men, will scarcely stand before the citations made from Mr. Livesey's

---

* *Moral Reformer*, vol. ii. (1832), pp. 111, 112.

† Abundant evidence disproving this allegation will be found in subsequent chapters.

‡ *Ibid.*, vol. ii. (1832), p. 114.

§ *Ibid.*, vol. ii. (1832), p. 115. || *Ibid.*, vol. ii. (1832), p. 116.

¶ But for the statement of Mr. Teare that "in the month of July, 1833, Mr. Livesey devoted part of the *Moral Reformer* to the advocacy of Temperance," the references to the question in that periodical would not have been so minutely referred to. The examination makes evident how unsafe it would be to follow Mr. Teare, or to rely upon his statements, and it also discloses the fact that before even the Preston Temperance Society was founded, Mr. Livesey had printed and published more information on the subject than Mr. Teare did throughout his entire life. What really did happen in July, 1833, was this,—Mr. Livesey then placed all Temperance information under the one heading, 'The Temperance Advocate.'

writings in this and preceding chapters. Mr. Livesey was a well (if self) educated man, nay further, with the evidences now before him, the reader will be of the opinion of Dr. F. R. Lees—that he was truly a man of culture.

As the reader will find a large amount of information regarding the establishment of the Temperance Society and the early labours of the Preston advocates in Chapters XII. and XIV. of the "Autobiography," and in Mr. Dearden's "Dawn," it is unnecessary to pursue the subject further here, indeed space will not permit it; but I would remark that Mr. Livesey munificently provided a home for the young society. Before the Society was formed he had taken the Cock-pit, which for seven years he generously allowed to be used as a Temperance Hall rent free; and his tongue, pen, and purse, were always at command. In his *Moral Reformer*, and afterwards in his *Advocate*, the Preston movement enjoyed all the advantages of an organ of rare ability, while he not only wrote their most effective tracts, but, according to Mr. Dearden, supplied them at the mere cost of the paper * His influence pervaded the Society, and his rare and remarkable talents, and sterling qualities made it famous; in fact his relationship to the movement can only be fittingly described as that of Pioneer and Founder.

Mr. Edward Grubb, the only surviving member of the Preston advocates, in the letter quoted on page x., refers to the statement made in some of the Temperance papers at the time of Mr. Livesey's death, that there were in Preston abstainers before Mr. Livesey †—not an extraordinary circumstance, seeing that there always have been persons who, from one cause or another, did not drink. About these persons, whom Mr. Grubb knew, he remarks :

" These men had nothing to say against the drink, or the use of it by others; they never spoke against it, nor wrote against it, nor invited any one to follow their practice. How is it that men having no resemblance to Mr. Livesey, should be named before him? Tell us of a teetotaler *before* him ; ‡ the originator of a *teetotal* SOCIETY *before* him; a teetotal speaker or demonstrator before, or a writer 'before or equal to him; that did the same work, did it as well, or so much of it—and then we shall be able to say what is befitting us to say."

In the same communication Mr. Grubb says, and we think we have abundantly made clear his contention :

" Mr. Livesey was the first man in the first period; that is, the great man in the greatest and best period ever known since the Temperance Reformation began in England; and the popular estimation of his character, now, is not greater than he had with us at the beginning."

* "Autobiography," p. 101.

† The persons here specially alluded to abstained from alcoholic drinks, not on account of their deleterious character, but because they were taxed. They abstained on political and patriotic grounds, as others did in various parts of the British Isles.

‡ Mr. Grubb does not mean simply an *abstainer*, but a *real teetotaler* which is something more than that.

CHAPTER VII.

TEMPERANCE: THE PRESTON MOVEMENT.

As Providence prepares the thought in the reformer, so it prepares it less consciously in kindred souls; and thus it happens that when the master speaks, the disciple answers, as thought responds to thought, and heart to heart.—Dr. F. R. LEES.

The most remarkable instance of a combined movement in society which history perhaps will be summoned to notice, is that which in our own days has applied itself to the abatement of intemperance.—THOMAS DE QUINCEY.

Nothing awakens our sleeping virtues like the noble acts of our predecessors. They are flaming beacons that fame has set on the hills.—OWEN FELTHAM.

THE PRESTON TEMPERANCE MOVEMENT stands alone. Nothing like it had preceded it, and nothing equal to it has since appeared. It possessed distinctive characteristics and singular merits, and the more closely these are examined and inquired into, the more striking and unique they appear. In fact, the movement loses nothing, but gains at every point, from a comparison with other efforts.

The first pledge of the Society, as we have seen, was based on the most advanced declaration then published. True, it did not go far enough to satisfy Mr. Livesey and some of his disciples; but if vigorous and systematic effort could make a society based upon the old lines successful, the experiment was now in a way of being fairly tried. The founders of the Society from the first adopted Mr. Livesey's method of visitation, and devised an almost perfect system for bringing the subject of Temperance under the notice of the people in their own homes.* But where the Preston Society possessed advantages superior to all others, was in having *men*, prepared by tuition and training, ready to set its machinery in motion. In spite of a defective constitution, wonders were wrought, and the town was thoroughly aroused upon the question. The meetings in the Cock-pit were crowded and enthusiastic. The Society had barely been three months in active operation before Mr. W. Pollard (who had been the chief speaker at the inaugural meeting, and whose principles were rendered more robust by coming into contact with

* Mr. William Livesey, in his paper "Fifty Years Ago," read at the Crystal Palace Jubilee, September 5th, 1882, has the following pointed reference to visitation: "Besides holding an average two meetings a week throughout the year, the dissemination of Temperance teaching by means of tracts and extensive visitation of the people at their own homes were two marked features in the Society's operations; indeed, the rules of the Society required a systematic weekly visitation. The third rule of the Society also required that all pledge-breakers should be visited by one or more of the committee. The extensive visitation, which was thoroughly and continuously carried out in those early days, led to the best results, not only in strengthening the hands of the weak, but in converting those who had not joined the Society. This work of sympathy and self-sacrifice was a most potent instrument in building up the Society. Of late years we have had articles in all the daily papers, from the *Times* downwards, and also in a large number of weekly ones, on 'How to Reach the Masses.' This problem the men of Preston solved at the first sitting of their committee; they saw the way and walked therein. Nothing is easier than reaching the masses, but people nowadays won't adopt the Preston plan of going directly to the people, visiting them at their own homes, and talking kindly to them at their own firesides."

Preston) took part in the first Tea Party, held in the Cloth Hall on July 11th, 1832, and declared—"and," says Mr. Livesey, "he is a competent judge"—"That what he had seen and heard at Preston, convinced him that no society in the kingdom had made the same progress as this had." * And a few months later, Mr. Edward Morris, of Glasgow—who, as a traveller, had exceptional opportunities of learning the condition of the movement in the principal cities and towns in Scotland and the North of England—in a letter dated October 29th, remarks: "There is, perhaps, no town in the empire (not even excepting Glasgow and Manchester) which shows more zeal in the Temperance cause than Preston." † These gratifying results Mr. Livesey was not slow in accounting for.

"This success," he says, "has been principally owing to the committee-ship and management being entirely in the hands of good-hearted, *plain, working* men, whose efforts have not been cramped and paralyzed by a splendid patronage." ‡

The Preston Society was not started merely to prevent, but to cure, drunkenness. The reader of the first and second of these introductory chapters will be familiar with Mr. Livesey's belief in the possible reclamation of the most degraded of his fellow-creatures, and that his Temperance associates entertained the same idea is made clear by the following citation from the July *Moral Reformer:*

"I could fill the whole of this number with detailing the statements and confessions of reformed drunkards, which have been delivered in a manner calculated to delight every man who feels for the good of his species. In this respect, I believe, we go beyond what most other societies have marked out as the course of operation: they seem to think that the conversion of old and hardened drinkers is hopeless, and, therefore, trust more in the efficacy of *preserving the temperate*, in order to secure a better race of men for the next generation. We are not so passive, nor so distant in our prospects; the number of reformed drunkards, the most notorious in the town, who now do honour, by their consistent conduct, to our Society, are a sufficient assurance that, with appropriate efforts, and with the blessing of God, the chief of drunkards may be reclaimed. It is true, we have had some relapses; and it would be strange, out of so many, if this were not the case; but they are not abandoned—they are visited by those who speak to them with charity and kindness, and whose efforts, I believe, in no instance have yet been known to fail in restoring them. They are not upbraided, but counselled to steadfastness, and warned to keep from temptation. In every case it has been the 'first glass' to which they could trace their fall, and often to the misguided entreaties of a friend; but the result has generally been, that, seeing the danger, they have now resolved *never to taste either ale or spirits*." §

Of course Mr. Livesey, who for years had systematically visited the poor, undertook his share in this interesting work. || As a total abstainer, he would be an efficient counsellor and friend to the poor backslider, who had fallen a victim to ale drinking, since he could plead his own practice, and point out the advantages resulting to health from the entire abandonment of all intoxicants. The vigour with which the Preston crusade was prosecuted, speedily disclosed the fallacy of attempting a Temperance reform upon any other basis than that of abstinence from fermented as well as distilled liquor; and the Preston men were not long in

---

* *Moral Reformer*, vol. ii. (1832), p. 247.   † *Ibid.*, vol. ii. (1832), p. 384.

‡ *Ibid.*, vol. ii. (1832), p. 247.   § *Ibid.*, vol. ii. (1832), p. 210.

|| This is no mere surmise. On the 19th of June, 1834, Mr. Livesey was examined before the famous Parliamentary Committee on Drunkenness, and in reply to a question (994) as to his opportunities of observing the causes, etc., of drinking, said: "During the last two years *I have made it my regular employment on a Sunday morning to go and visit the poor part of the population, and especially the houses of those who are addicted to the vice of drunkenness*" (p. 117).

making their movement thus comprehensive. The task of tracing, step by step, the development of this the most interesting reform of the age, is a tempting one, but cannot be pursued here. The reader is, however, referred for many interesting particulars and details to the "Autobiography," which, from page 62 to the end, is more or less occupied with the subject.*

The spirit in which the work was entered upon is evinced by the opening paragraph of the first Annual Report of the Society, which is as follows:

"In presenting the first Report of the Preston Temperance Society, the Committee cannot withhold an acknowledgment of their great obligations to the great God and Father of us all, for the signal results with which He has crowned their labours. Small in its origin, and unpatronized, the Society has swelled to its present magnitude ; has excited an interest in this town unprecedented in the history of any other society, except in that of the Christian religion."

The old Preston Cock-pit was the scene of some of the most enthusiastic Temperance meetings ever held. The converts were encouraged to relate their experience, which many of them did in a most effective and graphic manner. The building has been called a school of eloquence, and certainly it was a place—

> Where all spake
> According to their sorts, and the occasion. †

Mr. Livesey, when writing upon 'Home Speakers,' gives the following description of the method of the Cock-pit meetings :

"At Preston we have no select place for speakers, no platform; and the meeting-place being in the form of an amphitheatre, every person can command a view of the whole congregation ; hence the speakers rise up in their different places, and tell their plain and honest tales to the great delight and benefit of the audience." ‡

Mr. Livesey's first coadjutors in the work had previously had the benefit of his instruction, and he resolved that the new converts to Temperance should have

---

* Although the space at my disposal will not allow me to give a sequential narration of the progress of the Preston reformers, I cannot forbear presenting the following items of historic interest :—In the *Moral Reformer* for June, 1832, Mr. Livesey protests against the term 'moderate' being applied to *any* use of poison. In the July *Moral Reformer* he reports progress: the meetings are well attended and enthusiastic ; several thousand tracts are ordered ; "the town is divided into twenty-eight districts, and a captain is appointed to circulate tracts and to superintend each district." About fifteen pages of this number are occupied with Temperance articles, including one by Dr. Harrison, on 'Ale and other Fermented Liquors.' In the August number Mr. Livesey reports that the meetings are overflowing. "It deserves to be remarked," he says, "that at a late civic feast given by the mayor of this borough, *three* gentlemen present *drank* water, and were honoured *as water drinkers*, by having their healths drank." It is reported that on July 11th, 540 persons attended the first Tea Party, held in the Cloth Hall. Altogether eleven pages are devoted to this topic. In the September *Moral Reformer* Mr. Livesey refers to the difficulties arising from ale drinking, but has "no fear that perseverance in diffusing *correct information*" will not overcome them. He cautions societies against admitting persons as members indiscriminately, and in another article he says: "What an immense increase in the home trade we should have if the money now spent in ale, wine, and spirits, was spent in different articles of clothing and furniture, produced by our own labourers, and in rational enjoyments." In the October number he says : "The great current against which we have to contend is the mischievous practice of *ale drinking*"; and one of his hints for the improvement of Temperance Societies is, "That the pledges be framed *to meet the habits of the people* in the places where they are adopted." His remark that "in this respect we have not, in Preston, perhaps, made the best choice," indicates that the first pledge of the Society did not come up to his idea of what was needful. And it is also evident that the limitation of one year in the teetotal pledge first adopted by the Society was not approved by Mr. Livesey; for in an article in the *Preston Advocate* for January, 1835, on Youths' Societies, he says : "The pledge should be one of total abstinence, without any limitation of time. The words 'for one year,' I consider to be dangerous, and calculated to make the young people look upon the pledge as a burden to be borne for a time, instead of what it really is, a declaration of independence from the disgraceful and slavish yoke which custom, backed by erroneous opinion, has palmed upon society " (p. 2).

† Bailey's "Festus."   ‡ *The Preston Temperance Advocate*, vol. iv. (1837), p. 62.

similar advantages. A room at the Cock-pit was fitted up as an academy, where men redeemed from the degradation of drink, and anxious for self-improvement, were taught the rudiments of education, and the precepts of wisdom.* This school was well calculated to improve the public advocacy of the reclaimed drunkard, and therefore helpful both to the men and the movement. The first Annual Report of the Society speaks of this class of speakers as follows:

" With very few exceptions, the speakers are persons who have been reclaimed from drunkenness by the efforts of this Society, and their advocacy is found to produce the most powerful impressions, for they speak with the eloquence of facts, and the genuine pathos of truth." †

The obstacle to Temperance progress, presented by the universal belief in the virtues of malt liquor, was of so serious a nature that it paralyzed the movement throughout the country. The Preston friends were confronted with the same difficulty, and no one felt its importance more keenly than Mr. Livesey, who, in the early part of 1833, entered upon a complete examination of the Malt Liquor question. He took Franklin's famous experience and declaration (which he had published in his *Moral Reformer*, in June, 1832) as his starting-point, and collected information on the subject from various sources, actually laying a friendly brewer under contribution. He found not only that the use of ale and beer could be abandoned with advantage—his own experience for upwards of two years had taught him that—but that fermented liquors were positively prejudicial and injurious, while their supposed nutritious qualities were all a delusion. The results of his inquiries were embodied in a lecture delivered on Thursday, February 28th, in the Cock-pit. Mr. Livesey pursued his inquiries further upon the subject, never resting until he had completed his famous indictment against malt liquors, which for upwards of half a century has been known to the world as " The Malt Liquor Lecture."

Again and again was Mr. Livesey induced to re-deliver his famous lecture in the Cock-pit, where the audience seemed never to tire of listening to it. The reclaimed drunkards, who had been rescued from the perils of malt liquor, delighted in seeing the 'old thief' anatomized; but the lecture not only gave them unanswerable reasons for their new faith, it exposed to view more completely than had ever before been attempted, the wickedness involved in a system which transformed the bounties of a gracious Providence into a withering curse. While the rescued ones were shown the perils of the 'great delusion' from which they had escaped, they were reminded that the world at large was still living beneath its pestilent shadow; and in this way the missionary spirit for which Preston was so famous was encouraged and advanced. It was thus too that Preston teetotalism acquired its robust character; the zeal of the Preston abstainers was born of knowledge, and therein lay its strength.

Not content with lecturing upon the subject, Mr. Livesey published an epitome

* Mr. John Brodbelt, writing in the *Preston Temperance Advocate*, for March, 1837, bears testimony to the utility and value of this institution. "In Preston," he says, "we have academies formed by members of the Temperance Society,—men, some of whom a short time ago were wallowing in the filth of drunkenness, but whose leisure time is now spent in intellectual enjoyment" (p. 20).

† *Moral Reformer*, vol. iii. (1833), p. 125.

of his discourse in the *Moral Reformer* for June, 1833, as an address to Ale Drinkers, headed "The Great Delusion," under which title the article was immediately reprinted, and widely circulated as a tract.* Mr. Livesey did not, however, allow the matter to rest here. The 'great delusion' had both infected and affected the rich and poor alike, and he was anxious to enlighten the upper classes, especially those legislators who had passed the Beer Act ostensibly as a measure of relief to the working man. In the August issue of the *Reformer* consequently appears the following notice:

"ALE DRINKING.

" So important do I consider the subject discussed in the tract entitled ' The Great Delusion,' addressed to ale drinkers, that I intend forwarding a copy, printed on purpose, to every member of the House of Commons, and the House of Lords. The agricultural interest keep employing the Press to sing the praises of ale drinking as a source of health, national prosperity, and good morals. All those interested in the Temperance cause should expose the delusion." †

The need of this splendid effort of Mr. Livesey's—a piece of work of which he speaks modestly enough, and merely as an incentive to others to go and do likewise, but which no then existing society would have undertaken—is apparent from the following quotations from Parliamentary utterances on the Beer question. Mr. James Silk Buckingham, in his *Parliamentary Review and Magazine* for 1833, wrote: "We should rejoice to see the duties on malt and hops entirely removed, *a wholesome* and *nutritious* beverage, without tax or restraint, in the power of every man to brew for his own use." When such views were held by a Temperance legislator, we need not be surprised to find Mr. Joseph Hume, M.P., saying about the same time: " The malt tax might be reduced with advantage to the morals of the people; " or Sir W. Ingleby, that "In *a moral point of view*, the malt tax was calculated to brutalize the people ; " or Sir Robert Peel, that " The comforts of the labouring classes were proved to have increased by the augmented consumption of malt." ‡

Mr. Livesey's spirited act was responded to by one Member of Parliament— Mr. George Williams—who, on August 20th, 1833, addressed to him an interesting letter, the opening sentence of which is as follows :

" Your printed letter on the subject of ale drinking corresponds exactly with the language I myself hold with the victims of this indulgence. I have been a water drinker (only) for twenty-three years, and am as able as any man to illustrate its advantages." §

The circulation of the " Great Delusion " in Preston had a most beneficial result. Testimonies to its usefulness abounded on every hand. Its fame rapidly became national, and before many months had elapsed the facts it contained were widely disseminated in America. The circulation of the " Great Delusion," and the remarkable progress of the Preston Society, brought Mr. Livesey innumerable calls from places near and remote to lecture on the subject, which he responded to according to his ability.

* " The Great Delusion " was also reprinted at Birmingham, London, Bristol, and in many other towns.
† *Moral Reformer*, vol. iii. (1833), p. 259.   ‡ *Ibid.*, vol. iii. (1833), p. 289.
§ *Ibid.*, vol. iii. (1833), p. 321.

The first delivery of the Malt Liquor Lecture outside Preston occurred on Monday, February 17th, 1834, at the Independent Chapel, Bolton.* It was very effective, and one gentleman, a leader in the Society, who kept ' home brewed ' in his house, observed to his wife after the meeting, " no more brewing *at our house*." † The lecture was, however, brought more prominently into notice from being delivered in connexion with the Second Annual Festival of the Preston Society, on Thursday, February 27th, 1834, in the theatre of that town, where it produced " an extraordinary impression." ‡ On the 30th of September of the same year it was repeated to a crowded audience in the theatre. Robert Guest White, Esq., was chairman ; and the Rev. John Clay, in moving a vote of thanks, characterized Mr. Livesey's effort as being " one of the most interesting and convincing lectures he had ever attended." §

The Preston Temperance Society became a centre of almost universal interest. Its heroic band of devoted workers, led on by Mr. Livesey, completely transformed the town, and the beneficial effects of the new system were everywhere apparent. In short, a social, moral, and spiritual reformation was induced. The influence of the Society in promoting *real* piety was visible on every hand. From the individual testimonies of reformed characters on this point, made at a single meeting at Preston (Oct. 3rd, 1834), the following are selected :

J. Johnson declared : " I am indeed a brand plucked from the fire ; " and after describing his wretched condition as a drunkard and his complete deliverance by teetotalism, added, " I was now led to a place of worship, and have united myself with a religious body."

Henry Newton said : " I go regularly to a place of worship, and feel quite satisfied."

Richard Turner—the earnest, simple-hearted ' Dicky,' to whom we owe the term ' Teetotal,'—avowed : " When I go through the streets on a Sunday, it does my soul good to meet so many reformed drunkards, well dressed, and going to their places of worship."

R. Catton : " My house, which was a house of cursing and swearing, is now a house of prayer."

W. Kennedy referred to a meeting, addressed by Mr. Livesey and Mr. Swindlehurst, which he had attended as a wretched drunkard, and said : " The following morning I felt more happy, and offered up my prayer to God for protection."

J. Whatmough, eight years a drunkard : " I can now send my children to school, and go to a place of worship myself." ||

The attendance at all the places of worship in the town was greatly improved, and we read that " at Preston a particular church became so far noticed by the attendance of reclaimed characters as to acquire the name of the Reformed Drunkards' Church." ¶ The Rev. John Clay, the celebrated prison chaplain of

* It would perhaps be more correct to say the first time Mr. Livesey was reported to have delivered the Malt Lecture outside Preston. .

† *The Preston Temperance Advocate*, vol. i. (1834), p. 21.   ‡ *Ibid.*, vol. i. (1834), p. 25.

§ *Ibid.*, vol. i. (1834), p. 81. || *Ibid.*, vol. i. (1834), pp. 83, 84.

¶ " The Permanent Temperance Documents," First part, Douglas, 1839. Note to p. 95.

Preston, bore repeated and emphatic testimony to the Society's influence in increasing the comforts and happiness of the people, in filling the churches and chapels, and in practically extinguishing crime. Speaking at the Temperance festival, held in the Preston theatre on Wednesday, October 1st, 1834, he declared:

"The Temperance Society has conferred more benefits upon the community than any other; it may be said, indeed, that it has become the basis and strength of society. . . . The benefits of Temperance are inestimable; it tends to unite all classes in benevolence and good fellowship, which all ought to promote; to carry comfort into the poor man's cottage; to produce peace where dissension formerly reigned; and, above all, to convert the ignorant, the profligate, and the infidel, into the instructed, the decent, the sober believer. This glorious society of ours tends to raise infatuated men from the wretched slavery of drunkenness, and place them in that elevated rank amongst God's creatures for which He Himself designed them." *

Mr. Justice Alderson, early in the same year, had already directed public attention to the absence of crime in Preston, as the following citation from the *Preston Advocate* for April, 1834, shows:

"Mr. Justice Alderson, on hearing the case, Brown *v.* Smith for breach of covenant (one party having fallen into drunken habits), said, 'Why don't you bind him to the Temperance Society? I am sure the Temperance Societies do much good; for from Preston, where they are in operation, *there has not been a single criminal case* at these assizes.' It may be added that this is the fourth assizes to which this remark will apply, including the whole period that the Preston Society has been in operation." †

Mr. Clay, in his report for 1834, thus summarises the beneficial results of the Society's work:

"I write with circumspection and advisedly when I state my belief that no Society, instituted for the good of the operative classes, has, within the same period, produced such cheering and undoubted evidence of its value. I know of no institution which has worked so great an amount of unalloyed good; none which, with such apparent humble means, has brought about such wonderful changes for the better—carrying peace into households from which habitual intoxication had long banished it; competency and comfort where poverty and wretchedness seemed irrevocably fixed; and converting the ignorant and drunken infidel into a serious and sober Christian." ‡

And the following year he again reverts to the subject:

"It has been doubted," he says, "that such beneficial consequences as I have pointed out could have arisen from the cause assigned. In answer to such doubts, I can only again advert to the fact that this remarkable decrease in felonious offences is contemporaneous *with a powerful* society founded for the express purpose of closing the greatest inlet to crime. In fact, every one who has inquired into the subject knows that intemperance is the direct or remote cause of almost every offence against the law; and it is therefore a necessary consequence that where, as in this case, intemperance is greatly diminished these offences will diminish too." §

It will most likely be asked, "Did the Temperance Society in Preston continue to exert upon the town as marked an influence as that which followed its early operations?" To such a question the answer must be given that the high-water mark was *not* maintained, and the reasons are not far to seek. Teetotalism was

---

* *Preston Temperance Advocate*, vol. i. (1834), p. 82.   † *Ibid.* (1834), p. 30.
‡ "The Chaplain's Report on the Preston House of Correction, 1834."   § *Ibid.*, 1835.

a principle needed by mankind, and it could not be narrowed down or confined to one town. Consequently, after the reform had been fairly set going in Preston, the chief actors in the enterprise became absorbed in *a national movement*. The cause in Preston of course suffered; but what that town lost, the world at large may be said to have gained.

Regarding the movement in Preston, it may be safely affirmed that the principle has never lost its hold upon the town; and whenever the early plans and methods have been applied with anything like the old energy and devotion, corresponding good results have always been achieved.

The history of the Preston Society shows that great things are possible. It is a heritage of which the young men of that town may well be proud. May they be worthy successors of worthy progenitors. If they are, they will resolve, in the language of one of the early Temperance periodicals, that "what *has been* done, *can be* done again; yea, and by the blessing of God it *shall be* done, until our country and the world are free from the power of the destroyer."[*]

[*] *British Temperance Advocate and Journal*, 1839, p. 87.

CHAPTER VIII.

TEMPERANCE: HOW THE LIGHT SPREAD.

The seed,
The little seed they laughed at in the dark,
Has risen and cleft the soil, and grown a bulk
Of spanless girth, that lays on every side
A thousand arms, and rushes to the sun.—TENNYSON.

ENGLAND:
    The zeal and energy of the Preston teetotalers first lit up that beacon in the land whose light has streamed far and wide.—FIRST REPORT OF NEW BRITISH AND FOREIGN TEMPERANCE SOCIETY (1837).

SCOTLAND:
    I trust the Temperance reformers of Scotland will, at no distant time, have to return acknowledgments in a body to the wisdom and determination of their southern brethren in this matter.—JOHN DUNLOP (1836).

IRELAND:
    The Editor of the *Preston Advocate* has done more to advance the cause than any man living.—PROFESSOR JOHN EDGAR (1838).

AMERICA:
    The impulse given from Preston is precisely the one wanted.—*The Temperance Intelligencer* (American), October, 1834.

HITHERTO, excepting the mention of Mr. Livesey's lecture at Bolton, reference has been confined to the work in Preston and the results which attended it there. But it will be obvious that benefits so marked and striking could not be long confined to one spot, and this would especially be the case where men, banded together for a beneficent object, were animated by the ideas and spirit which Mr. Livesey had for years taught and exemplified. And the Preston men had no wish to keep such advantages to themselves; in the first Annual Report of their Society we find it stated that:

> "So many zealous and active friends have come forward in the support of this great cause in Preston, that the Committee have ventured to extend their efforts to surrounding villages; and societies are now formed in the villages of Walton, Penwortham, Leyland, Lytham, Longridge, Garstang, and Ribchester; some of which are making rapid progress. And such is the great strength of the Society, that as its labours have been extended abroad its vigour has increased at home." *

Such was the humble beginning of that grand missionary enterprise which, within two or three years, successfully planted the new doctrine of abstinence throughout the United Kingdom, practically superseding the first Anti-Spirit Societies, and setting up a system at once efficient, safe, and complete. From neighbouring villages, the Preston reformers extended their operations to the towns of Lancashire and Yorkshire, and subsequently to more distant places. Mr. Livesey was one of the earliest of the band to engage in this work. "I made a tour," he says, "to Liverpool, Bolton, Bury, and Manchester, at the commencement of the

---

* *Moral Reformer,* vol. iii. (1833), p. 126.

new year ; " * and he and his colleagues having once put their "hands to the plough," never looked back.   They had discovered a remedy for 'the national disgrace,' and for the numerous evils arising from the drinking system ; and their resolve was that, so far as they were concerned, the people should no longer perish for lack of knowledge.   Their missionary tours and visits to remote places are described in the "Autobiography," and more fully in the "Reminiscences"; and if ever we had a genuine Gospel Temperance Movement in operation, it was during the active labours of the Preston pioneers.   In motive, means, and spirit, this Preston missionary enterprise was more thoroughly in accord with the Gospel, and the precepts and methods of its Founder, than any subsequent movement, however designated by its promoters.   But with these heroic and devoted men neither religion nor teetotalism was a marketable article.   The injunction to "buy the truth and sell it not," was one they not only understood, but acted upon.   They did not profess to be better or more religious than other people, and they avoided "praying in the market-places," nor did they, "for a pretence," offer up long petitions ; they rather preferred, as being more in harmony with Gospel teaching, to retire into the closet and "pray in secret." †   With their earnest and eloquent colleague, Henry Anderton,‡ they could say—

> Bend reverently, my spirit,
> Before that Being fall,
> Whose wisdom first created,
> Whose power sustaineth all.

From a discussion which took place at the Annual Conference of the British Temperance League (1885) it would seem that these truly Gospel ideas are too antiquated and unobtrusive for some present-day friends of Temperance, who evidently dissent from James Montgomery's view that—

> Prayer is the soul's sincere desire,
> Uttered or unexpressed ;
> The motion of a hidden fire,
> That trembles in the breast.

But what besides a genuine trust in the Almighty, and a complete reliance upon Him, could have sustained these men ?   Possessing this, and burning with a love

---

* *Moral Reformer*, vol. iii. (1833), p. 53.

† In this preference they acted in accordance with Mr. Livesey's known predilections. In one of his private note books occurs the following : "I *do like to see* a man praying in his closet, when he supposes no human eye beholds him."

‡ It may be useful here to give an extract from a letter of Anderton's, written March 23rd, 1836, in reply to an invitation to take part in the Wilsden (Yorkshire) Temperance Festival for that year. Mr. Anderton explains that owing to the recent death of his father the responsibilities of the business devolved upon himself, and hence he was precluded from attending. His father was a trophy of the Preston movement, and of his death Henry says: "I wish, sir, some of your moderate-drinking professors could have witnessed the happiness of my father in the 'trying hour.' I wish they could have listened to his dying ejaculations to Heaven in favour of that cause which had been instrumental in rescuing him from the 'horrible pit of drunkenness,' and of leading him to the

> 'Fountain fill'd with blood,
> Drawn from Immanuel's veins.'

I wish they could have heard his earnest entreaties to his family and friends not to forget, but to spread, those principles of truth which we have advocated, and which proved to him the 'savour of life unto life.' When I told him that it was my intention to preach abstinence and Jesus as long as God spared me, I wish they could have seen him—unable to speak— wave his thin arm around his head three times, in token of encouragement and triumph. . . . I thought it would please you to hear that the cause we have espoused has, under God, led another drunkard—a forty years' drunkard—to Zion."—*Report of Wilsden Festival*, 1836, p. 15.

for their fellows, as a matter of Christian duty, they went out without " purse or scrip"—at their own charge—and everywhere " the common people heard them gladly." It has been said that " sincerity has always a breath and spirit of its own," and none discover that quality more readily than the poor. By instinct, the masses recognised their true friends in these primitive Christian missionaries, to whose teaching they gladly responded. And so the torch of true Temperance, lit in Preston, was passed on from hand to hand.

Mr. William Hoyle, in a paper read at the Preston Conference of the British League, July, 1882, after referring to the work of the Preston men of 1832, who were " led on " by Mr. Livesey, remarks :

" For men to go forth and hoist the flag of total abstinence—to proclaim to the world the doctrine that intoxicating liquors were not only useless, but hurtful —was to cross the path not merely of the beliefs and prejudices of the age, but also of the interests of large masses of the community; it was to expose one's self to the charge, not simply of ignorance and folly, but often to contempt and persecution. To do this work in those days, therefore, required much greater courage than simply to abstain; it required men who were so imbued with a desire to benefit others as to be willing to sacrifice themselves, and endure obloquy and disgrace, if need be, to secure this end. Those who, without fee or reward, or without the prospect of securing such, are willing thus to labour and suffer, are among the world's great heroes. Such were the men who in this town of Preston in 1832 banded themselves together and started on the high and Christ-like mission of blessing others; who went forth to redeem their country from the sin and misery of intemperance." *

And he thus emphasizes the fact of Mr. Livesey's leadership :

" For two or three years, the [national or missionary] movement went on without the institution of any special organization. Mr. Livesey *headed the work, and was general of the forces*, not only aiding and directing them by words of counsel, but when expense was involved, *finding the needful;* and further, he sent forth from the press literature that carried the truths of Temperance into multitudes of homes where the voice of the missionary could never reach." †

MR. EDWARD GRUBB ON THE PRESTON ADVOCATES.

Mr. Edward Grubb, the only survivor of the original band of Preston Temperance advocates, a man of marked genius and power, and the disciple of Mr. Livesey who seems more than any other to have imbibed his master's spirit, has occasionally given to the world pen portraits of his associates,—studies drawn by the hand of a master. The only attribute in Mr. Grubb's literary efforts calling for regret is brevity, and it is hoped that he may yet see fit to publish a more extensive account of the remarkable movement with which his life has been associated. Mr. Grubb is very properly jealous of the history of the Preston movement, and the memories of the remarkable group of men who figured in it, and justly impatient with the method of treatment the subject has received at the hands of professional writers who have attempted to deal with it. Writing in 1858, he thus refers to the condition of things when they commenced their work:

" Temperance was then an unexamined question; the advocates had no authority to quote in its favour, no model to copy in their speeches. Every one was thrown upon his own resources, and they soon made it evident that if denied the

---

* *The British Temperance Advocate*, 1882, p. 728.   † *Ibid*, p. 728.

help of established precepts, they possessed the endowment of an original genius for the work they had undertaken. This peculiarity began to display its character in the invention of their topics, and in their indefatigable industry in collecting and arranging facts. The applause bestowed upon these advocates was as genuine as their own friendship, and will last as long as gratitude exists among men, as the reward for singular public benefits. They *commanded* attention—the originality of their views, the wonderful demonstrations they gave of the truth of their doctrine; the just, forcible, and eloquent character of their addresses; excited and called into full play an intellectual activity such as no man remembered before. . . . It was no reproach to them that they lived by their own labour, and not by their wits. If the cares and toils of business did not furnish them the means of a soft and indolent life, neither was that a ground of reproach to them. The Temperance cause was regarded by these men as a sacred obligation; it had not then become a commercial speculation in the hands of needy adventurers. These men went to the villages and towns *without stipulating for reward*—they needed no letters of recommendation, and when they had discharged their consciences by doing their duty, they returned, with exhausted means and wearied limbs, like good citizens, to the duties of active life." *

Five years later, in the " Memoir of Henry Anderton," prefixed to the poet's works, Mr. Grubb returns to the subject, and favours us with the following picture of the workers and their work:

" When we survey the situation and circumstances of the early advocates," he says, " we find their duties and comforts altogether different to anything now existing. The difficulties they had to contend against demanded unremitting activity, and the brutal opposition by which they were assailed required the most vigorous exertion to overcome it. Those common enjoyments, which unite and foster the ties of friendship, were put beyond their reach. In this state of things, the allurements of ease or peace could no more charm them than the inhabitants of the desert; and yet, great as the discouragements were, the progress of the cause was as much accelerated by the opposition of its enemies as the zealous and disinterested efforts of its friends. It is a duty to remind those who sometimes condescend to allude to the Preston men, that there is nothing in the present state of things that resembles, in the least particular, the times when Anderton laboured for the cause. The word ' advocate' then did not denote what the word signifies at present. In the Preston sense, that term applied to every one who maintained the doctrine of total abstinence; the advocacy had not then become a profession. In this general sense there were many of the rough-and-ready class, but, even in its most restricted meaning, there were no men who subsisted by their own advocacy. The Preston men gave their time, and spent their own money; they entered towns and villages without invitation, made their speeches, and scattered their tracts by the way. For a long time they kept alive what they had created at home and in other places. The Preston society was not established for the support of its advocates, but the cause; the society did not create them, but they created the society. There never was an institution in modern times like that original and brave confederacy. There was no unmerited preference given—the motive power to mischief was excluded from their noble design. Every one, from the least to the greatest, was ready for his work according to his ability. Those whose talents gave them the highest place in public esteem, made no sport of their humble brethren. Preston did not derive its men, any more than its means, from other places—they had a man for every kind of work, and fit for home or foreign service. They were the best men I have ever known in the cause; their loyalty to truth and to each other was worthy the age of heroes; they were above fear, and, therefore, dreaded no man; like good men who knew their duty, they did it without regard to consequences. They had less talk and more work than falls to the lot of some folk now-a-days, but what they said would ' bide the reckoning.' " †

* " Old and New Temperance Advocacy," 1858, pp. 12, 13.

† " The Temperance and other Poems of the late Henry Anderton." Preston: W. and J. Dobson, 1863, pp. xxv., xxvi.

This is not the occasion to particularise and detail the labours of this true missionary band of Temperance reformers,* but it may be admissible to quote a few lines from Mr. John Finch's "Portraiture of Teetotalism" (1836). Its author, although not a Preston man, was closely identified with that town owing to his partnership with Mr. T. Swindlehurst, with whom he signed the teetotal pledge in the autumn of 1832.

"It would be impossible for me," he says, "or any other individual to enumerate all the societies which have sprung from it (the Preston Society), the number of their members, or the names of the individuals who have honourably distinguished themselves in forming them; therefore, let no person or society be offended that I mention only a very small number of them: Livesey, prince among reformers, Anderton, Grubb, Teare, 'Slender Billy,'† 'Tallyrand,' 'Dicky' Turner, Bradley, 'His Majesty' (Mr. Swindlehurst), myself, and about twenty others in Preston and Liverpool, have stood in the front of the battle from the beginning and slain our thousands." ‡

It may be here observed, notwithstanding the ingenuity of writers and speakers who have endeavoured to trace the cause to other places and persons, that not a scintilla of evidence exists which connects *teetotalism as a national movement* with any place, person, or society, outside Preston. It is a curious coincidence too, that in no place where it is alleged an abstinence pledge was drawn up, or an abstinence society established, prior to those of Preston, has any contemporary account of the same, either in newspaper, periodical, pamphlet, or tract (or printed document or record of any kind), been yet produced to substantiate the claim. But even if it is conceded that such pledges and societies existed, their influence was so purely local, that they were in no sense factors in the establishment of teetotalism, and had neither part nor lot in the matter. The Preston men not only established the principle of true Temperance, they created a propaganda for its dissemination,—the importance of which most history makers have overlooked. Dr. Lees, however, pointed this out years ago in "Meliora;" and in his "Science Temperance Text Book" he has since emphasized the fact; while he fittingly describes Preston as having been "the cradle of the movement." § The propaganda consisted of the platform and the press; and while Mr. Livesey took his share of work in connexion with the former, he entirely projected, maintained, and sustained the latter. His *Moral Reformer* (1832-3), and his *Preston Temperance Advocate* (1834-7), carried the new doctrines to English-speaking people everywhere; while the numerous pamphlets and tracts which he published on the topic, awakened thought, stimulated inquiry, confirmed waverers, and built up new converts in the faith. In order

* For a striking representation of the work of these heroes see "A Chart of the First Ten Years' Labours of the Early Workers"—being the *Jubilee Temperance Almanac*—compiled and arranged by John Pearce. London: National Temperance League.

† 'Slender Billy' was William Howarth, a remarkably fine-looking and very stout man.

‡ "A Portraiture and the Ancient and Modern History of Teetotalism:" Liverpool, 1836, p. 7.

§ Dr. Lees says: "Foremost, as chief and propagandist, stands Joseph Livesey. It was he who, by his admirable malt liquor lecture on 'The Great Delusion,' and his plain Saxon speech, first planted the teetotal standard in London, and in the great provincial towns of Birmingham, Leeds, Bradford, Darlington, Newcastle, and Sunderland. It was he who, through the might of the press, firmly fixed the new ideas in the intelligence of the thoughtful disciples throughout the land, and who laid those goodly foundations on which many later minds have built noble structures of art, eloquence, and science. Of the name of 'the Patriarch of the movement' he is surely most worthy" (*Science Temperance Text Book*, London: National Temperance League, 1884, vol. ii. p. 7).

to substantiate the position taken, that Preston was the great centre of the movement (which was never questioned in the early days, and which nobody doubted until 'histories' began to appear), the following citations are given as a sample of the testimonies which may be found in the early records of the movement. They will also give the reader a pretty good idea of how the reform spread, and bear out Mr. Grubb's remark regarding the high esteem in which Mr. Livesey was held in the beginning.

ORIGIN OF TEETOTALISM IN LONDON.

On pages 69–71 of the "Autobiography" will be found Mr. Livesey's account of the establishment of teetotalism in London.* His statements are supported by Mr. Hart, in his "Truth Unfolded," and by Mr. Frederick Grosjean, of Regent Street—from whose house emanated the invitation given to the Preston Advocates to visit London—in his short article on the ' Origin of Total Abstinence in London,' published in the *Intelligencer* of December 3rd, 1836. No words could more forcibly represent the leadership of Mr. Livesey than the following, used by Mr. Grosjean: "We formed ourselves into a provisional committee, and passed several resolutions, one of which was to invite Mr. Livesey, of Preston, to visit London—*as we were determined to begin well.*" † The New British and Foreign Temperance Society, established August 29th, 1836, which may be said to have been founded by Mr. Livesey, ‡ acknowledges the Preston movement thus:

" Mr. Livesey, of Preston, was the first who, clearly seeing the state of the country, ventured on the bold innovation of introducing a pledge of total abstinence from all intoxicating drinks, in the promotion of which he has laboured up to the present time with untiring energy and astonishing success, and has deserved a foremost place in the gratitude of his country." §

The Second Report acknowledges a donation of thirty thousand publications, anonymously conveyed through the medium of Mr. Livesey; and the Second Report of the British and Foreign Society for the Suppression of Intemperance—the other large Metropolitan association—declares that: "Much good has been done by an extensive circulation of Livesey's Lecture, which may be regarded as a text-book of total abstinence principles." ||

THE BEGINNING OF TEETOTALISM IN MANCHESTER.

At Manchester, the Rev. Francis Beardsall, who had previously been identified with the ' moderation' movement in Market Harborough, was the chief agent in

---

* Mr. James Silk Buckingham erroneously describes a meeting held in Wellclose Square, London, as having taken place in 1834, and which he contends was the first teetotal meeting held in London. But Mr. Couling reprints in his " History" the bill calling the meeting, and proves that Mr. Buckingham's memory failed him, the date being August 13th, 1835 (See Buckingham's " Coming Era of Reform," 1854, p. 439, and Couling's " History of Temperance Movement," 1862, p. 74).

† *London Temperance Intelligencer* (1836-7), vol. i., p. 35.

‡ As a result of the visit of Mr. Livesey and his colleagues in September, 1835, the British Teetotal Temperance Society was formed; and on August the 29th, 1836, Mr. Livesey—who had been in London several days addressing meetings and conferring with friends—took part in the first meeting held under the new name. He also assisted at subsequent anniversaries.

§ " First Report of the New British and Foreign Society for the Suppression of Intemperance " (London: J. Pascoe, 1837), p. 13.

|| " Second Report." London: J. Pascoe, 1841, p. 3.

introducing teetotalism.* He had presided at a meeting addressed by the Preston advocates, and a week later signed the teetotal pledge. In a communication addressed to Mr. Livesey, dated November 22nd, 1834, he announces :

"After deliberately considering the subject, I have been compelled to adopt the pledge of total abstinence from all intoxicating liquors. . . .

"I have begun to hold a weekly Temperance meeting on a Thursday night, in the General Baptist Chapel, Oak Street [of which he had become pastor in the previous July]. The special object of this meeting is to promote the principles you so ably advocate, viz. total abstinence from all intoxicating liquors. We receive signatures to the moderation pledge. . . . Our rule is total abstinence ; the exception is moderation." †

In a letter dated December 23rd, in reply to one from Mr. Livesey, Mr. Beardsall says : "In your last letter to me you suggested the propriety of forming a society of teetotal men," which, he says, "is done," adding that both pledges are used.‡ In the first number of Mr. Beardsall's periodical—*The Star of Temperance*

---

* Towards the close of his life, Dr. Grindrod was evidently misled by his memory, into believing that his own teetotal career began two or three years earlier than it really did. Mr. Winskill, in his history, states on the authority of an anonymous biographical sketch of the doctor, and private memoranda supplied to him, that Dr. Grindrod, who had previously been living at Halton Castle, joined the Manchester Temperance committee, and in 1832 or 1833 both practised and advocated total abstinence. It is also stated that on 20th February, 1834, Dr. Grindrod founded at Manchester the first exclusively teetotal society in England ; and Mr. Winskill mentions the doctor's discussion with Mr. Youil, ale brewer, in a manner that leads to the erroneous inference that it took place in 1834, instead of 1835 ("History of the Temperance Reformation," by P. T. Winskill, Warrington ; 1881, pp. 60, 61, and 69). In the first number of the *Temperance Penny Magazine* (Manchester), dated August 1st, 1835, Mr. Youil's lecture in reply to Dr. Grindrod is announced to be delivered on the following Thursday (August 6th), and in the second number the proceedings are reported at considerable length. This *Penny Magazine*, of which only eight numbers appeared, is deserving of mention as having been the first weekly teetotal publication issued in Great Britain. The earliest notices of Dr. Grindrod's connexion with Temperance work which I have been able to trace occur on pages 37 and 96 of *The Preston Temperance Advocate*. On the former page, Mr. S. Cundy, in a communication dated April 11th, 1834, states that on Easter Monday Dr. Grindrod had taken part in a Sunday School tea party, at Bennet Street, Manchester ; and on page 96 it is recorded that on Nov. 19th, he spoke at the festival of the Angel Street Temperance Association, presided over by Dr. Warren. These were both meetings of the moderation movement. The date of the commencement of Dr. Grindrod's teetotal career happens, however, to be settled beyond controversy in the first number of the *Star of Temperance* (Manchester), published Saturday, September 12th, 1835. In an article on the "Rise and Progress of Temperance Principles," containing several important facts and dates, it is stated that "The use of the Tabernacle, a large and commodious building (for meetings) was kindly granted in May last, when Mr. R. B. Grindrod, surgeon, *commenced his glorious and triumphant career in the Temperance cause*" (p. 4), an announcement, which in view of the cordial relationship that existed between the Rev. Francis Beardsall (editor of the *Star*), and Dr. Grindrod, must be taken as authoritatively settling the vexed point. It is also worthy of remark that the society which Dr. Grindrod is credited with having founded is not mentioned in the article in question, although a detailed and circumstantial narration of the progress of Temperance in Manchester is given. In a letter written August 30th, 1838, Mr. Beardsall says :—"I have been in the workings of the Temperance Society in Manchester and neighbourhood from its beginning on the moderation scheme. I was a gratuitous agent of the B. & F. T. S., and pleaded for ale, porter, wine, etc. . . . I was the first in Manchester to adopt the principles of teetotalism apart from the moderation scheme." (Letter in "Report of Public Meeting at Plymouth." Devonport, 1838, p. 14.) Mr. Beardsall signed the Teetotal pledge, September 6th, 1834, and if he was, as he asserted (and was never contradicted), "the first in Manchester to adopt teetotal principles," Dr. Grindrod's connexion must have been of a later date. I have only to add that the statement in the *Star* agrees with the recollection of Mr. James Baxendale, of Norton Selsey, near Chichester, who until recently had for many years resided at Greenwich. Mr. Baxendale was a resident at Manchester at the time referred to by Mr. Beardsall, and he then became interested in Temperance work. All existing records indicate that Manchester looked to Preston for aid and direction in the new movement.

Mr. Winskill asserts that it is questionable whether even the Preston men were "at the outset of the work so indefatigable, able, and powerful, as Dr. Grindrod." Regarding this statement, I have only to remark that there is no evidence of Dr. Grindrod having been in the movement at the outset ; and before he was known *outside* Manchester, teetotalism had been successfully and firmly planted by the Preston propaganda, not only in the British Isles, but in America. Dr. Grindrod did a great work, but at a much later period ; indeed, he was not known nationally until after the publication of "Bacchus." The attempt to give him precedence of the Preston men is calculated to damage his *legitimate* reputation. The fact is that teetotalism was half-way round the world before Dr. Grindrod had become a national influence.

† *Preston Temperance Advocate*, vol. ii. (1835), p. 5.　　‡ *Ibid.*, vol. ii. (1835), p. 11.

(Sept. 12th, 1835)—appears an article on ' The Rise and Progress of Temperance Principles.' After giving particulars of the introduction of the first Temperance movement into Manchester (May 12th, 1830), the following reference is made to the source whence Manchester Teetotalism was derived :

"The teetotal pledge, which enjoined abstinence from all intoxicating drinks, had been, for some time, supported by that indefatigable and able advocate of Temperance, Mr. J. Livesey, of Preston. The adoption of this pledge at the last conference, and the introduction of it into the regular meetings, led to discussion, etc. etc." *

THE BRITISH TEMPERANCE LEAGUE.

This organization, or rather a Union of the Lancashire societies as was at first contemplated, was suggested by Mr. Livesey. In December, 1833, he says :

"It occurs to me, as Lancashire contains about a third of the number of all the members in the kingdom, and as there are men in every town anxious to carry on the work with spirit, a meeting of Temperance friends from different towns, convened in some central town in this county, would be likely to promote the prosperity of the cause. I merely throw out the suggestion." †

In the July (1834) number of the *Advocate* Mr. Livesey again reverts to the subject :

"A conference of the Societies in Lancashire," he says, "has been frequently spoken of and recommended. If fixed upon at a suitable time and place, and suitable arrangements are made, no doubt it would be of great service. No time so suitable as summer. I should be glad if some of the central Societies would move in it." ‡

Such a conference was held at Manchester on September 24th, 1834, Dr. Hall presiding, when a resolution was passed recommending to the local societies the adoption of a total abstinence pledge in addition to the anti-spirit pledge then in use. At a similar gathering the following year, held September 15th and 16th, at Oak Street Chapel, the first national association recognising teetotalism—The British Association for the Promotion of Temperance—was formed. Delegates from twenty-four towns attended, and Mr. Livesey delivered his Malt Lecture. Mr. Samuel Thompson, of Darlington, who, through an outrage perpetrated upon him by a publican, was unable to be present, wrote (Sept. 11th, 1835) to the committee of management, making important suggestions. He also bore the following testimony to the value of the *Advocate :*

"I beg leave to say a few words respecting the *Preston Temperance Advocate*, a publication which ought to be in the possession of every family in the kingdom. The Temperance Societies are much indebted to Mr. Livesey for his periodical, which in my opinion has done more for the cause of Temperance in the North of England than all the other publications put together. I distribute 1,000 copies monthly of this interesting and cheap work, and I hope next year to double that number in the county of Durham. From a firm conviction of the great utility of the *Preston Advocate*, I would respectfully but earnestly recommend to the members of every Temperance Society the necessity and importance of extending its circulation to the utmost bounds." §

It would appear from Mr. Thompson's letter that Mr. Livesey sent out the notices convening this conference, as he speaks of having been informed of it by

* *Star of Temperance*, 1835, p. 4. ' † *Moral Reformer*, vol. iii. (1833), p. 382.
‡ *Preston Temperance Advocate*, vol. i. (1834), p. 56. § *Star of Temperance*, 1835, p. 14.

Mr. Livesey. The assembled delegates, from all the principal towns in the North of England, were evidently of Mr. Thompson's opinion respecting the *Advocate*, and they also fully appreciated the value of Mr. Livesey's general services to temperance, as may be seen from the following resolution unanimously adopted by them and carried—according to the *Penny Magazine*—"with three rounds of applause:"

"That the cordial thanks of this Conference be presented to Mr. Livesey, of Preston, for his indefatigable exertions in the cause of Temperance; and that he be requested to continue his valuable services, both by his personal exertions and by the continuation of his excellent publication, *The Preston Temperance Advocate.*" [*]

It is suggestive that Mr. Livesey was the only person to whom a compliment of the kind was paid; [†] indeed, at that time no one else had rendered similar services to the cause. In the very meagre report given in the *Temperance Penny Magazine*—the only periodical which attempted a report of the discussion—Mr. Livesey figures as the champion of all the most advanced proposals submitted. At the request of the Conference, he wrote the address issued to members of Temperance Societies, inviting support to the new Association, and he was elected one of its Hon. Secretaries, an office he sustained until 1839.

NEWCASTLE, BIRMINGHAM, AND LEEDS.

The *Northern Temperance Almanack* for 1838, compiled and published by James Rewcastle, of Newcastle-on-Tyne, declared that "What Luther was in the time of the Reformation, and Wesley in the early days of Methodism, Joseph Livesey is in the era of Temperance Reform." [‡] And Mr. John Cadbury, of Birmingham, in a letter dated Sept. 1st, 1840, referring to the visit from Preston, said: "Teetotalism acted like an electric shock on the working classes, who at once saw the truth, safety, and certainty of the remedy; and very soon the moderation society sank into oblivion." [§] In an article in the *Leeds Temperance Herald* for December 23rd, 1837, the editors, referring to the amalgamation of the *Preston Advocate* with the *Leeds Herald* which took effect the following year, say:

"Stepping into the position of the *Preston Advocate*, which has hitherto been the great medium through which the societies in this part of the kingdom have made known their difficulties and successes. . . . Most especially we desire to make it known that our continued existence is mainly owing to the generous and disinterested conduct of Mr. Joseph Livesey." [‖]

THE WEST OF ENGLAND.

Mr. Stephen Cudlip, of Exeter, writing to the author of the "History of Teetotalism in Devonshire," gives some interesting particulars of how the first Temperance Society in that city (formed in 1834) became a teetotal society. He relates that in 1835 a member of their society paid a visit to a relative in Birmingham, and that on his return home he brought with him several *Preston Advocates.* "I

[*] *Star of Temperance* (1835), p. 19.

[†] A similar resolution was passed at the first anniversary of the Association, held at Preston, Tuesday, July 5th, 1836—"That the thanks of this meeting be given to Mr. Livesey for his indefatigable labours in promoting the Temperance cause."—*Temp. Journal*, 1836, p. 156.

[‡] *Northern Temperance Almanack* (1838), p. 8.

[§] "Report of a Meeting, etc., Plymouth." Devonport, 1838, p. 13.

[‖] *Leeds Temperance Herald*, p. 202.

obtained," he says, " a number which gave a most interesting account of a week's festival, held in the theatre of that place ; " and the reading of this copy of Mr. Livesey's famous periodical made him a teetotaler, and led to the Society gradually adopting the same principle.   Mr. Cudlip remarks : " This, then, is the fact, that a little *Preston Advocate* was the first spark,—of what has since increased to a large flame of true and pure Temperance light."* At Tavistock, we are told, " The wide circulation of *Livesey's Lecture* on the malt question, proved very useful in the early history of the society." † At Torrington that, " Some of the members of the old society read *Livesey's Lecture :* " this was at the close of 1837, and in the January following " a total abstinence society was formed." ‡ And in the first number of the *Western Temperance Luminary* (January, 1838), edited by Dr. H. Mudge, appears an article on " Progress of Temperance," which is opened with the following acknowledgment of indebtedness to Preston :

"What we consider ourselves justified in designating Temperance *in reality*, began to be publicly enforced in the North of England in 1833.   Mr. Livesey, of Preston, was the first to expose the great delusion which prevails as to the nature and properties of malt liquor.   His lecture is a masterpiece of strong if not eloquent reasoning, and is worthy of the notice of all well wishers to the cause." §

TEETOTALISM IN IRELAND.—FATHER MATHEW.

Robert Guest White, Esq., of Dublin, visited Preston in 1834, and signed the teetotal pledge.   Afterwards he became the first President of the British Temperance Association, and used his influence to promote the new movement in Ireland. In a letter, dated November 24th, 1834, addressed to Mr. Livesey, Mr. White informs him that he " remains a real teetotaler," and adds :

"Having attended the meetings [at Dublin] of every Temperance Society since my return, when I go in they say, ' Here comes Preston—the real teetotal Preston ; ' and I assure you I never omit telling them the happiness I experienced, and the good effected at Preston." ‖

Mr. John Finch, of Liverpool, who, as partner to Mr. Thomas Swindlehurst, came into close contact with the Preston reformers, did excellent work in establishing teetotalism in Ireland.   Mr. Finch was a man of originality and power, and, like his friend Joseph Livesey, interested in every plan of bettering the condition of the people.   As a Temperance reformer, Mr. Finch unquestionably derived his inspiration from Preston.   In June, 1835, he established a Teetotal Society in Strabane,¶ and subsequently Mr. Swindlehurst addressed a very successful meeting

---

* " History of Teetotalism in Devonshire " (Devonport, 1841), p. 82.

† *Ibid.*, p. 121.   ‡ *Ibid.*, p. 134.   § *Western Temperance Luminary* (1838), p. 5.

‖ *Preston Temperance Advocate*, vol. ii. (1835), p. 4.

¶ This was the first *active* and aggressive Teetotal Society formed in Ireland.   A Temperance Society is said to have been established at Skibbereen, Cork, as early as 1817.   It has been alleged that the rules of this society, from the first, imposed abstinence from fermented as well as distilled liquors ; and some persons have gone so far even as to say that its members were called *teetotalers*.   According to other accounts, the original basis of the society was the anti-spirit, but in consequence of failure, it was afterwards extended to fermented drinks.   There is no contemporary record of the Skibbereen society, nor does it appear to have had any pledge.   The earliest published account of it occurs in Mr. John Finch's "Portraiture" (1836) already quoted from ; and he evidently wrote from information obtained on the spot.   He says : " There is now in Skibbereen a Teetotal Society.   For some years it numbered *not more than about half-a-dozen members*, but at the time that the dreadful disease, cholera, visited Skibbereen, its number was about sixty or seventy [this would be

at Waterford.* In one of a series of articles on the " Irish Temperance Reformation," in the *Great Western*—a teetotal paper edited by Mr. Edmund Fry, and published at Plymouth—Mr. Robert McCurdy connects the conversion of William Martin to teetotalism with the Preston literature. Mr. McCurdy was one of the early advocates of teetotalism in Ireland. He says:

. " Mr. William Martin, of Cork, had early adopted the principles of the old Temperance Society. . . . Some of the Preston publications fell in his way, and he was encouraged to attempt the formation of a society on total abstinence principles. It was the good done by that society, and the untiring persuasion of Mr. Martin, which induced *the Rev. T. Mathew to become a teetotaler.*" †

Mr. Livesey had a very high appreciation of Father Mathew, as will be seen from the following reference to the good Franciscan's visit to Manchester :

" It is long since I experienced as much pleasure as I did this week by a visit to Father Mathew. It is gratifying to find one's self in the company of the *greatest Reformer* of the age. And it is increasingly so to find him a plain, unassuming individual, aiming at nothing but removing the wretchedness and misery of the people, and bringing them into a condition to enjoy life, and be a blessing to others. I met him at Manchester, and there, on the ground adjoining St. Patrick's Chapel, stood the good man, bareheaded, with an honest, homely countenance, smiling upon the people, and pouring into their ears the words of truth and soberness.

in 1832], and it is worthy of remark, that, whilst hundreds were falling victims all around them, scarcely one of their members was attacked by it, *and none were lost.* It was evident that the ' wisdom of these poor men in abstaining from the drunkard's drink' was better than the folly ' of their neighbours in drinking,' yet no man remembered these same poor men, their counsel was disregarded, and *their light was hid*" (pp. 3, 4). If this society had been as numerous, flourishing, and successful as some have represented it to have been, it must have exerted an influence outside Skibbereen; but its light was feeble and hidden, and to credit it with having exerted any appreciable influence in establishing teetotalism in Ireland, would indeed be to exalt tradition above history. No reference is made to this society in any of the early Temperance periodicals.

* In November and December, 1836, Mr. Finch made an extended tour, visiting most of the principal towns, and forming many societies. In places where he could get no assistance, he got up his own meetings, and his services throughout were rendered without fee or reward. The character of Mr. Finch's labours can be gathered from the annexed abbreviated extract from the full report of his proceedings printed in the *Preston Advocate :*
" Dublin, Nov. 6th, 1836.—Attended a tea party of about 400, half of them females, spoke three quarters of an hour. A meeting was to take place next evening to form a teetotal society —all the speeches, including a good one from Mr. McCurdy, of Halifax, were teetotal. Left a copy of my tracts with Daniel O'Connell, Esq., M.P., Earl Mulgrave, R. G. White, Esq., and all my customers. A good feeling exists in Dublin towards the teetotal cause."——" Newry.—Had a meeting on Sunday afternoon, in the Court-house, which was well attended—the M.P. for Newry was present—had a most attentive audience. The last time I spoke here, had one of the most disorderly assemblages I ever met in any town in Ireland."——" Belfast.—Called on Professors Edgar and Hincks, and challenged all the professors and students in the academy, all the advocates of moderation, and all the maltsters, brewers, distillers, and publicans of Belfast, to the public discussion of teetotalism : but the challenge was declined, nor would Professors E. or H. give me any assistance in procuring a place for a public meeting. I was thus prevented from speaking in this stronghold of moderate drinking.——" Castlebar.— Delivered a lecture here on Saturday night (market day), to a large and one of the most attentive audiences I ever spoke to, which was the first temperance or teetotal address ever delivered in this town. At the close of a two hours' discourse, 32 persons, many of whom acknowledged that they came for the purpose of ridiculing and opposing me, entered their names as members of the Castlebar Teetotal Society."——" Galway.—I delivered my third lecture, on Monday night, to one of the largest meetings ever assembled, in Mr. Kilroy's large and elegant ball-room at his hotel. Thirty-eight signed the teetotal pledge at the close of the meeting; and on the following evening when we met to choose visitors, committee, and officers, the number was increased to fifty-five."——" Cork.—Spoke at Mr. W. Martin's Teetotal Society, held in his store in Fish Street. The two pledges are mixed in Cork, in all the societies except Mr. Martin's, which destroys unity of purpose, and prevents that active exertion which is necessary to ensure great success. There are a great number of teetotalers and sincere friends to temperance in Cork; the Rev. Mr. Dunscomb, Protestant clergyman, and the Rev. Mr. Scanlan, Roman Catholic priest, Blackrock, are still most active in the cause." ——" Wexford.—I called a meeting here, in the Court-house, which was the third I have held there—great numbers attended " (*Preston Advocate*, 1837, p. 43).

†. *The Great Western*, Oct, 31st (1840), p. 34.

Without any priestly attire, or clerical forms, on the plain ground he stood, surrounded by a multitude anxious to catch a glance of his countenance, to touch his hand, and especially to hear the consoling words which fell from his lips. . . . Happy man! too humble to think anything of himself, and too anxious to save drunkards to rest while one remains. His memory will be cherished throughout all generations; Ireland, and millions unborn, will bless his name. He is truly a Rational Reformer; without Church restraint, or Church sanction, he is going about doing good. May his life be long spared!"*

TEETOTALISM IN SCOTLAND.

Mr. Robert Reid, in his paper upon "The Rise and Progress of the Total Abstinence Movement in Scotland," fixes the date of the beginning of teetotalism as a national movement in North Britain. "The total abstinence principle," he says, "first attracted public attention in Scotland, in September, 1836. Societies were then formed, first in Glasgow and then in Edinburgh, and with marvellous rapidity the movement thereafter spread in every direction."† The Preston publications had, however, reached Paisley about November, 1834, where their circulation aroused a number of the members of the society from the "general lethargy" which had crept over them. Mr. William Brough, secretary of the society, in a letter (dated April 15th, 1836) addressed to Mr. Livesey, reports:

"At this period [eighteen months before] your noble publication appeared here for the first time, and tended materially to fan the flame of exertion and enthusiasm. . . . A large number of meetings have been held; . . . tracts (*principally your own admirable series*) have been distributed. *Since the appearance of your Advocate, the greater part of our societies' leading members have advocated the principle of teetotalism.* The pledge based on these principles, however, was not formally adopted until our monthly meeting for March last. It was

* *The Struggle*, No. 83.

† "The Temperance Congress of 1862," London, p. 157.—Mr. Reid's statement that abstinence from all intoxicants "first attracted public attention in Scotland in 1836," is in strict accordance with the facts of the case. The alleged existence of isolated societies, based on abstinence, is no contradiction to it. The societies at Dunfermline, Paisley, and Greenlaw, although not without interest, exerted no influence in the establishment of teetotalism in Scotland. Mr. Davie's Dunfermline pledge (Dec. 21st, 1830) made an exception in favour of 'table-beer,' and consequently did not strike at the entire drinking system. The society itself does not appear, from the reports of its proceedings, to have differed from the ordinary societies; it gratefully accepted the services of the lecturers of the Scottish Society, and was evidently satisfied with their anti-spirit doctrine; it also subscribed liberally to the fund of the parent society. It exerted no influence in educating surrounding societies, and appears to have died a natural death about the time the moderation societies expired throughout the country. A report from Dunfermline, in the *Scottish Temperance Journal* for September, 1839, states: "It is only two years past the 12th of July last, since we constituted ourselves into a society, our number at that time did not exceed thirty" (p. 126). This fixes July 12th, 1837, as the date of the establishment of the Dunfermline Total Abstinence Society; while the fact that only thirty persons could then be found to associate themselves together as abstainers, proves that the influence exerted on the town by the first society was of a very feeble character. The Greenlaw Abstinence Society (January 19th, 1832)—according to the account of its founder, the Rev. John Parker—speedily died out (see "Logan's Early Heroes," p. 85). In fact, neither of the Scottish experiments was sufficiently vigorous to attract and compel attention, and no mention whatever of their distinctive features is made in the Glasgow *Temperance Society Record*. It has been stated that the conductors of this able magazine refused to report the special features of these societies, but its editor reproved Mr. Buckingham for advocating cheaper beer. If, however, such was the case, the fact in itself affords a striking corroboration of our position, since the doings and doctrines of the Preston Society at once found their way into all the 'moderation' periodicals, especially into the *Record*. It is only necessary to examine the claims of these societies to see how different in every respect they were from the Preston movement, and to arrive at the conclusion respecting them expressed by Mr. Robert Rae in 1862, at the conference of the British Temperance League, that while in January, 1832, there may have existed in Scotland "at least three societies based upon total abstinence, they had not much fire at that time, and therefore *we must look to Preston as the place from which emanated that energy and enthusiasm which* CONVERTED THE MOVEMENT INTO A NATIONAL ONE." —*British Temperance Advocate Supt.*, September, 1882, p. 7.

then unanimously resolved that it should be adopted in addition to our present pledge." *

The Rev. Wm. Reid, in his Life of Robert Kettle, after referring to the origin of teetotalism at Preston, says : " Foremost in Scotland in this new movement were Mr. Edward Morris, Mr. John Dunlop," † etc. Mr. Morris, who is mentioned in a previous chapter, visited Preston in October, 1832, and signed the teetotal pledge there. He subsequently took the lead in introducing teetotalism into Scotland. His visit to Preston produced an impression on his mind which was never effaced. More than twenty years afterwards he thus refers to it in his " History of the Temperance and Teetotal Societies in Glasgow : "

" Preston was the next place of note to which I directed my footsteps. There I first became acquainted with Mr. Joseph Livesey, and his excellent spouse and family. The newspapers on all the line of my journey had taken up the subject, on the occasion of my various discourses, and about an hour after arriving at this town, *the birthplace of teetotalism in England*, a message was sent to me, to the temperance hotel where I stopped, from Mr. Livesey, to take tea at his house that evening, and stating that he and the temperance committee wished me to address their society at their weekly meeting that night. I wished to have avoided this, and to have entered their hall and listened in silence to the ' Preston lions,' but they had already intimated my name, and I could not in courtesy refuse complying to the kind message of a truly good man. A select few of the leaders met me at tea, and we formed at once our plan of battle during my stay in their spirited town, where I attended altogether about a dozen meetings. In no place since I quitted Glasgow did I find the temperance cause so flourishing as in Preston. The teetotal principle was then rising and showing its buds in that town. I found that Mr. Livesey was the life of the Preston society, and he was ably and zealously supported by Messrs. Dearden, King, Teare, Swindlehurst, and other worthies, whose names, I fondly believe, are written in the Lamb's book of life. Pleasant were the days of my tarriance in this town, and the vivid recollection of the animated scenes of our meetings in 1832, there, gives fire to my pen, and it may be, to my muse, which will add to the utility of this work. To Preston and its temperance heroes I retain strong attachment." ‡

For some time previously Mr. Morris had been an active Temperance worker, but having embraced the " new doctrine," his teaching became more thorough. In a lecture delivered in the Seamen's Chapel, Brown Street, Glasgow (October, 1834), he strongly urged the adoption of the teetotal pledge. A young man named Scott, from Preston, followed him in " a brief but pointed address ; " and although " the teetotal principle got a good lift from this meeting," and some individuals embraced the new views, no public action was taken or society was formed. Two years passed away without further progress. " There was a hanging back," Mr. Morris says, " and the old societies were in a very rickety state—the ship was sinking in spite of its best pilots." § But the needed spur came, and Preston supplied the lacking element. Early in the month of September Mr. John Finch, to whom the movement in Ireland was so deeply indebted, succeeded in forming a Teetotal Society at Annan. He then sought out Mr. Morris, to whom he had a

* *Preston Temperance Advocate*, 1836, p. 37.—The Paisley Youths' Society, formed 14th January, 1832, with a pledge against the use of "all liquors containing any quantity of alcohol, except when absolutely necessary," does not appear to have inspired the Paisley Society to take the step forward. Here again Mr. Livesey's publications were the chief educators.

† " Temperance Memorials of the late Robert Kettle," Glasgow, 1853, p. xxx.

‡ " History of Temperance and Teetotal Societies in Glasgow." By Edward Morris, Glasgow, 1850, p. 33.   § *Ibid.*, p. 52.

letter of introduction from Mr. Livesey. " On the 16th of September, 1836," says Mr. Morris, " Mr. John Finch called upon me, . . . with a letter from our mutual friend, the well-known Mr. Joseph Livesey, the ' founder of teetotalism in Preston.' " Mr. Morris had heard of Mr. Finch as an earnest, zealous, and eloquent advocate of the Preston doctrines, and he gladly arranged for him to occupy the platform at the Temperance Society meeting in the Lyceum Rooms, Nelson Street; and, says Mr. Morris, " well did he discharge his duty—wit, pure and beautiful, such as Addison abounds in, flashed through his brilliant lecture." At the close Mr. Morris proposed, and the meeting unanimously adopted, this Resolution: " That the old society pledge be abandoned, and the society meeting here adopt the clean pledge of the Preston friends, viz.: not to take or give any drinks, of whatever kind, that can cause intoxication." The Glasgow Radical Temperance Society, based on the above resolution, was thus formed, and thirty-seven names affixed to its declaration, Mr. Finch heading the list as ' honorary member,' while Mr. E. Morris's name stands second.*

During this visit to Scotland, Mr. Finch pressed the adoption of teetotalism upon Mr. John Dunlop, the founder of Temperance Societies in Great Britain. Up to this time Mr. Dunlop had not favoured the " new doctrine," but Mr. Finch was successful in securing his interest, and ultimate adhesion. The *Liverpool Temperance Advocate* for November 26th, 1836, contains a long letter from Mr. Dunlop to Mr. Finch. It is headed, " The Great Northern Champion of Moderation Converted to Total Abstinence ! " and the editor prefixes a short paragraph, in which these words occur : " What a glorious triumph has the zeal and perseverance of Mr. Finch obtained for our cause ; for to him is entirely owing Mr. Dunlop's adoption of total abstinence." In this most interesting letter, written from ' Glen, Greenock,' and dated November 19th, 1836, Mr. Dunlop says :

" You may remember that I acquiesced in your views regarding the first branch of the entire abstinence obligation, but demurred as to the second part, which excludes the giving or offering of intoxicating liquor to others. On considering the subject, however, in the most deliberate manner, I am now satisfied that you and your friends are right ; and, in fact, I believe that you have in one point, by this clause, effectually struck at the system of ' *drinking usage* ' which it has been for some years a great object with me to get exposed and abrogated. My sincere thanks, therefore, are due to you for being instrumental in bringing practice to this decided state ; and I trust the Temperance reformers of Scotland will, at no distant time, have to return acknowledgments in a body to the wisdom and determination of their southern brethren in this matter. . . . I have put myself into correspondence with a variety of places on the subject, and made two pilgrimages to Glasgow, where superior local knowledge has, I trust, enabled me somewhat to strengthen and enlarge *the foundation you made there*. It appears to me that the strict regulations adopted by you and your friends are not the result of a temporary flash of Temperance enthusiasm, but the legitimate fruit of the advance and progress of sound views on this important subject. Our people in Scotland have lately, it appears, fallen into a habit of drinking porter and ale to intoxication, which was not their wont formerly ; indeed, the proscription of whisky by the present Temperance Societies has had the effect of introducing here a large consumption of fermented malt liquor.† . . . Our Temperance members resort to the public-house, and use ale and porter for awhile, but in the course of

---

* Morris's " History," pp. 52–55.

† This is a striking example of the futility of attempting to effect a Temperance reform by substituting the weaker for the stronger forms of alcoholic liquids.

a few months very frequently break their pledge, and resume drinking whisky as before.* If gentlemen call upon operatives to abandon ale and whisky, it follows that they themselves ought to abandon wine in the present crisis, and if they summon the inhabitants to abrogate the artificial drinking usages, they must, in consistency, commence in their own houses to withhold liquor in compliment, etiquette, or for any but medical purposes." †

No apology is offered for making this rather lengthy citation from Mr. Dunlop's letter. It is worthy of remark, however, that it clears up several points, and destroys more than one hypothesis regarding the origin of teetotalism in Scotland. It conclusively shows the important part played by Mr. Finch in enforcing the claims of teetotalism on Mr. Dunlop, who immediately set to work to extend the principles of true Temperance throughout Scotland.

At a subsequent important occasion, Mr. Livesey rendered efficient service to his Scotch friends. In June, 1839, he took part in the anniversary of the Scottish Temperance Union, delivering his Malt Liquor Lecture in Edinburgh, Glasgow, Paisley, and Greenock. *The Scottish Temperance Journal* followed an account of the lecture at Glasgow, on June 11th, with these words:

" Mr. Livesey has done more for the advancement of this cause, not only by his writings and speeches, but by many years' personal labour in visiting the abodes of the poor and wretched, conversing, sympathising, remonstrating, and advising with them, than has perhaps fallen to the opportunity of any other man in this country. We understood Mr. Livesey to say, that the greatest obstacle to our success in Scotland, was the want of a properly organized system of visitation, without which the good accomplished by our public meetings would, in a great measure, be lost." ‡

And it is evident that the Edinburgh Society profited by Mr. Livesey's visit and advice upon visitation, for in the October issue of the *Journal* a report from that city states that:

" Since Mr. Livesey's visit in the month of June, the cause has been rapidly advancing. . . . . The Society has adopted the suggestion of Mr. Livesey, *and commenced a Sabbath morning visitation,* in those localities where intemperance has hitherto ruled supreme. . . . This plan promises, if efficiently pursued, to be one of the most successful schemes for the accomplishment of our object." §

DR. EDGAR, AND JAMES SILK BUCKINGHAM.

Dr. J. Edgar, the zealous promoter of the first Anti-Spirit Societies in the North of Ireland, viewed the introduction and spread of total abstinence with suspicion, and as a corruption of Temperance. He vigorously opposed teetotalism, but he admired Mr. Livesey. In his famous discourse on " The Intoxicating Drinks of the Hebrews," Dr. Edgar speaks of the *Preston Advocate* as being the " best conducted and most widely circulated periodical advocating teetotalism in the United Kingdom; " and he describes Mr. Livesey himself as a " man who has done more to advance the cause than any man living." ‖ Mr. J. S. Bucking-

---

* The Editor of the Glasgow *Record,* after issuing his magazine for six years, had announced in December, 1835, its discontinuance. " For a considerable time," he says, " there has been a gradual declension in its circulation. In a number of places where the societies have become extinct, the demand for the *Record* has altogether ceased." And at the time Mr. Dunlop wrote, most of the Societies were either dead or in a moribund state.

† *The Liverpool Temperance Advocate,* 1836, pp. 163, 164.

‡ *Scottish Temperance Journal,* 1839, p. 107.   § *Ibid.,* p. 137.

‖ *The Temperance Advocate* (Belfast), 1838, p. 136.

ham, M.P., at a meeting at Kennington, London, May 22nd, 1837, speaking of the two systems—that of moderation and total abstinence—used Mr. Livesey's figure of "the two bridges," introducing its author's name as follows: "Mr. Livesey, whose name must never be mentioned without respect and honour." *   And in his "History" he remarks of the Lancashire movement that, "Mr. Joseph Livesey, of Preston, was its chief originator, as he has been ever since its zealous and able advocate." †

AMERICA REACHED FROM PRESTON.

One of the most interesting chapters of American Temperance history—that detailing the transition from the anti-spirit to the anti-alcoholic platform—has never been fully written.   The resolutions of conventions announcing the change have been repeatedly given, but the means by which the more radical sentiment was brought about appear to have been altogether overlooked.   One of the most recent and important works dealing with Temperance in the United States—Dr. Daniel Dorchester's "Liquor Problem in All Ages," the preface to the second edition of which is dated December 15th, 1883—has a chapter upon the "Development of the Principle of Total Abstinence (1826–40)."   The writer succinctly narrates the action taken by conventions and associations, but, like all other Trans-Atlantic authors who have dealt with the subject, he altogether ignores the inspirers and teachers who prepared the way for action, and indeed rendered it practicable.   Beyond all dispute Mr. E. C. Delavan ‡ was the foremost actor in this important development; but Dr. Dorchester only once mentions his name in the chapter, and then merely to notify that at the Boston convention of 1835, a letter was received from him "strenuously advocating the principle of total abstinence." §   If, however, the

* *London Temperance Intelligencer,* vol. i. p. 248.

† "The Coming Era of Practical Reform," 1854, p. 438.

‡ The spirit and energy of the early Temperance efforts in America were largely due to Mr. Delavan. Like Mr. Livesey on this side of the Atlantic, Mr. Delavan in his own country created a *propaganda.* It ought not to be necessary to quote authorities to enlighten the reader regarding Mr. Delavan, but the world moves so rapidly, and 'modern instances' labour so persistently to make it appear that very little or nothing had been done prior to their own efforts, that a citation or two may be pardoned. Dr. Marsh, in his "Recollections," says: "Edward C. Delavan, a young and enterprising merchant of Albany, having retired early from business, with a fortune at his command, was induced, in connexion with John T. Norton and other spirited gentlemen, to throw his whole soul into the enterprise, and give it all his power. In 1829–30 he became chairman of the Executive Committee, and in less than three years, flooded the State with MILLIONS OF PUBLICATIONS" (p. 41). According to a statement prefixed to the Annual Report of the American Union for 1837–8, " at the establishment of the *Journal* [the Union's Official Organ], Mr. Delavan generously placed at the disposal of the Committee the sum of TEN THOUSAND DOLLARS;" and from the same document we learn that when he resigned the position of chairman to the State Society, he placed at the disposal of his late colleagues a like magnificent sum (p. 91). At the time he visited Europe in 1838–9, it was understood that he had then expended altogether £10,000 upon Temperance propaganda. Throughout his long life, Mr. Delavan continued a most munificent supporter of true Temperance principles. He died at Albany, January 15th, 1871.

§ "The Liquor Problem in All Ages." New York: Phillips and Hunt, p. 263.—The only other reference made by Dr. Dorchester to Mr. Delavan's interest in the fermented drinks question, occurs on page 254 of his elaborate work, and it relates to the famous libel action of the Albany brewers against Mr. Delavan. In 1835 Mr. Delavan stated in the Albany *Evening Journal* that the water used by the brewers was drawn from ponds which were the common receptacles for dead animals. Whereupon the brewers claimed damages to the extent of three hundred thousand dollars; but Mr. Delavan abundantly proved his allegations, and triumphed. The case excited a great deal of interest, and Dr. Dorchester's conclusions thereon illustrate how prone our American Temperance friends are to follow mere side issues, to the neglect of the main question. He says: "The character of the Albany ale and beer was scathingly exposed by Mr. Delavan." Really, however, nothing of the kind happened; as the only thing exposed was the water from which the beer was made.

An examination of Trans-Atlantic Temperance literature discloses the fact that the position at that time is to be clearly understood, appeal must be made to those who were conversant with the facts; and the Rev. Dr. John Marsh, who from his long official connexion with the cause in America * was well qualified to speak, thus represents the dilemma in which the early reformers there found themselves:

"Men saw," he says, "enough of the evil to move them to the conflict. They also saw clearly that entire abstinence from the drunkard's drink was the only infallible antidote. But what was 'the drunkard's drink?' Was it wine, beer, cider, metheglin? No, by no means. The doctrine of Rush yet prevailed, that wine was a blessing; that fermented liquors ' contained so little spirit, and that so intimately connected with other matters, that they would seldom be drank in sufficient quantities to produce intoxication, and, when drank moderately, were generally innocent. The first reformers built a brewery in Boston for the accommodation of members of the Temperance Society. No. No. Ardent spirit was the drink of the drunkard. †

"For ten years [*i.e.*, from 1826 to 1836] the battle raged with fury. The triumphs were glorious: 20,000 distilleries were abandoned. Ardent spirits were driven from our sideboards, and fields, and workshops, and social gatherings. But in the very moment of victory, the enemy rushed upon us in a thousand serpentine forms; our very captives were stolen from our hands; through cider and beer reformed men went back by thousands, and, in the use of wine and cordials, the refined and wealthy rapidly prepared themselves and their children for abundant sorrow. A new battle was to be fought, and it was a hard one. It was a battle with friends, and with men by whose side many had fought the old serpent; ay, with men who planted their defence in the very word of God.

American Temperance reformers have busied themselves far too much with the fabrication, sophistication, and adulteration of alcoholic liquids; a question which properly belongs to the drinker and not to the Temperance man. For instance, the Rev. T. P. Hunt, an able and devoted lecturer, known as the "Liquor Sellers' Vexation," mainly directed his inquiries and energies to the exposure of the frauds of the trade. Dr. Dorchester tells us with what result: "The thought that they were taking logwood, sulphuric acid, arsenic, *nux vomica*, gypsum, and *cocculus indicus*, into their stomachs, not for their own good, only for the good of manufacturers and vendors, alarmed many, and helped to advance the Temperance cause" (p. 281).

But whatever the immediate results of such teaching might be, it is obvious that those who had "advanced the cause of Temperance," by giving up adulterated liquor, would be likely to retrograde it as soon as they were satisfied they could get the 'genuine article.' And unfortunately indications are not wanting of this course being extensively followed.

What is the condition of things in the States to-day regarding fermented drinks? Dr. Dorchester tells us that America is suffering from a 'beer invasion,' and from other sources we learn that the manufacture of 'native wines' is increasing so rapidly that very shortly America will lead the way as a wine-producing country. Dr. Dorchester thus opens his chapter on the beer invasion: "We have before alluded to some changes in the drinking habits of the American people, a vacillation of some in their devotion to the principle of total abstinence, and a tendency to the use of malt liquors. . . . Specious pleadings have been made for beer, as promotive of health, constitutional development, and even of Temperance. . . . Many American people have easily yielded to these sophistries, and betaken themselves to beer drinking. . . . Brewers have multiplied, and beer wagons, beer barrels, and beer bottles are all around us" (p. 452), and he further remarks upon the increased consumption of beer: "We believe it to be one of the saddest phases of American life during the last thirty years, that these liquors have come so generally into use. Numberless youths, and older persons also, have by such means been led to form habits of intemperance, who, but for these, would have remained true to total abstinence. *The beer theory has been demoralizing in its whole influence, reconstructing the theory of Temperance in many minds on a false and pernicious basis*" (p. 464).

It is clear that what is most needed in America, and the only thing that can prevent the Temperance sentiment there from being generally 'reconstructed on the beer theory,' is sound teaching upon the A B C of the question; and nothing would more contribute to the *real* advancement of Temperance in the States, than the vigorous and systematic circulation of Mr. Livesey's writings upon malt liquor. Unless some such means are adopted, American Temperance is in danger of succumbing altogether to the 'beer invasion.'

* Dr. Marsh's official connexion with the movement dates from May, 1829. He became an agent of the American Temperance Society in April, 1833, and laboured chiefly in Pennsylvania. At the Saratoga Convention, August 4th, 1836, the 'Society' became the 'Union;' a new departure recognising abstinence from fermented liquors was taken, and Dr. Marsh became secretary of the new Teetotal movement, and, subsequently, editor of its official organ. He died August 4th, 1868, aged 80 years.

† In 1830, wine, unless it was 'fortified' with spirit, was not regarded as being 'intoxicating drink.' Professor Moses Stuart in his famous essay says: "Our wines, . . . in consequence of *having distilled spirit mixed with them*, . . . may fairly come under the denomination of intoxicating drinks." ("Footprints of Temperance Pioneers," New York, 1885, p. 23.)

" It was in 1835 and 1836 that we *came up to the broad and consistent principle of total abstinence from all intoxicating drinks as a beverage.** Here we gained firm footing. Here we became possessed of truths *which none of the wise and good of former days knew ;* for, had they known them, they would have rejoiced in them, and transmitted them, a precious inheritance, to those who came after.† This was one [and the most important truth too] : *Alcohol is the fruit of fermentation,* and not, *as was generally supposed, of distillation ;* and wherever found, whether in fermented or distilled liquor, is a subtle poison, never needful in health, and in all its tendencies at war with the whole physical and moral system as God has made it."‡

It will be interesting to trace the means by which the important advance referred to by Dr. Marsh was brought about. Mr. Dearden says that American Temperance reformers " asked for information from England," § and as one result of the answer to their inquiry, a circular, urging abstinence from *all* intoxicants, addressed to clergymen, was issued (by the New York State Temperance Society), signed by E. C. Delavan, John F. Bacon, Israel Harris, Israel Williams, Azor Taber, and Anthony Gould. In it Preston is thus referred to :

"Accounts were constantly reaching us from England, showing facts there to be precisely such as our own country exhibited. The Societies of that country which adhere to the old pledge are accomplishing little or nothing ; while Preston and the neighbouring districts, where the thorough pledge was the first and only pledge known, is advancing most rapidly, in securing the pure, unadulterated, and unendangered reform of all classes, and Preston has now become a fountain of life and redemption to the whole region around." ||

Mr. Dearden does not give the date of this important circular, neither can I find it in any American work at hand, but he quotes it in a connexion which warrants the inference that it was issued prior to the Albany Convention of 1834.

While there may have been in America, as in Great Britain, as some allege, an isolated society existing, based on the total abstinence principle, prior to the establishment of the Preston Society, it is certain that the great truth that a successful Temperance movement can only be based upon abstinence from fermented as well as distilled liquors was first conveyed to the States by Mr. Livesey's publications.¶

---

* Dr. Dorchester states that in 1833 "the principle of total abstinence from *all* alcoholic liquor was *quite extensively* adopted " (p. 638) ; but he adduces no evidence of this, neither do the contemporary reports, etc., support it.

† Writing in 1836, upon this very point, and referring to the earlier opinions, Mr. Delavan says : " The great physiological truth, that alcohol, under all names and in all admixtures, when taken into the healthful human system, is a disturbing and unfriendly agent, that under no circumstances can contribute to nourish or invigorate the human body, was unknown, or at least disregarded." (*Report of American Union,* 1837–8, appendix p. 90.)

‡ " A Half Century Tribute to the Cause of Temperance." By Rev. John Marsh, D.D. New York, 1851, pp. 6, 7, 8.

§ " A Brief History of the Commencement and Success of Teetotalism," Preston, 1840, p. 36.

|| *Ibid.,* p. 37.

¶ There is no reference in American Temperance literature to any movement in the States during the Anti-Spirit period at all analogous to that of Preston ; and if here and there a total abstinence society existed, as some have contended, it was not aggressive, and exerted no perceptible influence upon the general agitation there. But the term 'total abstinence' may be found in some of the early American literature, and it is therefore necessary to understand what the words were meant to imply. Indeed, it should be remembered that 'total abstinence' was often used both in America and Britain to denote the total disuse of distilled spirit. In America, however, the words " *entire* abstinence from everything intoxicating " (a phrase which most readers would regard as equivalent to teetotalism) simply implied abstinence from the products of the still ! An illustration of this use of the term may be found in " When will the Day Come ? " p. 10. (Massachusetts Temperance Society, Boston.)

The London correspondent of the *Alliance News* (Feb. 17th, 1893) gave credence and circulation to the following account of the establishment of a *Teetotal* Society in America in 1827, based entirely on the recollection of its founder, an old man of eighty : " The origin of the

One of the earliest notices in America of the more radical Temperance reform inaugurated at Preston occurs in the *Temperance Intelligencer* (published at Albany, N.Y.) for October, 1834, where the work at Preston is referred to as being totally unlike anything existing in America.

" *Where, in America*," inquires the writer, " have you a society formed in the heart of a population of thirty or forty thousand souls, in which, for four assizes, no criminal has been tried? ·Where a town in which a cock-pit has been hired and turned into a place for Temperance meetings, wherein several hundred working men meet several times a week . . holding meetings . . which bid fair to revolutionize the sentiments of the whole north of England? This scene is going on at Preston in Lancashire; and to what is it owing? To the honesty of their proceedings; their leaders at once saw the fallacy of preaching moderation, where intoxicating liquors were used, and they have anathematized them all, *as mere delusions !* Here total abstinence reigns supreme, and the great monster ALE is held up to unsparing horror and detestation, and this feeling is making progress elsewhere. The impulse given from Preston is precisely the one wanted."

It was Mr. E. C. Delavan, the most munificent supporter of Temperance operations and propaganda the great Republic has yet produced, who had the discrimination to recognise that Preston supplied precisely " the impulse " needed to perfect the American movement. Hearing of the Preston work, Mr. Delavan became a correspondent of Mr. Livesey, from whom he not only received the *Moral Reformer* and *Preston Advocate*, together with all other tracts and pamphlets issued from Preston, but Mr. Livesey for years wrote him a monthly letter of suggestion, advice, and encouragement. Abundant evidence exists showing how much' Mr. Delavan profited, and how greatly he was stimulated in his exertions—and also how deeply America is indebted to Mr. Livesey and the Preston movement—by this pleasant connexion. Mr. Delavan's own letters, quoted from below, fully disclose

word ' Teetotal ' has been often discussed. Those who contend that ' teetotal ' and ' teetotally ' were colloquially used in a general sense before R. Turner applied the term in September, 1833, to total abstinence from all strong drink may be right, but no printed evidence to support the earlier use has been presented. What is very strange, however, is the *fact* [!] that R. Turner has been anticipated in the very special application of the word hitherto supposed to have originated with him. It appears that in 1819 the Hector Temperance Society was formed in the State of New York on the anti-spirit principle, and that, dissatisfied with this principle as too narrow, some of the members abstained from all intoxicants. In 1827, the Lansing Temperance Society was formed, and two pledges were introduced—one against distilled spirits, the other against all alcoholic liquors. The first was marked ' O. P.'—old pledge ; [The pledge of the American Temperance Society, involving *total abstinence* from distilled spirits, was only adopted the previous year; it soon, however, became an *old pledge*, according to this account.] the second ' T,' meaning total. A goodly number signed the latter, and they were spoken of as ' T—totalers '—the initial letter, ' T,' and the explanation ' Total,' being pronounced as one word. The witness to this point is the Rev. Joel Jewel, of Troy, Bradford Co., Pennsylvania, who was the secretary of the Lansing Temperance Society, and is now about eighty years of age. I do not suppose that the nickname lasted long, or was widely known ; but that it should have arisen at all is one of the curiosities that come unexpectedly to sight in the course of historial research."

It is worthy of remark that the Lansing Teetotalers do not appear to have been known either to Dr. Justin Edwards, Dr. Marsh, or Mr. Delavan, nor are they mentioned by the Rev. L. Armstrong, the Rev. J. B. Dunn, or Dr. Dorchester, who have all written on the history of the American movement. The Fifth Report of the American Temperance Society, however, contains information from West Lansing, but mentions no peculiarity about the Society there. It is singular that Mr. Delavan, who travelled Europe to inquire into the condition of Temperance Societies, should have overlooked a novel Society in his own State, which had by six years anticipated even the distinctive name of the Preston Society! But it is incredible that 14,082,010 Temperance periodicals and publications could have been issued between 1828 and 1838 by the New York Temperance Society, without finding, and evoking a response from, the conductors of this particular Lansing Society. This is all the more striking, too, when we find that in the Report of the State Temperance Society for 1833, five Societies are reported from Lansing, with an aggregate membership of 553; but Mr. Jewel's name does not appear either as president or secretary. Altogether, 1538 Societies are reported in the State of New York. The circulation of a doubtful case like this tends to fog rather than to elucidate history. It is extremely probable that Mr. Jewel has made a mistake of several years. Nothing is more uncertain and unreliable than the memory of old persons, and statements similar to the above, when unsupported by collateral evidence, ought not to be received as history.

all this; they also indicate how scrupulously and promptly he advised his teetotal mentor of every important step taken.

In a letter addressed to Mr. C. Chapman, of Birmingham, dated March 24th, 1834, Mr. Delavan says: " Let your citizens generally follow the example of the Society at Preston, in Lancashire, and the work will soon be accomplished."* In a letter addressed to Mr. Livesey, dated Jan. 23rd, 1835, he says: " We begin to feel the influence of your noble example. Our people by thousands are becoming *teetotalers.* . . . We rejoice at the cheering aspect of things in your country: the *influence* upon us and our people will be *mighty.*" † On the 20th March following he again wrote expressing his gratitude for the timely arrival of a supply of the Preston ammunition:

" Your letter of Feb. 1st, with the first volume, and the Jan. and Feb. numbers of *The Advocate* are received. Your excellent paper affords me timely assistance in the ' fermented drinks ' question, which is now emphatically *the Temperance question* in this country.‡ The old pledge has done all that it was destined to do of good, and is now doing injury among us. . . . The pledge you adopt at Preston is the only one that is any longer deserving the attention of the friends of Temperance anywhere." §

Writing to Mr. Livesey on April 17th, Mr. Delavan specially refers to the good effected by the *Preston Advocate*, and mentions the means he adopts for putting the paper into the right hands. He says:

" It always gives me joy to receive a letter from you: your successes in and near Preston react on our country with great power and benefit. The 100 *Advocates* you send me monthly, I direct to as many individuals, and those individuals send them to others; so that their influence is felt far and wide. No Societies but those who adopt the Preston principle can stand,—in the very nature of the case they must go down. . . . We are gaining daily here; within a few days, about 300 clergymen, of all denominations, have sent me their names to the teetotal. . . . Send us even 200 of your *Advocates: they do us good.*" ||

The fight is now becoming serious, and on May 20th Mr. Delavan writes: " I go to Boston to-morrow, to attend the annual meeting of the American Society, which has not yet *come up to your standard*, but I think it will soon." ¶ We find that Mr. Delavan's forecast was speedily realized. Six days later he wrote Mr. Livesey from Boston, with noticeable promptitude, the following welcome intelligence:

" The American Temperance Society has now, blessed be God, taken the high and tenable ground, on which there is perfect safety. At a large, talented, and most respectable meeting, held this day, the following preamble and resolution was UNANIMOUSLY adopted by this noble society." **

The resolution declared that abstinence from all kinds of intoxicating liquors as a drink, is not only safe, but salutary. The *Moral Reformer* (American), a magazine largely devoted to Health, edited by Dr. W. A. Alcott, in its issue for

---

* *Preston Temperance Advocate*, vol. i. (1834), p. 59.   † *Ibid.*, vol. ii. (1835), p. 29.

‡ At the sixth anniversary of the New York State Society, 3rd and 4th of Feb., 1835, we find, mainly owing to Mr. Delavan's influence, that the question of abstinence from all intoxicating liquors was discussed, and it was fully agreed to devote both the *Recorder* and *Intelligencer* to its advocacy.

§ *Preston Temperance Advocate*, vol. ii. (1835), p. 37.

|| *Ibid.*, vol. ii. (1835), p. 44.   ¶ *Ibid.*, vol. ii. (1835), p. 51.   ** *Ibid.*, vol. ii. (1835), p. 60.

September, 1835, contains a description of the principles and methods of the Preston teetotalers, in which the following statement appears:

"Although our brethren on the other side of the water were rather slow to move in the cause of Temperance at first, yet they are now outstripping us in the race, because they have the good sense to see that nothing short of *total abstinence from all that intoxicates* will ever answer the purpose." *

On August 6th, of the same year, Mr. Delavan writes: "We look forward to the regular receipt of your paper with much interest. It advocates the only principles that will in the end do your countrymen or mine solid good." †　And Mr. E. James, Corresponding Secretary of the New York State Temperance Society, writing June 1st, informs Mr. Livesey that the American Temperance Society, at a meeting recently held at Boston, officially and regularly adopted the true ground of total abstinence, and he remarks: "The Eighth Report of the American Society I have not yet seen, but a gentleman who has heard portions of it read states that it advocates, fully and clearly, *the Preston doctrines.*" ‡　A reference to the Report (for the year 1835), mentioned by Mr. James, fully substantiates his statement. Eleven closely printed pages of that document are occupied with reports of the doings of the Preston Society, and the experiences of its members.§ This was the critical year with our trans-atlantic friends, who very widely circulated throughout the Union the Preston statements and experiences.‖　The fact is especially noteworthy that in the Report for 1835, in which the Preston movement so prominently figures, the term 'alcohol' takes the place 'ardent spirit' had occupied in previous reports. The extensive circulation of information upon the fermented drink question by Mr. Delavan speedily bore fruit, and on February 20th, 1836, he was able to report a further and important step forward. Writing to Mr. Livesey from Albany, he says:

"The great contest for total abstinence has been decided in this State. On the 11th we held our annual meeting, and forty-five out of fifty-four counties were represented. The debate continued two days and a half. . . . I consider the question of moderation in Temperance now settled in this country. The argument is complete and unanswerable. . . . *Your publications and example have had a great influence on our country, and we thank you for all you have done for us.* . . . Much has been done with the old pledge; it was a good pioneer, but your *teetotal* is the finisher." ¶

On March 22nd, 1836, the Rev. Dr. Justin Edwards, author of the masterly reports of the American Temperance Society, in writing to Mr. Livesey, says: "We rejoice exceedingly in your success with the *total* pledge, which is the only one that will render the cause entirely triumphant, and is now, in this country, rapidly gaining upon the *partial* pledge." **　On August 24th, 1836, Mr. Delavan implores of Mr. Livesey: "Hold on, my dear sir; let what will come, hold on, and

---

* *Moral Reformer* (Boston, U.S.A., 1835), p. 291.

† *Preston Temperance Advocate*, vol. ii. (1835), p. 76.　　‡ *Ibid.*, vol. ii. (1835), p. 85.

§ See American "Permanent Temperance Documents" (Boston, U.S.A., 1835), pp. 476–486.

‖ Dr. Marsh, referring to this incident, speaks of the reclaimed men, relating "their experience, in a manner similar to the reformed men *afterwards* in the United States" (" Recollections," p. 147).

¶ *Preston Temperance Advocate* (1836), p. 28.　　** *The Trial of Alcohol* (Preston), p. 8.

God will prosper you." * Personally, Mr. Delavan had thoroughly imbibed the Preston doctrines. At this time he regarded teetotalism as a principle, not a mere expedient; and while he gave credit to those of his brethren who abstained on the ground of expediency, he set his own view of the matter in the strongest possible light.

" To me," he declares, " it seems *morally wrong* to drink anything that tends to abridge our own lives, or injure our neighbour. I am convinced that the use of intoxicating liquors as a beverage, while in health, is *always* injurious and never *useful*, and that while using it in any quantity, I am accessary and co-operative in keeping up all that dreadful machinery of making and vending, which is filling our world with misery, and destroying in this country alone, directly or indirectly, at this time, *one hundred thousand* annually. Feeling thus, for myself, I cannot put this question on any ground but *duty*—duty to myself and to my neighbour." †

The Ninth Report of the American Society (for 1836) contains a number of very interesting letters from persons of distinction, including one from Robert Guest White, Esq., of Dublin, who states that in 1834, when in London, he heard from Mr. James S. Buckingham of the doings at Preston, and proceeds:

" Having visited it (Preston) at the end of August, was present at a festival held in the theatre five successive nights. . . . I became a pledged member of the society, by signing the *total abstinence pledge* upon the spot. . . . As to the capability of a teetotaler's exertions, permit me to mention those made by my dear and worthy friend, Mr. Joseph Livesey, of Preston, who in October last travelled upwards of three hundred miles in six days [before railway facilities, this], in which time he attended five evening and one noon Temperance meetings, speaking upwards of two hours at each of them, without feeling the least inconvenience or fatigue; and thus he is able and willing to repeat, whenever opportunity offers, or the cause of Temperance requires." ‡

During 1838-9, Mr. Delavan spent several months in Europe, principally employing himself in investigating the results of wine-drinking in France and Italy, and posting himself up in all that related to the Temperance enterprise in Britain. How heartily Mr. Delavan appreciated the spirit and genius of the Preston movement—which he evidently thoroughly understood—will be seen by the following quotation from a letter on the condition of Temperance in England, addressed to the Rev. Dr. J. Marsh, Secretary of the American Temperance Union. The letter, written from Paris, is dated November 20th, 1838. Mr. Delavan says:

" In Preston and the neighbouring county our excellent fellow-labourer, Mr. Livesey, by his indefatigable efforts, has produced a most astonishing change; and it only requires the same amount of labour and action in other sections of the country to produce the like results." §

Writing to Dr. Marsh from London, May 17th, 1839, Mr. Delavan describes a visit to Preston, from which it will be seen that he had learned to "love Mr. Livesey as a brother" for his work's sake. He says:

" Preston being within thirty miles of Liverpool, I paid Mr. Livesey a visit. You know that this gentleman was the first individual who raised the total abstinence banner. He was the first individual that prepared and signed the total

* "The Temperance Doctor" (Preston, 1836), p. 8.

† "Report of American Temperance Union," 1838, p. 91.

‡ "American Permanent Temperance Documents," pp. 561-3.

§ *Journal of the American Temperance Union* (February, 1839), p. 18; and also *The Temperance Journal* (London, 1839), p. 146.

abstinence pledge. The results of his labours can never be known in this world—
he has done too much good to be popular. I hear much evil said of him ; but I
love him as a brother, from whom, in the early stages of the great work we have in
hand, I took *much* counsel and support. A more devoted and intelligent, and at
the same time unpretending advocate of temperance, I have nowhere seen." *

" In June, 1839, Mr. Delavan visited Scotland, and attended the meetings of
the Scottish Union, at Edinburgh. He reports to Dr. Marsh that "some of the
delegates wished to reserve small beer and home-brewed ale ; † but only on the
belief that it contained no alcohol,—but on investigation [explanation] it was ex·
cluded." ‡

On June 12th, 1839, an address from the Newcastle Temperance Society,
signed by John Priestman, was presented to Mr. Delavan. After admitting our
indebtedness to America, it declared that : "The citizens of America, and the
philanthropists of the world, owe much to the men of Preston, who taught by
decided example the genuine principles of a Temperance reform ; " §—a sentiment
in which Mr. Delavan heartily concurred. Its citation is also useful as showing
how the Newcastle Society at that time regarded the Preston movement.

A direct acknowledgment of the indebtedness of America to England for the
teetotal pledge was made at the fourth annual meeting of the American Temperance
Union, on May 14th, 1840, by the Rev. Dr. William Patton, who in the previous
year had been a delegate to England. Dr. Patton said :

" Total abstinence from all intoxicating drinks is a principle of English manufacture. We sent over the old ardent spirit pledge ; but after all, it did not touch
the English beer, the good old brown stout, wine, nor delicate cordials for ladies.
All these were untouched, and the graves of the drunkards were filling up as fast as
ever. . . So they adopted what they called the *teetotal* pledge (though I don't
like the name) ; ‖ and they sent that back to us." ¶

The conclusion then is irresistible that not only the British Isles, but America,
and, through these lands, the world at large, is indebted to Preston for the only
successful system of Temperance reform : a system which, after a test extending
to half a century, can point to evidences of its efficiency in all climes, among all
races, and in every rank and sphere in life. And it is also equally conclusive that
Joseph Livesey was the founder and inspirer of the remarkable Preston movement,
and the chief director of its effective-propaganda.

* *Journal of the American Temperance Union* (August, 1839), p. 125.

† Mr. Davie's *total abstinence* pledge of 1830 allowed a similar exception,—it did not strike
at the entire system.

‡ *Journal of the American Temperance Union* (1839), p. 127.   § *Ibid.* (October, 1839), p. 158.

‖ Why not, Doctor ? If the grotesque word was in use in New York State in 1827, it
would surely have familiarised itself to the American ear by 1840 !

¶ *Journal of the American Temperance Union* (June, 1840), p. 87.

CHAPTER IX.

TEMPERANCE: TEACHINGS.

MR. LIVESEY was recognised as *the* teacher at the outset of the Temperance enterprise. We have Cobden's testimony to his "happy art of putting questions of a difficult and complex character into a simple and lucid form;" and to that valuable and not too common faculty the Temperance cause in Europe and America is much indebted for its advancement. After a thorough examination of the drink question from its very foundation, he came to the conclusion that the entire system was a mistake. There was no accident in the drunkenness, the physical and social disorder, the moral turpitude and spiritual decadence arising from drinking; these evils were the natural and logical outcome of a system which, by turning food into poison, violated the laws of Nature, and defeated the designs of Providence. And just as surely as an individual who systematically breaks the laws of health will suffer pain, so a State, community, or people, which perverts the bounties of Providence from their true and natural use, will pay the penalty in physical, moral, and spiritual evil. This truth, which is the foundation of all real Temperance reform, and was the distinguishing characteristic of the Preston platform, Mr. Livesey in the beginning did more than any one else to popularize, by setting it forth in a "simple and lucid form."

The oral delivery of the Malt Liquor Lecture produced very remarkable results, and as Mr. Livesey was not ubiquitous, he could not be in Preston directing an important propaganda, and at the same time lecturing to the people at John O'Groat's or Land's End. Dr. Mudge and others repeatedly urged the publication of the full text of the discourse, but for some time Mr. Livesey's energies were too much taxed to permit of its preparation. The Birmingham Society published it from the shorthand writer's notes in April, 1836; and in or about June of that year Mr. Livesey issued an authorized edition of his famous lecture as a closely printed demy 8vo pamphlet of 32 pages. The production has never been superseded, and it entirely merits the opinion expressed of it by Mr. Thomas Beggs, one of the most thoughtful and philosophical writers on Temperance, whose judgment is of considerable weight and value.

"That Lecture," says Mr. Beggs, "contained the whole philosophy of the

Temperance movement in its domestic, social, and political aspect, and left little to those who followed Mr. Livesey but enforcement and illustration of the propositions laid down." *

THE TEACHINGS OF THE ORIGINAL MALT LIQUOR LECTURE.

"The Malt Liquor Lecture," as originally published, in 1836, was, as Mr. Beggs has described it, a thoroughly comprehensive review of the whole question of Temperance. The Lecture appended to this volume is a reprint of an abridged edition, prepared for extensive circulation, and restricted to the discussion of the manufacture, nature, character, and effects of malt liquor. It cannot be too carefully studied by the reader. During the last half-century, Mr. Livesey's views on malt liquor have been extensively circulated in Great Britain, America, and the colonies, and his positions have never been successfully controverted; indeed, they were too clearly demonstrated ever to have been seriously assailed. Mr. Livesey's general teachings on Temperance, in 1836, in his published lecture, and several years earlier in his spoken addresses, were comprehensive and complete. In the original lecture he sets out with a statement regarding the extent and consequences of drinking, and calls attention to the fact that the greater part of the alcohol consumed in Britain is swallowed under the disguise of malt liquor. The causes of intemperance, he then classifies under five heads—"INTEREST, APPETITE, FASHION, IGNORANCE, and DEEP DEPRAVITY;" and the thoroughness with which he treated the question is made evident by the following citations from the lecture: †

Interest.

"It is an unfortunate circumstance," says Mr. Livesey, "for society when the interests of perhaps a majority are in a state of conflict with the happiness of the rest. I will not ask who *are*, but who are *not* interested in the *manufacture, sale,* or *use* of intoxicating liquors? *The trade*—including all who make, sell, or *assist* in this nefarious traffic—includes a vast number of foreigners, who make or supply all our wines, hollands, rum, and brandy; the merchants who import the same; the first and second class of wholesale dealers in this country; the brewers and the distillers at home; the owners of public-house property; the maltsters and the hop-merchants; the barley and the hop-growers; the licensed victuallers, beer-shop and dram-shop keepers; with almost an innumerable host of servants, travellers, and clerks attached to every branch of the trade. Whilst we have all these *directly* benefiting by intemperance; whilst every street is disgraced with these 'vaults' of death; and whilst interest throws open the door of temptation in the middle and at the end of every street,—is it any wonder that we are this day a nation of drunkards?

"Every person engaged in the outfit of the gin palaces and public-houses, in the outfit of breweries, distilleries, etc., is likely to be on the side of drinking. The coopers, glass, pot, chair, and pipe makers, and many others will incline to support the public-house system. Landlords being so numerous, and being among the best of customers for butchers' meat, drapery, newspapers, etc., it is easy to conceive that many who are not friends to drunkenness, are likely, at least, to connive at the habits of drinking, from which their profits, to some extent, seem to proceed. Sickness and crime are the common results of intemperance. Those who profit by either of these (and they are not a few) are almost certain to connive, to some extent, at this prevailing vice. In estimating the number of those who are likely

---

* "Life and Labours of Alderman John Guest." London, 1881, p. 16.

† The quotations are taken from the first edition of Mr. Livesey's Lecture, the full title of which runs as follows: "A Temperance Lecture based on the Teetotal Principle; including an Exposure of the Great Delusion as to the Properties of Malt Liquor; *The substance of which has been delivered in the principal towns of England.* By Joseph Livesey. 'All great things subsist more by FAME than real strength.'"—*Preston, 1836.*

to countenance it *from interest*, it would be unfair to omit even the Government itself; for were it not for the revenue derived from intoxicating liquors, it is impossible to believe that Government could have approved of some late legislative measures, or that it would encourage the legal demoralization of the people. Indeed, it requires an extensive knowledge of society to form any adequate idea of the *interest* which is allied with the manufacture and sale of intoxicating liquor.

Appetite.

"When we look at the inveterate habit acquired by many in the use of snuff and tobacco, I scarcely need to tell you, ladies and gentlemen, that what at first is unpalatable and nauseous, becomes by repetition agreeable and tempting; and this applies with great force to all kinds of alcoholic stimulants. They are capable of producing almost immediate excitation; and being always followed by a corresponding depression, the drunkard longs for another glass, to regain his spirits, and thus becomes the slave of appetite. Many become drunkards against their better judgment, and go on, labouring under remorse of conscience, and the apprehension of death, drinking the liquor, which they know will prove their ruin. Thus our national intemperance is perpetuated, for old topers become leaders of bands, and serve as decoy ducks to others, who soon become like themselves, the slaves of appetite. Thousands and tens of thousands, who began with a social glass to please a friend, or to relieve some ailment, have gone on, increasing the quantity, till you see them sacrificing both themselves and their families to their insatiate thirst for drink. How painful to see fathers or mothers, whose love of ale or spirits will even lead them to rob their children both of food and clothing, in order to procure for themselves intoxicating liquor! How painful to stand at the front of the dram-shop, and observe the wreck of health, fortune, intelligence, and virtue, floating through these infernal doors! When a man begins to *like* the liquor, he is half undone, and he is fortunate indeed if he do not finish his course in the drunkard's grave. Some drink for interest, some for fashion, and some through ignorance; but, if the truth were known, a vast number drink *because they like it.*

Fashion.

"To this I beg your serious attention. Because our mammas and papas drank a certain sort of drink, we adopt the same practice, without entering into any inquiry whether it be good or bad. The fashion of drinking begins with us at our birth, and follows us till we are laid in the grave. So soon as a child is born into the world, the event must be celebrated by the use of some kind of intoxicating drink. The largest table and the best china are procured, and in the centre stands the cream jug with the cork in, well supplied with Jamaica cream. Here the parties enjoy themselves, and drink to the health of the new-born babe, the doctor being president of the feast. The mother being put to bed, every visitor who enters the room is treated with a glass out of the stock provided for the occasion; and then, after all the tittle-tattle common on such occasions, she is handed another glass before she goes, to keep the cold out.

"The *christening* is the next season for drinking, and Sunday is usually selected for the ceremony, because it affords a greater opportunity for drinking.

"Both *weddings* and *funerals* are conducted on the same principle; and on the latter occasion we find, where the parties are assembled to pay their respects to the departed, that the tables are covered with hot ale and cold ale, pipes and tobacco; nay, such is the absurdity of the drinking fashions at funerals, that so soon as you touch the latch of the door, you are presented by a female, suitably attired, with a smoking hot tankard of poison and water.

"Christmas, Shrovetide, Easter, Whitsuntide, every memorable day in the history of our religion; every national holiday; races, fairs, and especially *elections*, are all seasons for destroying reason, impairing health, and demoralizing character, by the use of strong drink.

"In respectable life, it is the fashion on all social occasions to drink stimulating liquors. At dinner, it is supposed that the food would not digest unless accompanied with wine or brandy; and the afternoons are so tediously long, that each gentleman has to take his pint of wine in order to kill time! When one friend calls to see another, the common invitation is, 'What will you have to drink?' It rarely happens that persons are asked what they will have to eat; but always, 'What will you have to drink ?' Calling lately on a friend in Everton, near Liverpool, I was shown into the parlour, and waited till the gentleman came in. With scarcely any preliminary conversation, he instantly fetched out the decanters, and said, 'What sort will you take ?' He did not say, 'Will you take a beef steak ?' or 'Will you take anything to eat ?' but 'What sort of drink will you take ?' 'None of these sorts,' was my reply; 'but if your good lady will favour me with a cup of tea, I have no objections to join her'; which was immediately supplied, with plenty of good bread and butter. I was in London a few months ago, and having to call with my friends upon the Duke of Wellington's steward, the usual question was put—not, 'What will you have to eat ?' but, 'What *sort* do you drink—ale or porter, or half-and-half ?' 'Have you nothing better ?' I asked, looking rather gravely. 'No, sir,' he rejoined; 'we are not allowed anything better.' 'What ! can you furnish us with neither water nor milk ?' He seemed to treat our remarks as a joke ; but we assured him that, being Lancashire teetotalers, we were really in earnest ; and that we had too much respect for our stomachs to pour into them any such dirty, deleterious liquors.—In commercial life, the fashion of drinking awfully prevails. Buying, selling, paying, settling, every commercial transaction associates itself with drinking. How strange it seems, that persons should happen to be thirsty when they have business to transact ! When your travellers come for orders, they perhaps step into your shop, and finding you busy, they invite you to come up to their inn in the evening. There the parties sit and drink till they have emptied several bottles ; and I need not say what kind of bargains are usually made on these occasions.—The fashion of drinking among mechanics is kept up in every establishment. Footings, rearings, and apprentice fees are all spent in intoxicating drink. The effects of these footings, etc., clearly show that this is no idle picture. —All the sick club meetings, funeral societies, and trades societies' meetings are held at public-houses, and the business is uniformly accompanied with drinking. And, indeed, most of these societies are got up by the landlords entirely to 'bring custom to their houses, and to tempt men to buy their liquor.—The foundation of all our buildings, even our churches and chapels, are laid in drink ; and the flag which you see upon a building that has just been reared may be regarded as a *flag of distress*. The men who raised the building are drinking in some public-house or jerry shop.—The same fashion prevails at sales, and especially at agricultural sales ; the auctioneer may cry for bids, but the attendants seem destitute of the power of speech till their mouths are moistened, and their spirits inspired with this '*water of life*.' With the assistance of this stimulant, they begin to appreciate the full value of every article. Their expanded imaginations lead them frequently to fancy that a calf is a cow, or that a horse is several hands higher than it really is ; and they bid and buy at prices of which they are ashamed next morning. I remember a joiner who attended a sale, and who, I suppose, fancied he had been a working man long enough, and that for once he would be a gentleman. An old chaise was brought to the hammer ; bidding went on smartly, till it was struck off to him at eight pounds and a shilling. He was so drunk that he could scarcely walk home ; they therefore put him into the chaise, dragged him home, and carried him to bed. Next morning, when he opened his casement, he had the exquisite pleasure of beholding his own carriage at his door ! In fact, turn which way you will, the poisoned bowl meets us everywhere ; and imperious fashion has forced this evil custom into every department of society.

"But cannot these fashions be changed ? And what is the change for which we ask ? We do not ask you to part with any of the necessaries or of the harmless pleasures of life. We do not say, give over eating, or give over drinking. The simple change we ask is, that all your drinks shall be free from poison. You may have them of any colour, of almost any flavour, and at any cost ; you may ransack the French language, if you please, for names ; all, I repeat, that we ask is, that your drinks be free from that ingredient which the laws of our physical nature have forbidden to be taken by any person in a state of health. Why should there be any difficulty in changing fashions in drinking ? If in reference to our clothing —a mere external matter—we can submit to a change of fashion, why not in reference to that, which, entering our stomach, has a general influence upon our health and happiness ? In this respect, the ladies afford us a fine example. There was a time when a lady's dress was longer than herself ; but now, such has been the change of fashion, that, in my opinion, they are indelicately short. Formerly, ladies wore large, huge, ugly bonnets, which bade defiance at any attempt to get a glance at their countenances ; but these have been supplanted by the little pretty cottage bonnets, which now grace the ladies' heads. The upper part of the arm for a ladies' dress, according to the rule of reason, was at one time measured by the arm ; but now it is an axiom with milliners to measure that part of the arm by the body ! If such changes as these can be made, why then continue the abominable old fashion of drinking intoxicating drinks ? Why persist in swallowing maddle-brain in preference to every other sort of liquor ? On this change depends the progress of the temperance reformation ; and those who are not willing to submit to it have yet to learn the true principle of patriotism, and are even strangers to real self love. My friends ! change the fashions—*be determined to change the fashions !* If the customs of your country be bad, somebody must originate a change, and who would not seize the present opportunity, and make every sacrifice, to wrest his country from the despotic grasp of imperious fashion !

Ignorance.

"The next cause of intemperance, unhappily prevalent in this country, is *ignorance.* By the efforts of the Temperance advocates, the ignorance long existing respecting the properties of ardent spirits is in a great measure removed. But as to the properties of MALT LIQUOR, this country still labours under a GREAT DELUSION. Ale has been celebrated as our national beverage, and all classes have seemed to agree that it was the proper drink of the working man. Wiser heads than yours have proclaimed a thousand times, even in the senate, that ' ale was a highly nutritious beverage ; ' and whilst this sentiment has everywhere been responded to, whilst the press has circulated the same opinion, no wonder that the common people should still labour under this serious mistake. The regulations of the legislature have also been made upon this false principle ; and hence, while asserting that malt liquor is necessary for the working man, and while increasing the facilities for his obtaining it, Government has been changing and multiplying the restraints which they seemed anxious to impose to prevent drunkenness. The magistrates license thousands of *drunkeries,* and yet levy a fine upon those who become what the liquor was sure to make them. In one room, they are giving leave to sell the drunkard's drink, and in the other busily engaged in fining the drunkard, and the man they licensed to make him such !

" The first method of ascertaining the property of malt liquor, is, by its *effects* upon those who drink it. This is a test which all men of common sense can adopt. The tree is known by its fruits, and ale is known by *its* fruits. The application of this principle was clearly set forth by a poor man who attended one of my lectures. At the conclusion, his brother approached the platform, and attempted to put several questions, when the man came behind him, pulled at his coat, and said : ' Bill, until tha cun prove that ale's done more good than it's done ill, I'd ha tha to let it aluun.' This, my working friends, is a test which you can all apply. Take a sheet of paper, and write down on the one side all the good that ale has done, and on the other side all the evil that it has done ; and I am quite willing the quality of the liquor shall be determined by the balance. Apply the same rule to every other article of meat and drink that you have in your houses (excepting alcoholic drinks)—bread, beef, butter, milk, water, or any other article of food ; and you will see what a difference there will be in the result. Every article which God intended us to use, is in the aggregate productive of good, and not of evil ; but if there were any article in my house calculated to produce a hundredth part of the poverty, and misery, and crime, which ale is producing, I would insist upon its being entirely banished. And this brings to my mind the observations of Tommy Lord at one of our meetings : ' If my porridge (and I loike my porridge as weel 's I like onything else) sent hoaf as mony to hell as ale has done, I'd drop my spoon.' Judge also by the rule of comparison ; see what a striking difference there is betwixt the ale-drinking man and the man who abstains entirely from it ; and also, in reference to the same individual, betwixt his condition at the time when he indulged in malt liquor, and now that he has begun to practise abstinence. If it be said, the effects of drinking ale here referred to arise not from the proper use of the article, but from the abuse ; I answer, *the use involves the abuse ;* and I affirm, that whilst ale continues to be an alcoholic drink, capable of producing intoxication, and whilst the excitability of the human system continues to be what God has made it, the professed moderate use of this liquor is absolutely certain to produce those effects denominated excess. When you recollect that we have no occasion to complain of excess from the use of tea or coffee, milk or water, you will clearly perceive that the blame is often cast upon the drinker which belongs to the deceitful properties of the liquor. To reason otherwise betrays either a spirit of bigotry, or a decided inattention to matter of fact. The truth is, that alcohol, in certain combinations, has its use in chemical, mechanical, and medical operations; but, were it not for national prejudices, it would be difficult to find that it had any use whatever in its combination with coloured hop-water, excepting that of filling the asylums, the workhouses, and the prisons, and diffusing misery, immorality, and crime through the land.*

Deep Depravity.

" This is the last general *cause* which I have named in the arrangement of this lecture. I have noticed frequently that persons possessing the fullest information as to the properties of intoxicating liquors, and carrying in their own circumstances the most decided evidence of their bad tendency, persons who care nothing for the fashion of drinking, who have neither liking for the liquor nor any interest in the traffic, after all, frequent the ale-house, and indulge in most of the excesses of intemperance. In such cases the love of sin and sinful practices is the prevailing motive. Everything that is wicked and debasing associates, in this country, with the use of strong drink : and hence, men drink for the purpose of indulging in other vices. Idleness, swearing, lying, revenge, gaming, cruelty, debauchery, and all kinds of folly, are allowed and practised in public-houses. These and drinking reciprocally influence each other ; and hence, vicious characters, finding that intoxicating liquor introduces them to various scenes of iniquity, and gives a zest to animal indulgences, drink the poisoned draught from no other motive than the love of evil. Hence we account for the apostasy of so many temperance converts, who have no liking for the liquor itself. Being unrenewed in the spirit of their minds—being insensible of the wickedness of their past lives, they become abstainers from intoxicating liquors from motives of mere worldly policy, but they never duly repent ; their hearts remain unrenewed, and, being strangers to a real Christian life, they frequently break their vows. And from the same cause, persons, instead of trusting in God in the midst of affliction, and meeting disappointment and trouble with pious resignation ; instead of looking at all earthly good as a shadow, and rising on the wings of faith and hope to more lasting enjoyments, they fly to the bottle, drink the momentarily care-destroying drink, and give that homage to a relentless idol which is due to the God of heaven. The alehouse, instead of the throne of grace, is the asylum of all such. When abstinence is accompanied with true penitence of soul, and leads to an attendance upon the means of grace, and to a religious life, there is a fair hope of perseverance ; but not otherwise. Hence, as temperance, in the first instance, is the restorer of reason, and a deliverer from the shackles of the ale bench, all who feel interested in the completion of our temperance reformation, should, at proper times and places, endeavour to bring every reformed drunkard under the influence of that gospel which is the power of God to complete salvation. And perhaps no stronger recommendation could be given of our system than this, that an increased attendance at churches and chapels and a revival of religion have generally followed the successful establishment of Teetotal Societies.†

The Mystery of Ale Drinking Explained.

" This bottle, ‡ containing the spirit from the same quart of ale, develops the whole mystery. Men mistake stimulation for strength, and because after drinking

* Under the second head of 'Ignorance,' Mr. Livesey gives an elaborate description of the processes of malting and brewing, which the reader will find embodied in the lecture at the end of this volume.

† Is this putting teetotalism in the place of religion ? The fact is there is more genuine piety in the Malt Liquor Lecture than in many of the so-called Gospel Temperance publications.

‡ The exhibition of the *extract* [solid matter, taken from the ale] in one hand and the *spirit* in the other—all the rest being water—served very much to simplify the argument. – J. L.

a quantity of ale they feel a little excited, they really think it does them good. They judge from present feelings, instead of permanent effects. We shall often hear workmen say, after taking a pint of ale in the forenoon, how much better they feel; and yet it is equally true, that we hear them complain of its *dying* in them; and hence, instead of its being a source of strength, it becomes a cause of weakness; for it not only injures the system by constantly exciting it, but by being taken as a substitute for proper food. If drinking ale really gives strength and vigour to the body, the man who gets his quart on a Saturday night ought to be full of blood and quite active on a Sunday morning; instead of which, we find him *thirsty, depressed*, and scarcely able to get from his bed to his big chair, where he usually sits unwashed till after dinner. It is the same delusion which leads our females to the dram-shops. You may see two women, after pawning an article for threepence, proceed to the dram-shop, call for a noggin, and after throwing it down their throats (for the palate cannot bear so fiery an article long enough to taste it), they come out wiping their mouths, declaring, 'It is the best I ever tasted in my life; it goes to my finger ends and my toe ends.' The truth is, spirit, like the bellows, blows up the fire, but does not add one single particle of fuel. Feel a man's pulse after taking a few glasses of ale, and you will find that the circulation is considerably quickened. And it is an invariable law in reference to the human body, that if you force the blood faster than its natural speed, a corresponding depression is certain to follow. If men would endeavour to ascertain what part of the ale it is which produces those feelings that they call strength, they would find that it is the *whisky* part, and no other; and, consequently, if the stimulation of a glass of ale be strength, that of whisky and water must be equally so. Without further remarks, I will afford you an opportunity of forming your own opinion as to the properties of the spirit which is found in the best ale.* The effect of the alcohol, which you now see burning on the plate, is to destroy the coats of the stomach and to injure the livers of those who drink it, and to produce externally a red-hot face and a nose covered with brandy blossoms. Though there may be many working men, who, perhaps, have never suffered in this way, I much mistake my audience if there are not hundreds here, the bottom of whose pockets it has burned out many a time. I remember, when lecturing at Burnley, a man observed, when he saw the spirit on fire, 'I have drunk as much of that as would have lit all the lamps in Manchester.' There is, my drinking friends, one consolation on this subject for you, that if from your ale you do not get much *food*, you get plenty of *fire*.

Are Drinkers Strengthened or Stimulated?

"If, again, you plead for a pint of ale as a source of *strength*, I hope the exposition given to-night will fully show the futility of such a plea. It is the *solids*, and not the *liquids*, upon which labouring men are to work. I have often been asked, 'Can a man perform his labour on cold water?' to which I answer, 'No, nor on cold ale either.' What is it that gives strength to the miller's horse, *which drinks nothing but cold water*, and makes its ribs wrinkle with fat? It is the *food* which he eats. And it is good food, my working friends, good roast beef and barley pudding, from which you are to derive your strength. Water is most useful as a diluent, and the best that nature has provided. It serves to supply the waste of fluid which is continually going on in the body. But still it is nutritious food which must support the strength and repair the waste of the solid parts of the human frame.

"If you drink your ale for the purpose of *stimulation*, I agree that it will answer that purpose; but the effect of this stimulation, in most cases, is to injure the human system. To work by stimulation is to draw upon the constitution, and to avail yourselves of muscular power before it is fairly due. Ale may lift you higher than yourselves, but it is sure to let you fall again. Working by stimulation is like pawning the constitution in order to get premature power; † and not unlike

* Here about four ounces of proof spirit, taken from the quart of ale, were burnt on a plate, to the astonishment and conviction of many who saw it.—J. L.

† Mr. Livesey thus anticipates, by several years, the conclusions of Baron Liebig; who in his "Letters on Chemistry" declares: "Spirits, by their action on the nerves, enables the drinker to make up the deficient power at *the expense of his body;* to consume to-day that quan-

the conduct of those families who get a prime dinner for Sunday, a good dinner on Monday, very bare towards the middle of the week, and towards the latter end nothing at all. You have a full development of the truth of this in the Saturday night drinker. He lives twice too fast; he gets Sunday morning's life on Saturday night. And such is the excitement, that were he even to refrain from his cups on the Sunday, the rest of the Sabbath is insufficient to restore nature to her equilibrium by the hour of labour on Monday morning. Stimulation is incipient madness; and every one who seeks after it, less or more, seems to aim a blow at that noble and heavenly gift of God,—the gift of reason.

The Scriptural Argument.

"Christianity teaches us to deny ourselves, in order to promote the happiness of others, and gives us a splendid example in the conduct of its founder.   .   .   .

"The Scriptures not only promulgate the truth itself, but approve of every measure which is requisite in *preparing the way* for its success. The preparation most needed in this country, and at this time, is the removal of all intoxication and intoxicating drinks; and this the Temperance Society is trying to effect. The word of God universally reprobates drunkenness, and states distinctly, that no drunkard can inherit the kingdom of heaven. Situated as we are in this country, with our present fashionable drinks, it is found that no system but the teetotal one can save the drunkards, or prevent the rising generation from becoming such; and where, then, I ask, are the principles of our Society at variance with the Scriptures?

"But it will be replied, Did not Christ Himself make wine, and is it not also frequently spoken of in terms of approbation? but you forbid wine altogether. In reply to this, I beg to ask, What kind of wine did Christ make, and what kind of wine do we find sanctioned in Scripture? Was it Port, or Sherry, or Hock, or Claret? Was it fermented, or unfermented? Was it intoxicating, or not intoxicating? For it ought to be distinctly understood that we are not warring against the term '*wine*,' nor against the good qualities which liquor bearing that name may contain. We do not object to the *name*, the colour, the flavour, or the cost of any kind of liquor; all we object to is the ALCOHOL, or the intoxicating property which they may contain. The mere English scholar is apt to be misled by the word 'wine' in our translation, and to suppose that it uniformly stands for a liquor like that used by the wine-bibbers of this country. In the Hebrew there are nine different words, some referring to the grape itself, others to the unfermented juice of the grape, others to a liquor of a doubtful character, and in other cases to liquor that was eminently intoxicating, all represented in the English translation by the terms 'wine,' or 'strong drink.' Nothing is more common in the Prophets than the terms ' corn, and oil, and wine,' evidently referring to these articles as the blessings of Providence; but I appeal to any of you, whether you would not consider the grapes themselves, either in a moist or a dried state, or the juice of the grape in a state of perfection, better than when that juice was suffered to run into the vinous fermentation to produce alcohol? Pharaoh drank his wine in a state of the greatest perfection (Gen. xl. 11); and to a liquor like this, calculated to 'cheer the heart of man,' but not to inebriate his brain, we have no objection. To show the uncertainty of deciding the qualities of a liquor by its name, and especially at places distant from each other, I may remind you of the various sorts of liquor to which the term *beer* is applied. It is used by some to denote the strongest malt liquor; by others, as a name for that which is drunk at dinner, of an inferior strength; and in this part of the country, it is commonly used as the appropriate name for a very weak malt liquor sold at a penny a quart. And not only so, but we have ginger *beer*, spruce *beer*, nettle *beer*, and treacle *beer*, as well as malt beer;

tity which ought naturally to have been employed a day later. He draws, so to speak, a bill on his health, which must be always renewed, because, for want of means, he cannot take it up. He consumes his capital instead of his interest, and the result is the inevitable bankruptcy of his body" (3rd ed., 1851, p. 455). The learned German employs an illustrative figure exactly similar to that used by Mr. Livesey. It may be also mentioned that Baron Liebig fully sustains Mr. Livesey's position regarding the innutritiousness of malt liquors. Supposing a man to consume daily eight or ten quarts of "the best Bavarian beer,"—according to the Professor—he will, in the course of a year, obtain from it nutriment about equal to that contained in a five-pound loaf of bread!

and when it is proved that *these* are intoxicating, then we may believe that the same conclusion may be drawn as to the term *wine* used in Scripture.*

An Appeal to Drunkards.

"Drunkards! We are your best friends. Your own companions despise you, the landlords deride you, and you are even shunned by many religious people as worthless characters. *We are your friends:* we pity your case, and are trying to save you. Degraded as you are in the estimation of others, you are not less so in your own estimation; yet we behold you with the eye of pity and benevolence, and will do all in our power to rescue you from your misery. Drunkards! It is you we want to reform, for the whole need not a physician. Hitherto you have struggled for deliverance, but struggled in vain. Moderate drinking was the cause of your ruin, and yet this by some is offered you as a remedy. Avoid taking too much, is their advice: but with all your endeavours, on this principle, you find it impossible to succeed, for you are never able to get enough. The only safe and efficacious plan is to avoid the *first*—yes, the *first*—to many, the *fatal* glass. No matter how desperate your disease, if you will come to Doctor Teetotal, he will cure you, and charge nothing for it. Thousands have applied, and in no single case has his medicine failed to effect a complete cure. Poor drunkard! thine enemies, even the 'blue devils' themselves, pursue thee almost to death; thou art the subject of a tormenting conscience. Look! here is our city of refuge; the gates stand wide open; flee into it, and thou art safe! Thou art on a stormy ocean, ready every moment to be ingulfed in the great deep. See! here comes our lifeboat: step into it, and thou wilt land safely on the shore of abstinence. Drunkards! I am your friend; I am delighted to meet you, and I hope you will profit by my advice. Thousands, thousands of drunkards have already been saved: why not you? Do you doubt the efficacy of the system? Try it. You have tried drinking, perhaps for twenty years, and you have felt its dreadful effects. Try abstinence as many months as I have tried it years; and if you suffer in your health or strength, in your pocket or conscience, if you sink in the estimation of yourselves, your wives, your children, or your employers, send me an account of the loss, and I will pay the amount to the utmost farthing. God destined that we should be happy; and who are more entitled to enjoy this happiness than the working classes, the producers of all our wealth? By joining our ranks, miserable as you are, you may still be happy. Sobriety will make you into new men. It will remove from your faces those scars and scratches and pimples which you are obliged to exhibit to the public. It will put new shoes on your feet, and new clothes on your backs. It will put a white or yellow lining in your pockets, and comfort in your breasts; it will make you contented servants, kind fathers, and loving husbands; and, what is better than all, convinced of the notoriously wicked lives which you have led, it may induce you to prepare for another and a better world. The publican's prayer will then be yours—'God be merciful to me a sinner!' Do come, then, to-night, sign our teetotal pledge, and be determined to keep it as long as you live."

Readers of the lecture from which the foregoing citations have been made, in every part of the world, were converted by it to abstinence. Evidence of this continually crops up. For instance, within a few months of its publication, we find Mr. James Teare writing to Mr. Livesey: "Your Malt Lecture has been the means of converting hundreds, if not thousands, to teetotalism;"† and on the 22nd May, ·

---

* Writing upon wine drinking, in the *Temperance Advocate*, as early as June, 1834, Mr. Livesey had said: "It may not be improper here to make a few observations in reference to the qualities of the wine mentioned in the Scriptures, to show how erroneous we are in identifying our Port and Madeira with the wine generally used in Judea. The term *wine* appears to have been used in Judea with the same latitude as the term *beer* among us. We have various sorts of beer—treacle beer, ginger beer, as well as *malt beer*; and in reference to the latter, we have 'small beer,' 'table beer,' 'strong beer,' as well as 'John Bull' and 'brown stout.' It was exactly the same in reference to the Judean wine. 'The fruit of the vine' was used in various ways. The grapes were eaten, sometimes in a 'moist,' sometimes in a 'dried' state, like our raisins. The most harmless state of the *juice* of the *grape* was that when the grapes were pressed into the cup (Gen. xl. 11), and being unfermented could not intoxicate" (*Preston Advocate*, 1834, p. 41). Is not this the germ of the generic theory of Scriptural wines, elaborated and perfected by Dr. F. R. Lees, the writer who more than any one else has succeeded in harmonizing the teachings of the Bible and science upon this topic?

† *Preston Advocate*, vol. iv. (1837), p. 21.

1862, Mr. Livesey was present at a public meeting in Exeter Hall when two of the speakers—the Rev. Wm. Roaf and Mr. John Phillips—incidentally declared themselves to have been converted by the same means. The Rev. Wm. Roaf, of Wigan, an active worker in the movement, and author of the "Pastor's Pledge," said:

" Soon after I entered the Christian ministry I heard about teetotalism; but what ' ism ' it was I really could not understand. I was all in a mist and fog about it until a kind friend put into my hand a pamphlet by that good man sitting there—Mr. Joseph Livesey, of Preston—(great applause) entitled, ' The Malt Lecture.' I well remember the spot where I stood and read it. When I got to the end, thinks I, ' I shall sign the teetotal pledge to-day.' I then called my wife up to my library, and I read it to her, and said, ' Will you sign the pledge? ' She said, ' Will you ? ' ' Certainly,' I said, and she agreed. When the evening came, I called up the two servants, and read it to them ; and as I read it, I expounded a little bit. I said to them, ' Will you sign the pledge? ' ' Oh l certainly,' they said. So the next morning I sent fourpence down to the Temperance Office for four penny cards, and we all signed the pledge, and sent them to the secretary. He called on me soon after; his heart was in his mouth. He was so glad, he could not express the joy he felt." *

And Mr. John Phillips bore the following testimony :

" I went into a coffee house in the West End of London some twenty-five and a half years ago, and on the table of the coffee room I read Joseph Livesey's " Malt Lecture." Like my rev. friend, Mr. Roaf, I was deeply impressed with the strong common sense, and the sterling cogent arguments of the Lecture, . . . and I could do nothing else than take the course laid down. ' Mr. Livesey ' (addressing that gentleman), ' I have been twenty-five years an honest teetotaler, and in a very humble way an earnest labourer in the cause. Whatever good I may have done, may the recollection of it rest upon your snowy, puritan, honoured head.' . . . I cannot tell you with what joy I meet Mr. Livesey to-night. I have so much to thank him for." †

TEMPERANCE APHORISMS.

Mr. Livesey's happy faculty of stating an important truth in a few words made his Temperance Sheet Almanacs both interesting and useful. He gave his readers a motto for each day in the year. The subjoined examples of his aphoristic teachings are taken from " The Temperance Almanac for 1839 (the sixth year of teetotalism), by Joseph Livesey ":

> Teetotalers, beware of ' except as medicine.'
> A little ' as medicine ' more to *please* than *cure.*
> ' The last shift,' a suitable sign for a jerry shop.
> Every Temperance Society should keep a teetotal rattle.
> Landlords' victuals are of a wet kind.
> Cold water will cure a pimpled nose.
> Join Temperance, knowledge, and charity together.
> Fire in the stomach, but none in the grate.
> No Society can prosper without a weekly meeting.
> Sell Temperance papers at the close of every meeting.
> *Religious* newspapers advertise *strong drink !*
> Temperance hotels should be kept clean and orderly.
> Teetotalers, see that ye fall not out by the way.
> *Bad coffee* brings no custom to the Temperance house.
> Avoid sectarianism in your speeches.
> The first glass is *one* ' over the line ' of sobriety.
> Let us work more and profess less.
> If there were no *buyers,* there would be no *sellers.*
> The public house is the starting chair for the gallows.

---

* *The Weekly Record,* May 30th, 1862, p. 230.   † *Ibid.,* p. 232.

Whisky-craft is the greatest tyrant of Ireland.
The best side of a public house is the outside.
Religious grog-sellers serve Christ and Belial.
'Come and sign '—example is better than precept.
A reformed drunkard's speech is a second pledge.
I am a member of the Never-touch-lads-Society.
Wanted ! new recreation for ex-tavern customers.
A teetotaler with a ' little drop ' wife is but half a member.
Every drunkard's hovel should be visited.
Malt liquor for nurses is the *forcing* system.
Dr. Teetotal gives advice *gratis* to rich and poor.
Drinking whisky is rasping with a new file.
' It will do you no harm,'—a poor compliment.
Speak ' nothing but the truth ' at your meetings.
Up and be doing—stop all this brewing.
' Treasure in heaven ? '   No ; it is in the *cellar !*
Every man should at least reform *one.*
Temperance is not opposed to religion, but is a part of it.
Brewers' horses are fatter than their customers.
The barrel and the Bible are sent out in the same ship.
Christ's ministers ought to attack our besetting sin.''

THE MEDICINAL USE OF ALCOHOL.

The use of alcoholic liquors as medicine is a fallacy which has done much to retard the progress of Temperance.   Weak-kneed abstainers, whose teetotal standard was no higher than their pledge, have largely availed themselves of the exception in the ordinary abstinence pledge.   Multitudes of reclaimed drunkards have been again drawn into the old quagmire and irrecoverably lost by ' medical prescription.'   Mr. Livesey's principle was always in advance of his pledge, and he was one of the earliest Temperance teachers to raise a note of warning against this source of danger ; while he published, at a price within the reach of all, the most thorough and advanced medical and physiological teaching upon the subject.   His *Advocate* contains letters and articles from the pens of Dr. J. Fothergill, Dr. Beaumont, and other of the earliest medical adherents of the movement.   " The Temperance Doctor," published in the autumn of 1836—containing important papers by Dr. J. Fothergill, Dr. Mussey, Dr. C. A. Lee, and quotations from other authorities—was in a few months followed by " The New Temperance Doctor," comprising important contributions by Dr. E. Johnson, Dr. C. A. Lee, of New York, and other medical writers.   The question was further advanced by a judicious abbreviation of the famous Essays of Dr. Mussey and Mr. Lindsly, issued, uniform with the preceding publications, as " The Physiological Influence of Alcohol."   Each of these pamphlets contained as much matter as is frequently given in a shilling volume ; they were well printed on good paper, published at the low price of one penny, and commanded a very extensive circulation.

Articles from Mr. Livesey's own pen, addressed to nursing mothers and other classes, pointing out the fallacy of resorting to alcoholic stimulus, or cautioning teetotalers against succumbing to ' medical advise,' are plentiful in his own publications, and may also be found in the periodical literature of the movement.   In 1852, he uttered a timely protest against the 'bitter beer craze.'   Of this popular form of medicinal drinking, he says :

" If the swelling out of the doctors' bill and the tantalizing of his patients were the only evils, they were bad enough ; but there is one far greater, and that is, assisting in making and keeping up a nation of drunkards. I know not of any influence that has ruined so many ignorant, timid, and ailing people as the doctors' advice to take intoxicating stimulants, and especially those under the ensnaring character of porter and bitter ale. Hundreds of teetotalers have been ruined by this advice. They began to take this ale tonic, and after receiving fancied good for months and years, they are still taking it. The truth is, the love of stimulation is created, till they easily fall into the ranks of the intemperate. . . . Oh ! what a wreck of health, fortune, and character is to be found in our prisons and asylums, and in the wretched obscure homes of the inebriate, originated and matured by the alcoholic tonics recommended by doctors. It is really time we met the medical foe of the abstinence cause face to face. We have given it quarter too long." *

How Mr. Livesey practised what he taught should never be forgotten by his teetotal disciples. Many a man who has been brave upon the platform when denouncing the drink, has cowardly yielded to the enemy upon a sick-bed. But not so Mr. Livesey when the day of trial came to him, as it will to everybody sooner or later. In 1869 he lay prostrated with rheumatic fever at Windermere, and his medical attendant, altogether baffled and believing the patient at death's door, announced that brandy afforded the only hope of recovery. In that condition, what did Mr. Livesey do ? Did he avail himself of the exception in the pledge, until the results of a *sufficiently extensive* experiment at the Temperance Hospital had demonstrated that it would be *safer* to defy the doctor than to follow his advice ? No ! that course might be adopted by a weak-kneed abstainer : it was not the one followed by the Father of Teetotalism. What did Mr. Livesey do in this crisis ? Teetotal reader, fix upon your mind the answer to this question, as it is given in the *Preston Herald :*

" ' Raise me up,' he whispered to his son, who was present ; and when that had been gently done—' Bring me the looking glass, and let me see my face,' he said to a lady present, and that was done too. He looked at himself for a while in silence, and then said : ' Well, there is a look there I don't like. I believe, however, I shall get well again ; but *whether I do or not,* I WILL NOT DRINK THE STUFF. Put me down again, and if I am to die, *I will die now.*'" †

On pages 89 and 90 of the " Autobiography " will be found Mr. Livesey's own remarks upon this incident ; and we are informed that the circumstance so impressed the doctor that he ultimately became a teetotaler.

ADULTERATION AND SOPHISTICATION ARE NOT QUESTIONS IN DISPUTE.

Mr. Livesey always contended, and wisely so, that the questions of the adulteration and fabrication of inebriating drinks were of little importance in the Temperance argument ; and that by pursuing them, the main object was in danger of being lost sight of. The whole question of teetotalism turns upon the inherent qualities of alcoholic liquors, and their fitness as articles of diet ; points which must not be obscured by the discussion of mere side issues. The following quotation, besides tersely dealing with adulteration, affords some very useful information respecting the properties of ' genuine alcoholic wine,' and forms a fitting sequel to Mr. Livesey's teachings on malt liquor.

" Our Temperance writers," he says, " are constantly dwelling upon ' adulteration' of wines.   They tell us that millions of gallons are made up of cider, sloes, log-wood, and such-like ingredients, without any juice of the grape.   Now, if pure alcoholic wines were *wholesome* and *uninjurious*, there would be some force in denouncing these adulterations.   But the fact is, nothing used in these fabrications is so injurious as the alcohol in genuine wines.   We are told that the adulterated article does not contain a drop of the real juice of the grape.   Well, granted, and where is the juice of the grape in those wines that are said to be pure, yet heavily charged with alcohol?   By the fermenting and fining processes, the properties of the grape either sink to the bottom of the vessels, or are changed into other substances. Almost the only part remaining unaltered is the water, amounting to about 75 per cent.   You cannot frighten wine-drinkers by telling them of elder-berries or logwood ; they get what 'cheers' and 'inebriates,' and that is what they like.   When our friends talk and write so much about adulterations, it seems to imply that they regard unadulterated wine as unobjectionable, and people will infer as much. Looking at the free use of brandy in making up the best wines, I doubt very much whether that made from cider and its accompaniments is not less injurious.   It is evident that we make two mistakes.   The first is that in this country we form an extravagant estimate of the 'juice of the grape,' an estimate that would soon sober down if we were living in countries abounding in vineyards.   The next is, we conceive that our 'good wine' *is* the juice of the grape (it is sometimes called the 'blood of the grape ').   Would it not be more correct to call it 'brandy and water?'   After undergoing all the operations of pressing, fermenting, fining, and keeping, what do we find?   *Water*, 75 per cent. ; *alcohol*, 20 per cent. ; and the other five made up of acids, fixed and volatile, including colouring matter and the essential oils from which the peculiar odours are obtained.   The great importing firm of Gilbey, in their Annual Circular for 1867, admit that the fermentation of grapes ' throws off much of the body and richness of the fruit, so much so, indeed, that it must be admitted that the similarity of the juice of the grape, before and after fermentation, is scarcely discernible.'   And the *Lancet* states that in every 1000 grains of the Clarets and Burgundies tested, the mean amount of albuminous matter present was only 1½ grains !   I speak now of our orthodox wines, those for instance that secure the praise of poets, and for which parties do not hesitate to pay an extravagant price.   Those manufactured with less care have more of the extractive matter." *

THE CASE STATED IN A FEW WORDS.

Mr. Livesey's Temperance creed occupies but little space.   It is thus stated in the *Preston Advocate* for June, 1834, and he never subsequently either departed from it or modified it :

" The making of alcoholic liquor is the chief cause of misery, disease, crime, disorder, madness, and death.   Is not, then, this immense destruction of good barley, which God has sent as food for man and beast, wantonness of the worst character? and ought it not to be discountenanced and condemned by every lover of his kind?   Every man who touches, tastes, or handles, is an accessory to this evil.   The call of the Temperance Society is,—MALT NOT—BREW NOT—DISTIL NOT—SELL NOT—DRINK NOT,—and [if it is responded to] England will be the happiest country in the world ! "†

The teachings of Mr. Livesey on many other points will be found in the next chapter.   There they are interspersed with the chief plans and methods of aggressive action pursued by himself throughout his Temperance career—plans and methods which in his hands or under his direction were productive of so much good to the race—and which eminently deserve a fair trial at the hands of all persons anxious to extend amongst their fellows the blessings of Temperance.

* *The Staunch Teetotaler*, 1868, p. 278.
† *The Preston Temperance Advocate*, vol. i. (1834), p. 42.

CHAPTER X.

TEMPERANCE: METHODS (AND, INCIDENTALLY, TEACHINGS).

A man must also have a certain readiness and fitness for teaching, and a certain quality of body, and above all things he must have God to advise him, as God advised Socrates to occupy the place of one who confutes error.—EPICTETUS.

Sectarianism in Temperance, or politics, or ecclesiasticism, is the antagonist of all organization *as an army*; that is, as moved by one impulse and one plan to one purpose and one end.—Dr. F. R. LEES.

The wise man goes forward apace, because the right way is always the shortest; on the contrary, the crafty politician arrives later at his end, because he walks in by-ways and crooked paths.—CONFUCIUS.

WITHOUT a doubt Mr. Livesey was in the habit of doing things in his own way, and sometimes perhaps he was rather impatient of the methods of other people; but then if this had not been the case, he would not have been Joseph Livesey. His individuality was strongly developed, and its influence pervaded all his public work, that of Temperance being no exception. While he formed, aided, and co-operated with societies and associations of various kinds, he never allowed himself to be merged in the mass, neither did he expect his associates to lose themselves in the crowd. One truth which Mr. Livesey saw clearly and never failed to act on himself, or impress upon others, was this,—that each person in the world has an allotted task, and no man can do another's work. And hence whatever may be done in promoting Temperance or any other beneficent object in association with others, forms but part of one's duty, and can in no case supersede personal and individual duties and responsibilities.

At the outset of the Temperance enterprise in Preston, Mr. Livesey applied to its promotion those plans, agencies, and methods by which he had previously endeavoured to extend education, moral reform, and true piety among the people. It was in every way a great advantage to the new movement, that he was an original and experienced teacher and reformer; and a man whose sympathies were deep, whose benevolence was extensive, and whose Christianity was of the most practical kind. The fact that he was a ready and agreeable speaker, and a practised writer at the time the society started, was also highly advantageous.

MR. LIVESEY AS A SPEAKER AND LECTURER.

Antoninus has said that "a man may be rigid in his principles, yet easy and affable in his manners, and free from any moroseness in delivering the precepts of his philosophy;" and Mr. Livesey was a practical demonstration of the truth of the axiom. Very few speakers on Temperance equalled him in persuasiveness. There was no trick in his advocacy, no stage effects were sought after; neither did he sacrifice reason to rhetoric. He was sparing of his appeals to the emotions, always

cxxix

k

keeping them in due subserviency to his addresses to the understanding; while he chiefly relied upon the force of truth presented to the intellect and conscience in a plain straightforward manner. Mr. Morris mentions that as Mr. Livesey was once speaking at an open-air meeting in Scotland, two gentlemen were attracted by "the silvery tones of the orator," [*] a remark which is in strict accord with other opinions regarding Mr. Livesey's voice.

While the quotations given in the previous chapter from the Malt Liquor Lecture as published give a good idea of Mr. Livesey's matter, they do not help us much regarding his manner on the platform. It is a written rather than a spoken discourse; fortunately, however, a verbatim report of the lecture was taken and published at Birmingham; [†] and that enables us better to understand the extraordinary results which everywhere attended its delivery. The words as spoken seem instinct with life, and there is altogether a *verve* about the Birmingham edition which we do not get in others. In his famous lecture Mr. Livesey not only convinced men in spite of their prejudices and appetites, but in the very teeth of their interests. Even the manufacturers of intoxicants themselves, listened and succumbed. A notable instance of this happened at Mr. Livesey's first lecture in London, and is recorded on page 70 of the " Autobiography." Nothing could be more depressing to the speaker than the circumstances on that occasion. He was utterly alone, so far as human help, or even sympathy, was concerned, and very little practical good seemed likely to result from the effort; but shortly afterwards, Mr. Livesey was gladdened by a note informing him that "an ale brewer, and partner of Dr. Epps, has given up the use and sale of it from what he heard at your lecture." Thus was a convert secured from the class of all others the least likely to contribute one. But another parallel case may be cited. When in Scotland, attending the anniversary of the Scottish Union in 1839, Mr. Livesey delivered his lecture at Edinburgh. The Rev. W. R. Baker, referring to it in an article in the *Temperance Journal*, says: " The following morning a young lady informed me that her father, who was present, and who is a porter, wine, and spirit merchant, was fully convinced by the lecture of the truth of teetotalism." [‡] On this occasion Mr. Livesey had a very distinguished auditor in the person of Mr. E. C. Delavan, who thus speaks to Dr. Marsh of the lecture:

" On the evening of the 5th, I heard Mr. Livesey, of Preston, give what is called his *Malt Liquor Lecture*. I shall not be able to give you any idea of it. You have read it, I presume; but the effect in delivery was very great, as the experiments and quantities were all placed before the eye, and thus more readily affected the mind. I will try and give a little analysis before I close, which you can put in [the *Journal*] [§] if you think proper. [||]

One other testimony as to the effect produced by the delivery of the lecture may be cited. The late Mr. T. B. Smithies regarded it not only as the most con-

---

[*] " Morris's History," p. 89.

[†] " The Great Delusion : Mr. Joseph Livesey's celebrated Lecture on Malt Liquor; delivered in the Town Hall, Birmingham, on Tuesday and Wednesday evenings, the 5th and 6th of April, 1836, With several important statements connected with the Temperance Reformation. Birmingham, printed and published by B. Hudson, at the office of the ' Philanthropist,' Bull Street, 1836." Such is the title page of a closely printed pamphlet of sixty pages, entirely occupied by Mr. Livesey's Lecture, which took two evenings in delivery.

[‡] *Temperance Journal*, London, vol. i. (1839), p. 231.

[§] A synopsis of the lecture, occupying about *half a column*, appears in next issue.

[||] *Journal of the American Temperance Union* (1839), p. 127.

vincing of all the utterances on Temperance of the time of its delivery, but was strongly impressed with its permanent value. Writing in his *Welcome* for July, 1882, he says:

" It was our privilege to hear this popular lecture in the city of York, and we shall never forget the marvellous effect produced on the audience as Mr. Livesey poured out the various measures of barley on a large white sheet on the platform. If Joseph Livesey had done nothing more than his frequent repetition of this most convincing lecture in the chief towns of the land he would have merited national thanks. It is perhaps not too much to say that this lecture, which was printed above forty [really forty-six, now forty-nine] years ago, is to-day regarded by the old Temperance workers as one of *the best and most useful* Temperance tracts ever issued. It cannot be too widely circulated. It is a fact worthy of note that to the delivery of this lecture was due not a few of the early adherents to the Temperance cause." *

And it may be truly said that these early adherents—converts of Mr. Livesey's —have been throughout the standard-bearers of the movement. Their teetotalism was of the sturdiest type, and they remained true to it in spite of the blandishments of society, the adverse influence of the medical profession, and even the temptations of the 'traffic.' The career of the late Mr. George Charlton, J.P., of Gateshead, who —after having laboured with rare devotion and singleness of heart for upwards of half a century in promoting Temperance—died September 15th, 1885, presents a striking illustration of this. The *Newcastle Chronicle* of September 16th, in sketching Mr. Charlton's useful life, states that he joined the ' moderation' society in 1834, but that:

" In 1835, Joseph Livesey visited Newcastle, and delivered his celebrated ' Malt Lecture,' in the old Music Hall, Blackett Street ; and from that point may be dated the vivication of teetotalism in this district. A society was formed, . . . and among its earliest members was Mr. Charlton."

It is difficult at this time to appraise the true value of Mr. Livesey's services to Temperance during the period of transition from ' moderation' to teetotalism. The more radical members of the old Temperance Societies throughout the country, anxious to effect the change from the partial to the complete system, looked to Mr. Livesey as the great exponent of the new principle. His publications constituted their ammunition and enabled them to effect great things ; but they needed his inspiring presence, and hence the invitations from all parts of the land which poured in upon him. To these he responded as he was able, visiting all the great centres of population, and effectively exposing 'the great delusion' of ale drinking. It was found that one lecture from Mr. Livesey was sufficient either to engraft the new idea into the old society, or, when the conservative element within the society was too strong for this, to establish a new Society upon the sounder basis.

It should be remembered that this important work—details of which will be found in the " Autobiography "—was undertaken entirely and completely upon the terms laid down for Apostles in the Gospels. Not only did Mr. Livesey lecture without fee or reward,† it was his rule to pay his own expenses. Hence his strength as a teacher, and his independence of patronage or favour. In this

* *The Welcome*, 1882, p. 424.

† Mr. Livesey deprecated making an admission charge to Temperance meetings. In the *Advocate*, for March, 1837, appears the following: " CHARGE FOR ADMISSION.—J. Livesey gives this notice, that he will attend no meetings when there is any charge made for admission " (p. 24).

crusade he " courted no man's smile, feared no man's frown," but laboured to establish the truth, and promote universal well-being. Often, as in London, he had to make his own arrangements, and prosecute his labours in spite of the opposition of the nominal friends of Temperance. Mr. Livesey's task in breaking the ice in Birmingham presents a striking illustration of this difficulty, but the opposition was encountered and overcome. Nothing in the history of Temperance in Birmingham has ever equalled that incident, and yet a parallel has been attempted to be drawn between the first meeting addressed by Mr. Livesey, and a meeting addressed by Mr. R. T. Booth, of Gospel Temperance celebrity. But no two incidents could really be more unlike.*

Mr. Livesey's visit to Birmingham, in 1836, may be mentioned as forming another important event in the history of Temperance in that town. A festival was held in the Town Hall on the evenings of the 6th and 7th of April, and he lectured each evening. The published report of the proceedings has already been mentioned. From the *Preston Advocate*, we learn that Mr. John Cadbury presided on the first, and Mr. James on the second evening. The results were very gratifying, and as Mr. Livesey had rendered the Society services so invaluable without fee or reward, the friends wished to acknowledge their indebtedness in a manner which would not be distasteful to him. They accordingly arranged for a silver medal (of not much intrinsic value) to be presented to him by the Rev. John

---

* Briefly, Mr. Livesey visited Birmingham on June 17th, 1834, where, according to pre-arrangement, he was to lecture in the evening. He called upon Mr. Cadbury, who was the recognised leader of the movement, but when it was understood that Mr. Livesey's lecture would be directed against fermented liquor, Mr. Cadbury declined to sanction it, and said its delivery would not be allowed. Whereupon Mr. Livesey remarked that as he had come to lecture, he should do so; and if the chapel announced for it was not allowed to be used, he should " make the street his meeting place." His earnestness and determination were evidenced by the bell man being at once sent round to announce a mid-day meeting for working-men, in St. Luke's church-yard, which was accordingly addressed by Mr. Livesey. As the time for the evening meeting approached, the opposition to it was withdrawn, and the lecturer was allowed to take his own course. The result was that Mr. Cadbury—whose mind would naturally be somewhat preju-diced against Mr. Livesey's teachings—was convinced of the soundness of the views pro-pounded, and immediately invited him to pay a second visit to Birmingham as soon as possible, and repeat his lecture.

Very different indeed were the circumstances under which Mr. Booth visited Birmingham. Mr. Ernest Blackwell, Mr. Booth's secretary, in his elaborate prospectus of Mr. Booth, " Booth; or, the Factory Boy who became a Gospel Temperance Evangelist, London, 1883 " (pp. 49-52), describes the preliminaries to the meeting; the crowd, the choir, the ribbons and pincushions; and by-and-by the hero, " with his dark brown hair, and blue eyes," walking on to the plat-form leaning upon the arm of his host, Mr. John Cadbury (son of Mr. Livesey's friend), whose " silvery locks " were covered by a broad-brimmed hat. Of course the reception was grand. After singing and prayer, Mr. Cadbury, who presides, rises; but perhaps Mr. Blackwell had better speak for himself: "Mr. Booth rises also, and the mass-congregation follow his example. The old gentleman tries to speak, but the people cheer; and being more in numbers, whilst averaging fewer years, they have the advantage. The clapping of hands is succeeded by the stamping of feet, and shouts of joy seem to be crowning the demonstration, when Mr. Booth's keen eye descries a young woman waving a white handkerchief, far away towards the back of the hall. He fumbles in his coat pocket for his own, and can't find it. Anybody else's will answer as well, so he helps himself,—perhaps takes the chairman's,—and waving it high above his head, signals for the whole congregation to do likewise. Then the wave of enthu-siasm rolls higher and higher and the sea of heads becomes capped as though with white-crested breakers. Tears are brought to the chairman's eyes, and when he attempts to address the thousands before him, only a few, seated upon forms near the platform, can catch his words." It is noteworthy that up to this point, Mr. Booth had done nothing, except walk the platform, slap " a rheumatic (*sic*) old clergyman upon the back," and go through the perform-ance with the chairman's handkerchief; and yet the audience is psychologized, and the vener-able chairman in tears. Persons in that condition will readily sign the pledge; but all that has been effected, in the case of those who have acquired a liking for the drink at least, has been to exchange one form of excitement for another; and friends who hope to rear a permanent Tem-perance reform with such materials are sadly wanting in a knowledge of the causes of drink-ing, proximate and remote. But for Mr. Blackwell's mention of Mr. Livesey's first Birmingham meeting, Mr. Booth's name would not have been introduced into this volume.

Angell James, to whom was entrusted the task of proposing a vote of thanks to Mr. Livesey. The medal was inscribed—

"Presented to Joseph Livesey, of Preston, at a Temperance Meeting held in the Town Hall, Birmingham, on Wednesday, April 6th, 1836, as a small token of grateful acknowledgment for his steady zeal and uncompromising advocacy of the principles of Temperance." [*]

Mr. James in the course of a eulogistic speech said:

"I have only to express my earnest hope, that those energies with which God has endowed you, may long continue; may God spare your life and strength to continue your exertions in this cause; may you be enabled to go on, followed in your career, as you doubtless are, by the tears of gratitude and smiles of joy of reclaimed drunkards' wives and children; followed by what I am sure you will always value, the blessings of society, the approving testimony of your own conscience, and the smile of an approving world." [†]

PRESENTATIONS NOT TO BE ENCOURAGED.

Mr. Livesey accepted the medal at the time, but he viewed presentations with suspicion, and regarded such tokens as rewards which no true reformer should look for. Subsequently he explained his part in the transaction as follows:

"I was invited to deliver my Malt Lecture, in the Town Hall, in Birmingham, which I did to an overflowing audience; and up to the moment I pronounced the last word of my address, I had not the most distant idea of the intention of my Birmingham friends. But so soon as I took my seat, to my surprise, and, I may add, to my confusion, the Rev. Angell James rose, and, after an appropriate address, delivered into my hands a silver medal. Respect for the kindness of my friends, and a desire that the harmony of the meeting should not be interrupted, led to the acceptance of this present; but this I can say sincerely, that if I had been apprised of their design before the meeting commenced, I should have resolutely insisted upon my friends relinquishing their intention. And in proof of my settled principle upon this point, I will here state, what otherwise would have remained generally unknown, that a kind friend and a warm supporter of the Temperance cause wrote, some time ago, begging my acceptance of a silver tea service, which he would have come and presented at a public meeting, in Preston, but which for the reasons assigned in this paper I respectfully declined." [‡]

THE PRESS AS A MEANS OF ENLIGHTENMENT.

Douglas Jerrold somewhere remarks, "When Luther wished to crush the devil—didn't he throw *ink* at him?" And *ink* was the great weapon with which Mr. Livesey attacked the current belief in the supposed good qualities of the '*Devil in Solution*'—alcohol. We have seen that he commenced this mode of warfare at least sixty years ago, and as long as he could wield a pen he prosecuted the crusade. Active in every department of Temperance labour, and himself the inventor of many of the best plans and methods of action ever devised, Mr. Livesey always regarded the printing press as being the most efficient engine for the dissemination of Temperance truth. And he fully acted up to his belief. His own magazines and periodicals are filled with teachings judiciously expressed in the plainest Saxon. His Temperance pamphlets are models of their kind, while his smaller tracts and leaflets are pointed and effective and like a "nail driven into a sure place." His *Struggle*, although a Free Trade paper, was permeated with Temperance teachings. Indeed, it was rare for a number to be issued without an

---

[*] *Preston Temperance Advocate*, vol. iii., Apl. Sup. (1836), p. 6.
[†] *Ibid.*, vol. iii. (1836), p. 37. [‡] *Ibid.*, vol. iv. (1837), p. 66.

incidental reference to the question, while in some issues Temperance was brought into striking prominence. But this was so wisely and judiciously done, that no reader could feel aggrieved, and the gain to Temperance must have been very great. Quite apart from his own publications, he was a prolific writer, and the periodical literature of the movement is largely enriched with articles and letters from his pen.

Great was his faith in truth and in its adaptability to man. When no national Temperance organization existed, he founded and sustained a *national* organ; and after that had been handed over to his spirited young disciples, he continued his press propaganda in another form. For nearly half a century he wrote, printed, and distributed Temperance tracts. His famous Tract Depôt supplied persons willing to buy with literature at the mere cost of paper and machining; while those who could not afford to buy, but were anxious to be the distributers of Temperance information, were furnished with weapons free of charge. And after fifty years of unceasing effort in this sphere of usefulness, when the debtor and creditor account came to be examined it was found that Mr. Livesey's receipts from Temperance publications were less by £7,000 than the sum he had expended upon them. Here is perhaps the most munificent contribution to Temperance propaganda ever made: and it would be altogether impossible to suggest any other channel in which £7,000, or, indeed, even five times that amount, could have been as profitably expended.*

HOW MR. LIVESEY WORKED AS EDITOR.

Information regarding the manner of literary men in their work is greedily sought after, especially now-a-days. A writer in the *Preston Advocate*, who uses the initials " A. T. T.," favours us with the following view of Mr. Livesey at work:

" Being at Preston, I was introduced to the editor of the *Temperance Advocate*, seated in his arm chair. It was about nine o'clock in the evening, when his son happened to step in from the post-office with a bundle of letters, which he placed upon the table; among the rest was a newspaper tied round with a shop thread. I was just near enough to glance at the title, which I perceived to be *The Watchman*, and in several parts of the paper appeared blots, or rather crosses, intended as marks of reference. He first looked at the marks on the four outside pages, and, folding the paper afresh, then at those on the other side. He wrinkled his brow, pouched his lips, placed the paper on the table and gave himself a jerk in his chair; and then, taking it up again, made marks in several places. With a significant rubbing up of his hair, he then set to, after asking my pardon for his inattention to myself, and wrote apparently a lengthy article. I was rather curious to know the contents of the paper, but good manners at the time prevented me making any inquiries. Next morning, I was through the printing-office, and happening to see a paper on the case of one of the compositors, I took the liberty of reading it, which was *verbatim et literatim* as follows:

* Were this the only contribution made to the cause, it would be munificent. In truth, however, the £7,000 in question merely represents Mr. Livesey's out of pocket expenses in producing and circulating Temperance literature. But when to this is added the negative loss involved in such a work, especially the loss sustained during the first seven or eight years of the Temperance reform, he stands out as *the most princely supporter the movement has yet had*. It should be remembered that Mr. Livesey was a man of remarkable business abilities and uncommon judgment; and that for seven years during the best part of his manhood he practically abstracted himself from his business to devote himself to the establishment of teetotalism, travelling to all parts of the kingdom at his own charge. It has been estimated that had Mr. Livesey gone in for money-making during these years, he could have realized several thousand pounds yearly. If he had done so his family would have been materially richer to-day, but the world would have been immeasurably poorer! Truly, he *was* the Father and Founder of the movement!

IF RIGHT IN A RELIGIOUS PAPER, WHY NOT IN THE PULPIT?

" I have just received from some working friend *The Watchman*, dated December 28th, 1836, in which I find no fewer than seven advertisements marked with a cross, in order, I suppose, to fix my attention to the contents. This is a religious paper, and of course nothing is said in it, any more than in a chapel, which is not calculated to promote the best interests of religion. The first article I fixed my eyes upon in the editorial column was one recommending prayer meetings throughout the kingdom on the first Monday in the New Year,—' FOR THE OUTPOURING OF THE HOLY SPIRIT.' Now, who would expect in the self-same paper seven laboured, bombastic, barefaced advertisements of all kinds of intoxicating liquor? Advertisements drawn up and well seasoned with cant and puffery. Here is the outpouring of the *evil spirit* with a witness. But surely *The Watchman* must have been from home, perhaps on a Christmas visit, or perhaps asleep, it being dull weather. One thing is certain, he was not on his ' guard' when he admitted these advertisements.

" Supposing on the preceding Sunday the minister of some Wesleyan chapel, having announced a prayer meeting ' for the outpouring of the Holy Spirit,' after a pause had said, ' I have something else to tell you : there are several places in this town which I am requested to point out to you. I would not like certainly to be held accountable for the tendency of this notice ; but as I have received a fee from each place, I beg you will listen. At the first you will get ' choice Highland whiskey,' which, for delicacy of flavour and purity, will be found the finest ever submitted to the connoisseurs of that *delightful* beverage. The second is a wine establishment, which has enjoyed an extensive patronage for nearly thirty years (and of course must have done an immense deal of good !). At this place you may purchase ' Crusted Port,' ' Sherries,' ' Brandies,' ' Jamaica Rum,' ' British Spirits,' ' Scotch and Irish Whiskey,' of superior quality and flavour. At the next place you will get the celebrated ' Patent Brandy,' recommended by the faculty, and declared by chemists to be more pure than the finest samples of French brandy. Four others yet remain to be noticed ; but as I perceive you are impatient to be gone, I will just read to you the number and street of each place (which he did from the paper in his hand), briefly observing that at these vaults you will be supplied on liberal terms for *cash*, with an article of ' purity and excellence,' ' purity and genuineness,' with ' good sound wines,' ' recommended to families for general use,' and with ' Lochnagar whiskey ten per cent. over proof ! ' At the conclusion of this announcement, would the people say Amen ? And I maintain that if the *tendency* of these advertisements be bad, the difference betwixt saying a thing in the pulpit and in a paper cannot make it good. If half the poverty, misery, crime, wretchedness, disease, impiety, and death, which have proceeded from the liquor sold by any one of these establishments, could be collected and placed in front of the *Watchman's* office, he would then see the tendency (and I hope the wickedness) of every step calculated to invite persons to purchase and to drink these body and soul-destroying liquors.' "[*]

TIMELY AND JUDICIOUS ADVICE TO SPEAKERS.

As a public speaker, Mr. Livesey was a model. Clear, distinctive, persuasive, he always had a truth to tell, or a principle to enforce, and he disdained to resort to extraneous aids. Especially he avoided exaggeration, and was never betrayed into uncharitableness. But he felt that some of his disciples occasionally allowed their zeal to get the better of their judgment, and he therefore admonished them.

" It betrays great ignorance of human nature," he remarks, " to expect to *bully* men into an approval of the Temperance cause. Where we gain one by these means, we shall win over five hundred by *sound reasoning, kindness,* and *love.* I do hope the Temperance speakers will take these hints in the spirit in which they are given, and that in future we shall try to avoid those extravagances into which an inconsiderate zeal has too frequently betrayed us." [†]

The evil complained of, however, required further checking ; and, as it has not yet altogether abated, but may still be found in connexion with Temperance and other popular movements, it may be useful to quote Mr. Livesey further :

[*] *Preston Temperance Advocate,* vol. ii. (1835), p. 10.   [†] *Ibid.,* vol. iv. (1837), p. 26.

, "It becomes more and more necessary," he says, "to caution our friends who deliver Temperance addresses at public meetings, to be on their guard in reference to using offensive language. Various complaints have recently come to hand, from different parts of the country, of the *personal attacks* and *violent denunciations* of various speakers at Temperance meetings. No doubt our friends are influenced by their zeal for the cause on these occasions, but discretion is wanted as well as zeal. No good can arise from this kind of advocacy; it can neither enlighten nor convince, and instead of attracting the attention of candid hearers, it is the most certain mode of driving them away. We ourselves never like to be attacked, either by name or character, and if we would treat others as we would like to be treated ourselves, we should certainly forbear to use any violent language, or to drag individuals before the meetings for the purpose of exposure. And in reference to religious professors, and others who appear to be slow to learn, we should not impugn their motives; God alone is their Judge. Our duty is, by patience and perseverance, by kindness and a consistent example, to win them over; these are our only chances of success; and even if we should fail by these means, instead of abusing them, either as individuals or as bodies, we should console ourselves with having done our duty in a Christian spirit. If our public advocates will judge of the merit of the practices here complained of, by the *effects* generally produced, I think they will be led, independently of duty, to see the *impolicy* of dealing in personalities and offensive language." *

And what can be more kind and considerate towards opponents than this?

"We are always in danger of judging too harshly of others. For instance, if the ministers and religious professors do not come forward and help us, is it not better to let them alone and to work on, in our own way, without them, than to be constantly denouncing them for not doing what we wish? Nearly twenty years' experience has settled the matter in my mind upon this point. There may be unworthy motives prevailing, such as the love of the liquor, conformity to the fashions, or the fear of man; but we are not their judges, and, in not a few instances, I know that their doctrinal views are not compatible with teetotalism. Besides, the really devoted give so much time to their own meetings and the affairs of their denominations that we cannot expect them to do much for us." †

Temperance speakers and writers would do well to listen and attend to the ollowing suggestion:

"Do we not in our addresses and publications dwell too little upon the beauties and blessings of teetotalism? Might we not allure men to abstinence, quite as much, if not more, by showing the loveliness of a sober life, the happiness of a teetotal family, as by a representation of the horrors of drunkenness? I sometimes think we dwell too much upon one and too little upon the other." ‡

HOME SPEAKERS AND PROFESSIONAL ADVOCATES.

The reader will have learned from the first chapter the ideas of Mr. Livesey regarding hireling religious teachers. He applied the same principle to the abstinence movement, and always urged the employment of unpaid services.

"Societies," he wrote, "should depend as much as possible on their own resources for carrying on their meetings, without relying upon foreign aid; and several societies within a convenient distance should associate together for mutual assistance, for supplying their respective meetings with speakers. . . . Constant dependence upon foreign aid prevents the home members from exerting themselves and improving their own talents. . . . Every speaker should store his mind with *facts*, which, if well told, are sure to be acceptable—and otherwise try, not merely to occupy the time of a meeting, but to produce a lasting impression. Travelling [professional] advocates, it is to be feared, for a long time will be indispensable, yet we should guard against making a *distinct order* of them. . . .

* *The Preston Temperance Advocate*, vol. iv. (1837), p. 58.
† *Livesey's Progressionist*, 1852, p. 12.   ‡ *Staunch Teetotaler*, 1867, p. 47.

In the Temperance cause it is hoped there never will be such a distinction as 'clergy and laity.' Temperance pauperism, or an unreasonable dependence upon others, should be diligently guarded against; no district will prosper long if influenced by this spirit." *

Fifteen years later, he laments:

"We are getting too much in the way of religious people, depending upon a few set meetings and authorized speakers. Instead of going into the highways and byways, and visiting the worst parts of our towns, each working according to his means and ability, we selfishly sit down with the good we have obtained, leaving the world to perish. My teetotal friends, let us feel and act as if we belonged to the *age of progress.* We need no statistics to tell us of the work we have to do. Intemperance rages like a devouring flame all around. Let every one consider how he can best aid and put forth all his energies to extinguish it. No one should be idle; no one needs be idle. With a heart to feel and a tongue to speak, every teetotaler should be a missionary. Never wait for orders. Delay not for the decision of committees. Begin to WORK, and continue to work from a consciousness of duty and the love of doing good. Never be discouraged because ministers stand aloof, and rich people give you little support: like others, they are, in a great measure, the creatures of circumstances, and if you were in their place, you would probably act the same." †

And after the lapse of several months, he further remarks:

"What I dread is, the Temperance cause dwindling into a mere formal service; the work to be done merely speaking at the 'hall,' and that chiefly by a paid agent. In many places it has come to this. All the efforts are confined to an occasional meeting, and that only when some paid agent comes round." ‡

According to Mr. Livesey's views, if a 'distinct order of advocates' were considered necessary, it should be composed of men who, from a sense of duty to their fellows, are prepared to make sacrifices for the truth. The friends among whom they labour would supply their necessities, but the remuneration ought not to be more than they could realize from their legitimate calling. If a shoemaker took up the work of a Temperance apostle, he should be satisfied with a shoemaker's pay; and if he were what he professed to be, he would be satisfied with it. And the same of a carpenter, or a barber, etc. Mr. Livesey's idea of the kind of work a real Temperance Missionary should be prepared to undertake, may be gathered from an entry—headed 'Advice to Agents'—in one of his private memorandum books; made probably about the time James Teare and Thomas Whittaker went out as travelling advocates:

"1. Direct your inquiries principally to the nature of the drink.
2. Give something tangible at meetings.
3. Make an outline of a week's work.
4. Don't fly from the place.
5. If no preparation has been made, set to work and do it yourself.
6. Go and visit the principal backsliders, or other likely persons."

Had Mr. Livesey's advice upon this important department of effort been followed, the probabilities are that the cause would have been to-day in a far healthier condition than it is. The course which has been followed is mainly responsible for the fact that from first to last the movement has been repeatedly preyed upon by designing persons. The Temperance people have been regarded as 'fair game' by a set of adventurers who were not slow in discovering that a

* *Preston Temperance Advocate,* vol. iv. (1837), p. 51.   † *Livesey's Progressionist,* 1852, p. 2.
‡ *The Teetotal Progressionist,* 1853, p. 222.

given amount of pretension was all that was needed to enable them successfully to prosecute their designs.

BEWARE OF IMPOSTORS.

" In the early stages of teetotalism," says Mr. Livesey, " our cause suffered much from these characters. If a man professed to be a reformed drunkard, and began to speak at the meetings, he was caressed, trusted with money, and often introduced to confidential situations. Not a few abused this confidence. . . . The cause had to bear all the disgrace, and is suffering from it to this present day."[*]

These men were soon at their work ; and Mr. Livesey did not hesitate to expose them. One instance may be cited; it will not occupy much space, and as every species of the genus adopts similar tactics, it may be useful in putting friends on their guard. In the *Preston Advocate* for March, 1837, appears these brief and suggestive words : " Magnus Klien should learn to pay for his postages, *as well as puffs in the papers.*" And in the following issue the reader is informed that : " Impostors are going about, and the societies have been much disgraced by needy adventurers assuming the garb of Temperance, for disreputable purposes."[†] In the May number a more pointed reference is made to Mr. Magnus Klien in these words, which follow a general caution :

" There is a person now constantly *puffing* in the *papers*, a *foreigner*, for whom a subscription has been raised.[‡] He contrives to get letters of introduction from unsuspecting persons. He has been here; and it might be useful to ask him wherever he applies—' Have you any recommendation from Preston?' Nothing but a strong desire to defend the societies against imposition could have produced these remarks." [§]

SOCIETIES AND ORGANIZATIONS NEEDFUL.

While Mr. Livesey was emphatically an independent individual worker for the promotion of Temperance and other reforms; and while he endeavoured to encourage and stimulate independent labourers in their efforts, he believed in organization, favouring, however, like Dr. Lees, ' an organization of spirit' rather than a ' spirit of organization.' In Mr. Livesey's view, the health of a Temperance movement depends upon the vitality of a large number of local self-contained, self-managed, independent, and unpatronized Temperance societies ; which might be affiliated to a district organization or National League for national objects, with great advantage. But the leagues and larger associations should draw their chief support and derive their power from the smaller societies ; instead of the local Temperance societies, as is too often the case, depending on the larger societies for assistance. Under an arrangement of this kind we should have local societies, free from

---

[*] *The Teetotal Progressionist*, 1852, p. 67.

[†] *Preston Temperance Advocate*, vol. iv. (1837), p. 28.

[‡] When will English Temperance people cease to allow themselves to be victimized by the ' pretentious ' foreigner class? They all commence as Mr. Klien did, by ' *puffing* in the papers ' —*i.e.*, either by writing the puffs themselves or *inspiring* them,—or they adopt some other plan of self-laudation. When the British Temperance public exercise discrimination on this subject, equal to that displayed by Mr. E. C. Delavan in 1839, they will not be thus so easily imposed upon. Writing to Dr. Marsh regarding a project for ' missioning ' England by American advocates, he said: " Such a measure [that of sending American speakers to England] is not required, as there are already in this country numbers of lecturers of the most commanding powers, fully acquainted with the subject, and *quite equal* to any we have at home."—(Letter from Glasgow, June 10th, 1839 : *Journal A. T. Union*, 1839, p.126.)

[§] *Preston Temperance Advocate*, vol. iv. (1837), p. 40.

leading strings, composed of members thoroughly devoted to the work, and on them the task of permeating their own neighbourhoods with Temperance teaching would devolve : and the aggregate national Temperance sentiment would be gathered up, expressed, and demonstrated by the central association or associations. Perhaps the most perfect plan of a local Temperance Society ever produced was suggested by Mr. Livesey, and published in his *Moral Reformer* for January, 1833.* And regarding the larger organizations, Mr. Livesey remarks :

"It is the useful and not the ornamental that we should care about. I would rather have one good plain disinterested teetotaler, who gives every week what time he has to spare to the cause, than fifty vice-presidents who do little or nothing, —perhaps not even subscribing more than five shillings a year! Talk about getting every teetotal minister in the vicinity ' to preach a Temperance sermon *once a year!* ' Three times a week would be more likely—once in the church, once in the school-room, and once in ' Paddy's rookery.' One society, after speaking of ' a sermon once a year,' reports that they would have had ' more sermons ' but they were afraid of ' increasing their debt.' Where such notions as these prevail, no wonder that the cause goes down. ' Unions ' may be strength *if the materials be genuine ;* but there may be too much union. Without always depending on the slow arrangements of an executive committee, I like individuals to devise their own methods of acting, and to go ahead on their own account. Where there is too much dependence on the authority of managers and committees (unless they are first-rate men), the work is apt to be retarded. And if a ' Union ' or a ' League ' get so embarrassed as to devote all their energies to keeping up the ' establishment,' instead of working for the world, this is sure to be the case."†

Mr. Livesey particularly cautions Temperance people not to rest satisfied with progress on paper—with the progress of " Annual Reports "—and reminds them that :

"Large funds and fine buildings are no more symptoms of prosperity in the Temperance cause than they are in the religious world, where in fact the very contrary is often the case. Christianity has been working, amidst reported prosperity, for eighteen hundred years, and its outward forms and monuments, its temples and wealth, dazzle in many parts of the earth and astonish the world ; but when we look for its practical power upon the people, alas ! alas ! we are confounded. Let the Temperance Societies be warned by this. While our streets are filled with drunkards, let them consider that nothing comparatively has been done ; and that without honest-hearted labour, indefatigable exertion, in a plain straightforward way, among the masses of the people, we shall be in the same position twenty years after this." ‡

Writing in 1852, Mr. Livesey says :

"It seems to me that the abstinence principle is becoming less and less exclusively attached to the outward form and organization of Temperance societies. It is, happily, diffusing itself among all ranks ; and, like honesty, truthfulness, chastity, and other moral virtues, is receiving attention, less or more from all parties, and is being practised by numbers who are not, and will not be, members of any society. In this we ought to rejoice ; and the happiest day for England will be that on which perfect sobriety has become so general as to render distinct organizations no longer necessary.

"But we must have *societies*, or the Temperance reformation would soon be extinct ; and a *pledge* of personal abstinence must be an indispensable condition of membership. Other conditions, I think, should be added, such as contributing to the funds, attending meetings, and assisting in the work. If these were insisted upon, our members might not be numerous, but they would be consistent and

---

* In the plan referred to provision is made for teaching, visitation, and organization ; nor are the social needs and political requirements of the movement overlooked.

† *The Staunch Teetotaler*, 1867, p. 165.　　　‡ *Livesey's Progressionist*, 1852, p. 12.

select ; they would generally be known, and could be relied upon for forwarding the cause ; and I certainly would prefer a society of fifty *such persons* to a thousand names in a book without any rational or practical bond of union. Like other societies, we should then have our *members' meetings*, and at these meetings only should new members be admitted." *

SECTARIAN THEOLOGY AND TEMPERANCE MEETINGS.

With Mr. Livesey, Temperance work was in its very nature religious work. Temperance could only be taken up and prosecuted in his way, as a matter of religious duty. Innumerable quotations proving this could be given from his writings ; but the *fac-simile* reproduction from the *Preston Advocate* here introduced.

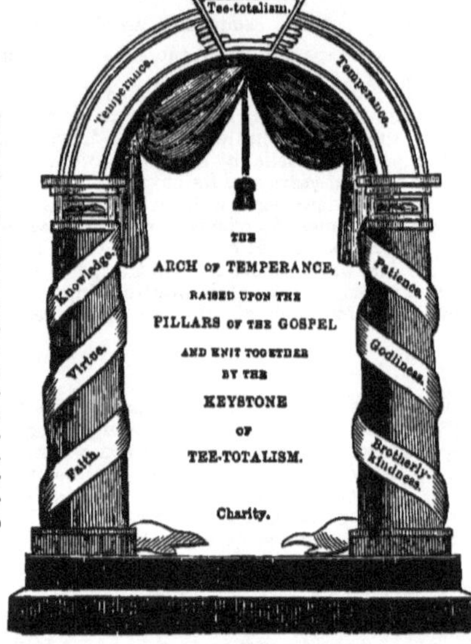

of a pictorial allegorical representation of Teetotalism as the keystone of the arch of Temperance, which is supported by the pillars of religion, will perhaps suffice. The cut, with the heading of the *Advocate*, will also give the reader an

* *Livesey's Progressionist*, 1852, pp. 43–4.

idea of the 'get up' and appearance of that paper, which, it should be remembered, was the same size as the *Struggle*.

Mr. Livesey, however, strongly opposed, in the interests of both Temperance and religion, the introduction of religious teaching into Temperance meetings.* He is very explicit on this point, and with a view of promoting genuine union, he says :

"'Behold how good and pleasant a thing it is for brethren to dwell together in unity!' This is best effected among Temperance people, by cultivating that *kindness* and charity which Christianity inculcates; and avoiding every religious peculiarity which is likely to give offence to others. If men of all creeds are invited to join, we should avoid doing injury to the feelings of any, by putting forward notions in which it is well known they cannot agree. In all mixed societies, introducing *prayer* into the meeting is sure to give offence; and *singing* should always be confined to Temperance songs." †

Regarding singing at ordinary Temperance meetings, Mr. Livesey advises :

"Temperance melodies and good moral songs, especially if sung as solos, would be attractive to many; and it is after the feelings have been thus charmed, that the understanding is most ready to listen to argument, and the conscience to command attention to its promptings. As much as possible this singing should be considered a medium for *instruction*, excitement, and amusement, and not as *worship*, for I consider this too sacred to introduce into an ordinary Temperance meeting; and hence, the melodies selected should not be those which appeal to the Almighty, and express feelings, wishes, and resolves which are really not expected to be felt by a mixed company on such occasions."‡

The case against obtruding religious peculiarities into Temperance meetings is unanswerably put as follows :

"The principle upon which persons have hitherto entered Temperance Societies is this,—that *all sects and parties are equal*, and that *no religious peculiarities* should be introduced into the tracts or *the meetings*. Our Society in Preston, and all others, so far as I am acquainted with them, have a rule expressly to this effect.

Supposing a thousand persons join together upon this distinct understanding, what person, or what number of persons, has any right to set that rule at defiance by introducing any peculiarity, either in the shape of prayer, singing, or in his addresses? If one person has a right to introduce *his* form, another has the same *right*; and it is not difficult to perceive the contention and confusion that would necessarily ensue.§ A member of the Society of Friends has as much right to demand *silence* as the Primitive Methodist has to call for a ranting hymn; the Churchman for one of his *forms* of prayer, or the Catholic for his *mass*, as the Independent an extempore *prayer*; the Armenian for his *universal grace*, as the Calvinist for his more *restricted* views; and the Unitarian for *his notions* of Christianity, as well as those who claim to be *orthodox*. Indeed, Temperance would be in great danger of becoming a secondary matter,—every partisan wishing to press

* But Mr. Livesey viewed with favour the establishment of Denominational Temperance Societies, or societies in connexion with places of worship. He held, indeed, that every Christian Church should itself be a Temperance society.

† *The Preston Temperance Advocate*, vol. iii. (1836), p. 50.

‡ *The Teetotal Progressionist*, 1852, p. 49.

§ M. Houzeau de Lehaie, president of the International Temperance Congress at Antwerp, September, 1885, in concluding his able address re-echoed Mr. Livesey's idea that Temperance teaching should not be mixed up with theology. He said: "It is not too much to gather in one band the forces of all those who are interested in the well-being and the progress of humanity. Let us work, then, altogether, whatever may be our creed—Christian, Israelite, or Materialist. We are united, in one same thought, to free man from alcoholic slavery, which weighs so heavily upon him, and we have in common to sustain us, an ardent love of humanity" (*Church of England Temperance Chronicle*, Sept. 19th, 1885, p. 448).

forward his own peculiarities, or to counteract the attempts of others in doing so."*

OPEN-AIR TEMPERANCE MEETINGS

Were aided and encouraged by Mr. Livesey, who was himself an effective out-of-doors speaker. In his *Advocate* for May, 1837, he thus refers to May-day :

> "Let every Society start this day with out-door meetings, and be determined to carry them on regularly throughout the summer. The least society in the country should hold one meeting weekly ; in towns of the size of Preston there ought, at least, to be a meeting *every night ;* and in large towns the number of meetings should be in proportion. To ensure the continuance of these meetings, in the first place, make out a list of every teetotaler who is able and willing to assist in carrying them on. Next, draw out a plan of time, place, and hour of commencing ; to every meeting attach a name, but not without the consent of the individual, and let that person be considered responsible for providing speakers, and carrying on the meeting. These plans should be hung up in the Temperance houses, and distributed about. A simultaneous movement like this is calculated to produce an extraordinary revival." †

But a meeting for an hour or two, when a longer one could be conveniently held, was not enough to satisfy Mr. Livesey :

> "A perpetual Temperance meeting," he says, "I think might be attempted in summer, in many towns, with great advantage. On public occasions, in fair weather, when a great number of speakers are at hand, I would fix upon some very central situation, and, beginning in the morning, would carry it on till a late hour in the evening. A rattle should be out during the whole day, apprising the people, so that by this means the whole town might know of the meeting, and all parties might attend at the most convenient time. Singing and music, if possible, should be interspersed with the speeches, which would very much relieve and enliven the whole. I offer this merely as a suggestion,‡ which may perhaps be matured by the next summer. §

Upon the more extensive introduction of singing into meetings he elsewhere remarks :

> "Make your meetings more attractive by introducing singing, especially solo singing. You cannot keep up the interest by abstract reasoning, nor even by facts and anecdotes, so well as by adding singing. It is pleasing and acceptable to nearly all, and after the labours of the day, working men require a little of something light and amusing, and the youthful teetotalers should be encouraged to learn to sing." ‖

---

* *The Preston Temperance Advocate*, vol. iii. (1836), p. 57.   † *Ibid.*, vol. iv. (1837), p. 35.

‡ In his "Reminiscences," Mr. Livesey gives practical illustrations of this idea. He says : "I remember being present at a meeting of Temperance delegates at Edinburgh [this would be in 1839], many of them accustomed to platform work. After the business was over, I suggested that the next day we should hold what I called a *Perpetual Meeting.* Fixing upon a piece of ground adjoining High Street, we commenced at nine o'clock in the morning, and continued the meeting till about the same hour in the evening. Having so many speakers, we arranged by relays to keep the meeting on without a break for about twelve hours. I delivered my Malt Liquor Lecture last, in the dusk of the evening. At Leeds, I remember, myself and friends on one occasion occupied a whole Sunday forenoon in holding what I may call a *Movable Meeting.* We started in one of the slums by singing a few verses ; we then borrowed a chair ; the people came out of their houses, and we occupied about half an hour with short speeches (and speeches from reformed drunkards are often on such occasions the most impressive) to those who crowded around us. We moved to a few streets further, and continued this work till dinner time. Most of our out-door meetings formerly were never advertised. Our plan used to be this—to send a man round all the streets in the locality with a watchman's rattle for an hour or so before the time. The children were specially attracted, and would follow the man in his round, carrying home the announcement. By these inexpensive means meetings get well-known and well-attended. Many such gatherings has our old friend Dicky Turner (author of the word teetotal) announced with his rattle." (p. 39.)

§ *Livesey's Moral Reformer*, 1838-9, p. 200.   ‖ *The Teetotal Progressionist*, 1852, p. 67.

FREE AND EASY CONCERTS.

Mr. Livesey never lost sight of the vital necessity of instituting counteractives to the customs and institutions, which, by virtue of ' the social principle,' feed and foster drinking habits and practices. Indeed, he was always great with counteractives. The Preston Races evil, he at first dealt with by setting up something else attractive for the young people, and using his best endeavours to induce them to choose the safer of the two courses. He found that a Saturday evening concert was highly useful in keeping teetotalers away from entertainments usually more or less associated with drink, and he warmly urged the adoption of the plan generally. Mr. Livesey's idea of a Saturday evening social meeting is well expressed in the following lines of the late Mr. John Guest, of Rotherham :

> From drink and discord blithely free,
> With wife and bairns we share our glee;
> Together gaily laugh, yet learn
> Life's true, grave interests to discern.
>
> Free from the drink that drains the purse;
> Free from the coarse blasphemer's curse;
> Free from the smutty song and tale;
> Free from the broil that brings the jail.*

Mr. Livesey thus urged the establishment of Saturday concerts :

"I would earnestly urge upon the teetotalers in every town to establish social Saturday night meetings. They are sure to answer. After working hard through the week, many teototalers want a little amusement; and if no suitable provision be made, not a few of them are weak enough to go with their comrades to the public-house. These meetings will be highly prized by all such. It is here that the talents of many of our members are first discovered. Our cottage meetings are chiefly addressed by persons brought out at these social gatherings; and the spirit of zeal and co-operation as to all our movements is kept alive by this ' social intercourse.' " †

Two or three months later Mr. Livesey reported that the experiment had succeeded far beyond his expectations:

" So successful," he says, " has been our experiment of a Saturday night singing meeting, that our Temperance Hall, which has served our ordinary meetings for twenty years, threatens to be too small to accommodate the numbers who attend. At our first meeting we had thirty present; we have increased every week, till we have now upwards of 400. I look upon this as a valuable auxiliary to our cause. It brings teetotalers together in good spirits; it affords a retreat to those who are in danger of public-house temptations ; and it elevates the feelings of our members, and stimulates their zeal for additional efforts." ‡

The mode of procedure described by Mr. Livesey was simple enough :

" Our charge of admission is only one penny, and the people often get a Temperance paper in at that price ; and this is about the maximum charge that will secure a large attendance of the proper sort of people. . . . Instead of having any deficiency of singers, we have had rather more than could be accommodated. First one starts up, and then another ; some singing, some giving recitations ; many of them persons snatched from the public-house; and we occasionally admit a single short speech from some new convert. . . . We spend the proceeds of

* "Life and Labours of John Guest," p. 150.

† Mr. George Ling, at the Great Central Hall, London, and the Rev. G. M. Murphy, at the Lambeth Baths, have for years practically tested the utility of these evenings for the people, with results in every way satisfactory. The Help-Myself societies, promoted by Mr. William Palmer, of Reading, have also adopted a similar course, with corresponding success.

‡ *The Teetotal Progressionist*, 1852, p. 50.

our meetings upon tracts, and these are delivered to our visitors and speakers at the close of the meeting. We are now distributing at the rate of 16,000 per week of our small handbills, or in that proportion where larger ones are given away." [*]

TEETOTAL AMUSEMENTS.

What the friends of Temperance have comparatively but recently turned their attention to, in such experiments as the Victoria Music Hall for instance, Mr. Livesey nearly fifty years ago advocated as an essential requisite to success. He says :

"In the Temperance cause we have hitherto been working to a great extent on a negative principle, striving to make people sober, and to secure to them their reason ; but it has occurred to many of our friends, from the defection which frequently takes place among reformed drunkards, that other efforts ought to be made of a more positive character ; that in fact, having deprived the inebriate of the pleasures of the bottle and the public-house, we ought to substitute other pleasures suited to the changed habits of the individual. Man is a social being, and nobody participates more, though in a very boisterous manner, in the feelings of sociality than they who frequent the tavern. When such become teetotalers, a substitute is wanted to fill up the vacant desire, and to occupy the leisure time. Fortunately some, having families, and others forming religious connexions, need no further substitutes ; but when neither of these, nor anything similar, offer themselves as a stay to their wandering minds, which is the case with many teetotalers who, notwithstanding, receive much temporary benefit from the system, what is the general result ? The strength of their principles sustains them for a time, but the love of company leads them to public-houses, where, for a while, they drink peppermint or gingerbeer, till, led on either by the tempting appearance of the liquor, or bantered by their associates, they resume the use of drinks which intoxicate, and the latter end with these is worse than the beginning." [†]

TEMPERANCE HOUSES AND HOTELS.

From the outset of the Temperance movement, Mr. Livesey recognised how important and necessary it was to "*outbid* the house of gin ; " [‡] and in the *Moral Reformer* for December, 1832, he makes the following announcement :

"A Temperance House, I understand, will be shortly opened in one of our principal streets, and, I hope, many others in every part of the town. Oh ! if we could substitute *coffee* for *jerry* [ale], *soup* for *gin*, reading for cards, and rational conversation for brawling and balderdash, the intervals of leisure would cease to be, as they are at present, a great curse to our working men. I am just upon the point of starting a ' Working Man's Reading Room,' which will be furnished with forty fresh newspapers and other periodicals weekly, at 1*s*. 7½*d*. per quarter, equal to 1½*d*. per week. With this, the Temperance Houses, and the Institution for the Diffusion of Knowledge, there can be no excuse for any one going to spend his time in a public-house, where, being almost compelled to drink intoxicating liquors, so many have been ruined." [§]

The establishment of a house of resort, where non-intoxicating drinks were provided, would of course be a great boon to the members of the Temperance society ; but that alone was hardly sufficient for Mr. Livesey, who, it will be seen, personally undertook at the same time to provide a reading-room, liberally furnished with newspapers and periodicals. These adjuncts to, or rather integral parts of, Temperance effort, have scarcely received the attention they deserve. It is, comparatively speaking, but recently that the promoters of Temperance have

[*] *The Teetotal Progressionist*, 1852, p. 79.
[†] *The Preston Temperance Advocate*, vol. iv. (1837), p. 42.   [‡] Ebenezer Elliott.
[§] *Moral Reformer*, vol. ii. (1832), p. 375.

realized what Mr. Livesey saw from the beginning in this respect.   And all efforts hitherto made have fallen sadly short of the obvious requirements.   The Coffee-house was superseded by the British Workman public-house; then the latter made way for the more imposing Coffee Palace, which in its turn has (in London, at least) been supplanted by the *Reformed* Coffee Palace; but the great weakness in all these attempts has lain in the inferior quality of the provisions supplied, in the want of cleanliness and neatness in the establishments, and in the uncouth and slovenly character of the employés.*   Mr. Livesey has repeatedly pointed out the weaknesses to be guarded against in efforts of this kind.   For instance, in 1835 he gave the following ' word to keepers of Temperance hotels':

" Keep everything clean, and give an air of *neatness* and *comfort* to every part of your establishment.   Let every article you sell, not forgetting *coffee*, be of the *best quality.*   Serve every customer with what he may want in the least possible time; for this purpose always have water ready boiling.   Make a distinction in your rooms, beds, etc., and consequently in the prices of your articles, to suit the different classes of your customers.   If your own family be small, and you have plenty of beds, and other accommodations, it is an advantage to keep two or three boarders; inasmuch as by enabling you to have a fresh joint every day to dinner, travellers and callers may be better accommodated.   For a time you must reconcile yourselves to many foul aspersions, both from enemies and inconsiderate friends. Many are so unreasonable as to think that if they buy three-pennyworth of anything, they should have it as cheap as if they got it out of a person's basket in the street.   They forget the expenses of rent, lighting, fire, servant's wages, interest of money, and wear and tear; and they also forget that these houses have not, like public-houses, the profits of intoxicating liquors to make up what may be deficient on the articles of food.   Allow me also to advise you, in order to assist in spreading the principles of Temperance, to procure a board, and post all the Temperance bills on it you can get, and place it at the door every fine day." †

And thirty-two years later he pointed out defects in the management of refreshment houses, glaring enough to ruin such places, but which are still too prevalent. He says:

" I wish ' Refreshment Houses' were better managed.   I mean those where no drink is sold.   I went into one the other day about noon.   I asked for a cup of coffee and a chop, but there was no fire, the room was in bad order, the table-cover dirty, and on the side table there were newspapers torn and soiled, the newest a fortnight old, and some of them months past date.   This is not the way to get custom, nor to obtain for our refreshment houses anything like a good reputation." ‡

Mr. Livesey's hints and suggestions might be profitably studied by many Temperance Hotel keepers of to-day, and also by the directors, proprietors, and managers of not a few of our Coffee Palaces.

CAUTIONS TO TEETOTALERS.

There could be no warmer friend of Youths' Societies and the juvenile Temperance movement generally than Mr. Livesey.   He efficiently aided the earliest attempts made in Preston to interest and instruct the young in true

---

* The management of these establishments in Liverpool and the north of England generally is much better than in London and the south.   Lockhart's Cocoa Houses are by far the best institutions of the kind; they are evidently under careful supervision, and free from the above mentioned defects; while in many places the so-called Coffee Palaces—owned by Limited Companies—are striking examples of the " cheap and nasty."

† *The Preston Temperance Advocate*, vol. ii. (1835), p. 41.

‡ *The Staunch Teetotaler* (1867), p. 14.

sobriety, and in his later years had always a good word for the Band of Hope movement. But surveying the whole field of Temperance, he was exceedingly jealous of any one department being worked unduly, and at the expense of the general cause. And this was specially the case when doubts were expressed regarding the possible reclamation of the victims of drink, as may be seen from the following:

"Of late I have heard it expressed by many leading teetotalers that there is little chance with the present generation of adults, and that our only hope is from the young. Now, I should be sorry to detract from the importance of imbuing the rising generation with the principle of abstinence, and uniting them in Bands of Hope for this purpose; but to rely upon these either as a substitute for labour among the adults, or as being of greater importance, I think is a decided mistake. I am not willing to abandon the grown-up drinker, and if the plans hitherto tried have not proved effectual, we must try to discover others that may be so. I have heard people talk of all the old drunkards dying off. To me it is a horrible idea, and altogether discordant with the views I hold of the arrangements of the Deity,— that there is no acquired evil without a remedy.* . . While I would say, establish Youths' Temperance Societies by all means, do not on their account relax one iota as to your exertions with the adults. To retreat from the great world of grown drinkers in order to teach boys and girls merely, is, to my mind, an indication of weakness, and rather a symptom of despair. †

HOW TO INTEREST THE VICTIMS OF DRINK.

Various devices and suggestions were made by Mr. Livesey from time to time to interest the victims of drink, some of which were exceedingly practical. He *well* knew the power of sympathy, and as one means of bringing it to bear upon those who had either fallen through drink, or were in danger of falling, proposes:

"I think if, in every town, we had one or two influential friends to whom penitents could be referred to as 'confessors,' this might do much good. Supposing a teetotaler, who is well known and respected, had cards printed with some such notice as the following: 'Mr. Little would be glad to see you at his room, 28, Church Street, on Friday, at any time from three to four, or from seven to eight o'clock, as he wishes to speak to you.' These cards could be entrusted to the members, to place in the hands of persons whom they meet in liquor, or whom they know to be given to drinking. I doubt not but many would be induced to embrace the opportunity of unbosoming their feelings and obtaining encouragement to overcome their temptations. Possibly a plan like this might lead to the formation of regular classes, in which parties could be admonished and strengthened together under the guidance of some friend." ‡

But Mr. Livesey never lost sight of his own individual responsibility towards the drunkard. Notwithstanding his splendid services to the Temperance movement, his incessant circulation of light on the subject, and his unremitting visitations, he continually reproached himself that he had not done more. Upon this point he remarks:

"I scarcely ever hear of the death of a hard drinker but I feel some remorse

* Dr. Lees, in one of his latest and acutest works—"Lord Bramwell as 'Drinker' and 'Thinker'"—expresses the same idea: "We would exhort the reader," he says, "not to fail into that deplorable condition of feeling which looks upon the victim of drink as worthless and hopeless! Such a Pagan indifference is unworthy of the age, and is founded moreover upon the altogether false conception that it is chiefly the worse and weaker men and women who become inebriates. The contrary is the fact. Men of genius and power, women of refinement and culture, once given to narcotics, are more susceptible to their fascination and influence than persons of ordinary mind and temperament. They *can* be reclaimed, however; and what is more important, they can be *prevented* from treading on the fatal decline."—(" Selected Works," 1885, vol. iv. p. 73.)

† *Livesey's Progressionist*, 1852, p. 12.   ‡ *The Staunch Teetotaler*, 1867, p. 165.

that I did not take more pains, if possible, to have stopped him in his mad career. There is one now, just dead; he was at the tavern on the Friday, drinking the fatal liquor; on the Monday morning he was a corpse, and the last words that a friend heard him say were, that if he did recover he would become an abstainer. I often spoke to him, and so did my wife, but we did nothing more. Now I think, if, in addition, we had invited him to our house to take a cup of tea, or shown some more special concern for his welfare, this sudden and fatal end might have been prevented. Society seems to have little feeling but that of contempt for the poor inebriate, although it is *their* habits and *their* fashions that have made him such. I know how difficult it is to cure a drunkard, and that by far the most important part of our work is to *prevent* the young from becoming such; but still, it is not impossible. They require a great deal of nursing; and I think a teetotaler's parlour might be put to a far worse purpose than entertaining a 'Mary Magdalen' or a dissipated 'Colin.'" *

HOW TO RECLAIM BACKSLIDERS. ,

One of the leading characteristics of Mr. Livesey was his unbounded faith in the possible reclamation of even the most degraded victim of drink and vicious habits. He rarely despaired of cases considered by others as hopeless. But then his plans were so different from those of other persons that it is no wonder that he often succeeded where they failed.

"Deal gently with those who break their pledge and go astray," he advises; "draw them back by love and persuasion. A kiss is worth a thousand kicks. A kind word is more valuable to the lost than a mine of gold. Think of this, and be on your guard, ye who would chase to the grave an erring brother." †

The repeated relapses of his *protegés* into drink and degradation did not dishearten Mr. Livesey, and 'again and again' he repeated his efforts to rescue them. Sometimes, when he felt that the physical condition of a man who had relapsed into drunkenness had operated as a predisposing cause to the evil, he would attempt to improve the victim's general health; and in such cases Mr. Livesey's knowledge of hydropathy often enabled him to render essential service to a despairing fellow-creature. Accordingly, he might be seen, with a bath and other necessary appliances, wending his way to the forlorn habitation of a poor fellow prostrated by a drunken debauch. The good Samaritan would carefully attend to him, administering the bath; alleviating in every possible way his distresses and improving his surroundings. In the subject of all this care and solicitude most people could only see a disreputable vagabond, but Mr. Livesey recognised a brother. Time after time would he rescue a man from the mire of intemperance, and place him in a condition to do better: and if, after repeated relapses, Mr. Livesey's son ventured to suggest that the backslider was abusing good nature, the father would reply, "Ay, William, but the Master said we were to forgive our brother not only seven times, but seventy times seven; *and it is far short of that number yet.*"

Amongst the various physical causes predisposing to drinking, Mr. Livesey ranked improper food and eating to excess, and hence his interest in

THE GREAT QUESTION OF FOOD REFORM.

The food reformers and vegetarians have much to thank Mr. Livesey for. By many persons, the association of dietetic reform with Temperance is considered a new phase of the question; but, as a matter of fact, the Preston reformers were

---

* *The Staunch Teetotaler*, 1867, p. 164.　　　† *Livesey's Progressionist*, 1852, p. 40.

pioneer investigators of the food question. An article by Mr. Livesey, entitled
'Moderation in Food,' in the *Moral Reformer* for March 10th, 1838, discusses the
subject in that kindly and suggestive manner which so distinguishes him, and which
may be imitated with advantage by some present-day advocates of vegetarianism.

"The Temperance Societies," says Mr. Livesey, "have thrown out a new light
in reference to what is most proper to drink. The same spirit of inquiry will, doubtless, elicit the best information as to our food. . . . As an experiment, I have
not eaten fish, flesh, or fowl for about six months. Mr. Bradley, secretary of the
temperance society, and others, act on the same rule; and I must say, for myself,
that I am very agreeably surprised with the result. I believe a fair trial would convince most of the *carving* gentry that sound health, and a regular flow of spirits,
are not to be obtained by indulging in the varieties of the table." [*]

In the same article, Mr. Livesey reproduces a letter which had been addressed
to a friend of his own by Sir Richard Phillips, of Chelsea. And that worthy
baronet states that he had lived exclusively upon vegetable food since 1780, and
that up to the time of writing the letter in question (October 25th, 1837) he had
enjoyed "uninterrupted good health." The spirit of Mr. Livesey's article—would
that it more generally animated temperance, dietetic, and other teachings—may be
gathered from the following:

"This article is written not to dictate to, nor censure those who follow the
usual mode of living, but rather to state the views which others have adopted, and
to submit the subject as one of interesting investigation. Let man become less
animal in his indulgences; let him cease to pursue his epicurean [in the generally
understood sense] pleasures, and he will be led most likely, by an intellectual advancement, to seek those refined and noble pleasures which consist in denying
ourselves and doing the will of God." [†]

THE SYSTEMATIC CIRCULATION OF TRACTS AND LITERATURE

was always warmly advocated by Mr. Livesey, who never grew tired himself of this
unobtrusive but effective method of spreading the truth. In an early number of
his *Staunch Teetotaler* he thus advises the reader: "When you have read this
number, hand it to some of your neighbours; *keep it going* while it sticks together."
But the circulation of literature was regarded by Mr. Livesey as the duty not
only of individuals but of societies.

"I think no society," he says, "should feel content unless it occasionally
speaks to *every house* either by the agency of cottage meetings or the distribution of
tracts, or both. And it has always appeared to me that expenses incurred upon far
inferior objects might be saved sufficient to cover the cost of a house-to-house distribution. For instance, I see in one report, 'A new silk banner, £5,' while the
cost of 'Tracts and other publications' for a whole year was only £4 4s. 7d." [‡]

It is to be feared, however, that the case is far worse than the above represents it, and that but too many reports would show *pounds* expended in banners,
flags, and the other paraphernalia of 'demonstrating,' for *shillings* laid out in
literature and similar educational agencies. We want less of the former and more
of the latter; and when this change is made, *real* progress may be expected.

* *Livesey's Moral Reformer*, 1838-9, p. 73.　　　　　† *Ibid.*, p. 74.
‡ *The Staunch Teetotaler*, 1867, p. 24.

VISITATION AN ESSENTIAL PART OF TEMPERANCE WORK.

Chapter xvi. of the "Autobiography" Mr. Livesey devotes to visitation—a distinctive feature in the work of the Preston Society in its best days—and a form of Temperance effort in which his faith continued strong to the last. In his advice to the managers of Temperance societies (1834), referring to the experience of the Preston Society, he says :

" Among the means adopted, *personal visitation* has been distinguished by the best results. Your committees should meet weekly, and receive reports of all delinquents; that is, of persons who have broken their pledges; and appoint some of the members to visit and admonish them. Where this is neglected, societies cannot flourish. But besides this, every reformed drunkard, as well as every friend of Temperance, should visit the victims of intemperance in his neighbourhood, and endeavour, by persuasion, and bringing them to the meetings, to induce them to become sober, and join the Society. There are hundreds of drunkards, who are lamenting their fate, and who are glad of the assistance and advice of a friend, to lift them out of the mire. The doctrine that old drunkards cannot be reformed is false, and has been proved to be so in hundreds of instances. To act thus is the real spirit of Christianity ; it is going to the people, and seeking that which is lost." *

Mr. Livesey had a happy knack or method of securing the attention and interest of men who were under the influence of drink in the streets. The following extract from an article on visitation, will be read with interest. It well illustrates his methods, which were in striking contrast to those of certain kid-gloved reformers. He has been passing through the streets, calling in here and speaking to a man there, and he relates :

" Proceeding a little farther into another street, I met a man very drunk, carrying a jug of ale (I can never get past these men—they know me so well), and, as usual, he made a stand, exclaiming ' Ah, it is old Mr. Livesey,' and then, as drunkards often do, he began with all kinds of blessings and good wishes upon me and my family, telling of sundry adventures he once had with one of my sons. ' You have been a good friend to me,' he repeated. ' Don't you remember once meeting me in Lord Street, and taking me into the Working Men's Club, and treating me to a cup of coffee? and you then gave me good advice ; but I have not kept it.' I then called to mind once picking him off the pavement, where he had fallen in a scuffle with another drunken man. He belongs to a respectable family, but for some time he has been totally given up to drinking. It would take pages to rehearse all that he said, and all the exclamations he made ; among the rest he referred to the case of one of his companions, who finished his career as a drunkard not long ago, observing, ' I kept him for fourteen months.' After talking some time, I attempted to get away, but he insisted upon my going with him to the house where a number of men were waiting for the beer. There I found them all more or less in liquor. They were startled at my entrance, but were remarkably civil, and insisted on my taking the arm-chair and talking to them. This I did willingly, but it was impossible to keep my leading friend quiet ; he would be on his feet expatiating on all sorts of topics. It was Friday, and in reply to what I said as to it being a sorry sight to see a number of clever men drinking and losing their time, they all condemned their own conduct, and agreed that what I said was true. The old man of the house at one time had kept the Dog Inn, but he acknowledged it was a bad business. Two of the party said they had been teetotalers, one seven and the other nine months. After spending nearly half an hour with them, and giving each of them a teetotal paper, I left ; but my beer friend was determined to go with me, and, seizing my arm, stuck to it and said, ' Now you shall go home with me,' and after traversing several streets, keeping him up as well as I could, the passers-by laughing at us, we entered a plain neat cottage, his mother being the only one at home. I need not say how distressed she was, and soon began to relate the long

* *The Preston Temperance Advocate*, vol. i. (1834), p. 17.

tale of sorrow which filled her heart as to the conduct of her unhappy, her only son. She felt, I could see, as only mothers can in such a case. The poor fellow seemed unable to contain himself, he was so delighted that I had, as he termed it, ' condescended to come with him,' and to his mother he exclaimed, ' You ought to be proud of such a guest ! ' After trying to console her with a hope of his reformation, I managed to get away. I sent a pledge paper to her in the evening and marked it ' for her son.' This is one of those cases that are seldom cured except by much nursing, and by surrounding them with the best temperance influence. I have called since ; he has kept off drink about seven weeks, but has not yet signed the pledge. . . .

" In Church Street were standing six young men, all of whom had evidently been drinking. They were hard up, and as I passed, one said : ' I wish I had a sup of ale.' I turned back, and presenting them each two papers, one containing the teetotal pledge for 1867, I said : ' These are what you want.' One begged I would give them 2*d.*, and another said it was for something to eat. ' Young men,' said I, ' what a pity it is to see you in this plight ; it is Wednesday, and you have been idling all the week. You could earn your 30/- a week ('Aye, 33/-: we are all mechanics'), and might be well off. Instead of this you are robbing the tailor, and (pointing to their ragged clothing) bringing yourselves to ruin. Why don't you go and ask the publicans to help you, with whom you have spent all your money ? ' ' They would not give us a bite, but put us out.' ' Well, I'll do better for you than you request,' and stepping into a shop, I wrote as follows :—' To the Steward of the Working Men's Club. Give each of these men a bowl of soup and bread, or a cup of coffee and bread, and I will pay for it. The publicans have got all their money, and will do nothing for them.—J. L.' I gave them the paper ; they were delighted, looked one at another, shook me by the hand, and said, ' You *are* a teetotaler.' If only one out of the six should be benefited, I shall be well rewarded. We cannot do too much of this kind of work. It has been awfully neglected by our members. It was this that gave the Preston Society so much success during the first seven years. Temperance men seek now-a-days to do their work by proxy : they give a subscription, take their ease, and foolishly expect that a hired missionary can do all that is required." *

MR. LIVESEY ON PROHIBITION AND THE ALLIANCE AGITATION.

Mr. P. T. Winskill rightly says that Mr. Livesey has been misrepresented " as being altogether opposed to legislation in favour of Temperance principles," and he quotes from a private letter (dated July 3rd, 1880), in which Mr. Livesey says :

" While we have ten drinkers to one abstainer, we cannot expect *prohibition* to be extensively adopted. Our people should work as they never worked, and instead of ' compensation,' if the drinkers can be induced to *cease buying*, the houses will shut up of themselves without compensation. This is the policy we should always have pursued. Parliament will be right, when the makers of Parliament are right themselves." †

The Preston men uniformly denounced the liquor traffic, contending that an enlightened State would never tolerate it ; and Mr. Livesey was no exception to the rule. Indeed, he was one of the earliest among them to take that ground. In his *Malt Liquor Lecture,* he says :

" If a hundredth part of the evil were produced from a druggist's or any other shop which springs from a public-house, you would be called upon to suppress it at once ; and the principal reason why public-houses are not thus odious is, the *legal* character they sustain in the eyes of the public, in consequence of their *license.* We might as well expect a healthy town if every twentieth dwelling were made the storehouse of the seeds of contagious disease,—clean streets, if, at the interval of every hundred yards, there was a mud pool constantly casting up mire and dirt,—as to expect general sobriety while about every twentieth house is meta· morphosed into a *drunkery !* " ‡

---

* *The Staunch Teetotaler* (1867), pp. 27, 28, and 29.   † Winskill's " History," p. 311.
‡ *The Malt Lecture,* 1st edition (1836), p. 34.

There can be no doubt about this teaching, nor about his subsequent utterances upon the subject. But these and similar sentiments were the logical outcome of the Preston platform, which declared the entire drinking system to be a mistake, nay, more than a mistake—a gigantic wrong. Writing in the *Staunch Teetotaler*, in 1867, Mr. Livesey thus refers to the commencement of the Prohibition movement in this country:

"When the reports, some fifteen years ago, reached us across the Atlantic, of the wonderful effects of the Maine Law, we were in ecstasies. Here was a ' short cut,' we thought, to the finish of our work ; we had only to pass the law, and all was done.* We believed the law would be passed, and soon. The result has shown how much we were mistaken." †

When, in 1853, the United Kingdom Alliance for the Total and Immediate Suppression of the Liquor Traffic, was founded, Mr. Livesey joined the movement ; but on reflection, and after several years' experience of the Alliance agitation, he came to the conclusion that it was futile to expect a people who believed in the virtues of the drink to hold the views of the Alliance regarding the traffic ; and, consequently, that the shortest and only safe way to reach Prohibition would be by permeating society with teetotal teaching. For some time he hoped that other friends associated with the Alliance would be driven by events to the same conclusion, and remained silent. But, as Browning says—

> In every man's career are certain points
> Whereon he dares not be indifferent ;

and in a speech delivered at the Anniversary of the Scottish Temperance League, in May, 1862, Mr. Livesey broke silence. Feeling that efforts were being made in the wrong direction, and that the Temperance reformers who were working to obtain a Permissive Bill were on the wrong track, he believed it to be his duty to sound a note of warning. This was the more needful since he had rendered considerable aid to the Alliance. "I assisted in their first publication," he said, "and rendered them a good deal of help in the earlier stages of their movement." ‡ He avowed

---

* Notwithstanding the enactment of Prohibitory and Local Option laws in many States of the Union, America consumes more alcohol per head than Great Britain. Dr. Dorchester, in his ", Liquor Problem," quotes, without questioning their accuracy, statistics presented to the Sanitary Congress in Geneva, in 1882, according to which the consumption of alcohol per head in the United States was 7¼ *litres*, while in England it was but 6 (p. 573). In truth the ' liquor problem' in America will never be satisfactorily solved until more *teaching* upon the *drink* is imported into the controversy. Even where prohibition has been successfully applied, but where moral suasion efforts have slackened, a retrograde step to license has been taken. Dr. Dorchester thus accounts for this check : "A new generation, who reached the functions of citizenship at the time when the Prohibitory laws had fallen into neglect and reproach, and knew them only as weak and comparatively inoperative; . . . the younger class of voters had not passed through what their fathers had" (p. 407). Regarding the prohibitory movement in Massachusetts, the same writer, after stating that the law was restored in that State in 1869, explains : "But the *current sentiment in favour of beer* was so strong that in 1870 a clause was attached to the Prohibitory law allowing the sale of beer, porter, and ale,—the practical effect of which was to *nullify prohibition*" (p. 405). Unless the American Temperance reformers meet the rising invasion of beer and native wines with *specific* teaching, the movement is likely to be swamped, and their prohibitory El Dorados are in danger of becoming Pandemoniums. Fortunately, however, the truth is perceived there, as the most influential organ of Temperance in the States, *The National Temperance Advocate*, in its issue for September, 1885, declares that : "An enlightened total abstinence public opinion is the only basis for the successful, enduring prohibition of the liquor traffic " (p. 160).

† *The Staunch Teetotaler* (1867), p. 124.

‡ Shallow critics may twit Mr. Livesey with having changed his opinions. Not so, however, Mr. Washington Wilks, who, in 1862, replied to Mr. Livesey's pamphlet. He said : "I do not taunt our respected friend with a change of opinion. He would be less worthy of our respect if he had never submitted his mind to the influence of time and circumstance." And on this

himself still a friend of prohibition, but differed altogether from the Alliance methods of obtaining it.

" The friends of the Alliance, I fear," he said, "have not looked upon the question in all its bearings; and I know quite well that many of its supporters and contributors are beginning to have their misgivings. They know quite well how the temperance reformation stands to-day; how it is owing to moral suasion that multitudes of men, who do honour to our towns and villages as teetotalers, were brought in, not by law, but by persuasion. I dislike the agitation more particularly for this reason—I found that many of my friends. as soon as the Permissive Bill was launched, slid away from our meetings, and declared that their attendance was unnecessary, as everything would be done by a *coup d'état*, and if we insisted upon that law, the work would be done. It is a terrible mistake. We shall by-and-by recover our senses, and all our teetotalers will put their shoulders to the wheel. If our good Alliance friends would work and spend their money in converting the people to teetotalism, as they have worked and demonstrated their attachment to a hopeless measure—I say, if they would spend their money in making teetotal converts, they would ten thousand times sooner bring about important legislation." *

These were strong words, as also were others uttered by Mr. Livesey at the same time. He declared that he had never previously spoken so plainly on the question, having been restrained by the fear of creating divisions and offending old friends; but that the day had come for speaking out. Shortly after the Scottish speech, Mr. Livesey's views upon the question were more fully stated in a pamphlet entitled " Free and Friendly Remarks upon the Permissive Bill," the publication of which created considerable excitement. He there pointed out that the citizen basis of the Alliance had not answered the end its promoters hoped for. It was anticipated, he says, " that a great extension of strength, personal and pecuniary [drawn from the ranks of the drinkers], would be secured;" but nine years' experience, he contended, had shown the inconclusiveness of early notions, and exposed the source both of the weakness and strength of the institution. And as teetotalers were the backbone of the movement, the more effective way of promoting prohibition would be to make the Alliance a teetotal organization.

The Permissive Bill, and the electoral machinery set in motion to secure its passage through Parliament, Mr. Livesey regarded as grave mistakes, and he urged the Council of the Alliance to carefully reconsider the subject, and abandon its Permissive Bill policy for something " which would consolidate its strength, and give greater hopes of practical results."† The Bill itself he pronounced unattainable; besides which, it was open to strong objection because " it offers no choice but the *present system* or *absolute extinction*." He altogether denied the parallel often attempted between Permissive Acts on the Statute Book, which dealt with objects " easily to be secured," and the proposal of the Alliance, which involved " the greatest revolution in social affairs that this age has witnessed, and affected

point M. Antoninus may be quoted: " Never think it any disgrace to change your opinion and correct an error, it being equally liberal, and the part of an ingenious mind, as to follow any one who would direct you the right road. It is still your own act and you only pursue your first intention,—to discover the truth, and to arrive at the point intended.' Mr. Livesey believed some of his friends were on the wrong road, and, consequently, he endeavoured to direct them aright.

* *The Scottish League Journal*, May 17th, 1862, p. 165.

† Nearly twenty years afterwards this was done, when the Permissive Bill was withdrawn, and the Local Option Resolution substituted for it.

property to the extent, it is said, of sixty millions." * Mr. Livesey's attitude to
the electoral policy of the Alliance may be gathered from the following :

" Temperance men may *act* politically at election times and seasons, and in
such a way as promises to secure an advantage to their cause, and does not tend
to increase divisions among themselves, or create a hurtful feeling against them with
the public; but for so comparatively feeble a body to assume the character of a
distinct political and parliamentary power, will, I believe, result in disappointment,
if not in direct injury, to the Temperance cause. . . . To set up ourselves as a
distinct party, or to *pledge* the *support* or *opposition* of Temperance electors, is going
too far.† . . . No one section of the Temperance body ought, or can, dictate
to the whole." ‡

Mr. Livesey contended that the better way would be to proceed upon the
'bit-by-bit' plan; every advance made to be secured by imperial legislation,
taking effect simultaneously throughout the entire kingdom. In short, he would
apply to the drink question, what Mr. Edwin Chadwick calls Bentham's "master
principle of legislative and judicial organization," viz., "*always to do the same
thing in the same way, choosing the best, and always to call the same thing by the
same name.*" § And this idea clearly pervades the following citations.

" Whatever change is made in the laws respecting drink-selling, it ought not
to be of a permissive, but of an imperial character; it must be such as will extend
to every nook and corner of the land, laying its hand upon the leviathan of the
metropolis as well as the country village ; a mandate that will not say, ' If you can
make a successful fight with the giant monster of liquordom in your little parish
or town, you shall be cleared of its yoke,' but one that thunders in the ears of the
140,000 drink-sellers, ' Thus far shall you all go, and no farther.' Whatever is done
to curb or to destroy this business must not be left to the puny efforts of private individuals, nor to the doubtful and ever-varying decisions of the fickle multitude.
. . . Only one hour cut off the Saturday and Sunday nights' drinking in all the
140,000 houses throughout the kingdom would far exceed in lessening the evil
than the closing of a few country public houses."

" If a council had been convened to decide upon the likeliest course for ruin-
ing the Temperance cause, it would not have recommended a surer step than
that of embroiling the people in elections where the drink interest was to be one of
the contending parties. . . . God forbid that I should ever witness the holy
cause of teetotalism—that cause which stands associated with all that is peaceful,
and quiet, and elevating—dragged into electioneering rows ; or that its friends
should suppose that measures calculated to provoke so much drunkenness and
wickedness are required to secure its prosperity and success."

" The Permissive franchise is an entire novelty : has at present no footing in
the country, and no connexion with our social or political system ; ‖ and, moreover,
the objects it seeks to obtain—so far as they are attainable—can be secured by
other and far more likely means." ¶

Mr. Livesey knew that a criticism of this sort would call out defences of
the policy attacked, more or less embittered by party feeling ; but he did not

---

* " Free and Friendly Remarks upon the Permissive Bill," Preston, 1862, p. 3.

† Twenty-three years have elapsed, and we find Mr. J. H. Raper, at the Conference of the
British Temperance League (July 7th and 8th, 1885), reported in the *Advocate* as follows :
" Mr. Raper wished all honour to those who thought they could make a separate Temperance
party to act politically. He was sorry to say, however, that so far as he could see, there was
no machinery adequate for that, apart from the other two great parties. He asked them,
however, not to be discouraged. . . . They would have to permeate the existing political
parties."—*British Temperance Advocate*, 1885, p. 128.

‡ " Free and Friendly Remarks upon the Permissive Bill," Preston, 1862, p. 11.

§ Chadwick on " The Evils of Disunity," London, 1885, p. 2.

‖ This is exactly the view of the matter at present taken by Mr. Joseph Chamberlain, M.P.,
Mr. Joseph Cowen, M.P., and other supporters of Local Option.

¶ " Free and Friendly Remarks upon the Permissive Bill." Preston, 1862, pp. 3, 9, 10.

enter upon the task without first counting the cost. He remarks, that while prepared to defend his positions when assailed by argument, "scurrilous and personal abuse" will not be noticed.

As might have been expected, he was rather severely handled by the representatives of the organization thus placed on the defensive. He received, what every man who attacks a considerable party must expect, unfair treatment. Indeed, every possible attempt was made to detract from the value of his work and lessen his influence. The *Temperance Spectator*—an able magazine issued in the interests of the Alliance—which in April, 1860, had published a laudatory biographical sketch of Mr. Livesey (quoted from on page xxvii.), in its issue for October, 1862, speaks of him as "wakening up, after a quarter of a century's somnolency, varied only by starts and spasms, and assuming the onerous position of Adviser-general to the Temperance army," and states that he had "been raised to vitality and activity by the aid of the galvanic batteries of the two leagues." [*] Mr. Livesey was also compared to Dr. Edgar and others who had not kept pace with the reform. These statements, and many similar ones, made about him at this time, were evidently intended to lead the people to suppose that he had been asleep on the Temperance question since 1837,[†] and that, being a Rip Van Winkle, his utterances were made without a knowledge of the then condition of things, and consequently were unworthy of regard.

Throughout the *Staunch Teetotaler* (1867–8) Mr. Livesey urged Temperance people not to put too much faith in legislative remedies, but to redouble their energies in teaching the people the doctrines of teetotalism. He seemed deeply impressed with the idea that, failing to get what they desired by the Permissive Bill or some other enactment, their interest in the general Temperance question would flag or die out altogether, and he sought to prepare them for the disappointment which he believed to be inevitable. His general views on Temperance legislation, and how best to get it, are expressed in the following quotation :

"If past experience be worth anything, it should teach us not to depend too much upon LEGISLATION. Neither magistrates as administrators, nor the legislature as the maker of our laws, have ever done much for Temperance. From the first we have been agitating for more restriction and prohibition, but with very unsatisfactory results. The sale of beer is free, wine is free, and the limit to selling applies only to spirits. I am a more thorough-going prohibitionist than many of my friends, but I am convinced that so long as the legislature is chosen by drinking constituences, it will support the drinking system; and therefore, before we can expect beneficial changes in the laws, we must have a great change among the men who make them; and as nothing will be done towards this change by the drinking party, it can only be brought about by teetotalizing the country far more than it is at present. The character of the House of Commons is formed by the constituencies, and it is quite obvious that they have not created a Parliament well disposed towards prohibition. Nobody knows better than I the advantage to the cause of

* *Temperance Spectator*, vol. 4, 1862, p. 149.

† Mr. William Hoyle, however, allows that Mr. Livesey's active services extended to 1847. According to the *Alliance News*, Sept. 6th, 1884, in proposing the resolution given on page 169 —after speaking in very high terms of Mr. Livesey's Anti-Corn-Law labours—he said: "During the first fifteen years of the Total Abstinence movement his labours and services to it were exceedingly important, and of the very highest value. It was impossible to measure the amount of influence for good which he then put forth." In reality, however, Mr. Livesey's interest in the movement never waned, and he worked on his own lines to the end of his days.

sobriety, religion, and everything that is good, of closing the liquor shops, but the question is, How are we to do this?   After much experience, my opinion is that if ever the liquor traffic is subdued, it will be by the spread of teetotalism in the country." *

Of course Mr. Livesey's outspoken utterances regarding efforts which he considered well meant, but misdirected, brought down upon him much censure from the warmest friends of the Alliance.   Of the remonstrances addressed to him part were published, while the rest took the shape of private correspondence.   Among those who thus addressed Mr. Livesey of course there would be one whose letters in the days of his vigour were as numerous as they were scathing,—the redoubtable and energetic secretary of the Alliance, Mr. T. H. Barker.   Like other correspondents of Mr. Livesey, Mr. Barker always admitted the thorough disinterestedness and honesty of purpose of the Father of teetotalism, whose long, unceasing, and gratuitous labours in the promotion of 'True Temperance Teaching,' afforded him a high vantage-ground in controversy.   The words with which Mr. Livesey concluded a rather caustic correspondence with Mr. Barker in 1870 are quite characteristic of the man : "It is *time*, not *argument*, I believe, that is to arbitrate betwixt us." †   And without doubt, *time* will arbitrate upon the matter.   Indeed, it has already settled several points then in dispute, and the future will fully disclose the true value of Mr. Livesey's ideas regarding Temperance legislation, and the necessary preliminaries to it.

In 1872, the Alliance reached the zenith of its power, and resolved upon the heroic policy, now generally described as 'a vote for a vote, and nothing for nothing.'   Its General Council, at the Twentieth Annual Meeting, resolved upon a bolder electoral policy ; recommended its supporters, in case of a vacancy in the representation of any constituency, " to put in nomination a candidate favourable to the Permissive Bill ; " and pledged itself to supply candidates in cases where local friends failed to find suitable ones, so as to enable every elector to vote for the Permissive Bill, "until the question be decided."   By this act, the Alliance virtually constituted itself a third party, and Mr. Livesey returned to the discussion of the subject.   He issued another note of warning in the form of a a pamphlet entitled, "True Temperance Teaching," the opening paragraph of which is as follows :

" When Mr. Washington Wilks and others in 1862 were attempting to answer my pamphlet and to write me down, he used these words : ' He (Mr. Livesey) urges a threefold objection to the Permissive Bill ; first, that *it is impossible to be obtained ;* secondly, if obtained and attempted to be put in force *the attempt would be a failure,* and do more harm than good ; and, thirdly, the *agitation for the Bill is diverting the attention of Temperance reformers from other measures* of an imperial character more likely to be carried, and of *far more practical importance.*   If the *first* of these objections can be sustained, THERE IS AN END OF THE CONTROVERSY. The town that had neither gun nor gunpowder was excused, by the king in the story, from making any other apologies for not firing a salute.   If a Permissive Bill be impossible of attainment, we may as well *say no more about it.*'   Eleven more years of agitation, vast expenditure of money, and great exertions point only in one direction, and that is to a *confirmation* of *all* I then asserted.   I have ever since considered the measure carefully, and do sincerely believe that it would be difficult to invent a scheme calculated to serve the temperance cause so little, and

* *The Staunch Teetotaler,* 1867, p. 35.
† "True Policy Vindicated."   Manchester, U.K.A., 1870, p. 11.

yet irritate its enemies so much as the Permissive Bill. I believe it to be unwise and impracticable, and if it could be adopted 'would grievously disappoint its most sanguine friends.'" *

Mr. Livesey re-stated most of the positions taken in his earlier pamphlet, criticised the electoral and Parliamentary policy adopted by the Alliance, and strongly advised Temperance reformers to redouble their efforts in teaching the people the foundation truths of Teetotalism. He appealed to his disciples in the following words:

"It was not by such far-fetched, ill-adapted means [as those devised by the Alliance] that teetotalism made its way and accomplished so much at the first; then there was no dallying with the enemy, but a *direct attack* was made *upon the drink* wherever we found it : explaining its pernicious effects upon the human system, and urging upon the hearts and consciences of every one the importance of *personal and entire abstinence.* It was by these honest, consistent, straightforward, and practical means that the good old cause of teetotalism spread throughout this country, into America, and throughout every part of the civilized world, scattering blessings at every step, leaving nothing but peace and goodwill in its train. In truth, it is the good old doctrine of total abstinence that has done all the good yet accomplished." †

Mr. Livesey, in raising a warning voice against a policy of action which he believed was prejudicial to the cause he had served so faithfully and so well, was actuated by a desire for its true advancement; and the motive which led him to issue his pamphlets in opposition to the Permissive Bill movement was precisely the same as that which induced him to publish his *Malt Lecture.* He had but one object—the extension of the Temperance movement. His leading contention, that it will be futile to expect the enforcement and respect of prohibitory laws in a community the great majority of whom believes in the goodness of the article prohibited, is one eminently deserving the consideration of the Temperance party, not only in Great Britain and her colonies, but also in the United States. *Time,* which Mr. Livesey invoked to arbitrate between himself and the Alliance party, had pronounced upon several points at issue before his death. He did not live, however, to see the greatest concession made to his views; but his body was scarcely buried before Mr. Raper (who represented the Alliance) declared, at the memorial meeting reported in the Appendix, that—

"'Their controversy was with the brewers,' and he recommended all local committees of Temperance Societies to possess themselves of Mr. Livesey's Malt Liquor Lectures, and get them distributed from house to house. If they could get 6,000,000 of these distributed during the next twelve months, it would do more good than anything else could do." ‡

Excellent advice, which the Temperance world cannot do better than seriously lay to heart, and vigorously act upon. For without a doubt, not only in Great Britain and the United States, but throughout the civilized world, the brewers will remain the most formidable opponents to the Temperance movement until their customers are enlightened upon the nature and properties of their brewage; and Mr. Raper clearly sees that the best, if not the only, way to fight the brewers, is

* "True Temperance Teaching, showing the Errors of the Alliance and the Permissive Bill." London, 1873, p. 2.
† *Ibid.,* p. 10.
‡ Appendix, p. 151.

by educating their customers.* And when that work has been done effectively and completely, the victory will be won.

It was due both to Mr. Livesey and to the great Temperance movement inaugurated by him, that his views upon such an important phase as the prohibitory agitation should be fairly stated; and they are commended to the free and friendly consideration of reformers of all shades of opinion who are interested in a solution of the 'liquor problem.'

DID MR. LIVESEY LOSE HEART OR FAITH?

It has been represented that Mr. Livesey, during the later years of his life, lost faith in the ultimate success of Temperance. A careful examination of his writings, however, does not support that conclusion. It is true that he gave up a hope he once entertained of securing the triumph of the Temperance reformation by the 'short cut' of a legislative enactment: and he ceased to hope for any aid from legislation until the ideas regarding the nature of drink, entertained by the people who make Parliament, were radically changed. His faith, however, in moral suasion—in the power of truth and in the possible redemption of the most abject victim of alcohol—was well-nigh sublime. Indeed, in this respect, he sets his disciples a worthy and noble example. He saw signs of progress, and in these he took encouragement. They were not, however, so discernible to him in the excitement of 'missions' and the display of 'demonstrations,' as in the gradual though sure recognition of the truths of teetotalism in scientific circles; since in his view a stable and abiding Temperance reformation could only result from the general adoption by the public of sound views regarding the nature and properties of alcoholic drinks. He had spent his life largely in instructing the masses upon the question, and when he found practically the same teachings propounded and enforced by Dr. Richardson and other scientists, it was to him a matter of supreme satisfaction; for he felt that as a teacher he had not lived in vain.

* That Mr. Raper accurately gauged the present situation was made evident by the reception accorded to Mr. Childers' Budget. The noise made by the believers in beer was so much louder than that made by the Temperance party that a proposal to add about ¾d. a gallon to the beer tax was withdrawn. As the *Echo* of June 6th, 1885, said: "Notwithstanding the persistent propaganda of the teetotalers, beer is still the national drink of Englishmen." And we have since seen a Cabinet Minister, Lord Randolph Churchill, pronouncing beer to be as important an article of food as bread! Speaking at Wimborne, August 12th, 1885, Lord Churchill said: "We defeated the late Government in their attempt to place a heavy tax upon beer, and I hold that that great national drink is as much the food of the people as bread" (*vide Standard*, August 13th). Mr. Disraeli, when Chancellor of the Exchequer, in 1852, had expressed similar sentiments, which appear to have been 'resurrected' by Lord Randolph. Mr. Livesey has the following comment upon Mr. Disraeli's views: "It is true, Disraeli asserted that 'malt liquor was a prime necessity of life,' and 'one of the principal sources of health and strength.' When I read these statements, I could not but recall to my mind the observation once made by a great man, that 'the nation was governed by the *ignorance* of the nation.' . . . These old notions being reproduced by such an authority shows how necessary it is to bend our attention to this special point, and on every occasion to fully expose all such baseless assumptions" (*Teetotal Progressionist*, 1852, p. 189). And, unquestionably, teaching on malt liquor is *still* required.

CHAPTER XI.

PUBLICATIONS,—CLOSING YEARS.

As the reader may find it convenient to have at hand a brief account of Mr. Livesey's writings arranged chronologically, the following bibliographical information is here supplied.

Passing over with the mere mention his numerous letters upon religious and social subjects, addressed to the Preston papers, and his placards upon a variety of topics, some of which are very striking and effective, we commence with his first pamphlet.

"A Friendly Address to the Poorer Classes on the important Points of Economy, Cleanliness, Industry, Honesty, Religion, etc. ; with an Attempt to Correct some of the evils which produce so much misery among them. Preston : L. Clarke. London : Wightman and Cramp." Such is the title of the second edition of Mr. Livesey's pamphlet, which is dated 1826, and consisted of 24 fcap. 8vo pages. The first edition, he tells us, was issued in the previous year.[*] The first and second editions were published anonymously and signed "A Sincere Friend." A third edition, with a slightly altered title-page, on which the author's name appears, was published in 1836. Its contents, however, were then re-arranged, and in great part re-written, the Temperance teaching being much more pronounced. The price was twopence.—(*Not in Brit. Mus. Library.*)

"The Besetting Sin"—a pamphlet mentioned by Mr. Livesey on page 45 of the "Autobiography"—was devoted to the question of Drunkenness, and most probably published either in 1825 or 1826. —(*Not in Brit. Mus. Library.*)

"Remarks on the Rite of Confirmation, and the Use of Sponsors in Baptism ; intended to prove that they are Unreasonable, Unscriptural, and Dangerous. By J. Livesey. Preston : I. Wilcockson. London : Simpkin & Marshall." Not dated, but probably issued about 1827. Contents and scope are indicated by title. Size fcap. 8vo, pp. 14. Price twopence.—(*Not in Brit. Mus. Library.*)

"Remarks on the Present State of Sunday Schools, with Hints for their Improvement. Also a recommendation of Youths' Schools, and of Dr. Chalmers'

* "Autobiography," p. 45.

' Local System,' as best adapted to Counteract the present Progress of Juvenile Depravity. By J. Livesey. Preston: I. Wilcockson, 1829." Size, fcap. 8vo, pp. 11. Price not stated. This interesting little work treats upon the education of the neglected classes. It deals primarily with Sunday Schools, but incidentally it takes a much wider range. Like all Mr. Livesey's productions, this little treatise is marked with sagacity, and displays considerable insight into the subject discussed. In the opening paragraph a sentiment is expressed which is in remarkable agreement with the conclusions arrived at by Dr. B. W. Richardson, after three years' experience on the London School Board. "If we brighten the intellect," says Mr. Livesey, "without at the same time strengthening the *moral feeling*, we are only capacitating individuals for greater mischief, and increasing their facilities for the commission of vice." *—(Not in Brit. Mus. Library.)

"The First Book" for persons learning to read, referred to on page 45 of the "Autobiography," was most likely published very shortly after the little pamphlet on Sunday Schools, as the deficiencies of the primers and reading books then in general use in schools are therein remarked upon. It is evident that the "First Book" had not then been issued, or it would have been mentioned by Mr. Livesey. —(Not in Brit. Mus. Library.)

Mr. Livesey's first periodical—the *Moral Reformer*—commenced in January.

* As this pamphlet has come to light since the chapter on education was printed off, it may interest the reader to learn that it contains some particulars of Mr. Livesey's Youths' School referred to on page xxxvi. Mr. Livesey says: "In this school from forty to fifty boys, from fourteen to twenty-one years of age, are regularly taught every Sunday. No compulsion, no coercion, is used, and yet the lads seem quite happy to forego their play to attend school, and are much more orderly than could be expected. The teachers take into consideration their age, and suit their system of teaching to it; they lead them on by affection, encourage them by every prospective advantage, and conduct their teaching upon a plan which seems always to interest them. As some may feel wishful to know more of this system, I will give a brief detail of it. They meet but once in the day, from half-past 9 till 12; of course, in the afternoon their parents are at liberty to take them to any place of worship they please. They commence by reading a portion of the Scriptures; the classes are then furnished with teachers, and about forty minutes are occupied in reading and spelling. Their names being called over, every boy is furnished with a slate or book, and writes a copy, every single line of which is examined as he proceeds. This being finished, the writing is laid before an impartial person, and the boys change seats, higher or lower, till the next week, according as he judges of its execution. They then clean their slates, and are required to write, without copies, any passage of Scripture which they may have committed to memory. This is an interesting process, and, attended as it is by a subsequent examination, is well calculated to produce good impressions. It leads them to a correct orthography, to a proper use of capitals and stops, and to a taste for composition, as well as impressing the subject upon their minds. Some out of each class are requested (but not compelled) to read what they have written, which, from the great variety, is both entertaining and highly instructive. From these passages, as they are read, admonitions and exhortations are given by one of the teachers in as plain a manner as possible, and the scholars are sometimes led on by questions to make their own remarks. If any passage should refer to natural history, or to any part of creation, they always endeavour to make their ideas subservient to their conviction. In these exercises their countenances will sometimes indicate an elevation of mind, which cannot be mistaken. Advantage is taken of seasons or events; they are told the meaning of Christmas, Easter, etc., and are informed how differently they were originally celebrated to what they are now. If a man be drowned, or murdered, or executed, the event is improved by such observations as are likely to be useful. These instructions occupy nearly half an hour. The school concludes with prayer. On these principles the school has been conducted for several years, but the teachers have no Medial law among them, for if any improvement can be suggested it is adopted; and what may be regarded of some little advantage, in order to do this they have no person's consent to obtain beyond their own circle. This school got on tardily at first, and it was not till the plan of writing, and the subsequent application of it to religious instruction, was adopted, that they found a principle which would keep the youths together with ease. Some persons object to teaching children to write on Sundays, and generally, for the same reasons that led men to clamour against the venerable Raikes, when he first attempted to establish Sunday Schools. If, instead of being led by prepossession, men would reason candidly, I think they would come to a different conclusion. On no subject, perhaps, is that saying more verified, 'Ye strain at a gnat and swallow a camel'" (pp. 7, 8). Such were some of the plans followed in this Sunday school. A subsequent adult school, conducted by Mr. Livesey, gave Preston its first Temperance Society, and furnished to the world many useful reformers.

1831, and was concluded in December, 1833. Each number consisted of thirty-two demy 8vo pages. The price of the _Moral Reformer_ was sixpence, but Mr. Livesey supplied it at half-price to persons who agreed to take the magazine regularly for a year. By this plan a really valuable work was brought within reach of everybody who could afford the sum of _three farthings a week._ Mr. Livesey thus preceded, as a purveyor of cheap literature of an instructive and elevating character, both the publishers of _Chambers' Journal_ (issued at three-halfpence weekly) and the _Penny Magazine;_ as the first number of the former appeared on February 4th, 1832, while the latter was commenced on March 31st of the same year. At that time, and until 1836, the duty upon paper was threepence per pound, a sum which is about equal to the cost of the paper upon which most of the cheap periodicals of the present day are printed! When this fact is remembered, the difficulties of establishing a cheap periodical in 1831, and subsequently of sustaining a popular Temperance literature, will be better understood. From its commencement, the _Moral Reformer_ was got up in a neat and creditable manner; but its appearance very much improved from March 1832, when Mr. Livesey became his own printer.* The _Moral Reformer_ was in every way a remarkable production. It discussed with intelligence and power a great variety of topics; its spirit and tone were admirable. The originality of its editor (and indeed author) is very noticeable, it being quite an exception to find him quoting authorities, while he frequently wrote articles extending to twelve or sixteen pages without any further citations, than a few lines of Scripture.—(_Not in Brit. Mus. Library._)

The _Preston Temperance Advocate_, the first teetotal publication ever issued, was commenced in January, 1834, and published monthly by Mr. Livesey for four years, when it was handed over to Messrs. F. R. Lees, John Andrew, and Barnabas Crossley; and it still survives as the organ of the British Temperance League. As a medium for the diffusion of Temperance truth, the _Preston Advocate_ has never been surpassed. It contained no offensive personalities, and was in every way admirably designed to inform and instruct the reader upon the question. In short, it may be said to have effected for Temperance what the _Struggle_ subsequently did for Free Trade. The size of the _Advocate_ was crown 4to, and each number consisted of eight pages. Its price was one penny. In November, 1835, Mr. Livesey commenced to illustrate it, and throughout the years 1836–7, a wood-cut appeared on the first page of each number. Writing subsequently upon Temperance periodicals, Mr. Livesey thus refers to the cost of these illustrations: " I know that the sale of the _Preston Advocate_ was kept up very much by this means. It is true the expense of these cuts was considerable; . . . the _Advocate_ cuts varied in cost from £1 to £5; " † but this extra expense was more than covered by increased sales. In the issue for May, 1836, appears a notice to the effect that on the 28th of that month the _Advocate_ would appear as a weekly, but in the June number Mr. Livesey announced that after mature consideration he

---

* Mr. Livesey ceased to be his own printer at the end of 1859, when, owing to the illness of his eldest son, he disposed of the business.

† _Livesey's Moral Reformer_, 1838–9, p. 179.

had decided to abandon the idea of a weekly publication, resolving instead to issue on the 15th of each month a supplement, containing matter of permanent interest, uniform in size and price with the *Advocate*. In this way Temperance literature of sterling value was produced at the lowest possible cost, to the great advantage of the movement. Each of these supplementary numbers was complete in itself, and the series comprised "The Temperance Doctor," "The Trial of Alcohol," "Physiological Influence of Alcohol," "The Wine Question," "Temperance Poetry," "Temperance Picture Gallery," "American Reports," "Temperance Tales," and a number of similar productions, forming altogether the cheapest Temperance library ever produced. Whenever the *Advocate* contained matter of more than ordinary interest, Mr. Livesey's habit was to notify that the forme of type would be kept intact until a given date, up to which societies or persons could be supplied with quantities of the publication for distribution at £2 per 1000 copies; and similar facilities were offered regarding the supplements. These points are mentioned as illustrations of Mr. Livesey's sagacity as the conductor of a press propaganda worked upon the principle of pure benevolence. At the time the bulk of these publications were issued, the duty on paper was threepence per pound ; in 1836 it was reduced to three-halfpence. —(*Not in Brit. Mus. Library.*)

"The Sheet Almanacs," issued by Mr. Livesey at a penny, were very widely circulated. The first, published in November, 1834, for the following year, was unquestionably the pioneer Teetotal Almanac.—(*Not in Brit. Mus. Library.*)

"The Malt Liquor Lecture."—In June, 1836, appeared the first edition of this famous discourse or treatise, the full title of which is given on page cxvii. It was well got up and comprised thirty-two demy 8vo solid pages of type. Its retail price was sixpence, but a very large reduction was made upon quantities. A cheaper edition having been inquired for, Mr. Livesey announced that he was prepared to issue one in sixteen pages crown 4to, to sell at twopence, as soon as orders for 7000 copies at £5 per 1000 were forthcoming. In the *Advocate* for December, 1837, he acknowledges the following orders : London Society, 1000 ; Bradford ditto, 1000; Clithero ditto, 200; Stroud ditto, 100 ; Huddersfield ditto, 100. Whether the stipulated number were ordered or not does not appear ; but the lecture was published in the form and at the price promised, and subsequently the stereotype plates were handed over to Mr. Pascoe, of London, who printed a large penny edition from them. The full text of the original lecture was also published in Edinburgh, Birmingham, Dumfries and Ipswich ; * and in 1864 Mr. Livesey reprinted it verbatim as a crown 8vo pamphlet of 32 pages, which was published at one penny, but supplied in quantities of fifty and upwards at half-price.* Several abridged editions of the lecture were issued by Mr. Livesey on various occasions, one of which is bound up at the end of this volume. In 1870 Mr. Livesey issued "A New Lecture on Malt Liquor " * at a penny, which was an adaptation of the original lecture to that time. The lecture was also reprinted extensively by publishers and benevolent persons, † and altogether its circulation must have

† Mr. Livesey gave a general permission to reprint any of his publications ; he never retained any copyrights.

exceeded two millions.—(*Only the editions marked with an asterisk are in Brit. Mus. Library.*)

Livesey's Moral Reformer was commenced as a penny weekly in January, 1838. Its size and appearance were similar to *Chambers' Journal;* and it was continued as a weekly publication until March 31st, when its pages and price were doubled, and it became a monthly. In this form the *Reformer* was continued until February, 1839, when it ceased. An examination of this work discloses Mr. Livesey's chief motive in issuing it. He had a large number of Temperance disciples throughout the United Kingdom, and he was evidently anxious for their mental improvement. Knowing that the human mind cannot stand still, and feeling that the adherents of Temperance needed something to supply the place of the old associations connected with drinking, which had previously engrossed their attention, he endeavoured to lead them into a more elevated atmosphere. This second series of the *Moral Reformer* was admirably adapted to such an end; but a sufficient number of Mr. Livesey's teetotal disciples failed to avail themselves of its benefits, and consequently a publication of great merit was discontinued. The numbers issued make a volume of 220 pages.—(*Not in Brit. Mus. Library.*)

The Struggle, a weekly illustrated paper, issued in support of the Free Trade movement, will be found very fully described in chapter v. (on pages lxi., lxii., lxxi.), and on pages 21–3 of the "Autobiography," 1841–6.

The Preston Guardian, a weekly newspaper, started Feb. 10th, 1844, and conducted by Mr. Livesey or his sons until the end of 1859, was indeed a 'guardian' of the rights and best interests of the public. The get up of the paper was admirable, and its contents varied and excellent. Local occurrences of interest were pictorially illustrated in the *Guardian* by woodcuts, which were greatly superior in definition to the 'process' blocks now so common in newspapers. The *Guardian*, which in every respect merited the recognition accorded it by Mr. Cobden, was the leading paper in North Lancashire.

Livesey's Progressionist. In August, 1851, the *Teetotal Times*, which had been conducted for upwards of five years as an independent Temperance paper by the late John Cassell, was incorporated with the *Temperance Chronicle*. Feeling the need of an independent journal, Mr. Livesey in January, 1852, issued the first number of *Livesey's Progressionist; or, Advocate of Temperance, and Physical, Moral, Social, and Religious Reform*. Each number of the *Progressionist* consisted of 16 pages, and the price was one penny. The preliminary notice, which indicates the scope of the work, was as follows:

" In bringing out the first number of the PROGRESSIONIST, I may briefly state, that the work is primarily intended to advocate the teetotal cause, and to enforce its claims upon the public; but, at the same time, as circumstances may occur, it will take up any question in which the world's progressive improvement is involved. I wish it to be distinctly understood that no individual or society, none but myself, must be considered responsible for the articles contained in this periodical."

J. LIVESEY.

The *Progressionist*, which discussed many topics allied to Temperance, was a strenuous advocate of progress. In April, 1852, the title was changed to the *Teetotal Progressionist*, and in the following month, owing to failing health, Mr. Livesey handed the periodical over to the late Mr. Horsell, who conducted it until the close of 1853. Mr. Livesey contributed to the *Progressionist* numerous articles on a variety of subjects during the years 1852 and '53, and his communications have either his signature or initials appended to them. The work was similar in size to the *Preston Advocate*, and the numbers for the two years make a goodly volume of 372 pages.

The Staunch Teetotaler, by Joseph Livesey, was commenced as a penny monthly in January, 1867. In size and appearance it resembles *The Moral Reformer*. In his Prefatory Remarks, Mr. Livesey reminded the reader that he was then in his 73rd year. " I feel it a task to leave home and lecture," he says, " but can pleasantly fill up part of my time in writing for the press." *The Staunch Teetotaler* continued in the field for two years ; at the close of 1868 Mr. Livesey was compelled to relinquish it in consequence of the failure of his wife's health. The great excellence of this magazine has been elsewhere remarked upon ; indeed the entire work merits republication. In order to promote the circulation of Temperance truth, the monthly numbers of *The Staunch Teetotaler* were supplied in parcels of 250, for 10*s*. The complete work makes a volume of 384 pages.

" Reminiscences of Early Teetotalism. Preston, 1868." A demy 8vo pamphlet of 40 pages. A third edition of this work was issued by Mr. Livesey as recently as April, 1884.

" The Autobiography of Joseph Livesey. Preston, 1881." A work of 98 demy 8vo pages, the second edition of which forms part of the present volume.

It is unfortunate that copies cannot be obtained of the very numerous pamphlets issued by Mr. Livesey, who was in the habit of promptly seizing upon, and thus dealing with, passing events. It is quite impossible to give a complete list of the titles of Mr. Livesey's latter pamphlets, but the following may be named : " A Letter to Wilson Patten, Esq., M.P., on the Drinking System, the Late Sunday Bill, and the Maine Law, 1855." A demy 8vo pamphlet of 16 pages, issued at one penny.—" Free and Friendly Remarks upon the Permissive Bill, Temperance Legislation, and the Alliance, 1862." A 16 pp. imp. pamphlet ; price one penny. (*Not in Brit. Mus. Library*.)—" Malt, Malt Liquor, and the Malt Tax, 1865." 16 pp. demy 8vo ; price one penny.—" A Word to Publicans, 1868." Demy 8vo.—" True Temperance Teaching ; showing the Errors of the Alliance and the Permissive Bill, 1873." A 16 pp. demy 8vo pamphlet published at one penny. (*Not in Brit. Mus. Library*.)—Mr. Livesey published a very powerful letter addressed to Mr. Gladstone upon the fearful evils resulting from the Grocers' and Confectioners' License Scheme of that statesman. His last effort in pamphlet form was a small work entitled *The Temperance Teacher*, issued at irregular intervals in 4 pages demy 8vo, and so arranged that each number, by a slight alteration, could be circulated as a tract. Ill health limited the *Teacher* to about a dozen numbers.

" The Temperance Tracts," written, neatly printed, and issued at the lowest possible price, by Mr. Livesey, were so numerous that anything like a complete list of them is impossible. For upwards of half a century he was continuously engaged in this important sphere of usefulness. " Livesey's Temperance Leaflets," the cheapest tracts ever issued, comprised 32 varieties, and were sold at 10*d*. per

1,000 ! Mr. Livesey's publications were all issued under his own responsibility. The rule announced in the following notice, inserted in the *Preston Advocate* for January, 1835, was strictly adhered to throughout his subsequent career :

"It may be proper to state, that although the *Temperance Advocate* and the 'Preston Temperance Tracts' are drawn up with a strict regard to the principles and rules of the Temperance Society, yet they are solely under the control of the publisher, and that neither the committee nor any other person is answerable for what they contain." *

CLOSING YEARS.

In the *Moral Reformer* for January, 1831, Mr. Livesey—then in his thirty-seventh year—expressed his determination to devote himself to the service of his fellows. "The remnant of my life," he said, "is pledged to the welfare of my species, and in pursuing this object, disappointments will not discourage me." † Disappointments repeatedly came, but they failed to dishearten him ; and for upwards of half a century he bravely pursued the career of usefulness he had marked out for himself.

To the very last, his interest in the cause of Temperance never waned ; and when age had incapacitated him from attending meetings, or visiting the homes of drunkards, he busied himself among his tracts and publications. Surrounded by these silent messengers of truth and mercy, he passed his declining years ; occupying his time either in preparing for the press new appeals on his favourite topic, replenishing his stock of tracts, or in dispatching parcels of literature to all parts of the world. When the genial and kind-hearted Jabez Inwards visited Preston in 1868, he found Mr. Livesey thus employed.

"Passing down the street," says Mr. Inwards, " I saw in large black letters the name of Joseph Livesey. We entered his place of business, and walking up a somewhat old and rather darkened staircase, we found in the front room over the warehouse this well-known Temperance reformer *in the midst of his literature* and his letters. And although he has seen more than threescore years and ten, he still reads well and writes much. He has a very ruddy, healthy-looking face. His hair is quite white, and his eyes beam with light and intelligence. The facial development is expressive of thought, humour, and love. Our stay was short, and all our conversation was upon the subject of Temperance ; and we mutually expressed our abiding conviction that moral suasion is the most effective implement that can be used to put down drunkenness and drinking. And when we shook hands with this venerable patriarch, we expressed a wish for ourselves, and all true friends of Temperance, that his valuable life might be spared for many years to come." ‡

For sixteen years afterwards, almost every day Mr. Livesey might be found amongst his tracts and papers, employed exactly as Mr. Inwards described him.

During the last year of his life, he prepared and issued a new series of tracts, called the "Autograph Series;" his last published declaration upon the subject of Temperance apparently being the concluding paragraph in the third edition of his "Reminiscences," which is dated April, 1884. On page lxxix. of the present work the reader will find Mr. Livesey's first testimony to the benefits resulting from abstinence from *all* alcoholic liquors, made after a year's trial of the principle ; and it is fitting that his verdict upon the system, after trying it for more than

* *Preston Temperance Advocate*, vol. ii. (1835), p. 8.   † *Moral Reformer*, vol. i. (1831), p. 18.
‡ *Temperance Record*, Feb. 28th, 1868, p. 74.

half a century, should be here recorded.   It is a valuable and truly noble declaration.

"For fifty-three years," writes Mr. Livesey, "I have enjoyed teetotalism as a great blessing; and having received so much good myself, I feel it a pleasure and a duty to endeavour to confer the same good upon others.   I live in a world of sin, sorrow, and suffering, and I find that in this country one of the greatest causes of these is taking intoxicating drink.   It is a deplorable fact that in the face of all the efforts that are made to ameliorate the condition of the people, this habit is growing worse.   *I therefore abstain, first for my own sake, and next for the good of others;* for my own *family* and *kin*, and for my neighbours, associates, countrymen, and fellow creatures at large.   By uniting *example* to precept, I have been able to influence a great many others to abandon the drink, and have assisted in disseminating truth all over the world.   Strong drink has no resting-place under my roof, and my table always reads a safe lesson in favour of sobriety.   Having now entered my 91st year, I am, if possible, more determined than ever to stick—as Cobden said—to 'the pump and the tea-pot,' and do all I can to persuade others to do the same." *

In 1882, when the British Temperance League held a Jubilee Conference at Preston, Mr. Livesey was in very feeble health.   He was able, however, just to look in upon the friends on Wednesday, July 5th, the third day of their sitting.   It was the last view he ever had of a Temperance gathering, with his material eyes.   The meeting was held in the Lancaster Road Congregational Chapel, and Mr. Livesey's visit is thus described in the *Advocate:*

"At a few minutes before twelve o'clock, the chairman announced that Mr. Livesey was in front of the chapel, in a cab, and intended visiting the Conference, on condition that they were perfectly still, and that not a word was said by any one.   A minute afterwards, the venerable apostle of teetotalism entered the building, and, amidst perfect silence, assisted by his son, Mr. William Livesey, and Mrs. William Livesey, he walked round the chapel.   On arriving in front of the rostrum, and facing the audience, his eye fell upon an old and dear friend (Councillor J. Sergeant, of Southport), with whom he shook hands.   Several others were desirous of clasping Mr. Livesey's hand, but they refrained from doing so, seeing that the effort would be more than he could bear.   He then walked down the aisle, and on nearing the door, met Mrs. Dorothy Hodgson, of Bolton, near Bradford, who had come to Preston for the sole purpose of seeing him.   This lady signed the moderation pledge at the first meeting held in the Bradford Friends' Meeting House, and subsequently took the total abstinence pledge at the first meeting held in the town addressed by Mr. Livesey.   After they had shaken hands, Mr. Livesey remarked [and this was his last public utterance on temperance]:

'I SHOULD LIKE TO HAVE SAID A FEW WORDS, IF I HAD NOT BEEN SO POORLY.'

He then withdrew.   The audience were deeply touched by the appearance of the old gentleman, who on the 5th of March had completed his 88th year, many persons being moved to tears, and manifesting emotions they were unable to subdue.   At the suggestion of Mr. Thomas Whittaker, the verse commencing 'Praise God, from whom all blessings flow,' was sung.   This concluded, a delegate's suggestion that a minute be spent in asking God to carry on the work commenced by Mr. Livesey was acted upon." †

From the foregoing report of the impressive and affecting visit of the veteran Temperance reformer to the Conference at Preston in 1882, the reader may possibly infer that after that time he was quite unfitted for even suggesting, much less doing, anything to further the cause to which his life had been mainly devoted;

---

* "Reminiscences," 3rd edition, 1884, p. 40.
† *British Temperance Advocate* Supplement, August, 1882, p. 16.

but such was not the case. Of course a long and active life of ninety years, during which Mr. Livesey may be truly said to have done double duty in every kind of work he undertook—especially when it is remembered that he had passed through four if not five attacks of rheumatic fever—would preclude the expectation that in his latter days he would be equal to personal exertion ; but his ability to suggest, direct, and stimulate others, and cheer and urge them on to ' work harder than ever '—advice he never omitted—continued up to the latest hour he was able to occupy his old arm-chair, which was really within a fortnight of his death. A peep into the privacy of Mr. Livesey's home is afforded by the following description of it, which, on urgent solicitation, has been furnished by a favoured friend of the father of teetotalism.

" Mr. Livesey's residence at Bank Parade was very well suited to his tastes ; it is one of the last row of houses on that side of the town, is very sheltered and retired, not being a much frequented thoroughfare, and has a very sunny aspect ; indeed, I was told that it is the warmest road in the town, and that when the old warrior on the battle-fields of reform was only able to ' paddle ' to and fro twice or thrice the length of the parapet of the Parade, that little walk which he took when the mid-day sun was shining always revived him. Fronting his residence was his garden, a very long strip of land running down almost to the bank of the Ribble. So long as he had sufficient physical strength, he devoted much personal labour to the cultivation of flowers, an occupation of which he was passionately fond. I was informed that in those years his garden was the centre of attraction to children, whom he delighted to supply with flowers ; in that department, as in all others, he seemed ever filled with pleasure at being able to give pleasure to others, and especially so to children, who, as one has well observed, were ' drawn to him as by a magnet.' Indeed, who that has ever been in his company, old or young, could help being so drawn to him ; for, to use a most homely phrase, he was ' truly a lovable man.'

" Entering his home on the last occasion, I was ushered into the dining-room, and the first object to strike my view was a remarkable life-like (and life-size) photograph, taken in his 88th year ; it was really a ' speaking likeness.' * A momentary survey of the portrait was broken in upon by the appearance of Mr. Wm. Livesey, the eldest son, who with his wife and daughter—to whom I was introduced—then resided with the venerable old man,—a happy arrangement in his declining years, for all concerned ; as it was evident from what I saw that the pleasure of serving and being served was equally distributed. The son said to me, " You have come at a very fortunate time, for dear father has just finished one of his refreshing little ' naps,' and will be just ready to talk with you." I was then taken to the drawing-room and duly introduced, when the dear old man, grasping both my hands, gave them such a hearty shake as to send a thrill of joy at the happy opportunity I had of once more and the last time—for it was in the year he was removed from amongst us—of speaking to one who is as worthily entitled to the appellation of ' Grand Old Man ' as any reformer of the present generation.

" The drawing-room was unlike most apartments which get that name ; I might describe it as a compound of counting-house, tract depôt, and a roomy but cosy-looking sitting room. In one corner sat the patriarch, and opposite to him was a large table and desk covered with papers, indicating a considerable correspondence work—these were occupied by his eldest son, who was sitting near enough to his father to constantly receive his instructions ; ay, and reproof too, unless ' dispatch was the order of the day,' in everything that was being done. The old man did not hesitate, even in my presence, to push on work. He said, ' I can't bear to see time wasted—our William takes twice the time to tie up a parcel that I could do it in ; of course he does it neater, but then my way would serve all the purpose and thus leave him time to do something of more importance !' This

---

* The portrait we give in this volume, printed by the Woodbury process, is from a photograph taken at the same sitting as the one here referred to ; it is equally faithful as to features, but lacks the genial smile which always beamed when Mr. Livesey was in health.

referred to a parcel of pamphlets, tracts, and handbills, which Mr. Livesey instructed his son to select and present to me.* I ought to say that at the extreme
end of the room from that at which father and son were sitting, was a lofty open
sideboard with several shelves, on which were piled pamphlets, tracts, and handbills, and from this large stock I got a copy of every publication, including of course
the invaluable ' Malt Liquor Lecture.'

"You do not expect me to report fully the short but interesting conversation I had with the old man ; suffice it to say it was wonderful how he grasped the
exact position of the Temperance movement, and how clear he was as to the present
duties of its leaders.   At parting, he burst into tears, regretting he had not laboured
even harder than he had done, and earnestly urging me to ' *work harder than ever.*'†
A farewell ' *God bless you* ' from myself ended a most interesting and affecting
interview."

It has been well said that ' the soul never grows old.'   The body—the
material instrument through which the soul manifests itself in this life—droops,
decays, and finally returns to its native dust; but mind, being superior to the
deteriorating influences of time, is unaffected by those changes which weaken the
body and incapacitate it for labour.   Mr. Livesey's latter days fully illustrated
the truth that mind is superior to matter.   Lecturing at the Great Central
Hall, London, on the 20th of October, 1885, Mr. Edward Grubb mentioned that
the last time he called upon Mr. Livesey he found the old gentleman sitting in
his easy chair, carefully wrapped up.   During the interview, the old veteran lifted
up his hands, which were encased in warm gloves, and remarked that although
they now failed him, and refused to do his bidding, his mind was as clear and
as active as ever.   And in this condition he continued until the crisis came.
Towards the end of August, 1884, certain difficulties which had troubled him for
years culminated, and necessitated a surgical operation.   Mr. Livesey, who submitted to the ordeal without demur, was found by his professional attendants
to be otherwise in perfect health.   For a few days it was hoped by his family
and friends that his long life might be still further protracted ; but the advantages
gained by the operation proved to be only temporary, and on the 1st of September
it became apparent that the end was at hand.   Calm and cheerful, and mindful
to the last of the comforts of his children, relatives, and friends who were
in attendance upon him, Mr. Livesey awaited the great change which is the
common lot of mankind.   "As the end approached," says the Rev. Charles
Garrett, "he fell asleep ; and as the death-dews gathered upon his brow, all was
calmness and peace.   When the end came, the eyes opened for a moment, and
the voice whispered, ' *Glory*, glory,' and he was not, for God took him." ‡

In such manner Joseph Livesey—reformer and teacher—passed from earth to
the higher life, during the afternoon of Tuesday, the 2nd of September, 1884.

* I am told that this was a standing jocular remark with the townspeople who went to visit
the old man. On one person saying he had been to see Mr. Livesey, the other would remark,
"I know two things you would get." "How do you know that?" "Why, every one gets a
double dose,—a kindly lecture and a parcel of tracts." "That's just what I got." At the Post
Office also, when the servant, of an evening, used to take up a large basketful of book-post
packets of tracts (Mr. Livesey being frequently in the habit of dispatching 50 or 100 a day,
addressed by himself), the officials would remark, "Another lot."

† At the London Conference of the British Temperance League (1884) Mr. Thomas Walmsley,
an old Prestonian worker, related that Mr. Livesey, whom he had visited shortly before, seized
hold of his hands, and exclaimed—"Thomas, what I regret the most is *the little I have done in
my life.* Oh! do work as much as ever you possibly can." (See Appendix, 138.)

‡ "The Faithful Servant and His Reward." London : 1884.

As Mr. Livesey was born on the 5th of March, 1794, he died in his 91st year. 'The friend of the poor' would perhaps be his most appropriate epitaph. His life was productive of great good in his own day; but the full measure of its beneficent influence will only be realized by a future generation, wise enough to put his precepts into general practice.

WHEN Faith and Love, which parted from thee never,
    Had ripened thy just soul to dwell with God,
    Meekly thou didst resign this earthly load
Of death, called life, which us from life doth sever.
Thy works, and alms, and all thy good endeavour,
    Stayed not behind, nor in the grave were trod;
    But, as Faith pointed with her golden rod,
    Followed thee up to joy and bliss for ever.
Love led them on; and Faith, who knew them best
    Thy handmaids, clad them o'er with purple beams
    And azure wings, that up they flew so drest,
And speak the truth of thee on glorious themes
    Before the Judge; who thenceforth bid thee rest,
    And drink thy fill of pure immortal streams.—MILTON.

AUTOBIOGRAPHY OF JOSEPH LIVESEY.

CHAPTER I.

In sitting down to write my autobiography, as promised, I feel several discouragements. In going over the events and collecting the incidents connected with so long a life, it is very difficult to make a selection such as shall not omit what would be deemed by my friends as important, and yet not to tire them with details of little moment ; and to do this without exposing myself to the charge of vanity and egotism is still more difficult. Next, my memory of late has become very much impaired, and this increases the labour required, to be certain that facts, events, and dates are truly narrated. Fortunately, I have the benefit of a very copious memoranda, which I made while residing nine weeks at a Water Cure Establishment on the Rhine, in the year 1853, which has been laid by, unperused till now. The following is the first paragraph, giving the reasons for drawing up the sketch, which was not intended to appear during my lifetime, and little did I think that fourteen years would elapse before it would be disturbed.

" My experience of sixty years may possibly, if placed upon record, be of some service to those who are but just beginning to tread the active stage of existence. If it should convey to such, useful hints that may enable them to escape any of the ills of life, and prompt to a course of virtue and usefulness, I shall be well rewarded for the trouble of my narrative ; and, if not, the writing will beguile away a few hours, which I now find myself, from infirmity, unable to appropriate to a more useful purpose ; and, at any rate, these memoirs will be read with some interest by a few whose friendship I have had the happiness to enjoy. It may also be pleasing to my numerous family to have condensed, ready to their hands, the most striking incidents of my life, some of which they may have never heard of or forgotten ; and, possibly, they may here trace some of the advantages which they at present enjoy over the children of many other families."

I drew my first breath in a humble cottage in the village of Walton, on the 5th March, 1794. This village is beautifully situated on the banks of the Ribble, one mile and a half from Preston. I was born in that part called "Walton Cop," and there I resided in three different houses, almost contiguous, till after my marriage, when I came to Preston, in the winter of 1815. I was named after my grandfather, Joseph Livesey, my other grandfather being William Ainsworth. They were both small farmers in the township of Walton ; the former occupying a farm in Toad House Lane ; the latter, one called " Water-

ing Pool," near Tardy Gate. My father's name was John ; my mother's Jennet.
I never had a sister, and only one brother—William, who died early. My
parents both died of consumption, in the year 1801, within ten weeks of each
other, leaving me at the age of seven without father or mother, sister or brother.
I was taken by my grandfather, Livesey, whose family consisted of my grandmother, and one uncle, Thomas, and I remained with him, as I shall show, till
I was married.

My father, from the time of his marriage, resided in the same row of houses
in which I was born. He was a hand-loom cloth manufacturer, had his warehouse close by, and, of course, was among the earliest makers of cotton goods
in this district. He had received a good education, as is evident from his productions at school, which I have still in my keeping. Being taken away in the
prime of life, at a short notice, nothing remained but for my grandfather to
carry on the business in which he had already invested all he could spare. I
was taken to my grandfather's farm, but as he had now the cotton business in
hand, he shortly relinquished farming, and came and resided at my late father's
house in the village. Here, his troubles, poor old man ! commenced. He knew
nothing of the business, and my uncle, upon whom most of the management
devolved, knew as little. Either from "bad times" or bad management, or
both, the concern came to grief. I don't recollect how long, but I suppose they
did not carry on the business more than three or four years. Their embarrassments kept increasing ; and I remember well the old man, on a Tuesday night,
upon the return of Thomas with unfavourable reports from Manchester market,
crying like a child. Young as I was, I busied myself in the warehouse, sometimes at the warping-mill, sometimes helping to hook pieces, or weighing out
the weft. The "moutre" trade was then carried on to a great extent, and the
disputes with weavers and threats of " bating" were frequent. Both yarn and
cloth were enormously dear, so there was a great temptation for weavers to sell
cops, to take off "half beers," and, by obliterating the "smits," to get longer
fents than they were allowed. Not long ago, there resided in Preston a female
who had a cambric petticoat, the material of which she said she bought of my
father, at seven shillings a yard. Warping only was done on the premises ;
winding, sizing, and weaving were all done out. Ridgway's and Ainsworth's
waggons (bleachers) used to call weekly for the goods. It was about this time
that Mr. Bashall commenced manufacturing at Bamber Bridge, and he and my
father, I understand, were on friendly terms ; and the success of one family
compared with the other, having about equal means to start with, forms an
instructive contrast. My poor old grandfather lost all he had—the savings of
his farming and his industry—and the only consolation that remained connected with his misfortunes was, that he was just able to pay, in full, all his
creditors. In those days, all the small farms in Walton, Penwortham, and the
adjoining country places, were "weaving farms," having a "shop" attached, to
hold a certain number of looms ; and as grandfather and uncle had both learned
the trade, nothing now remained for them but to return to the loom, and for
many years they had to rely on this alone for a livelihood.

From this period, being then about ten or eleven years of age, I remained with them till I was twenty-one. For sometime my chief employment was winding weavers' bobbins. My grandmother grew infirm and died soon after, and as we were too poor to keep a servant, and having no female help except to wash the clothes, and occasionally to clean up, I may be said to have been the housekeeper. We lived in a house of £5 a year. From necessity I became pretty proficient in all kinds of labour connected with domestic life, and I never regretted this, for in speaking to the poor during my visitations, I have found my early experience of great service; and in the event of any reverse of fortune, I always felt that I was prepared to live where others would be beset with difficulties, or perhaps starve. The cellar where my grandfather and uncle worked held three looms, and so soon as I was able I was put to weaving; and for seven years I worked in a corner of that damp cellar, really unfit for any human being to work in—the fact that from the day it was plastered to the day I left it the mortar was soft—water remaining in the walls—was proof of this. And to make it worse, the Ribble and the Darwen sometimes overflowed their banks, and inundated this and all the cellars adjoining. It has to me often been a subject of perfect surprise how I bore up and escaped with my life, sitting all the long day close to a damp wall. And I can only suppose that this was counteracted, in a great measure, by the incessant action of almost every muscle of the body, required in weaving. "All fours" never cease action on the part of the hand-loom weaver. Yet, it is very probable that the four rheumatic fevers that I have had to endure, and the seven years' chronic rheumatism in my lower joints—rendering me unable to walk without great pain —which followed, had their remote cause in that miserable place. I remember taking our pieces to Messrs. Horrocks and Jacson's warehouse, and I never wove for any firm but this, and the late Mr. Timothy France, of Mount Street.

I never regretted that poverty was my early lot, and that I was left to make my own way in the world. It was here, I believe, I learned to feel for the poor, to acquire the first lessons of humanity, and to cultivate my own energies as the best means (in my case the only means) of self-advancement. Up to this time I had had little schooling, only about sufficient to read the Testament, and write, and count a little. This cellar was my college, the "breast-beam" was my desk, and I was my own tutor. Many a day and night have I laboured to understand Lindley Murray, and at last, by indomitable perseverance, what long appeared a hopeless task, was accomplished without aid from any human being. Anxious for information, and having no companions from whom I could learn anything, I longed for books, but had no means with which to procure them. There was no public library, and publications of all kinds were expensive; and, if I could succeed in borrowing one, I would devour it like a hungry man would his first meal. Indeed, few of our young men can have any idea of the contrast betwixt the present and the past, as to the advantages of gaining knowledge. At the period I refer to there were no National Schools, no Sunday Schools, no Mechanics' Institutions, no Penny Publications, no cheap Newspapers, no Free Libraries, no Penny Postage, no Temperance Societies, no Tea Parties, no

Young Men's Christian Associations, no People's Parks, no Railways, no gas, no anything in fact that distinguishes the present time in favour of the improvement and enjoyment of the masses. Most of the articles of necessity for a poor man's home, during the war with France, were nearly double their present price, and all felt the pressure of the times. My only pocket money, when a lad, was "the Sunday penny;" and I have a distinct recollection how proud I felt when I went among my companions on the Sunday afternoon with three-pence in my pocket, which was my increased weekly allowance.

In a few years after I was tasked to do so much, and all that I could earn over I was allowed for myself. It was then I got my grammar, exercises, and key, Cann's Bible with references, and a few other books, as my means would allow. I seldom got a meal without a book open before me at the same time, and I managed to do what I have never seen any other weaver attempt—to read and weave at the same time. For hours together I have done this, and without making bad work. The book was laid on the breast-beam, with a cord slipped on to keep the leaves from rising. Head, hands, and feet, all busy at the same time! I had a restless mind, panting for knowledge, and incapable of inaction; and I remember that sometimes—there being nothing else that I could see out of my window—counting the number of people that passed in an hour, distinguishing males from females. That part of the loom and the wall nearest my seat were covered with marks, which I had made to assist me to remember certain facts, and these hieroglyphics were there when I left. This cellar is only a short walk from where I am now writing, and I feel a pleasure in making a call at this hallowed spot. The privations connected with poverty, in my case, admitted of no exceptions. The day seemed too short for my love of reading, and as often as I could, I remained to read after uncle and grandfather had retired to bed; but I was allowed no candle, and for hours I have read by the glare of the few embers left in the fire-grate, with my head close to the bars. It was a fault I had then, and which has continued with me through life, to skim over a book. If I took one up I seldom felt content to lay it down till I had reached the last page. Looking back sixty years, I cannot help constantly exclaiming "What a contrast there is betwixt the present advantages of poor people and their children compared to that period!" And, I may add, "How little do the wealthy really know of the suffering and adversities of those who all their lives have to toil for their daily bread!" While thousands of costly volumes lie dormant, unopened and unread by their owners, the backless volume of a borrowed book was read by me with eagerness; and this doubtless has been the case with many others. What would I not have given at that day to have had the opportunity afforded by the Preston Institution—to have availed myself of its valuable library—a privilege too much undervalued by the working-classes of the present time. And yet it is a question, in many cases, whether want or plenty makes the most sterling character. My first bookcase consisted of two slips of wood, value about eightpence, hung to the wall by a cord at each end, and the first work placed upon these anti-aristocrat shelves was "Jones' Theological Repository," a periodical of a number of volumes, which I had got at second-hand. I shall never forget, as I descended the cellar stairs, how I sometimes turned back to look and admire my newly-acquired treasure !

So far my history is of a cold and chilling character, and the reader will feel it more than I did myself. I had always a hope that better days would come. Surely, thought I, when looking at my condition, I am not doomed always to spend my days on the loom ; and brighter days *did come*, as my subsequent history will show. I made several early efforts to get off the loom. I went to learn the shuttle making business, but did not succeed. I followed, at one time, " twisting in " for weavers, and in this I succeeded better. Once I tried for a situation as jobber, lost a week, but got no wages. Naturally precocious, I was always thinking of the future. When reading the Scriptures, I often pictured myself in the pulpit dividing the text after the manner of ministers ; and, at a very premature age, I thought of the miseries of single blessedness, and wished for a house of my own. With the country habits of my uncle and grandfather, there was little that was interesting in the way of social intercourse among us, and not caring to mix much with the lads of the village, I was a good deal isolated and left to my own resources. I never could join them in their rough sports; and by the fighting parties, for which the village was famous, I was always put upon and called " soft," and, of course, had to endure many humiliations. I generally made the girls my companions, in preference to the boys.

Still, at the earlier part of this period, I had my play and favourite amusements as well as others. With the present Mr. George Longworth (late cryer of the court), and the late Mr. Robert Snell, and others, I used to play marbles, but nearly always to a disadvantage. Lads and lasses together, we used to romp, and play at " hare and hounds," " prison bars," " hide and seek," " tig and touchwood," and in-doors at " forfeits." We used to beguile the evening hours in telling about " Jack the giant killer," and all the other legendary tales. We all believed in the existence of bogies, and the exploits of the " Bannister Doll," a noted Walton bogie that had some connection with the Bannister Hall Printworks. Thomas Jolly's house was our chief rendezvous ; with their own large family, and the collection of so many other children, the crowding and the noise was such that Mrs. Jolly many a time got out of patience with us, and drove us all home. We use to go a nutting in Cuerdale woods, but always in fear of the keeper. I once had a day's hunting, and only once ; following the hounds all day in my clogs, I never desired a repetition of this sport. I delighted to wade in the river, and fishing was my favourite sport. For hours together I could sit at the Ribble side watching the swimmer, if I did not get a single bite. In the season, I laid night-lines in different parts of the river—at Cuerdale, at the " Church deeps," and above and below Walton Bridge ; but sometimes I had the mortification to find that both lines and fish had been taken away. During my boyhood, I remember one visit to Preston which had a special interest. It was at the Guild of 1802. I was then eight years of age, and in Cheapside, a relative of mine seated me on his shoulder while the imposing procession passed by. Mr. Watson and Mr. John Horrocks had then introduced cotton spinning into the town, and this rising and profitable business was strikingly represented at this gala. The following notice is from Mr. Hardwick's "History of Preston :"—

The gentlemen's procession commenced on Monday morning, immediately after breakfast; it was preceded by the Marshal, armed cap-a-pie, on horse-back, trumpeters on horse-back, &c.; then came twenty-four young, blooming, handsome women, belonging to the different cotton mills, dressed in a uniform of peculiar beauty and simplicity. Their dress consisted wholly of the manufacture of the town. Their petticoats were of fine white calico; the head-dress was a kind of blue feathered wreath, formed very ingeniously of cotton, so as to look like a garland; each girl carried in her hand the branch of an artificial cotton tree, as the symbol of her profession. The gentlemen walked in pairs, preceded by Lord Derby and the Hon. T. Erskine. They amounted to about four hundred, consisting of all the principal noblemen, gentlemen, merchants, and manufacturers of this and the neighbouring counties. On Tuesday was the ladies' procession. A numerous body of gentlemen, holding white rods in their hands, walked before, and filed off, making a line on each side of the street, through which the ladies were to pass. The girls from the cotton manufactory led the van as before; afterwards came the ladies, two and two. The Rev. Mr. Shuttleworth, rector, and Mrs. Grimshaw, the mayoress, and queen of the guild, walked first; after them came the Countess of Derby and Lady Charlotte Hornby; Lady Stanley, daughter of the Earl of Derby, and Lady Ann Lindsay; Lady Susan Carpenter, and the Hon. Mrs. Cawthorne; Lady Gerard, and Lady Houghton; Lady Jerningham, and Lady Fitzgerald. Several other baronets' ladies, and the rest of the other ladies, followed, walking in pairs; in all, near four hundred in number, consisting of the most distinguished ladies in this and the neighbouring counties. They were all superbly dressed, and adorned with a profusion of the richest jewels.

It has been this *cotton* which has converted our aristocratic town of six or seven thousand into a hive of industry, with a population now approaching 100,000.

Among the places where drunkenness prevailed, I am sorry to say, Walton was no exception. The weavers crowded the public-houses, and they regularly kept " St. Monday." The villagers all thought well of drink, and at the dame's school, kept by Jenny Holmes, to which I was first sent, there was spiced ale or wine 'at the Christmas banquet, and the little folks, I remember, were showing off by imitating the drunkard. We had a sad wet lot connected with the Church. The grave-digger and his father were both drunkards; ringers and singers, both were hard drinkers, and I remember the latter singing in my father's kitchen, one Christmas Day morning, in a most disgraceful condition. The parish clerk was no exception. When the Church clock was standing for want of winding-up in a morning, as was often the case, the remark was " the clerk was drunk again last night." The hospitality of my father's house always included the bottle. One of my uncles (Ainsworth), a timber dealer in the village, a fine healthy man, killed himself in the prime of life with drinking, and left a large family unprovided for.

I was surrounded by mental darkness and vice, without the companionship of congenial spirits, but, cherishing the aspirations of future advancement, it was to me a great consolation and a source of future hope to become acquainted with a family of the name of Portlock, the heads of which and some of the members were decidedly religious. I began then, when about sixteen, to feel the value of existence, the importance of sacred things, and to enjoy the comforts of religious and friendly intercourse.

CHAPTER II.

I must bespeak the patience of my readers while I linger a little longer in my native village, Walton. From the time I lost my parents to my removal to "Proud Preston" was fourteen years, and it is not easy to cram the incidents of such a period into a few pages. It will already have been seen that I had hard exercising ground; but still, I think, well fitted, in a case like mine, to qualify for the battle of life I had to fight. I referred in my last to the total absence of those conveniences, comforts, and advantages now enjoyed by the working classes, and I may here take up the same tale. For instance, in my young days, there was no water-supply from any public works, and I had to fetch all we needed, for common purposes, from the river; and, as a beverage, from a neighbour's pump. "Kitting" milk had not then been invented, and I had to fetch it daily—about a mile and a half—from "Cockshot Farm," not far from the Brownedge Catholic Chapel. I remember the first coach that ran through Walton; it was called a "boat coach," from its form, and a Mr. Cooper was the proprietor. The inside was not unlike our omnibuses, and the passengers sat on the top without seats. At that time the travelling luxury for common people was the hind part of a waggon drawn by eight horses with stumped tails, at the rate of about two and a half miles in the hour. The wisdom of those times decided that if you cut off the tails of the horses you increased their strength; and though this was an act of great cruelty, having only to be done once, I don't think it was so cruel as the modern fashion of punishing these noble animals, by always "reining up" their heads when at work. A pack of hounds was kept at Walton Hall, by Sir Henry Bold Hoghton, and our gentlemen hunters always cut a dash by appearing in red coats, but our parson always retained his canonical black. At church we had some singular practices. At the close of the forenoon service the sales and other notices were read out in the church-yard. At a wedding the minister was privileged to salute the bride as soon as the ceremony was over, but whether he *always* availed himself of this favour I am not certain. In anticipation of the old ringers being done up (and their habits were no guarantee against this), a new set was formed, and, though only sixteen, I joined them; I rang the second bell. We had fines for being too late, and for other offences, and these accumulated till Christmas. We had no one to teach us better, so we decided to spend the money in a jollification at the White Bull. We had a supper, and afterwards, as much liquor as we pleased; mulled-ale, rum-shrub, and raspberry-brandy, and whatever we pleased to call for. I need not say what was the effect. It is very much to be regretted that even now, for want of better guidance and better instruction, young men in such cases are left to themselves, to indulge in drinking practices that often end in their ruin. Every Sunday, "Watson's Apprentices," as they were called, attended Walton Church. They were workers in the cotton mill, known as "Penwortham Factory," and came in order, under suitable superintendence, wearing a uniform of brown coats, with cuffs and collars of yellow. It was said they were obtained from a Foundling Hospital in London. Many of them were crooked-legged, becoming deformed with having to stop the machinery by placing their knees against it. Sir Henry Bold Hoghton, who resided at Walton Hall, was afflicted with gout, and could scarcely walk. He always came to Church on a cob, but Lady Houghton came in the carriage. When the carriage drove up, we boys, who were sauntering in the church-yard, always ran to see her get out. We had several distinguished families in the village, some of whom will still be remembered. After Sir Henry, who resided at Walton Hall, we had "Squire Ashton," of Walton Lodge; Mr. Charles Swainson, of Cooper Hill; Mr. E. Pedder, of Darwen Bank; Mr. Jacson, father of the late Mr. Charles Jacson, of Preston; Mr. Tongue, father of the late Mr. Tongue, of Forton Cottage; Mr. Fisher, father of the late Mr. John Fisher, of the Lancaster Bank, and his brother Samuel, and others. The most distinguished ladies, all unmarried, were the Misses Sergeant, three sisters, noted for their kindness and benevolence to the poor; the Misses Cooper, the Misses Woodacre, Miss Rhodes, and Miss Barton.

When very young, I remember the Methodists attempting to get a footing in Walton, but with little or no success. They held their meetings in the house of Joseph King, clogger, and I attended some of them. Mrs. King and other females belonging the Society, wore "Quaker bonnets," and I presume, at that time, more respect was paid to the advice of Wesley, by his followers, as to ribbons and dress, and, I hope, smoking and drinking too, than at the present day. I was about seventeen when I became acquainted with Portlock's family. They were Baptists, and very kind to me. I was soon impressed with the importance of religion, and began to attend the Baptist Chapel (Leeming Street, Preston), sometimes the Independent's (then at the North end of Chapel Street), sometimes the Methodist's (then in Back Lane.) Charles, one of their sons, and Thomas Jolly, jun., and I, became close companions. Our souls seemed knit together, and many a happy night have we spent in talking upon religious subjects. The result was that Charles and I were baptized together, I believe, in the year 1811, in the Baptist Chapel, which stood where St. Saviour's has been newly erected. Thomas Jolly was baptized some time after. I felt a strong conviction that I was doing the will of God in this service, though it was in opposition to the wishes and entreaties of my grandfather and other relatives. To me it was a day of great enjoyment. I remember well, after the baptism was over, joining with great fervour in singing the hymn—

> "Jesus, and shall it ever be,
> A mortal man ashamed of Thee;
> Ashamed of Thee whom angels praise,
> Whose glory shines to endless days."

The return of Sunday was to me a feast of good things; all the fervency of youth and the zeal of a new convert were added to a deep conviction of the importance of religion. With what delight did I use to go, in my clogs, to Preston, to the evening prayer meetings held in the vestry! I have still, in my possession, Watt's hymn-book, which I bought at the time. On the inside of the front cover is written, "Joseph Livesey's Book, 1811." On a blank leaf is

the following, " Is any merry, let him sing Psalms. *James v.* 13." And, at the
end, is this verse—

> " Hope is my helmet, faith my shield,
> Thy word, my God—the sword I wield ;
> With sacred truth my loins are girt,
> And holy zeal inspires my heart."

The congregation was too poor to pay a minister; and, at that time, a Mr.
Baker, tailor and draper, regularly officiated as such ; but, unfortunately (I don't
exactly remember the cause), a division ensued ; one part of the people adhering
to Mr. Baker, and the other wishing to get without him ; and this divison
became so strong that, one Sunday morning, the chapel having been locked up
by one party, was broken open with violence by the other. The ordination of
the Rev. Mr. Edwards was about to take place at Accrington, and it was then
agreed to refer the quarrel to the decision of the ministers who would then be
assembled ; but this was attended with no satisfactory result. Sometime after
this I left the Society, and joined what were then called the " Scotch Baptists,"
whose meeting place was in Mr. Charnock's school-room, over the " Horse Shoe
smithy," in Church Street.

I cannot refrain dwelling a moment upon our mission to Accrington on this
unpleasant business. Along with others I walked from Walton ; the distance
would be about 14 miles. The Rev. Mr. Stephens preached the Ordination
Sermon from the text " One is your Master even Christ, and all ye are brethren."
Equality was what I admired, and I was much pleased with the discourse. At
the close of the service it was announced that any one who wished to take
dinner could be accommodated at a certain inn, at 1s. each. But I learnt that
there was a free dinner for the ministers and other rich friends. I felt as one of
the poor who really needed a dinner, and not having a shilling to spare, that the
doctrine of equal brotherhood, though brilliant in the pulpit was not so in " word
and deed." But what offended me most was, that, being allowed to enter the
large room after the dinner, I saw the ministers and other friends enjoying
themselves with their long pipes amid the fumes of tobacco, drinking spirits and
other liquors. Though physically feeble, I was never deficient in moral courage,
and when we were introduced to the rev. gentlemen who were to hear our case,
I could not forbear giving vent to my feelings. I protested against this eating
and drinking, and said that in primitive times men were ordained to the ministry
with " prayer and fasting." A poor, simple, ill-dressed, illiterate, unknown lad
lecturing divines on the primitive duties of self-denial ! A regular laugh was
the response, and indeed what else could be expected ? I believe this exhibition
gave a cast to my mind of which I have never got clear, and I should be glad to
believe that nothing similar is to be met with in the present day.

My mind from this time was directed to religious subjects, and whilst my
connection with the Scotch Baptists was a valuable defence against all the
worldly temptations with which youth is surrounded, in another respect it was
rather a misfortune. They attached so much importance to what they called
" soundness in the faith," that it was with reluctance they held fellowship with
others who did not hold the same belief. There were but a few in the society,

and imbibing the same views, my religious intercourse was greatly circumscribed. I became the zealous advocate of opinions rather than the promoter of charity among all good people. At any cost I would "stand up for the truth." I gave my mind to controversial theology, and spent far too much time in settling (as I thought) disputed points—especially those betwixt Calvinists and Arminians, Unitarians and Trinitarians—points which have occupied polemic champions through all ages and are yet unsettled. There was what would be called a "self-confidence" about me that was not inviting to others. I remember getting a severe rebuke from a minister in Manchester. In a long controversial letter I wrote to him, I used the words, "I never see anything wrong, but I am determined to set it right." Coming from a youth of about 18, it was not very modest, and the minister at that time performed a friendly service in giving me a check which I never forgot.

I now come to an interesting period. Whatever people may say, I believe there are very few who don't think something of wedding before they are out of their teens, however long it may be before their wishes are accomplished. My habit was always to act with promptitude : some would say with precipitancy. I never could endure delays with anything in prospect. No doubt there are reasons,—in some cases strong reasons—against early marriages ; but on the other hand, there are stronger against late ones. No age can be fixed upon as a standard, for almost in every case there are peculiar circumstances that have to be considered. But with some experience, and a long range of observation, I have come to the conclusion that the advantages are greatly in favour of persons marrying young ; of course, making a judicious choice, and being prepared with means to start with comfort, out of debt, and with a fair prospect of resources to meet eventualities. It was not personal acquaintance that decided my choice. I heard of Miss Williams as an amiable, religious girl, and before seeing her, my choice was decided, provided I could obtain her consent. I don't recommend such a course to others, for though in my case it turned out everything I could wish, to decide so momentous a question without a more extensive knowledge and more opportunities of knowing each other, would in many cases be attended with the worst results. Her father was a Welshman, a master rigger, in Liverpool ; he had married a second time, and as the daughter had no peace or comfort at home with her stepmother, she left, and when I first heard of her, she was living at Mr. Jackson's, an intimate friend of her father's, who kept an earthenware warehouse and china shop in Swan Street, Manchester. The family were "Scotch Baptists," worshipping in Cold House Chapel, Shude Hill, and she was a member of the same church. Thus, as it were, exiled from home, she might almost be considered an orphan like myself. On my first visit I attended their meeting, and as I was in the habit of giving exhortations at Preston, I was invited to do the same, and she has often told me since, that it was my speaking that prepared her more than anything else, to give a favourable response when I "popped the question." We were thus fixed 30 miles from each other, and with the exception of about three visits, all the "love-making," which lasted about a year, was done by long sheets of paper filled to every corner.

There were no railways then; I had to walk all that distance, and I well remember one of the times that, having got as far as Bolton, 20 miles, and it was getting late, I felt unable to proceed. There was a mail coach, and the question was betwixt taking the mail, and staying at Bolton and proceeding next morning. Of course I wanted to reach Manchester, and out of my poor means I had to pay 5s. for riding outside the mail, a distance of only 11 miles. Having no means to furnish a house, if there had been no other reason, I was obliged to wait until I came of age. A relation of mine had bequeathed to me about £30 to be paid then, and with this I furnished a nice little cottage in Walton, rent £7 a year, with a garden attached. I used to attend sales and purchase articles of furniture as cheap as I could, regardless of the jokes and taunts that neigh-bours would pass upon me; and I hold it to be right that no man should take a wife till he has a house furnished ready for her to come to. To commence in lodgings, as some newly married pairs do, is abominable. The time was fixed, and on the 30th May, 1815, without the attendance of "ten carriages," or even "one," the display of "orange blossoms," or "Honiton lace," in St. Peter's Church, Liverpool, the knot was tied. It was a very quiet affair; the parson took us into the vestry, which is a very unusual thing, and gabbled over the service as quickly as possible. I remember paying him with a 5s. piece, and afterwards remarking what a cheap wife.I had got. Mr. Williams, her father, gave a supper in the evening to a few friends. I was turned 21, and Miss Williams 19 and a half; and though very delicate looking at the time, it has surprised us both, how much she improved and the great amount of work she has gone through. There was no driving off to spend the "honeymoon;" our "wedding tour" was from Liverpool to Walton next morning; and I need not say that when we made our appearance in the village we received the congratu-lations of our neighbours, and no doubt many strange remarks were made by the females, looking on, as to the wisdom of my choice. Here we both settled down to our work, Joseph to his loom, and Jane to her wheel; and though as low in means as most people to start with, we have "lived and loved together," now more than 52 years, never once having reason to regret the step we took. Some of the incidents connected with this long period, the large family we have brought up, and the favourable change which took place in our circumstances and position will be-noticed in future chapters.

CHAPTER III.

The last chapter left me at Walton, just settled with my dear wife, who has been a treasure to me, as I stated, for nearly fifty-three years. Our cottage, though small, was like a palace, for none could excel my "Jenny" for cleanli-ness and order. I renovated the garden, and made it a pleasant place to walk in. On the loom I was most industrious, working from early in the morning often till ten, and sometimes later, at night; and she not only did all the house work, but wound the bobbins for three weavers—myself, uncle, and grandfather; and yet, with all this apparently hard lot, these were happy days. Hope springs eternal in the human breast; and young people just beginning life, however poor, if they are united and affectionate, sober and industrious, feel its inspiration, and work on with joyful anticipations of better days. I soon learnt the truth of the old saying, " In taking a wife you had better have a fortune *in* her than *with* her;" and if all men were guided by this, and the females knew it, we should have happier marriages, and the girls would aim to acquire *substantial* instead of *artificial* attractions.

Living in Walton, for various reasons, was found to be inconvenient, and we removed to Preston in less than a year. Our first house was in Park Street (at the back of Paradise Street), at 2s. 6d. a week. Here our first child was born, bringing with him a little brother. It was in our wedding year that the cursed Corn Laws were passed, the House of Commons being surrounded by soldiers with drawn bayonets. Under the blighting influence of this measure, food was enormously dear, and the price of labour much depressed. In such circumstances, to have *two* additional mouths to fill all at once was rather discouraging, but one died soon after birth, and the other is now in his fifty-second year. We struggled on for some months, when unexpectedly, in the autumn of 1816, an incident occurred which gave an important turn to our affairs.' My health was bad, the house was not adapted for weaving in, and a family coming on, our prospects just then were very gloomy. The turning point was a trivial circumstance, which it may be interesting to relate, as it has led to results of which I had not the remotest idea. The doctor I consulted said I ought to live better, and that a little cheese and bread and a sup of malt liquor (the old remedy !) about eleven o'clock in the forenoon, would be of great service. I forget whether we got the malt liquor, but I distinctly recollect our purchasing a bit of cheese. It was of a common quality, sold at 7d. or 8d. a pound. Just at that time (Oct. 11) was the Lancaster cheese fair, and I heard some people stating that prices had declined to about 50s. the cwt. Calculating this, I found it was only 5d. per lb.; and it occurred to me, that if I could purchase a whole cheese and divide it among our neighbours, it would be doing them a good turn and be a saving to ourselves. Farmers then stood with cheese in the market. I went to enquire the prices, and met with a farmer of the name of Bradley, from the Hill House, Wheeton, who had just two cheeses unsold. To finish, he offered to take 4¾d. per lb. for them. This, I thought, was a fine chance, but where was the money to pay for them? I had none; indeed, I remember on one occasion, that we had to wait till I returned from the warehouse with my piece money before we could raise the necessaries for our next meal. John Burnett (a good friend to everybody in time of need) kept a draper's shop in Friargate, and I stepped down to tell him the case, and he at once lent me a sovereign, with which I paid for the two cheeses. In a short time these were in Park Street, and what a sight! Two whole cheeses on a weaver's table ! What was to be done as to the division and distribution ? 1

told the neighbours of my achievement; each consented to take a piece, and in order to cover any loss by weighing out, they paid me 5½d. per lb. John Burnett also kindly lent me a scale and weights. Persevering as I always was, after the neighbours were served, I took a stool, with the scale and cheese, and stood during the remainder of the Saturday afternoon at the bottom of Vauxhall Road, and sold a quantity in small pieces. I had still some left; but, in the evening, I counted up my money and weighed what was remaining, and found to my surprise that I had made about eighteen-pence profit. Being more than I could have made by weaving in the time, I was quite lifted up, and on the Monday morning, determined to finish, I went hawking the remnant till all was sold. I then resumed my weaving, but the people in the town came through the week for my cheap cheese, so that I was induced the next Saturday to renew the attempt, Mr. Burnett finding me the means.

For some time I continued weaving through the week, and cut cheese out on the Saturday, first at a corner of Syke Hill, and then in the Market Place. Here I fixed my table, and produced considerable excitement by cutting out cheese at 5½d. per lb., the general price being 7d. I soon succeeded in retailing as much as three hundred-weight in a day. Shortly after this my wife took the table, and I became a sort of wholesale man, selling whole cheeses, and some-times a hundred-weight. She was quite as active, as persevering, and as successful as myself. Winter though it was, we stood out in all weathers, caring little for present comfort, in hope of future success. I then began to attend Chorley, Blackburn, and Wigan markets, and thus filled up the week. I gave up the loom, and made a present of it to a poor man in Queen Street, named Joseph Woodruff, and some years after I sought it out, gave him a sovereign for it, and out of the various parts a writing table was made, on which I am now correcting this article. Turn it over and you will see the several pieces that constituted the cradle of my future usefulness; and when I am in the grave, may this remind my children that their father was a poor man, and that of all the duties incumbent upon them they should never forget the poor! Seeing my success, I had two or three friends who lent me money on interest, with which to keep up my stock. It will be remembered that there were then no railways, and when, in addition to the other markets, I began to attend Bolton, (20 miles,) I walked there, stood market, got dinner in the street, and walked back the same day. By and bye, I got a pony ("Billy,") and began to go into the country among the farmers to buy their cheese. I was my own ostler, for I did not spend a penny that I could spare; and I remember I used to think it very hard, after returning from Bolton quite fatigued, when seated in the corner, to have to go to the stable to clean and feed the pony. For twenty years I scarcely missed a Monday going to Bolton, first walking, then on horseback, and afterwards in a gig; for, next to Preston, it was the best market I had. Till 1824, when a part of the Preston new Corn Exchange was allotted for the sale of cheese, I stood on the Saturday for eight years, along with other cheese dealers, in the street, near the Castle Inn, Cheapside. Imbued as we all were with the old delusive notion that drink would keep the cold out, we used to run across the Market Place to Mrs. Rigby's, the Blue Anchor, who was noted for her good twopence-halfpenny ale. While on the one hand I was kept from going to excess, on the other I fear that my example induced the others to go, and once there, they would sometimes remain till they were intoxicated. Cheese buying in the country, too, was a dangerous business, the farmers generally keeping the bottle to bring out over making a bargain. Many have been ruined, and it is a mercy that neither I nor any of my sons were ever overcome by it. Sometimes I would make a venture to a distant place, to Ulverston for instance; and I remember leaving Ulverston one evening to catch a coach at Levens Bridge, when I had to go through a district in which I was quite a stranger. It came on dark, with a heavy dew. Not knowing where I was, nor what course to pursue, I kept on the road till I came to a farm house. I was afraid to knock at the door lest I should be misunderstood, and lest some dog might be within, so I quietly got into an outbuilding, and laid on the hay (I cannot say I slept) till break of day, when I crept out, nobody being the wiser, and found my way to Levens Bridge. On another occasion, going on foot over the Eleven-mile Sands, from Hest Bank, where so many have been drowned, I had nearly been overtaken by the tide. I saw it rolling in westward, and I ran east with all the speed of which I was capable, and recovered the land, but had a very narrow escape. These are a few incidents connected with my early experience in the cheese trade. This business for fifty-one years has gradually increased, especially since several of my sons have taken a part, and whose exertions have contributed very much to our success. For most of that time, it has had a larger connection than any similar establishment in North Lancashire.

Though almost interdicted, I cannot do justice to my feelings if I do not say a few words as to the excellencies of my dear wife. In our early struggles, when commencing business out of nothing, she was not only my counsellor in difficulties, but an active and efficient helper to the extent of, and even beyond her power. She was no lady wife; though respectably connected, and accustomed to plenty before marriage, she willingly shared my poverty and privations, and bore a full part of our burdens. She shared my joys and more than shared my sorrows, for she wiped them away. Whenever I was cast down she was the one to revive my spirits. For a long time she did all the house work as well as attending to business, and she would sit up past midnight making and mending the children's clothes. And when she first got a servant, and, indeed, ever since, her ideas of cleanliness are so extreme, that she would always put a hand to herself. No pen could do justice in describing the sympathy she showed towards every sufferer that came within her reach; nor set forth her willingness to undergo any toil to give them relief. If ever a " good mother " existed she deserves that name. No labour was ever too much, no anxiety too great, or sacrifice too severe to provide for the wants of her children, to get them well ducated, and to bring them up respectably. Her motherly kindness never waned, and never will; for, to this day, her happiness is bound up with the happiness and well-doing of her family. Though delicate from the first, the amount of endurance she has manifested is truly wonderful. If ever we had a bit of a tiff (and these are sometimes useful in clearing the connubial atmosphere), it was almost always about her working too hard ; and yet, I am strongly inclined to think that this exercise, and the pleasure she had in seeing her house and children nice, have contributed far more to her lengthened life than the opposite would have done. A lady's life of soft indulgence, rising late in the morning, lolling on a sofa most of the forenoon reading novels, with little exercise, fed with rich food, and pampered with delicacies—these have killed many a thousand with better constitutions than Mother Livesey's. One day I received this positive injunction from her : " See thou sayest nothing about *me*." We always *thou'd* each other, and, for equals, I am fond of this Quaker's style. However, I have ventured to state the above, for which I may perhaps get a " curtain lecture," but I know it will be short and sweet.

This may not be an improper time for noticing our family. I was always fond of children, and am so to the present day, and hence, I was not like some fathers, who are troubled when the "little strangers " make their appearance. If the man is "blessed that has his quiver full of them," I may, at any rate, claim a share in that blessing. Every two years, as a rule, brought an addition to our numbers—thirteen in all—and, without any choice, the boys greatly predominated—ten of one sort and three of the other. Four died in infancy, and nine remain, eight sons and one daughter. Mother often used to pray that she might be spared to see her youngest child grown up, and all settled in life ; and her desire in these respects has been realized. However, I find I must curb any inclination to enter upon details, for a full narrative of all the events and circumstances, enjoyments and disappointments, successes and reverses, connected with half a century's experience in bringing up so large a family, would more than fill a three-volume treatise. Suffice it to say that the good has greatly predominated over the evil ; the bright over the gloomy. Mother is proud of her family, and well she may ; there are not many at our age who have eight sons, all grown up, the youngest thirty-two, and the eldest nearly fifty-two, and all doing well ; and the position of our daughter, the ninth, is equally satisfactory. Seven out of the nine are married, and, counting the grand-children, we find they number twenty-seven. I enter this week upon my 75th year, and Mrs. L. is less than two years of the same age. I said the four we lost died in their infancy, and it is remarkable that since 1840, now twenty-seven years, we have not had a single death in our family, either of children or grand-children. Some couples feel it a hard task to have the charge of a small family of three or four children, and some parents I have known almost at their wit's end with a single son, as to fixing him to a trade. How would such manage if they had eight boys to provide for? Our last little girl, Priscilla, was a great favourite, and as I was proud of them all, I got a friend one day, Mr. Edward Finch, to make a sketch of the family group—then ten in number—in the drawing-room ; the father sitting, with nine children, round the table, according to ages, reading, and the mother close by, in the rocking-chair, with her little darling on her knee. This I have preserved, and, if I am spared to finish this memoir, I intend to get it engraved as a frontispiece.

There are very few families, even among the wealthy, which have not had to lament the profligacy of some of their sons, and I don't know a greater trouble that can come to parents than to see the objects of their brightest hopes become pests in society, the reputation of the family being tarnished by those who ought to do it honour. We have, fortunately, been saved any such infliction. If I were to name what I think has mostly contributed to this result, so far as we have been concerned, I would say that, in the first place, as soon as ever their progress in education would admit, if not before, I accustomed them all to *work*. Every one, so soon as he was able to do anything, was put to some kind of employment, and this, in training children, I deem of great importance. Idleness, whether in young or old, nearly always leads to evil. Next; they were not sent from home, either to get educated or learn professions or businesses; and hence they were not exposed to the numerous temptations which are always surrounding young people, unshielded by the watchful care of parents. To this there was a slight exception, but not of long continuance. I deem the watchful eye of the parents of great importance as a protection to youth, and I can trace the ruin of numerous young men, most promising at one time, entirely to their being sent from home at an age the most dangerous—some to college, and some to trades. In the third place, at home, they had not only good lessons given them but good examples; and, as it respects drink, even before we became teetotalers, we kept none in the house, and it was scarcely ever seen on the table. Water or milk was our invariable beverage at meals. Since then my 37 and Mrs. L.'s 35 years' teetotalism have benefited them much. Being so numerous, they were company for each other, without seeking for companions elsewhere; and perhaps I ought to add that I myself was their companion. I always took delight in their company; I used to play with them, run with them, romp with them, and, when sitting by the fireside, sometimes I should have one on each knee, and one or two climbing up the chair back, perhaps combing my hair or pulling my whiskers. While we allowed nothing that was vicious or unseemly, we put as few restraints as possible upon their youthful vivacity; no doubt, this endeared them more to home. Thus, being in contact with us constantly, they naturally imbibed, to some extent, the habits of carefulness, economy, steadiness, and industry which they saw in their parents. Then as to businesses; I created trades for most of them myself. The cheese trade kept expanding, so that it afforded an opening for at least three, or more of them, as they grew up. In 1832, I commenced the printing business, and in 1844, the *Preston Guardian* newspaper, and these found employment for others. One learnt to be an engineer, and the rest have been provided for without much inconvenience. I intended to refer to the great change which has taken place in the town of Preston since my first coming to it, and to some other topics, but these must stand over till next chapter.

CHAPTER IV.

It was my fortune, or perhaps misfortune, to commence married life at a time of all others the least encouraging to persons in the humble walks of life, dependent upon their own exertions. It would be difficult to convince the present generation of the hardships endured in the past—from about the years 1810 to 1832, and indeed, with the interval of a few good harvest years, to 1846. When the temporary peace was made in 1813, and after the defeat of Napoleon at Waterloo, the final one, in 1815, instead of "peace and plenty," as everybody expected, it turned out to be *peace and poverty*. The long Peninsular war, and the war with America, had exhausted the resources of the nation; and what was worse than all, just at the time when we might have been benefitted by the free intercourse of nations, extension of trade, and a supply of cheap food for the people, the ruling party resolved upon the mad policy of protection, which goaded on a starving people almost to rebellion. At one time, oatmeal was £6 a load, and I well remember flour selling at 2lbs. for a shilling. The average prices of wheat were—

In 1810........	106s. per quarter.	In 1812........	125s. per quarter.
In 1811........	94s. ,,	In 1813........	108s. ,,

When peace was made prices came down rapidly, and the landed interest being in the ascendant in Parliament, the Corn Laws were passed to keep up prices by preventing foreign importations. The indecent haste with which the bill was passed was calculated to arouse the opposition of the people as much as the measure itself. If we want a proof of the wantonness of *class legislation*, of the regardlessness of the rights of the people, and of the sacrifice, even of common decency at the shrine of *selfishness*, we find it in the history of the passing of the Corn Bill. Bills embracing matters of little moment will frequently be months under discussion; but this which seriously affected the interests of every tradesman, and every working-man, and every eater of food in the kingdom, was passed with an almost unexampled precipitancy, as the following statement will show:—

1815.   HOUSE OF COMMONS.
March 1 .... Corn Bill read *first* time.
,,   3 ....   Ditto   *second* time.
,,   6 .... Committee on the Bill.
,, 10 .... Read *third* time and passed !

(Riots in London, and the House of Commons surrounded with soldiers).

HOUSE OF LORDS.
March 13 .... Bill read *first* time.
,, 15 ....   Ditto   *second* time.
,, 20 ....   Ditto   *third* time and passed ! !
,, 23 .... The Bill received the *Royal assent ! ! !*

Thus it was *ten days* only in the *Commons; eight days* in the *Lords;* and, three days after, this monstrous enactment became law by a dash of the *Royal pen !*

The harvest of 1816 was said to be "one of the worst ever known in England, both for quantity and quality." No loaves could be baked, all the wheat being unsound, and flour could only be used by being made into cakes. It was by military force that the people were kept down, mobbing and rioting taking place all over the country. The Luddites, in 1811 and 1812, committed sad depredations in breaking machinery. They mistook the cause of their sufferings; being led to believe that the depression in trade and the reduction in wages were caused by the introduction of machinery. There were alarming riots in Westminster when the Corn Bill passed; at Dartmouth, seven were killed and thirty-five wounded. We, in Preston, had great radical meetings in Taylor's Gardens (where William Street, Oak Street, &c., now stand). In Peter's Field, Manchester, on the very spot where the Free Trade Hall now stands, the "Peterloo" tragedy was enacted. The meeting consisted of people from all the adjacent towns, estimated at from 60,000 to 100,000. This assembly of unarmed people was suddenly assailed, by order of the magistrates, with the Manchester and Cheshire Cavalry, assisted by a regiment of Hussars, who rode in among the people with drawn sabres. Eleven were killed and six hundred wounded; Mr· Hunt, the chairman, was taken prisoner, and committed to take his trial at the York assizes, where he was sentenced to two and a half years' imprisonment in Ilchester gaol.

It would be difficult to convey to the present generation an adequate idea of the sufferings of the people, or of the distracted state and revolutionary feeling of the country at this period. Public subscriptions and charities, distributions of bread and soup, and various modes of relief, from time to time, were devised by the benevolent. In all those for Preston I took a part, and in a future chapter I think it may be desirable to enter into the details of our operations. At one of the distributions in 1811, although it seems never to have occurred to the committees to advise the people to abstain from brewing and using intoxicating liquors, by which so great a waste of good food is induced, they issued the following advice:—"That it be strongly recommended to all housekeepers to be economical in the use of bread and potatoes, to abstain altogether from pastry, and not to use any bread until after the expiration of twenty-four hours from the time of its being baked; and that it be also strongly recommended to all persons who keep horses to be economical in the feeding of them, by diminishing the quantity as much as possible." Even in the days of my poverty I contrived to spare something for those poorer than myself, and that which seems natural to me has been greatly matured by my constant connection, in one shape or another, with those who are the poorest and the greatest sufferers among the people.

Though not a professed political agitator, I took a share in every movement which had for its object the freedom of trade and the untaxing of the people's food. It was impossible for me to remain a mere spectator, when I saw my fellow-creatures suffering so severely from a removable cause, and on every occasion I endeavoured to expose the cruel tendency of the Corn Laws; the wickedness of excluding foreign food when the people were starving, for the selfish purpose of keeping up the value of land. Ten years before the Anti-Corn League was fairly at work, in my *Moral Reformer*, I wrote strong articles upon this subject. The following, which appeared in the March number, 1831, will show my sympathy for the poor weavers, and my denunciation of the wicked Corn Laws, under which they were suffering :—

"WEAVERS' WAGES, AND CORN LAWS.—To me it is quite clear, after the opening of the budget, that, in the present circumstances of the country, to expect an efficient relief for the poor and labouring classes from a reduction of taxes merely, would be the greatest delusion. What relief is there offered to the poor weaver? About a penny a week in candles! Is this likely to concilate the country? To live like human beings, the weaver's wages must be doubled ; but as that is not practicable, the price of his bread ought to be balanced with his wages. *The curse of the country is the Corn Law*, and till that is repealed, persons may drag their weary limbs about, may beset the dispensary for physic, crowd the workhouse to excess, may sink beneath their sufferings, and die from hunger; but there will be no relief. I could fill a volume with detailing the most miserable and wretched cases which have come before me during the past month. Oh! how hard, that honest and industrious men should hunger, while God gives bread enough and to spare! The following is a correct statement of the respective earnings of nine weavers, upon an average of the last six weeks, after deducting for candles, winding, sowin, &c. These persons devote the whole of their time to weaving, and some of them work from five in the morning to nine or ten at night. This statement is taken from the books of a respectable manufacturer, and to which reference at any time may be made. The first on the list gets the most money of any weaver he has, and the list itself may be considered as a fair specimen of all his weavers. So many exaggerated statements are abroad that I thought this might be useful :—

W. M.......8s. 7d.	W. N.......6s. 8½d.	R. G.......4s. 10d.
R. H. ......7s. 3d.	R. M.......6s. 0½d.	J. P. ......4s. 6d.
J. B. ......6s. 9d.	J. H. ......5s. 0d.	T. G. ......4s. 2d.

Making an average of 5s. 11¾d. each per week. Such is the miserable pittance of the weaver, and with provisions at the present exorbitant price, if any man in the country can behold this state of things without raising his determined voice against it, he must be destitute of the common feelings of humanity."

This extract will show how well I was prepared to join the Anti-Corn Law League, and to engage in the work of giving to the nation free access to the markets of the world for the sale of its manufactures and for the purchase of its food. I never engaged in a work with more earnestness, or with a deeper conviction of its justice ; and a strong belief that suffering humanity would be greatly benefited, stimulated me to make extraordinary exertions. And though, at that time, an increasing business and the cares of a large family pressed hard upon my time and energies, I still found opportunities to write, to lecture, and to agitate for the repeal of the Corn Laws. Though I never assumed the character of a political agitator, yet, I feel it no slight honour to have stood with "Cobden and Bright," on a platform in the open-air, denouncing monopoly, and pleading for the people's rights. And, comparing the last twenty with the previous thirty years, I don't hesitate to say that the free trade policy advocated so long by Colonel Thompson, Villiers, Cobden, and Bright, and at last taken up by Sir Robert Peel, has saved this country from revolution ; and, in fact, has been the forerunner of that contentment, tranquillity, and progress which have marked this latter period. It would be difficult for me to narrate all that I did in this good cause, but I will name some of my labours. Perhaps the greatest service I rendered was in the publication of *The Struggle*. For four years and a half I brought out this little work every Saturday morning, price one halfpenny, commencing with 1842, and closing in June, 1846, the very week that Her

Majesty signed the Repeal Bill. Every issue had engravings, after the fashion of *Punch*, but rudely executed. These, with the pithy articles, illustrating the principles of commercial freedom, and especially proving that free trade was for the interest of the farmer and farm labourer, were perused with intense interest, and were circulated extensively in the rural districts. A friend of the name of Christy, spent much of his time in travelling among the agriculturists distributing my *Struggle*. The engravings, of which there were altogether 378, attracted their attention, the arguments convincing them that all pretence for excluding foreign provisions for the labourer's and farmer's benefit was a delusion. I don't remember the average circulation, but I know at one time it was 15,000 weekly. I was indebted to Mr. Harvey, of Liverpool, especially, for the design of many of the engravings. It is quite refreshing for me, now and then, to take down the *Struggle* and look at the "pictures." To give a slight idea of the engravings, I may mention two. The advice of the protectionists to the people was, that they should emigrate, and schemes and plans of all sorts were afloat for promoting this. To expose this notion, one of the engravings represented parties pulling a cow by the tail on to a house, to eat the grass that had grown among the thatch, instead of cutting the grass and bringing it to the cow. It was well know that for some time before the repeal, Sir Robert Peel had his misgivings as to the effect of the Corn Laws, and another of the engravings, entitled "Peel's Meditation among the Tombs," exhibited him in a solemn mood, seated on a gravestone in the Church Yard, calculating the number of deaths by starvation which the famine laws had produced. My space will not allow of extracts from the numerous articles which made up this little missionary for free trade, but I give the following, as showing the spirit in which they were written :—

"THE DINNER AGITATION!—It is pleasant to have a clean table and everything in good order; it may be flattering to be called by great names, and to be looked upon as wise; but after all, it is mortifying to be *without a dinner*. A table, but *no dinner;* plates, but *nothing on them;* a stomach in the best order, but *nothing for it*. Oh! plague on such pleasures; let me rather have *a dinner*, although I submit to Paddy's style of eating it. Nothing is so difficult to dispense with as *the dinner*, especially when it is to answer the place of a late breakfast. So says John Bull. It's pleasant no doubt to advance in arts and sciences; to excel in writing and printing books; to carry one reform after another. All this may show how we progress in modern "civilisation;" but still these are not *bread*. Catholic emancipation, repeal of the test and corporation acts, cheap knowledge and cheap postage; all these are progressive reforms; but John says they do not *fill his belly*, and he begins sadly to grumble, because he finds that of all his demands, the claims of the *belly* are the least regarded, and the last to be granted. John did at one time pride himself as he walked abroad in seeing the country studded with mansions and new churches; in beholding prisons enlarged, and new workhouses erected; but he was mortified when he looked upon his numerous family and found that they had *no dinner*. In plain truth, next to the air we breathe, our first want is *food*, and the *first* act of every legislature should be to secure *an abundant supply to every human being*. It is truly vexing to read over the titles of the bills brought before Parliament every Session for the exercise of the collective wisdom of the nation, and not to find one solitary bill for supplying all the people with *food*. The nation should listen to nothing else till *this* be done. The people should set their minds upon it, and be determined to have it. The *dinner agitation* should be the *first*, and every other question regarded as of inferior moment. What inconsistency to build new churches, and yet never attempt to provide *daily bread!* What is the use of enactments for draining and ventilation when people cannot get enough to *eat*, soap to wash with, or good houses to live in? Every kind of medicine for the sickly horse is thought of but *corn*, and every kind of national reform but that of giving *bread* to the people. Look at our miserable hunger-bitten population, and then think that though you have 'British and foreign societies' of every sort, and a concentration of professed religion and humanity in every shape, you have not one society for supplying the *staff of life!* Till *bread* is secured for the whole people, I would neither petition nor pray for any other measure whatsoever. In our Father's house there is *bread enough* and to spare; the earth is God's table, and it is abundantly spread; why should any perish with hunger? Let us see that everyone has a chance of plenty, and then, and not till then, if they abuse it or act unworthily, may we adopt other means for their correction. When anyone asks you to subscribe to some new public building, ask him, have the people in the neighbourhood *enough to eat;* when they ask for taxes to enlarge prisons, put the question—was it not the *want of food* that increased the number of inmates and made this necessary? When asked to subscribe to convert heathens and Jews, reply, 'I will do so when I have succeeded in *feeding the hungry* of my *own land.*' When you step into the cottages, keep your eye fixed on the poor man's *cupboard*, and when you find the family compelled to make three meals into two, and to dilute the porridge with water instead of milk; when you find dogs and horses far better fed than human beings, I trust you will adopt my resolution—to command all the power you possess in favour of *the dinner agitation.*"

And among other curiosities in *The Struggle*, I may add the following petition, forwarded in 1843 :—

FAMILY PETITION.

To the Honourable the Commons of Great Britain and Ireland in Parliament assembled.

The Petition of Joseph Livesey (and family), cheese factor, Preston, in the County of Lancaster,

Humbly Sheweth,

That they regard the Corn and Provision Laws of this country as unjust, cruel, impolitic, deceitful, and impious, and fast tending in their influence to ruin the whole country.

They, therefore, humbly beg your Honourable House IMMEDIATELY *to* REPEAL *the same, and your Petitioners will ever pray.*

Joseph Livesey,	Howard Livesey,
Jane Livesey,	Jane Livesey, the younger,
William Livesey,	James Livesey,
Joseph Livesey, junior,	Alfred Livesey,
John Livesey,	Franklin Livesey.
Newton Livesey,	

Looking back, I scarcely know how I managed to get through all I had in hand at that time; and, if Peel's bill had not passed, I should have had to give up *The Struggle*, for I remember I was so near being exhausted that I could not arrange for an engraving for the last number (No. 235), but inserted that which had appeared in the preceding one; and I had to ask the aid of one of my sons to write a leading article. This work soon became scarce, and my last spare copy I forwarded, bound, to Mr. Cobden, which is now, I dare say, in the library of him whom I regard as one of the greatest statesmen that modern times have produced. Mrs. L. and myself had a stall in the great Free Trade Bazaar which was held in Covent Garden Theatre, where we remained a fortnight, in which place we never saw daylight. This was held in July, 1844, to assist in raising the £100,000 fund of that year to carry on the agitation. Those who have been pressed into the service of begging and providing materials for a bazaar stall, and have had to superintend the sale of the articles, can easily understand the anxiety and fatigue of such a position, and of the mortification often felt at seeing their goods sold below their value. I formed one of a large deputation that waited upon Sir Robert Peel at Whitehall Buildings. The worthy baronet was not then converted to the principles which, to his everlasting fame, he afterwards so lucidly explained, and so vigorously carried into effect. There were three causes that brought about the repeal of which he at last became the advocate—to the disruption of the tory party. First, the great change in public opinion as to the policy of protection; secondly, the failure of the harvest, including the loss of the potato crop in Ireland; and thirdly (and some think principally), the movement for increasing the freeholds, so as to qualify free rade voters in the counties. For this, it was proposed to raise (and had not the repeal been granted every farthing of it would have been raised) a "quarter million fund." I have kept two of the collecting books as a memento of this effort. I assisted to purchase £17,600 worth of property for freeholds in Preston, for which Mr. Ascroft was agent, and with purchases made by others, it is probable that £20,000 worth of property was obtained in this borough for making freehold votes. The same efforts were made in Cheshire, the West Riding of Yorkshire, and in most of the counties where there was a chance of carrying a free trader. I purchased freeholds for myself and sons in North and South Lancashire, and in North Cheshire, and I have had a freehold vote for five different counties or divisions. Our great financier was "George Wilson," and about the most liberal giver was "John Brooks." Though no orator, he was always ready with his "thousand pounds," and he would go round to Stalybridge, Ashton, Hyde, &c., and had only to say the word, and the "thousands" were ready. It was this *money power*, more than the arguments, that confounded the protectionists, and compelled them at last to relinquish the law for crippling trade and making food dear. Though there is nothing I dislike more than mixing up with electioneering contests, yet, viewing the repeal of the Corn Laws as a question of humanity, I never hesitated when an opportunity offered. I always encouraged our friends to hoist up the "big loaf," as the best banner to fight under; there are many that will remember *this*, and the cry of "sour pie," which we raised in this borough against those who opposed the reduction of the sugar duties, and by which we succeeded. At Walsall, I spent ten days, assisting at the election of Mr. John B. Smith, president of the Manchester Chamber of Commerce, and President of the Anti-Corn Law League. Mr. Rawson, Mr. Hickin, Mr. Acland, and others from Manchester were there. Believing in the power of the press, I suggested and superintended the issuing of a small paper every morning, called "The Alarm." It was an anxious time; the contest was severe, and we were beaten by 27 votes, though in five months there was another contest, when a free trader, Mr. Scott, was carried by 23 votes. At one of the

County elections, I attended, at the Court House, Lancaster, with **Mr. John** Brooks, and nominated Sir Thomas Potter. We had no intention of going to the poll, but embraced this opportunity for promulgating the free trade doctrines, though in a great measure prevented by the "hooting" of a great lot of roughs hired for the purpose. After this, such was the change produced in North Lancashire by the purchase of property for qualifying County voters, that though the County had been represented by tories from time immemorial, and had had no contest for a century, on this occasion, Mr. James Heywood, a liberal and a free trader, was returned without the protectionist party daring to nominate a candidate. At the nomination I addressed the electors in reply to Mr. Townley Parker, and was loudly cheered, in that same hall where, on the previous occasion, at the nomination of Mr. Talbot Clifton, I could scarcely get a hearing.

I have been connected with many public institutions and philanthropic movements, local and general, but I feel convinced that I have never rendered as much service to the cause of humanity and national good, as by my labours in promoting free trade and the temperance movement. The one serves to provide liberally the necessaries and comforts of life, and the other teaches the people the rational way of enjoying them. If there be one day in the year which I should like to celebrate as a day of thanksgiving and gladness, it would be the 26th of June, the day on which Queen Victoria, in 1846, placed her Royal name to the charter of our commercial liberties. The Prayer Book speaks gratefully in favour of "cheapness and plenty," and if ever there is another thanksgiving service added it ought to be for the repeal of the Corn Laws. I have often wondered that no monument worthy of the event has as yet been erected in any part of Lacashire.

CHAPTER V.

If "order is Heaven's first law," I may feel thankful that I have not been altogether disobedient to it. From a boy I had a strong feeling for keeping everything tidy, in good repair, and in order. For some time after our marriage we changed residences frequently, and we have lived altogether in ten different houses. It was my habit always to be making alterations, and improving the appearance of the places. I am fond of fields and flowers, and there is nothing I have prided myself in more than a nice garden in good order. I have always tried to get a house, however humble, where we had trees and fields to look out upon, and not bricks and mortar and other people's windows, or, if possible, as Mr. Cobden expressed it, a house that the wind could blow round. Attached to our first cottage was a garden, which, when we entered, might have belonged to one of Solomon's sluggards. I soon metamorphosed it—made a nice walk, planted flowers, and for a poor man's garden made it charming to look upon.

At the front of the next I levelled the street, a work not belonging to a tenant, and planted flowers behind, though they withered and died for want of sun and air. At a little farm we occupied, at Holme Slack, I spent a deal of money in ridding up hedges, draining, planting shrubs, and re-modelling the gardens, and we were often complimented by visitors for the nice order in which everything was kept. This place was to me a most pleasant retreat, especially in the evenings on returning from the town, weary with the toils of business, or distracted with the turmoil of some conflict on public affairs. Oh how I did enjoy the tranquillity of those delightful walks, and the perfumes of those over enchanting flowers! I felt a sense of repose as I opened the gate, and the quiet of walking under those shady trees, how it seemed to obliterate the recollection of crowded streets and long chimneys. For about 20 years we remained there, and long before the end of that period I beheld the ivy covering the walls to the eaves, which I had planted with my own hand. There were also the fine Portugal laurels, the tall Irish yew, the holly bush, the acuba, with a variety of roses, forming a pleasant avenue, and rendered ten-fold more interesting from the recollection that all these were put down tiny plants by myself at moments stolen from the calls of business. It was some time before we erected a dwelling of our own at Windermere, and there I have had the credit of good taste and a love of order in laying out the grounds with shrubs and flowers. The last little service I did in this way was, the presentation of a dozen choice Araucaria plants to our Park about two years ago, one of which I assisted to plant myself.

I thought it not inappropriate to mention the above as an introduction to a statement I have to make of my exertions, at different times, in assisting to carry out improvements in this borough. A residence of more than fifty years, with a connection with public bodies, has given me many opportunities of effecting improvements, of following up my inclination to remove nuisances, and adding to the enjoyments and conveniences of the inhabitants. Before entering upon these, it may not be amiss to say a few words as to the town itself. As a manufacturing town, Preston is considered second to no other in Lancashire. It is "Proud Preston," not because the people are noted for their pride above others, but because of the eminence of its situation, having to be approached on all sides by advancing ground. Its staple trade is spinning and the manufacture of cotton cloth, and so exclusively so that, during the "cotton famine," it was among the greatest sufferers in the county. To show its progress, a year before I became an inhabitant it had only a piece of a Church, the steeple built of red sandstone, being in a dilapidated condition; it has now thirteen. It then comprised little more than three main streets, Churchgate, Friargate, and Fishergate, and in each was fixed a bar where a toll was collected, there being no ingress or egress for horses and conveyances but through these. I remember well the channels in Church Street running down the middle. The changes which have taken place are not less in the extent of the streets and buildings, and the increase of population, than in the *personnel* of those who were connected with its business. With the exception of Mr. John Taylor, druggist, it is stated that I am the oldest tradesman. Mr. D. Longworth, in his *Monthly*

Advertiser, places me second, and says: " Mr. Joseph Livesey, cheesemonger, Church Street, has been in business fifty-two years, and presents a bright example of how a person placed in the humblest walk of life may, by patient and steady perseverance, rise up to a position honourable to himself and useful to his fellow-men." To remember the former occupants of our long streets and shops, and to find that they have disappeared in one's own time, and numbered with the dead, impresses one's mind strongly with the fleeting tenure of human life, and the importance of "numbering our days and applying our hearts to wisdom." Looking back also to the names of those who, at that time, were considered the " heads of the town," it is painful to think of the changes which have taken place—to think of so many names of high standing, either extinct or scarcely to be met with, and so many of their families gone into obscurity. It is still more painful to know that this great change is not traceable to any act of Providence. I once had a list of gentlemen, tradesmen, and professional men who had killed or ruined themselves by dissipation, but I abandoned it, finding that I could not turn it to any practical purpose without hurting the feelings of surviving friends.

Many foolish practices prevailed here when I was young. I never saw the "ducking stool," but I have seen—what I never wish to see again—a bull baited, near the House of Correction. I witnessed, before I was married, the leaping of the colt-hole on " Collop Monday." This was a large hole, some yards across, on the Marsh ; and persons called " Colts," who had been elected freemen or bailiffs, had to leap it. It being too large for any man to leap over, substitutes were hired, who, for a consideration, did the leaping, but, of course, leaped in and got a good wetting. On this occasion there was a succession of follies. The colt hole performance being over, the crowd proceeded to Water Lane End, where, by stopping the courses, all the filthy water was thrown across the road ; coppers were thrown in—the boys and roughs all scrambling in the dirty water to pick out as much as they could. Next, they came to the Castle Inn, and threw out of the window to the crowd a quantity of pence heated in the fire. After this, I remember, they made to the top of Lord Street, where there was a pump, and the " Colts" were made to run round the pump, the people laying on with hands, hats, or other convenient instruments. Edward Toy, grocer, in Cheapside, I distinctly recollect, was one who was thus honoured in his initiation to municipal honours. Great changes have taken place ; bull-baiting, cock-fighting, and the races have all been given up. The time of the latter was a great holiday, and the Derby family paid an annual visit to Preston at the races. The old Earl (grandfather to the present Earl), was strongly attached to the sport of cock-fighting, but both this and the races, and also their visits, were given up upon the defeat of the Hon. E. G. Stanley (the present Earl), at the election in 1830, by Henry Hunt. The Mansion was razed to the ground, and the stables made into shops. The Mansion in Church Street was nearly opposite a shop we then occupied (No. 107), and on the occasion of the races we witnessed the great excitement which used to prevail in this part. The Earl took his airing in an open carriage, with a pair of ponies; but the Countess had a splendid equipage—a coach and six, with the attendants in livery. When the Derby family took offence and left Preston, it was thought by many that its sun had set for ever : but we have survived, and almost forgotten the shock then felt ; and I presume we have learnt this useful lesson—that self-reliance is far better than dependence on patronage and favour.

In the course of my long residence in this borough, I have served the offices of Select Vestry-man, Member of the Board of Guardians, Commissioner for the Improvement of the Borough, and Town Councillor. In connection with the Commissioners, I tried to effect several improvements. I was on the general committee, and every Thursday we had a tour of inspection, and here it was that I found scope for my desire to remove nuisances, promote cleanliness, and to recommend such alterations as I thought the town required, especially in the back streets. I would often go ahead of my coadjutors, and but for them holding back, I should have incurred more expense than was justifiable ; though what I proposed was not in the way of ornament, but for purposes of real utility. The office of " Inspector of Nuisances" was just the one I should like to have filled. Hence, when I have visited Edinburgh, Glasgow, Dublin, Liverpool, or London, unlike those who are taken with the rich parts of the towns and with the splendid buildings, my " lions" were generally found in the streets where poverty, misery, and vice were most conspicuous. I have visited some of the worst places in these towns ; for instance, I have visited some of the cellars in Dublin, the miserable holes in St. Giles, and similar places in Westminster, Edinburgh, and Glasgow ; and I have hence a pretty correct knowledge how the people live who reside there. Though when in office as an Improvement Commissioner I got on much slower than I wished, yet I did accomplish something. The opening out of Orchard Street, joining Friargate to the Orchard, was effected chiefly by my perseverance ; and I got the shops, erected where Lord Derby's stables stood, placed a yard back, after the walls were up about three feet, thus widening the street to that extent. Many a dirty corner I got cleaned out—pig-styes and other nuisances removed ; I took considerable interest in the regulation of the markets and the sweeping of the streets ; but when on the one hand you have parties to deal with who are conservators of dirt, and on the other, persons who are afraid of incurring expense, you can only get on slowly.

I was elected one of the Councillors for St. John's Ward in 1835, at the first election under the Municipal Reform Bill. I began in good earnest to attempt such reforms as the abuses under the old *regime* had made most urgent. At the second meeting of the Council, Mr. Swindlehurst and I carried a motion to sell all the wine which the old Corporation had left, and which produced the sum of £226 3s. 7d. At a subsequent meeting, among other " articles not necessary to carry into effect the Municipal Corporation Bill," " two japanned wine waggons, five dozen wine glasses, ten decanters, and cork-screw," were also ordered to be sold. I succeeded in carrying a motion for fixing seats along the Ladies' Walk, in Moor Park, though it was strongly opposed by some who alleged that they would only be useful to the young men and young women who frequented that part. At my recommendation a scale was fixed just within the entrance of the

Town Hall, to be used, without charge, by persons to weigh their purchases ; but, though it is so important to the poor to be sure that they get proper weight, this scale was very little used. I committed a great mistake in persuading the Council to consent to a motion for abolishing the small tolls—my object being to induce the country people to increase their market supplies of vegetables and fruit—but the payment was restored the following year. As all tradespeople have to pay rents for their premises, it is but reasonable that the country people should pay for the accommodation they get in the market. I proposed to abolish the Mayor's salary, as an unnecessary expenditure, and, from a return I obtained from all the boroughs in Lancashire, I found that there was only one borough besides Preston (Liverpool) which gave a salary to the Mayor. In this, as in an attempt to abolish the Sunday processions of the Mayor to the Church, I was unsuccessful. The Council chamber is not exactly the place that I seem fitted for. My notions of personal duty, and of despatch, don't find much countenance in municipal bodies. At the end of my term of office, I did not ask for re-election, though some years after I was unwise enough to make the attempt, but was beaten, not by any superior qualification or experience on the part of my opponent, but by that mighty electioneering lever—cash and beer. The Council consisted of forty-eight—thirty-six Councillors and twelve Aldermen, and in looking over the names at its first meeting, thirty-two years ago, I find but one of the same gentlemen now in the Council, Mr. William Humber. And out of the whole forty-eight, there are, besides myself, only three living, Mr. Monk, Mr. W. Humber, and Mr. R. Threlfall. Either nine or ten Magistrates were then appointed for the borough, and out of these there is but one living, Mr. John Bairstow. In the good old Corporation times eating and drinking were orthodox duties ; and although Councillors now-a-days, when invited to a Mayor's dinner or other celebrations, do not "with one consent begin to make excuse," yet no part of the corporate funds is applied to these purposes, and upon the whole, there is an improvement in favour of temperance.

We are proud of our two Parks—Avenham Park and Moor Park—for there is no town in Lancashire where the people have the same outlets for health and recreation as are afforded by these Parks, and by the walks on both sides of the river Ribble. Many persons now living will remember how difficult it was for pedestrians to make their way along the margin of the river from Jackson's Gardens to Penwortham Bridge. I long felt anxious to put this path into thorough repair. The Corporation had neglected it, and I was the means of making it a pleasant footpath. In 1847 trade was bad ; great numbers of people were out of work, and both male and female beggars abounded. Large subscriptions were being raised for the relief in Ireland, and this suggested to me the advantage of making an effort to get these poor people some relief through the medium of employment. I mooted the project of making a walk along the Ribble ; a public meeting was convened, and a "Labour Association" formed A subscription was commenced, Mr. Isherwood being treasurer, and Mr. Edward Smith secretary. A number of unemployed able-bodied men were set to work, under the superintendence of William Shepherd, and, besides help from the

Corporation, £445 14s. 7d. was raised and expended. I don't know that I was ever connected with any undertaking that gave me more satisfaction. The following extract from the closing report of the Association will give an idea of the extent and kind of work we undertook, and will be read with interest by many Preston people :—

"Preparatory to commencing the Ribble Walks, your committee levelled Pottery Hill, and also the vacant ground adjoining Bridge Street and Mount Pleasant. They cleared and cindered a large square of open land at the front of Hammond's Row, now enclosed. Vacant pieces of ground in Glover Street and at the top of Great Avenham Street were cleared of rubbish, levelled, and made tidy. A large pit of stagnant water was filled at the bottom of Chapel Walks, and the ground made level. New footpaths were made and cindered on the South side of Meadow Street, on the West side of East View Street, and across the vacant ground from the latter to St. Paul's Square. The East side of St. Paul's Square was levelled, sidestones set, the stagnant water removed, and the whole cindered. After these jobs were completed, the embanking, staking, levelling, and laying out of the Ribble Walk from the corner of Mr. Jackson's garden to Penwortham Bridge was undertaken. At this the men were employed less or more fifteen months, and the great satisfaction expressed by their townsmen as to this improvement assures your committee that in this undertaking they have had the approbation of the public. They very much improved and beautified the walks leading from Ribblesdale Place along Mr. Wyse's garden to the river, and also that from the Tramroad along Mr. Jackson's garden, where they fixed three flights of stone steps. At Swillbrook, at the foot of Avenham Terrace, where the Improvement Commissioners had built a tunnel, your committee removed an immense quantity of earth from a distance, filling up the chasm, and making it into land as at present, which is admitted by all to be a great improvement. The whole length of South Meadow Lane, from Fishergate to Mr. Dent's (New Bridge Inn), was cleaned, levelled, and gravelled. The new walk along the East boundary of the Marsh was undertaken and finished by your committee; also the re-gravelling of the oblique one running across the Marsh towards Ashton, and the foot-roads connected with the Spa Brow were all put into good order. One of their last undertakings was to level, re-lay, and cinder the foot-road leading from the top of King Street, past Frenchwood, all the way to Walton Bridge. This road, which had been almost impassable, they made into a good road."

I have always felt it a pleasure—as I think every citizen ought—to render any little service I could for the improvement of our town. Formerly we had a number of pumps in the public streets for the use of the inhabitants, but they are nearly all removed, and so far their only substitutes are the eight fountains which I have provided in different parts of the town. These are preachers of temperance day and night to all the passers by, and thousands slake their thirst at these constantly running streams, who might otherwise be tempted into the beer-house. I felt anxious to erect a superior one in Avenham Park, but after naming it several times I met with very little encouragement. I placed a small drinking fountain in the Temperance Hall, another in Walker Street School; and in the Spinners' Institute I fixed a fountain, lavatory, and bath, and the same in the Weavers' Institute. At Bowness Bay, near the landing of the Windermere steamers, I erected a beautiful fountain which is supplied with excellent water from the grounds of Messrs. Crossley, of Halifax. There is a nice fountain on Douglas pier erected by my eldest son. I name these that others, possessing means, may be induced to do the same; and if temperance men were sufficiently alive to the advantages of water fountains there would not be a town or a village, or any public grounds or buildings without them.

CHAPTER VI.

Every additional paper I write under this head seems to be an increasing task, having to dwell so much upon myself and my own doings. But feeling unable now to draw back, all I have to crave of my readers is, that they will forgive any appearance of vanity or self-praise of which I may appear to be chargeable. This paper will refer to some of my dealings with the poor. Naturally I cling to them; I feel a pleasure in their company, and when I meet persons drunk or in rags—a sight forbidding to most people,—I seem drawn towards them, and never pass them without a feeling of pity. These feelings, perhaps natural, were, I believe, very much matured by my early reading of the New Testament, my attention often being arrested with the kindly, benevolent, sympathising, charitable, forgiving spirit of Jesus as manifested in all His teaching and in all His works. Many a time have I pictured to myself the scene of the woman washing His feet with her tears, and wiping them with the hairs of her head, and the kindly words He spoke to her in opposition to the rebukes of the Scribes and Pharisees. And then, again, the words He spoke to "the women taken in adultery,"—"Hath no man condemned thee?" "No man, Lord." "Neither do *I* condemn thee, go, and sin no more!" Mine has been an unpretending, humble course, trying, in a limited sphere, to relieve and serve the sons and daughters of poverty. It has always appeared to me that a man who devises plans for benefiting his fellow creatures, and carries them into effect himself—who disposes of his bounty with his own hands—can do much more good than one who gives far larger sums, but leaves the distribution entirely to others, and whose liberality, too often, after his death, is wrongly appropriated. No doubt I have been often imposed upon, but in this, as in all other human affair I would balance the good of relieving a number against the evil of occasionally being cheated. I think it is Paley who says he preferred giving occasionally when he knew he was being imposed upon rather than check the current of benevolence which it was important to encourage. But, at the same time, I have spared no pains in visiting people's houses and testing their real condition. There are very few poor streets or courts or yards, in Preston, where I have not been. And among those who, a long time ago, laboured in the same way, I have the pleasure to name the late Mrs. German, and Miss Whitehead (now Mrs. Dr. Stavert). On most, if not on all occasions when we had, during our depression in trade, public subscriptions for the relief of the poor, I took a part. It seems natural to me to enjoy myself among the poor; and if my present means were doubled or trebled, I think it would make no difference. I feel happier at any time at the fireside of a poor man's cottage, chatting with his family, than in the drawing-room of my richest friend. I shall not go into details, nor dwell upon visits to "the widows and fatherless in their afflictions," which is the duty of all, as part of "pure and undefiled religion," but refer to instances of a more public character, where I have originated and carried out plans, apparently simple in themselves, which conferred great good upon the needy poor. I may however, just name one case, quite forgotten to myself, but brought to my mind by a letter I have received from a lady. Speaking of her father, who was an old friend of] mine, she says: " He calls to mind an incident soon after your marriage, which exhibits the kindliness of your nature in the case of a poor man, who resided in a cellar in Vauxhall Road, sick, and full of putrifying sores, and to whom you sent the best feather-bed you had. Doubtless, if he were talking to you, many interesting events would be elicited."

In my intercourse with the poor, I found the greatest symptoms of misery, as it struck me, in their bedrooms. Many a score of beds have I seen without a single blanket; sometime with no covering but a thin cotton sheet or two, perhaps a few wrappers, or a piece of old carpet. These, and their body clothes, being all the covering they had during the winter nights. Few could believe how poor families sleep unless they saw it. And it seldom happens that lady visitors, or others who call, go up stairs. Everything there is alike wretched. Beds filled with straw or old chaff. The ticks dirty, and sometimes with holes in; the chaff wet, or running out. The floors not clean; the windows and fire-places closed; indeed, the air is so bad, that it is a wonder how they pass the night. In many cases, and generally where the parties have been " sold up," there are no bedsteads, but they sleep on the floor. Five in a bed, I have often met with—three in the usual position, and two youngsters at the feet. Visiting late at night, I once found seven persons in one bed, four little ones across at the bottom, feet to feet. It is true enough that one half of the world does not know how the other half lives. I was always so impressed with the discomforts of the bedrooms, that I turned my special attention to this. There is nothing, at a small cost, that is more comfortable for a poor family than a new chaff bed; and, I have heard a poor woman say, " it warms three sides." This I seem to have made my special study. One hard winter (I think it was about 1826), I distributed, on my own account, 900 sacks of chaff. Assisted by a few friends, we visited many of the poorest houses and cellars in the town. After making all inquiries, I decided to whom I would give two, three, or more sacks of chaff, according to their needs; but, as a condition, they were all, after throwing away their old chaff, to wash their bed ticks. I purchased the chaff from the farmers, at about 8d. a sack, and they brought it in cart-loads of about 30 or 40 sacks at a time. I gave them a list of names and streets, and sent a man to assist in delivering the chaff at the poor people's houses. On several occasions afterwards, in connection with our public charities, I may be said to have had the office of chaff distributor and bed inspector.

Formerly, working people, as a rule, were poorer than they are at present. Food was dear, work scarce, and wages low. The competition among work-people was so severe that emigration, for a long time, was looked upon as the chief remedy. We had many public subscriptions in times of distress—in 1816, 1830, 1840, and 1842, &c. In these, the distribution of soup and bedding generally formed the most prominent features. In the year 1830, the soup was made in the kitchen of Lord Derby's house, in Church Street, on a large scale. The chaff was stored in, and given out, at a warehouse in Fox Street. At another time, Lord Derby's stables were engaged for the same good work. We had, in 1858, a distribution called distinctly, " The Bedding Charity," and its history is worthy of being referred to. Mr. Isaac Whitwell, of Kendal, a truly benevolent man, had an exhibition in the Temperance Hall of the " Magic Lantern," to Sunday School children and others, which left a balance of £11 19s. 2d. He left it with me to decide how the balance should be appropriated. It was then a time of distress, and after consulting some friends, I said, if we could raise £30 or £40 more, we might replenish a number of poor people's beds. We made application to a few benevolent persons, and the project was so well received, that we resolved to form a " Bedding Charity." The following are the first and concluding paragraphs of the Appeal we issued for carrying this into effect :

" It is much to be lamented that among other privations, the bedding of a great number of the working people of Preston, especially the aged, is in a deplorable condition. They have but little covering—many not a single blanket —but, worse than all, their beds are in a very bad state, not having been renewed for many years. The chaff is reduced to dust, a deal of it very dirty, and in many cases it has become so wasted that the bed-cords are often felt through it. The high price of provisions has prevented them from being able to purchase new chaff ; and now that an inclement season is at hand, it has been thought no greater service could be rendered to the poor, at a moderate expense, than to renew a considerable number of these beds with new chaff. It is also intended to supply new bed-ticks, cotton sheets, and coverlets at a low charge.

" To the rich and benevolent we appeal to assist us in this good work ; and we trust, considering the present lamentable depression in trade, the approaching inclement season of the year, and the orderly behaviour of the poor of the town, that this appeal will not be made in vain.

" J. OWEN PARR, Chairman.   J. J. MYRES, Treasurer.
" J. LIVESEY, Vice-Chairman.   J. SHAW, Secretary."

A warehouse was taken as a depôt for chaff and bedding ; a great number of persons were employed in making bed-ticks and filling them. Every part of the town was visited ; and it was really a sight to see new beds and old beds, filled with new chaff, being trucked and carted through the town daily for a long time during these operations. It was a condition that the old bed-ticks should always be cleaned. Lime was also furnished to the people for whitewashing their houses, and sometimes soap ; and in cases, owing to sickness or old age, where the parties were not able to clean their rooms, women, some from the workhouse, were sent to do it. There was such a cleaning out on this occasion as had never been seen before, and thousands of clean beds were secured to the poor. For many weeks I never went home to dine, but remained at the depôt, quite happy in taking a bun and a glass of water, or a basin of soup for dinner. The Rev. J. Shaw, curate of the Parish Church, rendered invaluable service, and instead of the £30 or £40, we raised and expended upwards of £1,100, besides the amount which the people paid for Bolton sheets and quilts, at a reduced price. We had collections in the Churches and Chapels, and I may here quote two paragraphs from a printed sermon of the Rev. Cannon Parr, M.A., vicar of Preston, preached in the Parish Church on the 14th February, 1858, on behalf of this charity:—

"The Bedding Charity has been organized with a view to mitigate the extremity of distress known to exist. Honour be to Mr. Livesey, the prime mover in it—honour to the first and most munificent contributors to it—honour above all to the laborious and self-denying visitors, and to the *honorary* and earnest efficient secretary, the Rev. J. Shaw. Thanks to all these ; much has been done to relieve, and *more* to *discover*, an extent and depth of suffering which must be seen to be adequately understood and felt."

"The visitors have been struck with the amount of uncomplaining patience, unmurmuring endurance, which they have witnessed. The poor have felt comforted, and cheered, and honoured by the notice taken of them, and the sympathy expressed for them ; and in many it seemed to lay the foundation of a hope, that being thus seasonably helped, they might now be able to help themselves, and to do away with that feeling of desperation and self-abandonment, which extinguishes all exertion, and offers those who sink under it, a ready prey to every evil influence."

All classes, excepting the very poorest, could enjoy themselves every summer by going with the cheap railway trips. This led me to conceive the idea of arranging one for this class, which was eminently successful. Every summer the poorest in the town, "the halt, the lame, and the blind," the scavengers, the sweeps, and workhouse people, have been treated by a railway trip to Blackpool, Southport, Fleetwood, or some other sea bathing place. This annual treat commenced in 1845; it was entirely my own conception, and has been continued ever since, generally in the month of August. It has been called the "Poor People's Trip," the "Old Women's Trip," and the "Butter-milk Trip," the latter because, for number of years, we took a truck load of butter-milk with us for the use of our guests. The trip numbered at first 2,000 to 2,500, but in time it increased to 4,000. We arranged with the railway companies to take them for 6d. a head, and we issued tickets in packets at 8d., including for each person a bun, and milk *ad libitum*. Latterly coffee was substituted for milk. Benevolent persons and employers purchased the packets and distributed them among the poor, and the demand, I may say, always exceeded the supply. It was managed by a committee, of whom Mr. Joseph Dearden is one of the oldest. This low charge continued for 20 years; but for the last two years the railway companies have demanded 1s. I don't blame them for this, for it had become impossible to discriminate sufficiently so as to prevent numbers of persons taking advantage of the charity trip who were well able to pay a full fare. The trips however, have gone as before though at the higher charge, except that refreshments are not supplied ; and it is not looked upon now as an exclusively charitable arrangement. It used to be an interesting sight to me to see the trains start one after another, every carriage crammed with the poor people as "happy as princes." It was the only "out" many of them got during the whole year, and they would talk of it many a long day. Long before the time arrives the old women will call to ask when the trip will come off, and describe their ailments, telling marvellous tales how much they were benefited the year before. I often think how much friendship and good will might be diffused among the poor, if the rich would but only mix more with them, and contrive for their enjoyments. They little think of the store of gratitude that is lodged in breasts covered with rags, for anyone who becomes their benefactor.

My attention at one time was directed to the way in which the poorest classes were served with coals, which was by bags containing a hundred-weight each, or what should have been a hundred-weight, for I found upon weighing some bags that they did not contain more than 90 to 100lbs., instead of 112lbs. I determined to introduce an entire new system, so as not only to secure honest weight, but to reduce the price. Instead of bags filled at the coal yards by so many spadefuls, I fixed upon different points in the town, contiguous to the residences of the poor, and had cart loads of coals laid down in the streets. They were weighed on the spot, and wheeled in baskets to the people's houses. When one load was served out, the men employed moved the scale, which went on wheels, to another point and did the same there ; and it soon became known in each locality on what day the coal men would come. A great advantage was gained to the poor, and the bagging system became abolished. We sold at a price to cover expenses, for ready money. This plan worked most beneficially. After seeing it fully established, I induced a friend of mine, William Toulmin, to carry it on, which he did for many years, establishing small retail coal yards in different parts of the town, a system which now generally prevails.

In my visitations the conviction was forced upon me that but for their drinking and improvident habits, a great many families would not have been in the wretched condition in which we found them. In 1824, I wrote a pamphlet of 24 pages, entitled "A Friendly Address to the Poorer Classes," which went through several editions, but is now out of print. In this I spoke of industry, cleanliness, economy, sobriety,—against smoking, shopping, pledging, dealing with tallymen, and generally on better domestic management. Before I heard of temperance societies, I wrote and circulated, for the same classes, a pamphlet headed "The Besetting Sin." This dealt with the question of temperance as many deal with it in the present day, showing the horrid evils of "drunkenness" merely, urging great moderation, but saying nothing against the drink itself, or against its dangerous tendencies in small quantities. I had a restless spirit ; I was generally inventing something, as I thought, for bettering the condition of the poor. This will further appear when I speak of the schools and institutes which I either originated or assisted in promoting. I had fully intended, in this chapter, to give a sketch of my labours in connection with the Relief Fund during the Cotton Famine, which in magnitude and length of time eclipsed all the charitable distributions we ever had in Preston ; but this, for want of space, I must defer till my next.

CHAPTER VII.

In the last chapter I omitted, from want of room, noticing my labours in connection with the Preston Relief Fund, during the Cotton Famine. This was by far the largest of our public distributions. Commencing in January, 1862, it continued till May, 1865, three years and three months, without intermission. The fact that £131,000 was distributed in the various forms of bread, soup, flour, employment, coals, bedding, clothing, &c., shows the magnitude of the undertaking. The number of tickets given out for bread, soup, coals, clothing, &c., amounted to 5,141,418; and the number of persons, including all the branches of the families relieved amounted, at one time, to 40,627. This was a gigantic undertaking, and was managed so as to secure the praise of visitors from all parts of the world. Preston, being almost entirely dependent on the cotton trade, probably suffered more than any other town. For about two years I devoted most of my spare time to this important charity. There were so many mills stopped, and so many people out of work, that I and a few friends projected the first public meeting to originate a subscription, and which was called by the mayor. The general impression, however, was, that we were too hasty, and that it was premature to commence giving relief, though the result proved that we did not move a day too soon. We had prepared resolutions, and got the consent of parties to move and second them. The Rev. J. Owen Parr, the vicar, with a short speech moved the first resolution recommending a public subscription, which was seconded by Mr. Bairstow, upon which Mr. T. B. Addison rose, and made an elaborate speech against the resolution, urging that relief should be given only through the Board of Guardians. He seemed to have made a great impression upon the meeting; a pause ensued; no one rose to reply, although the meeting called by circular was attended both by ministers and private gentlemen. With me it was a moment of intense anxiety; I had laboured hard to bring this meeting about, and I feared that the ingenious appeal of the learned Recorder had frustrated all my hopes. Just as the motion was going to be put to the vote, I felt impelled to speak, (though according to arrangement I was to speak to a later motion,) and once on my legs, I felt no difficulty in replying to Mr. Addison. Warming up as I proceeded, I carried the meeting with me. Several others then followed, and the resolution was carried with only two dissentients, Mr. Addison and another. If ever I felt that I had rendered a service to humanity, it was by coming forward at this critical moment. A committee was appointed, the Vicar being chairman, and I vice-chairman, and afterwards all went on successfully. Mr. Philip Park and I were deputed to look out for premises in which to carry on our operations, and we were fortunate in meeting with a building in Crooked Lane, one with five storeys, resembling a cotton factory, belonging to Mr. James German, the use of which he granted us freely. This was fitted up chiefly under my superintendence. On the ground floor we had seven boilers making soup, and store rooms for the meat, bread, and flour. On the next floor was stored the clothing sent from all parts of the country, in quantities almost incredible, a part of this room being

allotted to the females employed in making and mending all sorts of garments.
In the next storey was deposited an immense quantity of chaff and cut straw
(cut by steam-power), and here the poor people's beds were filled, and a vast
number of new ones given out Above this, on the next floor, we had joiners,
tailors, and shoemakers at work. Altogether it was a busy place; our operations
extending also to a number of coal yards and schools in various parts of the
town. Speaking of our busiest time, the report puts down the number of persons
employed at 489, in the following departments :—Bread room, 5; soup room, 20;
clothing room, 13; joiners, 9; chaff room, 20; tailors, 66; shoemakers, 27; coal
distributors, 10; assistants, or odd hands, 7; dressmakers, 54; potato peelers,
50; visitors and messengers, 18; to which may be added 160 female sewers.
We had offices close by, where I attended daily, and for months I rarely went
home to dinner. In one part of the large building I made arrangements for
washing the children who generally came very dirty, and to many were given
tickets containing the following :—"To promote cleanliness and decency, Mr.
Livesey will pay to any hairdresser one penny who cuts the hair of this poor
boy. This ticket will be his claim for payment any time he may wish." Mixing
daily with the hundreds and thousands of the poor and the unemployed, if I
had not previously been familiar with every phase of poverty, I should have
become so here. The old enemy, drink, plagued us here as it does everywhere.
One Saturday, after paying our "gangers,"—men who took the lead in the out-
door labour department,—nine in number, I watched them all make off to a
public-house. The next week, after receiving their wages, I called them into an
adjoining room and spoke to them of their conduct, of which they professed to
be ashamed, and promised not to do so again. I got a person appointed paid
secretary, the son of a teetotaler. He had never tasted drink up to 28 years of
age; but having had a fever, was induced to take porter by the advice of the
doctor. This was the first step of his becoming a drunkard. He signed the
pledge, and we hoped he was reformed, but while in the office he broke out, got
behind with his cash, which I had to make good, and he was dismissed. He is
since dead. Many visitors to our establishment from the higher ranks saw more
of the condition of the "million" on this occasion than they had ever done
before. The gifts in the shape of clothing from every part of the kingdom were
extraordinary; I have seen as many as 50 bales of new material and cast-off
clothes received in one day. The devoted labour and liberality of the gentlemen
of the town, and the handsome subscriptions that were sent by numerous
parties, especially those through the Manchester Central, and the London
Mansion House Committees, proved equal to the emergency, and had it not
been for these during this protracted period of suffering, it would have been
impossible to have preserved the peace of the town. I hope no one living may
ever see another "cotton famine."

The new Poor Law, which passed in 1834, was very unpopular. The parishes
in the north felt that they did not require it, for though abuses existed, the
rates had not, as in some parts of the south, risen from 10s. to 18s. in the pound.
The starvation of the agricultural labourers, the heavy burden of the poor upon

the farmers, and the consequent losses to the landowners were the natural effects of the Corn Laws, and yet instead of seeing this and repealing them, a remedy was sought in a more stringent Poor Law, which equally affected north and south. From the first I was opposed to this measure, and did my best to prevent its being enforced in Preston. I foresaw that it would be a most expensive change, that the poor would be dealt with more harshly, and the liberty of the parishes sacrificed to a central authority. It would be difficult for me to recount the amount of labour I undertook, and the time I spent in opposing this measure. And though some of the absurd provisions have been repealed, and the orders of the Poor Law Board modified, or allowed to remain in abeyance, even yet it is a crude, expensive, and oppressive measure; and an interference with the liberty of local authorities such as would not be borne with in any other department. We had Assistant Commissioners, appointed at £700 and £800 a year, and whose expenses amounted to about the same sum, coming on visits of inspection, who knew very little of poor law administration. Where the law was enforced, and the authority of the Poor Law Board submitted to, the old fashioned *work*-houses, which corresponded to their names, were broken up; looms and implements of labour of all kinds made away, and new expensive Union houses ("Bastiles") were erected in their stead, whose tests are not *work*, but confinement and division of families. For more than 20 years I successfully opposed the erection of a new workhouse for the Preston Union—at the Board while I remained a member, and afterwards through the columns of the *Guardian* and other mediums; and I don't hesitate to say that I have saved this Union many thousand pounds by my opposition. While in office I could secure a majority of the Guardians against this measure, and at one time when the Poor Law Board at London had actually issued an order for building a Union Workhouse, I raised such an opposition and disputed the legality of the order in such a way that the work was not proceeded with. At last, however, I got tired out, and in the face of the labours and statistics of Mr. C. R. Jacson, industriously got up, I made no further attempt at resistance, and the new house, which was to cost £32,000, but which will amount to about the moderate sum of £42,000, is just about to be opened.

Mr. T. B. Addison was from the first a strenuous advocate of the new Poor Law. He and I could never agree; he would carry out the measure in all its rigour, and for five years at the Board we were constantly in opposition. Though he was a barrister, I also was well read as it respected the law and the orders of the commissioners (which were equivalent to law), and did frequently and successfully dispute his statements. Every year we had a warm contest about the chairmanship of the Board of Guardians. The magistrates and the country guardians generally supported Mr. Addison for chairman, and I and others as constantly opposed him, for we were better able to thwart his measures when we kept him out of the chair. Either twice or three times he was rejected, and in some of the instances by a majority of one. Once we certainly stretched a point to gain the majority of one, his opponent, Mr. Lomas, being persuaded to vote for himself. Mr. Addison's views and mine, as to the character and merits of the poor, were so utterly at variance that it was impossible we could work well together. I knew their condition from actual visitation, and he did not. He was very severe, and I was lenient, so much so that had I not been checked by him and others, I should often have committed errors by being too indulgent. Mr. A. was always hard upon the poor women who had been " unfortunate," or who had married young, and many a contention have we had about giving relief to such. His award was uniformly " the house " for such, and indeed for many others who were more deserving. I always set my face against urging poor families to break up their little homes by forcing them into the workhouses, the husband to one, the wife to another, and the elder children to a third. All this was inflicted under the soft name of " classification." My heart has bled many a time to see the poor pleading for a small pittance of out-door relief, where nothing but the workhouse was offered. Formerly the poor were relieved in the spirit of Christianity by the churchwardens and overseers; the shadow of such a thing never enters the administration now; the practice with many is to get rid of the poor every way and any way at the least expense, and for this the Union house is the readiest. Formerly the services of parish administrators were generally unpaid, but now a vast amount of the poor rate is absorbed in salaries, and townships that have few, if any poor, are yet heavily taxed for what are called " establishment expenses."

The new Poor Law for some time was so unpopular that resistance was frequently offered to its introduction. Mr. James Acland, said to be employed by government, went through the country lecturing in its favour. Coming to Preston, and knowing my opposition to the measure, he placarded the walls, challenging me to a public discussion. Though reluctant to appear in this character I accepted the challenge; the theatre was engaged, and the whole town was in a state of excitement. Every corner of the building was crammed. I had about the cleverest antagonist that could have been selected; but the feeling of the people was against him, and having made myself well acquainted with the law and the orders upon it, I was well able to dispute his positions. The discussion continued three nights, each speaking a given time. I carried the audience with me, and at the close, upon the question being put to the vote, Mr. A. had from 20 to 80 hands, all the rest being raised for me, followed by an extraordinary burst of feeling in my favour, and against the new Poor Law.

From causes which these papers will explain, I have always been mixed up with the poor and their affairs, and taken an interest in anything that contributed to their welfare. Several times I have raised subscriptions for noted persons who have been reduced, and thus secured to them a weekly allowance which proved a great help, and in no instance do I remember ever failing in getting assistance for persons whom I could recommend. Several times have I attempted to set poor men up in a little way of business as hawkers—selling books, blacking, caps, &c., but with one exception, I think, they were all failures, so clear is it that success depends far more upon personal qualifications than upon other circumstances. Often have I caused a little unpleasantness at home by introducing persons—strangers, who were in distress; for whilst on the one hand I was too credulous in believing their distressing tales, my family, from what they had seen, were apt to regard them as imposters.

I have still all the feelings of a poor man; I prefer the company of poor people; and if misfortune should render it necessary, I think I could fall back into that humble sphere of living with which I commenced without feeling the shock as most people would do. I have tried two or three times to be a gentleman; that is, to leave off work and to enjoy myself, but it never answered. I always felt desirous of coming back to busy and useful life, employing my time as I am doing at present. My notions of life are very simple, for man, I believe, is the happiest when removed from either poverty or riches, has tolerable health, and is pursuing day by day a useful object. An order to "live upon sixpence a day and to earn it" would not alarm me as it would most men. The plainest fare is what I like and what I prefer, and, as a rule, I should feel quite as happy at the poor man's table as I have done in France or Germany, where we had seven or eight courses to dinner.

<hr>

CHAPTER VIII.

In order to refresh my memory I was induced to look through my collection of private papers, and I find that I have upwards of ninety memorandum books, a few large, but mostly penny ones, in which I have made entries and remarks in connection with the various movements, agitations, subscriptions, societies, institutions, &c., in which I have been engaged during the last fifty years. One of the oldest, dated 1817, was my ledger, which I carried in my breast pocket, and which was deemed quite bulky enough for my business at that time. Some day, perhaps not distant, my friends and survivors may feel interested in reading a number of the remarks to be found in these books.

My aim was always to devise something that would improve the condition of the working people; and in those early times so little was thought of or attempted in this line, compared to the present day, that I never was at a loss for an opening in which to employ my inventive faculty or absorb my youthful energies. One of my earliest efforts which I can recollect, either just before or just after my marriage, was to assist in Mr. Dilworth's adult school at Walton. Mr. James Dilworth resided there and was what they called a "fester-out;" that is he gave out weaving for some other employer; this was before he started the commission business in Preston. He built the house in Ribblesdale Place now owned and occupied by Mr. John Horrocks, and his name is still retained in the Manchester firm of "J. Dilworth and Son." Soon after our marriage my wife and I devoted as much of our time and means as we could spare to instructing our neighbours. We started an adult Sunday School of our own, she teaching the females and I the males, in a cottage at the west end of Paradise Street, the rent being about 2s. a week. Afterwards I took a large room in Shepherd Street for a similar object, and the following printed bill will briefly explain the character of the school:—

Poor people in Preston and the neighbourhood are kindly informed, that a Sunday school, for youth of both sexes, from fourteen to twenty-one years of age, is kept in a commodious room, No. 4, Shepherd Street.

The scholars are confined to those of the above age; and as every attention is paid to their instruction, with the liberty of going to their own places of worship, parents and guardians of youth will find this a favourable opportunity of providing for the education of those who are obliged to labour through the week—such as have no learning, or are in danger of losing that which they have. School hours from half-past eight to a quarter past ten in the morning, and from a quarter past one to a quarter past two in the afternoon. All Gratuitous.— *Preston, February 1st, 1825.*

This room in Shepherd Street was used for various purposes. I have a placard announcing a "Weekly meeting for Religious Investigation" in this place; and among the rules by which it was to be guided I may give the following:—

1.—A subject to be proposed and agreed upon the week before it is discussed, to be decidedly of a religious cast. Any person engaging in the discussion, to have the liberty of proposing a subject.

2.—Meekness and charity are especially to be cultivated, and to form a prominent feature in every discussion.

3.—As an increase of knowledge and the promotion of Godliness must always be kept in view, the discussions of the meeting are not intended as matters of entertainment, or for the displaying of ability—in this respect it will differ from what are called "Debating Societies."

At that day there were few opportunities for the working people to see a newspaper, excepting at the public-house. Owing to the three-fold duty—that upon paper, upon the stamp, (3d.), and the advertisements—the general price was 7d., and the charge at the newsrooms was made by the year. In a prospectus dated January 16th, 1827, I announced that a "General Reading Room" would be opened in Shepherd Street, to be supplied with all the leading newspapers and periodicals, the charge to be 3s. 3d. per quarter. I took the whole responsibility upon myself; it was a success, and sometime after it was removed to more respectable premises, a large room over the *Chronicle* office in the Market Place, where it remained for many years. Though this project secured sufficient support to make it permanent, it did not meet with the support of the class for whom I specially intended it. The operatives fell off, and it became more a newsroom for the middle class, the members consisting of shop-keepers, clerks, &c. I have at least six times fit up or helped to fit up small places for the operative classes, as reading rooms, some quite free and some at a low charge, and I confess with grief that in every instance I have been disappointed. It is true that men who labour hard are not in a condition after work for reading; but the numbers who attend the public-houses and beershops, especially on the Saturday nights and Sundays, show that their love of liquor is far stronger than their love of mental improvement; and as it respects the reformed characters, those who are saved from drink, they are generally fully engaged with their trades and family matters, and if not, as a body they seldom manifest much disposition for reading.

A few years after this I took a large room over the "Cock-pit" (the place where the temperance meetings were held for twenty years) and for seven years I kept a Youth's Sunday School here at my own expense, assisted by clever devoted young men. The ages of the scholars and general rules were much the same as the above ; but perhaps the greatest attraction which secured a regular attendance on the part of the young people was that, in addition to reading and instruction, we taught them to write. It was either here or at my own house, that I taught a grammar class certain nights in the week, the rules of which I find in one of my books, and to this class probably some persons may have been indebted, in part, for their rise in the world. Among the list of members, the names of whom I still retain, I notice that of Mr. George Toulmin, the present proprietor of the *Preston Guardian*. As I have said before, I had a restless spirit, and was always projecting something new, not for my own case or gratification, but for the improvement and elevation of the poorer classes. I seldom chimed in with existing institutions, or felt disposed to act in a subordinate character, and consequently was frequently trying to initiate something, as I thought, in advance of what was then in operation. And I had this peculiar characteristic (some might call it a weakness) which has followed me through life, that in starting any project I would go into it at first with all the energy I could command, difficulties seeming rather to be an advantage. After seeing an institution fairly and successfully started, I generally began to feel indifferent, leaving its management to others. The temperance cause may be considered the only exception, but I dare say if I had seen this as successful as I could have wished, I might have felt here also a disposition to retire and engage in something else in its place.

In 1827 I was renting rooms in Cannon Street, now occupied for printing and machining the *Preston Guardian*. These rooms were used for various educational and progressional purposes. A Mr. Templeton about this time came to Preston in low water, and appearing to be a man of genius as to teaching, I got up a subscription for him, and one room was fit up as a school, in which he introduced the " arithmetical rods," and a peculiar copy book. Not succeeding so well, he was taken by the hand by Mr. John Smith, of the *Liverpool Mercury*. They brought out " Smith and Dolier's copy book," and the white enamelled tablets to write upon with the pencil. Mr. Smith delivered lectures on education, assisted by Mr. Dolier, at which the utility of these and other inventions were illustrated. On one occasion I induced the Town Council to engage Mr. Smith, who lectured several nights in the theatre to all the school children of the town. A " Mechanics' Institution " had often been spoken of, and letters recommending one, had from time to time appeared in the papers. I sympathized strongly with this feeling, and one day without consulting any other person I sat down, wrote a circular, sent it to the printer and caused it to be delivered to the most likely persons in the town, inviting them to attend a preliminary meeting for starting such an institution. It was to be held in one of the Cannon Street rooms. This circular was responded to by six individuals! If the reader of this will imagine half-a-dozen persons seated on a form, with a single candle to enlighten their proceedings, and the writer of this opening out his plans, he will have a view of the origin of that Institution whose building is now among the first in the town, an ornament to Avenham Walks and the vicinity, with a library of 8,000 volumes. This meeting was held on the 11th September, 1828, and the original circular is now framed in the institution. It was agreed to call it "The Institution for the Diffusion of Knowledge." Great efforts were made to collect subscriptions, to get a library and museum, in which I took my share. The making of the first catalogue was my sole work during my convalescence following a rheumatic fever. No other gentleman gave so much time at the beginning as the late Mr. Gilbertson, surgeon, and next to him I may name Mr. Ascroft, attorney. Many a long evening did we spend till a late hour, numbering and labelling the books, arranging the library, planning the museum, forming the classes, and providing for the lectures. The Institution soon secured the support of the town, but still not the support of the operatives to the extent we expected, much less that class technically called "mechanics." Yet to meet the condition of these we fixed the subscription as low as 1s. 7½d. per quarter, or 6s. 6d. per year. I well remember when this was discussed, observing in favour of this low charge, that it was just 1½d. per week, the price of a glass of ale. A considerable sum was spent in purchasing first-class books in the arts and sciences, but few of these were ever asked for. At the present time but few of the working classes are members of this Institution. The operations were carried on in Cannon Street for twenty-one years, the present building being entered upon in 1849, which, though for many years it laboured under pecuniary embarrassment, is now out of debt, with funds in hand, the proceeds of the last Exhibition.

My last effort of any magnitude in this line, was in connection with "The Working Men's Club," at No. 3, Lord Street. This building had been a gentleman's large house, but being much out of repair and in an undesirable situation, had been shut up for some time. I long had my eye upon it as suitable for some public purpose, and ventured to take it to try the experiment of starting a working men's club. The Rev. R. Macnamara, the curate of the Parish Church, was a warm advocate for these clubs, and with his and the assistance of others, a sufficient fund was raised to put the premises into first-rate order. In a pecuniary sense it has been quite successful, yet it has not attracted the drinking men from the public-house as many expected. In the eating department it has excelled, and in this way, no doubt, it has been very useful in preventing great numbers going to the public-house for their victuals, where they would be expected to drink. I was chosen president from the first, which I resigned a few months ago. This Institution now comprises the eating department, an excellent reading room, a gymnasium, a room for meetings, and several smaller ones for amusements. Mr. Geo. Penny, junior, has been the secretary from the beginning. My experience as the proprietor of a temperance hotel may appear hereafter.

It may occur to some to ask the question, how I could find the time or spare the expense necessarily required by my connection with these undertakings, especially the earlier ones, considering that I had to start out of nothing, and with a large family always to provide for. I may explain, first, that in all these movements I adhered strictly to the principle of utility and economy in every detail; I sought for nothing fine, nothing dazzling, and hence the expenses were always far less than where persons are guided by fashion and appearances. And, next, being successful in business and always careful and saving, in which I was joined by my wife, I always had something to spare for what I deemed a good purpose. I avoided all speculations, and with one exception, I believe, I have been invariably better off at the end of the year than at the beginning. This exception, however, was a serious one, and had well nigh upset me. By great exertions and perseverance I had got a little money beforehand, more than I regularly required in the cheese business. A person with whom I became friendly was in the cotton business as a manufacturer, and afterwards as a commission agent. He often repeated to me how profitable his business was, and, with additional capital how much he could make. With little experience of the treachery of the world I was tempted by the offer to become a partner, to let him have a considerable amount. This was in 1827; and under the influence of misplaced confidence I foolishly left the management of the business to himself, and became a sleeping partner. Believing his assurances from time to time that we were fast making money, I let him have all I could possibly spare. The sequel may be shortly told. Trade became depressed; I could get no satisfactory explanation as to the position of the concern; creditors became pressing, and he left the concern, and the town also, for me to do with as I pleased. It was a trying time; after emancipating myself from the weaver's cellar, and labouring and toiling, both of us, almost night and day, with half-a-dozen children about our feet, to find as we feared all gone at once by the treachery of one in whom we had confided as a friend, was a condition which experience alone will enable anyone to realise. I was left to wind up a business of which I was ignorant, and to provide for all its liabilities, the creditors pressing to be settled with. At such a moment it is cheering to have a partner to share your burden, and keep up your spirits. "Never mind," said my dear wife when she saw me cast down, "we shall get through; we worked hard for what we had; it is lost, but we can work for more." Mr. George Cooper, father to Mr. John Cooper, of the Oaks, was the largest creditor. Time was given me; I turned the stock into money, and by either two or three instalments I paid every creditor the full amount of his claim. By this unfortunate business I lost in money £1,600, and adding the disadvantage of robbing my own business of capital, and the time I was taken from it, I always considered the loss was equal to £2,000. It was a lesson on the question of partnerships which has lasted me for life. On the payment of the last instalment Mr. Cooper proposed that a silver cup should be presented to me by the creditors as a mark of respect for my honourable conduct, but I respectfully declined the offer, considering that I had done nothing more than an honest man ought to do. With our wonted diligence, industry, and carefulness we soon found ourselves prosperous again. I have not the same reason to think so well of the cotton trade as some fortunate ones. As I stated before, my father and grandfather, betwixt them, lost all they had in the cotton trade, and I had to go to the loom as the consequence. My sons will have defective memories if they forget these two lessons.

CHAPTER IX.

This chapter will contain a sketch of my labours in connection with the press. From a youth I had a strong inclination for scribbling, and, no doubt, like many young people, I formed an over estimate of my talent for this work. I was not wanting in the ambition to see one's self in print; and there are cases, unquestionably, where this turns out to be useful. Long before I attained my majority I wrote many letters to the newspapers, and it would be difficult for me to form any estimate as to the extent of space I have occupied in the correspondent's columns, especially in the local papers. Sometimes I would follow my inclination by writing "addresses" and "appeals," generally condemnatory of some popular vice, and publishing these as posters on the walls. A few of these are still preserved. From placards I got to pamphlets; one, I remember, was entitled "The Besetting Sin," directed against drunkenness, but, as I then knew no better, it recognized the moderate use of strong drink. There was one on "Confirmation;" another on "Sunday Schools;" also, a "First Book," for persons learning to read, which, I believe, had some merit. Each lesson filled a page, and finished with a verse of poetry of my own composition, for which, I confess, I have no talent. Commencing with short words, without silent letters, the lessons were better adapted for beginners than those in any elementary work I have seen. I published also in 1825, "An Address to the poorest classes," price 2d., which contained advice upon almost every topic connected with domestic management. This had a considerable sale, and went through several editions. In January, 1831, I commenced *The Moral Reformer*, price 6d., which was continued monthly, forming, at its conclusion, three yearly volumes. The contents of this work are miscellaneous; but bearing chiefly on moral questions, domestic management, and practical religion. The second and third volumes took up, and was the first periodical to advocate, the teetotal doctrine. This publication was superseded by my *Temperance Advocate*, which commenced in January, 1834, and was published monthly for four years. In no work of that period, I may venture to say, was there the same amount of clear reasoning, strong arguments, powerful facts, and interesting narratives and intelligence, as in this periodical. If I could procure a perfect copy, or a few copies, I should not object to give three times the published price for them. It was the first and the only teetotal periodical issued till the *Temperance Star*, *Herald*, &c., made their appearance. At the close of 1837, I handed over this work, and the connection, to "The British Association" (now "League"), and it has been continued by this body, with some changes in its form, ever since. I then commenced, in January, 1838, a new series of the *Moral Reformer;* but, owing to bad health, it was abruptly brought to a close in February the following year.

The Anti-Corn Law agitation, in which I took an active part, required a periodical adapted for the working-classes. I therefore commenced, in 1841, an illustrated paper, called *The Struggle*, which I brought out every Saturday morning for four and a half years, price one half-penny. The questions of free trade, corn law repeal, cheap bread, and collateral subjects, were discussed and illustrated in all their phases; and, for the designs and drawings, I was much indebted to Messrs. Harvey and Aspland, of Liverpool. The illustrations, though by no means first-rate, were well adapted to influence the popular mind. A considerable number of these were engraved by my son Howard. This little work was said to have produced deep impressions upon the agricultural labourers, amongst whom and other classes it had a large circulation. When I state that these periodicals, extending over the years 1832 to 1847, were got out amidst the toils of business, that most of the articles were written by myself, and that my general health at that time was not good, my friends may well join me in surprise as to how I was able to accomplish so much. But the fact is, whatever I engaged in, I pursued with as much energy as if the success depended upon my exertions alone. I occasionally glance over the 940 pages of *The Struggle*, and the 370 engravings, and read with great interest, now that the struggle is over, some of the pithy striking articles which they contain; and, looking back, I often wonder how I got through all this labour. On closing this work, I remember, I was so "done up," that I could not make an effort to get an engraving for the last number, and hence I had to order that which had appeared in No. 234 to be repeated in 235, the first pages appearing now with the same design. About this time I fortunately became acquainted with the "Water Treatment;" and, with this and rest, I shortly seemed fit for another campaign. For some time I had cherished a wish to start a newspaper, some of my sons having become acquainted with the printing business. I sent for my son John, and made a proposition to commence a Preston paper, although it was supposed that the ground was fully occupied. The first issue was in February, 1844. It was called the *Preston Guardian*, and in face of many difficulties it succeeded far beyond my expectation. Indeed, on one occasion, Mr. Cobden, referring to it, said he never remembered a case of a local paper succeeding as this had done in so short a time, and subject to the same competition. I should like here to record the fact which I have often stated in private, that *had it not been for cold water, there would not have been any Preston Guardian*. For some years my son John was the editor, commencing when only twenty-one, I writing occasionally the leaders on local matters; and to his talent the success might in a great measure be attributed. My eldest son, William, in addition to sub-editing and writing occasional leaders, had the management of the business department for many years, until compelled to relinquish it by ill-health. My youngest son, Franklin Livesey, was for some time connected with the paper, and my son Howard gave occasional assistance. It became a good property, and was sold to Mr. George Toulmin, the present proprietor, in 1859. During all this time the superintendence devolved in a great measure upon myself, and I need not inform those who have had any experience in connection with the newspaper press, of the labour and anxiety which were inseparable from such an undertaking.

My intense application often brought me down, but upon recovering I never felt easy without making some new effort to forward the moral and social improvement of the masses. In every agitation I recognised the power of the press, and felt the importance of enlisting its services in the object. In January, 1853, I commenced another monthly periodical, called "The Progressionist," but after the issue of six or seven numbers I was obliged, for want of health, to hand it over to other hands, I being an occasional contributor. I may also name that, at one time, I issued a series of what I called "Letter Linings," neatly printed on writing paper, so as to be enclosed with letters in a fair sized envelope without being folded. They were about ten in number, all of a practical character. The following headings will give an idea of them :—"For the parlour table ;" " Remember the poor ;" " Pay your debts." Economy, as I have hinted before, was always practised in our housekeeping. I felt convinced that many people are little aware of the amount of their expenditure for want of keeping a record of it, and are at a loss how and in what to save when they find their means inadequate. Not satisfied with the arrangement of the "Housekeeper's Registers" then in circulation, I got one up to my own mind, and published it, price one shilling. I was disappointed as to its sale, and I have always found, for some reason or other, that wives are very unwilling to use a register. If they are supplied with one the entries are generally irregular or neglected.

Of my publications in connection with the temperance movement, it will be difficult to give any adequate idea. I have already spoken of my "Advocate." For some time after the commencement of teetotalism, in 1832, the whole country was supplied with tracts from my office. I started a small printing establishment in that year, and, besides tracts of my own writing, I reprinted many others, including valuable documents from America, such as " Thou shalt not kill," " Physiological influence of alcohol," " Temperance Doctor," &c. I have never since been without temperance tracts or bills in some shape. I published a sheet of the latter containing thirty-two in number, which were sold at 10d. a 1,000 Most of my bills have been published in London by others, and some in America, and I am sometimes amused to find these same bills reprinted in our periodicals at home, and acknowledged as belonging to American publications. Not long since, I noticed one of them, headed "I don't drink wine." Latterly I have brought out a fresh series of bills, larger and on good paper which I sell at 1s. 6d. per 1,000, the mere price of the paper and machining ; and these I am anxious to see circulated in millions. They are excellent for visiting with, and, without house to house visitation, I don't think any society can be said to do its duty. I believe I drew up and published the first teetotal almanac, and our Preston book of " melodies" is of my selecting. The chief parts of my lecture, generally known as the " Malt Liquor lecture," first appeared in the *Moral Reformer ;* but was published as a pamphlet (price 6d.) in 1835 or 1836. Soon after, penny editions were issued from London, Birmingham, Edinburgh, &c. In this latter form, stereotyped, I have continued it ever since; and I suppose the circulation of this lecture has equalled, if not exceeded, any that has ever appeared in defence of teetotal principles. In emergencies, I seem always to have been able to make an effort to defend what I considered the truth. I brought out a pamphlet of 16 pages, in defence of Wilson Patton's bill on Sunday closing, when it was threatened to be repealed. Every member of the House of Commons and Lords was supplied with a copy. I addressed a letter to Mr. Gladstone, when he introduced his wine and grocers' licenses. Preferring, as I do, imperial to permissive legislation in coping with the drink traffic, so powerful in numbers, wealth, and audacity, I published a pamphlet in 1862, entitled " Free and friendly remarks upon the Permissive Bill, Temperance Legislation, and the Alliance." When the repeal of the malt tax was threatened, in 1864, I entered fully into every branch of the question in a pamphlet, entitled " Malt, Malt Liquor, Malt Tax, Beer, and Barley," being a reply to Sir Fitzroy Kelly, M.P. for East Suffolk, Mr. Everett, Mr. Smee, and other gentlemen, on the Repeal of the Malt Tax, and which had a large circulation. In fact, I never seemed as if I could sit down and be quiet when I saw work wanted doing, and felt able to render any assistance. I have always taken great interest in the establishment and circulation of temperance periodicals. I gave considerable time in assisting to start the " Alliance News." From the first I have watched with concern the progress of the " Temperance Advocate ;" and in order to raise the circulation I consented, in 1862, again to undertake the editorship, and to commence a " new series," on which occasion the following note was sent by our friend, Thomas Whittaker :—" You may send twelve copies of the paper weekly, for which I will try to get subscribers among my neighbours. I am made young again by the intelligence that Mr. Joseph Livesey, the father of the *Temperance Advocate*, has consented once again to revive and discipline his somewhat wayward child. Many besides myself will rejoice at this arrangement." After adding considerably to the number of subscribers, at the end of nine weeks I was, owing to being overworked, obliged to relinquish my duties. And now, feeling indisposed to leave home, and for the last year and nine months having been compelled to forego any inclination to do so on account of the infirmities of my wife, almost the only means left me to serve the cause to any extent is the press. Of my present undertaking I need say little. The *Staunch Teetotaler* was commenced with much misgiving; but having brought it to its twenty-first number, I rejoice that during these 20 months I have been able, in this way, to be among the hosts of our noble army, combating the greatest tyrant that ever ruled on God's earth. Of the execution of this work I have only to say that my teetotal friends generally seem well pleased. I constantly receive letters of commendation too flattering for me to publish. My chief aim, from the first, was to stimulate our friends to increased efforts, and to convince them of the folly of relying upon patronage, plausible reports, legislation, or anything else in place of their own labours.

With the sale of the copyright of the *Preston Guardian*, was coupled the whole of the plant, so that my printing establishment, started in 1832, closed with the year 1859, and, since then, I have got all my work done at other offices. Although unfavourable to testimonials, and having several times opposed the wishes of my friends in that direction in reference to myself, I felt, in parting with the office, that I ought to allow the men an opportunity of expressing their feelings on that occasion. This they did by presenting, engraved on vellum and beautifully framed, the following address :—

AN ADDRESS PRESENTED TO JOSEPH LIVESEY, ESQ., AT HIS RESIDENCE, BANK
PARADE, ON WEDNESDAY, FEBRUARY 1, 1860, BY THE PERSONS IN HIS
LATE EMPLOY.

Dear Sir,

We, the undersigned persons, employed upon the *Preston Guardian* newspaper, (from the management and proprietorship of which you have just retired)
are anxious to express our grateful sense of the numerous favours received by us
from your hands, and to record our conviction of the extended usefulness of
your labours, and the purity of motive by which your conduct in public and
private has been regulated.

Your example cannot fail to exercise a great influence upon the young men
of the present and next generations, as the leading events of your extraordinary
career are well known throughout England ; but, in Lancashire—especially that
part of the County which has had the benefit of your personal service—your
name has become, and must for a long time remain, a household word of esteem
and reverence. The domestic virtues have been enforced by your tongue and
pen, and beautifully illustrated in your practice. The obligations and duties of
a public man have been taught and exemplified in you with rare consistency.
Your biography when written will exhibit one of the most notable instances of
"the pursuit of knowledge under difficulties," and of its true application.
Patient industry, singleness of purpose, directness of aim, modesty and confidence, unostentatious charity, and practical benevolence, are the salient traits
of character which your long life has embodied. These qualities have won for
you the respect of all earnest men, and have enlisted the affection of those who
have been immediately associated with you in various undertakings ; your
anxiety on all occasions, and by every means which you considered legitimate,
to promote the comfort and happiness of the persons in your employment,
establishes a claim on their gratitude, and we fully recognise and admit our
share of these benefits.

It is usually the fate of public men to have their intentions and motives
questioned by ungenerous contemporaries, but we can assure you that the results
of your labours are not undervalued by the great bulk of the community. And
it cannot be otherwise than satisfactory for you to observe how many habits and
institutions have been amended, reformed, and established—some partially,
others chiefly, some entirely—through your exertions.

Although your retirement is not a matter that we can regard with indifference, or indeed without some regret, we cannot deny that the repose you now
seek has been fairly earned by a long period of successful toil for the public
good. We do not, therefore, feel that, if we had the power, we should be justified
in trying to alter your decision. We only venture to ask that you will continue
by your precept and example, so far as may be compatible with your own free
and full enjoyment of existence, to aid the endeavours of the poor to amend
their lives and circumstances. We also wish, by this address, to convey our
sincere and heartfelt desire that you may be spared many years to witness the
further realisation of those political and social reforms which you have helped
to create ; and we fervently hope that in retirement, you and your family may
experience a degree of happiness, not to be derived from such arduous and
anxious pursuits as those in which you have been, until very recently, engaged.

We are, dear sir, yours very faithfully and sincerely,

J. A. DENHAM.	GEORGE TAYLOR.	JOHN CASH.
WALTER BOND.	GEORGE COULTHARD.	THOS. H. HEALD.
RICHARD CLARKSON.	W. A. WATTS.	CHARLES GREENALL.
THOMAS BUTCHER.	JOHN CRAGG.	THOMAS BREWER.
THOMAS POOLE.	ISAAC HENDERSON.	JONATHAN SHEPHERD.
RICHARD SHEPHERD.	MARK PARKINSON.	A. V. MYRES.

CHAPTER X.

I now pass from the *press* to the *platform*. This has been from the carpeted stage of a theatre to a table, a chair, a cart, the fishstones, a gravestone, or an elevated sod. I have never disliked the "stumping" expedient where any good could be done. And observing at the present time the sort of meetings that lords and squires are holding to forward their own electioneering interests, our teetotalers never need be ashamed of standing up in the field or in the market place, or anywhere to plead the cause of temperance. My platform labours nave been chiefly in connection with this movement, ranging over full 36 years, though at times I have spoken and given lectures on other topics. I remember the titles of some of them :—"Health and Happiness," "Cottage Economy," "Hydropathy," "Forty years ago," &c. I should have been asked oftener to lecture for our public institutions, but the parties were afraid of my introducing too much teetotalism into them. One of my clerical correspondents after reading some of these papers, writes, " You have been a man of war from your youth." If so, I am glad to say the weapons of my warfare have been bloodless, and I trust generally calculated to produce peace and good-will among men. Wrong, oppression, corruption, would at any time bring me out to contend against them. If my friend had said "You have been an agitator from your youth," he would not have been far from the truth; though not so much a political as a social agitator, for in meddling with the former it was under a conviction that the welfare of the masses would be benefited by it. No one in Preston laboured harder than I did to promote the carrying of the Reform Bill in 1832. Turning to the *Preston Chronicle* of that year, I find reports of our meetings in the Orchard, and of the speeches delivered by myself, and by the late Mr. Segar, barrister, and Mr. R. Ascroft. I had been a witness of and to some extent a sharer in the sufferings which the people of England endured from the peace of 1815 to the above period, under the corn laws and the reign of protection ; and I hoped that a reformed Parliament would give us free trade, and other measures that would relieve and pacify the country. Nobody wrote more strongly on this subject than I did in my *Moral Reformer*. I seem at present to have little taste for politics, but during my earlier career I was always at my post supporting the Liberal party. I have witnessed many hardly contested elections in Preston, and taken part in a few ; but unless they could be contested with greater purity and less violence, it would be difficult to persuade me to do the same again. Our borough had the singular privilege of " universal suffrage ;" every man of 21 years of age with a six months residence, unless a pauper, had a right to vote; hence the constituency was always large in proportion to the population. Violence and rioting were seldom wanting, and bribery and corruption were rampant. Mr. Dobson, in his "History of the Elections of Preston," examined the bills of three of the elections of "Horrocks and Hornby," held in 1812, 1818, and 1820. In the first, for polling 1,379 votes, the expenses on their side only, were £5,671 17s. 6d. There were 56 public-house bills amounting to £3,807 13s. 7d. ! The expenses of the next election exceeded this, and the public-house bills amounted to £4,111 4s. 7d. The next in 1820, was still more severe, and the expenses of the one party amounted to £11,559 12s. 8d., the public-house bills being £8,203 19s. 4d.! There seems to be no record of the expenses of the opposing party, but at this last election it was stated that Mr. Williams's (the opposition candidate) expenses were £6,000. It will be seen that the publicans at that period, as at present, came in for the lion's share of the prey. Such was the corruption that, without "open houses," as they were called, it was difficult to get on in electioneering. The polling at that time lasted 15 days; it was subsequently reduced to eight, and by the Reform Bill to two, and since to only one—quite long enough unless the people and their patrons could learn to behave better and be more honest. At "Wood's election," as it is called, in 1826, I rendered considerable help in securing his return. His representation of Preston secured him the appointment of Recorder for York. He afterwards became chairman of Stamps and Taxes, and subsequently chairman of the Inland Revenue Department. At one of the elections (I think it was in 1830) when the Hon. E. G. Stanley, the present Earl of Derby, was a candidate, I remember his addressing the crowd from one of the Bull windows, and I replied to him from one of the Red Lion windows nearly opposite. I had not spoken long before half a brick, thrown by some one in the crowd, caught the window frame where I was speaking. On some of these occasions "bludgeon men" were organised and trained to do the fighting; and I have seen, by the entrance of a party of this class, the Area of the Exchange, containing perhaps 4,000 people, cleared in a few minutes. We had both Cobbett and Hunt as candidates in our borough, and the defeat of Stanley, (the present Earl of Derby) by the latter, was a very remarkable event, though by no means the result of fair play. The races were abandoned, the Cock-pit closed, subscriptions were withdrawn, and the family mansion was levelled to the ground. I assisted at several of the subsequent elections, and at none with more devotion and energy than at that in 1841, when free trade and the repeal of the corn laws were the great questions. At this contest we returned "Fleetwood and Strickland," in opposition to "Parker and Swainson," (the present R. T. Parker, Esq., of Cuerden Hall). There are many who will still remember the election cry of "sour pie," raised to show the evil of high sugar duties, which our protectionist candidates defended. My sons, William and John, were also warm electioneerers, and the success of more than one contest was, in no small measure, owing to their exertions. I always viewed the repeal of the corn laws as a question of humanity, and besides agitating at Preston, I visited Lancaster, and spent nearly a fortnight at Walsall. At "Crawford's election" in 1837, by speaking from the windows in the rain, I caught a severe cold and was laid up of rheumatic fever nearly two months. At these elections, I often felt much mortified at being mixed up with persons whose practices were anything but reputable, a course I never could undertake again; and yet it is difficult to say, according to the present system, how measures for the welfare of the nation are to be carried if persons of character and influence keep aloof from these contests.

Always a friend of religious equality, I disapproved of Church rates and Easter dues. I cannot recollect that I ever paid either. On these points I adhered to the opinion of the Quakers, that it was better to suffer as a protest against what I considered quite as injurious to the Church itself as unjust to those who never required its services. And it is some consolation to know that the principles I so long advocated, have been recognised by the legislature ; for even in the case of Easter dues it has recently been decided that in Preston the payment cannot be legally enforced. I could never see the justice of a minister of religion having the power to lay a tax upon every family in his parish ; charging the poor widow as much as the richest lady, and all independent of any services rendered or required. An Anti-Easter Dues Association was formed to resist this demand. Notices were followed by summonses, and summonses by warrants, and warrants on different occasions by seizure of goods. At one of these distraints made upon seven householders whose goods and furniture were taken, two cheese weighing 51lbs. were taken from our warehouse, for a demand upon me for 6½d. The sale of all the articles was advertised to take place at the Obelisk in the Market Place. Great excitement prevailed, and on this occasion some thousands of people were present. The cheese, chairs, bedding, &c., were brought out under the protection of the police ; the hour arrived and passed, but no one appeared to sell, the auctioneer who had been engaged, having proved faint-hearted. I addressed the people in the meantime from the Obelisk, and I confess that I felt thankful after that a riot had not taken place. The goods could not be sold in Preston, and after being kept for a long time, were sent to Liverpool to be disposed of. On the occasion of another seizure, my cheese taken for Easter dues were sold on the lockup steps, without opposition. Finding that it was of no use contending with me, and that I preferred suffering to paying, and that my refusal only brought on agitation, I was let alone, and I should say, for more than 20 years, no compulsory proceedings have been taken. I have no doubt many good Church people see now, how impolitic it has been to sustain their religion by such means, and for which no defence could ever be made, beyond this, that " it was the law."

It would be difficult for me to enumerate all the smaller matters in which I have been engaged generally as a speaker. Having always had a fair amount of self-possession, and a tolerable facility for speaking in public, my help was often solicited ; and considering the good feeling that I find existing towards me, even by parties that I have had occasion to oppose, it is evident that however they may have disapproved of my actions, they have given me credit for having been uninfluenced by bad motives.

One of my last efforts for the public good has been well spoken of by all. The suspension of the Preston Bank in July, 1866, will be well remembered. No hope of its resuscitation seemed to be entertained by any one for some time. I believe I was the first to express a belief that it could be done. Repeated meetings of the shareholders were held at which I was appointed chairman ; and gradually they became hopeful that the catastrophe of a winding-up,—with all the distress and misery to families and tradesmen and the town, which were sure to follow,—might be averted. I never felt the importance of making a desperate effort so much as I did on this occasion, though I was only the holder of five shares myself. Without going into particulars, for some weeks I gave myself wholly to this business. Meetings of depositors were called at different towns. I attended and spoke at them all; I was at three in one day—at Lytham, Blackpool, and Fleetwood. Under the advice of Mr. D. Chadwick, of Manchester, and with the assistance of Mr. R. Ascroft, and other friends and shareholders, arrangements were satisfactorily made with the creditors, all of whom are now paid, and the bank put upon a footing which, with proper management, cannot fail to be prosperous. At its resuscitation I was pressed to become one of the directors; and at the end of two years' service, contrary to my strong desire, I have just been re-elected for three more years. In looking back upon this successful affair, my satisfaction seems only equal to the gratitude of my townsmen. And what deserves to be remarked is, that with this additional duty, and the getting out of the *Staunch Teetotaler*, both occurring at the same time, my health during these last two years seems better than it was before.

All the time I have been writing these papers, I have felt it disagreeable to be speaking so much of myself; but if some of my readers, especially the young men, should be induced by my example to forego their own ease and pleasure, and devote their time and talents and means, in any enlarged measure, to the public good, I shall feel well rewarded.

CHAPTER XI.

I may now speak of my health. At the death of my parents, when only seven years of age, I was very delicate and weakly, and being left in the care of my grandfather, who was a small farmer, I was recommended to go into the shippon every morning for a cup of new milk from the cow, which did me a great deal of good, and all through life milk has been my favourite beverage. I was set early to work, but often felt unequal to what I had to perform. After leaving the loom and commencing the cheese business, I had to travel the country many days in the week, and my constitution being unable to resist the cold and wet I was seized the first or second year with rheumatic fever. On my mother's side there was an hereditary tendency to rheumatism. It would be difficult to describe the sufferings I endured, and such was the exhaustion of my poor weak frame that it was a quarter of a year before I was thoroughly recovered. The joints of both hands and feet were swollen, and quite fast, and I endured the most excruciating pains. For weeks I got little or no sleep. The slightest motion occasioned by my attendants walking over the floor was more than my poor nerves could bear. Sometimes I was delirious, and I saw, as I fancied, the most horrid spectres in the room. Though covered only with a single sheet, the heat of my body was almost unbearable, and such was the agony I endured that the vapour could be seen rising visibly from under the sheet. My business suffered much, and my dear wife who had to attend to it, and also to attend upon me, was worn down with anxiety and fatigue. I had afterwards, at intervals, rheumatic fever three other times, confining me to the room or keeping me from business from two to three months each time. It is impossible to describe what I have suffered, and considering how my constitution must have been impaired by these repeated attacks, it is a cause for deep thankfulness that I should be here recounting and detailing the events of my past life.

Like most people who are ignorant of the working and wants of the human frame, I not only implicitly followed the advice and took the medicines of my medical attendants, but was at all times ready to listen to the persuasions of kind friends who came with numberless prescriptions, some for curing and some for preventing my complaint. At each of the four rheumatic fevers I had a different doctor, and, beyond keeping my bowels more regular, I don't believe that their medicines did me a particle of good. Their general remark was, "it must have its time." Our drawers and cupboards were stored with physic bottles and pill boxes, and it was a happy day for me when I discovered their comparative uselessness, and learnt that nature is always curing, and that physic oftener retards than assists her wonderful conservative operations. For years I was seldom without severe colds and often ailing. During the winter of 1842-3 I was worse than usual, feeble, spiritless, and so susceptible of cold that if I went out in hazy weather I was almost sure to be laid up. About this time I met with Claridge's sixpenny pamphlet on the water cure, and was so struck with his statements and the cures he had seen at Grafenberg, that I was induced to make a partial trial of the water applications. Getting no relief from medicine, I was willing to try anything. Having already described my experience and practice of the hydropathic treatment, and my present plan of using the hand bath every morning, in chapters 4 and 5, I need not here repeat the same. Some consider me an enthusiast in my unceasing practice and recommendation of water inside and out, but if a man gets 15 or 20 years usefulness added to his life ; gets rid of rheumatic fevers and other sufferings, he may well be an enthusiast. Whether all the hydropathic baths have the virtues attributed to them I am not prepared to say, but of this I feel confident, that there is scarcely a person living who, having neglected his skin, never washing perhaps more than hands and face, will not be benefited by a fair trial. Though my health was generally improved, and though after adopting the water treatment I never had rheumatic *fever*, yet I was not quite free afterwards from rheumatic pains. We were so unfortunate as to move into the country, where we had a cold clay soil, and this and other exposures brought on chronic rheumatism in the ankle joints, from which I suffered severely for seven years, so much so that at one time I had to have recourse to the use of crutches. Moving to a warmer situation and a dryer sub-soil, about seven or eight years ago the swelling began to subside, and gradually left me, and it is really wonderful that now I am quite free from it, and walk as well as I did when I was young. Considering the long standing of this chronic affection, and my advanced age, many persons in the medical profession say that such a recovery is very uncommon. Very few persons commence the water treatment who don't get a strong dislike to physic, and lose faith in its efficacy. This has been so much the case with me that I have not taken a particle of medicine, not so much as an aperient pill, for 14 years. To this and to my abstinence from alcoholic liquors, and my other abstemious habits, I mainly attribute the improved health I have enjoyed during these later years. Still, I feel that the hand of time is not to be bribed. If I write too much or too long at a time, or read too long any matter leading to thought and reflection, I feel that the nervous power is too severely tasked, and indigestion, with its depressing consequences, is sure to follow. A change of pursuits, sometimes mental, sometimes physical, and relaxation if you can get it, enables a person to do much more than if he were always following one and the same thing. This is one great advantage I have always had. I was never without a good many irons in the fire, though some of them might be in danger of burning. Restless, of independent feelings, and never idle, it would be difficult to say how many things I have been engaged in, and this variety no doubt has been beneficial. Losing faith in physic, and learning the benefits of open-air exercise, cheerfulness, and temperance in eating as well as drinking, all of which are inculcated in the water treatment, I began to study the laws of health with great profit. It is very much to be regretted that even educated persons know so little of physiology, that they are daily violating these laws, and, as regards health, are entirely at the mercy of doctors or "quacks."

About 20 years ago I bought a piece of land at Bowness, the chief village included in the district of Windermere. I built two houses, one of which has afforded us a nice change in the course of the summer. I also erected a small Temperance Hall and other buildings, and lastly, four good houses, allowed to be the best of the kind in the village, so I have had some experience of "bricks (or rather stones) and mortar." Many a time, when quite overdone with the turmoil and anxiety of unavoidable engagements in the town, have I run down there for a little quiet, and being fond of shrubs and flowers, this place, with solitude as a change, seemed for a short time almost a Paradise. The front grounds of these houses adjoin the public road. Cheap trips to Windermere, "the Queen of the English lakes," are numerous every summer, and from the walks I often converse with the people over the railings. Of course, I warn them against drinking, and sometimes, to startle the topers, I point upwards to the four houses with mahogany window frames and plate-glass bay windows, and say, "you see those four houses." "Yes." "Well, I have cheated the landlords out of these!" Teetotalism, if it did nothing more than give a man a retreat like this in his old age is well worth embracing.

It would be difficult to live seventy years in this world of accidents ever occuring, without being exposed to some of them one's self. I have been thrown off a coach, pitched off a horse at full trot, and upset in driving a horse and gig down a hill. These are casualties that few who travel can escape; but I have had two very narrow escapes for my life, and both arose from the wanton conduct of men under the influence of drink. The first was in crossing the river Wyre, at Wardless, when it was very much swollen. I was in that district buying cheese, and stayed all night at the old inn, now used as a cottage. My son William was with me, then only a boy. It is a place where they ferry people over. Applying to the landlady to be taken across, early in the morning, she called upon a man then sitting in the house to take us. He appeared to be one who had been drinking all night. He went out and got a little flat-bottomed boat, so light that he wheeled it on a wheelbarrow. We (very foolishly, I must now confess) got into the boat and balanced ourselves. He appeared fresh, but we did not suspect but what he would be able to steer us over. When about midway he began to stagger, and fell over into the river. I felt sure we were upset and should be both drowned. The water was high and the stream rapid. The frail barque, however, righted itself, and the man either bottomed the river with his feet or he could swim. Alarmed as I was at his fall, I was still more so at his attempt to regain his place; he had well nigh capsized the boat with his attempts to get in. I was in a terrible fright; the drowning of us both seemed imminent, but I kept him at bay till he moved to the hinder part of the boat, and then pushed us forward. How thankful was I when I set foot on land! The next narrow escape was on the highroad from Chorley to Clayton, about half a mile from the Clayton toll bar. I was returning from Bolton market, in company with my friend, John Pomfret, in his gig. The evening was very dark. We were just at the bottom of a rather steep incline. Two of the bleacher's carters had been stopping to drink at the public-house at the top of the brow. On their coming out they had set their horses off at full trot, one against the other. Each cart had two or three horses and very heavy loads. We were at the bottom of the incline when they were at the top, and by our lamps we could see the perilous position we were in. There was little time to think or to act. I saw nothing but a certainty of our vehicle and horse and ourselves all being destroyed. They seemed to be abreast, each cart taking one side of the road. There was no chance of drawing to our own side, and I perceived that my friend was aiming, if possible, to drive between. Feeling impressed with a certainty of a collision I jumped out of the gig, with a view of reaching the parapet for safety; but in doing so fell on the road, and was so stunned as to be unable to rise, nor was there time to recover my legs. Oh! what a moment of suspense and terror! I expected nothing but to be crushed to death. There I lay while the carts passed, the wheel of one just missing my head. My friend got betwixt them safely. To describe the feeling I then experienced, and what I have experienced a hundred times ever since when I have thought of the awful situation I was then in, is impossible. Well may I, on personal grounds (and, indeed, who is there that may not?), swear eternal enmity to this cursed drink!

Some have expressed surprise how I have been able to give my attention and labour to so many matters. Well, in the first place, I seem as if I had never given myself rest or relaxation like other people. I have known very little of what is usually termed recreation; duty has been my pleasure, especially when engaged in something productive of good to the masses or the castaways. For years together I have never attended a "party," though often invited, and when the mayors of the borough have sent me invitations to their "dinners" or festive gatherings, I have always declined going. I had a strong objection to be found at any gathering where wine drinking was sure to be prominent, and where I could not with propriety protest against it. Indeed, I have carried this objection so far as always to refuse attendance at the wedding breakfasts of my own sons, when the lady's parents or friends would have wine on the table. I am not sure but I have carried this feeling too far; it has tended to separate me so much from the influential classes that the temperance cause may have gained less than it would have done by my mixing more with them. But I have always felt happiest among the poor—far happier sitting at a drunkard's fireside than in the drawing-room of my richest friend.

And, another reason of my getting through so much work is, that I have been greatly helped by my family. For the first 15 years after our marriage I had to struggle hard (for, even then, I could not refrain doing something for the public), but I never can sufficiently appreciate the assistance I received from the industry, carefulness, and good management of my wife. And the same I may say of all our children; without exception, they have all been active and industrious. When confined by one of my rheumatic fevers—kept from business for more than two months—my eldest son, William, then only 13 years of age, was a great help to us in the cheese warehouse; and as they have grown up they have all made themselves useful, and never, like many children, brought disgrace upon their parents, or entailed burdens upon us by their misconduct. I owe more than I can express to several of my sons, eight of whom are still living, the eldest turned 52, and the youngest 33. And what is most gratifying, five of them are avowed abstainers, and the others, if not so, are considerably influenced by their father's teaching upon this subject. Remembering the early days of these, when they walked before us two and two, admired by many, or when on every Good Friday I gave them a country ride, the interval affords matter for grave reflection, and reminds me forcibly of Job's saying that "his days were swifter than a weaver's shuttle."

I was always fond of children, and even now as I pass them in groups in the street, especially those that can just "toddle" about, I feel as if I could form one of the party. I could still drive the hoop, play the ball, or strike the shuttle-cock, and I do think if we could mix more with them we might save many from the sad state of degradation into which they fall. I hope, in concluding this chapter, I may be excused for appending the following extract from an article I wrote more than 30 years ago, relative to our youngsters :—

A real family man always takes delight in his children; and when everything around seems clothed with gloom and embarrassment, the smile of one child, the prattling of another, and the skipping of a third, create a source of enjoyment, and often lead him to forget his troubles. With myself, I confess, this has frequently been the case; and were it not for parental fondness, aided by the fascinations of children, how could we so gladly toil for their support, and spend upon them years of labour, without the least pecuniary return? But upon this subject a man must be a parent before he can feel as parents feel.

Who can love and admire Frank like Frank's father? He espies the parlour door open, and in he runs; and if I am on my feet he takes me by the hand and turns me to a chair. He then fetches my shoes, and does his best to put them on. He climbs my knee, takes my comb out of my waistcoat pocket, gets me to open it, combs my hair, now and then looking cunningly into my face to see if I am pleased. His next move is to climb up the chair back; perhaps he hurts his thumb, and I have to kiss it, which is an infallible cure. Children soon learn to like money; and hence he will perhaps venture to ask, in his own way, for a penny. The watch is a pretty plaything, so he will have it placed first to one ear and then to the other. If the days were ever so long, Frank would be my companion, were I disposed to play with him, till he fell fast asleep on my knee. I am exceedingly fond of children; and whatever others may think, I know that those who deserve to be called *parents*, will bear with me in relating these incidents. "Father, have you forgotten to bring those papers to give to poor people?" said Jem, as we were walking together, alluding to a quantity of Temperance papers which I had laid out for distribution. "No, I have got them in my pocket." "How many have you?" he again inquired. "I have plenty." "But how many is plenty?" "Perhaps about fifty." Jem, still scarcely satisfied with the answer, further inquired, "Would it not take a million to be *plenty* of some things?" "Indeed, I dare say it would; plenty is a very indefinite term." "I could not touch brown bread," said one of the boys at the breakfast table, as the plate went round, both sorts being usually supplied. "Now if I were to introduce one single regulation," I replied, "I know you would not only *touch* brown bread, but *eat* it, and not only *eat* it, but *like* it; and not only *like* it, but *ask for more*." Some surprise being expressed at this declaration, I continued—"This would be effected simply by keeping you for some time without food, and then giving you this bread to eat." I illustrated this by the following remark—"As I passed by a farm yard the other day, I saw some stirks eating *straw*, and apparently enjoying it. Now if these had been allowed meal and potatoes, or good hay every day, they would all have said, as you have said of bread, 'I cannot touch straw.' "—The young children have each a money box, with a little hole in the lid, always kept locked, and I keep the keys. One of them kept his box wrong side up, and when asked the reason, I was much amused with the answer. He said, "it was to prevent the mice getting in at the hole to eat the money."—"How many fathers have you?" said I to the children one morning. "Two," was the answer from some of the children; "one here and one in heaven." "Then have we not two mothers?" rejoined a little one who had been listening to the conversation.

CHAPTER XII.

When a man is induced to take a survey of his life, and of the part he may have played in the world, he is apt to consider what has led him into the peculiar line of action he has adopted. I was tempted the other day to refer to a "Phrenological" description of my character, presented to me by Mr. L. T. Fowler, as we are all curious to know what others say of us. And, I confess, my whole experience confirms what Mr. Fowler has stated in almost every particular. I will only instance two or three points. "You have the spirit of independence," say he, "and desire to have your own way—to rely upon your own strength and resources, and to carry out your own plans." Regardless of organization, my training from youth easily accounts for this. I had, so to speak, when young, to fight the world alone. Without help, and without association, my character and disposition must have chiefly grown out of my own reflections, arising from my isolated position. I was with my aged grandfather from my seventh to the twenty-first year of my age, whose only family consisted of himself, wife, and one son; and, for some time, of the son only, who was a person from whom I could learn nothing. Unlike those who are sent to mills or workshops, where character is formed in a great measure from associations, I had no companions to work with but my grandfather, much advanced in years, and who died at the age of 96. And I was equally destitute of books as I was of instructive companions. Even when I had chances I never cared to keep the company of the lads of the village. The consequence was, that almost upon every subject I have been unguided, and have had to form my own opinions; and this independence, commencing in youth, seems to have continued with me through life. Few have had more of the spirit of self-reliance than I have had; and seldom have I undertaken any enterprise but I have succeeded. With such antecedents, it might be expected that I should have "a way of my own" almost upon every matter. Even on the subject of temperance, though I have always tried to act in unison with those who are engaged in promoting the same object, I have seldom been able to commit myself to their policy and modes of action. I have been invited to become a vice-president by all our leading organizations, but I always refused, although at the same time I subscribe to their funds and wish them every success. I may say the same as to religious connexions, for, while I wish well to every party, whatever their form of faith, worship, or discipline may be, who really fear God and try to bless and benefit their fellow creatures, since I left the Baptists, I have not joined any particular denomination. In social undertakings the same independence seems to have guided me. I was always bent upon projecting something fresh—some new undertaking—and to resolutely follow it up, with such help as I could command, until it had become a success. This feeling of "individuality" seems to have stuck to me even in every day matters. Passing over others, I may just mention one point, because I conceive it bears upon one of our national habits, which an increase of intelligence, I hope, may tend to alter. I have long been convinced that there is as great a delusion existing in reference to the nutritious qualities of animal food as of beer. All our leading water doctors advise that flesh meat should be taken in greater moderation, but their advice is seldom regarded. Most people believe they could not live, at least they could not keep up their strength, without animal food. And many who have been accustomed to it and try, like a number who begin to abstain from alcoholic drinks, break down. Having read and thought a good deal upon this subject, I have long since come to the conclusion that the general belief in the highly nutritious properties of flesh meat is a mistake, and I have not arrived at this opinion without putting it to the test in my own case. I have abstained six months at a time without any loss of weight or strength, and I am now in my twelfth month without tasting fish, flesh, or fowl. I undertook this as an experiment, and, as before, I find no loss of weight or strength, but rather the contrary. And if ever I required a " generous diet," owing to the amount of labour and anxiety

I have been subject to, it has been during this period. There is, I feel certain, more nutriment in a pound of bread (the staff of life) than in a pound of flesh, and the difference in price is considerable. I cannot here enter into the argument at any length, but there is one advantage in the vegetarian diet (though that is scarcely a correct term) which I cannot omit. All medical authorities agree that people in the middle and upper ranks of life eat too much. In fact, they say more people kill themselves by over eating than over drinking. "Stuffing" is the greatest source of indigestion, for which I should say poverty was the best remedy. What is there that ministers more to over eating than those tempting and savoury dishes of which the English are so proud, made up of all kinds of animal food? Let *these* be abandoned, and there is far less danger of over eating. And, as a question of economy, there cannot be two opinions. My dinner, at home, as a rule, say three potatoes and a little butter, followed by a little pudding or roasted apples, or something equally simple, never costs more than 6d. And, it is a fact, if I did not occasionally check myself npon this diet I should get more corpulent than I like. I need no "castors;" mustard and pepper and spices are far better out of the stomach. Nature requires them not, and they only stimulate to weaken and do mischief. I should not have dwelt thus upon my own case if I did not believe that my countrymen have much to learn upon this subject; and, if they wish for information, they could not do better than to read the various publications in favour of a vegetarian diet; sold by J. Burns, 1, Wellington Road, Camberwell, London. Parents are very often blamed, and are blamable, for giving their children tea instead of milk; but they are equally mistaken in giving them flesh meat to make them strong.

If Mr. Fowler's chart can be relied upon, my organ of "acquisitiveness" is largely developed; and, in my experience, this seems to be fully confirmed. From my earliest years I had a strong inclination to *acquire* and to *save*, even in matters that others would have thought too trifling to care for. And when, in after life, opportunities were presented on a larger scale, I was never reluctant to embrace them. In business, nobody could strike a harder or more profitable bargain; and if this feeling had not been counteracted by "benevolence being large and active," as Mr. Fowler puts it, it is difficult to say the evils to which it might have led. A fondness for acquiring, and a not unwillingness to give when occasion required, seem to have marked my path through life. I was at one time fond of attending auctions, and sometimes my desire for "bargains" led me to make foolish purchases. I have got many a lecture at home, and deservedly so, for buying lots of lumber, and incommoding the house with useless things. I once bought a farm which I had never seen. Entering the auction room, it was hanging under the hammer at £1,700, and I immediately bid another £100. I knew the distance it was from the town, and the measurement of the land, but nothing more. Some other person offered another £100, and I followed, when it was knocked down to me at £2,000. I could ill spare the money, but, before the day of payment arrived, a friend of mine, fancying the place, took it off my hands, giving me a couple of sovereigns for my trouble.

Mr. Fowler gives me credit for being "free in the use of language, and with a little excitement you can talk quite copiously." In speaking I never tried to be eloquent, my aim always was to make myself understood—to render everything I wished to teach as plain as possible, and in this I seldom failed. I sometimes felt a little anxious before I commenced an address, but once on my feet, I experienced no difficulty in proceeding, and had always a remarkable amount of self-possession. In writing, my great aim has always been to make everything plain and easy to be understood, and without this no permanent impression can be expected. Some authors boast of writing their sheets and sending them off hand, direct to the printers. I cannot do this. Perhaps I am too fastidious; but every article I write is afterwards read over and corrected twice. If there is a weak expression I try to strengthen it; if a confused sentence I alter it, or write it afresh; and for this extra labour I have always been rewarded by the appreciation and approval of my readers. Even in corresponding with an individual, it is pleasant to receive a plain, well-constructed letter, but when you expect your productions to be read by thousands, it would seem criminal not to make them as perfect as you can. And after all, I seldom read one of my own articles in print but I could improve it. If the penmanship was as plain as my diction, my printer would have less occasion to complain.

In concluding these memoirs, it might be expected that I should give a lengthened account of my labours in connection with the temperance cause; but I have so often had occasion to refer to these, and having also published a series of papers entitled "Reminiscences of Early Teetotalism," in which my earliest efforts are specially noticed, I think it unnecessary to refer again to them at any length. I may, however, be excused for giving the following extract from notes which I made in the year 1853. They were written when I was very lame, at a water establishment in Germany, and with little expectation that I should ever be able to do much more work for the temperance cause.

"To the temperance cause I have devoted more time and more labour than to any other. I always saw that it lay at the foundation of all personal and domestic happiness, and of every social and political reform. In fact, without sobriety—and sobriety in the highest sense—you can do nothing. You may, indeed, project various systems of amelioration; but unless you can get both rulers, teachers, and people to be the decided enemies, not of drunkenness merely, but of intoxicating liquors, you can never carry these out with effect. To this good cause I can sincerely say I have devoted days and nights and years of labour, without any consideration but the pleasure of seeing people and families being made better and happier by it. Though often pained at the effects produced by drink, yet up to the year 1830 I took it myself, though in great moderation—say a glass or two when travelling, and a glass or two on a market day; but, I think, we never kept any in the house to treat our friends with—our habits of economy, if there had been no other reason, not admitting of this. Up to this period, like all other mistaken persons, I considered that the liquor was good; that it was the gift of Providence, and that the error of mankind lay in taking it to excess. . . . It would be tedious to advert in detail to the interesting incidents which have occurred to me during my connection with the temperance cause—since its commencement. The first seven years was a period of hard work and devotedness to the cause. The next seven reminded me that I had a large family growing up, but not over well provided for, so that my labours in this work were at periods only as convenience served, my time and attention being more thoroughly engaged in business. During the last seven years I have found my capabilities for hard labour giving way to the influence of years, and perhaps to previous over exertion. Still, I have stuck to the old ship, and by correspondence and occasional addresses have helped it forward. Within these few years I have several times organized visiting parties, but unless I could attend myself I always found them go down. Two years ago I started a temperance singing meeting on the Saturday evenings, which proved highly beneficial. It afforded amusement for the leisure hours of our teetotalers, especially the young, and induced many others to come to the meeting whom nothing else could have attracted. It was conducted with great simplicity. Five or six hundred people would frequently attend, and perhaps eight or ten different persons, promiscuously and voluntarily, would sing for the meeting, besides the singing of several temperance melodies, in which all would join. The proceeds were expended in temperance publications, and an immense quantity was distributed in the town and country. I generally attended myself every Saturday night. When want of health called me away from Preston, I regretted to find that the meetings fell off, and are now discontinued."

It is important that the reader should remember that the matter contained in the foregoing pages was all published in the *Staunch Teetotaler* 13 years ago. During so long an interval (from 1868 to 1881), many persons are dead who are referred to, and there are some facts named which will require to be modified. Page 16 will explain what I mean. The remarks made about my wife can not apply to the present time. She died on the 19th May, 1869, 12 years ago. Had she lived 19 more days, our married life would have extended to 54 years. In page 59 I speak of having eight sons, but two are since dead, and hence at present I have only six sons and one daughter; the eldest aged 64 and the youngest 48. Many other cases similar will strike the reader, where important changes have taken place during the past 13 years.

CHAPTER XIII.

It is well the foregoing was drawn up when I was better able than at present of giving more details. However, I shall pursue the same track, always keeping in view such facts and illustrations as will serve to promote the correct remembrance, and the prosperity of the good old cause of total abstinence. If I were to continue the thread of former statements, I should have to give an extended detail of the work of a vast number of good men who fortunately came forward in Preston and elsewhere, and laboured hard to uproot the evil that has long afflicted our land. This, in a great measure, is already done to my hand in the pamphlet entitled *Reminiscences of Early Teetotalism*, in which is given the *beginning* of teetotalism as an organized system, and the means, efforts, and letters of many of the principal workers. Hence I shall pass over, in a great measure, the period of time covered by *The Reminiscences*, and my narrative will be less regular, consisting of a variety of statements and commentaries from different sources with which I have been connected. There are, however, a few *historical* facts which I deem important, and to them I shall first advert. The *time* I have been an *abstainer* I refer to first. The following brief statement I take from my New Year's Address, recently published :—

It is now fifty years since I took my last glass. It was early in 1831, at Mr. Mc.Kie's, Lune Street, Preston. It was only one glass of whiskey and water. I often say it was the best I ever drank ; the *best* because it was the *last* ; and if I remain in my senses I shall never take another. I did not then understand the properties of alcoholic liquors, though I ought to have done, being 37 years of age. I have often said "there is *outside* drunkenness and *inside* drunkenness." I don't think any one noticed the effect which the liquor produced, but it led me to reflect, having six children, five of them boys, about whose future welfare I was very anxious, whether I ought not to *abstain* altogether. I resolved there and then that I would never taste again, and this resolution I have kept religiously to the present moment. It has been no self-denial, but a great *self-enjoyment*, for though I have spent much time and no little money in promoting the cause of temperance, I have been amply rewarded, first in my own personal enjoyments, and next in the sobriety and successes of my family. And I have also this pleasant assurance, that by my exertions thousands of families, here and elsewhere, have been made happy. I don't wish to boast, but my intense anxiety to rouse the feelings of my fellow townsmen and others against this cursed drinking system has induced me to refer to my own case.

From the first I have been an out and out advocate of *abstinence* from *alcohol*, and so convinced were I and my fellow workers of the soundness of our principles, and so delighted with the results of our early advocacy, we flattered ourselves that in about seven years the drinking system would be destroyed root and branch. We were simple enough to believe all this, and for a time worked as we have never done since. The novelty subsided, and many of our converts fell away ; workers cooled down, and some who had served the cause gratuitously began to look for remuneration. As usual, sectional divisions sprung up, and from time to time the progress has been retarded so much that the annual drink bill has kept increasing till at one time it amounted to 142 millions !

After so long a season of anticipation it is pleasant to believe that the signs of progress are now more favourable. Both doctors and clergy are rendering far more help than formerly, and with so much sound teaching I cannot resist the belief that a large portion of the masses will soon have courage to announce themselves as converts to teetotalism. It is to them I look chiefly, and when I see them animated with the same zeal and labour and self-denial that inspired the workers of early times, I shall feel sure that we are going to "win the day."

Often have I longed to see a *revival* of the good old cause—to witness the zeal, devotedness, disinterestedness, and labour of early days—and as often been disappointed. I do hope that better times are at hand—preludes of a temperance victory. And why should there be any doubt as to this ? Why should drink reign, and drink selling tread national prosperity, domestic peace, morality, and religion under its feet ? Nothing, I believe, is wanting but a strong combined resolution ; unity of action among all lovers of sobriety and goodness, and a willingness to sacrifice present and personal pleasures for the deliverance and happiness of our fellow-creatures. A *revival* like this would not remain as a light under a bushel. Diffusive teetotalism and agitating teetotalism are what I long to see, and what I try to promote to the utmost of my present limited power.

The statement as to my having been 50 *years a teetotaler* being a matter of memory, I was glad to find the following in the July number of my *Moral Reformer*, published in 1831 :—"So shocked have I been with the effects of intemperance, and so convinced of the evil tendency of moderate drinking, that since the commencement of 1831, I have never tasted ale, wine, or ardent spirits. I know others who are pursuing the same resolution, and whose only regret is, that they did not adopt this course twenty years since." And in the preface to the same volume, I remark—"I am often asked how I find time for all my work, and my answer is, the time which others spend at the pot house, or in visiting and attending parties, I spend in active pursuits ; and *never taking any liquor* at home or elsewhere, my head is seldom out of order ; I lose no time in the evenings to extinguish my reason, or in the mornings to try to regain it.

The former paragraphs state the time I commenced my *personal* abstinence; the next will explain its *official* commencement, and how it was brought about in Preston. The following from Dearden's "Forty Years Ago," may be regarded as a suitable introduction :—

In the year 1826, the philanthropists of America began to organise their forces to battle against the, then, main curse of their country—the drinking of "Ardent Spirits." These efforts were extended, and in 1829 the movement commenced in some parts of the United Kingdom. From that year up to 1831 societies pledging their members to abstinence from spirituous liquors began to multiply in our country, until they reached our town, which soon became the BIRTH PLACE OF TEETOTALISM! That there have been teetotalers in every age of the world no one doubts ; here and there teetotalism had been put forth by individuals, but it was at Preston it first took "a form and shape ;" at Preston it was, that the first organisation of forces was made for the dissemination of the true temperance principle of PERSONAL ABSTINENCE amongst our town's people ; it was from Preston that the first Apostles of Teetotalism set out to convert the people of this kingdom to the belief that *all intoxicating liquors, as beverages, are not only unnecessary but injurious.* Dr. Lees, in his work, the "Text Book of Temperance," after noticing the movements in other places, speaking of Preston, says—"Here things were ripening to a head ; here lived a well known local Franklin, Mr. Joseph Livesey, who, having risen by self-denial, culture and industry, from the working-classes, sought to extend to them the blessings of education, and of social and moral reform. With a keen Saxon insight he perceived the evil in their midst, and with cautious, persevering common sense sought to apply the cure. A well-to-do tradesman, he by-and-by became the proprietor of a printing press and the conductor of a little periodical called *The Moral Reformer.* No wonder the seeds of truth falling into such genial soil, should speedily germinate into power and fruitfulness."

It was, however, soon discovered that the liberty to take ale and wine in moderation, was a fatal source of backsliding. And hence, arose a fierce controversy, which lasted for some time as to the pledge, many, who had become thorough abstainers, maintaining that all the liquors alike containing alcohol should be excluded. To others at that time, and especially among the middle classes, this was considered a dangerous doctrine, and likely to break up the Society. The temperance reformers of the present day have no idea of the conflict that was kept up on this subject. To forbid wine and beer was declared an innovation upon both English and American temperance orthodoxy. I, with many others, felt that there was no safety for our members without this, and we were determined to bring about the change. One Thursday (Aug. 28, 1832), John King was passing my shop in Church Street, and I invited him in, and after discussing this question, upon which we were both agreed, I asked him if he would sign a pledge of *total* abstinence, to which he consented. I then went to the desk and wrote one out (the precise words of which I don't remember). He came up to the desk, and I said, "Thee sign it first." He did so, and I signed after him. This first step led to the next, for in the course of a few days, notice of a special meeting was given, to be held in the Temperance Hall (the Cock-pit), the following Saturday night, Sept. 1st, at which this subject was warmly discussed. At the close of the meeting, I remember well a group of us gathering together, still further debating the matter, which ended in *seven* persons signing a new pledge, it being opposed by others. I subjoin the pledge and the names :—

"*We agree to abstain from all liquors of an intoxicating quality, whether Ale, Porter, Wine, or Ardent Spirits, except as Medicines.*"

JOHN GRATRIX,	JOSEPH LIVESEY.
EDWD. DICKINSON.	DAVID ANDERTON.
JNO. BROADBELT.	JNO. KING.
JNO. SMITH.	

To us, at this day, there seems nothing striking in such a pledge as the above, but at that time, there were many that thought it unsafe to advance so fast. These, then, were the "seven men of Preston" so often referred to; but, it is but justice to say, that though their signing, no doubt, gave a great impetus to the cause, there were many others who did more to forward its interests and secure its success than some of these seven. Among those who really deserved to be called "the men of Preston" for their early devotion to this noble enterprise, I may mention the following:—James Teare, Edward Grubb, Thomas Swindlehurst, William Howarth ("Slender Billy"), James Broughton, Henry Anderton (Poet), Isaac Grundy (Treasurer), Henry Bradley (Secretary), Joseph Richardson, Richard Turner ("Dicky Turner"), William Gregory, Jonathan Simpson (Secretary), Robert Jolly, George Cartwright, Joseph Dearden, John Bimson, Thomas Osbaldeston, John Barton, Robert Charnley, Thomas Walmsley, James Stephenson, George Toulmin, Samuel Smalley, John Waller, Miles Pennington, John Brade, and some others.

The above were those I can recollect as warmly devoted to the cause, and served it faithfully as speakers, visitors, tract distributors, or in any way in which they could make themselves useful. With two or three exceptions they were all working men, and about one half of the number were reformed drunkards. By this band of humble, disinterested labourers, I believe more good was done than has ever been accomplished since by any similar agency.

I cannot advert to the commencement of my abstinence career without a deep feeling of thankfulness that, hasty as it seemed to have been, it was a wise step, and though not attended with the extended results that it deserved, it has secured untold blessings to millions who had been enslaved by drink. It has often been a subject of deep reflection—of hope and uncertainty. Sometimes we thought we were going to win the day; again we have been almost ready to give up in despair. Still the cause was so good; the argument so true; the blessing conferred upon those who were faithful, so decisive—supported by hope, we have persevered; and here we are, the once despised disciples of the *pump*, now regarded by many as leading the way, which but for ignorance and fashion, would be considered as worthy of the support of all good men.

The next historical fact to which I would advert is a brief notice of the man who gave the name to our cause; and, as it is sure to remain, it cannot but be interesting to my readers :—

Every one must feel an interest in knowing as much as possible the character and history of the man who gave to the world and to posterity the *name* that now represents abstinence from all kinds of intoxicating liquors. Up to the memorable evening when the word dropped from Richard Turner's lips we had to phrase the principle as well as we could. It should be remembered that at that time there was great contention betwixt two parties, one insisting upon a pledge of abstinence from spirits only and moderation in fermented liquors, the other upon entire abstinence from both. Richard Turner belonged to the latter party, and in a fervid speech delivered in the Temperance Hall (the old Cock-pit) about September, 1833, after his usual fashion he coined a new word and affirmed that "nothing but the tee-total would do." I remember well crying out "that shall be the name," amid great cheering in the meeting. When Dicky used this word it was intended to affirm that *moderation in beer and wine was delusive*, and that nothing but the teetotal, that is entire abstinence *from all kinds of alcoholic liquors*, would do. It has been attributed to his habit of stuttering, which is a decided mistake. The truth is that Dicky was never at a loss for a word; if a suitable one was not at his tongue end he coined a new one. He was a *worker*, and that, with us, covered a multitude of other defects. He never could do too much. To the sound of his rattle through the streets we often owed the attendance at the meetings we held in the town and villages, in schools and other places. At one time Richard undertook a mission on his own account to the South, preaching teetotal all the way to London, where he attended the World's Temperance Convention.

Richard Turner was born on the 25th July, 1790, at Bilsborough, about eight miles from Preston. His parents removed to this town, and he was sent, when young, to work in a cotton factory. He afterwards learnt to be a plasterer, and then a hawker of fish; and while patroling the streets, in the evening, on the second Thursday in October, 1832, much the worse for liquor, he walked into St. Peter's School Room, where a temperance meeting was being held, for (as he expressed himself) the purpose of having a little fun. At the very urgent request of Mr. T. Swindlehurst and Mr. J. Dearden, he signed the pledge of abstinence from all intoxicating liquors. He was 5 feet 4 inches in height, with a darkish ruddy complexion, and an earnest gaze. He was married to a person named Betty Cook, about the year 1818, who became the mother of two daughters, but it was not a happy match. During the morning of the 27th of October, 1846, he was seized with a severe fit of coughing, which broke a blood vessel in the stomach, from the effects of which he only survived about eighteen hours. To the last moment of his earthly pilgrimage, he maintained his teetotal pledge. On Sunday, the 1st of November, his mortal remains were interred in St. Peter's Churchyard, ground having been purchased for that purpose through the exertions of a few zealous friends of the cause, being within a very short distance of the place where he signed the pledge. A very large number of teetotalers attended the funeral, amounting to about four hundred. The streets through which the procession passed were thronged by spectators, upon whom the solemn scene appeared to make a favourable impression in favour of the noble cause which Richard Turner, for fourteen years, so zealously laboured to promote. The following is the inscription over his grave :—" Beneath this stone are deposited the remains of Richard Turner, author of the word Teetotal, as applied to abstinence from all intoxicating liquors, who departed this life on the 27th day of October, 1846, aged 56 years."

Preston was soon recognised as the Jerusalem of teetotalism, from which the word went forth in every direction. During the race week, 1833, seven of us projected a missionary tour to the chief towns in Lancashire, in order to establish societies on the teetotal principle, or bring those up to that point that were pledged to moderation only in fermented liquors. The names of the party were Thomas Swindlehurst, senior, and his son Randell, James Teare, Henry Anderton, Jonathan Howarth, George Stead, and myself. We took a horse and car, supplied with 9,500 tracts, and Mrs. Livesey presented us with a neat small white silk flag, containing a temperance motto. We started on Monday morning, July 8th, and visited Blackburn, Haslingden, Bury, Heywood, Rochdale, Oldham, Ashton, Stockport, Manchester, and Bolton, besides halting at intermediate villages as we passed through. We divided our party so that we could hold two meetings each night, some in buildings and some in the open air; and as there were then no railways, some of our party had often to walk a considerable distance. It would occupy more room than I can spare to relate half of the incidents connected with this excursion. Scarcely any previous arrangements had been made, or proper placards printed and posted. One of our party usually went before the rest to fix upon places, and we never failed in getting an audience. At Bury, for instance, a cart was procured and sent through the town, containing the bellman who announced the meeting, another who carried a placard stating the time and place, and a third who showered tracts as they went along. The Rev. Franklin Howarth, still at Bury, and true to his principles, presided at this meeting. At Rochdale we drove through the main streets with our car, and our flag flying, on which was gilt "Temperance Meeting." The bellman was not at home, so we left his fee and took the bell and rang it ourselves in the car ; James Teare, who had a powerful voice, announced the meeting to be held on the ground called "The Butts," at twelve o'clock at noon. A large congregation was collected; several powerful addresses were delivered, and although sneered at by a lawyer and openly opposed by a liquor merchant, it was evident that many of the people were deeply affected. It is not too much to say that the success of co-operation in Rochdale owes something of its vitality to the results of this meeting. An evening meeting was held at Heywood, but before leaving next morning, another meeting was convened in the main street by sending the bellman round, and one of the mills stopped working in order to allow the workpeople the opportunity of attending. At Ashton, the Superintendent Wesleyan Minister presided; and early next morning Charles Hindley, Esq., afterwards M.P. for Ashton, sent for us to breakfast with him, and we were very much pleased with the interest both he and Mrs. Hindley evinced in the object of our mission. It was three o'clock in the afternoon before we entered Stockport, and by some mistake no place had been secured for the meeting, and it was not until half-past six that the Primitive Methodist Chapel was obtained. Up to this time no notice had been given of any meeting. What was to be done? "Have you a drum," said I, "and a man that can beat it?" "Yes." Both were immediately procured; I ordered the car out, and off we started. We drove rapidly through the streets, stopping at every crossing, one beat the drum, another called out the meeting, and the rest of us showered out the tracts. The fact is, such an excitement of the kind I never saw before or since. Our purpose was answered, and an hour and a half seemed on this occasion sufficient to accomplish what, on our modern slow going system, would require a fortnight. Mr. Harrison, schoolmaster, took the chair. At Manchester the meeting was held in the theatre of the Mechanics' Institution, and was addressed by six of us, who were constantly interrupted by the plaudits of the assembly, consisting in a fair proportion of the upper and working-classes. At this meeting a man named Kennedy was made a teetotaler, and he afterwards came to Preston once every year, while he was able, to express his gratitude for the blessings he had received. Our last place was Bolton, and the meeting was held there in the Independent Methodist Chapel on the Saturday night. The effect of the addresses by our reformed drunkards was shown by the tears that were shed, and by every other demonstration of feeling. The chapel was granted for me to deliver a regular lecture in, on the following afternoon, Sunday. It commenced at a quarter to five, and continued about an hour and a quarter, listened to by a large audience with great attention. Up to this time, like all the rest, the Bolton Society was on the basis of abstinence from spirits only, the vicar being the president; but in the following week "The Bolton New Temperance Society" was inaugurated, I and two others from Preston assisting on the occasion. After the meeting was over we had to drive to Preston, 20 miles. Thus ended a hard but a glorious week's work, and which served to show how much may be done by few hands and humble instruments where right principles have taken deep root, and where regard for respectable appearances, and the fear of man, are entirely abandoned.

Mr. Brearley, of Rochdale, became an abstainer by hearing our addresses at "The Butts," and remained so to the day of his death. The following are letters from him and his wife out of many other similar ones which I received :—

My dear father and friend in the God-like cause.—It is a long time since I either saw you or heard from you; but the first week Mr. Gladstone brought out the budget, the spark of love you have in you was kindled toward your fellow-man, and I saw your name in the newspapers calling us all up to duty; and this week I see you have written to Mr. Gladstone. It did me good to read your name, and I blessed the paper and kissed it for your sake. Believe me, I never lay me down in my good bed but I think of you coming to Rochdale. I can never pay you for what you have done for me. I should like to see you once more before we die. When you have a tea party, or a move of any sort in this good work, I would gladly come over. We are doing a great work at our hall. It would do you good to be among us; I am almost worked to death in this good cause. You will see by those small slips what I have to do. God bless you and your wife, and all your children, and forgive me troubling you in this way.

I remain, yours truly, JOHN BREARLEY.

Closses Bamford, near Rochdale, March 22, 1860.

My dear father and mother in the Heaven-born cause.—I was very glad to see you look so well the other day in the neighbourhood of Lancaster. Oh I did rejoice on your behalf. May God ever bless you and mother in your health, in your basket and store, in your down-lying and up-rising, in your out-going and in-coming. I am still president of the Total Abstinence Society at Rochdale, and I can assure you I am almost worked to death during this cotton panic. Last night, I had to walk seven miles and a half from where I live to a meeting, at a place called Royton, and after having spoken an hour and a quarter, had to walk that length back by myself. On Sunday night last, I had to speak at Rochdale, and I shall have to go to a meeting there to-night, and to-morrow night I shall have to go again to take the chair at a tea meeting. Rochdale is more than two miles from my house, so you see how they work me up. I bless God a thousand times over that I ever heard your voice and saw your face, and I hope God will bless you and mother with good health and long life. I should be glad to hear from you soon. My wife and children send their love to you and mother, with ten thousand thanks, and pray that God will bless all you take in hand.—We remain, yours in love, JOHN AND BETTY BREARLEY.

Closses Bamford, near Rochdale, Oct. 13, 1863.

For three or four years after we at Preston had adopted the teetotal pledge, we were battling with the adverse party, who contended for a liberty to drink beer and wine in moderation, and most places were unwilling to surrender. As Christianity was fettered a long time with Judaism, and found it difficult to get clear of its traditions, so was teetotalism with the universally received doctrine of abstinence from spirits only. The towns in Lancashire and Yorkshire, and other counties, having become indoctrinated with teetotalism, the great centres of Birmingham and London had to be attacked. It fell to my lot to be the first to visit each of these places single-handed. All our meetings at that time went by the common name of "Temperance," and sometimes parties were thus taken in who attended them.

The following is a brief notice of my first visit to BIRMINGHAM :—

I arranged to visit Birmingham in 1834, and a meeting was announced to take place in the Friends' Meeting House, on Tuesday evening, the 17th June. But when I arrived, I found there was a "hitch" which had nearly prevented the meeting taking place. I shall never forget Mr. Cadbury (who died in 1860, aged 91) coming into his son John's counting-house, and stating that it had been told him that I intended to lecture against both wine and beer, adding, that if I did so, it would ruin their society; and he referred feelingly to his good wife, who had nearly all her life taken her glass of beer. My reply was that I could preach no other doctrine, and if the chapel was withheld, as was intimated, I should make the street my meeting place. Not liking to be idle, at the dinner time I gave an address to a number of working-men, in St. Luke's churchyard, for about half an hour. "To be or not to be," was now the question as to the evening's meeting in the chapel; but before the hour arrived, the bills having been out and expectation raised, I was told that I might take my own course. I repeated my lecture, and gave the illustrations on the malt liquor question, and such was the impression and such the effect upon Mr. Cadbury himself, that a letter followed me to London the next day, requesting that I would return that way, and re-deliver the same, which I did to a crowded and enthusiastic meeting. I scarcely need add that few families have been more true to the teetotal cause than the Cadbury's. Following upon this, our friends Swindlehurst, Teare, and Grubb visited Birmingham two months after, and held four meetings in Livery Street Chapel, commencing on Tuesday evening, August 11th, and which were also addressed by Messrs. Chapman and Cadbury, and three or four reformed drunkards, all of Birmingham. They were opposed by a medical gentleman, who on the last evening was answered in such a powerful address from James Teare, including copious extracts from medical writers, that upon the formation of their Teetotal Society, this same gentleman, it is said, expressed his willingness to sign the pledge. In the autumn of the same year, Birmingham was visited by Mr. Buckingham, M.P. for Sheffield, who warmly advocated the cause; and in the following February, a crowded meeting was held in the Town Hall, at which a report was read attributing the prosperity of the society to the visits of the men from Preston. This meeting was addressed by the Rev. J. Allport, Messrs. Buckingham, M.P., Chapman, Barlow, and others, whilst numbers who could not get admission were addressed on the Wharf steps by Mr. E. Brittain and other speakers. Mr. James Stubbins, solicitor, took great interest in the progress of the cause, and assisted much in its advocacy through the medium of the press.

LONDON was the seat and centre of The British and Foreign Temperance Society, under royal, noble, and sacerdotal patronage, and contended for the moderate use of fermented drinks; but, like other places, was compelled at last to yield to the teetotal doctrine, "pure and simple." I proceeded alone to the great metropolis direct from Birmingham, on Wednesday, the 18th of June, 1834. One of my earliest visits was to the Society's room in Aldine Chambers, where I saw Dr. Edgar and others, but received no encouragement from them, it being pretty well understood that I had come to advocate the teetotal heresy. Help or no help, I was determined to have a meeting, and after many applications for a place to lecture in without success, at last, after the loss of more than a week, I got the promise of a preaching room in Providence Row, Finsbury Square, then occupied by a Rev. — Campbell, who had lately seceded from one of the dissenting bodies. It was several steps below the level of the street; I got a number of posters, but they were lost among the flaring bills on the London walls; also, a quantity of small bills, which, in my simplicity, I went up and down affixing to the walls with wafers in various places, and, among the rest, I remember, in the passages of the Bank of England. The meeting should have taken place on the Friday evening, the 27th, but it turned out, by some mistake, that there was to be preaching that evening, and so I was put off till the next night—Saturday. I then posted the front of the building, and got men to parade with notices during the day. It was the malt liquor lecture I intended to deliver, and I had to see after all the preparations myself. I applied to a chemist to distil me a quart of ale, for which he charged me half a guinea, but

I got him to deduct 2s. 6d. I engaged an aged man named Phillips, who was the Society's porter or messenger, to procure me barley, scales, weights, &c.; but one day he called at Mr. Mark Moore's, where I lodged, and I was both vexed and amused when I was told that he had brought the basket, bottle, ale, scales, barley, and all the rest, with change out of a sovereign which I had given him, and placed them on the parlour floor, with this message,—"Tell Mr. Livesey I am very sorry, but I dare not do anything more for him, for the committee have intimated to me that if I give him any assistance it is as much as my place is worth." Well, Saturday night came, and after all this loss of time (some ten days), labour, and expense, my audience consisted of about thirty persons! It was, however, the beginning of the good cause for London. Shortly after my return I received the following note from Mr. Pascoe: "Sir,—Temperance, I think, is gaining ground in London. I am informed that much good has resulted from your lecture in Providence Row. The proprietor, who is an ale brewer and partner of Dr. Epps, has given up the use and sale of it from what he heard at your lecture." I met with a few temperance friends who were in favour of the new doctrine, and who continued to adhere to it. Mr. and Mrs. Grosjean took up the question, and after a lapse of some time, he invited a number of practical teetotalers to meet at his home, which they did on the 10th of August, 1835, including himself, Mrs. Grosjean, Messrs. Nichols, Perkins, Pascoe, Giles, Corley, Busil, Yerbury, Boyd, Young, and Boatswain Smith. These formed themselves into a provisional committee, adding the name of Morris, Mr. Nichols being appointed secretary. Having determined to establish a teetotal society, they invited myself, Messrs. Swindlehurst and Howarth, to come to London to assist them. We arrived on Monday, August 31, and the next night we held our first meeting in Theobald's Road, Red Lion Square, in a room then occupied by the Owenites. At this meeting, attended by from three to four hundred persons, a society was formed, called "The British Teetotal Temperance Society," with the following pledge: "I voluntarily promise that I will abstain from ale, porter, wine, ardent spirits, and all intoxicating liquors, and will not give nor offer them to others, except under medical prescription, or in a religious ordinance." I can scarcely pass over one incident connected with this meeting. When it was getting near the time to commence the attendance seemed very slender, and feeling rather cast down, I said to Swindlehurst and Howarth, "We must try to get more people to hear us;" and with this, Howarth and I went out and borrowed a small bell, and started through the adjoining streets, ringing the bell, and calling the meeting. We had not gone far when a policeman came up and told us that that sort of work was not allowed in London, intimating that if we did not instantly desist, he would have to do his duty. Of course we did as requested, but it will be seen that our conduct was productive of good results. We all spoke, and evidently astonished the people, and especially Mr. Howarth, who, from his being about the stoutest man in Preston, was generally known as "Slender Billy." We held three other meetings on the succeeding nights; agitating and distributing tracts during the day. That on the Wednesday evening was held in the National School Room, Quaker Street, Spitalfields, at which our friend John Andrew, of Leeds, gave us help. That on Thursday night was in Humphrey's Riding School, Waterloo Road. At these two meetings I delivered the malt liquor lecture, and at the latter it was said that three brewers and about twenty publicans were present. The others also addressed the meeting, and at the close I challenged any present to come forward to dispute my statements, but no one responded. The Friday night's meeting was held in the Mariners' Church, Willclose Square. Mr. Swindlehurst impressively urged the importance of the cause, and Mr. Andrew also; but what is remarkable, so far as I can remember, no Londoner came forward to speak excepting a working man or two. My own visit in 1834, and this in 1835, were the means of starting a new organization, in the face of "The British· and Foreign Temperance Society." The conflict for a time was severe, but the truth prevailed.

Being told that Mr. Inwards, who kept a shop in the neighbourhood, dated his teetotalism from our first meeting, I wrote to enquire if this were so, and which of the Inwards it was. The following is the reply :—

Houghton Cottage, Leamington, May 2nd, 1867.

My dear Sir,—Your first meeting, announced by yourself and the other two noble pioneers in the temperance cause, with the bell in Theobald's-road, I so well remember that I can never forget it. Both myself and neighbours made sport of the whole affair, and thought the men were mad. I and my next door neighbour (a poor dissipated drunkard) went. The meeting commenced, and I was offered a seat but would not take it. I began to feel interested; we both remained standing until the meeting was over, when you made an appeal to all to try the system, if only for a month. My neighbour said to me, "Inwards, what do you think of it?" I replied, "Well, what do *you* think of it?" "Why," says he, "*we are beat;* I will have a month if you will." I at once saw the good of it, if it would only keep him sober a month, and I replied, "I will." That night we both signed and commenced; the man was completely changed; his wife rejoiced, and his family were blessed. From that moment I saw and felt the *glory* and the *greatness* of *this holy cause.* Some of the worst drunkards in the neighbourhood were reclaimed, and brought under the sound of the word of life. They gladly received it, and of those who were added to the churches in the vicinity, many are now living ornaments to the cause, or added to "the just men made perfect." Eternity alone can reveal the infinite importance of the early operations of this movement. I soon after went into Bedfordshire, and pressed the subject on all my family. My brothers and sisters heard with attention—were amazed, but having reflected, *pronounced it right.* They adopted it, and commenced advocating it faithfully. I wish to be very modest in this statement, but cannot help referring with pleasure to the long, faithful, and useful advocacy of my dear brother Jabez, as one of the results of your first meeting. I am happy to inform you that myself and all my family have been true to the good cause ever since, and I have reasons for stating, that my journeyings through the country as an ardent teetotaler, defending and advocating it in almost all the *commercial rooms* in the *North and Midland counties,* have been attended with the most cheering results. Rejoicing to know that you are still labouring in the great work,—may the remaining journey of your pathway through life be illumined by the sun of righteousness, and its healing beams enjoyed until all your labours shall end in the paradise of God.—I am, yours very sincerely,   W. INWARDS.

I have avoided giving many details of my own labours during the early days, but as I often took tours for a week or so at once, a report of the following, I think, may be useful :—

COLNE.—On Monday Night, March 2, I attended a meeting held in the Piece Hall, consisting of about 1700 persons, the Rev. J. Henderson, in the chair. My friend Anderton commenced and finished with powerful appeals, and the recitation of pieces of poetry. To a person who had not heard of Colne, the number and manifest zeal of the friends here would appear extraordinary. I delivered my lecture on malt liquor, the effect of which was rendered still more impressive by the opposition of two gentlemen present. Their arguments were so futile and so foreign to the subject, as to confirm the hearers in the truth of what they had heard. Many of the higher classes in Colne set a good example, by giving the Society their decided support. I cannot but mention the kindness of Mr. Bolton, Solicitor and Clerk to the Magistrates, who sent his horse and gig with us all the way to Halifax.

HALIFAX.—Social Tea Meetings were held here next day, being Shrove Tuesday. About 650 persons sat down to tea in two of the Sunday schools. A public meeting was held in the evening, in Zion Chapel, G. B. Browne, Esq., in the chair. The cause in this place appears to have been in a languishing state for some time, but from the speeches of the gentlemen on the occasion, it appeared that the beginning of a revival had been experienced. After the addresses of the Rev. Messrs. Hawkins, Turner, Preston, Whitewood, Mr. Thompson, and Mr. Anderton, I delivered the usual explanations respecting malt liquor, which seemed to produce a good impression. Mr. Cartwright, from Preston, a reclaimed character, gave an affecting detail of his past habits, and of his change to a sober life.

HUDDERSFIELD.—The meeting, the following evening, was held in the New Connexion Methodist Chapel, and was addressed by Mr. Thompson, of Halifax, Cartwright, Anderton, and myself. Among the good effects produced, it is said, that many of the workmen belonging to Mr. Brooks's Iron Foundry, Longroyd Bridge, have determined to test the truth of my doctrine in their own experience. The Society for some time has been holding weekly meetings, the advantage of which was beginning manifestly to appear.

LEEDS.—On the Thursday evening, we held a most interesting meeting at Leeds, in the Music Hall. Every part of the place was crowded, and many could not obtain admission. Mr. Bulman, surgeon, was called to the chair, and after a few introductory remarks, explaining that the Leeds Society was not pledged to the statements which would be made that night, Mr. Thompson, from Halifax, gave an explanation of his labour, as a cloth presser, and stated that at one time he believed it was impossible for such as he to do without home brewed beer; but having tried it for three or four months, he could sincerely state, that he could do his work better, was less fatigued, less thirsty, and instead of being heavy and sleepy in an evening, he could sit up reading for several hours. My lecture followed, and the meeting was concluded by an address from Mr. Anderton, which was much cheered. At the conclusion 26 names were added to the abstinence pledge. The following note from a friend at Leeds, since received, has reference to this meeting : " Your visit to Leeds has been productive of much good. Several drunkards have signed, the objections of many moderate men removed, and the conviction has been produced in the minds of many, that the *teetotal* plan is the only sure and effective remedy for the evil to be removed."

BRADFORD.—The cause at Bradford seems to have been languid for some time, although there are many decided friends to the cause who have made great sacrifices to promote its prosperity. But as in most of the towns in Yorkshire, there seems to be indications of a speedy revival. Our meeting on Friday evening was in the Friends' Meeting House, which was well filled by a very well behaved audience ; Mr. Wm. Cole, Bowling, in the chair. We were met here by our zealous champion, Swindlehurst, who delivered an address, the effects of which were seen on the cheeks of many of his hearers. My lecture on the great delusion, and the danger and inconsistency of moderate drinking, was here repeated. Anderton followed by a display of wit and sarcasm, such as astonished many of the people. At the conclusion of the meeting, 43 names were obtained to the abstinence pledge.

STOCKTON.—The meeting was fixed here for the Friends' Meeting House, but upon arriving in the town, I was told that the meetings had been thinly attended, and that fears were entertained that there would be a slender attendance. Feeling anxious to prevent the mortification of speaking to empty benches, I adopted the following expedient to excite the attention of the town. Furnishing myself with a large quantity of tracts, and having applied to the bellman to hire me a small cart, we both took our seats, drove first into the Market Place —the bellman having an advertisement in his hat—showering tracts in every direction. He rang his bell, and I delivered the following announcement, "This is to give notice, that Mr. Livesey, from Preston, is going to deliver a lecture this evening, in the Friends' Meeting House, on malt liquors, at seven o'clock, in which he engages to prove that there is more food in a pennyworth of bread than there is in a gallon of ale. All the drunkards and tipplers, and those who have their clothes at the pop shop, are requested to attend." We proceeded first through the main street, then through the back streets, halting at every suitable place, throwing out the tracts and giving the same notice.—One week I travelled above 300 miles in six days (there were then no railways), attended five evening meetings, and spoke nearly two hours each evening, besides a noon meeting at Sunderland.

CHAPTER XIV.

Among our various schemes for inducing the hard drinkers to cast in their lot with us by becoming teetotalers, has been that of making *feasts*—say a knife and fork tea party—inviting a selected number, and after tea addressing them in the most urgent and affectionate manner to change their course of living. We had several got up by Mr. Bruckshaw, now of Bolton, and others. Perhaps the results were not always satisfactory; still some good was done, and our friends can point now to individuals whose change by these treats has been remarkable. The feasts, I think, were on too small a scale, but the greatest defects were these: the invitations were confined to drinkers, and were not followed by repeated visitation; hence many of the parties gave way before temptation. On the approach of Shrove Tuesday last, it was determined to renew these attempts, with some improvements. The improvements were, that females, the drinker's wives as well as the husbands, should have tickets given them; that the number should at least be doubled, and that instead of the expense being thrown upon *one* individual, others should be allowed to purchase either personal or presentation tickets at 1s. each. The result has given great satisfaction. A capital tea, with sandwiches and other accompaniments, was made; about 60 drinkers were invited, who, along with a number of abstaining friends, enjoyed a pleasant evening. Every arrangement was made to prevent any of the invited thinking that they were brought to the meeting to be gazed at, or treated in any respect different to others because of their habits. A great object to be kept in view in getting up these tea parties is, to *create more cordiality* between the classes. As in religion so in teetotalism, there should be as much *equality* as possible; the drinkers should feel that they are cared for, and that it is for *their* benefit that our efforts are constantly directed. Indeed, "Pity for the drinkers" should dwell in every abstainer's heart, and it should never be concealed that the blame does not belong exclusively to any one, but that if justice were properly meted out, it ought to be distributed to the drinkers, the parents, the teachers, and all others who had contributed in any way to the wrong-doing of drinking men or women. Several females treated the company with songs and music; stirring speeches were delivered, principally by old fuddlers, and the alcohol in intoxicating liquor was burnt before the audience. Judging from the conduct of the guests, some of whom had never been in the Temperance Hall before, they were highly delighted, and the hope is, that some at least will forever forsake their ale guzzle, and begin to live a new life. It is very important that we should learn not to be so severe, either in our censures or conduct, towards those who have fallen from a sober life. In many cases the cause is a misfortune rather than a crime. If they had been looked well after when young, and if their teachers and parents had been watchful and had supplied a good example, a world of misery and suffering might have been prevented. At any rate, I feel no misgiving in strongly recommending all our societies to imitate what is here set before them.

The following address was read, and copies given out for distribution :

An Address to all who are invited to the Temperance Shrove Tuesday Tea Party,
March 1st, 1881.

Dear Friends,—You will excuse the liberty I am taking in addressing you. I assume that most of you are *not* teetotalers ; at the same time you know that *I* am warmly attached to that party. I have adopted their principles, and followed them faithfully for 50 years. Not a drop of intoxicating liquor, neither gin, rum, brandy, whiskey, ale, or wine has gone down my throat ; I keep none in the house, and would not allow so destructive an article to enter my doors ; and I am enjoying all the benefit of this. Just think for a moment what a gain it must have been to my family in health, wealth, comfort, and happiness ; and what blessings my example and efforts have conferred upon thousands of others who have read my papers. What an old man just entering upon his 88th year can do, surely you can do the same. What hinders you ? Nothing, I venture to say, upon which you can for shame to dwell. I know what drinkers, even moderate drinkers, feel ; and still more, what those who go to excess have to endure. Now let me say to you all,—*let bygones be bygones*; make up your minds to live as God intended you to live. Keep ALCOHOL, the intoxicating stuff, out of your mouths; *never touch it*. Let your wages be spent upon your families, your houses, and yourselves. You who are working men, beware of Saturday afternoons ; this is the time when the temptation is often very strong. Some men will run to the drinkshop the moment they get out of the workshop or mill. They only intend to get a glass or so, but they don't leave till they have spent a great part of their wages. Oh ! what madness ! What folly to go on in this way, which leads to nothing but misery and wickedness, and to setting a shameful example all around them !

You have been invited here to let you see how teetotalers enjoy themselves, and to help you to decide at once to *give up your drinking habits*, to begin to live like men, to care for your families, and to lead a new life.—I am, Your old friend,   J. LIVESEY.

18, Bank Parade, Preston.

In looking over my *Moral Reformer, The Preston Temperance Advocate*, and the various pamphlets and tracts which were issued in the early days of our enterprize, I cannot help remembering with delight the zeal and devotedness of those with whom I had the pleasure to work ; and am apt to contrast these with the boasted activities of the present day. Judging from what we hear and read, many are apt to think we are now doing wonders, but these are mostly young converts or persons who are taken with the laudatory reports which appear in our periodicals. Impressed with this truth, that *alcoholic drink* is the stumbling block in the way of every good thing, and that *personal abstinence* is the starting point in the enjoyment of individual, domestic, and national happiness, our primitive men made the advocacy of teetotalism *pure and simple* their first and most important duty. Money, influence, labour, were incessantly devoted to the work, not making it only a matter of convenience, nor allowing themselves to be diverted from their proper work by side issues. Gradually this zealous devotion cooled down; and the love of ease, so common to a state of prosperity, soon created a disposition to rely upon proxy instead of personal labour. The employment of missionaries and agents is good in its place ; but when we depend upon these, instead of working ourselves, we make a great mistake.

I feel thankful for the measure of success which has been attained, but still I am anxious that it should be of a more decisive character. The only *true test of progress* in the abstinence cause is the returns of Government as to the "home consumption" of intoxicating liquors. When the present yearly consumption is reduced by 10 millions, we shall have proof that we are succeeding, and when the amount is reduced to one half, as it ought to be, then we might proclaim the hope of a decided victory. It is true our *principles* have made, and are making, great progress; but the *practice* of abstinence does not keep pace with it ; and if the societies and the teetotalers as individuals could be aroused to do their duty, as in primitive times, a more cheering prospect would ensue.

If our cause is to succeed, we must try to enlighten the whole people as to the nature and properties of all our popular drinks. Never till the public are sufficiently enlightened as to the worthlessness of alcoholic liquors, and their injurious influence upon the human system, will the temperance cause make that progress which all teetotalers are anxious to witness. We should incessantly work at this, and try by every means to impress correct views upon the minds of those who are the teachers and leaders of the people. There should not be a minister or a man of any position uninformed on this question. It is by the *press*, chiefly, that we can reach this class; and we should spare no pains or cost, in circulating sound information among them. Declaiming merely against "drunkenness," and its horrid effects upon society, is comparatively a loss of time, so long as "drinking" is passed over in silence. Until we have convinced the public that it is the *alcohol in the drink*, and neither the assumed "adulterations," the "house," nor the "man" that sells it, which is the cause of the evil, we are making no headway, and deceiving ourselves with hopes that will never be realized. I repeat, we must *concentrate* our labours and our best energies upon *the drink* and its *alcoholic properties*, and show that it is the moderate and fashionable use which constitutes the greatest obstruction to the success of our labours. I seem like one of the "ancient men," who, at the building of the second Jewish Temple, "wept" on beholding its inferiority compared to that which was erected by Solomon.

In the early days every meeting we went to in town or village was crowded. Those engaged at present, whose teetotal experience does not reach beyond ten or twenty years, think they are doing a great deal; and if we read the reports of fifty societies, including the large organizations, we always find a laudatory tone—an enumeration of great efforts; but, when we apply to the true test—the quantity of liquor consumed and the number of places that sell it—we find the facts are against us. This should arouse our societies from their slumbers, and warn them against complacency and self-deception. In the early days we felt that we were really engaged in a "Temperance *reformation.*" We gave heart and soul to it. The conflict was fierce; and the resistance manifested in hostile opposition, served only to fire our zeal. We seemed as if we would turn the world upside down.

The following address, which was largely circulated, shows so forcibly the spirit and earnestness of our early workers in Preston, that I feel anxious to have it preserved, especially as it contains the names of thirty of our reformed drunkards.

TO TIPPLERS, DRUNKARDS, AND BACKSLIDERS.

Friends!—You are miserable and wretched, both in body, soul, and circumstances; your families and friends are suffering through your folly; you have no peace here, and can have no peace hereafter; and all this proceeds from the delusive, maddening habit of drinking intoxicating liquors. You are told that these liquors do you good. *It is a falsehood, invented and propagated for the purpose of getting your money.* Judge of the good they have done by the *effects* which they have produced upon *yourselves* and *others.* Oh! shun the public-house as you would do a plague, and the company of drunkards as you would a gang of robbers.

Friends!—We were once drunkards, and most of us were in the same wretched condition as yourselves; but being reclaimed, we are anxious for you to enjoy the same liberty and blessings which we enjoy. *We are now happy:* our wives are comfortable; our children are provided for; we are better in health, better in circumstances; we have peace of mind; and no tongue can tell the comfort we have enjoyed since we became consistent members of the Temperance Society. Ale and strong drink have slain more than war or pestilence; and while we refuse no kind of food or drink which God hath sent, we *abstain* from all diluted poison, *manufactured* to ruin mankind, and to rob our country of its greatness. *We have seen our delusion: and we now drink neither ale, wine, gin, rum, nor brandy, nor any kind of intoxicating liquor. There is no safety for you nor us but in giving it up entirely.* Come forward then, ye tipplers, drunkards, and backsliders! attend our meetings, and be resolved to cast off the fetters of intemperance; *and once and for ever determine to be free!*

John Billington, Weaver.	William Parkinson, Clogger.
John Brade, Joiner.	Joseph Richardson, Shoemaker.
Richard Bray, Fishmonger.	Richard Rhodes, Weaver.
Robert Caton, Spinner.	James Ryan, Spinner.
William Caton, Spinner.	Richard Shackleton, Spinner.
William Gregory, Tailor.	Samuel Smalley, Spinner.
George Gregson, Plasterer.	Joseph Smirk, Moulder.
John Gregson, Mechanic.	James Smith, Spinner.
William Howarth, Sizer.	George Stead, Broker.
Robert Jolly, Sawyer.	Thos. Swindlehurst, Roller Maker.
William Moss, Mechanic.	Randal Swindlehurst, Mechanic.
Mark Myers, Shoemaker.	John Thornhill, Cabinet Maker.
Henry Newton, Mole Catcher.	Richard Turner, Plasterer.
Thomas Osbaldeston, Moulder.	Joseph Yates, Shopkeeper.
Robert Parker, Moulder.	William Yates, Weaver.

Preston, Dec. 27th, 1833.

The following report of a week's proceedings at Blackburn in the year 1835, (abridged from the *Temperance Advocate*) will give an idea of the zeal and enthusiasm which characterised the advocacy of total abstinence at that date. It would be a blessing if that and other towns could now be stirred up after the same fashion:—

An extraordinary effort **was** made in Blackburn during tho week preceding Easter week, (1835) in order to form a New Temperance Society on the *teetotal* principles, and to produce an impression in its favour ; and it is pleasing to add, with the most extraordinary success. The Committee of the Preston Temperance Society, anxious to spread the principles of their Society, engaged tho Theatre for six successive nights, in order that the blessings which had accompanied the labours of their friends in Preston might be extended to Blackburn. On Monday evening, Messrs. Swindlehurst, Broughton, Stagg, Speakman, Spencer, and H. Clitheroe, proceeded from Preston to Blackburn in the *"teetotal car,"* and addressed the meeting, Mr. Swindlehurst in the chair. On Tuesday, Messrs. Livesey, Osbaldeston, and Richardson, from Preston ; Gardner, Blackburn ; and R. Threlfall, from Moon's Mill, were the speakers. The chair was taken by tho Rev. J. Cheadle, from Colne. Mr. Livesey delivered his Lecture on the great delusion respecting the properties of malt liquor. The other advocates related their conversion to Temperance, and the blessings connected with a sober life. On Wednesday, the chair was occupied by a reverend gentleman of Blackburn ; and Messrs. Teare, Bradley, Jolly, Bimson, Caton, and Johnston, from Preston, addressed the meeting. On Thursday, the Rev. J. Fielding, of Preston, was called to the chair, when Messrs. H. Anderton, J. Johnson, G. Gregson, D. Crossthwaite, and — Greers, from Preston, addressed the meeting. On this evening the new Society was formed, and a Committee appointed, consisting of persons who had signed the previous evenings. On Friday, Messrs. Broughton, Swindlehurst, Brade, Moon, Howarth, and Mrs. M. Grime, from Preston, addressed the meeting, Mr. Baxendale in the chair. On Saturday, Mr. J. Finch, from Liverpool, took the chair. Messrs. Cartwright, Walmsley, J. Whitehead, R. Swindlehurst, J. Livesey, (a boy 13 years old) J. Whatmough, and H. Bradley, from Preston, and J. Margerson, of Blackburn, addressed the meeting. I have attended many Temperance meetings in different parts of the country, but never witnessed so much zeal and good feeling as pervaded these meetings. The result of the week's meetings is, 330 persons, including a considerable number of the most degraded characters in the town, have signed the pledge.

John Cassell was a grand worker in our cause, and honoured it in practice during his life. It was a subject of deep regret that he should have had so many other engagements. It was when lecturing in Mr. Beardsall's Chapel, Oak Street, Manchester, that I first saw him, standing just below, or on the steps of the platform, in his working attire, with a fustian jacket and a white apron on. He was then an apprentice, and, without serving his time, he left Manchester, a raw, uncultivated youth. "It was in October, 1836, that young Cassell arrived in London, in quest of employment as a carpenter, and shortly after spoke at a temperance meeting in the New Jerusalem School Room, near the Westminster Road. Mr. J. Parker, who was present, describes him as a gaunt stripling, poorly clad, and travel-stained ; plain, straightforward, and earnest in speech, but very broad in provincialism. Shortly after this, on the 17th of November, he spoke in Milton Street, Barbican, with an energy and effect, despite his provincial brogue, which gained him friends on the spot, and stamped an epoch in his onward and upward career. He is said to have frankly owned, on some of these occasions, that he carried his worldly all in his wallet, and had only a few pence in his pocket. Mr. Meredith became his friend, and enrolled him among the temperance agents whom he was generously maintaining at his own expense." In the *Advocate* for April, 1837, it is said, "John Cassell, the Manchester carpenter, has been labouring amidst many privations with great success in the county of Norfolk. He is passing through Essex on his way to London. He carries his watchman's rattle, an excellent accompaniment of temperance labour." It deserves to be recorded that the Rev. C. Garrett, now a giant in the cause, and Mr. T. H. Barker, secretary of the *Alliance*, were converted to teetotalism by hearing John Cassell; so that *their* temperance genealogy brings them back to Preston. The following note refers to the former :—

"Dear Sir,—On the evening of November 24th and 25th, 1840, Mr. John Cassell, as the agent of the New British and Foreign Temperance Society, delivered lectures at the Town Hall, Shaftesbury. After the second lecture, the Shaftesbury Total Abstinence Society was formed; several persons having signed the pledge, among them Charles Garrett, then a lad; the Rev. Thomas Evans, Congregational minister of this place, still living; and John Rutter, Esq., a solicitor of the town, who was one of the speakers at Covent Garden Theatre at the first world's convention. I signed on the 27th, and it was at a small members' meeting, sometime afterwards, in a School Room, that I, as the chairman, induced Charles Garrett to speak, for the first time, on teetotalism. James Teare had previously (in 1836) visited this neighbourhood, but his labours in this town were, I believe unsuccessful."—Yours truly,   G. E. NORTON.

Alluding to this meeting, Mr. Garrett says, "I remember the excitement caused by the publication of Cassell's bills—the wonder what 'teetotalism' meant, and the amazement with which everybody regarded the proposal to abstain from ale and cider. The publicans sent men to upset the meeting, and, amidst the row, I was the first to sign." The *Teetotal Times*, issued by our lamented friend, was one of the best periodicals ever printed; and in the *Standard of Freedom* and other publications teeming from the press in Belle Sauvage Yard, he always advocated our principles. His portrait (given with *Cassell's Illustrated Family Paper* of May 20, 1865), now lies before me, and calls up recollections hard to endure. Many a time have I wished that his large mind had been less burdened with the cares of business. The last time I saw him was at the Hydropathic Establishment, Benrhydding, Ilkley, and the marks of declining health were then but too visible. He died on the 2nd of April, 1865, cut off at the early age of forty-six, leaving his widow and daughter (still living) to mourn their loss. His name will always be honoured as the first of the firm in the great printing and publishing house of "Cassell, Petter, and Galpin, Ludgate Hill, London."

CHAPTER XV.

During our early years there was no topic I dwelt upon so much as what I denominated the "Great Delusion!" A delusion it was, and after 50 years labour, it has still a great hold upon the minds of the nation; in Lancashire no kind of intoxicating liquor is consumed so much as beer, and it is universally drunk in London and the suburbs. In my lecture I made it as plain as possible that the prevailing idea about this beverage was a desperate delusion, but the love of this coloured water, turned into beer or ale, has been, to a great extent, proof against all my arguments. However, I have the consolation of knowing that my lecture against Malt Liquor, delivered in almost every part of England, was well received, and since printed in various editions, has had a circulation unequalled by any other publication connected with the cause of temperance. It is constantly referred to, and has formed the basis of many lectures delivered by our agents. This lecture was first issued in the form of tracts, but soon took the form of a pamphlet of 32 pages, and as the privilege of printing was always open, editions were issued from various towns. The neatest edition that I have met with was the one issued by our late friend R. Dykes Alexander, of Ipswich, and now sold by the National Temperance League, 337, Strand, London, and at the office of the British Temperance League, 50, Norfolk Street, Sheffield, price 1d. Later on I remodelled it, and it is sold as the "New Malt Liquor Lecture." I send this out at 5s. per 100, or 250 for 10s., carriage free. It should be read by every teetotaler, and the delusion there exhibited is so universally plain that it ought to be enforced by all our speakers. This is quite necessary, for a large number of half and half teetotalers are quite ready to denounce alcohol in its distilled shape, but are ready to allow this poison as it leaves the brewery. This part of the teetotal question cannot be made too plain. Besides the lecture, I have published the arguments it contains in the shape of tracts and bills, two of which I subjoin ; the latter is the latest I have issued, and is at the present largely circulated :—

THE MALT LIQUOR DELUSION.—Some are so simple as to think that ale is the very "juice of the malt," and that it is nourishing on account of the malt it contains, whereas, it is the object of the brewers to retain as little of the malt as possible, but as much alcohol as they can secure. A good part of the malt remains in the "grains," and the other part, like meal or flour, sinks to the bottom of the barrels; so that if you want the greatest amount of nutriment in your ale, you must purchase *barrel bottoms!* The essence of ale-making consists, first, in *creating* and *developing* the *saccharine principle* in barley by the process of *malting;* secondly, in *washing out* this sugary substance by *mashing;* thirdly, in *changing this sweet liquor* into *spirit* or alcohol by *fermentation;* and fourthly, in allowing the remaining nutritive parts of the barley to *settle down* to the bottom of the barley in *fining.* These are the essential processes of ale-making, and the *colouring* from the *charcoal* of the malt, and *flavouring* by the *hops*, and the securing of *carbonic acid gas*, by bunging up the barrels, are all secondary matters, the chief thing being to produce not a feeding, but an *alcoholic* liquor, which will stimulate the nervous system. Ale, indeed, is simply the juice of the pump, *coloured, flavoured,* and *fired ;* in fact, a pint of ale is a *pint of water,* with about a meat-spoonful of alcohol, a pinch of hop, and a few particles of the worst parts of the barleys. The whole process of malting, mashing, fermenting, and fining, is not to make the ale feeding, but as intoxicating as possible.

It is a most difficult task to combat national beliefs. To many there is a charm in the very sound of "malt liquor ;" and hence, while our legislators and our great men are loud in their denunciations of *beerhouses*, they are careful not to say a word against *beer*. Yet it is the *beer*, and the *beer only*, that makes these houses so obnoxious. Change these houses into milk shops, or coffee shops, and all the evils of which they are accused would vanish at once. I have a tract entitled, "The testimony of forty-four chaplains of gaols against beer-houses," in which, though every bad thing is said against the *houses*, not one word occurs against the *beer* itself. Even Lord Shaftesbury, who often appears at religious meetings, and as a friend of the temperance cause too, was recently noticed to treat his labourers with "good old ale !" These gentlemen are all hampered with the prejudice that ale of itself is good ; it was Lord Brougham's error, it was Joseph Hume's error, and when puzzled with the fearful conse- quences which result from this favourite beverage, they have recourse to the assumption that it is *adulterated!* The fact is, that gentlemen's ale, which is certainly *not adulterated*, sometimes twenty-one years of age, is capable of doing more mischief, and is often known to do more, than any other, because it is made to contain the greatest amount of alcohol. On this point our legislators are as ignorant as others, and hence they are everlastingly trying to grapple with the *effects* of the drink, without attacking the *drink* itself. All the clamour and fruitless legislation about beershops arise from ignorance of the nature of the liquor. With a world of evil before them, they cannot believe that it is in the very nature of the drink to produce it. Only cast out the demon Alcohol, and no other measure would be required.

Instead of perceiving that the dreadful evils of the public-house system are concentrated in the *drink*, our legislators are constantly making a fuss about the *size* and *rating* of the houses, the *character* of the landlord, the *hours* of doing business, the *company* allowed, the *games* and *amusements* introduced, the *adulteration* of the liquors, the want of *police inspection*—all these, and many other matters, are made the subjects of legislation, and fresh regulations and restraints are imposed accordingly. Everything, in fact, but the right thing, seems to have been discovered. Starting with the belief that the drinks themselves are good, it appears never to have occurred to them that there is a stimulating, narcotic poison in all licensed drinks—ALCOHOL—which is the sole cause of all the evils complained of, and that any collateral evils are mere trickling streams proceeding from this polluted fountain. One single legislative measure—and that is to decree that *no liquors containing alcohol shall be sold*—would *set all right*, and upon this, *every other restraint might be abandoned*, and the trade of licensed victuallers be made perfectly free to all, accessible to every man that chooses to enter it.

THE BEER DELUSION.—*What is Beer?* Beer is the name given to all kinds of malt liquor, including ale, porter, and stout. It is, in fact, nothing but coloured, flavoured, and fired water. A pint of beer is a pint of water with a pinch of hops, a spoonful of alcohol (coarse whisky), and a few particles of the worst parts of the malted barley. Talk about this beer being the "juice of the malt;" the fact is, it is the *juice of the pump:* and the proper name for beer would be *adulterated water.* It is all water to begin with, but by the process of brewing it gets coloured, flavoured, and whiskied, and then it is puffed off as our "National beverage," as the working-man's drink. I have carefully gone over all the processes connected with beer making, consisting of malting, mashing, fermenting, and fining, and I am prepared to prove that it is still only water—spoiled water—though coloured, bittered, and whiskified. In its natural state water is one of Heaven's best gifts; it quenches thirst, dilutes our food, supplies the secretions of the body, and like all God's best gifts is plentiful and cheap. There is nothing so good as "honest water" for quenching thirst; in fact, in whatever shape you take it, whether as tea, ginger beer, lemonade, or in fruit, it is the water these contain that quenches thirst. Look at that beautiful sparkling glass of water as it stands beside your plate; it costs you nothing, it will do you good and no harm; it will assist digestion; it will not excite and then depress; you will drink no more of this fluid than is proper. And will you then, instead of drinking the clear, nice, transparent element, in its natural state, insist upon it being coloured with malt charcoal, bittered with hop, and fired with whiskey; and instead of having it for nothing, consent to purchase it at 4d., 5d., or 6d. per quart? Could folly go further than this?

Beer not only intoxicates, but often makes people unwell, and then they are apt to say, "Oh, there was something in it," or to charge it with being "doctored" or adulterated; they think that beer made only from malt and hops *must be good* and will not intoxicate nor injure those who drink it. They are profoundly ignorant that *the purest beer is whiskey and hop water*, coloured and flavoured; and until they are disabused of their unfounded notions, they will continue to go on reiterating these silly tales about adulterations. The people's belief that beer imparts strength, that it is feeding or nutritious, is a great delusion. It contains nothing that can give strength; it stimulates just in proportion to the whiskey it contains; but it gives no real power to the body. I have no hesitation in saying that *there is more food in a pennyworth of bread than in a gallon of beer.* It is the solids (digested) and not the liquids that gives strength to both men and animals. Millions of individuals work without beer. The testimony of masons, bricksetters, labourers, furnacemen, moulders, glass-blowers, sawyers, porters, plasterers, haymakers, shearers—in fact, all trades, and of persons both on sea or land, even those who have been exposed in the most northern latitudes, to the hardest work and the severest cold—these all work, and do their work better without beer. Malt liquor cannot give what it does not contain. You might as well ask the clouds to create sunshine, or the sun to freeze the ponds, as to hope for true muscular strength from beer drinking.

But even if beer were worth drinking, and contained the nourishment attributed to it, yet when you consider what evils it leads to, you will see strong reasons why you should never touch it. If it were as nutritious as bread, beef, or milk, yet so long as it contains the intoxicating principle, and brings so many to ruin, every good man should abstain from it. Beer is a deceitful drink. When men invite each other to go into a public-house, they never say, "Come, let us go in and have a fuddle," but always "Come, let us go in and have a glass," but the one glass taken, they want another, and often stop till they are unfit for work. In the whole list of intoxicants, I regard beer as the worst. First, because public opinion runs so strongly in its favour in preference to what are called "spirituous liquors." Next, because it is usually looked upon as "food," and hence it is not reserved for special occasions, but is on the table of many families daily. And thirdly, because, while wine is taken in small glasses, and ardent spirits by "bottoms," "squibs," and "nips," beer is drunk in the largest quantities, seldom less than tumblers.

If any impartial person will examine this beer as I have done, or if he will carefully consider what it leads to, he can come to no rational conclusion but that it is wise to abstain from it altogether. Beer making and beer drinking causes an immense loss of good barley, suitable as food for man and beast; it is the beginning of a great part of the intoxication of this country and the dreadful effects which follow. Taking the "one glass" of beer has led to the ruin of thousands, both males and females. If you will enquire of all the hard drinkers, men or women, how they commenced, you will find that in most cases it was with a glass of beer, or a glass of ale, or a glass of porter, and generally at the family table. It is pitiful to see women with their jugs, even on Sundays at dinner time, fetching beer. If you want to make your children drunkards, there is no likelier method than giving them beer to their meals.

It would seem, then, no great hardship to "rob the poor man of his beer?" It would be the greatest blessing that ever came to him. More than fifty millions of money are annually spent in beer, and as much grain destroyed in making it as would be bread for six millions of people. Six weeks' labour out of 52, at least, is lost to the country; and poverty, misery, violence, vice, and crime are multiplied—all from beer drinking.—J. LIVESEY.

I may show how it happened that I should be so fortunate as to discover, at a time when darkness upon the subject was misleading the nation at large, the prevailing error as to Malt Liquors. It was from Franklin (of America) I got the first hint as to the trifling amount of nutrition contained in malt liquor; and from enquiries as to the amount of barley generally used in making a given quantity of beer, and an examination of the abstraction of nutritious matter in the processes of malting, mashing, fermenting, and fining, I found that though Franklin was correct in principle, the loss was far more than he made it. He stated that there was a "larger portion of flour in a penny loaf" than "a pint of beer;" while the fact is, that there is more nutritious "flour" in a penny loaf than in a gallon of beer. This was truly a discovery at the commencement of our reformation; it formed the leading idea in my "Malt Liquor Lecture," which has had a world wide circulation. I cheerfully acknowledge my obligations to Dr. Franklin, and in the following quotation from his works, will be seen the passage which I siezed upon with delight, and also how useful he made himself among the printers, his workfellows.   What a blessing it would be if there was a young Franklin in every printing office.

"On my entrance upon work at the printing house of Watts, near Lincoln's Inn Fields, I worked at first as a pressman, conceiving that I had need of bodily exercise, to which I had been accustomed in America, where the printers work alternately as compositors and at the press. *I drank nothing but water;* the other workmen, to the number of about fifty, were *great drinkers of beer.* I carried occasionally a large forme of letters in *each hand,* up and down stairs, while the rest employed *both hands* to carry one.   They were surprised to see by this and many other examples, that the American aquatic, as they used to call me, was stronger than those who drank porter.   The beer-boy had sufficient employment during the whole day in serving that house alone.   My fellow-pressman drank every day a pint of beer before breakfast, a pint with bread and cheese for breakfast, one between breakfast and dinner, one again about six o'clock in the afternoon, and another after he had finished his work.   This custom appeared to me to be abominable ; but he had need, he said, of all this beer in order to acquire strength to work.   I endeavoured to convince him that *the bodily strength furnished by the beer could only be in proportion to the solid part of the barley dissolved in the water, of which the beer was composed : that there was a larger portion of flour in a penny loaf, and that consequently if he ate this loaf, and drank a pint of water with it, he would derive more strength from it than from a pint of beer.*   This reasoning, however, did not prevent him drinking his accustomed quantity of beer, and paying every Saturday night, a score of more than four or five shillings a week for this cursed beverage, an expense from which I was solely exempt.   Thus do these poor devils continue all their lives in a state of voluntary wretchedness and poverty.   After this, I lived in the utmost harmony with my fellow workmen, and soon acquired considerable influence among them.   I proposed some alterations in the laws of the *Chapel,** which I carried without opposition.   My *example* prevailed with several of them to *renounce their abominable practice of bread and cheese and beer,* and they procured, like me, from a neighbouring house, a good basin of warm gruel, in which was a small slice of butter, with toasted bread and nutmeg.   This was a much better breakfast, which did not cost more than a pint of beer, namely, three halfpence, and at the same time preserved the head clearer.   Those who continued to gorge themselves with beer, often lost their credit with the publican, from neglecting to pay their score.   They had recourse to me to become security for them, their light, as they used to call it, being out.   I attended at the pay table every Saturday evening, to take up the little sum which I had made myself answerable for, and which sometimes amounted to nearly thirty shillings a week."

There never was a plainer demonstration than this one opened out by young Franklin.   I know no greater blessing that could be conferred by our friends upon every printing office in England, and in London especially, than a supply of Franklin's remarks to every office, the cost of which would be no great burden.   Startling as were these remarks of Franklin, they were not more so than mine which followed—that there was "MORE FOOD IN A PENNYWORTH OF BREAD THAN IN A GALLON OF ALE !"

---

* Printing offices were then thus denominated, by reason of printing being first performed in England in the Chapel at the Sanctuary, Westminster.

CHAPTER XVI.

Our friends are always anxious to report *successes*, especially when they have received a large number of signatures to the *pledge*. Many hundreds, and in a recent case 7,000, was reported as the result of the labours of a clever speaker from America. It was currently stated that Father Mathew had pledged five millions to abstinence in Ireland, America, England, and Scotland. He did not take names in a book, but requested his converts to kneel and repeat the words after him. Everything about pledging has been done from the first very loosely. We have too often been misled by these reports, and when the individuals have been carefully visited a few weeks after, the numbers reported had to be greatly reduced, proving, in my opinion, the necessity of some modification in the pledge for professed new converts, if what might be called a pledge should be allowed to such. Many a time have I noticed how eagerly, at the close of our meetings, the people rush to the platform to sign the pledge, but when I have got the cases visited a few weeks after, I have been mortified at finding that great numbers had broken it. It is a question whether they should be allowed to sign there and then, under emotions such as are common to a large excited meeting; that if they sign at all, it should mean that they will *try* to abstain and become teetotalers. Such cases are very numerous; I will give one. A friend of mine, a very intelligent man, went to hear Gough; he was so excited with the address that, as supper was being brought in, he exclaimed, " No more porter, Betty, at this supper table here." He meant what he said, but before the week was over the porter jug was on as usual; and worse still, the same practice was continued to the day of his death. If intelligent men such as he can yield to their appetite for liquor, no wonder that the untaught crowd should do the same. No person, I am inclined to think, should be registered as a *member of the teetotal society* till after he has been visited, and afforded evidence of his consistent abstinence. Something of this sort I think should be attempted. There is nothing I have felt more anxious about than this *visiting*, and to go on taking names without it is building upon a rotten foundation. It is painful to confess how often I have been disappointed in the practical result of our meetings; I have adopted various arrangements of visitation for this work, and as often been disappointed. Many who had left their names in the book had changed their residence and could not be found, many had broken their pledges, and this work always got into arrears. I fear it is from this source that such conflicting statements as to the total number of teetotalers are allowed to appear in print.

There is need, again and again, to remind our teetotalers of this much neglected duty of *visitation*. Without frequent visitations, my decided opinion is that no society can be in a prosperous condition. Our ordinary meetings are too often thinly attended; people don't flock to them and crowd the doors as they did thirty or forty years ago; and unless *we go to the people*, the great mass will remain untaught and uncared for. In all our temperance labours we should get as *low down* as possible. It is not the righteous but *sinners* that need our help. Christ condensed all the commandments into *two*, one being this—"Thou shalt love thy neighbour as thyself." But how can we be said to love our neighbour whom we never see, never call upon, and never enquire after? Many teetotalers are fond of "demonstrations," but those who take a wider and more Christian view, delight more in visiting and teaching the residents of the *slums*, helping the downcasts, remembering that we are all of one flesh, children of the same Parent. Here indeed shines the bright example of the Lord Jesus. The interests of the poor, the wicked, the lost, the friendless, were ever near His heart. He delighted in the companionship of the lowly. The Jews would have condemned to death the woman taken in adultery, but what says Jesus? "Neither do *I* condemn thee, *go and sin no more*." Read His conversation with the woman of Samaria—one who had had five husbands, and was then living with a man who was not her husband. How different the tone of His discourse to that of many of His followers! The same kind and compassionate feeling was displayed at Simon's supper table, where the woman, a great "sinner," washed His feet with her tears, and wiped them with the hairs of her head. What a contrast is the teaching of Christ's parables with that of others! The prodigal son's return and the father's heart overflowing with compassion; the good Samaritan taking pity and relieving the man who had fallen among thieves, and who was passed by and left suffering by the Priest and the Levite ;—these are certain lessons of love and pity which we should all imitate. If one in a hundred go astray, He teaches us that we should seek him out and bring him back, rejoicing more over his restoration than over the ninety and nine who remained in the fold. It is a question for Temperance people to consider seriously how greatly behind they are in love, compassion, pity, kindness, and self-denial, their great Teacher, who went about doing good. We want more *practical religion;* more feeling, more sympathy for the sufferings of others. We should seek out and save, if possible, those who appear to be lost. "The want of sympathy," said a late judge, "is the sin of this age." The Temperance people should be pioneers in this work of universal charity. There should not be a drinking man untaught, uncared for, unlooked after, nor a drinker's house unvisited. If *visiting* was made a Christian duty, not merely the duty of a committee, but the duty of all, according to their time and opportunities, we should then have a full acquaintance with each other, learning to bear one another's burdens, and thus fulfil the law of Christ. The influence of *caste* seems to be getting worse. A change is greatly needed. As much as possible we should all mix together, the rich and the poor, the wise and the unwise, the good and the wicked. Not that we need to renounce either private property or private rights, but the mixing should be one of kindness, humility, love, charity, and good will.

I do deeply lament the indifference of many people in view of the over-spreading calamities of our country from the drinking system. Ignorance, poverty, vice, crime, lunacy, and irreligion abound; and yet how many persons are content with "attending their place of worship," and though they weekly— some daily—pass the doorsteps of thousands of poor souls, lost by taking drink, their "bowels of compassion" towards such seem wholly inactive. Some of the ministers, who ought, like their Master, to be the "friends of publicans and sinners;" who ought to exemplify the important fact that "visiting the fatherless and the widows in their affliction" is a great part of "pure and undefiled religion," seem satisfied with performing their pulpit services, and attending to the easier duties of their office, little concerning themselves with the condition of the masses outside. I once visited fifty miserable hovels in Cowgate, Edinburgh; only from one of which was any person gone to a place of worship; and to my inquiry, "Do the ministers of religion come and see you?" the answer was, "No, never!" What a lamentable state of things! If a minister wishes to be really useful, he should visit the "slums." If he wants to get a correct view of the morals and conduct of the people, he should be in the streets—the worst streets—on a Saturday night until public-house closing time. By such an example, members of his congregation would also be induced to labour and seek out and try to save those that are being lost. What should we say of our street-sweepers if they were always sweeping in the clean places, avoiding altogether the filth and dirt of the back streets, accumulating and spreading their pestiferous effects all around? What should we say of our medical men if infectious diseases were allowed to get so rife as to destroy thousands for want of their attendance, their time being taken up with those who least need them? I hold it equally important that quite as great efforts should be made to remove *moral* as physical evil, especially by those who are paid for doing the work. At a gathering which was held in Edinburgh, the Rev. William Arnot said:—"We must now strike a lower key-note. The Christian Church has been basking itself in the sunshine over an appalling mass of moral and spiritual degradation. The surface of it has yet barely been scratched. Women and children are being slowly and surely murdered within sound of our hymn-singing." Speaking of the great gulf existing betwixt the church and the masses of the common people, he says "they might as well be living in another planet." There ought not, in my opinion, to be, and there need not be, a drinking man untaught, nor a drinker's house unvisited. If the ministers of religion would determine upon this and take the lead, there are, I believe, in every congregation a number who would be glad to engage in the work. With true Christian zeal, with virtuous self-denial and perseverance, on the part of the religious and temperance people, I should have no doubt of a great change in the conduct and habits of the people. Multitudes of our fellow creatures are lost for want of being looked after by those who are able. Many live and die drunkards, nobody caring for them.

I know that we have a number of good men who delight in this work; and the number would be vastly increased if the leading spirits in each society would make a fresh start. It is to help such that I propose giving a few hints as to how they should proceed in their work. I said before that no time can be wrong for engaging in the work of *visitation*. But I always found Sunday forenoons the best of all times. The men are then at home and often on the stool of repentance from the previous night's fuddle. The drink-shops are closed, it is the publican's half-holiday, and we should take advantage of it. I will here suppose that we have only two hearty devoted persons from each place of worship (and this would make, say in such a town as Liverpool, the goodly number of at least 600 teetotal missionaries !) ; let these make their arrangements on the Saturday night as to the time and place of labour for the following forenoon, and provide themselves with plenty of handbills ; or, if more desirable, let them follow our old plan, meeting together and starting from a central room. Let these missionaries go to where the hard drinkers reside—and the difficulty is not to find where they do reside but a district without them, and I should always give preference to the neighbourhood of the church or chapel where the visitors attend. Their calls will have to be guided partly by what they learn in the neighbourhood (for if they ask to be shown the houses where the drinkers live there will be plenty ready to give the information), and partly by what they see, for dirty door-steps, broken windows, and other indications of the effects of drink, will not be long to seek. Of course in these visitations the backsliding teetotalers will be specially looked after. Our friends, with papers in hands, and a familiar " good morning," will soon get a hearing. In many cases they will not need to ask leave, but will be invited to come in. The poor fellows who are enslaved to drink are apt to cherish the idea that nobody cares for them ; and when you go and sit down by their fireside, and talk to them in a kind and sympathising spirit, they are delighted to find that they have some one who is still anxious for their welfare. The wife is sure to be with you, and to do all she can to make your words impressive, and the children listen with delight. In most cases you will find that these men have tried teetotalism, and they will tell you how happy they were when they kept it. If there should be opposition (as there will be in some places), let no hard words escape, or bad temper be shown, and avoid wasting time by any controversy, taking care to close the call by leaving them something to read, which is a good preparation for the next visit. These visitors will not go many times before they will be known, and their calls expected ; and the household improvements even by a few visits will soon be visible. This I would call the first part of our teetotal work among the masses.

Another work will unavoidably follow. In all the back streets on Sunday forenoons are groups of idlers, many of them young men, whose attention will be excited by the visitors with papers in their hands ; and in most cases they will not be allowed to pass without some observations. To stop and speak to these people is an important duty ; it is perhaps the only chance that can be had of meeting with them disengaged, and out of the drinkshop. This chance should always be embraced, and good tact, good temper, and great forbearance will be here required. Beware of long controversies, and avoid all offensive reference to religion. Keep to teetotalism, and to the benefits and happiness of abstaining from drink. These little gatherings are of great importance, and in such places as I have in view they can be improvised any time. Visits like these, conducted in a Christian spirit, cannot fail to benefit the masses, and they constitute the only agency by which we can reach a great majority of drinking people, and especially the young. Next, if we would do the work well, is to arrange as many plain, homely, public meetings as possible in the densely-populated parts of our towns. Every street should be made to feel the agitation in some shape or other. If it be winter, obtain the loan of schoolrooms, or outhouses, or cottages—if no better can be done. These meetings should be made well known, stating that a number of reformed characters will attend to give their experience. Our plan used to be this—to send a man round all the streets in the locality with a watchman's rattle for an hour or so before the time. The children were specially attracted, and would follow the man in his round, carrying home the announcement. By these inexpensive means meetings get well known and well attended. Many such gatherings has our old friend "Dicky Turner" (author of the word teetotal) announced with his rattle. Of course in summer buildings will seldom be wanted, as the meetings will be generally held in the open air. I never found a difficulty in getting a hearing in the "slums," especially from the females ; and *for their sakes alone* we should exert ourselves in every place. We keep complaining of the increase of female drinking, and what are we doing to lessen it ? Next to nothing, except denouncing "Gladstone's Wine Bill !" Let it, however, be distinctly understood that the plan I advocate is neither intended to supplant nor supplement the present modes of labour which have been proved to be really effective, but to take its proper place in the front rank of the agencies for a temperance reformation.

Now the kind of work I have referred to should not be spasmodic, similar to a "month's missions." We should go on the year round, all taking a part ; and such efforts would go on if we had the spirit of primitive teetotalism. With weekly meetings in central situations, constant agitations among the masses in the back streets, and Sunday labours similar to what I have described. Better days I hope are in prospect, but not without sound principles, and more energy in working them out. If Paul's spirit "was stirred in him" when he saw the city of Athens wholly given to idolatry, ought we not to feel the same when we see the worship of Bacchus eclipsing all others ? We should be like the early disciples, of whom it was said, "They that had turned the world upside down are come hither also." I recommend nothing but what I have practised myself, and of which I understand all the details. For three years consecutively I was engaged every Sunday forenoon in this important work, and at intervals ever since. These were glorious times, such as I fear I shall never see again ! We knew our work, and we did it, and if proof be wanting of the mighty change that was produced by these humble labours, it will at any time be forthcoming in the testimony of the late Rev. John Clay, chaplain of the gaol, an authority respected by everyone. Though at present drink seems to rule, it is a great encouragement to find that the old spirit is still alive, and *the only sound principle of entire abstinence* so extensively acknowledged. What we want is a *real revival*. When are we to have it ? and who will help to bring it about ?

Unpleasant as it seems to many to be mixed up with poor people, it always seemed to be my duty and pleasure to visit such. When I have travelled abroad, or visited the large towns at home, I never sought out "the lions of the place," but always preferred to see the state of the *Slums* where misery and destitution had taken up their abode. Though pained at what I witnessed, I always felt pleased that I had sought out the wretched and miserable, especially the great sufferers through drink, and had secured the opportunity of giving them good advice and encouragement amid their poverty. And the longer I live the more am I convinced that in this, both temperance people and religious people are coming far short of their duty. Ours is a mighty enterprise, but an uphill work; and yet it is the most important step in social reform that good men have attempted in our day. It lies at the basis of success in all other attempts to benefit our fellow-creatures. Meetings incessantly, indoors and outdoors; untiring visitations among the drinking classes; the distribution of temperance information, leaving no one untaught; the firm and faithful use of the press; denouncing every form of drinking, and keeping the whole question prominently before the world; all this done with a liberality worthy of such a cause, is the duty of every man and woman who claims the title of temperance reformer.

CHAPTER XVII.

Water for both inside and outside has been what I have long preached and practised. Hence I have always advocated Hydropathy, and have also largely availed myself, for my bodily ailments, of that mode of treatment. The first doctor practising Hydropathy which I consulted was Dr. Pasely at Bowness, Windermere. This was above thirty years ago, and his place was a most limited one compared with those which have been since erected in numerous parts of the kingdom, including the extensive establishment opened this year (1881) by the Windermere Hydropathic Company. This is situate on the slope of Biskey Howe, overlooking lake Windermere, and also the lovely lake-side village of Bowness, and immediately above my former residence at that place. Subsequently I visited most of the leading Hydropathic Establishments—Gully's and Wilson's, Malvern; the Wells and Ben Rhydding at Ilkley; and Smedley's I have visited several times. I have also been twice at the Hydropathic Establishment at Rolandseck on the Rhine—on one occasion remaining there nine weeks. No one has been more faithful to the use of Nature's best remedy, simplifying the water treatment in many respects. In the earlier days of Hydropathy the treatment was largely if not entirely by cold water applied in a variety of ways, but in later years the mode of treatment has considerably changed, warm and hot applications being largely in use besides the introduction of the Turkish Bath at some of the largest establishments. About this change in the mode of treatment I do not venture to give any opinion, but there is another change which is sadly for the worse, and which I am bound to condemn. In the early days of Hydropathy the establishments were curative ones, but as they began to multiply they became less and less so, until now many of them are more akin to hotels than places for the cure of disease. When they are conducted on Temperance principles, no objection can be offered ; indeed situate as they generally are on hill sides, where there is pure and bracing air, they offer advantages alike for pleasure and securing health independent of the baths. But it is lamentable to find in places ostensibly for the promotion of health, that there has been introduced the very substance—Alcohol—which undermines men's constitutions, and induces disease and every other evil. I regret to know that such is the power of appetite formed by moderate indulgence in alcohol, that even in establishments conducted, as they all ought to be, on strictly temperance principles, drink is sometimes surreptitiously introduced ; lamentable as is that practice, yet its evil influence on others is small compared with the sale of intoxicating liquors at such places; and in some others where not sold facilities are afforded for fetching it. The lesson to be learnt from all this is that the various temperance organizations need to put forth greater exertions than ever in the advocacy of total abstinence, for it might seem that concurrent with the extension of temperance principles, there has been a shifting of the sale and supply of liquors into perhaps more dangerous channels than the old ones, as in the case of hydropathic establishments and of social and political clubs, and worse than all, of grocers' shops.

The readers of this autobiography scarcely need to be told that my health during life has often been interrupted. I have suffered more from rheumatism than from any other cause. I have had rheumatic fever five times, and few have had more to endure from this than myself. It is an hereditary disease, and I have had several relatives who carried marks of the same to the grave. My last rheumatic fever laid me up at Windermere in 1869 ; it was very severe, and put a stop to my temperance work for a long time ; what rendered it most trying was that my dear wife was seriously ill at the same time—an illness which terminated in her death. We were both confined in the same house, but in different rooms, and never saw each other for seven weeks. I recovered slowly. I was unable to attend her funeral, and for a long time it was doubtful whether I should ever be able to render much more service to the temperance cause. One circumstance during this fever I shall never forget. Dr. Clowes was my medical adviser, and having attended upon me for some time my case was becoming serious, and one morning after a special examination, especially as to the action of my heart, he said :—"I know your principles, that you have a strong objection to stimulants, but I feel it my duty to be candid and to say that unless you consent I should not like to be responsible for the consequences." In reply, I answered—"Well, what is it you wish me to take?" He said—"I should recommend a little brandy, but perhaps in your case claret might answer." In my firmness against alcohol I was as unshaken as at the present time, but I replied—"I always understood that you could make up substitutes if required." He then said—"Well, I will send you a mixture," which he did at once. I only took one doze ; it was so bad, that calling for James—the man who attended upon me—I said to him—"This house has always been clear of drink and it shall now be clear of physic also, clear the room, take every bottle away"—speaking hastily at the time, being racked with pain. This he did at once as ordered, and I was left alone. There I was, I could scarcely move hand or foot, and I then began to think of the serious condition I was left in, for I did not know whether the doctor would call again, but if he did I was determined not to alter my decision. I said to myself—"If need be I am prepared to die, but I am not prepared to bring a scandal upon the good cause for which I have laboured so hard;" and this resolve I should repeat again if I were placed under similar circumstances. After some time I decided what to do. Remembering the reputation of Mr. Constantine, of Manchester, as a good bath-man, at my request he was telegraphed for, and after several visits and the application of the hydropathic treatment, in the best way my bed-ridden and painful condition would admit of, I began to improve, and though my recovery was slow, I ultimately recovered. I did not fail afterwards to "chaff" the doctor about my refusing to take any of his stimulants; I said—"If I had taken your claret, you would have repeated it all around that Mr. Livesey, notwithstanding his teetotalism, was obliged to take alcoholic liquor, and that it had saved his life, but as I did not take it—depending upon nature and assisted by water—and have recovered, you are quiet and say nothing." We have since discussed the question more fully, and what is a matter of great satisfaction to myself is, that he has since become a sound teetotaler, and has delivered—for the benefit of the Church of England Temperance Society—several lectures, some of which have been published. Since this period I have been compelled to be careful as to my health—to cease altogether taking journeys from home or to attend meetings, but my attachment to the good old cause has not abated, and I have continued to render all the help I could. Instead of keeping on my depôt of temperance tracts and bills in the town, which I found not convenient, I converted one of our bedrooms on the ground floor into a sort of stock and packing room, where I have all under my own management, and from which, with the help of some of the family, I despatch parcels almost daily to every part of the kingdom. Though I am now so closely confined to the house, yet I know as well as many others (perhaps more than some) what progress we are making. I get nearly all the periodicals that are published; my correspondence is still extensive, so much so that were it not for the help of my family I should disappoint many.

I have practised so many years washing every morning, that I have given the following details of my morning's operations as a *guide* to others. Once begun few will find any inclination to discontinue :—

I have always been an advocate for the free use of water to the skin; indeed, I may say that "water inside and out" has been a leading article in my hygienic faith. The people of this country are sadly too afraid of water; if they were as much afraid of beer it would be greatly to their advantage. One is the gift—among the best gifts—of heaven, "pure, sparkling, and bright," and can be had for nothing; the other is adulterated with whisky, and the people are such geese as to give for this unnatural mixture 4d. or 6d. a quart! There is one simple water operation that suits all cases, involves no loss of time, and is practicable in every bedroom, requiring nothing more than a large basin, a sponge, and two towels. This I call my "Morning Hand Bath;" and of its efficacy, when followed, I can not only speak from experience, but have received numerous testimonies of persons who have been benefited, but who could get no benefit from drugs. I have derived so much good myself that, as there are many that cannot afford the time or the expense of going to a water establishment, I will give a detail of the operation on my own person. All the appliances I require are, first, the usual wash-hand basin, into which I pour (sometimes before going to bed), say, two quarts of water. Into this I put a large coarse sponge, or, if I have not one at hand, a small towel, and next, something to stand on (simply to prevent wetting the floor), a piece of old carpet is sufficient, but I have a tin tray, 3ft. 3in. diameter, with a rim a few inches deep. These being provided, I get out of bed, the warmer the better, wet my head first with my hands, and then, taking the sponge full of water, I squeeze it on my shoulders, the water trickling down the body to the feet. If I want a good dose, I take a second spongeful in like manner, and sometimes a third; I have then at hand a couple of coarse towels, each about a yard long, and with them I rub myself vigorously for about a minute. Many persons, when commencing the practice, will require a longer rubbing—say two or three minutes; they need, however, to rub no longer than necessary to secure a reaction of warmth. It is important that the dressing should be quick, so as not to lose the heat which arises from the bounding of the blood to the surface. Ten minutes is the full time I take from leaving the bed to being in full dress. Of course this cannot be expected where much dandyism is attempted! At first it will be desirable for the amateur to take a brisk walk, for a quarter of an hour or so, immediately after, but in cold weather this should not be done without an overcoat; and as the walk is merely to secure reaction, when this can be obtained without it may be dispensed with. To persons who are only starting the practice I would say—if *cold* water be very disagreeable, by all means try *tepid*, and reduce it gradually to cold as soon as the body is able to bear it. For health, vigour, and physical happiness, I know nothing equal to " water inside and out." The latter I have practised, summer and winter, for above thirty and the former nearly fifty years. I have great faith in nature—in what physiologists call the *vis medicatrix naturæ*, and this conservative power has seldom disappointed me. If I am unwell I don't take physic; I wait, and recover much sooner, I observe, than those who dose themselves with drugs. I don't know any greater mistake made by most people than this—that as soon as they feel out of order, either the doctor or some quack medicine is sent for, and they are never satisfied unless they get something to " cure " them. Whereas the truth is, that most of our ailments are themselves a curative process, a remedial effort of nature to set the system right. To take physic, in most cases, is to interfere with, and often to defeat that remedial operation. The vitality of the system has then to exert itself both to get rid of the physic and to do its own proper work. We have a great deal to learn, and perhaps more to unlearn, as to what course is best for securing good health. Nobody knows the value of water and fresh air; I would that all preachers and teachers understood the water treatment, and would reduce it to practice on their own persons. To me it has been life itself: but for this morning ablution I should never have been able to do half the labour which has fallen to my lot. I have induced numbers to adopt the practice, and they have been greatly benefited.

CHAPTER XVIII.

My Autobiography would hardly be complete if it did not include a notice of the public celebration in Preston of my 80th Birthday, on March 5th, 1874. I feel, however, a greater difficulty in compiling this chapter than any of those which precede it. The occasion brought to Preston representatives from most of the great temperance organizations in the kingdom. The day's proceedings began with a Conference, held in the Corn Exchange, and amongst others present were Mr. Barlow, President of the British Temperance League; and also Mr. Crossley and Mr. T. Clegg; Mr. R. Rae, Secretary of the National Temperance League, with whom were Mr. Selway, Mr. Campbell, and Mr. Jabez Inwards. Mr. Logan, of Glasgow, represented the Scottish Temperance League. In the evening, the public meeting was preceded by a tea party, both held in the Corn Exchange. The public meeting was presided over by Mr. Robert Benson, and was addressed by about a dozen speakers from London, Glasgow, Manchester, Bolton, Preston, &c. The report of the proceedings of the day occupied nine lengthy columns in one of the Preston papers, and it is difficult to select from so much matter. I cannot spare space for even the merest outline of the many speeches delivered, but I give the following by the chairman, who said :—

We are met this evening to commemorate the 80th anniversary of the birth of our esteemed and venerable townsman, Joseph Livesey. There is no one amongst us that deserves our esteem and respect more than he does. Throughout the greater portion of his life he has not only been a political reformer, but, what is of much higher importance, he has been a social and moral reformer. We all know that he was one of the first who took a prominent part in raising the standard of teetotalism in our town and in this country. The principle of the abstinence from alcoholic drink lies very much at the root of all social reforms, and therefore, impressed with the importance of these truths, he has given us line upon line, tract upon tract, leaflet upon leaflet, lecture upon lecture,—spending his strength and his wealth in endeavouring to persuade his countrymen not to touch, taste, or handle these drinks, which have produced, and are still producing, by far the greatest amount of sin, misery, and woe. So much good seed cast broadcast over the length and breadth of our land has yielded, I have no doubt, an abundant harvest, and very many have cause to bless the name of Joseph Livesey. We must all rejoice that he has been enabled to carry on this work for so lengthened a period, and been permitted not only to attain the patriarchal age of three score years and ten, but ten years over ; and I do but express the earnest desire of all friends, that he may be favoured to enjoy the remaining years that may be granted him in the quiet and peaceful retrospect of a well-spent life.

The first speaker was Mr. Bradley, who presented the following address :—

To Joseph Livesey, Esq.

The Committee and members of the Preston Temperance Society have much pleasure in tendering their warmest congratulations to their old friend and fellow-townsman, Joseph Livesey, Esq., the venerable patriarch of the Temperance cause, on attaining his 80th natal day, with a fervent prayer that God, in His goodness, will spare and sustain him in health and strength for many years yet to come, so that he may continue his invaluable services to the good cause of Total Abstinence, in which he has so long and successfully been engaged.—March 5th, 1874.— (Signed)—Edward Edelston, James Duthie, Robert Benson, J.P., George Toulmin, J. A. Ferguson, Thomas Evans, David Irvin, J.P., William Bowker, Thomas Walmsley, Daniel Mayor, James Leech, Thomas Rawsthorne, J. J. Cockshott, John Proffitt, E. Dean, Joseph Dearden, Thomas Valiant, James Hodgson, W. R. Thorp, Joseph Jesper, Thomas Margerison, Richard Goring, George Garratt, Joseph Toulmin, William Blackburn, Rev. W. Hodges, James Toulmin, Thomas Hodgson, Robert Arkwright, William Coles, James Edelston, J. Archer Bowen, M.D., George Fish, Henry Garstang, Henry Bradley, W. Sowerbutts, James Garnett, John Irving, Henry Cartmell, Edward Smith.

Mr. Barlow, of Bolton, presented the address from the British Temperance League, the oldest of the many Leagues which we have now at work in furtherance of the cause. The following is a copy of the address :—

To Joseph Livesey, Esq., on his Eightieth Birthday.

DEAR MR. LIVESEY,—The Executive of the British Temperance League greets you on this your 80th birthday. The association with which we are connected, and which is somewhat fully represented here to-day, is not strange to you. Some of your earliest labours in the work of temperance principles and social reforms were in connection with the British Temperance League Association—now called the British Temperance League,—and from then till now—more than 40 years—your name and work have directly or indirectly been associated with it. The principles you hold so dear, and which you have so nobly advocated, are the foundation principles upon which our organization is built; and although our views and yours in reference to matters of detail have not always been in perfect harmony, yet, we have agreed to differ on many points, always maintaining the most perfect agreement in reference to the true basis of the movement, namely, total abstinence, pure and simple, for the individual, and restriction, with the view of the ultimate overthrow of the liquor traffic by legislative enactment. And now, dear sir, permit us to express our earnest hope, that although you have already passed the allotted age of man, your useful life may be spared yet many years; and that when your Master calls you, may you peacefully fall asleep, having the consciousness that you have done what you could to remove the curse of drunkenness from our land, and that your children may catch your mantle, and may go forward to the battle, and that to them may be graciously permitted to wear the laurels of victory.—We are, dear sir,

> JAS. BARLOW, President.
> WM. HOYLE, Treasurer.
> DAVID CROSSLEY, Chairman.
> E. B. DAWSON, Hon. Sec.
> T. ATKIN, Sec.

Mr. Logan, of Glasgow, next presented the following :—

Address from the Directors of the Scottish Temperance League to Joseph Livesey, Esq., of Preston, at the celebration of his 80th Birthday, 5th March, 1874.

Dear Friend,—Having learned that you are to be honoured by a public celebration of your 80th birthday, which occurs on the 5th of March, the Directors of the Scottish Temperance League gladly avail themselves of the occasion to express their high appreciation of the great services which you have rendered to the temperance movement, and their high admiration of your character as a man and a public benefactor.

To the town of Preston belongs the great honour of originating the total abstinence movement as a national and aggressive movement, and among its originators and early propagators no one was more prominent or more abundant in labour than yourself. Your name has been a household word in temperance circles throughout the length and breadth of England, Scotland, and Ireland, and far beyond these countries, since the very beginning of the movement. As an author and a lecturer, you did much to launch the infant cause upon the great sea of public opinion. Your visits to the principal towns and cities in the kingdom, and the delivery of your famous Malt Liquor Lecture attracted wide attention, and laid broad and deep the foundations of the movement that has now found a place in almost every town and village and hamlet in the land, and which is now all but universally admitted to be one of the greatest and most beneficent enterprises of the age. During the entire period of its existence your labours have been unremitting; for the last 42 years you have consecrated your talents, your time, your energies to the advancement of the cause. By means of your efforts the drunkard has been reclaimed, and the young and the sober have been shielded from temptation.—" The blessing of him that was ready to perish has come upon you."

You have edited and published newspapers and periodicals on your own responsibility; you have written and published and circulated tracts and pamphlets and lectures; you have lectured and visited from house to house, at all times and in all seasons, and all without fee or pecuniary reward; you have adhered to the practice of total abstinence in health and in sickness, in joy and in sorrow, and after an experience of 42 years, and with the weight of 80 summers and winters on your head, your faith in its adaptation to men and women at all ages and in all circumstances is unshaken. Your faith in the simple practice of total abstinence has never failed ; when others have become impatient of results, and have resorted to other methods of advancing the cause, you have preferred to walk in the old paths, and have refused to follow the multitude in what you believe to be mistaken and short-sighted policy.

We admire your talents, your courage, your faith, your patience, your labours of love. We honour you for your devotion to the temperance cause for the long period of 42 years, and for all the good that you have been enabled to accomplish. We congratulate you upon having attained to the advanced age of four score years, with your intellect unclouded, your affections warm and generous, and your enthusiasm, philanthropy, and patriotism unabated.

We hope that you may still be spared in the enjoyment of a hale and useful old age, and be privileged to witness still greater results from your efforts ; that the evening of your life may be calm and peaceful, and when your work is done, that you may receive the approval of the Great Master, to whose service you consecrated the best energies of your life.

Signed in name and on behalf of the Directors,

WILLIAM COLLINS, President.
NEIL M'NEILL, Chairman of Board.
WM. JOHNSTON, Secretary.

Mr. Selway, of London, speaking for the National Temperance League, explained that Mr. Bowly, the President, was unavoidably prevented from presenting their address. While the other addresses were in the usual form suited for framing, this of the National League was got up like a large folio album, in order to afford a sufficient number of pages for the large number of signatures, which, being executed in fac-simile, gives the book a greater interest and valuation, as including a selection of autographs of the leading temperance men throughout the kingdom. The following is a copy of the address :—

To Joseph Livesey, on completing his eightieth year, 5th March, 1874.

You have this day been permitted to accomplish fourscore of years, and from the vantage-ground thus attained can look back upon a life not only protracted beyond the average, but one that has been as useful as it has been long. The welfare of the people, the diffusion of knowledge and liberty, civil and religious, have ever found in you an ardent advocate and a stalwart champion ; but we would on this memorable day refer with especial pleasure and gratification to the years of unremitted toil which you have given to promote the great cause of Temperance, by inducing the people to abstain from those baneful drinks which produce drunkenness, with all its attendant evils and vices.

At a time when men were far more than now slaves to the habit of drinking, and when the belief in the necessity for alcoholic drinks was very great, the strong common-sense of your intellect grasped the idea that total abstinence from intoxicating liquors was the only cure for drunkenness, and with courage equal to the occasion, on the 23rd August, 1832, you originated and signed that pledge which has since become the bond of union of untold thousands, not only throughout the United Kingdom, but in every quarter of the globe, whose health, happiness, and prosperity have testified, and do testify to the advantages following upon the course you then adopted.

For more than forty years, a period greater than a generation of men, you have with unabated zeal and unswerving labour exerted the power of speech and the influence of your pen to promote the great work of Sobriety.

The earliest Temperance literature had you for its author, and the system of conveying truth in homely illustration and pithy sentences into every household by means of small printed messengers is largely indebted for its present great development to your earnest exertions.

Since the first inception of the Total Abstinence pledge how varied have been, and are, the agencies seeking to deal with the gigantic evils resulting from intoxicating drinks! Others may have sought new fields or to map other roads, but you have, amid many discouragements, doubtless, firmly held to your first and true course, unmoved by the lures of fashion or the hopes of ardent spirits who may have thought that they could obtain by change of action a more rapid result. You have ever been true to the cardinal doctrine of personal abstinence, the only true basis of national sobriety; and we feel that the happiest effects must follow on your example being pointed to as that of one who, under all circumstances of trial, disappointment, or success, never lost sight of his one aim, and pursued it with the energy and intelligence of a clear and vigorous mind.

The time has arrived when in the usual course of nature we must soon be called upon to say "Farewell!" Your name has been a household word, revered and respected alike by the child and the father, and it will be long indeed before Joseph Livesey is forgotten by those who have by his instrumentality been reclaimed from intemperance, or prevented from falling into its direful embrace. Their strong-nerved arms and those of their children shall combine to maintain the old flag in all its stateliness, and many a good man will seek to catch your falling mantle.

The day is far spent, the labour has been heavy, the rest shall be sweet; the light that shone more and more unto the perfect blaze of midday glory may somewhat wane, but "at eventide it shall be light." The presence of Him who has been your support in days of trouble will not leave you at the midnight hour, and when the joyful morning dawns, the greeting cry shall be, "Well done, thou good and faithful servant." That this may be so is alike the belief and the earnest prayer of the undersigned, who heartily congratulate you on this your 80th natal day.

[The address was signed by more than 220 representative temperance men in all parts of the United Kingdom, including the following:—Samuel Bowly, President of the National Temperance League; James Barlow, J.P., President of the British Temperance League; Samuel Morley, M.P., President of the United Kingdom Band of Hope Union; Sir Walter C. Trevelyan, Bart., President of the United Kingdom Alliance; William Collins, President of the Scottish Temperance League; Arthur Pease, President of the North of England Temperance League; John Harding, President of the Western Temperance League; Charles Sturge, J.P., President of the West Midland Temperance League; G. E. Norton, President of the Dorset County Temperance Association; W. S. Caine, President of the South Lancashire and North Cheshire Total Abstinence Union; Henry Munroe, M.D., F.L.S., Grand Worthy Vice-Templar of the Independent Order of Good Templars; J. A. Bowen, M.D., Chief Templar of the United Templar Order; Thomas Rooke, M.A., Honorary Secretary of the Church of England Temperance Society; Major-General F. Eardley-Wilmot, R.A., F.R.S., London; Rear-Admiral Sir William King Hall, K.C.B., Devonport; Major R. C. Stileman, J.P., Winchelsea; Rev. Canon Babington, M.A., Brighton; Rev. Newman Hall, L.L.B., London; Rev. Stenton Eardley, B.A., Streatham; Rev. Robert Maguire, M.A., London; Rev. Charles Stovel, London; Rev. William Reid, Edinburgh; Rev. Charles Garrett, Liverpool; Rev. William M'Kerrow, D.D., Manchester; Rev. Joseph Brown, D.D., Moderator of the United Presbyterian Synod; E. S. Ellis, J.P., Chairman of the Midland Railway Company; J. Ashworth, Rochdale; Edward Baines, Leeds; R. S. Bartleet, J.P., D.L., Redditch; J. D. Bassett, Leighton Buzzard; John Broomhall, J.P., Penge; J. Cadbury, Birmingham; T. Clegg, Manchester; Thos. Cook, Leicester; Joseph Crosfield, Reigate; George Cruikshank, London; W. H. Darby, J.P., Brymbo; James Edmunds, M.D., London; Charles Gilpin, M.P.; Jonathan Grubb, Sudbury; John Hughes, London; Charles Jupe, Mere; Alderman Lee, Wakefield; W. D. Lucas Shadwell, J.P., D.L., Hastings; Alderman Nicld, Warrington; Hugh Owen, London; George Palmer, J.P., Reading; W. I. Palmer, Reading; W. B. Robinson, Portsmouth; William Rowntree, Scarborough; T. B. Smithies, London; William Saunders, London; James Stubbin, Birmingham; William Tweedie, London; Edward Vivian, J.P., Torquay, &c., &c.]

A letter of congratulation was read from Mr. Thornton, Secretary of the Western Temperance League, as was also the following:—

Congratulatory address from the Committee of the United Kingdom Band of Hope Union to Joseph Livesey, Esq., on his eightieth birthday, March 5th, 1874.

Dear Sir,—We desire to congratulate you on the attainment of your eightieth year, and to express our admiration of your long and faithful labours on behalf of the Temperance movement and Bands of Hope. You have the distinguished honour of having been one of the founders of the Temperance reformation, and enjoy the felicity of living to see it established on a high and enduring basis. Your personal and gratuitous advocacy of total abstinence in days when advocates were few, and treated with contempt and persecution, was ever firm, gentle, wise, and powerful. Your sacrifices for the good cause were cheerfully made. Your publications the *Moral Reformer*, the *Staunch Teetotaler*, and the famous "Malt Lecture," attest the wisdom, clearness, and philanthropy of your mind and heart, and the "Malt Lecture" especially will long remain a text book in our literature. You have also always taken a deep interest in the young, and sought by many kindly efforts to prevent them becoming the victims of our national curse. For all this we, in common with all Band of Hope workers and other Temperance reformers, hold you in sincere esteem.

We trust that, in the providence of the Universal Father, your latter days may be full of peace, and we can assure you that when you have passed away from our presence to your reward we shall cherish your memory with tender regard, and enrol your name among the benefactors of mankind.

We remain, dear sir, on behalf of the Committee,

Yours faithfully,

SAMUEL MORLEY, President.
SILAS TUCKER, Chairman of Committee.
GEORGE W. M'CREE, } Secretaries.
FREDERIC T. SMITH, }

I had of course to acknowledge the presentation of the addresses, and also the many references to my labours in the cause which had been enlarged upon by the various speakers. I make a few extracts from the lengthened address I delivered on that, to me, very memorable occasion. I remarked :—I have long laboured to ward off such a celebration as that which has taken place this evening, but it appears that with all my caution and stratagem, and obstinacy I may add, I have been unable to be a match for the Preston, the London, the Scotch, and other Leagues upon this very important question. I never liked presentations. I have always written against and spoken against them, but I will not trouble you with my reasons excepting one, and I think that reason has weight in it. It is this—that a great deal too much honour is done to the individual, and others deserving either as much or nearly as much are over-looked. Persons who receive presentations, and to whose honour celebrations are got up, are often possessed of means and opportunities which do not fall to other obscure persons, poor persons, persons hampered with other engagements, who often labour as hard as I have done, and they are passed by, whilst I receive the congratulations from every part of the kingdom as well as from my Preston friends, and for which certainly I ought to feel extremely obliged. This is one reason, my friends, why I am opposed to these presentations. I could give other reasons, but then, perhaps, they would not tend to the edification of us on the present occasion. I did feel when I came into the room that I should feel embarrassed on this occasion, but when I came to look round me on the plat-form and see so many of my old friends, I felt in a great measure relieved from that embarrassment. * * * The total abstinence cause is the one to which I have given the greatest amount of my labour and attention, and it is the cause at the basis of which I do not hesitate to say every other cause owes its prosperity. Unless you can do away with the drink and the drinking system you neither can secure the education of the young nor the establishment of religion amongst the people. You can secure neither political liberty in its proper and highest sense, religious progress, nor anything else that is good, because so long as people drink they are in an unfit state either for individual improvement or for social progress. Worse than the public-house, bad as that is, the taking of intoxicating liquors is greatly spread in the homes of the people. What is termed a respectable drinker's house is the house for the spread of intoxication,—for the promotion of drinking. There is drink on the table in the morning, noon, and very often at night; and it is always in profusion on every social occasion. We have to labour to counteract all this, to say nothing of the inherent desire everyone brings into the world with them in favour of the drink. There was a time, my friends, some of you remember it—oh, I do remember it well, and if that time could come again I would really be like the Primitive Methodists—I would shout "Hallelujah." The time I refer to is from the year 1882 to 1837—five years, during which we laboured hard, and to which Mr. Clay, in his reports, again and again referred, showing that crime had diminished; five years, during which we had a number of demonstrations in favour of teetotalism at our procession meetings in the Theatre, when our anniversaries occupied six nights in the week, and when we had members of Parliament in the chair—great men every night. Our cause, my friends, has been going back. We have to start again, to begin again. Now, I want another beginning, another earnest start. Our organization may seem slender compared with those engaged in the opposite profession, yet with so much truth on our side, that gives us the advantage. The drink system is bad, and the arguments we use against it cannot be controverted. All who enjoy the blessings of perfect sobriety have a good word for teetotalism, but there are so many bound down by the chain of custom and usages, that they have not the courage to act according to their convictions. My friends, let us vigorously commence again; let us see if we cannot this Spring make a spring in favour of the old cause. You women can do a vast deal more than you do—infinitely more than you are now doing, in persuading people to leave that course of indulgence, idleness, and indifference to which they had been so much addicted. We should all try while we live, my friends, to do all that we can in the way of conferring blessings upon our fellow-creatures. We all profess to be Christians. Whether we be Catholics, Protestants, or Dissenters, no matter, we all like to be called Christians. Now, what is the character of a Christian? You will read it, my friends, in the parable of the prodigal son, also in the parable where the woman had ten pieces of silver and she lost one, and searched diligently until she found it; you will read it in another parable adjoining, where a man had a hundred sheep, one of which went astray, and he left the ninety and nine in the wilderness and was determined to find the one, and when he found it he put it on his shoulders and came home rejoicing, calling his friends and neighbours together. The meaning you all know. It is this—that there is greater joy in heaven over one sinner that repenteth than there is over the ninety and nine that need no repentance. We see men going to ruin; ministers of religion see and know individuals in their congregation, and also out of their congregation, who are drinking themselves to death, and yet they do not put up the warning hand. My dear friends, every one of you must try to pick out one that you know something about, and associate yourselves with them. It is not only for you to proclaim the teetotal doctrine from the platform, to enlighten the people, and to get their judgments informed accurately, but it is perhaps more influential and better in the long run that you should associate yourselves with them. There is not only light, but love wanted. No thorough teetotaller should live a day, should never sleep a night without considering—now, what can I do to benefit those people stricken or bowed down by the curse of strong drink? You must excuse me, my friends, but we do nothing compared with what we should do. We do nothing compared with what we did at the beginning of our enterprise, when our society prospered amazingly, and it was all because there was more attention, more zeal, more self-denial, more visiting, more determination to face the enemy, more carelessness as to what people said about us, and of us, and of our labours. And that which produced good results 40 years ago, the very same doctrine and the very same labour, will produce the same results at the present time.

Since the eventful celebration above noticed, more than seven years have elapsed, and on the recurrence of the 5th of March in each of those years, my kind friends at Preston have, through a deputation from the Committee of the Temperance Society, presented me with a congratulatory address. On each birthday since my 80th, friends in other towns have telegraphed me kind messages of congratulation; on some occasions these have been sent from public meetings held on the evenings of March 5th, in the respective years since 1874. In the present year (1881) amongst other letters which I received was one from Sir Edward Baines, formerly M.P. for Leeds, who, as chairman of the Leeds Temperance Society, forwarded a resolution of congratulation from that Association, adopted at a public meeting. On the morning of the 5th, a deputation, consisting of Mr. George Ling, representing the Central Temperance Association, and Mr. W. Walkley, president of the North London Temperance Society, and representing also the St. Pancras Total Abstinence Society, called upon me, having come from London for the express purpose of presenting the congratulations of those organizations, handing me a copy of the following resolution, passed at a meeting held in the Central Temperance Hall, Bishopgate Street, London, presided over by Wm. Saunders, Esq.:—"That this meeting of the members and friends, at the anniversary of the Central Temperance Association, hereby express their thanks and gratitude to God for the present position and power of the temperance movement, and desire to congratulate Mr. Joseph Livesey, of Preston, on attaining his 87th birthday, wishing him health and happiness further to witness the triumphs of that principle to which he has devoted with disinterested fidelity nearly 50 years of his long and honourable life."

The latter part of this work being undertaken in my 88th year, and when in enfeebled health, is necessarily less complete than the former portion written in 1867 and 1868. Those who desire a fuller history of the commencement and progress of the teetotal movement, I must refer them to my "Reminiscences of Early Teetotalism."

THE DAWN AND SPREAD OF TEETOTALISM.

For the reasons stated in the EXPLANATORY Notice prefixed to this work, the latter portion of my father's Autobiography is supplemented by the following abridgment of J. Dearden's *Dawn and Spread of Teetotalism*, published nine years ago, and long out of print.—W. LIVESEY [1881].

Total Abstinence from all intoxicating liquors is more briefly described by the one word Teetotalism, for which reason I shall use that term throughout, though strictly it ought not to come into use until I have reached the date of September, 1833, at which time it was coined, on the instant, by "Dicky" Turner, in the impetuosity of his earnestness, when he was addressing a public meeting in the Cock-pit. Of its origin and author there is no doubt, though some ingenious attempts have been made to trace it to other sources.

In the year 1826, the philanthropists of America began to organise their forces to battle against the, then, main curse of their country—the drinking of "Ardent Spirits." Through the succeeding year these efforts were extended, and in 1829 the movement commenced in some parts of the United Kingdom. From that year up to 1831 societies pledging their members to abstinence from spirituous liquors began to multiply in our country, until at length what became known as the "Moderation System," reached our town—PRESTON,—which soon after became the BIRTH-PLACE OF TEETOTALISM! That there have been Teetotalers in every age of the world no one doubts; nor is it at all unlikely that believers in its excellency and efficacy increased in numbers as the injurious effects of ardent spirits were brought more and more prominently before the public. Here and there Teetotalism had been put forth by individuals, but it was at Preston it first took "a form and shape;" at Preston it was, that the first organization of forces was made for the dissemination of the true Temperance principle of PERSONAL ABSTINENCE amongst our towns-people; it was from Preston that the first Apostles of Teetotalism set out to convert the people of this kingdom to the belief that *all intoxicating liquors, as beverages, are not only unnecessary but injurious.* Dr. Lees in his latest work, the "Text Book of Temperance," after noticing the movements in other places, speaking of Preston, says—"Here things were ripening to a head; here lived a well-known local Franklin, Mr. Joseph Livesey, who, having risen by self-denial, culture and industry, from the working classes, sought to extend to them the blessings of education, and of social and moral reform. With a keen Saxon insight he perceived the evil in their midst, and with cautious, persevering common sense sought to apply the cure. A well-to-do tradesman, he by-and-bye became the proprietor of a printing press and the conductor of a little periodical called *The Moral Reformer.** No wonder the seeds of truth falling into such genial soil, should speedily germinate into power and fruitfulness."

Going through the three volumes of the "Moral Reformer," I have been struck how gradually but early the principles of Teetotalism dawned upon the mind of its editor. The Beer Bill passed in 1830, and in the January number for 1831, he denounces it as "a great curse," and after condemning "cheap ale," he laments the repeal of the "beer tax," remarking that it would have been far wiser to have taken off the taxes upon candles and soap. In succeeding monthly numbers the repeal of the tax is denounced as "an egregious blunder," and the Beer Bill as "deluging the land with ale, and offering a bounty for drunkenness.'

* This work was published as a sixpenny Monthly Magazine in 1831, '32 and '33, making Vols. I., II. and III.

In the July number, we have the announcement that he had been then for some time a Teetotaler, as follows :—"So shocked have I been with the effects of intemperance, and so convinced of the evil tendency of *moderate* drinking, that since the commencement of 1831, I have never tasted ale, wine or ardent spirits." In the same number is given the opinions of some American physicians, and Teetotal principles are made striking by the following being printed in italics— " He is happy who considers *water the best drink*, and salt the best sauce." In the November number Teetotalism is advocated by a correspondent. Thus were Teetotal principles gradually being sent forth from Preston as early as 1831.

On the 1st of January, 1832, the teachers in Mr. Livesey's Adult School established a Temperance Society, when one of them, Mr. John Broadbelt, (afterwards a clergyman of the Church of England, and one of the "Seven men of Preston " who signed the first Teetotal Pledge,) urged upon them, on that 1st day of January, 1832,—the adoption of a Teetotal Pledge! He was over-ruled, otherwise *he* would have had the honour of first putting the Teetotal Pledge officially before the world. This Society afterwards merged into the Preston Temperance Society, which was established March 22nd. In the first number of the " Moral Reformer" for 1832, the editor in giving a fearful picture of the drunkenness in Preston on Christmas Day, (1831,) concludes thus : " At half-past three o'clock, I actually met a man trucking a barrel of beer on the parapet ; Oh ! the besetting sin of my unhappy country." The next number heralds the preparations for establishing a Temperance Society in Preston ; and the next, besides noticing a lecture delivered by Mr. Livesey, in the Cock-pit, on Temperance, early in March, gives the following as the fundamental principle agreed upon to be submitted to the public meeting :

" We, the undersigned, believe that the prevailing practice of using intoxicating liquors is most injurious, both to the temporal and spiritual interests of the people, by producing crime, poverty, and disease. We believe also, that decisive means of reformation, including example as well as precept, are loudly and imperatively called for. We do, therefore, voluntarily agree that we will totally abstain from the use of ardent spirits ourselves, and will not give nor offer them to others, except as medicines ; and if we use other liquors it shall be in great moderation, and we will endeavour to discountenance the causes and practices of intemperance."

The above was adopted at the meeting, which was held on March 22nd, at which Mr. Moses Holden presided, and amongst other speakers were the following —Rev. R. Slate, Rev. W. Moore, Rev. F. Skinner, from Blackburn, and Mr. Pollard, from Manchester. The address of the latter was very telling and was much spoken of at the time, in fact, he was one of the most effective, as well as the most useful, of the early advocates. At the close 90 persons joined the society.

The committee elected at the public meeting were no sooner installed in office than they made arrangements for holding meetings. The society was now without head-quarters or rallying-place. Mr. Livesey had, however, become tenant under the Earl of Derby, of the Cock-pit, a large and well adapted building, the rent of which he paid for eight years, and gave the society the free use of it for all their meetings. The first meeting was held in it on May 15th,—only seven weeks from the formation of the society. In that interval meetings were held in various school-rooms, the first on April 20th, which was addressed by the Rev. C. Radcliff, Rev. R. Slate, Jas. Teare, and others. The next meeting was held in the Primitive Methodist Chapel, in Lawson Street, which was addressed by Messrs. J. Livesey, T. Swindlehurst, J. Teare, and others. One of the oldest Teetotal members now alive has recorded in print the impressive character of Mr. Livesey's speech at this meeting, when he advocated Teetotalism in the strongest terms. Tuesday night was now the regular meeting night, and that in the Cock-pit ; still, extra meetings were also held in schools. All the Cock-pit meetings at this time were crowded and enthusiastic, intense earnestness prevailed, and reformed drunkards were soon proclaiming that they were practicing Teetotalism, though no Teetotal Pledge had yet been introduced.

Not only did the question of Teetotalism introduce itself very early upon the platform, but quite as early by the press, indeed the latter may to some extent be said to have anticipated the former. A writer in the " Moral Reformer," with the signature of " Juvenis," and under date March 27th, 1832, advocated Teetotal principles, and gave at considerable length an extract from the life of the celebrated Dr. Franklin, showing how, while drinking nothing stronger than water, he was more capable of fatigue and endurance than those of his fellow workmen who drank ale or other liquors; proving also the small quantity of actual nutritive matter ale contains. The "local Franklin"—as Dr. Lees styles Mr. Livesey—seized at once upon Dr. Franklin's facts and experience, thus brought so prominently before him in his own publication; and these laid the foundation for the well-known tract, "The Great Delusion," and the more elaborate and celebrated MALT LIQUOR LECTURE. Of this lecture Mr. Livesey has published many editions, besides conceding (as he does with all he writes,) liberty to anyone to re-publish. The total circulation of Mr. Livesey's lecture from all sources is now estimated at betwixt one and two million copies.* Nothing upon the Temperance question—from 1832 to 1873—has been presented to so many minds as that lecture, seeing that in addition to being issued by many publishers, it was delivered by Mr. Livesey at his own cost in most of the large towns of the kingdom. Dr. Harrison, Mr. Grundy, and Mr. Livesey were soon at work upon other tracts, for I find the following entry in the minute book of the society, as early as May 23rd,—"That Mr. Livesey's proposition as to printing 6,000 tracts, gratis, on condition that the society find the paper be accepted with thanks." There were no large funds in those days, for I notice that even the bare cost of the paper was obliged to be economised, as shortly afterwards the committee resolved "that the last 2,000 of the tracts shall be on inferior paper!" In addition to these 6,000 tracts, I find that in July 10,000 more were in circulation. Supplying the people with sound information appears to have been the great aim; and compared with the funds at command, more was done then than has ever been done since, for the total amount of subscriptions that year was only £25, nearly one-third of which was expended upon tracts (got on the reduced terms named,) and half as much expended in lectures. The earliest tracts are as strongly tinctured with Teetotalism as I have shown the active members of the committee to have been; the title of one shows this,—" Ale and other FERMENTED Liquors." This was written by Dr. Harrison, and was "No. 3" of the series, afterwards "The Great Delusion" superseded it, and was "No. 3." "No. 2" tract, "Cost of Intemperance," was written by Mr. Grundy, who also contributed some pieces of poetry, which became very popular. "No. 1" tract, "Addresses on Temperance Societies," was by Mr. Livesey. As early as June, 1832, I find J. Eden, of Chorley, writing in favour of Teetotalism, his advocacy of the principles being given to the public through the medium of the "Moral Reformer"; he also acknowledges having been impressed with the letter of "Juvenis," before referred to.

We now come to the month of July, 1832; on the 11th of that month was held the First Temperance Society's Tea Party, in the Exchange Rooms, at which 540 sat down. On the following day a large meeting was held on the Moor, it being the Races; the speaking was extended over four hours, and included the following—Rev. C. Radcliff (chairman,) Rev. S. Smith, Messrs. Livesey, Pollard, Teare, Holden, and Alston. In this month Dr. Harrison and Mr. Livesey were requested to write two additional tracts, and they were also requested to write an address to the Candidates for the Borough, requesting them to give no intoxicating liquor at the approaching election—the addresses to be printed and posted on the walls of the town. Though we may gather from the speeches delivered at this date by Reformed Drunkards,—many of whom were early snatched as brands from the burning,—that they had been acting upon Teetotal principles as early as May, yet up to September 1st no Teetotal *pledge* had ever been publicly introduced at any of the meetings. The question of ' ...ng a Teetotal *pledge*, in addition to the other, was the constant subject of discussion whenever any of the friends were met together; and as I have shown by the committee, early in June, requesting Dr. Harrison to lecture upon the use of *fermented* as well as distilled liquors, there can be no doubt how early the committee had become indoctrinated with Teetotal principles. This, however, was a critical period; for though the society was doing immense good in the reformation of drunkards, a portion of the committee could not move beyond "Moderation" in fermented liquors; hence caution was needed, lest any helpers should have felt too much

---

* This was nine years ago, it will now be much larger.

pressure was being put upon them, and so have retired from the work. Nine days previous to the 1st of Sept. a private pledge of Teetotalism was signed by two members ; this came about as follows :—John King (who had joined the society about three months after its establishment,) was passing Mr. Livesey's cheese warehouse, in Church Street, when Mr. L. invited him into the shop, and they commenced discussing Teetotalism and moderation,—which, indeed, was the uppermost subject when any of us met together. Both were of one opinion, and Mr. Livesey, on the spur of the moment, asked John King if he would sign a total abstinence pledge, if he (Mr. L.) drew one up. This he agreed to ; Mr. Livesey went to his desk and wrote the pledge. As the paper lay on the desk, John King came up to it, on which Mr. Livesey said to him, " Thee sign first," which he did, and Mr. L. then added his name.

From September 1st, 1832, dates the first Teetotal pledge offered to the people of Preston. That year it fell upon a Saturday, a rather unusual day to call a special meeting upon ; but one was called by Mr. Livesey. Most likely the fact of what had been done in the matter of the private pledge, which we have noticed, impelled him to try to launch the matter before the public. Be that as it may, I remember attending the meeting, and I may well remember the warm discussion which took place at it, for I was one who went in for more caution and less speed. As the earnest proceedings were drawing to a close, and some were leaving, a number got grouped together at one side of the room,—still debating the matter,— when at length Mr. Livesey resolved he would draw up a Total Abstinence Pledge. He pulled a small memorandum book out of his pocket, and having written the pledge with black lead, he read it over, and standing with the book in his hand said :—" Whose name shall I put down ?" Six gave their names, and Mr. Livesey made up the number to seven. Next day Mr. Livesey, finding the black lead writing not very good, copied in ink the pledge and the signatures, in the order in which they were given. " We agree to Abstain from all Liquors of an Intoxicating Quality, whether Ale, Porter, Wine, or Ardent Spirits, except as Medicine. John Gratrex, Edwd. Dickinson. Jno. Broadbelt, Jno. Smith, Joseph Livesey, David Anderton, Jno. King.* These, then, were " the seven men of Preston ;" not that they were more advanced than many others, but that they happened to be present at this special meeting. J. Broadbelt, as I have clearly shown, had actually proposed a like pledge as early as January in that year, 1832, and Mr. Livesey had been a Teetotaler from early in the previous year, 1831. J. Smith had been a very earnest worker before the society was established, for he had received some Temperance tracts from Mr. Swindlehurst early in 1832, which he (Mr. S.) had got from Mr. Finch, of Liverpool. The circulation of these tracts, followed by a visit from Mr. Jackson, agent of the Bradford society, no doubt led to the formation of the Preston society on the " Moderation Basis." Swindlehurst was not present at the special meeting, otherwise there is no doubt he would have been one of the first to give in his name ; and no doubt many others would, had they had the opportunity. Amongst others who were on the committee at this time (not included in the seven), who were active Teetotalers, were I. Grundy, Thos. Swindlehurst, J. Teare, Dr. Harrison, Rev. S. Smith, J. Dearden, H. Bradley, Robert Jolly, W. Sowerbutts, Jonathan Howarth, J. Brade, George Gratrex.

The advocates had now begun to spread the "glad tidings" of the means of deliverance from the evils of drinking in the neighbouring villages, and by October six country societies had been formed. It was in that month that " Dicky" Turner first signed any pledge. On the second Thursday in October he strolled into the meeting at St. Peter's School Room, where he signed the moderation pledge. I was present, and urgently pressed him to sign the pledge of total abstinence, which he then did, and kept it consistently to the day of his death, October 27th, 1846. During this month Preston was visited by Mr. E. Morris, of Glasgow, who became intensely interested in the proceedings. He composed one of the most favourite Temperance Hymns ever published ; it was " addressed to the members of the Preston society." He also wrote " an address to the young men and women of Preston." His visit to Preston led to his being the means of establishing the first Teetotal Society in Scotland. It is said that a few persons

---

* A fac-simile of this appears on page 109.

signed a total abstinence pledge in Scotland as early as 1830; if this be so, they must have hid their light under a bushel, and it was left to Mr. Morris, after his return from Preston, to uncover it. But I must pass over the rest of the year 1832, a year so pregnant with events, the good effects resulting from which it is difficult to estimate. I may just note that the first "Temperance Hotel" was opened at Preston on December 24th, 1832.

The first striking event in the year 1833 was a response to a circular received from America. There they had fixed to hold simultaneous meetings throughout the States, on the 26th February, and in Preston not only was a meeting held on that day, but on every day afterwards during the whole week. On the Tuesday and Wednesday twenty-four reformed drunkards addressed the two meetings; on Thursday, Joseph Livesey delivered his MALT LIQUOR LECTURE; on Friday there was a CHEMICAL LECTURE, by Mr. B. Barton, of Blackburn; on Saturday, the week was wound up by a singing entertainment; 260 signed the pledge at these meetings. Petitions to Parliament, by both males and females, were got up during this series of meetings, praying for a revision of the new Beer Bill and for other steps to "discountenance the causes and practices of intemperance." On the 16th of March, after several previous discussions, the committee decided that the time had come to *officially* recognize the Teetotal pledge, which up to now had only had a semi-official character, being pushed forward as the result of the action taken on September 1st, 1832. Mr. Livesey was requested to revise it, and also the rules, for adoption at the annual meeting, on March 26th, which was held in the Theatre, and crowded to excess. The pledge was as follows :—

"We do further voluntarily agree to abstain for one year, from ale, porter, wine, ardent spirits, and all intoxicating liquors, except used as a medicine, or in a religious ordinance."

A number who had signed the semi-official Teetotal pledge, on this night, signed the official pledge, amongst them were "Dicky" Turner, J. Livesey, T. Swindlehurst, J. King, myself and others. C. Swainson, Esq., presided at the meeting, which was addressed by Rev. S. Smith, Messrs. J. Livesey, T. Swindlehurst, I. Grundy, J. Teare, J. Fothergill, and others. In the course of his address, Mr Swindlehurst said he had not "drunk either ale or spirits" for twelve months. The number of members of the society up to that date was 2,060. The committee appointed at the meeting numbered 46, and 13 were added during the year, making a total of 59. The names of Henry Anderton (the poet) and James Broughton, were added to the committee during this year. Of the zeal and earnestness of these two advocates it would be impossible to speak too highly; their labours at home and in distant places were very great. Anderton was inimitable as a speaker. On Whit-Monday, June 3rd, the society had its first procession, which included 1,000 persons. The well-known "Jim" Duckworth, got up a mock procession, styled the "moderation and anti-hypocritical society." It was headed (says the *Preston Chronicle*,) "by a man in jockey cap and jacket, mounted on a wretched looking pony, in worse condition than the renowned Rozinate of Don Quixote. Then came two groups of fellows in two carts, some wearing old cocked hats and some masks, and other ridiculous appendages. There were some casks of ale and porter in the carts, to which they ever and anon made eager applications." The wretched affair ended by some of them getting into the hands of the police. It was by the doings of Duckworth at an out-door Sunday meeting about this time, that Grubb was brought to the front, and added afterwards by his powerful eloquence so much to the success of the cause. In July, Mr. Livesey commenced to devote a portion of his "Moral Reformer" specially to the movement under the heading of "THE TEMPERANCE ADVOCATE."

Some rough work had at this time to be done; the "fallow ground" had to be ploughed, and men were fortunately forthcoming for the fight; men who, regardless of all kinds of opposition, never faltered, never waited, but were ever ready in "season and out of season." The leaders of the movement were soon supported by a little army of advocates, in the persons of reformed drunkards, whose experience, as related by them, had great influence upon the masses. As early as this date there could be numbered 20 speakers engaged, not only in

Preston, but extending their labours to all the surrounding villages. Every village within nine miles of Preston had been visited, and Longton, Garstang, Kirkham, and Houghton, are named in Mr. Livesey's work as making the greatest progress. In September (as named at the commencement of this work,) the word TEETOTAL was first given to the world by "Dicky" Turner. He was an unlettered man, but intensely earnest of speech, never stopping in his fervency to correct any misplaced word. It was in this way that he coined on the instant the word Teetotal:—he wished to show how inconceivably superior to "moderation" was *total* abstinence; he wanted a word to express his feelings, and evidently had the word TOTAL upon his lips, but feeling how deficient it was to describe what he wanted, he tried to give it a prefix which would make its meaning stronger; he could not halt to fetch up a word,—he never did halt in his speech, he always went on,—and he out with the word TEE-TOTAL! Its sound was like magic upon the audience, who loudly cheered; I witnessed Mr. Livesey pat him on the back and say "that shall be the name, Dicky"! And that is the name to this day, and ever will be; for it now finds its place in every Dictionary, and in every country where the English tongue is spoken it is used to designate total abstinence from all intoxicating liquors. Just now (March, 1873,) the Malt Tax question is prominent before the public, a section of barley growers and brewers wanting to increase the flood of malt liquor which is creating such evil in our land, and I find in the September number, 1833, of "The Moral Reformer," that a similar movement was then on foot—just 40 years ago, and Mr. Livesey was opposing it then with just the same arguments as he has lately published in that valuable tract "Why Repeal the Malt Tax?" This year's Christmas Tea Party, the second one, was the most successful ever held in Preston, in connection with any cause,— 1,200 took tea; the rooms were decorated in a manner never since equalled; a large number of female and male members having spent night after night for weeks in the work of decoration.

On the 1st of January, 1834, was published, by Mr. Livesey, the first number of the first exclusively Teetotal periodical ever issued from the press. Its title was *The Preston Temperance Advocate;* its size and shape much like that of "Punch." It was issued monthly, at the price of one penny. Mr. Livesey continued this publication during the years 1834—35—36 and 1837, when he transferred it to the then "British Temperance Association." During the year 1835 it was published in Leeds, and conducted by Dr. Lees, under the title of "The Advocate and Herald;" after that date, for some time, it was published by Dr. Lees, in the Isle of Man. The reason for selecting that isolated spot for publishing was this—that all Manx Newspapers (and this was held to be one) were privileged to be posted without any stamp! They were thus delivered in all parts of England free of any charge. This too great privilege was suddenly withdrawn, and by it the Manx Newspapers were placed on the same footing as the English. After a lapse of nearly 40 years I do not think we have any paper but one which can be compared to this first Teetotal serial, for the amount of information of a character suited to inform those ignorant of the properties and qualities of intoxicating liquors, and their injurious effects upon the system; or of articles suited to stimulate labourers in the cause, or to build up and strengthen those who were weak; or so full of practical suggestions for furthering the work. This publication, coming so early into the field, was of great value, and soon began to give reports of the progress of the cause throughout Lancashire and Yorkshire, as well as more distant places. The "Temperance Advocate," in its pages for the year 1834, enable us to better trace the progress the cause was making than we have been able to do in the two previous years, for want of a publication wholly devoted to the cause. No "Missionaries" had yet been appointed or gone out from Preston; by "Missionaries," I mean persons deputed and set apart wholly to travel and lecture, and promote the cause—receiving remuneration directly or indirectly for their services. The setting out and labours of these will be recorded when my narrative arrives at the date of their doing so. Mr. Pollard, of Manchester, and Mr. Cundy, of the same place, had however, been some time at work as Missionaries; the latter in the past year, and the former ever since early in 1832. And the "Advocate" supplies us with records of their labours in 1834. In May Mr. Pollard made Carlisle his centre of operations for six weeks, having previously had Darlington for his head quarters. He reported the formation of 40 new societies previous to going to Carlisle. He thus wrote—that he " had only had two days rest in 56, and a deal of travelling, besides being engaged two or three times on the Sabbath, and good *unadulterated water* has been my only beverage, yet 1 have never been weary or exhausted." In November I find he was engaged five weeks around Leeds, in which his labours were greatly assisted by one of the most devoted labourers the cause ever had in Yorkshire—Mr. John Andrew, of Leeds, who has been " in harness" ever since.

Our Preston men were no less zealous or laborious than in the previous year. In the January number of the " Advocate" we have a report of a tour by Anderton to Chorley, Manchester, Oldham, and Eccles ; and later in the year,— along with Broughton,—to Colne, Marsden, Rawtenstall, and Manchester. I find Swindlehurst, or Teare, or Anderton, or Grubb, or Broughton, or Howarth, ("Slender Billy") reported as speaking at meetings at Haslingden, Todmorden, Burnley, Accrington, Bolton, Stockport, Birmingham, Lancaster, Dolphinholme, Garstang, Inglewhite, &c., &c. The villages around Preston were the scene of the labours of our reformed characters, of the members of the Youths' Society, as well as some of the popular advocates before-named. Wherever our Preston men went the " moderation" system was either at once suspended or left to linger and die by its own inherent uselessness for the prevention of intemperance. In many places—amongst others Bolton and Wigan—societies were formed desig- nated " The *new* Temperance Society ;" at Manchester the Rev. F. Beardsall says, that in adopting the Teetotal Pledge they reversed the order of things, putting the last (Teetotal) first ; he writes—"our *rule* is total abstinence, the *exception* is moderation, the result of five meetings is as follows, 76 teetotal, 24 moderation." The " Advocate," I need hardly say, always insisted upon the adoption of Teeto- talism, and the abandonment of " Moderation." It was the Rev. F. Beardsall who compiled the first Temperance Hymn Book. In the March number of the " Advocate" about 80 towns in Lancashire and Yorkshire are noticed, and the progress the cause was making reported. I name these to show how far and wide the principles of Teetotalism were spreading at that date.

In the last week in February, four meetings were held in the Theatre : simultaneous meetings being held at that date in America. Twenty-four reformed drunkards occupied two nights by their speeches. Mr. Livesey had one night for his lecture ; Anderton and Swindlehurst were amongst the other speakers. The second annual meeting was held in the Theatre on March 25th ; C. Swainson, Esq., in the chair. The moderation pledge, though fallen nearly into disuse, was not wholly discarded till the next anniversary ; but the Teetotal pledge was rendered more comprehensive by the addition of the words—" neither give nor offer." The good effects of the Preston Society were referred to by Judge Alderson, who during the hearing of a Civil case—(it transpiring that one of the parties had fallen into drunken habits)—remarked, " Why don't you bind him to the Temperance Society : I am sure Temperance Societies do much good, for from Preston, where they are in operation, there has not been a single criminal case this Assizes." I may add that this was the *fourth* Assizes there had been no case from Preston ! On April 18th, *the first exclusively Temperance Society in England was formed* by the young men of Preston. The pledge was signed the first night by 101 youths, including two sons of Mr. Livesey, and two sons of Mr. Swindle- hurst. This Society had its speakers, who visited the villages around Preston. On May 19th, the second Temperance Whit-Monday procession took place ; it included females, also the Youths' Society, and a large number of members from the village Societies. On that and the following evenings, meetings were held in the Theatre ; at this time the signatures to the Teetotal pledge were as 30 to 1 for the " Moderation" one. The most important meetings of this year were those of the half-yearly Festival, held for five successive nights in the Theatre, com- mencing on Tuesday, Sept. 30th. This festival was memorable from the visit of Robert Guest White, Esq., late one of the Sheriffs of Dublin, whose visit was of great value in promoting the cause on his return home. He presided on the first evening. He had heard the news of the Preston Teetotalers when on a visit to London, and resolved to come and see. The chairman for the next evening was the Rev. J. Clay, then Chaplain of Preston Jail, whose annual reports were world-famed for their valuable statistics ; he stated that since Teetotalism had been introduced into Preston, crime in it had decreased. The two following nights, P. H. Fleetwood, Esq., M.P., (afterwards Sir H. F.) filled the chair. The Christmas Tea Party was held in the Exchange, which, as in the former year, was well decorated ; the number present was near 1,000. Amongst the speakers were the following :—Mr. T. Entwistle, Bolton ; Mr. W. Haigh, near Huddersfield ; Mr. Proctor, Lancaster; Mr. and Mrs. Howson, Chorley ; Messrs. Margerson, Blackburn ; Brown, Leyland ; Gardner, Samlesbury.

On Sept. 24th, a conference of deputies from Lancashire and the adjoining counties was held in the Exchange Dining Rooms, Manchester. Various resolutions were passed for the better organization of the movement. Amongst other suggestions embodied in them was this—that the societies "be recommended to adopt the pledge of Total Abstinence." It was also resolved to raise a fund to send out agents to establish societies, and an agency committee was formed. The names of the deputies attending this conference are not published, but to show most of the places where societies had been formed, and those active in their progress, I have copied from " The Advocate " the names of those parties who sent reports of the proceedings of their societies during the year, viz. :—Manchester, F. Beardsall ; Leeds, J. Andrew ; Huddersfield, W. Haigh ; Sheffield, J. Edgar ; Birmingham, J. Wilkins and R. Davies ; London, J. Pascoe ; Darlington, S. Thompson ; Bolton, T. Ormerod and J. Rothwell ; Bury, J. Dearden ; Bacup, J. Haworth ; Heywood, T. Clegg and J. Heywood ; Stockport, J. Royle ; Oldham, J. Hawkshead ; Accrington, E. Bowker ; Colne, J. Douglas ; Barnoldswick, J. Spooner ; Settle, J. Wildman ; Keighley, R. Chester and A. Nichols ; Todmorden, J. Fielding ; Saddleworth, R. Tabraham ; Leigh, J. Fletcher ; Wigan, W. Barton ; Warrington, G. H. Crowther ; Chester, W. H. Darlington ; Liverpool, J. Clarkson ; Salford, S. Carter ; Kendal, E. Swinglehurst and W. Jolly ; Ulverston, J. Soulby, W. Brickal, and W. Benson. This year Preston was put in communication with America, principally by the commencement of a monthly correspondence betwixt that noble Teetotaler, E. C. Delaven, Esq., of Albany, New York, and Mr. Livesey.

The principal event at Preston in the year 1835 was the adoption, at the annual meeting in March, of the Teetotal pledge as the *only* pledge of the society. Up to that date the moderation pledge had not been *officially* discarded, though it had virtually been so for some time. The proceedings at this year's anniversary occupied five nights in the Theatre ; the chairmen presiding were as follows :—Rev. J. Cheadle, Colne ; Rev. J. Clay, Chaplain of Preston House of Correction ; Mr. T. Swindlehurst ; C. Swainson, Esq., Walton ; and the Rev. W. Riky. The annual report stated that the Rev. J. Clay had called attention to the diminution of crime at the Sessions since the society was established ; also, that not a single criminal case had been sent from Preston for trial at Lancaster for six consecutive Assizes. The pledge adopted was as follows :—

"I DO VOLUNTARILY PROMISE THAT I WILL ABSTAIN FROM ALE, PORTER, WINE, ARDENT SPIRITS, AND ALL INTOXICATING LIQUORS, AND WILL NOT GIVE NOR OFFER THEM TO OTHERS, EXCEPT AS MEDICINES, OR IN A RELIGIOUS ORDINANCE."

To celebrate the adoption of the above as the only pledge of the society, the bells of the Parish Church were rung on Thursday, March 26th, and there were other demonstrations of rejoicing, so that altogether this was a memorable week in Preston. The new pledge led to the re-signing of the members, upwards of 50 of whom did so on the evening of its adoption, which was the anniversary of the introduction of the abstinence pledge into England. All who did not re-sign, within three months ceased to be members of the society. The Whit-Monday procession took place on June 9th, and meetings were held on the Monday and Tuesday evenings, in the Theatre, which were addressed by friends from Blackburn, Chorley, Lancaster, Manchester and Liverpool. The half-yearly festival was held on Monday, October 12th, and continued every succeeding evening during the week, in the Theatre. Mr. R. G. White was present at these meetings, and at one of them a pint of tenpenny ale was distilled by Mr. Wm. Livesey, in the presence of the audience, who were afforded the opportunity of seeing the spirit produced from it burnt upon the stage. As usual, a Tea Party was held at Christmas ; the attendance this year was near 1,300 ; it was held in the rooms at the Corn Exchange.

In other towns in our own County, and also the neighbouring Counties, the principles of Teetotalism made great progress during this year. In January, I find the name of a man who has since attained a world-wide reputation as a statesman and an orator, even those opposed to him in his political creed giving him due honour,—I allude to John Bright. I find in "The Advocate," and also in the report of the Heywood Society, that he advocated the cause of Temperance at this early period of its history. It was at a Tea Party held on Monday, January 12th, in a large room of a mill belonging to Mr. Schofield, at Heywood, the Society at that place having only the Teetotal pledge. Thos. Clegg, Esq., (now of Manchester) was the Secretary of the Heywood Society at that time. One of the greatest Teetotal demonstrations ever held in this part of the country took place on Monday and Tuesday, April 21st and 22nd, at Wilsden, in Yorkshire. It was a grand festival of the Wilsden, Bradford, Keighley, Bingley, Thornton, Baildon, Cullingworth, Northowram, Shipley, Manningham, Hallas Bridge, Denholme, Clayton, Frizinghall, Morton, Cottingly, Allerton, and Harden Temperance Societies. There were present at it, J. S. Buckingham, Esq., M.P.; Mr. Edward Parsons, Author of "Anti-Bacchus;" Mr. Pollard, the agent of the Society for Yorkshire; Messrs. Livesey, Anderton, Swindlehurst, and Broughton, from Preston. All the roads and lanes leading to Wilsden were crowded with long processions. In a field, a short distance from the Church, a splendid booth had been erected for the tea party, the interior of which was gorgeously decorated. 2,500 persons took tea in it on the first day, and 1,000 on the second. Four meetings were held in the church, capable of holding 2,000 persons, at which, by the addresses of the above gentlemen and others, a deep impression was produced in favour of temperance. The Rev. J. Barber presided, and Rd. and Wm. S. Nicholls also spoke. It was by the exertions of these two brothers that the demonstration was so great a success. I must not omit to record the fact that Mr. Livesey delivered his Malt Liquor Lecture in the church! During the week preceding Easter, a great movement was made at Blackburn, when a new society was formed solely on Teetotal principles. The Committee of the Preston Temperance Society engaged the Blackburn Theatre for six nights, and all the leading advocates from Preston spoke at the various meetings. Mr. Livesey delivered his lecture, and one evening Mr. John Finch, of Liverpool, presided. During the week 330 persons signed the pledge, amongst whom was Thos. Whittaker, who afterwards became a zealous missionary of the cause. In a letter to Mr. Livesey, giving particulars of his commencing as an advocate of the cause, he says :—"By your advice, I went to the Conference of the British League, held at Manchester, in September, 1835. I spoke freely at several meetings in connection with that conference. I laboured mainly under your own direction from that time till the following May, chiefly in Lancashire. I was then sent out, by your recommendation, as the agent of the League, and visited Westmoreland, Cumberland, Northumberland, and Durham, and you know what followed. I have always looked upon you as my teetotal father. I signed the pledge with you. The first letter I ever wrote in my life I wrote to you, and it is printed in the 'Temperance Advocate' for July, 1836." Mr. Whittaker went out as Agent of the British Association early in the following year.

It was in this year that Dr. Lees was added to the list of Teetotalers, since which time he has,—by his powerful pen and eloquent voice,—done so much to spread sound information as to the nature and properties of intoxicating liquors. In May of this year, Teetotalism was introduced into the West of England by a deputation from Birmingham, who occupied ten nights in meetings at Bristol. At the close of last year Mr. R. G. White, carrying his inspiration from Preston, began to advocate Teetotalism at Dublin; in a letter to Mr. Livesey, under date Nov. 24th, 1834, he says :—"Having attended the meetings of every Temperance Society since my return, when I go in they say—'here comes Preston—the real tee-total Preston;' and I assure you I never omit telling them the happiness I experienced and the good effected at Preston." In June, this year, Mr. John Finch, of Liverpool, (who signed the teetotal pledge at Preston) established the first society on exclusively teetotal principles in Ireland, at Strabane, and subsequently established societies in other towns. On August 31st, Mr. Livesey paid his second visit to London, this time accompanied by Messrs. Swindlehurst and Howarth, and Mr. John Andrew, of Leeds.

The influence which the Teetotal teaching in Preston had upon the people of America at this day may be judged by a few extracts I give from a series of letters by E. C. Delaven, Esq., to Mr. Livesey. On January 23rd, he writes—"We begin to feel the influence of your noble example; our people by thousands are becoming teetotalers." On March 20th—"Your excellent paper affords me timely assistance in the '*fermented* drinks' question, which is now emphatically *the* temperance question in this country. The old pledge has done all it was destined to do of good, and is now doing injury among us." On April 17th—"Within a few days about 300 clergymen of all denominations have sent me their names to the teetotal." Mr. E. James, Secretary of the New York State Temperance Society, under date June 1st, reports as follows :—"It gives me unfeigned satisfaction to inform you that the American Temperance Society, at their eighth annual meeting, recently held in Boston, have officially and regularly taken the true ground of total abstinence from all intoxicating drinks, and their constitution has been amended accordingly, by striking out the words 'ardent spirits,' and substituting 'intoxicating drinks.'"

Of the progress of the movement in 1836 I must speak very briefly, for I have got to a period of its history when the proceedings throughout the kingdom were duly published; for besides "The Preston Temperance Advocate" there were now six other periodicals, some published monthly, others fortnightly, and one weekly. The principal event in Preston during the year was the holding of the third Annual Conference of the British Association, commencing on the 5th of July, in the then Temperance Hall (Cockpit.) There was a procession, which terminated its marching at Preston Marsh, where 10,000 people assembled, and four meetings were held simultaneously. R. G. White was present, and R. B. Grindrod (Author of "Bacchus") presided at the Conference. Two important resolutions were passed at this Conference, which dealt a death blow to "Moderation," if perchance it yet lingered in some societies—no society could be a branch of the Association if within three months it did not discard the moderation pledge; and no society could be a branch which did not, within six months, adopt the teetotal pledge. Throughout the whole of England, not excepting London, Teetotalism made great progress in 1836, for besides the voluntary and unpaid labourers, regularly appointed and paid agents were now travelling daily and nightly, informing, enlightening, convincing, and converting the people; moral suasion was then the sole power used, and the results of that year showed what a mighty power it is when used by sincere and earnest men. At this time and for many years following the people were being educated and informed by means of tracts and lectures and speeches, all confined to the one cardinal point, showing the nature and properties and injurious qualities of intoxicating liquors; *personal abstinence* was, of course, indispensable for all who were admitted into membership. The following list of names include the prominent advocates of Teetotalism in other places besides Preston :—London, T. A. Smith, (still labouring in connection with the National Temperance League in educating the people in sound teetotal principles by his chemical lectures,) Rev. J. Sherman, Rev. W. R. Baker, J. Meredith, J. W. Green, and M. B. Hart; Birmingham, Rev. J. A. James, J. Cadbury, J. Stubbins, J. Hocking (best known as the "Birmingham Blacksmith,") and W. Barlow; Bristol, J. Eaton and J. Thornton; Bath, J. H. Cotterill; Street, near Glastonbury, C. Clark; Bodmin, Dr. Mudge; Southampton, H. J. Pitts; Brighton, Rev. J. Edwards; Nottingham, Dr. Higginbottom; Norwich, S. Jarrold; Leicester, T. Cook ("Round the World" Tourist); Hull, F. Hopwood; Sheffield, W. C. Beardsall; Leeds, Joseph Andrew, W. Pallister, J. Kershaw, B. Crossley and T. Atkinson; Huddersfield, F. Schwann; Bradford, Dr. Beaumont, Rev. J. Bell, and Rev. W. Morgan; Halifax, J. Thompson; Keighley, T. Drury; York, J. Spence; Newcastle-upon-Tyne, J. Rewcastle and J. Priestman; Darlington, Dr. Fothergill; Manchester, Professor Greenbank, Rev. J. Bardsley, W. Ellerby, J. Cassell, and T. H. Barker; Chester, Rev. Jos. Barker; Nantwich, Rev. J. Hawkes; Wigan, Rev. W. Roaf, P. Grant, and J. Ramsdale; Southport, W. Mawdesley; Bury, Rev. F. Howarth and T. Hampton; Bolton, J. Cunliff and T. Entwistle; Blackburn, Jno. Thwaite; Heywood, B. Glazebrook; Rawtenstall, J. King; Colne, Rev. W. Henderson; Todmorden, J. Fielden; Lancaster, E. Dawson; Ulverston, A. B. Salmon. Without claiming for any one individual the honour of being the "originator" or "founder" of Teetotalism, (which some have unwisely wished to aspire to) every honest teetotaller will endorse what Dr. Lees has stated in his recent work, (Text Book) where he says:—Foremost, as chief and propagandist, stands Joseph Livesey. It was he who, by his admirable malt liquor lecture on 'The Great Delusion,' and his plain Saxon speech, first planted the teetotal standard in London, and in the great provincial towns of Birmingham, Leeds, Bradford, Darlington, Newcastle, and Sunderland. It was he who, through the might of the press, firmly fixed the new ideas in the intelligence of the thoughtful disciples throughout the empire, and who laid those goodly foundations on which many later minds have built noble structures of art, eloquence, and science. Of the name of 'the Patriarch of the movement' he is surely most worthy."

Subjoined is a *fac simile* of the pledge and signatures written by Joseph Livesey on September 1st, 1832. See pages 64 and 102.

We agree to Abstain from
All Liquors of an Intoxicating
Quality, whether Ale Porter
Wine or Ardent Spirits, except
as Medicine.
John Gratrix.
Edwᵈ Dickinson.
Jno: Broadbelt.
Jno: Smith.
Joseph Livesey.
David Anderton.
Jno: King.

JOSEPH LIVESEY.

BORN MARCH 5th, 1794. DIED SEPTEMBER 2nd, 1884.

By the REV. G. M. MURPHY, M.L.S.B.

MOURN, Preston ! for thy foremost man has gone,
Straight from the battle he has fought and won,
Right to the glory where the victor's song
Doth joy and gladness past all praise prolong.
Weep, England ! for an uncrowned king of thin
Has dropped the sceptre of earth's royal line ;
No more he treads the land he nobly trod,
He finds a nobler royalty with God.

Europe ! thy tears let fall and sadly moan,
Inscribe upon thy chief memorial stone
The name of Livesey, for his work and worth
Has blessed thy borders, and made glad the earth.
Great world of continents, and seas, and isles,
Just for a little space forego thy smiles,
And, mourning, sigh a moment for the man
Whose name stands foremost in the temperance van.

Ah ! weep and moan, and sigh and shed thy tears,
But through all ages and all coming years
Shall millions smile that Joseph Livesey stood,
And like a hero stemmed drink's cruel flood :
Unwavering, steadfast, true, amid the scorn
Begot of ignorance, of passion born,
And with approving glance surveyed the scene
Of smiling hearts and homes where woe had been.

Weep, yet rejoice, ye temperance men and true,
The leader fallen leaves the cause to you ;
With true emotion let each soul be moved,
And truly serve the cause our lost one loved.
Divinely aided, let us to the fight,
Till all the sins of drunkenness take flight ;
Till drink no more shall scatter death and shame,
And all the nations bless dear Livesey's name.

IN MEMORIAM—JOSEPH LIVESEY.

By J. F. NICHOLLS.

WHOM do we mourn ? a statesman, or a peer ?
A deep intriguer who could plot and plan ?
A mighty warrior, or a learned seer ?
No, no ; we mourn a self-denying man.

We mourn the loss of him who dared
To strive against drink's overwhelming tide ;
And introduce what since has been declared—
"A document that England views with pride."

We mourn his loss, acknowledging his worth—
An honour to the land that gave him birth !
The man whose heart was in his voice and pen ;
The man who deeply loved his fellow-men.

We mourn his loss—but wherefore our regret ?
He sleeps, but full of honour and of years ;
His race is run, and manfully he ran—
We'll praise his memory, and stay our tears.

APPENDIX.

EXPLANATORY NOTE.

ON the death of Mr. Livesey, his useful and honourable career was extensively and appreciatively commented upon by the Press and from the Pulpit. Lengthy biographical sketches, accompanied by editorial comments, appeared in the leading daily and weekly newspapers, and also in the principal temperance and religious journals.

As might have been expected, the Press in the town where he had resided for seventy years, and where his life—especially his inner life and deeds of benevolence —were best known, had the most lengthy biographical sketches and editorial notices; in the latter respect, the paper of opposite politics to Mr. Livesey's (the *Preston Herald*) paid a very high tribute to his worth. Two of the Manchester papers (the *Guardian* and *Examiner*) were scarcely behind those of Preston either as to the biographical sketches or appreciatory comments. Among other noteworthy articles deserving mention were the biographical sketch in "The National Temperance League's Year Book," written by one of the early band of teetotalers— Mr. John Andrew, of Leeds; the lengthy sketch in the *Church of England Temperance Chronicle* by Mr. Sherlock; the sketch by Dr. F. R. Lees in the *British Temperance Advocate*, together with the same writer's able review of Mr. Livesey's life in the *Alliance News;* and the sketch from the pen of the Rev. Charles Garrett in the *Sunday at Home* of Nov. 29. Several excellent notices also appeared in papers abroad, prominent amongst which were two lengthy articles in the *New Zealand Herald*, written by Mr. E. Cox, of Auckland, formerly a resident in Preston.

The following papers, amongst many others, contained articles on Mr. Livesey: *The Times*, Sept. 3rd; *Daily News*, Sept. 3rd; *Daily Chronicle*, Sept. 3rd; *Illustrated London News*, Sept. 6th; *Preston Guardian*, Sept. 6th and 10th; *Preston Chronicle*, Sept. 6th and 13th; *Preston Herald*, Sept. 6th and 10th; *Newcastle Daily Chronicle*, Sept. 3rd; *Leeds Mercury*, Sept. 3rd; *Manchester Guardian*, Sept. 3rd and 6th; *Manchester Examiner and Times*, Sept. 3rd; *Rotherham Observer*, Sept. 6th; *Blackpool Herald*, Sept. 5th; *Blackpool Gazette*, Sept. 12th; *Liverpool Porcupine*, Sept. 6th; *Penny Pictorial News*, Sept. 13th; *New Zealand Herald*, Oct. 4th and 11th; *Alliance News*, Sept. 6th and 13th; *Temperance Record*, Sept. 4th and 11th; *Scottish League Journal*, Sept. 6th and 13th; *Good Templar's Watchword*, Sept. 8th; *Church of England Temperance Chronicle*, Sept. 6th and 13th; *Blue Ribbon Chronicle*, Sept. 13th; *Blue Ribbon Gazette*, Sept. 10th; *Irish Temperance Banner*, Sept.; *British Temperance Advocate*, Oct.; *Band of Hope Chronicle*, Oct.; *Irish League Journal*, Oct.; *The Sunday at Home*, Nov.; *Western Temperance Herald*, Oct.; *The Abstainer* (Uxbridge), Oct.; "*National Temperance League's Year-book*," 1885; *Nonconformist*, Sept. 11th; *Christian World*, Sept. 4th; *Christian Chronicle*, Sept. 11th; *Christian Herald*, Sept. 10th; *Christian Globe*, Sept. 11th; *Christian Million*, Sept. 11th; *Family Churchman*, Sept. 11th; and *Medium and Daybreak*, Oct. 24th. The only adverse or unfriendly notice which we have seen appeared in the *Saturday Review*, Sept. 6th, and even in that it is admitted, that, but for his teetotalism and early surroundings, Mr. Livesey would have been a great man !

Believing that the preservation, in a permanent form, of the principal Press notices, Pulpit utterances, and Resolutions passed by Temperance bodies will be welcomed by Mr. Livesey's friends, and appreciated by the general reader desirous of understanding the wide-reaching influence wielded by the honoured "Father of Teetotalism," the appended selection has been made. Extra space has been devoted to the Preston articles and sermons, which are of exceptional interest and value coming as they do from fellow-townsmen among whom Mr. Livesey's long life was so well spent. They exhibit the high esteem in which the man and his work were held by those who lived in close contact with him. Owing to similarity of matter and treatment, considerable difficulty has been experienced in deciding what to print and what to omit. The selection has, however, been made without undue preference, and with the view of avoiding repetition as much as possible.

A.

PRESS NOTICES OF "THE STAUNCH TEETOTALER."

I.—*The Temperance Record, Jan. 30th, 1869.*

It was well for the Temperance cause that our veteran friend, Mr. Joseph Livesey, resolved to issue *The Staunch Teetotaler.* His name in thousands of families has long been a household word. We know that it was a joy to many of the Temperance friends when they knew that the father of this great social reformation had resolved to send forth a cheap and interesting serial; for it was quite clear to them that no man living was better qualified to speak of the origin and triumphs of the Temperance cause. Mr. Joseph Livesey, in all the virtues and principles which adorn and dignify the man, is a living success. He is alike a teacher to the poor and to the affluent. His early life is full of interest and instruction. He forgets not the days and the nights when he manfully laboured for his daily bread; and the scenes and the circumstances of his early days are deeply impressed upon his mind, and may be read by the young men of our country and of the world with the best possible results. The *Staunch Teetotaler* is a reflex of the feelings, thoughts, and sentiments of one who has been a great champion in the Temperance cause. The structure of the work evinces what we may call the executiveness of the editor's mind; for we venture to affirm that no volumes of Temperance literature of the same size contain so much real information interpersed with such a host of facts. In them you will find no diverging, no flying off at a tangent, no shrinking from the utterance of great and important truths, no coarse expressions, no uncalled-for or severe remarks; but a plain, earnest, straightforwardness which must secure the admiration and approval of all. There is a rich vein of pure Christian benevolence running through the whole. He has written as one who feels what an awful curse intemperance is. He has watched its terrible progress and power, and his soul is full of pity for the wretched and the fallen. In reading the *Staunch Teetotaler* we hardly know which to admire the most, the clearness of the head or the love of the heart. His thoughts are full of light, and we believe there is not a sentence which is not well and intelligibly expressed. He is never in a fog, no learned difficulties mar his pages. He reasons from facts, and his conclusions cannot be overthrown. In the earlier times, yea, in the first dawning of the Temperance light, he occupied the position of the patriot, the friend, the teacher, and the lecturer. At once he went to the origin of the evil, and his famous lecture on Malt Liquor has been of immense value to the Temperance cause. Standing upon such a sure foundation, he has turned neither to the right hand nor to the left. He saw what a shameful waste of corn was involved in the making of intoxicating drinks, and he also saw what useless things they were when they were made, and as a logical thinker he could not help but arrive at the conclusion that in the making of the drinks a great wrong was done. While his intellect clearly perceived these things, his heart was moved to commiserate the sufferings of our common humanity. Hence he writes to the moderate drinkers, and points out the danger they are in. Hence he implores the backsliders to return to the ways of temperance and truth. Hence he must have many kind words for his neighbours. He has written to the young men and to the young women in such a loving and practical manner as to secure from such their greatest respect and esteem. To husbands and fathers, to the wives of working men, to gentlemen of the middle class, and to the wives of the gentlemen of that class, he has spoken the words of soberness and truth. In these and other articles we read the deep feelings of his soul. In them there is an evidence of universal love. He passes by none, but embraces all; and in the clear thoughts and the deep sympathies which crowd the pages of the *Staunch Teetotaler* there are the beautiful minglings of light and of love. The " Reminiscences of Early Teetotalism " are an invaluable addition to our Temperance literature. They have been written by the only living man who could have done them justice. They furnish a faithful picture-history of our early teetotalism; and as none but a Cruikshank could have given us " The Worship of Bacchus," so we think, yea, we know, none but a Livesey could have given us such a faithful and valuable sketch of the struggle and successes of our glorious cause. Hence we have little points which are of the deepest interest, and nice delicate shades of thought which characterise the clear, terse style of the *Staunch Teetotaler;* and while through the whole there is the broad outline of rigid fact, there are the sweet and moral resonances of the heart's deep love. We are pointed to the source of intemperance, viz., the alcohol in the drink, and of the difficulties in the way. We are favoured with the signatures of the first noble seven, and an account of the early meetings, and of the intense enthusiasm, the earnest speeches, the profound attention, and the glorious results. The truth, like an arrow of light, found its way into the heart of the drunkard; he paused, considered, reflected, repented, and returned. There was a mingling of the moral and intellectual forces. The cries of the enslaved had ascended to heaven, the moral atmosphere was full of the poison of alcohol, and the evil was breaking the backs and the hearts of men. Poor suffering humanity could endure it no longer; a change must come, or the glory of the country would soon pass away. The light shone, and the heavenly truth of abstinence burst upon the soul, and it was lovingly received and faithfully proclaimed. And so in this respect began the healing of the nation. But, in addition to this and other good things in the *Staunch Teetotaler,* we are favoured with the editor's most interesting autobiography. It is crowded with telling facts. We see the poor frugal, thoughtful, hopeful boy. At night he sits by the ember fire to read his book; thus we find in his childhood and youth learning and labour shook hands. When he married it was for love, and all adown the future of his life he has enjoyed the great blessing of domestic happiness and peace. We shall not soon forget the well-told incident of the medical prescription of the bread and cheese and beer, of his youthful rambles, of his village life, of the flowing river, of the parish church, and of the bell-ringers, of his serious impressions, and of the day when he was baptized, and how kindly and tenderly he always speaks of his Jenny, and how she made his small cottage like a palace for its tidiness and cleanliness, and how he bought his first cheese, and sold it again, and of the fear he entertained, though he was a strictly moderate drinker, that his example might have led others to excess. He tells us that he has never seen the " ducking stool," but he has seen what he never wishes to see again, viz., " a bull baited." He was active and attentive to business, and success crowned his efforts. In the borough of Preston he has filled the offices of select vestryman, member of the Board of Guardians, commissioner for the improvement of the borough, and town-councillor; and he informs us that after the first election under the Municipal Reform Bill, that at the second meeting of the council, he and Mr. Swindlehurst carried a motion to sell all the wine which the old corporation had left, and which produced the sum of £226 3s. 7d.; and at a subsequent meeting two japanned wine-waggons, five dozen wine-glasses, ten decanters, and corkscrews were sold. There are but a few of the good things, and of the improvements which have taken place in the borough of Preston, which have either been suggested by, or have received the hearty co-operation of, Mr. Joseph Livesey. Young men of the Temperance reformation, we especially recommend to you the reading of this most interesting autobiography; you will find in every page useful and practical lessons. In the two volumes of the *Staunch Teetotaler,* you will find special addresses or letters to almost all classes. The " Varieties " are always pointed and pleasing, excepting it be when the details refer to the evils and crimes of intemperance. When we consider that the first number of the *Staunch Teetotaler* was issued when the venerable editor had attained his 73rd year, we must not complain that upon his attaining his 75th year he should have felt it necessary to discontinue its publication. But we feel assured our readers, with ourselves, all will regret, that firstly our great veteran finds that his health is unreliable, and secondly that his beloved wife has been so great a sufferer for two years as to require his constant attention. Brave and noble-minded man, tender-hearted and loving husband, we heartily wish, in the name of all the friends of Temperance, that every needful blessing may rest upon you and yours. And sincerely do we hope that, though in the weakness of affliction, your beloved partner may yet be spared to you; for from your writings it is manifest that she has ever been the light of your home and the joy of your heart. We thank you for the issue of these two volumes of the *Staunch Teetotaler*, and we rejoice to know that though you have laid down the pen of the Editor, that your heart is still full of love for that cause which has been the joy of your manhood, and will be the glory of your declining years. We feel assured that the heart which has ever been so deeply impressed with a desire to promote the happiness of others, will still cling to the great truths of Temperance. And whether your spirit shall feel the light of life, or the shadows of death, it will cling to the loving and the true, and repose its trust in God. Though we cannot follow our veteran reformer into the social and domestic sphere, our sympathies will be with him ; and we know of no nobler sight on this side of · the grave than is presented by those kind deeds and delicate attentions which pure love inspires, and which will cause the aged to forget his infirmities while ministering to the comfort of her whom he loves. We believe that as his day so shall his strength be. He is now full of honour and ripe with age, but still feels that he has a work to do, and, God helping him, he will do it.

II.—*The Preston Chronicle, Feb. 6th, 1869.*

A few weeks ago we announced that our respected townsman, Mr. Joseph Livesey, had decided, in consequence of advancing age and domestic illness, to discontinue the publication of *The Staunch Teetotaler*. This week we have received the whole of the numbers of that periodical, neatly bound in a single volume ; and to-day we have pleasure in making some comments upon both the book and its author. We admire a man, no matter what his views may be, if he is sincere ; and if his object is the elevation of the masses and the welfare of society. Such a man we believe Joseph Livesey to have been. We differ from him as to the merits of his favourite theory—teetotalism ; but we have always admired his consistency, his energy, have always recognised his sincerity, and have often had occasion to speak approvingly of his labours. To the victim of passion and the slave of appetite, to those incapable of using without abusing intoxicants—and there are many such persons in society—to men who have for years cursed themselves and families with strong drink, and cried out in the bitterness of their thraldom for emancipation—to these Joseph Livesey has been a blessing. There are numbers in this and other towns whose lives were once miserable, and whose homes were once wretched, through the unclean spirit of drink, who will always have reason to thank Joseph Livesey for his advice, encouragement, and assistance.

For a long series of years Mr. Livesey has been an energetic advocate of teetotalism, and this last effort of his, as manifested in the *Staunch Teetotaler*, is, although made in the " sere and yellow leaf " of his life, amongst the best, the most vigorous, he has ever put forth. The first number of the volume before us was issued in January, 1867. At that time Mr. Livesey had reached the long age of 73—an age when most hard workers have finished the fight ; an age when the generality of hard thinkers have closed their career or receded into a senility incompatible with vigorous intellectual labour. But Mr. Livesey is not to be ranked amongst the ordinary company of men. We dare say he attributes much of his buoyancy and vigour to total abstinence ; and if he does, we shall not find fault with him, for he, after all, must be the best judge in this matter. Whatever may be the cause of his mental freshness and physical energy—for there could not be the former without the latter—we can only say that they are marvellous, and that society would be infinitely better if it possessed the knowledge and power to attain and preserve more generally similar qualities. The *Staunch Teetotaler* is, we think, an invaluable *répertoire* for all Temperance men. It is not only well got up in its mechanical parts, but is, as a record of experience, as an expounder of facts, and as a compendium of all the best and most vital Temperance arguments, worthy of the most favourable criticism. The sole object which the author of it has had in view appears to have been this—the benefit of his fellow-men. It has not been a money-making affair ; it was not commenced as a pecuniary speculation ; it was not continued as a financial auxiliary ; its absolute aim was the inculcation of

Temperance principles; its only end was the manumission of society from what a brilliant orator once called "the deep damnation of the sin of drunkenness." And we believe that, to a considerable extent, Mr. Livesey has not laboured in vain in this respect. To all classes of drinkers—the moderate man who swallows his glass philosophically; the spreer who devours his liquor in a periodic fit of passionate appetite; the flying tippler who visits every public-house, who is always drinking and never seems drunk; the heavy "soaker" who begins every forenoon with bitter beer and cheese and bread, and every night with a stupid gin hiccup and a cap; the lady who sips her pale sherry sentimentally, and the unfortunate female who drowns her sin and her sorrow in the oblivion of alcohol; the seeming saint who drinks slyly and greedily, and the confirmed inebriate who has neither the policy to conceal nor the will to stop his violent orgies—to all these Mr. Livesey speaks. And his words have no uncertain sound. The burthen of them, the sin they condemn, is drinking and drunkenness; and their talisman is teetotalism. All the main arguments which can be fairly used on behalf of total abstinence, all the persuasion which the most devoted philanthropist can indulge in, are used in the *Staunch Teetotaler*. It is a thoroughly sober affair to the backbone. Its object is to make men and to keep men sober. The evil is exposed and denounced; the remedy is named and inculcated. All kinds of questions bearing upon the Temperance movement are referred to, ably commented upon, intelligently set before the reader in this volume. The experience, the thoughts of a long, laborious, and useful life are condensed into the pages of the *Staunch Teetotaler;* and we cannot but praise the ability, the good common sense, the broad humanity with which many of them sparkle. The language is plain and epigrammatic; it hits the nail on the head, and hits it soon; the thoughts are full of life and spirit; neither the brain nor the heart lack their olden force in the discussion of the various social matters with which the volume is crowded. The primal object, as we have before remarked, is total abstinence; but many other questions, interesting to those who do not, or cannot, subscribe to Mr. Livesey's views, are mentioned. The problem as to the origin of teetotalism is clearly solved—solved, too, by the only living man whose opinion is really worth taking on the subject. Mr. Livesey is an authority upon the Temperance question. We believe he knows more about its origin and history than any other man; and, from what he says, it would appear that the honour of starting the total abstinence movement can be claimed by no single man; that several persons had a hand in the inauguration and development of the cause; and we think that Mr. Livesey is entitled to as much of the honour as any man, and to more of it than several who took part in the early struggles of teetotalism. One of the most interesting parts of the *Staunch Teetotaler* is that which refers to the personal history of Mr. Livesey. He gives the story of his life in a manner excellent alike for its simplicity and candour. There is no attempt at literary ornament, no effort in the line of display; the history is plain and pointed, is characterized by an openness of thought, a frankness of detail, and a kindly, genial unburthening of the heart and mind which will give a lasting interest to all its utterances. It constitutes a rare story, and one all the more charming because true—a story beginning with humble life and severe trials, passing on to honest industry and wonderful perseverance, achieving commercial and moral triumphs of no ordinary description, and culminating in honour and opulence. To the lowly born and hard working, this story should be an incentive; and to all it will convey a moral, namely, that perseverance and sobriety are the sure agents of success and honour. Mr. Livesey was never what may be termed a very brilliant man; but he has had those qualities which invariably surpass brilliance—a large endowment of common sense, an industrious disposition, and a clear conception of his moral responsibilities and duties. With respect to his teetotalism, we may say that he has been one man in ten thousand. Teetotalism has not meant with him, as it has done with many, a simple doctrine of selfishness—a parsimonious puritanical whim, indulged in for the purpose of saving money, of getting and keeping, and of blowing the loud trumpet of self-righteousness. He has always been steady, consistent, and unflinching in his advocacy of it, and has ever put it forth as a doctrine calculated better than anything else, in its practical adoption, to improve the condition of the people socially, morally, and physically, and to rid modern society of one of its deadliest scourges. He has spent what many would call a good fortune in propagating his views on the Temperance question; and even in his last undertaking on behalf of that question—the publication of the *Staunch Teetotaler* —he has willingly sacrificed no inconsiderable sum of money. But not alone as a total abstainer is Mr. Livesey entitled to our regard. In his day and generation he has been a warm and energetic politician—one who always fought on the side of progress and popular freedom, and one who always struggled for the good of the cause, and for nothing else. Unlike some of our modern politicians—unlike certain local reforming spirits—who care more for lucre than principle, and infinitely more for popularity and personal aggrandisement than anything else, Mr. Livesey was in his political day a hard, earnest, disinterested worker, who thought he was well rewarded if the cause he fought for won. In his municipal and parochial capacities Mr. Livesey was also at one time, before age necessitated a relaxation of his efforts, a particularly useful man. He was an energetic exposer of abuses, a determined denouncer of extravagance, a zealous and unflinching economist. The money, the morals, and the health of the town—all of supreme and vital consequence— were matters which specially engaged his attention. He was an excellent counterpoise to those given to wastefulness, specious theorizing, and careless speculations at the expense of the public. A few Joseph Liveseys are wanted in our executive departments now ; they have been wanted long ; and, if we had them, every ratepayer would feel the benefit of their services. We could enumerate, if it were necessary, many acts done by Mr. Livesey which have been of great advantage to the public. We will just name one. It is not very long since the Preston Bank was in great difficulty ; the storm, however, was weathered ; and we attribute the bank's existence now very largely to the advice and assistance of Mr. Livesey. He studied the position of affairs carefully ; he took part in the reconstruction of the establishment earnestly, and for the sole sake of saving the town from a pecuniary disaster. The depositors had faith in him—believed what he had to say, relied upon his suggestions ; for they knew that his words and recommendations were thoroughly honest—and, in time, the confidence of the public was restored, and the bank re-established upon a footing calculated to ensure success. If Mr. Livesey had never done anything else for Preston, his labours in connection with the bank would have entitled him to the lasting respect and gratitude of Prestonians. We have yet another word to say concerning Mr. Livesey ere we close this review. There are few men who know how charitable he has been. We have heard it said, with a spice of sarcasm, that his benevolence, like that of the generality of teetotalers, was a very shrivelled and miserable affair. We know differently. He has spent large sums of money, has given articles of clothing, etc., times without number, in the relief of poor, destitute, and unfortunate people. Many persons have received from him weekly allowances of money or food, and we know that for years the late Mr. John Catterall was his private almoner. His charity never assumed an ostentatious character, and even the members of his own family will never know of many benevolent acts he has done. Life with Mr. Livesey has been a success ; and the good he has done in it makes it all the more successful. The *Staunch Teetotaler* is a fitting legacy to the people. The volume we have before us evokes feelings of mingled pleasure and sorrow—of pleasure because a good intention and a pure tone of morality pervade it, because it gives us, amongst many interesting things, the history of a great question, the life of a worthy man, and, collaterally, furnishes us with many local events of interest ; and of pain because it seems to close the literary career of a man who has been one of our most prolific moral and social writers, and because it has been ended through the serious illness of one near and dear to him, and loved by all acquainted with her. We sympathize with him in his sorrow ; we hope he will long be spared ; but whether his time be early or late, this is certain—that he will leave us with a consciousness of having done his duty, and of having used his best efforts for the welfare of humanity.

III.—*The Preston Herald, Feb. 13th, 1869.*

We have this week been favoured with a copy of the latest work of the gentleman whose name heads this article. It is a volume of some 400 pages, and consists of two years' numbers of a monthly publication entitled *The Staunch Teetotaler.* It is handsomely got up, and includes what will be highly valued by Mr. Livesey's friends and admirers –a photographic portrait of himself, with a *fac simile* of his autograph. If it had been simply a work on Teetotalism, we should have given less prominence to this notice, as a review of it would have been more appropriate in the many Temperance periodicals which now teem from the press. The volume, however, includes twelve chapters devoted wholly to Mr. Livesey's autobiography, and it is to that portion we give our attention.

It is almost a work of supererogation in us to say that both in political and Temperance matters our opinions do not coincide with those of Mr. Livesey; indeed in politics they are "as wide as the poles asunder." But when we come across—what is rather rare in our present Radical leaders—a man of high moral character, of steady independence, of sterling consistency, and of unselfish aims, he shall have justice at our hands, however much his opinions are opposed to our own. To the general public, no doubt, the autobiographical portion of the work will be the most interesting; but while it gives us very much information about one who has been more or less a public man for nearly half a century, we must confess we closed our perusal of it a little disappointed. The writer has hardly done justice to himself; he occupies too great a portion of his space with what we might term family matters, and too little with his doings in connection with local public affairs. Our townsmen need not be told that there has scarcely been a movement in Preston, social or political, for the last forty years, but what Mr. Livesey has been connected with it on one side or another; and certainly none for the relief of that class from whence he sprung, and with whom his autobiography shows his sympathies are as intense as ever. We learn that the village of Walton-le-Dale is Mr. Livesey's birthplace; at "Walton Cop," on March 5th, 1794, he first drew breath. The description of the poverty and struggles of his early life may be read by all young men with great advantage. They will learn how the Walton weaver lad, labouring in a damp, dismal cellar, struggled to educate himself; this place, he tells us, was "his college," and the "breast beam" of his loom his reading desk; toiling hard with hands and feet to earn a subsistence, racking head and brain to get a store of knowledge—without a schoolmaster and almost without books. A little later, in 1816, he gets to Preston, his first residence being in Park Street (a street running from Leeming Street to the top of Vauxhall Road), the rent of which we are told was 2s. 6d. per week. In that year he laid the foundation of his present extensive business as a cheese merchant, and here again his indomitable perseverance is shown. He borrowed a sovereign from a Mr. John Burnett, woollen draper, with which to purchase the first cheese he ever bought or sold. The same kind friend lent him a pair of scales, etc. We are reminded that Mr. Livesey is the oldest tradesman in Preston, with one exception. At that date we learn that the great apostle of teetotalism (now for 38 years) used to send across to Mrs. Rigby's, the Blue Anchor, Market Place, for some of her famed 2½d. (per glass) ale! A little earlier he tells what a wet lot the ringers of Walton Church were, and that, being one of them, he was once led into temptation. Amongst other business matters we have a short but affecting story of Mr. Livesey's losses when a "sleeping partner" in a cotton manufacturing concern; how he was ruined in it, but struggled on, and paid all the creditors in full. This matter brings out some strong cautions upon the dangers and difficulties of partnerships.

We must rapidly pass over Mr. Livesey's labours in connection with town affairs—as select vestryman, improvement commissioner, town councillor, poor-law guardian, etc. We learn that out of 48 persons who constituted the Town Council in 1835, when Mr. Livesey was elected, only one is now a member of that body, and only three, besides himself, are now alive. The autobiography gives us some little (but too little) information as to the establishment of the Preston Institution. About its origin Mr. Livesey says: "One day, without consulting any other person, I sat down and wrote a circular, sent it to the printer, and caused it to be delivered to the most likely persons in the town, inviting them to attend a preliminary meeting for starting such an institution." That meeting was held on September 11th, 1828, and was attended by six persons. Such was the small beginning of one of our most valuable institutions. The late Dr. Gilbertson and Mr. Robert Ascroft are named as being zealous workers in the early and struggling days of the now prosperous institution. We think Mr. Livesey has overlooked the late Mr. Moses Holden, for we know he was one who worked hard at the commencement. We cannot even allude by name to many other public institutions in connection with which Mr. Livesey has laboured, but must pass on to briefly notice what he says about himself as a public writer and author.

Without reservation, Mr. Livesey admits that he was early affected with *cacoethes scribendi ;* to use his candid words—" From a youth I had a strong inclination for scribbling, and, no doubt, like many young people, I formed an over estimate of my talents for this work." Then he proceeds to notice his contributions to the newspapers (1814), and subsequently also to his issue of handbills, tracts, pamphlets, etc., down to 1825, when he published his "Address to the Poorer Classes." We well remember this work ; it had an immense circulation, wealthy persons of every shade of politics and religion purchasing it for distribution. It contained some most excellent advice on every department of domestic management, the author being very warm in his denunciations of "shopping and popping." It is in works of this kind Mr. Livesey shines most. His strongest sympathies are with the class from whence he rose. He is quite at home in addressing those struggling to climb the ladder of life, and, whilst ever kindly, he is fearlessly honest in rebuking their shortcomings. This we take to be one secret of his powerful moral influence over the masses in times of agitation and excitement. Who is there now amongst the Radical party that could, either by pen or on the platform, influence the masses like Joseph Livesey? Not one. And why? Because the people don't believe in them. "Honest Joe Livesey," as the "Rads" used to call him ; and well he deserved the application, much as we believe he was mistaken in some of his political views. But we are digressing ; we are noticing his published works. This we can do very imperfectly ; indeed, we could not even enumerate those upon Temperance ; we doubt if he could tell himself half he has issued on that question. We understand that in his Temperance publishing department his pecuniary sacrifices have been very heavy—not alone in non-paying publications, but in the large gratuitous circulation he has ever had on foot, and which is still continued. Included amongst his political works are "The Moral Reformer" (two series), and his "Struggle," published during the Anti-Corn Law agitation. Mr. Livesey's most successful effort in the publishing line was the establishment of the *Preston Guardian*, commenced 1844, and continued by himself and sons till 1859 ; a paper which while in the Livesey family had powerful moral and political influence.

Our notice is unavoidably incomplete, but it would be sadly so if we omitted to notice Mr. Livesey's exertions in connection with the resuscitation of the Preston Banking Company. The closing of the doors of that bank on the 19th of July, 1866, caused such consternation amongst the commercial community of Preston as had never before been felt. At first its re-opening appeared hopeless, and then the consternation became still greater. In the hour of despair Mr. Livesey's advice and assistance were sought ; it was said, "If we can only get a man to lay a statement before the public whose word will be implicitly believed, we may calm over the excitement and tide over our difficulties." And Joseph Livesey was that man ; he was made the mouthpiece of those engaged in the work of revival ; and though wholly a stranger to banking affairs, when he set himself to the task in earnest (and it *is* in earnest he does always set to work) he displayed talents that few even of his friends have ever given him credit for. For his years and state of health, he surprised many—speaking one day at three meetings held in three different towns. To the confidence reposed in his utterances and the stimulant his exertions gave to others, may in a great measure be attributed the re-opening of the bank. The town at large owes him indeed a debt of gratitude for his labours at that time.

Upon those portions of the book bearing wholly upon teetotalism, we adopt the comments of one of its advocates,* but we may conclude this notice by remarking that the vexed question as to who was the founder of teetotalism is now clearly settled ; —*the first* teetotal pledge was drawn out by Joseph Livesey, and signed by John King and himself, on August 24, 1832 ; a few days later [Sept. 1st.] the pledge was copied into a penny memorandum book, and signed by the following seven persons:—John Gratix, Edward Dickinson, John Broadbelt, John Smith, Joseph Livesey, David Anderton, and John King. Such was the small beginning of an association about the fundamental principles of which men may, and do, widely differ ; but that its influence is now felt throughout the wide world, wherever the English tongue is spoken, none can deny.

* *Temperance Record*, ante p. 113.

B.

SELECTIONS FROM PRESS NOTICES OF
MR. LIVESEY'S CAREER, EVOKED BY HIS DEATH
AND FUNERAL.

I.—*The Preston Herald, Sept. 6th, 1884.*

Yesterday the mortal remains of our late venerable townsman, Mr. Joseph Livesey, were laid to rest in Preston cemetery, in the presence of mourners of all parties and of all creeds from far and near. This is as it should be. Though the grand old teetotal patriarch ranked himself as a Liberal in politics and a Nonconformist in faith, it was his peculiar glory to have shown throughout his long life that humanity is always better than its creeds, and the searchings of a noble soul always superior to mere party shibboleths. He was a reformer, and a staunch and true one, for more than the threescore years and ten which the Psalmist allots as the full span of human life; but his cry was—that above all and before all mere political amendments of the dead letter of the law, is the work that will infuse into every man and woman the spirit that will set them to reform in themselves whatever interferes, by their own acts, with their own happiness or with the joy and comfort of their neighbours. And though his whole career was informed and inspired by deep and sincere religious conviction, he was ill at rest within the narrow limits of any one communion, for he cared less for the dogmas and doctrines which so many hold as passports to heaven than for the signs and tokens by which the Founder of Christianity commended religion to the love of those who loved Him. To Mr. Livesey religion was nothing if he did not find it still to be what it was once reported to be by the Galilean "who came to seek and to save that which was lost," to "call sinners, and not the righteous, to repentance," to "bind up the wounds of the broken-hearted," to give liberty to the captive, light to those who sit in darkness, comfort to those who dwell in the shadow of death. Mr. Livesey expected to find in religion, by whatever Church or sect professed, all the sweet and reasonable and ennobling things "our great forefather Christ" pictured it to be while He dwelt on earth among His brethren, and he was often disappointed. Thus it came to pass that the Scotch Baptists, with whom he was in early life connected, lost their attractiveness to him when he found, after tramping with others to Accrington to attend to some church business, that he and his weaver companions, who were moneyless, notwithstanding the fatigue of their journey, were left to provide for themselves, while the lords of the congregation dined together. The lapse of years, however, only heaped disappointment upon disappointment so far as his connection with religious denominations as such were concerned; for if he sustained in the prime of his manhood a vigorous and well-directed warfare against the Easter dues and the Church rates, and the tithes of the Established religion, he frequently reserved his bitterest sarcasm, his keenest shafts of scorn, for the Wesleyans and Independents, who ventured to advertise that it would be expected of those who attended particular services to "give silver" at the door. Mr. Livesey conceived it to be the one grand purpose of Christianity to care for the poor, to seek them out in slums and alleys and crowded courts, to raise them from the dunghills, to breathe into them the breath of higher and purer and nobler life, and to this end to go out and in amongst them, doing good; and all this he looked for and yearned for much more than for the building of grand places of worship or the comfortable housing of the teachers of the congregation. Mr. Livesey's religion was essentially Catholic and essentially primitive in its cast. He saw that the world is still very sorrowful, still greatly burdened by sin and iniquity and care, and he felt with something of apostolic fervour that to the true Christian there can never be rest, and earthly comfort is not to be dreamed of while there are men ready to perish for lack of that which Christianity can alone supply. His demand therefore was, that the churches, instead of caring for silver at the doors, or tithes, or Easter dues, should go out, as their Master went out, into the highways and byways, carrying light and joy wherever they went. Men, of course, will talk to-day of Mr. Livesey's notions of religion being "impracticable" in an age so very different from that in which Christianity took its rise. But this answer was more generally given, and given with more emphasis forty years ago than it is now; and indeed the good time seems coming rapidly at last when Mr. Livesey's idea of true Christian worship will be realized—we have the assurance in the establishment of a University Mission in the East end of London, in the growth of the Salvation Army, in the growing popularity of the Church Army, and in many another agency set to work for the evangelization of the masses. The depth and the sincerity of Mr. Joseph Livesey's individuality in religion was quite as marked in the domain of politics. He was an Anti-Corn Law man, not because the movement was helpful to the Liberal party in a political emergency, but because he knew from his own bitter experience in his young days what a grim reality a dear loaf of bread is in a hungry family circle. He threw his whole heart and soul and mind and strength into the Free Trade movement because he believed it would make the homes of the poor happier. Circumstances made him a Liberal, but he was no blind, unreasoning partisan; he at all times preferred loyalty to conscience to party allegiance. He had a programme of his own, and a high and noble one it was; and for years and years his was the solitary voice crying out in the wilderness that the wretched, the forlorn, and the outcast are capable of amelioration in their lot if the attempt to improve them is only made in right good will. Mr. Livesey advocated the establishment of night schools before Lord Brougham; he urged the advantages of thrift long before Sir Arthur Helps had glorified the virtue; he preached of "Self Help" before Smiles had charmed the world with his book; and he was a sanitary reformer before sanitation had become a science. Indeed, to us Mr. Livesey has always been the personification of Goldsmith's grand doctrine, that the subject who has within him the instincts and aspirations of a true man can be held down, cribbed, cabined, and confined, by no laws; that under the most adverse circumstances the soul of such a man swells beyond the measure of the chains which burst from around him, and he stands redeemed, regenerated, and disenthralled without the help of any political party—

> Vain, very vain, my weary search to find
> That bliss which only centres in the mind;
> Why have I strayed from pleasure and repose
> To seek a good each government bestows?
> In every government, though terrors reign,
> Though tyrant kings or tyrant laws restrain,
> How small, of all that human hearts endure,
> That part which laws or kings can cause or cure.
> Still, to ourselves in every place consigned,
> Our own felicity we make or find;
> With secret course, which no loud storms annoy,
> Glides the smooth current of domestic joy.
> The lifted axe, the agonizing wheel,
> Luke's iron crown and Damien's bed of steel,
> To men remote from power but rarely known,
> Leave reason, faith, and conscience all our own.

To Mr. Livesey the whole end and purpose of politics was to further and help "the smooth current of domestic joy." To that end he gladly supported every measure that gave the poor the opportunity of being improved by school, that prevented fools and knaves from rising into power, and that made for the bettering of the condition of the people. So far he was a politician, and a keen and ardent one; and in such crusades of the kind as he joined, he did with all his might what his hand found to do. He took his part in the battle with tongue and pen, and, poor man as he was at the beginning, he never spared his purse while there was anything in it, to promote the cause he had at heart. In the Corn Law agitation he did yeoman's service before Cobden or Bright, and he did it in a way which not only showed his inventiveness and his determination, but his naturally deep insight into the springs which control popular action. He scoffed at Malthusian doctrines, and with great vigour and much humorous zest he ridiculed those who proposed emigration as a cure for poverty, as acting upon the same principle as the fools of Gotham, who with much waste of time and energy pulled the cow on the roof of the house to eat off the grass that was growing there, instead of bringing the available food from its inaccessible position to the point at which it could be used. The various efforts to improve the condition of the factory workers which were made in the first half of his lifetime had his eager support. But Mr. Joseph Livesey was no mere theorist, no specious but empty arguer, content to reel off sentences and then rest and be thankful. He practised what he preached. He enforced the good he could, without waiting for law by its slow processes to make the good work fashionable. He established week-night and Sunday classes, and taught in them; he helped to found Mechanics' Institutes, he provided reading-rooms for the working classes, he promoted cleanliness and decency and morality in crowded thoroughfares, he made the press a power among the multitude, and of Mr. Livesey it may be said confidently, that, notwithstanding his prolonged connection with journalism in one form and another, he never wrote a line which dying he could wish to blot out. But, to put the whole case shortly, the dream of Mr. Livesey's life was to raise the fallen, give strength to the halt, sight to the blind, and hope to the poverty-stricken. He found ministers and politicians ready enough in his young days, as they are now, to exclaim about the wretchedness of the poor, but to rest content with that easy exercise. It was not in his nature to so easily satisfy his conscience that he had done his duty. "Well, God mend them all," said the pious old Scotch minister; but the young deacon, with a spark of the fire of Christ in him, replied, "Na! Na! Donald; we must help God to mend them." And that was the feeling of Joseph Livesey. Other people might reconcile it to their sense of Christian duty to be content with joining in prayer and praise with the comfortable throng, but he was moved by that spirit which is above and before all Churches to take the good tidings to those who would not come to hear them; and he, moreover, was impelled to regard it as a further duty of a Christian to care for men's bodies as well as their souls. Seeing how often mind and frame, how body and soul, how purse and character were ruined by indulgence in intoxication, he invented the teetotal pledge. On the day he and his six companions took that step they commenced to make history. The tiny seed cast into the ground on that occasion has grown into a mighty tree, with roots firmly embedded in every scale of society, and branches which overshadow the whole round world, while its beneficent influence has wrought a silent but most perceptible revolution in the character of the age in which we live. Even in this matter of temperance, which commanded his fullest and warmest love, Mr. Livesey was from first to last true to his principles. He would never consent to be of those who would dare to take the kingdom of heaven by violence. He believed in moral suasion in philanthropy as well as in politics and religion; and hence, though as years went by the disciples outran the master, and clamoured for legal power to suppress the sale of intoxicating liquors, he would never give his countenance to the platform of the United Kingdom Alliance. His answer to all solicitations to join that movement was—"No, let us keep going to the people; if they will they can do all you want them to do without an Act of Parliament at all; only let every man apply the Permissive Bill for himself, and the thing will be done." It is impossible to honour too highly the sturdy British common sense exhibited by Mr. Livesey in his attitude towards every question with which he became confronted. And yet his shrewdness and common sense did not make him less the plucky hero which Englishmen invariably reverence. Lying nearly twenty years ago on a bed of sickness at Windermere, where his wife had died a few months before, the doctor told him he was at death's door, and the only hope of recovery lay in his taking brandy. "Raise me up," he whispered to his son who was present, and when that had been gently done, "Bring me the looking-glass and let me see my face," he said to a lady present, and that was done too. He looked at himself for awhile in silence, and then said, "Well, there is a look there I don't like; I believe, however, I shall get well again; but whether I do or not I will not drink the stuff; put me down again, and if I am to die I will die now." There was a touch of the real hero there. And the moral of the long and useful life of the grand old man who was laid to rest yesterday in the Preston cemetery was, it seems to us, this—That in the country of which we are citizens, however humble a man's origin may be, however limited his means, however little he may have enjoyed the great and precious advantages of University education, if his heart is set upon a noble cause, and he has the courage and perseverance of a man in his nature, he will in the end reap if he faint not. Probably no man, who begins life upon a lowly rung of the social ladder, will ever gather gear by his devotion to the public service; but he may safely lay his account to enjoy in his old age, when the nobility of his motives comes to be understood, honour and reverence and troops of friends and all that should accompany old age. Possibly before long one or other of the Preston parks will contain a statue of Joseph Livesey, for his admirers occupy all the civilized countries of the world. What more inspiring thought could a sculptor wish than that of Joseph Livesey, the founder of teetotalism, the moral reformer, the friend of the poor, sitting at work at a hand-loom in that damp, dark, miserable cellar at Walton-le-Dale, peering eagerly into the pages of a book fixed on his breast beam! The hoary head is a crown of glory, but the glory of the late Joseph Livesey is magnified when we remember his origin and the great odds against which he fought his noble, self-sacrificing fight for the good of mankind all through his long and most honourable and exemplary life.

II.—*The Preston Guardian, Sept. 6th, 1884.*

The public manifestation of sorrow and respect in the streets and in the cemetery of Preston, yesterday, during the funeral procession and burial of Mr. Joseph Livesey, was such as few who witnessed it have ever seen equalled, frequent as is the recurrence of these solemn occasions when the mortal remains of the eminent and the gifted of the human family are borne to their last resting-place. Not alone the entire mass of the inhabitants of this town, in which the departed Philanthropist has spent his long and laborious life, but millions of Englishmen and Englishwomen in every part of the Kingdom, have evidently felt that they had a personal share in the loss of him who by precept and example has been the polestar of their own lives, guiding them safely onward across the trackless stormy ocean of experience into safe havens; and those in distant places who could not themselves be present at Joseph Livesey's funeral have been moved to send hither as their representatives men who have been engaged for years in the same beneficent work as the revered leader who has closed his earthly record. The display of feeling in Preston yesterday was indeed most striking, both amongst the townspeople of all grades, who in thousands filled the streets traversed by the funeral procession, and in many cases followed it to the cemetery, and also amongst the many well-known co-workers in the Temperance cause who had come hither from London, Manchester, and many other centres of important organizations, to take part in the obsequies on their own account and on behalf of those associated with them. Thus the funeral, which the family of our deceased friend would have wished to be private, became, by the spontaneous concourse of townsmen and of strangers, public in the most significant and impressive sense. It could not be otherwise. All who attended it would have reproached themselves with neglect of a sacred duty if they had remained at home whilst the remains of Joseph Livesey were being carried to the grave. The funeral service was almost painfully pathetic, as one and another of those who were privileged to deliver brief addresses rose and pronounced his tremulous eulogium upon one whom each had regarded with all the affection of a son for his father. The effect of some of these addresses upon the throng of mourners was profound; and was enhanced by the thought that some of those who spoke were monuments of the early triumphs of our grand old Reformer in snatching from the grasp of the drink-demon some whom Providence had designed and qualified for spheres of distinguished usefulness. The re-appearance of " old familiar faces," like those of Thomas Whittaker and Edward Grubb, around the coffin of Mr. Livesey was a reminder, comforting even amidst these sorrowful circumstances, that although the first and foremost of the leaders in the social revolution inaugurated at Preston more than fifty years ago is at length taken from our midst, some yet are left who joined the ranks and fought in the first hard battles of the war, and who may be said to have been associated with the movement in its genesis. There were Waterloo veterans left when Wellington died, full of honours and of years, and there remained a few of Joseph Livesey's first recruits in the Temperance crusade to stand amongst the weepers at his tomb, and to render their tribute of loving regard to his memory. The younger captains and ensigns in the Temperance army can hardly be expected to enter fully into the feelings which swayed the old men of the organization who met over Joseph Livesey's grave yesterday, as all that had happened in the far distant years when they were fellow-soldiers under his leadership, fighting in the vanguard—one might say in the forlorn hope—sent to assault a fortress of social habit and usage which looked absolutely impregnable, rushed back to their memories. But, if the young generation of workers—all praise to them for their ardour and fidelity!—cannot realize the past, they can comprehend the present, and conceive by that what the future may be, if the powerful forces now engaged on the side of sobriety prove equal to the service devolving upon them. We shall never think of the spectacle at the funeral of Mr. Joseph Livesey, yesterday, without being encouraged by the conviction that a community which has been stirred by the death of the Founder of the Total Abstinence movement, as that of Preston has been, and the nation which has sent so many of its best citizens from every part to march in his funeral procession, must have been deeply influenced by the teachings of which he was the oldest and most distinguished apostle.

III.—The Preston Chronicle, Sept. 6th, 1884.

Mr. Joseph Livesey, the veteran teetotaler of Preston, died on Tuesday afternoon, in the 91st year of his age ; and his remains were interred yesterday afternoon, in Preston cemetery. The funeral was a great one—great, not in the commonly understood way, by means of spectacular funeral trappings or elaborate sepulchral pomp, but in a representative sense. There were persons present from all parts of the kingdom, and Temperance associations of every kind had deputations in attendance. Many tradespeople in the town, especially those located on the route of the cortège —including even publicans and dram-shop keepers—also showed their respect for the deceased patriarch by putting up shutters, drawing blinds, etc.

No one more than Mr. Livesey exemplified the truth of the old dramatic line— " A man is his own star ; " and than he no one more distinctly illustrated the words of the northern bard—" The rank is but the guinea stamp ; the man's the gowd for a' that." Mr. Livesey was born in a very humble, if not actually poor sphere of life ; he was fatherless and motherless when seven years of age ; he had afterwards to toil on, for years, in a gloomy cellar, as a hand-loom weaver ; he educated himself ; he became a tradesman, an author, a reformer ; by instinct and by reason he always followed the lines of thrift, industry, and progress—thrift in its old-fashioned and truest sense, industry in its most earnest and honest bearings, progress in its widest and most varied forms. In the face of all obstacles he pursued these lines ; and by all classes, by those who did not believe in Teetotalism as well as by its most tenacious adherents—he was greatly respected. He has died full of years and honours ; and to himself—to his own integrity and inherent energy, his own moral courage and indomitable perseverance—are mainly due the eminent position he attained, and the excellent, world-known name and fame which survive him.

In all kinds of movements—educational, social, sanitary, moral and political—Mr. Livesey was, in the days of his health and strength, always to the fore ; but, as a Temperance reformer he will chiefly live in history. When the adoption of Temperance was looked upon as a mere eccentricity, and when its advocacy was scouted as a delusion, Mr. Livesey took a distinguished place in the van of the movement. He went about the country lecturing on its behalf, and frequently at his own expense ; and ever afterwards, through good report and ill, he unswervingly adhered to its principles and unflinchingly supported its objects.

Irrespective of gratuitous services in the general cause of Temperance, Mr. Livesey spent, in the dissemination of Temperance literature alone, about £7,000. And he spent that sum out of his own resources. How many in the country are there now who would do that? To Teetotalism we do not pin our faith ; but we have always respected the method adopted by Mr. Livesey for its spread. He believed in moral suasion. Teetotalism by individual conviction, not by Act of Parliament, was his practical motto. Sobriety generated by sound reason and persuasion, not abstinence forced upon people by high legislative enactment, was the thing he believed in—the plan he persistently recognised to the last; and, if ever the cause of Temperance has to win—win truly, comprehensively, permanently—it will have to triumph on that basis, and on that alone. There have been more brilliant, more mentally sparkling men than Mr. Livesey; but we know of no one living or with the "great majority" who has been more industrious in the cause of general amelioration, more intrepid in the promulgation of his opinions, or more anxious to promote practical progress and make thoroughly happy the homes of the people.

IV.—The Times, Sept. 3rd.

Mr. Joseph Livesey, who for many years devoted himself to the Temperance movement, died yesterday at his residence, Bank Parade, Preston, in the 91st year of his age. Mr. Livesey may be said to have been the founder of the total abstinence movement, having, on the 1st of September, 1832, drafted for the signature of himself and six others the first teetotal pledge. From that date for a period of about 50 years his labours and sacrifices on behalf of his favourite cause were without parallel. Perhaps his most able production in connection with the Temperance movement was his celebrated "Malt Liquor Lecture," an ingenious demonstration of the fallacy of the nutritiousness of ale, etc., which had the approval of a large proportion of the medical faculty. Commencing among the humbler classes, Mr. Livesey lived to see his principles adopted and advocated in the highest and most influential circles of society. The Free Trade movement had in Mr. Livesey a most energetic and useful supporter, both on the platform and in the Press, and also by pecuniary contributions. During the four chief years of the League's agitation he published, at his own risk, and under his own editorship, an illustrated weekly paper called *The Struggle*, which rendered great service in the education of the people, especially among the agricultural districts, on the great question of the day. It was primarily also with the object of assisting the anti-protection movement in North Lancashire that he established, in 1844, the *Preston Guardian*, which became the leading organ of Free Trade and Liberalism in that district. With a long succession of local charitable movements Mr. Livesey was intimately identified.

V.—The Daily News, Sept. 3rd.

With the death of Mr. Joseph Livesey, there has passed away from our midst one of the most useful and unobtrusively noble men of our time. The usual commonplaces of regret are inapplicable to his case; for he has died in the extreme fulness of years, and after his unselfish and humane labours had produced their beneficent fruits. Men of Livesey's stamp are the backbone of a nation; and it is the boast of the English race that, more than any other, it has produced men of his kind. Born five years after the French Revolution, and dying yesterday, he has witnessed the greatest political and social changes which have ever passed over modern Europe. His own share in them was of more importance than was perhaps apparent on the surface. He anticipated Lord Brougham in the movement for the establishment of mechanics' institutes. He was a staunch soldier in the army of Free Trade. And he had written much and vigorously against the Corn Laws before Cobden and Bright inaugurated their great agitation. But Mr. Livesey's name will be more particularly and inseparably connected with the great Temperance movement, which, at the time of his death, is overspreading the world. Mr. Joseph Livesey and the six associates whom, on the 1st September, 1832, he induced to join him in signing the first "teetotal pledge"—a document drawn up by himself—were the pioneers, and the first apostles, of the Temperance cause. That was the beginning of the teetotal pledges; and for half a century after that date lectures and pamphlets were delivered and written by the million on the cause to which the reformer had determined to devote his time and his energies. Mr. Livesey was an effective writer, and a man of wide and various information. But he was his own teacher. Before he had entered on his teens he was thrown on his own resources; and he cultivated literature in the intervals of hard work at his handloom, and by the light of the kitchen fire—candles being a too expensive luxury. Mr. Livesey's life might afford Mr. Galton another instance of heredity. The elder Mr. Livesey was a man of original gifts, as was proved by his experiments in the substitution of machines for handlooms in his own trade of weaver. Some more particulars of Mr. Joseph Livesey's honourable career will be found in another column.

Mr. Livesey devoted himself most intensely to the Temperance movement, of which, in the form of total abstinence, he may be said to have been the founder, having on the 1st September, 1832, drafted for the signature of himself and six others the first teetotal pledge. From that date for a period of about fifty years his labours and sacrifices on behalf of his favourite cause were without parallel, comprising the delivery of thousands of lectures and addresses, the circulation of millions of pamphlets, tracts, and leaflets, the last of these being his annual temperance address on New Year's day, 1881. The Free Trade movement had also in Mr. Livesey a most energetic and useful supporter both on the platform and in the Press, and also by pecuniary contributions. Fully ten years before the organized agitation in which he was associated with Cobden, Bright, and others, he wrote against the corn laws in his *Moral Reformer* (a monthly magazine published in 1831-2-3), calling them " the curse of the country." During the four chief years of the league's agitation he published at his own risk and under his own editorship an illustrated weekly paper called *The Struggle*, which rendered immense service to the cause of the league. It was primarily also with the object of assisting the anti-Protection movement in North Lancashire that Mr. Livesey established in 1844 the *Preston Guardian*, which remained as a substantial property in his family until 1859. In the North of England there are still living some who will also remember Mr. Livesey's spirited campaign against the centralized constitution and despotic powers of the Poor Law Board, which was then brought into existence. Subsequent to, if not consequent upon, this agitation the " orders " of the Board underwent considerable relaxation. Mr. Livesey's services to his native town (for Walton is but a suburb of Preston) were of extraordinary duration and value. Few faces were more familiar than his in districts where sickness and suffering prevailed.—*Daily News.*

VI.—The Illustrated London News, Sept. 6th.

At his residence, Bank Parade, Preston, Lancashire, in his ninety-first year, has just died Mr. Joseph Livesey, whose name for more than two generations has been a household word among those men of the North-West Country who, according to Hugh Miller, " bulk large in the forefront of humanity." The late Mr. Joseph Livesey was something more than a man of patriarchal age, beloved and revered by all who knew him. He was a British Worthy of the type that old Fuller loved to draw—a type of the representatives of which in modern times no meaner writer than Dr. Samuel Smiles should be the historiographer. Mr. Joseph Livesey may be said to have been the founder of the Total Abstinence movement in England; having on the 1st of September, 1832, drafted, for the signature of himself and six other earnest men who thought as he did, the first teetotal pledge. Nor during the ensuing fifty years did he ever falter in fighting the good fight of Temperance. Of course he was an enthusiast, and hated Sir John Barleycorn as fiercely as Milton hated episcopacy and Butler puritanism. Without enthusiasm, this world would be a terribly humdrum one. The venerable Preston Worthy fought as bravely in favour of Free Trade as he did against Strong Drink. His tongue, his pen, his purse, were always at the service of those who held the once unfashionable doctrine that the toiling masses have a right to recruit their strength with abundant and untaxed food. Wherever there was injustice to be combated, corruption to be denounced, wrongs to be remedied, there was Joseph Livesey—self-sacrificing, single-minded, persistent, and courageous. When, half a century ago, the New

Poor Law came into operation, Mr. Livesey, all staunch Liberal, as he had ever been, was among the first to protest against the narrow-minded, heartless and cruel administration of the new code—the denial of outdoor relief, the pitiless rigour of "the workhouse test," the barbarous separation of husbands and wives for the crime of being poor, the insufficient diet, and the often brutal treatment of paupers by relieving-officers and workhouse-masters. Mr. Livesey did not approve of Church-rates, and consistently declined to pay them. He did approve of popular education and charitable works of all kinds; and his long and happy life was one great achievement of usefulness and beneficence.—G. A. SALA.

VII.—*The Daily Chronicle, Sept. 3rd.*

The career of a veteran social reformer has closed with the death of Mr. Joseph Livesey of Preston. As the father of the total abstinence movement, Mr. Livesey will long be gratefully remembered by the vast numbers of his countrymen who have been brought under its influence. He was also one of the fathers of the nation, for he had attained to the rank of a nonogenarian, and thus forcibly illustrated the physical advantages of the application of the principles he so successfully advocated. The great social reform of which he was the earliest promoter dates from the year of the great political reform to which may be traced the peaceful revolutions which have since taken place in the history of the English people. The total abstinence pledge instituted by Mr. Livesey was taken by him and the six other "wise men of Preston" in 1832. The enthusiasm with which the Temperance movement, thus inaugurated, was subsequently carried on affords a remarkable illustration of the great work which can be effected by a few humble workers possessed of earnestness and homely eloquence. It is quite possible that the progress of education and the general improvement of manners resulting from it would have contributed much to the diminution of drunkenness had Mr. Livesey's voice never been heard in the land; but it is nevertheless useless to deny that the greater sobriety which distinguishes the present generation as compared with the last has been in a great measure directly attributable to his untiring energy and devotion. Moderate men, conscious of the fact that the use of intoxicants is sanctioned by the highest authority, may differ in opinion as to the desirableness of converting England into a nation of teetotalers; but there can be no difference of opinion as to the value of total abstinence for those who cannot be moderate. All honour is due, therefore, to men who deny themselves a legitimate luxury for the sake of rescuing others from a life of degradation and infamy. In men actuated by the highest motives fanaticism is pardonable. The results of the movement inaugurated by Mr. Livesey, however, have been manifested not only in the emancipation of multitudes of men and women from their enthraldom to a vitiated appetite, but also in various legislative reforms for the better regulation of the drink traffic. Few will be prepared to deny that these reforms have been beneficial to the community.

VIII.—*The Manchester Guardian, Sept. 3rd.*

The announcement of the death of Mr. Joseph Livesey will be received with sincere regret, not only in his native county of Lancaster, not merely in his fatherland, but wherever the English language is spoken, and wherever men are disposed to render honour to sterling worth, force of character, and honest endeavour for the public good. There are some millions of "teetotalers" in the United Kingdom who regarded, and rightly regarded, Mr. Livesey as the father of the Temperance movement. It is sometimes urged against teetotalers that they are men of one idea, but the biography of their founder affords a good reply to the charge. Worthy of Defoe is the narrative of the struggles of this Lancashire lad, whose early years were passed in the damp cellar of a hand-loom weaver; whose early studies, for lack of candles, were pursued by the flickerings of the kitchen fire. He rose to competence by the severest economy and industry, only to see his well-won earnings swept away by misplaced confidence in another; but that which to some men might have been disaster was to him but a further incentive to exertion. Mr. Joseph Livesey was a successful man of business, but he never forgot the obligation which every citizen owes to the commonwealth. He did good service to his native town, and especially in the dark days of the Cotton Famine showed his foresight, and the power of individual exertion. He was a staunch Liberal, and an earnest and able opponent of the Corn Laws. He had great faith in the educational agency of the Press, and his work, whether as journalist or lecturer, had the unmistakable stamp of sincerity and good faith. Even those who did not share his views gladly recognise the good · that he has done and the benefits which his teaching and example have conferred upon the people of this country, and especially upon the working classes, from whose ranks he sprang.·

IX.—*Manchester Guardian, Sept. 6th.*

The funeral of Mr. Joseph Livesey was a striking evidence of the general regard in which he was held. The prophet was not without honour in his own country, and not only his fellow-citizens but disciples and comrades from afar joined in paying the last tribute of respect to a remarkable man. The gathering of temperance reformers yesterday was notable. It is known that Mr. Livesey's family would have preferred a private ceremonial, and in the homely character of the man there was something that might seem incongruous with a public funeral. Yet Manchester thought it necessary to pay this official honour to the unostentatious Dalton, and Preston could hardly fail to offer a tribute to one whose individuality had been so potent and whose long and useful life had made him one of the institutions of the town. Therefore, although the town made no official arrangements, the representatives of the municipality and of the public bodies as well as private citizens showed their sympathy by following him to the grave, and the long procession was swelled by deputations from temperance organizations in various parts of the country. The moral of a career of earnest usefulness was thus fittingly pointed. In the next few weeks the lessons of this life will be expounded from many thousands of platforms, and it may be hoped that Joseph Livesey, in his desire for the common welfare, in his struggle for education, and in his sympathy with the poor, will find many zealous imitators. He has himself told the story of his own life, and the narrative, like most autobiographies is one of great interest. He had the gift of sympathy, and by its aid transformed countless homes from misery to comfort. This was at once the object and the reward of his life.

X.—*Manchester Examiner and Times, Sept. 3rd.*

By the death of Mr. Joseph Livesey, of Preston, Lancashire loses one of the bravest and best of her sons, one indeed who will rank among the foremost philanthropists of his time. At a ripe age, in the fulness of honours, and in the enjoyment of the supreme satisfaction of knowing that his country and the world were the better for his labours, he has gone to his rest; and though those to whom Mr. Livesey was nearest and dearest, and the multitude of his personal friends, will lament the loss of one whose presence was always a delight to them, they have the consolation of knowing that the record of his life will be a continuous encouragement to unselfish devotion. If it were only the evil that men do that lives after them, the world would, indeed, be a miserable dwelling-place; but nothing is more certain than that no honest effort in the direction of practical charity is ever wasted; and because the whole world is really kin it is impossible to limit the influence of the sustained efforts of good men to benefit and elevate their fellow-creatures. And when men like Joseph Livesey cease from their labours, the faith that the good work which they did will still be carried on is the assured solace of the survivors. It has often been said that civilization is not less advanced by the disinterested operations of modest workers than by the achievements of those whose names are in everybody's mouth; and the career of Joseph Livesey admirably illustrates this truth. He was the son of a hand-loom weaver, and during many years of his life he literally toiled to support himself and his family; moreover, in all things and at all times practical, he never became honestly convinced of the soundness of a doctrine or of the necessity of a course of action, without being impelled to make his neighbours share his convictions ; and it was his happiness to be both a pioneer and successful champion in more than one beneficent popular movement.

The secret of Mr. Livesey's remarkable success as a great social reformer was not only in the strength of his convictions, but in his ability to read and be guided by the lessons of experience. A patient and diligent student of men and books he always was; but it was the recollection of his own sufferings, the memory of his own difficulties, that quickened his devotion and enlightened his intellect in the pursuit of the best means to help his neighbours. Because he remembered the untold disadvantages under which he laboured from the want of sound elementary education in his own early days, he was an earnest advocate of cheap and well-conducted schools and of a sound system of popular elementary education ; and it was his happiness to see the successful working of an Act of Parliament under which every child in the kingdom has the opportunity of easily acquiring the knowledge he had only been able to gain under enormous difficulties. The recollection, too, of terrible mistakes and even criminal blunders committed by his fellow-workmen at a time when the ignorance for which they were not responsible made them dupes of unscrupulous adventurers, led Mr. Livesey to promote, to the best of his ability, a cheap newspaper press. No one was ever more earnest in his advocacy of the repeal of the taxes on knowledge; and in all the social and political movements with which he was associated he never overlooked the influence of the Press. He was, in fact, the founder of more than one periodical, the most important of which was the *Preston Guardian*, with the management and editorship of which he was connected for nearly a quarter of a century. By his vigorous articles in his little newspaper, *The Struggle*, he did much to enlighten public opinion and to excite that public indignation against the bread tax, without which the labours of the Anti-corn-law League would have been in vain. And when the American war afflicted us with a famine which threatened to be as dire in its consequences as those which Free Trade had driven from our shores, the energies and resources of this good man were again excited by his far-reaching sympathy and the recollections of the miseries of half a century previously. During the cotton famine he was among the foremost to aid the sufferers in his native town ; and among the officers of that famous army of relief which volunteered so nobly and worked so vigorously, Joseph Livesey held a distinguished place.

But though Mr. Livesey's other claims on the gratitude of posterity are unquestionable, he will, without doubt, be chiefly remembered as the virtual founder of the Temperance movement in this country. He was one of the first to take the pledge, and to him and six friends in Preston must be awarded the chief honours of the Total Abstinence crusade ; nor is it too much to say that without their efforts and success the more recent developments and modifications of the movement would never have existed.

For thirty years after the teetotal movement was successfully inaugurated Mr. Livesey was indefatigable in promoting its extension. Shrewd, earnest, conscientious, and eloquent, he was universally recognised as the head and guide of the Total Abstinence body, and as the father of English Temperance. He attended meetings in all parts of the country. Great and enthusiastic audiences assembled to hear him in Birmingham, and there was also a meeting, not so successful, but not barren of good results, at London. Meetings were also held and societies formed at Manchester, Bolton, and many other Lancashire, as well as Cheshire, and Yorkshire towns. His " Malt Liquor Lecture " opened the eyes of thousands, and among others of that most popular teetotal advocate Dr. F. R. Lees.

The success of the efforts of Mr. Livesey and his colleagues was at first most distinctly apparent among the working classes, but the middle and higher classes did not long remain irresponsive. There is, indeed, much left for the Temperance reformers to accomplish ; but they have really effected a revolution in the drinking customs of the country. To them has been due the conversion of thousands of abodes of wretchedness into happy homes. They have made drunkenness disgraceful. The outrageous orgies in which kings and princes did not disdain to take part when Joseph Livesey was a young man, could not now take place within the confines of respectable society ; and the credit of no small share of this healthy change is due to the disinterested labours of the early Preston teetotalers. The importance of their work has, in fact, long been acknowledged, not merely by those who shared Mr. Livesey's opinions, but not less emphatically by those men who do not adopt his practice. And assuredly when the roll of the Lancashire worthies of the present century is complete, not the least honourable name in the list will be the pioneer of teetotalism, Joseph Livesey, the weaver's son of Walton-le-Dale.

XI.—The Leeds Mercury, Sept. 3rd.

Mr. Joseph Livesey, the oldest pledged teetotaler in the world, and a very exemplary worker in the domains of social, moral, and political reform, died yesterday afternoon, in the 91st year of his age, at his residence, on Bank Parade, Preston. . . When the Anti-Corn Law League was formed, Mr. Livesey was quite prepared to become a member of it. In his autobiography, he says he never assumed the character of a political agitator, but felt it no slight honour to have stood on a platform in the open air, denouncing monopoly and pleading for the people's rights. Messrs. Cobden and Bright pressed him to go out as a lecturer against the Corn Laws, but he found it impossible to comply. It must be matter of surprise to all who know anything of Mr. Livesey's early life, to learn how much he did in this way. He was then carrying on a large business, and had the cares of a family on his hands, yet we find that for four years and a half he brought out every Saturday morning a publication called *The Struggle*, which, at one part of its career, had a circulation of 15,000. *The Struggle* was devoted to the enunciation of the views of the Corn Law Leaguers, and its ably written articles, aided by the cartoons which accompanied it, undoubtedly did a great deal to bring before the public the great principles of the cause it advocated. Particularly in the southern agricultural districts of the country was *The Struggle* an effective agent in the cause of abolition. . . Though earnest and active in the promotion of many benevolent and philanthropic movements, it will be chiefly as a pioneer of the Temperance cause, and as an earnest, unwearied advocate of its principles, by speech and pen, that Mr. Livesey's name will be known to posterity. In his "Autobiography," and in his "Reminiscences of Early Teetotalism," full and interesting details of the part he took, and of the many arduous, self-sacrificing efforts he made in the Temperance cause, are given. . . In religion he was practically unsectarian; in politics he belonged to the school of Reformers. As a speaker, he was lucid and vigorous; as a writer, earnest and clear; and while he took the greatest interest in teetotalism, he was ever ready to encourage all movements calculated to enlighten the minds, improve the homes, and purify the lives of the people.

XII.—The Newcastle Chronicle, Sept. 3rd.

Temperance reformers and English Radicals will to-day learn with regret that Joseph Livesey is dead. Not long ago the veteran reached his ninetieth year. Joseph Livesey was a typical Englishman. Equally remarkable for decision of character and vigorous intellectual power, he exhibited many of the qualities which rendered Cobbett famous. Without Cobbett's egotism he had much of his tenacity of purpose, while his political record was more consistent. He had felt, in his own case, the difficulties which iniquitous enactments had created for the people; and, years before the Anti-Corn Law League existed, he argued vigorously for Free Trade. It was in this strain that he denounced the bread tax. "The curse of the country is the Corn Law, and till that is repealed, persons may drag their weary limbs about, may beset the dispensary for physic, crowd the workhouse to excess, may sink beneath their sufferings, and die from hunger, but there will be no relief." When this was written the average wage of weavers in England, working from five in the morning until nine or ten at night, was rather under than over six shillings per week. The necessity of dealing with legal wrongs induced Mr. Livesey to turn printer, and almost coincident with his entering on this business, he identified himself with the Temperance movement. From the date of his connection with this movement, onward, throughout his entire career, Joseph Livesey was a zealous apostle of abstinence. His "Malt Liquor Lecture" and his annual Temperance addresses bear witness to the energy and intelligence which he brought to the advocacy of this cause. It was to "a diffusive and agitating teetotalism" that his heart went forth. Without combating other forms of attacking the vice of intemperance, the veteran abstainer clung throughout to moral suasion as the true panacea for drunkenness. His ideas on this point were thus expressed: "It is not more law, but more labour that we want; not Parliamentary parchments, but feeling, sympathizing hearts; not prayers to Government, but appeals to the masses—mixing with them, teaching them, and inducing them to leave the public-house and drinking companions, holding lively meetings and forming brotherly associations."

Mr. Livesey never lost sight of temperance principles. To him the country is indebted for the association with the cause of not a few of its most eminent advocates. Many imagine that a man who abstains from intoxicants must be utterly lacking in the social qualities which lend a special charm to life. No idea of Joseph Livesey's character could be more unjust. He was throughout his entire career distinguished not more for business shrewdness than intense sympathy. His exertions during the Cotton Famine are to-day gratefully remembered by the men of Preston. It was ever his aim to lift even the lowest and most unfortunate of his fellow creatures from the Slough of Despond into which they had sunk. His own personal career had been one of considerable vicissitude. After a severe struggle, in which he had amassed a competence, he suddenly found the earnings of his life swept away by an injudicious partnership. But with the resolute energy that ever distinguished him, he began the world anew, and fortune, which favours the brave, again smiled on his efforts. After a life extending over ninety years, he has sunk like a victorious summer sun, leaving a name destined to be remembered as that of one of the noblest workers in the cause of social and political progress which the age has produced.

XIII.—The Porcupine (Liverpool), Sept. 6th.

Amongst the illustrious abstainers of the present generation, none stand out with greater prominence in the Temperance cause than the name of Joseph Livesey, who this week has gone to a well-earned repose, wept, honoured, and sung. A philanthropist of the most chivalrous nature, with a heart as easily touched as a child's, an ear ever open to the cry of oppression and sorrow, a hand ever ready to assist the helpless, and a strong irresistible will to carry his schemes to a successful issue, "Teetotal Joe," as he was generally called amongst those who almost worshipped him, stood out pre-eminent as a reformer, a teetotaler, and a genuine, self-made man.

There are many lessons in his adventurous life—struggles overcome and obstacles surmounted, perseverance never daunted and energy never relaxed—from which not a few of us might learn a valuable lesson. . . . Well, he has gone at a ripe old age to a well-earned repose after a useful life; and many a bright home, with its joyous wife, happy husband, and bonny children mourn him.

And thus the curtain falls on a career of practical usefulness, devoted to what is perhaps the noblest work of philanthropic reform ever inaugurated by man. But though the standard is struck from the grasp of the veteran, there are not lacking strong and brave hands to raise it in the forefront of battle. . . . Most of these stood by the open grave yesterday, and with heartfelt sighs, and manly tears in their eyes, took their part in the solemn requiem of the dead.

XIV.—The Blackpool Gazette and News, Sept. 12th.

Mr. Livesey's whole life was full of the promotion of agencies for the spread of knowledge and the better education of the masses; and the motive which fired him to the spread of his anti-drink Gospel was simply a wish to improve the homes and purify the lives of the people. It was in the furtherance of this aim that Joseph Livesey discovered his teetotal panacea. Temperance workers and Temperance societies had preceded him, but the duty of total abstinence seems to have come as a moral revelation, to one whose practical labours amongst the poor had disclosed the worst phases of the debauched drinking habits of the people. In all his labour, however, the father of teetotalism was practical : he was not constantly pining after Acts of Parliament in order to enforce his precepts. . . But the real charm of Joseph Livesey's life will best be revealed when some kindly hand takes the biographical pen, and gives us a sympathetic record of its noble achievements outside the pale of a one-idead enthusiasm. Mr. Livesey was more than a teetotaler—how much more we shall never rightly know, unless some clear-headed biographer tells us the story of his life, without the glamour of an overbearing prejudice, but with all the inspiration which comes from a life teeming with incidents of an ennobling character.

XV.—The Blackpool Herald, Sept. 5th.

For some short time Mr. Livesey's death had been daily expected, and it is not too much to say that his last illness has occasioned an amount of feeling such as is extended to very few men at the present time. The cause is not far to seek. Of all men, the life of Mr. Livesey has been a model of excellency, philanthropy, and self-denying incessant work for the good of his fellows and the elevation of the people, socially, morally, and politically. Not alone as a Temperance advocate, but long before that great social movement had its existence by his creative genius, he had written and published many addresses of great social value for the advancement of the labouring classes ; and his *Moral Reformer*, given to the world as a periodical, was not only the pioneer of cheap literature, but it touched and enforced every moral and Christian virtue as a prelude to the happiness of home life. Nor did the enforcement of these principles depend upon his efforts through the Press alone, for they were personally advocated by house-to-house visitation amongst the poorest of the poor. For years and years every Sunday morning, starting so early on his philanthropic mission as to catch the dissipated husbands before they had gone out, he was there to speak the words of truth and soberness to the erring ones, and to relieve their distress. "He chid their wanderings, but relieved their pain." His sympathy with the struggles of the poor had no bounds, and his practical charity in relief of their needs, exhibited during these weekly perambulations, carried a comfort and blessing in its long train to numberless destitute homes. But Joseph Livesey was his own almoner, and he knew how great and how frequent were these acts of kindness and of love towards the abject poor. So far as it may be said of any man, it may be said of him, that "he visited the fatherless and the widows in their affliction, and kept himself unspotted from the world." When he himself was poor, and early in his married life, he was so much shocked with the state of a poor sick woman whom he visited and who lay "full of sores," that he took his only bed, one filled with feathers, for this poor creature to lie on ; and this incident may be truly taken to be the prelude of that deep sympathy with and for suffering humanity which was the key to his long life of usefulness.

XVI.—The Rochdale Observer, Sept. 6th.

In glancing back at Mr. Livesey's career we are struck with wonder that one man should have lived through such changes and vicissitudes. His birth almost carries us back to the Reign of Terror; and the experiences of his early manhood recall a dark period in our social and industrial history, the mere attempt to realize which causes us an involuntary shudder. In these days of universal education and largely curtailed hours of labour, the story of Livesey's early struggle for existence reads like some freak of a disordered imagination. It requires, indeed, a vivid fancy to enable us to picture Livesey's early surroundings, and it is with a feeling of inexpressible gratitude that we thank God for the happier lot of the present generation. Men like Livesey confer credit, and even lustre, on their native land ; and if intellectually they rank below statesmen of the type of Cobden and Bright and Gladstone, it must in all honour be said of them that they exert a scarcely less important influence in shaping the destinies of their country. Livesey himself was one of the pioneers of Free Trade ; and Bright and Cobden, if we are not mistaken, were most cordial in recognition of his valuable services to the great cause which they made peculiarly their own.

If we were asked to account for the great influence exercised by Livesey over his fellow-men we should be inclined to mention as the chief cause the wholeness and sincerity of his character. There was nothing small or crabbed about him. He was a profound believer in the brotherhood of man, and this belief led him to devote his energies to the amelioration of the lot of his humble brethren in every possible direction. Perhaps we want more men of this stamp now than at any former period, not because our needs are more pressing, which they certainly are not, but because there is too great a tendency to convert our public men into "specialists," with their inevitably contracted sympathies. Livesey at any rate was an all round reformer; and Lancashire, which has so greatly respected the man while living, would do well to honour his memory now that he is dead. Preston especially would do well to take this matter into its consideration. Livesey was one of its greatest citizens; he spent all his life there, closely identifying himself with its welfare, and he has just died there, "full of years and full of honours." Let Preston resolve to do something worthy of its distinguished townsman, and all Lancashire, to say nothing of more remote districts, will be proud to assist in the undertaking.

XVII.—The Alliance News (Dr. F. R. Lees), Sept. 6th.

The life of the Temperance reformer, Joseph Livesey, written with the skill, power, and insight which mark Mr. Morley's Life of Cobden, would, owing to the long stretch of time which it covers, furnish an interesting and instructive picture of the life and changes of the waning century. We, however, must mainly confine ourselves to the relations it bears to the principles and objects of the Alliance. We knew him intimately, not only from his writing and his work, but in private life and familiar intercourse, and our verdict is, that, "Take him for all in all, we may not look upon his like again." Outsiders, even, must be impressed with the fact that he was one of the most remarkable figures of this generation, closing, in the 91st year of his age, a career of extraordinary usefulness, not only to the locality of his birth, but to his country and his kind. And yet Mr. Livesey was but a type of many a true-born Englishman—not greater than they by any single faculty or trait, but greater by harmonious combination of powers united with happy accidents of circumstance. In him the Englishman is seen in all his best, if common, characteristics—his benevolence, his aptitude, his industry, his perseverance, his sterling honesty, and his broad common sense. He was at once a pure man, a kind father and affectionate husband, an earnest citizen, a clever industrious tradesman, an enlightened Christian, and a fervent patriot. In many regards (philosophical faculty excepted) the life, labours, and writings of Mr. Livesey, and even his personal traits, bore a singular resemblance to those of Benjamin Franklin; and up to a certain point, the comparison holds even of his intellectual character, though circumstances never favoured its development into the philosopher and statesman. Mr. Livesey was not, and never could be, indeed, a ruler of men; for all his peculiarities, his excellences and defects alike, kept him within the sphere of individual action. Yet, in a lesser measure and a lower sphere, he possessed, if not the mesmeric power of some men, or the commanding influence of others, much persuasive influence and no inconsiderable diplomatic power. Lesser men than himself delighted to honour him, and men greater than himself gladly paid a tribute to his wisdom and his worth.

Mr. Livesey, of course, will be chiefly and lastingly known by the great work of his life, not as the first abstainer by many, not even as the founder of the first local Teetotal Society, but as the first great missionary and successful founder of the Teetotal Movement. Other persons may have taught the same truths, as indeed they did, but it was he, and he alone, who gave to them that impulse which made them successful in the nation. From his sowing, and that of his first followers, we trace the great harvest. He was the Napoleon of the movement who first crossed the Alps of Obstruction; and on the path which he trod great armies have followed into the fruitful Italy of Success. To abandon metaphor, it was Joseph Livesey who, in this country, initiated the Teetotal Movement, and in this relation of missionary he was first and, within the limits to which he wisely confined himself, peerless. We always judge of fitness and force by their results. Success is the measure of applied fitness. He was, therefore, tried by this standard, the man for the time and the work he did. And, indeed, the secret is an open one; it is seen in his mental and physical attributes. His fair and florid countenance, beaming with earnestness and good nature, his plain Saxon style of speech, his homely metaphors and telling illustrations, were exactly fitted for a pioneer of a truth which could only be unfolded by degrees, and were especially adapted to win the confidence and reach the understanding of the classes he most delighted to address. He never went beyond his knowledge, never uttered empty verbiage, never appealed to mere sensational feeling; and so it comes to pass that his early writings and lectures are as true and telling to-day as when they were first delivered fifty years ago. . .

In his character of a politican and controversialist, Mr. Livesey never lowered himself to the level of a partisan. He was at all times tolerant, scrupulously truth-ful, and even respectful. He erred liked other men, but evidently not wilfully, or in a spirit of bigotry. Attached to the party of Liberals himself, he was fair to-wards the Conservatives; and so he always won their good word. This is what, in 1869, the *Preston Herald* said of him :—"'Honest Joe Livesey,' as the Rads used to call him; and well he deserved the application [of the epithet], much as we believe he was mistaken in some of his political views."

To our young men, the life of Joseph Livesey should be full of instruction and encouragement, if not inspiration. It teaches, by a consistent and illustrious example, temperance, tolerance, thrift, prudence, self-denial, economy, benevolence, perseverance; and it confirms the lesson by exhibiting as the result, health, honour, usefulness, competence, and long life. If, in the first half of this 19th century, so much good has been done by the rightly directed efforts of one man, and so much incitement to good in others, what, with all the wonderful advantages now opened out to us at the close of this century, may not, inspired with earnest aim and guarded by simplicity of life, the young men of the future accomplish! Oh for the zeal of the departed and fast-departing Fathers !

XVIII.—*The British Temperance Advocate (Dr. F. R. Lees), Oct. 1st.*

The new departure [in Temperance reform] commenced in that great year of reform, 1832, was taken up with extraordinary zeal. Many men were reformed, and, leaving their employments, went out full of love for the work, and a zeal which saw no difficulties, all over the town. Others also went, too, with their rough-spun eloquence, first through the towns of the North, and then over the Midlands. The story of that time—fairly and fully told, for example, by some of its survivors, as Mr. Edward Grubb, or Mr. Whittaker, would be one of the most graphic and inter-esting of works. Amongst these devoted pioneers must not be forgotten the striking figure of Mr. Swindlehurst, the lieutenant of Mr. Livesey. Many of these early men had been victims of drink; but instead of being weak-willed men, as the ignorant writer in *The Times* describes our reformed drunkards, they were men of firm will, heroic courage, mighty in overcoming the obstructions of the world, and in subduing opposition.

In this early stage of the Temperance Reform Movement, and for some years afterwards, Mr. Livesey, by virtue of his superior culture, his age, and experience, naturally led the movement. In 1832 he gave his famous "Malt Liquor Lecture" in many of the great towns, including Birmingham and Leeds. In the former place, the celebrated preacher, John Angel James, heard him, and became one of his converts; and in the latter he induced Mr. F. R. Lees to sign the *teetotal* pledge, though he had been trying entire abstinence for some time, and had abstained four years from spirits.

In the same year Mr. Livesey invaded London, that " great Babylon " of drink, and sowed the fully ripened seed of temperance truth, as told in his "Reminiscences of Early Teetotalism." He took small bills, some of which he pinned with wafers to the walls of the Bank of England, and other places. He held a meeting, and delivered his famous "Malt Liquor Lecture," inducing a brewer who was present to give up his business and join the movement. Shortly afterwards he again visited London. One of his fellow advocates went out with a bell, and rang in the streets, announcing the meetings at night. The constable stopped him, remarking that they did not permit that sort of thing there. One man, however, heard the bell, and attended the meeting, and the result was the bringing round to the side of teetotalism the brother of the well-known Jabez Inwards. The cause now spread rapidly, and teetotal societies were established all over the kingdom. A literature was beginning to appear in favour of the new opinion, which was worked even more vigorously than it is at present; and Mr. Livesey had the honour of starting it. In 1831 appeared " *The Moral Reformer*, or Protestor against the Vices of the Times," a 6*d*. monthly, which closed with Vol. III., in Dec., 1833. It was a remarkable work, and in the last number we find a letter from Mr. John Finch, of Liverpool, advocating as the remedy for intemperance, poverty, and crime, " National *Education*, and the altering the *circumstances* of Society "—the keynote of all that had been done, or can be done, in the way of reform. A volume known by nearly the same title—*Livesey's Moral Reformer*—was published in 1*d*. weekly numbers, size and style of *Chambers' Journal*. No. 1 was issued Jan. 6th, 1838, and when it finally closed, it formed an interesting volume of 222 pages devoted to moral, economic, and social reform. In the meanwhile, Mr. Livesey had published his notable *Preston Temperance Advocate*, the first number being dated Jan., 1834. This 1*d*. monthly closed in Dec., 1836, containing the illustration of the " Two Bridges "—one without battlements, over which men where continually slipping into the river below; the other, a high level, guarded as safely as that at Charing Cross. Mr. Livesey ceased this publication in favour of the *Leeds Temperance Advocate*, then conducted by Messrs. Crossley, Andrew, Lees, and Pallister, and which, some years afterwards, Dr. Lees (its then proprietor and editor) transferred to the British Temperance League. Mr. Livesey also wrote numerous pamphlets, and for decades of years, even up to last year, issued and circulated at his own expense, to every house in Preston, a New Year's Address on Temperance. His "Malt Liquor Lecture," it is computed, had a circulation of over two million copies. He founded the *Preston Guardian*, the success of which was commented on by Cobden, and for years worked with the Anti-Corn Law League. He and his wife had a stall at the great Bazaar in Covent Garden Theatre, in aid of the funds. He issued *The Struggle*, to promote the work of the League ; and this monthly paper, headed with cartoons conceived by a Liverpool gentleman, lasted from Jan., 1842, to June, 1846. In 1859, Mr. Livesey sold the *Preston Guardian*, and afterwards retired, but worked daily in temperance work up to a few weeks ago. Though Mr. Livesey was by disposition disinclined to work in corporations—his individuality being remarkable—he was an extremely useful citizen. Through his exertions and skill, the Preston Banking Co., which had closed on the 19th July, 1866, was resuscitated, his statement of affairs re-establishing confidence. For some years he has received deputations on his birthdays, and addresses from all parts of the kingdom, showing in what esteem he was held. The later thoughts and reflections of Mr. Livesey were put before the world in the periodical entitled the *Staunch Teetotaler*, which, beginning with No. 1 in Jan., 1867, ended with No. 24 in Dec., 1868.

An *instinct* to do good characterized Mr. Livesey ; and few but his relatives and personal friends know how constantly he was engaged in visiting and in works of charity amongst the poor. Notably, he was, during the Lancashire Cotton Famine, one of the most assiduous workers and wisest organizers ; and truly, in many regards, " his works do follow him."

XIX.—*The New Zealand Herald (Mr. E. Cox)*, Oct. 4th and 11th.

The honour of being " the Founder of Teetotalism " was enough, it might be thought, for one man's life ; but Mr. Livesey's Temperance work was only one—the greatest—yet but one, of many labours in a career literally abounding with deeds and enterprises of benevolence. He saw that the most powerful agencies of modern times were the Press and the platform, and he employed them to the utmost of his ability. He had begun to speak in public early in life ; had great self-possession, the utmost naturalness, and great facility of expression. As a writer, he is a model of plain, pure English, with the raciness and correctness of William Cobbett, without his occasional coarseness. He wrote and spoke with such simplicity and earnestness, with such point and ease, that no one could fail to understand him or to be moved by his power. . . . His devotion to the Temperance cause became proverbial ; he was said to be a man of one idea, " Old Joseph Livesey and his one idea, teetotalism." This judgment was superficial—yet, stay, it is true he had one idea, but broader, nobler : how and in what way he could do the most good to his fellow-men, above all to the poor and wretched. . . . How often he set up again some unfortunate tradesman ; what faith he had in the recovery of poor drunkards ; how he relieved the stranger, and pleaded for the fallen and forlorn ! The extent of his private generosity will never be known ; how often and how unostentatiously he sent aid to others in the 'time of extreme difficulty or sorrow he himself would be the last to acknowledge. To him " all earthly joys were less than this one joy of doing kindness." . . . And now, " the old man eloquent," and healthy, yielding at length to nature's decay, has passed to the unseen. Healthy, did we say? yes, almost to the last the picture of health ! To some of your readers his portrait is familiar ; to some, as to the writer, he was personally and well known : his kind benevolent expression ; his clear, ruddy complexion ; his open, keen, but kind blue eye, with its lofty arch of eyebrow ; sagacity, energy, sensibility, kindness, written upon his brow and strongly marked features. To the last his mind remained clear. The tranquillity of a conscience undefiled, the surrounding joys of happy memories, the love of all who knew him and of thousands who knew him not, the oft-expressed esteem of his fellow-townsmen and fellow-workers, the shouts of victory to the cause he loved so well, and the tender offices of faithful children ; these all waited upon and gladdened his declining years. Born of consumptive parents, his childhood exposed to great privations, and his life full of labour, that he attained to the ripe age of ninety can only be attributed to his extreme simplicity of taste, to his remarkable abstemiousness, his love of water " within and without," to the admirable balance of his mental powers, to his out-door employments, and his habitual peace of mind. In all parts of the civilized world his memory will be cherished with grateful regard, and his name enrolled among the benefactors of mankind.

XX.—*The Temperance Record, Sept. 4th.*

Mr. Livesey's long life, from its humble beginning to its triumphant close, was marked by a spirit of independent energy which could face difficulties and overcome them. The remarkable and interesting episodes in his life must be familiar to most of those who have made themselves acquainted with the growth of the Temperance reformation, which, so far as the total abstinence movement in England is concerned, had its birth when the seven Prestonians signed the pledge which Joseph Livesey penned. This was done on September 1, 1832, and the act indissolubly associates his name as the " father " of the grand movement which has been destined to bring peace and happiness to millions of his countrymen. It is worthy of note that Mr. Livesey had adopted the practice of teetotalism a year prior to his signature to the teetotal pledge, and had thus fully persuaded himself of the wisdom of the course he set himself to induce others to take. . . . Throughout his long-extended career of usefulness Mr. Livesey had a strong faith in the efficacy of house-to-house visitation, both in regard to the general relief of distress and for the promulgation of Temperance truths. He not only recommended this course, but pursued it, so long as he was able, to the benefit of many who were thus brought within the range of his personal influence. His teetotalism has ever manifested itself in practical efforts to ameliorate the condition of his fellow-men ; and his literary efforts have been characterized by persuasive eloquence and argumentative soundness. . . . He lived to make and to leave the world better than he found it. He was always restless in the presence of evil or distress. In his autobiography he says, " I never seemed as if I could sit down and be quiet when I saw work wanted doing, and I felt able to render any assistance ; " and it has been this irresistible longing to be doing something which kept him active to the end, and produced those inspiring "New Year Addresses," fitly designed to stimulate present workers to increased activity. The pioneer work of Joseph Livesey was not confined to Preston; he visited London, as well as many of the large Midland and Northern towns, under circumstances of hardship and difficulty almost insuperable, and was largely instrumental in arranging for other honoured labourers to sow the good seed.

XXI.—The Church of England Temperance Chronicle (Mr. F. Sherlock), Sept. 6th.

It is with a feeling of the deepest sorrow that we announce the death of Joseph Livesey, of Preston, a man whose name will ever be remembered for his noble services in the promotion of the Temperance Reformation. For the last few weeks he had been in a somewhat critical condition, and he sank peacefully to rest on Tuesday afternoon at his residence, Bank Parade, Preston, in the ninety-first year of his age. His long life was unselfishly devoted to the good of his fellow-men; and his eminently useful career—looked at from whatever standpoint we may—presents admirably suggestive lessons so legible that all may read them, and that with profit. In the limits at our disposal it is impossible to do anything like justice to the life-story of this typical Englishman. We must, therefore, content ourselves with briefly sketching some of the more prominent outlines. . . . .

In his early years Mr. Livesey devoted a large expenditure of time and money to platform advocacy. He delivered his "Malt Liquor Lecture" in most of the towns and villages of Lancashire and Yorkshire, in Edinburgh, Birmingham, London, and many other places. At that early period, when almost every one believed in the highly nutritious properties of beer, the statement that "there was more food in a pennyworth of bread than in a gallon of ale," supported as it was by such convincing evidence, proved most startling.

XXII.—The Irish Temperance League Journal (Mr. John Andrew), Oct. 1st.

Mr. Livesey had great faith in the power of the Press. Before he was twenty-one he had written many letters to the local papers; and sometimes he exercised his literary skill in writing addresses and appeals condemnatory of popular vices, and published them as posters on the walls. From placards he made a natural transition to pamphlets, one of the earliest of which was directed against drunkenness, and was entitled, "The Besetting Sin." In 1825 he published "An Address to the Poorest Classes," which contained advice upon almost every topic connected with domestic management. This pamphlet was published at twopence and went through several editions. . . .

It is always interesting, in reviewing the lives of persons who have risen to some distinction, to notice the various incidents and facts which exercised a salutary and stimulating effect upon their energies of body and mind, and roused them to efforts for the removal of great evils; and we think no one can read the brief recital we have given without seeing that each important change and event in Mr. Livesey's early life helped to fit him for his subsequent noble career, and his constant efforts to do good. He was never a man of one idea. His conduct clearly and unmistakably indicated that he might, without boasting, adopt the saying of the Roman poet—

"I am a man, and what concerns man, concerns me."

XXIII.—The League Journal (Scottish), Sept. 6th.

Mr. Livesey has thus been identified with the movement from its early beginning in this country, and with unflagging zeal has advocated it throughout his protracted career. In the prosecution of the Temperance movement he pre-eminently manifested those qualities and virtues which command admiration and win respect. Courage, consistency, faithfulness, honesty, simplicity of motive, combined with shrewdness and common sense, were some of the chief elements in his character which contributed to his success as a man of business and as an exponent of the Total Abstinence cause.

The great aim of all Joseph Livesey's lectures was to teach the people the nature and properties of all intoxicating drinks. Believing that the cause of Temperance will not prevail until the public are fully alive to the injurious effects of alcoholic liquors, he constantly insisted that the alcohol in the drink, and not the house in which it was sold, nor the man who sells it, was the cause of the evil. To this all his energies were directed and concentrated, and he did as much as any man to clear the subject of much misconception which long clung to it, and is not altogether swept away. This was the burden of his celebrated " Malt Liquor Lecture." . . .

The fathers, where are they? and the prophets, do they live for ever? are words which rush to the lips as we glance over the long list of names. And now the father of teetotalism in England, and the prophet of the new doctrine proclaimed by him and his compeers more than fifty years ago, has also passed away, leaving behind him a noble record of faithful service which will be an inspiration to Temperance workers for many years to come.

XXIV.—*The Band of Hope Chronicle, Oct.*

Few events in the history of Teetotalism have given rise to greater and more widespread regret than the death of this truly great man, who passed away on September the 2nd, in his 91st year. Wherever the Temperance movement has spread, Mr. Livesey's name has long been known and honoured ; and though it was not to be expected that his days would be greatly prolonged, the news that he had been called away came upon us all like a sharp and sudden shock, and filled us at once with surprise and grief.

It is not our purpose to follow the record of Mr. Livesey's long and useful life in detail, but reference must be made to the fact that his pen was turned to good account as well as his tongue. His famous lecture on malt was followed by other useful tracts and addresses, which were widely circulated and must have exercised an immense influence.

XXV.—*The Irish Temperance Banner, Sept.*

Almost up to the last Mr. Livesey issued pamphlets and leaflets entitled " The Preston Temperance Teacher," in which there were apt quotations occasionally from works and speeches, followed by comments by Mr. Livesey. One of his latest leaflets was a letter he sent to the great Temperance Conference in London in June, 1881, containing suggestions on the special means for reaching neglected classes. With all his labour, Mr. Livesey often lamented that he had done but little. When Mr. Thomas Walmsley, an old friend and unostentatious but vigorous Temperance worker, was with him one night, but a few months ago, he clasped his hands and said, " Thomas, what I regret the most is the little I have done in my life. Oh, do work as much as ever you possibly can." This indicated the humble estimate he took of his lifelong work.

XXVI.—*The Nonconformist, Sept. 11th.*

Mr. Livesey for many years served the Temperance cause with a spirit of self-sacrifice and energy which would demand a volume to do it justice. Let it suffice to say that for more than half a century the Temperance movement has had no more earnest or faithful friend than the man whose hand was the first put to the pledge of entire abstinence from intoxicating drinks. Mr. Livesey has never been a man of one idea. The story of his life is practically the history of the public movements—political, social, and religious—of the town of Preston. On the various governing bodies in the town he has, at different times, occupied a seat;

and when at length the weight of accumulated years compelled him to retire into the quietude of private life, there lived no man in all the place more sincerely honoured and revered for his work's sake. His house has long been the Mecca of teetotalers, who from all parts of the world found their way there to do honour to their venerated leader; and now that his long and useful life is ended, he has left behind him the reputation of a pure and blameless life, and a memory which will not readily be permitted to die.

XXVII.—The Christian World, Sept. 4th.

There passed away on Tuesday afternoon last, in his ninety-first year, like a "shock of corn fully ripe in its season," Joseph Livesey, of Preston, the veteran leader of a band of seven who, on the 1st of September, 1832, just fifty-two years ago, drafted the first Temperance pledge, the original of which, carefully preserved and framed, we saw on the fourth of July last as it was handed round the platform at the later Jubilee Meeting of the British Temperance League at Exeter Hall. But Joseph Livesey was not merely a Temperance reformer. The Free Trade movement enlisted his sympathies some ten years ere Richard Cobden and John Bright commenced the agitation, when he issued his illustrated weekly paper, *The Struggle*, which did such great service to the cause. In 1844 he established *The Preston Guardian*, the leading organ of Free Trade and Liberalism in the district. The despotic powers of the first Poor Law Board found in him as determined an antagonist as the late John Walter, the father of the present proprietor of *The Times*, and the agitation which subsequently took place led to the relaxation of many of the Board's most stringent "orders." Joseph Livesey was also the promoter of one of the first mechanics' institutions in the country, and every local and philanthropic movement in the district found in him a zealous friend and an energetic pleader. Preston is indebted to him for its drinking fountains, and it was mainly through his efforts that the Preston Banking Company re-opened its doors in 1866 after its temporary stoppage. He has now passed away to his reward.

XXVIII.—The Christian Chronicle, Sept. 11th.

The town of Preston claimed Joseph Livesey as one of its oldest tradesmen, as he had for more than half a century been prominent in every public movement for the benefit of the town, especially those of a benevolent character. But the reputation of Mr. Livesey is by no means local; all over the civilized world his name is honoured and loved as one of the most noble men of his age. He is probably best known as the "Father of Teetotalism," for in that cause his prolific pen was engaged for fifty years. The paragraphs which have appeared in the newspapers, for several days past, announcing his illness prepared his friends for what they must have expected, as his great age precluded any reasonable hope of his ultimate recovery. On Tuesday afternoon, the 2nd inst., he died, and on Friday last he was interred in the cemetery at Preston. Having served his generation, by the will of God, he has been gathered like a shock of corn fully ripe.

> " Now the labourer's task is o'er,
> Now the battle day is past;
> Now upon the farther shore
> Lands the voyager at last.
> Father, in Thy gracious keeping,
> Leave we now Thy servant sleeping."

XXIX.—The Christian Globe, Sept. 11th.

Mr. Livesey was permitted to live to see Temperance become popular. The attitude of the aristocracy when Temperance is the subject of discussion is now neither hostile nor even apathetic—rather may it be described as enthusiastically favourable. Mr. Livesey lived to read of, if not to take part in, a grand demonstration of aristocrats at Stafford House in favour of the Temperance movement, and that meeting was presided over by the Duke of Sutherland himself. Fifty years ago a nobleman who was an habitual drunkard might, perchance, have been looked upon as a "jolly good fellow": now he would not be tolerated in decent society. Our bishops and other ecclesiastical dignitaries are unwearied in their efforts in the good cause. "The Nation's Curse" has been denounced from the altars of the Church of Rome, and the pulpits of the Churches, Established and Nonconformist, which it is needless here to particularize. Mr. Livesey lived to see all this ere he departed in peace, and he had the glorious satisfaction of knowing that, with God's blessing on his labours, much of this was owing to his indefatigable energy. Truly it may be said that Joseph Livesey has not lived in vain, and his name is written on the hearts of thousands who, humanly speaking, owe to him, and such as him, their salvation from the dread embrace of the deadly demon—*Drink.*

XXX.—*The Sunday at Home (Rev. C. Garrett), Nov. 29th, 1884.*

A remarkable career ended when the late Joseph Livesey of Preston was laid to rest. Popularly known as "the Father of Teetotalism," he had a much wider claim to the respect which followed him. Brought early under religious impressions, his natural kindliness of heart was directed by Christian principle. Doing the duty that was next to him, his native town supplied him with a sphere for rare philanthropy. Those who could not accept all his opinions or approve of all his methods, yet found in them a powerful stimulus and wise suggestion. The life of such a man must be interesting to all who value the welfare and happiness of the community.

XXXI.—*The Christian Million, Sept. 11th.*

It is given but to few men to live to see the fruits of their labours to anything like the extent vouchsafed to the subject of this biographical sketch. Starting work during the darkest hours of the present century, Mr. Livesey lived to see the movement which he set on foot encouraged and aided by some of the greatest leaders of thought in the State, in science, and in literature.

XXXII.—*The Family Churchman, Sept. 10th.*

Ideas are slow of growth. A truth may take centuries to ripen into action: and it is rare that the customs of society are overturned or even rudely shaken in the lifetime of the iconoclast who first attacked them.

In this respect Joseph Livesey's name is almost unique amongst social reformers. When he died last week, full of years and full of honour, he had seen the cause which fifty years ago was unnoticed and unknown—its very name not to be found in the dictionaries—one of the factors of modern civilization, its principles advocated by the foremost thought of the day, and its influence felt in every department of life.

The lessons of such a life as Mr. Livesey's are "writ large" in modern history, and its power will remain with us as an abiding heritage.

XXXIII.—*The Christian Herald, Sept. 10th.*

From the year 1831, until his death, Mr. Livesey was unceasingly prosecuting the great campaign; indeed the whole story of the progress of Temperance in this country is inseparately associated with his name. Conferences and public meetings have again and again been stirred by his enthusiastic and patriotic utterances; and although during the past few years his appearances on the platform have been less frequent, his pen was actively employed to the last in enlightening the people as to the advantage which total abstinence confers.

C.

MR. LIVESEY'S FUNERAL AND THE MEMORIAL MEETING.

Abridged from the Preston Papers, Sept. 6th.

Yesterday afternoon the remains of Mr. Joseph Livesey were reverently committed to the earth, amid an imposing demonstration of popular respect. The desire of the family was that the obsequies should be of the quietest and most private nature possible, but so strong was the wish on the part of the great Temperance organizations throughout the kingdom, that the remains should be followed to the grave by a representative body of the disciples of the revered father of teetotalism, that they consented that the *cortège* should be followed by a procession of all who chose to come forward and show their love for the old leader. The processional arrangements were accordingly made by the Temperance Committee, who provided that Temperance friends should assemble at the Temperance Hall, and that the gentry and others should meet at the Guildhall. The funeral attracted one of the most numerous and representative bodies of Temperance leaders that has ever assembled in Preston, and a large gathering of men of all ranks and conditions from the town and district. There was the most universal expression of regret at the loss of one who led the van of Temperance and social reform over a half a century ago, and who had continued a central figure among the most distinguished Temperance writers and workers almost up to the last. During the afternoon crowds of people commenced assembling in the Market-place, Fishergate, Church Street, Stanley Street, and Newhall Lane, and by three o'clock a throng, estimated at about 10,000 people, lined these thoroughfares, waiting for the funeral procession to pass by. Many shops were closed; in others the shutters were put up, and the blinds were drawn at almost all houses on the route to the cemetery. In other portions of the town numerous places of business were closed during the funeral, and flags floated half-mast from the political clubs and other public buildings.

By half-past two o'clock a number of persons had assembled in front of deceased's residence, 13, Bank Parade. Many of them were of the working class, but the seriousness with which they viewed the conduct of the funeral arrangements served as an index to the feelings of respect they cherished. On all hands was heard testimony to the great good Mr. Livesey had accomplished. At a quarter to three the Rev. Charles Garrett (ex-President of the Wesleyan Conference) arrived at the house, and led the family in devotional exercises. Half an hour later the Rev. J. H. Rawdon, M.A. (Vicar of Preston), joined the bereaved. A few minutes after half-past three the coffin was borne from the house and placed in the hearse, which had arrived a short time previously. The *cortège* then moved on. Seated on the hearse with the driver was Mr. A. Bleasdale, Mr. Livesey's male attendant. Three mourning coaches followed. The first contained Mr. William Livesey, Mr. John Livesey (sons of deceased), the Rev. Charles Garrett, and the Rev. J. H. Rawdon, M.A. In the second were Mr. Howard Livesey, Mr. James Livesey, Mr. Alfred Livesey (sons), and Mr. Robert Lee (son-in-law); and in the third carriage were Mr. John Livesey Lee (grandson), Mr. Charles Greenall (one of deceased's executors), Mr. Edwin Nye (undertaker), and Mr. Thomas Evans. The following private carriages took up positions immediately behind:—Col. Goodair's, H. E. Sowerbutts', Esq., J.P., in which were J. Bowdler, Esq., J.P., and Mr. D. Crossley (Bolton); A. E. Eccles', Esq. (Chorley), containing Mrs. Eccles, as representing the British Women's Temperance Society of that town; Dr. Hammond's; a carriage in which were Messrs. James and William Toulmin; and another containing the Rev. D. F. Chapman, M.A. The procession moved by way of French-wood Street, along Avenham Lane, up Chaddock Street and Guildhall Street, into Fishergate, and thence to the Townhall, where it was joined by the Mayor's carriage (J. Forshaw, Esq.). There were also twelve other private carriages, in which were George Toulmin, Esq., J.P.; T. Whittaker, Esq., J.P. (ex-Mayor of Scarborough); J. Smith, Esq. (Cadley Bank); W. B. Roper, Esq., J.P.; J. Barlow, Esq., J.P.; T. Watson, Esq., J.P. (Rochdale); Mrs. Peake, and other representatives of the British Women's Temperance Association; Mr. John James Smith; representatives of the Independent Order of Rechabites—Councillors Roper and Cunliffe, and Messrs. Hodgson and Sharples, Manchester; Messrs. Thomas Hardy and E. D. King (Manchester); and Professor André.

THE GUILDHALL.

In accordance with arrangements which had of necessity been made hurriedly by the committee of the Preston Temperance Society, gentlemen not officially connected with the Total Abstinence organizations and others to whom it would be more convenient, were invited to meet at the Guildhall, which was placed at their disposal, and afterwards join the procession from the Temperance Hall. Taking advantage of this provision, many visitors from a distance and a number of leading townsmen assembled at the Guildhall about three o'clock. Amongst those who attended were many members of the Total Abstinence organizations, some of them appearing in official capacities. About half-past three the procession from the Temperance Hall arrived in the Market-place, and the gentlemen who had met at the Guildhall joined it.

THE TEMPERANCE HALL.

The Temperance Hall was the rendezvous of the delegates of the Temperance Associations of the kingdom, and of those who had come forward of their own free will to show their respect for one who, by the force of his example and power of his pen, energised the band of Temperance men throughout the country. It was a fitting idea to assemble the adherents of the grand old cause on ground consecrated by the early Reformers. The meeting in the Hall was a large one. In front of the platform was the framed portrait of Joseph Livesey, which is usually hung up on the wall at the back of the platform, and it was surrounded by a beautiful wreath of white flowers. Shortly before three o'clock it was announced that there would be a short service. All being seated,

The Rev. E. Franks gave out three verses of a hymn in which was beautifully paraphrased the passage commencing "The Lord is my Shepherd, I shall not want." This was sung to an old tune, and then the Rev. H. Gilmore read in slow and solemn tones the 103rd Psalm.

The Rev. Charles Williams offered up prayer. In his invocation he said they thanked God that He had led Joseph Livesey to be the first to take the pledge of total abstinence. They were thankful for the long fidelity of their deceased friend, and for the great benefits he had conferred on his fellow-men—for drunkards reclaimed—still more for the millions who had been prevented from going along the road that led to ruin. They, too, magnified His name that He allowed His servant to continue to live until, like a shock of corn fully ripe, he had been gathered into the heavenly garner. They prayed God to continue his succession. Might his mantle fall on every one of them; might they be as determined, faithful, and loyal as he was; and God grant that as he lived to see the day when millions became teetotalers, so many of them might live to see the day when drunkenness should be no more, and when this land of ours should be as sober as it was free. He, too, prayed most earnestly that the death of Joseph Livesey might give a greater impetus to the movement than even his great and noble life did give.

We are unable to give a complete list of the large number of representatives of the various Temperance organizations, and of the numerous friends of the deceased unconnected with them who were present at the funeral. An attempt was made by the reporters of the three Preston papers to obtain the names of the Temperance friends who assembled at the Temperance Hall, and also of the general public who assembled at the Guildhall (the use which had been offered by the Mayor for that purpose). The lists thus obtained were published, but as many joined in the procession to the cemetery, and attended the funeral, who had not assembled at either of the above Halls, the lists of persons published were unavoidably incomplete, therefore we deem it better not to republish them. We are able to supply the names of those officially deputed to represent the following organizations:— British Temperance League, Mr. J. S. Barlow and Mr. David Crossley; National Temperance League, Mr. R. Rae and Dr. Martin; Scottish Temperance League, Mr. W. Johnston and Mr. Jas. Johnston; United Kingdom Alliance, Mr. J. H. Raper and Mr. T. H. Barker; United Kingdom Band of Hope Union, Rev. G. M. Murphy and Mr. F. Smith; Order of Rechabites, Messrs. Roper, Hodgson, Cunliffe, and Sharples. In the large gathering at the grave were representatives of most Temperance organizations in existence in England, and also persons from the following places:—Accrington, Armley, Bamber Bridge, Barton, Barrow, Birkenhead, Birmingham, Birkenshaw, Blackburn, Blackpool, Blundell Sands, Bolton, Bowness, Bradford, Bury, Chorley, Clitheroe, Crewe, Cullompton, Denver, Devon, Dodworth, Earlstown, Fleetwood, Freckleton, Garstang, Glasgow, Halifax, Hapton, Hanley, Helmshore, Hoghton, Hoole, Horwich, Huddersfield, Kendal, Kirkham, Knowle Green, Lancaster, Lambeth, Leeds, Leyland, Liverpool, London, Longton, Longridge, Manchester, Padiham, Peckham, Pendleton, Poulton, Ramsbottom, Rawtenstall, Ribchester, Rochdale, Rotherham, Salford, Scarborough, Sheffield, Stockport, Southport, Tring, York, Warrington, Wigan, White Coppice, Withnell, Windermere.

SERVICE AT THE CEMETERY.—ADDRESSES AT THE GRAVE SIDE.

The funeral *cortège* passed into Fishergate shortly before four o'clock, and as it reached the Guildhall the amalgamated procession, which now comprised about four hundred gentlemen, took up a position in the rear of the carriages. The hearse was exceedingly plain, and quite devoid of plumes, or any of the trappings of woe. This class of hearse was provided in accordance with the wishes of deceased, who disliked ostentation in all its forms. As the procession passed through the streets, heads were reverently uncovered, and it was indeed felt that the country had lost one of her best sons. The cemetery was reached at about half-past four. Here a very large body of people had assembled, but Mr. Thorpe, the sexton of the Nonconformist ground (assisted by police, under Inspector Dawson) had made the most perfect arrangements, and Alderman Satterthwaite, J.P. (the chairman of the Burial Board) and Alderman Hallmark were present to render all the assistance in their power. It had been decided that the service should be conducted over the vault of the Livesey family, and a table, on which was a Bible and the Prayer-Book, was placed in the centre of the slab. The *cortège* having arrived at the cemetery, the coffin was taken from the hearse, covered with wreaths, and carried on the bier to the mouth of the vault, into which it was at once lowered. The vault contains: Jane Livesey, his wife, died at Bowness-on-Windermere, and interred June 22nd, 1869, aged 73 years; and Franklin Edwin Livesey, their son, died at Bank Parade, and interred January 18th, 1871, aged 35 years. The relatives of the deceased and immediate friends surrounded the vault, and for some distance around there was a dense and respectful throng. The sun shone in an unclouded sky, and the scene was indeed solemnly imposing. The body was inclosed in one of Smith's patent sanitary metallic coffins. The coffin was covered with black cloth and black mounting. A brass shield on the lid had the following inscription—" Joseph Livesey, died Sept. 2nd, 1884, aged 90 years." Wreaths were sent by the following friends:—Mrs. Robert Lee, Didsbury (only daughter of deceased), Messrs. Jas. and Alfred Livesey, Mrs. Reveley (granddaughter of deceased), Miss Myres (Bank Parade), Mr. J. Hargreaves (Liverpool) Mrs. Irvin (Longridge), Mrs. Brayshaw (Giggleswick), the Preston Temperance Society, Mr. Bleasdale and family, Mr. J. Wrigley and family (Holbeck, Windermere), the British Women's Temperance Association, and from other friends who failed to furnish their names.

The Rev. CHARLES GARRETT, ex-president of the Wesleyan Conference, read the chapel portion of the beautiful service of the Wesleyan body, and the chapters full of hope and comfort for the bereaved. He then offered up the following prayer: We are around the grave in which are deposited the mortal remains of one whom some of us have known long and well. We bless Thee for that life which Thou didst give. We bless Thee for the long years that Thou didst spare him to labour for the good of humanity, and, therefore, Thy glory; and we thank Thee to-day for the hope we have that, a long life of toil being ended, he has heard from Thy lips the words, 'Well done, good and faithful servant: thou hast been faithful over a few things, I will make thee ruler over many things.' We pray Thee to grant that we may learn the lesson which the solemnities of this day are designed to teach. May we endeavour to live for the good of others, seeking in all things to perfect Thy glory, tread in the steps of the Divine Master, catch His spirit, fight the good fight of faith, and at last may we have an abundant entrance into the eternal home. Let Thy blessing abundantly rest on the bereaved family. They have had the holy and the blessed influence of the stimulating life of our dear friend for a long period. Give them grace that they may catch their father's spirit, and that they may live to carry on their father's work. O Lord, we pray Thee, let Thy blessing rest on the Temperance movement. Grant, we beseech Thee, that the work begun under the teaching and the guidance of our departed friend may be abundantly prospered by the interference of Thy Almighty hand. Thou dost bury Thy workmen, but Thou dost carry on the work. So let it be with us. May the day soon come when the dark and sorrowful homes of our land shall be filled with the light of Temperance, purity, and true religion. May the day soon come when every slave of intemperance shall be free, and when this land, lifted up under Thy smile, shall teach the glad tidings of salvation to a perishing world.

Mr. JAMES BARLOW, the President of the British Temperance League, stepped to the front of the vault, and observed that it was a very sad occasion which had brought them together that afternoon. They were assembled to pay their last token of respect to that prince who had fallen, and whose remains were now laid to rest. Although they were interring his body his work would and must go on. He thought that they had all a great deal to learn when they considered the example that they had had now for more than fifty years in connection with the great Temperance movement. When they viewed that noble spirit of self-sacrifice ever manifested by Joseph Livesey, they might well say that he set a true and excellent example to each one of them. He did indeed echo the wish so beautifully expressed in the prayer of the Rev. Mr. Williams that afternoon, that in the death of Mr. Livesey more good might be done than in his long and active life. He trusted that all engaged in this work would be inspired by his noble example. They all knew that Mr. Livesey had a single eye; they never doubted anything he said. His whole frame was full of light and love, and he ever strove to benefit the great masses of his fellow-men, especially the poor. When they contemplated Mr. Livesey's life—how he was left when young an orphan and poor, how he had worked himself up, and what a part he had taken in the great work of Reform—he thought they would admit that the working-men could not have a more healthful example to follow. He trusted that they would have a worthy record of a life so noble, that it would be circulated from one end of the country to the other, and that it would be the means of influencing many future generations for good. He represented the British Temperance League that day, and he could tell them that from the time of that League being organized to its recent Jubilee in this town, Mr. Livesey was closely identified with them, and was always ready, not only with his pecuniary help, but with his counsel and devotion, so as to help forward one of the greatest movements of the day. It was a privilege for him to be associated with Mr. Livesey and to listen to his wise advice, and he believed that the result of his death would be to hasten the accomplishment of that work which he in the course of a long life ever had in view.

The Rev. G. M. MURPHY, of London, representative of the United Kingdom Band of Hope Union, said the service in which they were that afternoon engaged would, he doubted not, vibrate through a very large portion of the great heart of England; and not only that, but over the transatlantic dominions, over Canada, over Australia, and over other parts of the civilized world. In those far distant lands, as well as at home, the service in which they were engaged would call forth something like a sigh because of the departure of one so true, and noble, and useful; and also it would call forth feelings of thankfulness that God had spared for so long one who had done so much for the true moral well-being of his country. Mr. Barlow had told them truly that he represented one of the oldest Temperance organizations in the country. Now, he had been chosen to speak on behalf of the youngest of the organizations, and for it he could truly say that they felt Mr. Livesey's name would be revered, honoured, and beloved for ages yet to come, and the people would praise his memory and bless the cause that he was privileged to initiate. On behalf of the five or six million children of the kingdom, and of the million and a half who belonged to the Bands of Hope of this country, he could say that they revered Mr. Livesey as one of the great philanthropists of the century. They would grow up to know him and his work better, and to thank God that such a man as Joseph Livesey lived. A little while ago he stood by the grave-side of Richard Cobden, who gathered his first inspiration for good on the neighbouring hills at Sabden. It was said that Cobden gave the people bread, Joseph Livesey, by his lifelong action and constant and loving conduct, through the agency of the Temperance Reformation, had given to the people not only bread but clothing and housing, and thank God he had given many that bread which had led (through the mercy of the Redeemer) to that glory which he himself now realized. And as they had already prayed God for the family of their friend, he prayed that they would, after that afternoon's service, render to the cause to which they all owed so much an even greater measure of work. They were laying to rest one of the truest, bravest, noblest, and worthiest of men, and let them be baptized by his example, so that the cause they loved might be better served than it ever had been before ; and then as their noble friend and his co-workers looked over the battlements of heaven and saw their work they would have more of heaven's joy when they beheld the cause they loved so much and served so well and so truly, furthered by their increased action ; because he being dead yet spoke and lived through their action, and the cause of Christ, of truth, and of temperance was furthered by their more than self-denying energy. The millions of children in the kingdom would ever love and cherish the memory of him whom they had that afternoon laid to rest. He prayed that those who were left behind might serve as he served, truly and loyally to the end, so that they might have said to them :—

" Servant of God, well done ;
Rest from thy loved employ ;
The battle's fought, the victory's won :
Enter thy Master's joy."

(Cries of "Amen.")

Mr. J. H. Raper who represented the United Kingdom Alliance, said that he was privileged to say a few words to them. He fully recognised his connection with all the great organizations at work to carry on the great Temperance movement which was commenced by their dear friend. His sympathies and activities covered the whole of these movements, and he was there, with many hundreds around him, ready to acknowledge their indebtedness to the labours of their dear friend. He was one of those who were caught in the first five years of the movement by the striking activity of the Preston men, and he saw before him one of that band of early pioneers,—Mr. Edward Grubb—whose voice he should like to hear that afternoon. Those early men went through the country energised by the activities of their dear father, whose frame lay beneath them there. Many of them in those early days received the great truths of the Temperance Reformation, and their whole lives had been tinctured by the teaching of him who was now no more. He was there, just in a single sentence, to express, on behalf of millions of his fellow-countrymen and of the Anglo-Saxon race, their indebtedness to the band of noble men whose chief they that day committed to his tomb. He felt that the great duty of each one present was to consecrate himself, around the tomb of Joseph Livesey, to carry on his great work. Though much had been already accomplished, a great deal yet remained to be done, for they knew how many millions of homes were suffering in consequence of the drinking system which Mr. Livesey tried to uproot. It was for them that day to resolve by God's help that they would carry on the work that Joseph Livesey commenced. He pledged himself before heaven and before his fellow-men to do it, and he asked them to join with him in that fitting consecration. (Amen.) As he approached that grave one poor little ragged boy stood aside to let him pass, but he trusted that some of those young people before him would live to see a sober and happy country—a consummation which Joseph Livesey lived for, and for which he worked through a long and glorious life.

Mr. Thomas Whittaker, of Scarborough (as one of the oldest colleagues of Mr. Livesey in his great work) said : A man who lives well never dies. " I am," said Christ, " the resurrection and the Life, and whosoever believeth in Me, if he were dead yet he liveth." If men reaped as they sowed, then there was a grand harvest for the tenant who recently occupied the fabric then at their feet. They put his remains low in the grave, but 10,000 men that day with their faces lifted up to heaven thanked God that ever Joseph Livesey lived. (Amen.) He rested from his labours, and his works followed him. He spent his life—and the speaker had known him for fifty years—as the friend of the poor—the advocate of the oppressed, the sympathiser with the widow, and a father to the fatherless. "The poor ye have always with you," and Joseph Livesey lived among the poor, never forgot the poor, and the poor that day in thousands had watched his remains carried to the grave, and felt moved to bless his name and cherish his memory. On the plate on that coffin was recorded, "Joseph Livesey, died Sept. 2nd, 1884." On Sept. 1st, 1832, Joseph Livesey wrote out and signed the first total abstinence pledge in the world. So long as the God of truth lived—and He was from the beginning, and to His existence there was no limit—so long would truth be recognised in the pledge written out by the hand that was now cold and stiff in death, and which had been life and blessing and salvation to thousands of men. The inhabitant of those bones, and the breath that moved in that body, spoke to him (Mr. Whittaker) in Blackburn. He was living in a hole, buried while he lived, and in Joseph Livesey's voice Providence said, "Whittaker, come forth." And public opinion said, "Loose him and let him go," and Joseph Livesey said, "Thomas, go out as a missionary." He was Joseph Livesey's child. Joseph Livesey sent him out into the world to preach liberty to the captive, and the opening of the prison-doors to them that were in bonds, and for fifty years, thank God, he had been able to testify to the benefits of total abstinence. He had no sorrow, no darkness, no cloud, in the death of Joseph Livesey. If men reaped what they sowed; if men were in the future what they are here; if there be a just and an eternal and a merciful God—and there was; if there be a Heaven to gain and blessings to enjoy: if Joseph Livesey did not have it, no man who ever lived would have it—never! There was no doubt, no fear. Tell him the man Joseph Livesey ever hurt, the spirit he ever wounded, the smitten and oppressed child he ever passed by without sympathy and help! God bless his memory, and God preserve the work he did, and help those who were his disciples, and who had been co-workers with him for years, to be faithful until death, and then they would have a crown of eternal life. It was a grand thing to live. He believed in living. He believed in a man who once lived, and lived well, never dying. It was only passing away,—going to another country. "Our fathers, where are they; and the prophets, do they live for ever?" "It is appointed unto man once to die, and after death the judgment." They had life now; let it be a glorious life, a useful life, and a blessed life; and then like him they would go to their fathers and have the same reward and the same blessing. Ninety years! With long life they would honour him! No man could have fallen in Preston amid such loving esteem and such affectionate memory as did Joseph Livesey. Not only in this town, but in the whole country, in the whole of Europe, his name was a household word. Might they cherish and revere that name, and in the name of Christ carry on that great work to which he had set his hand for above fifty years.

Mr. Edward Grubb, the only surviving member of the original Preston workers, said he had been a witness that day of the manifestation of good feeling to a distinguished fellow-citizen, who had grown up amongst them and laboured for them through a long life; one who had not only shown himself good in public, but also in private life, and proved that he had been an Englishman of whom they might all well be proud. He was an example to moral and political reformers of sound views, of correct taste, of a genuine faith in principles. Those who talked about temperance to-day and honoured it, knew but little of that temperance which was originally inaugurated and secured in this country by the genius and ability of Mr. Livesey. As a spectator that day, his (the speaker's) heart had been greatly moved to see that the friend he had loved so much through life, whose instructions he enjoyed so much in youth, and with whose family he associated some of the sweetest pleasures of his existence, had passed away. When he thought that that voice would instruct them no more; its soothing tones allay the irritation of disquietude no more for them, he felt there was something taken from this world that left it a blank to him. In that grave they saw the first of that gallant body of men who heralded in the greatest movement of modern times. Mr. Livesey had not been merely the instructor of the poor, and the sympathiser with the widow, but the great Temperance Reform in Preston, in England, or in the world, was blessed by the fact that it had been associated with the name of Joseph Livesey. It was not alone for the ability and genius of Mr. Livesey shown in the cause of Temperance only, that he would be remembered. It was through the universality of his knowledge, of his benevolence; the broadness of his patriotism, that grand and expansive interest in humanity which recognised a brother in distant climes—it was through that that he knocked off the shackles from the slave, that he took away imposts on their food, that he opened their ports to free trade, and became an instructor to the statesmen and politicians of his day. He (the speaker) had known Mr. Livesey from that tender period of youth when instruction came to them in the best form. He had not only enjoyed Mr. Livesey's instruction through the Society for the Diffusion of Useful Knowledge; not only had it in the public expositions, in the services he had rendered in the old Cock-pit, but had it also in his family and among the friends of those who in early life heard him unfold the mysteries and wonders of the Word of God as no man had ever done before. When he looked back for the past fifty years and now saw his dear instructor lying there, it raised feelings of tenderness and love in his heart. Although he loved those who had been his contemporaries in the work of Temperance, and he had admired the zeal and ability with which they had prosecuted that Temperance cause, yet such was the love and admiration he had for that great man who was before them in the grave, and for those dear spirits who had gone before them and left him (the speaker) almost a solitary spectator of that day's proceedings, that he felt a heaviness of heart and a soreness of spirit that made him say he would almost rather be with those who had gone before than with those who were left behind. He could only say that much as they knew Joseph Livesey, they knew him only very imperfectly. They should bear in mind that they were on the spot where existed the man who laid bare for the first time in the history of the world the mysteries and horrors of alcohol, and gave forth a new philosophy, and started a new way of thinking, that had animated Preston, and, through Preston, had put life into the whole world. Mr. Livesey's young disciples had this singular merit—that among them was established the first original Temperance Society in England, Ireland, Scotland, and Wales; and its principles propagated by the Preston men at their own expense. And the man who was their teacher and leader lay in the grave before them. They therefore tendered to Almighty God not only their great thankfulness for every good and perfect gift He had vouchsafed to them, but also for giving them such a friend and counsellor as Joseph Livesey. Mr. Raper had consecrated himself anew to the work of Temperance, so he (the speaker) would consecrate himself at that graveside, that while he lived he would carry on the work of Mr. Livesey. He would carry on the old work in the old way—in the old spirit, and with the old disinterestedness, and with the old dignity, and, if needs be, with the old fire that animated Mr. Livesey and the early men. He pledged himself that, God helping him, he would never let that good work die as long as he lived. In conclusion, he tendered his love and sympathy to the members of Mr. Livesey's family in the great loss they had sustained. He entered most acutely into the private feelings of their dear friends. There was one there who had been to him as a brother, and who he knew would accept from him this declaration in the presence of his dead father, that neither that father's genius, nor his talents, nor his character, nor his services would go neglected or unrecorded.

The Rev. CHARLES GARRETT then read the grave-side portion of the burial service, concluding with the Benediction.

. A large number of persons then advanced and took a last look at the coffin. The wreaths which had been brought from the house were placed on the overlying slab of the vault. A few more wreaths and bouquets of flowers were reverently placed on the coffin by those who lingered around the tomb. One wreath was so placed by Mr. Perry for Mr. J. E. Lightfoot, J.P., of Accrington, and others were placed on the coffin on behalf of the Accrington branch of the British Women's Temperance Association, and the United Kingdom Band of Hope Union. The *cortège* afterwards returned to the residence of the deceased.

MEMORIAL MEETING AT THE TEMPERANCE HALL.

In the evening of September 5th a memorial meeting was held, at which there was a large attendance, when earnest addresses were delivered, the speakers giving their experiences of the benefits arising from the practice of total abstinence principles. Mr. T. Walmsley presided, and he was surrounded by the Rev. C. H. Murray, Councillor J. Toulmin, Mrs. Eccles, Messrs. A. E. Eccles, E. Edelston, J. Duthie, T. Scholfield, J. Shaw, S. Swindlehurst, S. Hoyland, J. H. Raper, T. Whittaker, E. Grubb, J. Garnett, J. Smith, Eddy, W. Gregson, R. Bannister, J. Buck, and T. Watson.

The CHAIRMAN, in commencing the proceedings, alluded to Mr. Livesey always being favourable to the old Cock-pit, because it was a building of a circular character, where there was no platform or aristocracy. He liked the plan of speaking as they were moved, and he always encouraged persons to deliver addresses. He thought that evening it would be advantageous if the proceedings took the shape of an experience meeting, for there were many friends who would like the opportunity of stringing a few sentences together, so that they could say they spoke at the funeral of the late Joseph Livesey. He would therefore ask the speakers not to take up more than five minutes each.

Mr. WATSON, Rochdale, said that on January 24th last, 50 years ago, Joseph Livesey, Thomas Swindlehurst, James Teare, and H. Anderton came to Galgate, his native village. He was sitting at home making ready to go to rest, when he heard a bell ringing. On looking out of the door he heard the announcement that there was to be a meeting in the village chapel. He went and heard a variety of speeches, some of which he remembered that day. At the close of the meeting it was announced that those who desired could sign the pledge, a pledge much different from that of to-day, inasmuch as it was only for a month, two months, or at the longest twelve months, and this because doctors had not stated that boys could grow to be men without beer. He took the pledge, and had since treasured it. He also took another pledge—he gave his heart to God. These two pledges had been his safeguard through life. He attributed what he was, the position he held, and the good he could do, to them. He held Joseph Livesey's memory with sacred trust. He looked upon him as his father in the temperance cause.

Mr. BARLOW, Bolton, stated that 49 years ago he attended a temperance meeting and signed the pledge. He thanked God that he took that step, and he could say that when he looked back upon those 49 years, he thanked God and took courage in the prosecution of their glorious work. There had been a great improvement during that period in the country at large, for at that time it was the exception for Christians, and especially ministers, to identify themselves in the temperance cause, whereas now the Christian Church and the clergy were to a very large extent on their side. This gave him very great encouragement. Their Christian brethren must engage in the cause, for any one who visited the slums, and saw the effects of intoxicating drinks, must make an effort to rescue the people from that which was their ruin. He did not think they were met in sorrow. God had preserved Mr. Livesey all these years, and he had gone to his grave with honour. Let them consecrate themselves afresh to their noble work, and do their utmost to vanquish from the land the enemy of all that was good, so that they might have a happy, contented, Christian people.

Mr. CARTER, Liverpool, said that he was a proof that men could grow old without using intoxicating drinks. He had to thank God for the benefits that had come to him through the instrumentality of Mr. Livesey, by whom he was induced to sign the pledge. He had signed it, and for fear of ever forgetting it he had had it engraved on his walking stick which he carried with him. At the request of a gentleman on the platform the speaker read the inscription, namely, "John Carter, teetotaller from intoxicating drinks, 1835." He had kept it for 49 years, and if he lived until next month he would be 75 years of age. Having referred to his work on behalf of temperance, he said they had no cause to hang their heads with reference to the death of their departed friend. They had reason to thank God that he had spared him so long to establish and diffuse temperance principles in the land that gave him birth and throughout the world.

Mr. WATSON, Halifax, said he thought it was in 1828 or 1829 that he signed the moderation pledge. Their efforts with this pledge proved of little avail, for men kept falling again into drunken habits. This condition of things was changed by the seven men of Preston who introduced the total abstinence pledge. He had been a teetotaller for 45 years. He wished them to learn the lesson that the cause in Preston commenced with seven men, and that number had increased to such an extent that to-day there were 5,000,000 total abstainers. If they to-day should prosper in the same proportion, they would have a teetotal nation by the end of the century. He asked them to think about this, act upon it, and they might rest assured that God would bless them.

Mrs. CAROLINE JOHN, Bolton, referred to the encouragement and kindness she had always received at the hands of Mr. Joseph Livesey, whose name she loved and honoured. She had heard his name and read his leaflets and writings many years before she had an opportunity of seeing him, but when she came to Preston for the first time and went to see him, she would never forget what a loving shake of the hand he gave her, and the kind remarks he made. He presented her with two books which she prized very much indeed, and she had also received letters from him encouraging her in the work she had been engaged in for so many years.

Mr. A. E. ECCLES, White Coppice, spoke of the encouragements he had received from him whose body they had that day interred, and mentioned that in 1856 he sent workers from Preston to where he resided. Since then they had kept the ball rolling. In three years they drove the liquor trade away, and now they had driven away tobacco. He hoped as temperance men they would now go against everything that intoxicated—opium, tobacco, and alcohol.

Mr. COLLINS, Manchester, spoke of Mr. Livesey's self-denying labours, and of his noble example.

Mr. WILD, Huddersfield, who had known Mr. Livesey for half a century, alluded to the great value of his Malt Liquor Lecture.

Mrs. LEWIS, Blackburn, who was carrying on a successful temperance work in that town, on the lines recommended by Mr. Livesey, especially in visiting the homes of the people, spoke of the great value of Mr. Livesey's writings.

The Rev. C. H. MURRAY at this point announced that letters of apology for inability to attend had been received from a number of gentlemen, including the Rev. Prebendary Cross, vicar of St. Andrew's, Southport, who was prominently associated with the Church of England Temperance Society; Rev. D. Burns, D.D., of London; Rev. S. MacNaughton, Preston; Mr. Hugh Davies, Wrexham; Mr. L. Ianson, Higher Walton; Rev. Father Kirwan, Wigan, formerly of Preston; Dr. Lees, of Leeds; and Sir Edward Baines, of the same town. The letter from Prebendary Cross was as follows :—

" St. Andrew's Vicarage, Southport, Sept. 4th, 1884.

" Dear Mr. Barlow,—I had earnestly hoped to have been present to pay the last tribute of respect to Mr. Livesey, but I find the funeral fixed for a time when I cannot possibly attend. May I ask you to convey to his relatives and friends my deep regret for my unavoidable absence, and at the same time may I give a feeble expression to my great and loyal admiration of the sterling integrity, the unfaltering energy, and the unswerving rectitude of our deceased friend and leader. But whilst we mourn his loss, we cannot call his death untimely, for God permitted him to live to see, from the seed he sowed in faith and prayer and tears, blessed and abundant fruit. The battle of temperance is not yet won; but surely the bright heritage of the memory of Joseph Livesey's labours and success will be no mean encouragement to us, his humble followers, to persevere until, in God's good time, the victory is assured and the land we love rejoices in a peace and prosperity of which it will be found that next to righteousness, temperance is the most potent factor.—Believe me, dear sir, very faithfully, THOS. H. CROSS, Vicar of St. Andrew's, Southport, Prebendary of Cloufert and Hon. Canon of Liverpool Cathedral."

The letter received by Mr. Robert Rae from Sir E. Baines was as follows :—

" St. Ann's Hill, Burley, Leeds, September 4th, 1884.

" My dear Sir,—I have more than half a century cherished a reverence for the character and gratitude for the public services of my lamented friend, Joseph Livesey, at whose funeral there will be so many sincere mourners to-morrow. If it had been in my power, I should have felt it my duty to attend the last rites in honour of the patriarchal leader of the patriotic and philanthropic body, the total abstainers. Such was the force and persuasiveness of his lectures and writings, and still more of his personal example, that we may justly regard him as having done more than any other man of our day to increase the happiness, the virtue, the health, the comfort, and the longevity of his fellow-men. It has pleased Providence to give its attestation to his doctrine by prolonging his years to their tenth decade, on which he entered last March. I remember his kindly calling upon me many years since, when he was crippled with rheumatism, and was setting out for a Continental journey. Whatever medicine or medicinal waters he tried, he never touched alcohol in any of its forms, and to our grateful surprise he returned fresh and strong, so as to be able to work out his ninetieth year. My personal obligations to him were very great. I became one of his disciples when 37 years of age, and I am now 84, having been an abstainer for 47 years; and I am able, with deep gratitude to God and to His human instrument, to tell of a degree of health and activity not often surpassed. But I am not proof against cold, damp, and out-of-doors exposure, and I have found it needful to refrain from attending funerals, which often involve such exposure for a considerable time. I am, therefore, prevented from attending the interment of this public benefactor at Preston. But I cannot refrain from expressing to you, who hath kindly informed me of the day and hour of the funeral, and who attend officially as the secretary of the National Temperance League, my sincere regret at being compelled, as a matter of prudence, to refrain from joining you, and earnest sympathy with Mr. Livesey's family and all his mourning friends on this public bereavement.—I am, dear sir, yours truly, EDWD. BAINES.—Robert Rae, Esq."

Mr. MURRAY also announced that they had received the following telegram from Mr. William Wilkinson, the secretary of the Irish Temperance League, Belfast:—"The Executive Committee of the Irish Temperance League in meeting assembled beg to join with the meeting in Preston in expressing their warm appreciation of the invaluable services of their departed friend Joseph Livesey, who during the past 50 years has done much to further the great temperance reform."

The Rev. SAMUEL KNELL, Birmingham, said he might venture to speak for the Western Temperance League and the Dorset County Temperance Society, but he would venture to say that the far south of England owed the introduction of the temperance movement to the Preston men. On behalf of the south, as an Isle of Wight lad, he ventured to express gratitude to God here in Preston for the work of the early Preston teetotallers. As a temperance worker, he had had occasion more than once to be thankful for Joseph Livesey's New Year's tracts, some thousands of which had been put into his hands in order that he might get a copy into every house. None of them could think how much had been accomplished by Joseph Livesey's writings alone. Let them remember their old friend, and, as they had promised at that grave away in the Cemetery, consecrate themselves anew to this great work.

Mr. KILSHAW (town missionary, Blackburn), who was associated with Mrs. Lewis in her temperance work, alluded to Mr. Livesey's work of personal visitation, and spoke of the great good which had resulted in Blackburn, from following Mr. Livesey's example in that respect.

Mrs. ECCLES (White Coppice, Chorley) spoke in very gratified terms of the encouragement that the late Mr. Livesey had given them in connection with the British Women's Temperance Society. He said to them, " Go on, and work." They intended to work, for a heavy responsibility rested upon them, and it behoved them to see that no time was " lost for the want of a word."

Mr. LINO, of London, having briefly spoken,

Mr. S. SWINDLEHURST, son of Mr. Thomas Swindlehurst, one of the early and zealous advocates of teetotalism, spoke of the doings of the men of Preston at the commencement of the movement. He alluded to the practice of wine drinking by the old Corporation, and narrated how Mr. Livesey and his father, who were members of the reformed Corporation, succeeded in getting a resolution passed by that body for selling all the paraphernalia connected with wine drinking.

Mr. S. HOLLAND, Sheffield, spoke of the great obligation he felt to Mr. Livesey and the Preston men for their early labours, and was followed to the same effect by Mr. WM. ENTWISTLE, of Bolton.

Councillor GREGSON, Blackburn, said he had been very pleased to be present that day, for he was encouraged by the earnestness that he had witnessed. The work of Joseph Livesey was not done yet. Joseph Livesey was a greater power in the country now than he had ever been, for they were all using his implements, and fighting with his weapons. Their path was now comparatively easy, yet they had a good deal to do, but it must be done, the traffic in strong drink must come to an end.

The next speakers were Mr. EDDIE, Manchester; Mr. JONATHAN SMITH, Leeds; and Mr. BENJAMIN WALKER, late of Earlstown.

Mr. J. H. RAPER said they were approaching the number of thirty speakers at that remarkable and memorable meeting. The occasion was, indeed, a very memorable one. It was remarkable that they had no tone of grief about that meeting; although they were met face to face with the fact that the time must come when they must lay down their arms on earth. The secrets of eternity they were not permitted to know, but he greatly indulged the idea of absent in body, present with the Lord; and in that idea he figured great nearness on the part of the departed, and he could almost fancy the spirit of their old friend was amongst them. After alluding to the suggestions by previous speakers as to some kind of memorial to Mr. Livesey, he said that a great feature of Mr. Livesey's (and the Preston men's) work was their opposition to alcohol in any form. What were called temperance men previous to them had gone simply against ardent spirits; but that, as Mr. Livesey showed, was a " great delusion." Now, to-day they were drinking two gallons of alcohol in the form of malt liquor for every gallon in all other forms. Last year they drank 25,000,000 gallons of pure alcohol in the form of spirits and wines, but they consumed above 50,000,000 gallons in malt liquor. Their controversy was with the brewers, and he recommended all local committees of temperance societies to possess themselves of Mr. Livesey's Malt Liquor Lectures and get them distributed from house to house. If they could get 6,000,000 of these distributed during the next twelve months, it would do more good than anything else could do.

Mr. ED. GRUBB at the outset manifested some slight depression, apparently by reason of the circumstances under which they were met, but as he proceeded he became animated with the spirit that characterized him in the early days of the movement, and gave an effective address. He told his audience that if temperance reformers wished to do the work commenced in Preston 50 years ago, they must have a definite and distinct object in view, and a determination to accomplish that end. He referred to the manner in which they now conducted the campaign as compared with the earnestness and devotion exercised by those who, by their individuality, succeeded in doing so much good in the early years of the movement. In conclusion, he urged them to work assiduously so that their cause might prove victorious, and that this country might be richly benefited.

Mr. ROBERT RAE said he thought the suggestion that had fallen from Mr. Raper a very important one. He thought there was a great deal to be said respecting taking a new departure in the temperance movement, and he wished that their friends might be impressed with the Livesey idea of educating the people and impressing them with the fact that there was no nutriment in intoxicants. It was true that many people had wrong opinions respecting strong drink, and until they had these eradicated, and until they became aware of its true nature, they would fail to vanquish the enemy which was injuring this country to such an alarming extent. He hoped that they would endeavour to get at the people by giving them something to read that demonstrated the unsatisfactory nature of alcoholic drinks, by house-to-house visitation, and by coming daily in contact with them, so that they could not plead ignorance on that great subject. If this should be the result, then that meeting would not have been in vain.

Mr. T. WHITTAKER also agreed with Mr. Raper's suggestion. He thought it not only a good one, but a practical one. He did not see how they could better show their respect for their dear departed friend, and how they could do greater good to the nation, than by resolving to recommend the temperance friends in every town and village throughout the kingdom to present to every house a copy of Joseph Livesey's Malt Liquor Lectures. Samson slew more by his death than during his life, and if they could through that pamphlet make known the life and labour of Mr. Livesey, it might be they would pull down the temple of drink.

It was a practical suggestion which was within their power to carry into execution. Proceeding, he argued that he belonged to Preston people, alluded to his experiences in this town, stated that the first letter he ever wrote was to Mr. Livesey, whose school he attended, and informed the audience that he became a temperance advocate through the kindness of him whose body they had just interred. He was not ashamed to be a teetotaler. He was thankful for his lot and condition in life; he esteemed and loved all his fellow-workers, but he could not get from the fact that for the first time he felt without Joseph Livesey. His bodily presence was gone, his benevolent face and kindly heart were gone, his intelligent and sympathetic letters gone—he did well, he did long, but he is gone. It was appointed for man once to die, and after that the judgment. Let them act well their part, for it was there the honour lay.

Mr. Walmsley, in responding to a vote of thanks, referred to the fact that the last time Mr. Livesey spoke in that room it was in connection with the Orphan school—an institution in which he took a deep interest—the outcome being that a gentleman had recently left £100,000 towards the object, and a great orphanage was to be built.—The pronouncing of the Benediction closed the meeting.

D.

PULPIT REFERENCES TO MR. LIVESEY.

(FROM THE PRESTON PAPERS.)

I.—Rev. Canon Rawdon, M.A.

At the Parish Church, Preston, on Sunday evening, September 7th, the preacher was the Vicar, the Rev. Canon Rawdon, M.A. There were appropriate hymns, and the 85th anthem was beautifully sung, " Blessed is the man that hath not walked in the counsel of the ungodly nor stood in the way of sinners, and hath not sat in the seat of the scornful. But his delight is in the law of the Lord," etc. (Sir John Goss). The preacher took his text from part of the 36th verse of the 13th chapter of the Acts of the Apostles, " David, after he had served his own generation by the will of God, fell on sleep." In the course of his sermon, the Rev. Canon said : The grave has just closed over one of the most remarkable men whom this neighbourhood—he might almost say this country—had produced ; one in whom they all felt a kindly interest in his old age, and in whom as their fellow-townsman they had a sort of pride. His name would be for ever connected with the commencement of one of the greatest moral and social reforms which had ever been set on foot in this land, and he was sure it would not be thought unfitting that he should invite their attention to one or two lessons which such a life might teach them. There was always something morally bracing and healthful in the contemplation of the life of one who had been useful and successful in spite of early difficulties. The history of an orphan boy, a handloom weaver—without education and almost without friends—bravely struggling to maintain and educate himself, raising himself eventually by character and perseverance far above his original level ; and then making his influence felt as a public man in various directions, was sufficiently interesting and instructive ; but in this wonderful country of ours such careers were not unfrequently to be met with, and they did not very closely concern them as Christians. But there was something better in that life on which he would rather ask them to dwell—he meant the high and the holy purpose, which, once formed, Mr. Livesey never ceased for a day to prosecute, and by which he was enabled to serve his generation in a most eminent degree at a time when intemperance was an almost universal sin in this country, and when neither the Church, nor any of the sects which had separated from her, were taking any effectual means to stay the evil. This man was led to deal with it by trenchant means, and he conceived the idea of uniting with his fellow men in a definite pledge to abstain wholly from that which was doing so much evil. How intense his conviction was ; how incessant his labours as a moral and social Reformer ; how honest his purpose, they all knew. They could see also how that purpose, that burning desire to benefit his fellow-men, ennobled and lifted his life, and how, side by side with his philanthropic labours, by God's blessing he was able to follow successfully the daily toil by which he earned his bread. And now look over England and see the fruits of that movement which he set on foot, and where will you not find his name known and honoured. He did not claim him as one of themselves. Mr. Livesey was not a Churchman, and few present would probably agree with all that he did and said, but none the less, he thought, were they bound to recognise the great good which, directly and indirectly, he was enabled to effect ; none the less were they bound to recognise the self-denying, laborious life which he lived to serve his generation in the way which he believed to be according to the will of God. And surely the principle which he advocated was in the main Christ's own—"If thy right hand offend thee, cut it off. If thy right eye offend thee, pluck it out." At least, we may all go thus far, and acknowledge that for those who have fallen under the yoke of this sin, no other cure is possible, and that to many the call to deny themselves, for others especially, must be hard and imperative. Yes, it was this principle of self-denial, this doctrine of the cross which they knew gave real faith and perseverance to Livesey's work, and there were two things which particularly distinguished him in connection with it, and which went far to explain the universal respect and regard in which he was held, not only by those who agreed with him, but by those who most widely differed from him. He did his work without provoking enmity. His aim was to persuade, not to coerce, and so he made friends where others with a like zeal, but with less of Christian gentleness, would have made enemies. This was one point. The other was his sympathy for the poor. His hand as well as his heart seemed to have been ever open as he went out amongst them in days gone by. No wonder that when he was carried forth to burial the streets were lined by their eager faces; no wonder that even those with whose occupation his teaching most interfered were not behind in showing their respect for his memory. Such a life as this should surely not have been lived in vain amongst us. Surely they would thankfully lay to heart its lessons, showing them, as they did, how singleness of heart and honesty of purpose to serve God by benefiting mankind could never go unrewarded and unblessed, and how it must win the praise of God and man. Once more. Let the grave which has just closed over one so universally respected, remind them of that end of their life here, which, though from one point of view was a penalty, was from another and a higher a reward. The Scriptures spoke of the rest which remained to all God's servants when the toils of life were over. "They rest from their labours," "They are fallen asleep,"—sweet and holy thoughts, so full of comfort and refreshment! What could they need more? What could be so blessed after the labours and disappointments of this mortal life? David fell asleep with his fathers, his work all done, its imperfections and errors lost in the mercy and loving kindness of his God. So they trusted it was with their departed friend. So they hoped it might be with themselves and all whom they loved. Be it then their aim to consecrate themselves to a life of usefulness and labour, to serve their generation according to the will of God, and then to go calmly and willingly to their rest. God grant that that might be said of each of them. If the soul was resting with Christ in Paradise, it booted not to them that the body was mouldering in the grave. They had the hope that in the last day they would rise entire and incorruptible, and with that hope before them the grave was indeed robbed of its terrors, and became but a temporary resting-place; and though there were some secrets connected with the intermediate state and with the life that stretched endlessly beyond, it mattered not, for faith rested contented on the full and gracious promise. They knew that when He should appear they should be like Him, and they would see Him as He was.

II.—*The Rev. J. P. Shepperd, M.A.*

At St. Thomas's Church, Preston, on Sunday evening, September 7th, at the conclusion of a sermon on the well-known text, "If God be for us, who can be against us?" the Vicar (the Rev. J. P. Shepperd, M.A.)—after explaining that man has only one great enemy, viz. moral evil, and that that enemy appeared in different forms and in divers ways—alluded to intemperance as the most successful confederate of the evil king. Then followed a description of some of the many efforts and organizations to combat this mighty giant, all of which obtained their origin and gathered their power and influence from the bold, self-denying action of one man, Joseph Livesey. Whenever we contemplate the history, or measure the height of a hero, said the preacher, it is only honest to consider the times in which he lived and the circumstances with which he was surrounded. In Mr. Livesey's day, every influence was against him, and hence the unpopularity of his startling proposal. He was indeed the youth who, 'mid the snow and ice of cold opposition, lifted high his banner with the strange device, "Abstain! Abstain!!" and led his friends to follow him far up the heights, from some of the lowest depths of drunkenness; so that now tens of thousands have cause to thank God and bless the name and memory of the man who rescued them. Any man who is the means of lifting the damning pall of intemperance out of the reach of his fellows, of rolling away the stone out of the road, so that those who come after may not stumble over it, and thus brings them into a state of mind and body in which they can appear at the House of God where Jesus of Nazareth passeth by, is doing God's work, and is worthy of the praise and honour of men. This Joseph Livesey has done in thousands of instances, by entering the battle-field single-handed against such fearful odds, and yet gained the victory and helped others to do the same. Do not, Mr. Shepperd continued, let them think that their share of honour was accomplished when they had heard that sermon, or perchance sent a wreath to the funeral. Such a man, after such a work, demanded of them, as Christians, something far more lasting and useful. Might the day shortly come when every member of our Temperance Societies and Bands of Hope will have the opportunity of contributing to some permanent memorial institution for rescuing the intemperate, and also some granite statue in our people's park, in front of the gaol, or in some other prominent part of the town, so that this patriot's name may be duly honoured and handed down to posterity as a household word. They might not agree with Mr. Livesey ecclesiastically, or politically, but as Christian men and women they could afford to sink all such differences and take the man as they found him, and honour him much for his very work's sake. Would that they could have stood at his graveside with their minister, and many of his reverend brethren, and representatives of most of the leading organizations; would that they could have listened to those soul-stirring addresses from Mr. Livesey's friends and coadjutors present,—their resolutions would have given the Amen to those of the speakers, "that though the man has gone, his principles, his work cannot, must not, suffer." Might they, as those men did, consecrate themselves afresh to God, and say from their very souls, "Lord, help us to do more in this cause, for the dear Master's sake."

III.—Rev. W. F. Newton, M.A.

At St. Mark's Church, Preston, the Rev. W. F. Newton discoursed on Sunday morning, September 7th, from Luke x. 33-35, and in urging upon his hearers to cultivate the "Good Samaritan" spirit commended in the Gospel narrative, he made allusion to Mr. Livesey. Here and there were spirits like this good Samaritan, and he believed the venerable Joseph Livesey, whose mortal remains were committed to the dust last Friday, was such a spirit. A noble, unselfish life was his, spent "not to please himself, but for his neighbours' good and edification." He (Mr. Newton) had not the privilege of a personal acquaintance with the deceased Mr. Livesey, who was far advanced in years when he came to Preston, but he had long learned to value very highly the deceased's character and work. "The hoary head," said the Preacher, in Proverbs xvi. 31, "is a crown of glory, if it be found in the way of righteousness." That head now lies in the dust, but his memory lives, will ever live. Joseph Livesey was the Good Samaritan in Preston, and perhaps it should be added, in the world. He took care of the poor, the suffering, the fallen, the perishing, the lost. The drunkard was a man "fallen among the thieves." Our most terrible, cruel, ruthless thieves were the drinking habits of our country. They robbed the poor man of his honest earnings; aye, and the rich of their wealth. They stripped their victims, not merely of the coats on their backs and their homes of all comfort, but their minds of peace, and their character of all that was manly, and noble, and Christian. The man who pitied and raised such a fallen, degraded fellow-man or woman; who gave his money, and time, and life to rescue and save the lost, was worthy of all honour, and his memory was blessed. Such a man was Mr. Joseph Livesey, the father of the temperance movement in Preston and this country. Mr. Livesey, Mr. Newton was informed, used to go out on Sunday mornings into the low haunts and wretched dwellings of drunkards, and with a Christ-like pity laboured to relaim them from their vicious habits, and win them to better ways. It was no light task, no easy mission he had set himself to do, and not enough had been said of the immense difficulties which beset his path in the early days of the temperance reformation. God was their helper in that great philanthropic work, and many were the hearts and homes that had learnt to bless his name and thank God for his life's work. Might God raise up amongst them other Joseph Liveseys! Might the blessed work he began fifty-two years ago be helped on by hearts and tongues like his! The Lord Jesus bade them that morning to "Go and do likewise." Take care of him—the fallen, the degraded, the lost through drink, through sin, by whatever name it is known.

IV.—The Rev. R. Firth, M.A.

On Sunday, September 7th, there were harvest thanksgiving services at Christ Church, Preston, which was effectively decorated with corn, flowers, grapes, and some magnificent plants from the conservatory of Mr. Councillor Harding. Mrs. H. V. Dixon, the Misses Bell, Hulton, Allison, and some other ladies had charge of the decorations. The Vicar, in his morning sermon, said the gift of plenty might be abused by extravagance and luxury, by waste, perversion, or ill-use. Such abuse was too frequent. Its most prominent form was, perhaps, the conversion of immense quantities of grain into stimulants. By such conversion the grain lost many of its most valuable properties, and acquired others of a dangerous and injurious character. It was this abuse of a gift in itself good, that caused the main drawback and misery of our times; a misery which, however great, would have been greater but for the efforts of earnest men to stay or mitigate the evil. It was hard to estimate with any approach to accuracy the good that had been done by teetotalism. It was easy to exaggerate it. Of those who were teetotalers, a large proportion—in his opinion the great majority—would have been, under any circumstances, temperate and moderate. Some because naturally predisposed to moderation; some by reason of their strong moral and religious principles; and some from the lower motives of prudence and economy. But allowing for all these cases, there was a remnant greater or less—not small in the aggregate—to whom teetotalism had been a refuge and stay, and who owed to it life, health, and prosperity. During the past week they had lost from their midst the man who, more than any other man, might claim to be the father of abstinence from strong drink —a man of natural gifts, of much perseverance, of force of character, of sincere philanthropic feeling, and of one idea. That to his eyes total abstinence loomed unduly large was likely enough. Had he had less faith in it, he would not have done so much for it. Born in a humble station, under circumstances little favourable, his name would go down to posterity as the parent and prophet of one of the widest and most vigorous social movements of the nineteenth century; a movement which, beginning in Preston, had spread over the civilised world, and millions were in the ranks of its advocates and disciples, amongst whom were not a few of the best and most generous spirits of our times.

V.—Rev. E. S. Murdoch, M.A.

On Sunday, September 7th, the Rev. E. S. Murdoch, M.A., Vicar of Emmanuel Church, Preston, made appropriate allusion to the late Mr. Livesey. Basing his remarks upon 1 Corinthians xv. 58—"Be ye steadfast, unmovable, always abounding in the works of the Lord"—the rev. gentleman, before concluding his discourse, said Joseph Livesey had been one of the very pioneers of the temperance movement. He was a man who had certainly done a great work in his day and generation for the benefit of the masses, and thrown himself thoroughly into the great and good work of battling with the giant evil of our day—the evil of intemperance. It was a matter of much encouragement to those who had the interests of the people at heart at the present day to know that there were hundreds and thousands of other men who, in their measure and degree, were endeavouring to do all they could not only to stamp out the evil of intemperance, but who were battling with other evils that abounded in our land. Mr. Murdoch observed that if they were to succeed in the great cause of temperance they must have the aid of religion, they must be helped on by the spirit of God. If they persevered in their own efforts, and were aided from power on high, they must succeed.

VI.—The Rev. D. F. Chapman, M.A.

In alluding, on Sunday, September 7th, to the death of Mr. Joseph Livesey, the Rev. D. F. Chapman, M.A., Vicar of St. Peter's, Preston, remarked that as he stood amongst that immense crowd of persons—persons of different ranks in society, of different political and religious opinions—who gathered around the grave on the previous Friday, he could not help asking himself—" What was the secret of the influence Mr. Livesey had in this country and in others ? " He thought it was because he had set before him a high and noble object—the welfare of his fellow-men. He had adopted the doctrines of total abstinence which were at one time regarded as unpopular and visionary, but which had since grown in public favour, until now they were as popular as any movement of the day. Although Joseph Livesey met with a great deal of opposition and innumerable difficulties at the outset, he had before he died the satisfaction of seeing the cause he loved triumphant, and thousands of his fellow countrymen advocating the principles which were once so unpopular. It was a gratifying thing to find that many others had been raised up by God to follow in the footsteps of Joseph Livesey, and who still remained to carry on the war against intemperance.

VII.—The Rev. T. Rippon.

At Moor Park Wesleyan Chapel, Preston, on Sunday, September 7th, the Rev. T. Rippon, at the conclusion of his morning's sermon, said that had he been a resident amongst them for some length of time, it would have been his duty to have preached a memorial sermon on a great man who during the past week had fallen— Mr. Joseph Livesey, While he lived he seemed to have been a practical exposition of their text, " Be thou faithful unto death, and I will give thee a crown of life." He (Mr. Rippon) pleaded guilty to hero worship ; he reverenced a true man, whether he was a Cabinet Minister or a costermonger. Character was everything. From his boyhood the name of Joseph Livesey had been a familiar one, and since he entered public life and gave himself to the work of temperance reform, he had used that name as a charm to stir the pulses of his countrymen in favour of those principles he held so dear. Mr. Livesey had gone, and with loving hands he laid a flower upon his grave. Before he came to Preston he anticipated the pleasure and honour of visiting the grand old man, and telling him how much he loved and honoured him, and it seemed sad and strange that the first service he had to conduct as their minister, should be the one in which he had to refer to Mr. Livesey's death and burial. But " we mourn not as do those who have no hope." He lived to a purpose, and God spared him to see, before his dying, the great cause he had in-augurated bear rich and blessed fruit. The pledge drawn up by the seven men of Preston was thought absurd and utopian—it was regarded as the spawn of a sickly sentimentality ; but its promoters held on their way undaunted. Their earnestness in time flashed conviction to the consciences of many, and now prejudice had gone. Abstinence now was popular and honourable, though strong drink had a fixed and firm hold upon the people. But the man who created a conscience on this matter might well be termed a hero, and his memory call forth their homage and respect, for such men lead the vanguard of true progress. For himself he would rather have Joseph Livesey's honours than a Wellington's or a Wolseley's ; there was greater credit due to a man whose victories reddened no rivers, whitened no plains, but who planted his victorious banner where men might rejoice in temperance, in brotherhood, and in God. He appealed to the young men especially, to learn of such a character as Joseph Livesey, and seek as he did to bless and save their country from every evil thing.

VIII.—Rev. W. Edmundson.

The Rev. W. Edmundson, preaching on Sunday evening, September 7th, in Orchard Chapel, Preston, founded his discourse on Acts xiii. 36, " David, after he had served his own generation by the will of God, fell on sleep." He said they had a grand inheritance in the past; poets, philosophers, and preachers made free and effective use of those who had left their footprints on the sands of time. Whilst setting forth the great truths of the Gospel, Paul introduced the historical reference of the text. By telling of the heroic deeds of the past, others might be led to endeavour to tread in their steps and emulate their spirits. David was a true man; though not free from faults and falls, he was a scholar in the school of truth and a soldier on the side of right, therefore after his grave had been covered for many generations, Paul made humble mention of him in his sermon nearly 2,000 years ago. Joseph Livesey was a true man; he was true to his God, true to himself, true to his race, and therefore he had pleasure in giving his life and work a place in his sermon that night. It was the place of every teacher to serve the Creator; He alone was absolute in His being, unlimited in His authority. Now pre-eminently Joseph Livesey was a servant. He delighted in work, he honoured workers. A friend of his one day introduced a stranger, remarking, "he is a total abstainer." In reply, Mr. Livesey said, "I do not want to hear that he is a total abstainer, I want to hear what he is doing." He firmly believed Joseph Livesey fought the fight and ran the race that heaven had set before him. He endeavoured, amid many disadvantages and hardships, to make the most of his life. He did this by much reading and by severe thinking. He recognised God's being, he revered God's word. In his youth he wrote on the fly-leaf of his hymn-book, "Hope is my helmet, faith my shield; Thy Word, my God, the sword I wield." Edward Grubb told them the other day how he used to hear Joseph Livesey in his family, and among his earlier disciples in temperance work, expound the Word of God as no one had ever done before. Joseph Livesey did not serve God according to the ideal of many religionists. He had been called a Christian unattached. Did they regret his separateness from the churches? *Possibly membership of a church would have lessened his influence and hindered his usefulness.* His mission was wider than any church—it embraced all churches and all the race. Did they think that they might do without church life because Joseph Livesey did? When they had a work in hand so vast and noble as the work of Mr. Livesey, perhaps they might. A true man served in his generation; he was not a slave of his generation. An age was often blind to its best interests; an age, like men, was often unwilling to receive the truth it needed. A true man must be prepared, he was prepared, to place himself at issue with the tendencies of his time. In his earlier years of public work, Joseph Livesey was out of harmony with his generation. Public opinion and customs were against him; ministers of churches were against him; doctors and chemists were against him; but like a true man he went on and on until he conquered. A true man in serving his own generation was of service to it.

Joseph Livesey saw the foes of his generation. A few months ago a late Prince of their royal house spoke of drink as the only terrible enemy England had to fear. Joseph Livesey fifty years ago saw that, and he hurled against the drink all the energies of his being and life. He saw how drink was imperilling the prosperity, the lives, and the salvation of men, hence he would not drink it, more out of regard to others than himself. In various ways, his tender sympathies were expressed. He was foremost in providing destitute homes with comfort, in finding entertainments, clubs, cheap trips, and pleasant walks for the people. Now, sympathy was influential. A man of heart was a man of power. Joseph Livesey gained power over men by going among them as a brother. He had been in life's lowest sphere, he had experienced the struggles and hardships of poverty, and he had always the feelings of a poor man. A man who led the thoughts and emotions of a people wielded tremendous influence. Did not Mr. Livesey do this? He did much by his pen and by his speech. It was said that he spent £7,000 of his own resources in spreading temperance literature. The words he uttered were words of truth, the statements he made were statements of fact. As a true man in doing a service to his own generation, he was of service to other generations. David's influence was felt to-day as they sang his psalms; Bunyan was not visibly seen amongst them, but as a living power he was still in the world; and Joseph Livesey had passed away as a bodily presence, but his example, his teaching, and his spirit would abide in that town and country for many years to come. The text contained a description of a true man's death, "He fell on sleep." Death was but an introduction to a higher life and nobler service, and Joseph Livesey would find service in the great eternity into which he had entered, and from the heavenly heights he would look down with gladness as he beheld the universal strength of the principles he taught. Here was a grand possibility, namely, that of living a true life, which meant a godly life, a useful life, a life that made the last enemy into an enriching friend. The possibility was before every one of them. None were too low to rise, as shown by the lives of Livingstone, John Howes, and the poor weaver of Walton-le-Dale, who became the author of total abstinence and one of the greatest philanthropists of his age.—Before the conclusion of the service the choir rendered in an effective manner, "Rest, oh, rest," adapted to Handel's "Dead March," in Saul.

IX.—The Rev. J. C. Kershaw, M.A.

Preaching at Walton-le-dale Church, the Rev. J. C. Kershaw said the death of a man like Mr. Joseph Livesey struck a note which made itself felt wherever his name was known. To Walton people it ought to be of the greatest possible interest. It certainly was the duty of all who had known him in those last days—when his influence was thoroughly won and established—to promote the welfare of his fellow-men, and especially to save them from one of the greatest standing curses of England, the love of strong drink; it was the duty of all who had seen that, not to let the grave close over him and his name pass away without taking home some lessons from his example. One thing which, to his (the preacher's) mind, stood out with most striking clearness about a life like Livesey's was the grand illustration which it afforded of the real power of a man's personal influence, independent of all accidents of wealth or position. No one could have a much more lowly or more humble start in life than Mr. Livesey had, and yet few indeed at the end of life could show stronger marks of his influence which moved not only poor men, but those in wealth and high position. The rev. gentleman then impressed upon his hearers the necessity for using their personal influence one on another, and concluded by saying that many a happy soul would rise up and bless them for the good which their good personal influence had been to them.

X.—The Rev. Thomas Evans.

On Sunday evening, September 7th, the Rev. Thomas Evans gave an address at the Congregational Chapel, Lancaster Road, Preston, on "The life and character of Joseph Livesey." He based his remarks on the words "Well done, good and faithful servant, enter thou into the joy of thy Lord." He said a few months ago Prince Leopold told the people living in that dark spot on the Mersey that strong drink was the only enemy England had to fear. In Joseph Livesey they had a man who faithfully laboured in season and out of season, teaching the people how to conquer their greatest enemy. Last Friday the people of Preston were eye-witnesses of the national esteem in which Mr. Livesey was held, for in the procession which followed his remains were the leaders of many important societies. They had been brought together by force of character, true worth, and to pay homage unto truth, rewarding honesty of action. These men loved to think of Joseph Livesey as one who never failed nor offended. He was one with freedom glowing in his eyes, nobleness of nature in his heart, and independence took a crown and fixed it on his head. So he stood in his integrity, just and firm of purpose; aiding many, fearing none—a spectacle to angels and to men. The leaders of the temperance movement were also privileged to see how the people of Preston loved and respected the one beloved by them. Joseph Livesey was faithful to the cause for 52 years. Many men were good at a short race, but it must be short. In Joseph Livesey they had one faithful unto death. Many people were tolerably faithful to a cause if the cause did not give them much trouble, but there they had one who was faithful in the face of almost incredible opposition. Who were the men of Preston, daring to sign a pledge and dictate to the world? Poor and unlearned. Most bitterly indeed did persecution come from an unexpected quarter. The Church of Christ was far from blameless in its conduct in the past with regard to that important movement. The Church of God in Wales had done ten times, if not fifty times, more during the last fifty years in the temperance cause than had the Church of the Lord in England. The opposition sprang from an idea that temperance was being put in the place of the Gospel. Well, it must be the forerunner in scores of cases, and if they put it as a forerunner they only followed the example of one of the greatest apostles. When the angel knocked off Paul's fetters and threw open the prison doors, and the gaoler was going to put himself to death, thinking the prisoners had escaped, Paul cried out, " Do thyself no harm." Total abstinence in all its work was simply a declaration to the people, " Do yourselves no harm. Do not injure yourselves in this way; do not put yourselves in a position by these alcoholic drinks that you are not fit to listen to the Gospel, and that we cannot reason with you." Locally they ought to be proud as a people that Preston was the birthplace of the founder of one of the finest movements for the benefit of their country that they knew of. But it was a poor compliment to boast of Preston as the birthplace of total abstinence and not be a total abstainer. Look at the change made during the last 52 years.

Look at the medical profession; look at the Church of Christ. See the power that the Church of England was now in the temperance field. He wished she would move to jealousy the Nonconformists. The Church of England had put in the temperance field more of its great men than any other religious body he knew of. Temperance was generally left with Nonconformists to those who were in the ranks; the captains and the generals did not take the active part they might. Of course, he was aware of Mr. Spurgeon and the Rev. C. Garrett, who had done a deal for the cause of temperance. If the signing of the temperance pledge by Livesey 52 years ago had done nothing more than lead the National Church to take the part she now did, it had accomplished a work that would be blessed indeed. Livesey went to London, and a member of Jabez Inwards' family listened to him. Next he went to Manchester, and there met with and impressed the carpenter, John Cassell, afterwards the great London publisher. Cassell afterwards spoke, Charles Garrett listened and was influenced, and who knew the work that that son of the Lord had been able to do? Then there was the question—What moved Livesey? Like the Master, he lived for others. Speaking of the Saviour, Livesey said, " It was the practice of Christ to be amongst the sinners : even the poor, the degraded, they never failed to secure the pity and compassion of the Saviour. Let us keep the example of Christ before us." Was not that practical Christianity? If it was not, where were they to go in search of it? And looking at Livesey's life, he (Mr. Evans) would emphasize the words of Christ, and say, " Which now, thinkest thou, was neighbour unto him that fell among thieves?" " He that showed mercy on him." It was said that Wilberforce went to heaven with the chains of the released slaves hanging about him. But when he (Mr. Evans) thought of the chains Wilberforce knocked off as chains immediately connected with the body, then passed from a work like that to the work of another Wilberforce and a Livesey in our time, striking off fetters not simply binding the body, but the mind and the soul— the whole man—he thought it would be a greater honour to pass into heaven with the chains of rescued drunkards, with the blessings of the widow and the orphan, with the kind expressions of the poor, and with the fact that they had done something, not simply to rescue the bodies of men, but to put them in a better position as men to praise and to bless God.

XI.—*The Rev. W. Dawkins.*

Preaching at the United Methodist Free Church, Moor Lane, Preston, on Sunday night, September 7th, the Rev. W. Dawkins spoke from the words, " The night cometh, when no man can work." Christ, he said, when asked whose fault it was that the man was born blind, instead of directly answering the question, sought to lead his hearers to a higher platform of thinking of such cases. Christ regarded it as an opportunity for service. " Never mind how he became blind; I have the power to help him, and I must help him." That was a principle of action which if adopted would remove the infinite burdens of ignorance, hunger, and misery. It was the principle that created the temperance movement. The early temperance men felt that they must speak, must do something, must go to the world. The day was the opportunity for doing this; night meant that the end of the opportunity was coming. In some countries night came quickly without any twilight; in others there was a long twilight. Joseph Livesey had a long twilight. But he could afford to wait, because he had worked well during the day. The lesson to be drawn from Joseph Livesey's life was that the proper business of life should be done with diligence and despatch, because the day was short and the night was coming. Mr. Dawkins had listened at Mr. Livesey's graveside to the appeal made to consecrate themselves to the work Livesey had in hand, and he now appealed to the young men of his congregation and asked them what they meant to do with respect to the temperance movement, and also with respect to the work for Christ.

XII.—Rev. E. Quine.

At Saul-street Primitive Methodist Chapel, Preston, on Sunday evening, September 7th, the Rev. E. Quine, taking as his text James i. 27, referred to the late Joseph Livesey. He remarked that Joseph Livesey was not a man that confined himself to his own home or to that grade of society to which he belonged, but spent his time amongst the masses, going from street to street, alley to alley, and house to house, doing good. During the days of his vigour and activity there was no man better known in this town than Joseph Livesey. He possessed a large heart, and it was always his intense desire to promote the welfare of the poor, and this was largely prompted by his earlier experiences. In alluding to the earlier portion of Mr. Livesey's life, the preacher showed the disadvantages under which he laboured compared with the advantages of the present day. Joseph Livesey's love for the poor was so strong that the further down a man was socially, morally, and spiritually, the more earnest were his efforts to uplift that man. But his most distinguishing trait was his philanthropic disposition, and it was this that led him to start that movement—the temperance organization—by which he was best known at the present day, and by which his name would be perpetuated as long as we had a country. In conclusion, the preacher expressed a hope that the time was coming when intemperance would be a thing of the past, and that the words spoken at the graveside of Joseph Livesey would have the desired effect— to induce all to take up the work and carry it on.

XIII.—The Rev. H. Gilmore.

At the Fylde-road Primitive Methodist Chapel, Preston, on Sunday, September 7th, the Rev. H. Gilmore preached from Psalm cxxvi. 5 and 6. The text, he said, taught them, first, that everything worth having gave anxiety and labour, and, secondly, that by labour and anxiety men might attain to everything that was worth having. After remarking that labour brought, firstly, success in the temporal pursuits of life, secondly, success in the intellectual pursuits of life, and thirdly, success in the relation to religious matters, he asked them how this was illustrated by the life of the late Joseph Livesey? He lived to a green old age. They all held long life, if usefully employed and health-fully enjoyed, to be a great blessing. Mr. Livesey had this, but not by inheritance. His parents died of consumption whilst he was young. Therefore, if he did not actually inherit the disease he was very susceptible to it, yet he lived to see ninety summers. How did he attain to that? Simply by great labour and the exercise of temperance principles, by the observance of the laws of health, by self-restraint and a careful use of his powers. He gained those blessings because he was willing to pay the price of them. How was Mr. Livesey in relation to his temporal affairs? The preacher did not know that he was a wealthy man, but evidently he was able to live in comfort during the declining years of life and spare something for his humanitarian mission. How did he obtain this? Not by inheritance. It was won by labour and saved by economy, and so in the best and earnest sense personal. The same thing might be said of his culture. He was a man of sound judgment and generally well informed. In some of his published works there was a clearness of reason which showed character and vigour, and if there was no great amount of literary training displayed, it was quite evident that he made a clear, correct, and vigorous use of his mother tongue. Mr. Livesey's usefulness and the power he had exercised for the good of man throughout the world, were next dwelt upon. What he had done, had been done for the love of humanity and at personal loss and sacrifice. Mr. Livesey had attained a prominence, and that was shown by the large gathering at the funeral, and by the fact that scarcely a newspaper in the civilized world had not recognised his position and done honour to his memory. Mr. Livesey had not attained to this height by some extraordinary accident, but by his persistent adherence to righteous principles and pursuit of the good of his fellows.

XIV.—The Rev. Charles Garrett.

On Sunday, September 14th, the Rev. Charles Garrett preached a funeral sermon on Mr. Livesey in Pitt Street Chapel, Liverpool. In his discourse (which has been published *) founded on Matt. xxv. 23 : Mr. Garrett said : Faith without works is dead, and from such faith the living God turns away with abhorrence, and cries, "Little children, let no man deceive you ; he that doeth righteousness is righteous." "He that loveth not his brother whom he hath seen, how can he love God Whom he hath not seen?" "Whoso hath this world's goods, and seeth his brother have need, and shutteth up his compassion from him, how dwelleth the love of God in him?" "Pure religion, and undefiled before God and the Father, is this, To visit the fatherless and widows in their affliction, and to keep himself unspotted from the world." In this way Mr. Livesey's religion was shown, and there is not a word in the recital of the good deeds of the faithful servant contained in the 35th and 36th verses that may not be addressed to him. In his efforts to lift up the fallen, and comfort the sorrowful, he was met at every step by the giant curse of intemperance. The drinking habits of the people frustrated all his attempts to place them in their right position. With his natural practical energy he set to work to find a remedy for the evil. Having found that remedy in total abstinence, he at once gave himself to its advocacy. Like the Apostle Paul, he could say, " This one thing I do ; " and for many years his supreme anxiety was for the spread of the Temperance cause. In this work he was greatly disappointed at the opposition he met with from the Christian Church. Hard and cruel things were said against both him and the movement he had inaugurated. Insult and persecution were employed ; and, irritated by the conduct of those who knew not what they did, Mr. Livesey disassociated himself from the visible church, and remained apart to the end of his life. . . . I have no doubt but that he did that which he thought best, and the wisest of us are not always wise. The Apostle John says, " He that dwelleth in love dwelleth in God, and God in him." And Coleridge says :

> " He prayeth best who loveth best,
> All things both great and small ;
> For the good Lord, that loveth us,
> He made and loveth all."

Judged by this test, Mr. Livesey's religion was of a high type. He loved all God's creatures. Loved flowers, and trees, and mountains and the mighty sea. Loved birds and horses, and all the dumb creatures around him. Especially he loved his fellow-man, and the weaker and poorer and the more degraded, the deeper and the more tender his love. Little children were drawn to him like particles of steel to a magnet, and no matter how poor or ignorant or miserable they were, he ever showed himself their friend, and spared no pains to elevate and bless them. . . . Every now and then some " bitter cry," like a yell of the lost, startles us from our sinful indifference to the post, and we form a Committee or appoint a Commission, or engage a Bible-woman, and then go quietly to sleep again. Convention after convention has been called to discuss the question, " How to reach the masses " ; while the Church could reach them all in a month. *A church of Joseph Liveseys would do it.* . . .

* "The Faithful Servant, and His Reward." London : Eliot Stock. Price Twopence.

Who that was privileged to see that wonderful funeral, when thousands of people, magistrates, ministers of all creeds, politicians of all opinions, the rich and poor, from all parts of the country, gathered in reverent sorrow around his grave, could help feeling that a ruler, a prince, and a great man had fallen? And who can doubt but that this honour went beyond the grave? and that, qualified by long and faithful service here, he has been exalted to engage in higher forms of blessed service in heaven? His reward consisted in his being admitted to his Master's presence. "Enter thou into the joy of thy Lord." That is an honour of which we know but little. It is beyond our comprehension. We cannot imagine what is meant by the joy of the Lord. It is often spoken of. It is the joy that was set before Christ when He undertook the redemption of man. It is a joy peculiarly His own; yet into that joy the faithful servant is admitted! I say we know little of it; but we do know that it is pure, and perfect, and permanent. Into that joy our departed friend has, I doubt not, been admitted. He was naturally reticent about spiritual matters. This reticence grew upon him as life advanced. As the end approached, he fell asleep; and as the death-dew gathered upon his brow, all was calmness and peace. When the end came, the eyes opened for a moment, and the voice whispered, "Glory, glory," and he was not, for God took him. Having served his generation by the will of God, he fell asleep, September 2nd, 1884.

The last point I wish to name is his generosity. I do not mean generosity in the sense of giving, though he was generous there, as was shown in many ways. I mean, however, generosity of spirit. Temperance men, from the outset, have been in danger of erring here. Seeing the path of duty clearly themselves, they became impatient with those who could not see as clearly, or move as fast, and sometimes they spoke more against persons than practices. Let us remember that others think as well as ourselves; and that though we may ascend the papal chair, others will not render to us the homage which we demand. No man is ever won by denunciation, or converted by bitter words. The "truth in love" is ever the most successful mode of propagating it; and as others bore with us, we must learn to bear with others. Mr. Livesey had this attribute in a remarkable degree. Hence all who knew him respected him. Though foremost in political contests, he had till his death the friendship and admiration of his political opponents; while the closed shutters and drawn blinds of the public-houses, as the funeral procession passed through the streets of Preston, showed that the firmest principles might exist in harmony with the most generous spirit. God and truth are with us, and they that are in the right can afford to be generous.

XV.—*The Rev. G. M. Murphy.*

On Sunday, September 7th, the Borough Road (London) Congregational Church was crowded, when Mr. Murphy preached from Eccles. xii. 5, "The almond tree shall flourish." After a description of the solemn and instructive scene at the funeral, he said, the almond tree was a fitting emblem of such a man, and such a life. 1. The almond blooms on a leafless bough; Livesey's pedigree was of the barest. 2. It flourishes before all other trees; so did Livesey, not only foremost in temperance reform, but in many reforms beside. 3. The almond tree was pleasant to look at; Livesey's face was an index of his generous heart, a joy to see. One of the sweetest pleasures of the preacher's life was to have known him, and to have had occasional intercourse with him in the privacy of his beautiful home. 4. Its fruit was much and precious. Livesey's was a fruitful life, ever pregnant with good to his country and the world; it continues, though he has passed away. 5. Flourishing almond trees denote that winter is over and the sweet spring-tide is coming; and surely for him, such a servant of God, loving his fellow-men so well, a pattern of purity of life, when the winter of earth was over, the eternal spring of heaven would be his. 6. The tree was most beautiful when in full bloom. And in this also the blossoming of glory for the father and founder of teetotalism would be seen in the largeness of heaven's reward. A life had passed away devoted to great and good purposes—noble in its utility, worthy of all honour, and of universal imitation.

XVI.—The Rev. C. Williams.

The Rev. Chas. Williams paid a tribute to the memory of Joseph Livesey in Cannon Street Chapel, Accrington, on Sunday evening, September 7th. Selecting as his text the words, " For he shall be great in the sight of the Lord, and shall drink neither wine nor strong drink" (Luke i. 15), the preacher urged that total abstinence had the approbation of the Lord. Could they honestly apply the language of their text to Joseph Livesey? In one particular the text was applicable to his life, at any rate to more than fifty years of his life—" he shall drink neither wine nor strong drink." He thought also the former part of the text was applicable—" he shall be great in the sight of the Lord." Joseph Livesey was a broad-minded as well as a whole-souled man. His very history, apart altogether from religion and temperance, was stimulative as well as interesting. From first to last he proved that he was in every respect in sympathy with mankind. But he desired that evening to draw attention mainly to his religiousness and to his temperance work. Joseph Livesey was a man thoroughly religious. Why, as far as he was concerned, the temperance movement originated in his Christian work. It was because so many of his Sunday scholars were debauched by drink and ruined by intemperance that he took the subject into serious consideration. It was to preserve them and to keep them from wandering along the broad road that Joseph Livesey commenced the temperance crusade. Mr. Williams, after referring to Mr. Livesey's religious work, went on to speak of his temperance work. That was a work which he said did not at first meet with that sympathy from others which it should have met with. Some were puzzled by this; he was not. Joseph Livesey did not believe in what he continually classed as a "hireling ministry," and he very frequently described the popular religion of the day as a mercenary religion. He thought it wrong for ministers to take payment for preaching the everlasting Gospel, and he said so. He always did say what he believed. It was his conviction that if all Christians were true to Jesus there would be no need for paying ministers. Quite right, and he (Mr. Williams) imagined that there was not a minister of the Gospel but would thank God if all Christians were so true to Jesus that there was no longer any need for their services. This peculiarity of Mr. Livesey's belief brought him into collision with clergymen and the Nonconformist ministers. He perhaps misunderstood them; it was certain they misunderstood him, and in consequence there was alienation, and Joseph Livesey did not work in co-operation with the organized churches, and the organized churches would not work in co-operation with him—a most lamentable state of things. He should think a paid minister of the Gospel should have been above taking offence at such sentiments, but should have said, " Say what you may about our receiving payment for preaching in the name of our Divine Master, we will cast our lot in with you and help to do God's will, and to benefit those by whom we are surrounded." But unfortunately they did not say so, and hence to a very large extent the breach between what were called the old teetotalers and the Christian Churches, between men like Joseph Livesey and the clergymen of the Established Church, and the Nonconformist ministers. Mr. Williams then referred to the great progress of the movement, and observed that he was very glad that Joseph Livesey lived to gather in not a little fruit from his labours, and to witness such a conversion of the public mind as to promise future triumph to the great temperance cause which would certainly triumph. And so he paid a tribute to Joseph Livesey. He paid his tribute to him as a man, for he respected his manliness; to him, as a patriot, and never did citizen love country with a purer love than he, or serve it with greater zeal; to him as a reformer, for with injustice and oppression and evil he waged a ceaseless war; to him still more as a temperance reformer, for to him more than to any other they owed the change that had taken place in the drinking customs of the world; but most of all, he paid his tribute to him as a Christian man, for he feared God, he loved the Saviour, and took the Bible for his guide; he was what a devout conscience made him, and he sought to serve the Christ in whom they trusted and whom they preached. Mr. Williams concluded by urging the young men to follow the example of Joseph Livesey

XVII.—The Rev. Richard Nicholls.

On Sunday afternoon, September 7th, the Rev. Richard Nicholls preached to a large congregation at Lower Chapel, Darwen, making special reference to the life and labours of the late Joseph Livesey. The text was taken from Matthew xxv. 40. After giving a brief sketch of the life of Mr. Livesey, the preacher observed : Many lessons may be gathered from his history. 1. We learn what can be accomplished by quiet, but vigorous and sustained determination. Poverty, difficulty, opposition, are the conditions under God by which the characters of men are disciplined, chastened, and purified. Many of the world's greatest teachers, many of the best men that have ever lived, have been trained in a hard school. The sufferings and struggles of his early life fitted Joseph Livesey for his subsequent work. He then learnt the lessons that prepared him for the great mission he afterwards undertook. 2. The true work of life can only be done when there is personal consecration to Christ. The highest and purest motives by which men can be ruled are those that are derived from a consideration of outward relationships. If a man is governed simply by a desire to please himself, his life will be of the most miserable and unworthy kind. The love of Christ constraining the heart is the noblest prompting power. 3. In trying to do men good we must have regard to their present as well as their future interests. This idea was prominent in the life of Joseph Livesey. He knew that poor dwellings and imperfect sanitary arrangements could not but be unfriendly to the true interests of the people. For this reason he was an earnest and sincere social and political reformer. But that which he saw to be the blot upon the fame of England, and which in his judgment was the chief evil in the land, was intemperance. Against this sin he brought all his strength to bear, and his name will be held in lasting memory as the Apostle of Temperance. We may further observe that in his character there were manifested those special features that should not only receive our attention, but should also excite our emulation.

1. His work was intelligently conducted. He knew what he was doing, why he was doing it, and how it should be done. He was not a fanatic. He adduced facts, and then appealed to the reason and judgment of men for their acceptance. A clear proof of this is given in the two celebrated tracts of his—" The Malt Liquor Lecture " and " The Great Delusion." 2. He displayed great decision of character in his work. He was not moved about with every wind of doctrine. He was no relation of Mr. Face-both-ways. He looked straight before him, and his steps moved in a consistent path. 3. He consecrated all his energies to the moral and religious work he had undertaken. Business success, money making, were made subservient to the higher and holier purposes of life. Still his regret was that he had done so little. For at least sixty years he was an earnest worker in the cause of Christ and humanity, sparing no pains, withholding no sacrifices. And now he is gone, it is for us to take up and carry on the work he and others commenced. We are called upon to enter into his labours. In a moment of weariness and depression, through which many a valiant heart has passed, Joseph Livesey once said, " I fear I have laboured in vain, and I shall die a disappointed man." But the star of hope rises above his grave to-day, and shed its kindly light upon his labours in the past and our work in the time to come.

On Sunday evening, by special request, the Rev. R. Nicholls repeated his sermon in the Congregational Chapel, Bolton Road, to a large congregation.

Numerous other sermons were preached on Mr. Livesey,—indeed, the lessons of his life were referred to by preachers throughout the land. Amongst those who gave special prominence to Mr. Livesey's life and labours may be mentioned the Rev. G. W. McCree, of the Borough Road Baptist Chapel, London ; the Rev. S. R. Antliff, of the Congregational Chapel, Cannon Street, Preston ; the Rev. Herbert Harris, of the Baptist Chapel, Fishersgate, Preston; and the Rev. George Goodchild, of the Baptist Chapel, Pole Street, Preston.

E.

OFFICIAL RESOLUTIONS ON MR. LIVESEY.

I.—The British Temperance League.

At the Executive Meeting of the British Temperance League, held Sept. 17th, 1884, it was resolved :—

" That the Executive of the British Temperance League, at its first meeting after the decease of the late Mr. Joseph Livesey, would place on record their deep sympathy with the family of their lamented friend. At the same time, they would rejoice in the great good which he was enabled to accomplish. Moved when young to act wisely in his personal life, he was enabled to exercise a vast influence for good over the minds of his fellow-men. By his firm adhesion to the Temperance pledge, his consistent and persistent advocacy of the truths of the Temperance cause, both by speech and press, his strong faith in the ultimate victory of the movement, and his unwearying encouragement of Temperance workers, he did so much to raise humanity that no one can estimate the value of his life. It is written that a good name is better than great riches, and this Committee would thank God that this inheritance is given first to all the family, and then to all teetotallers."

II.—The National Temperance League.

The Committee of the National Temperance League, at their meeting on Sept. 4th, 1884, passed the following resolution :—

" The Committee of the National Temperance League have received with much grief intimation of the death of their venerable and much respected friend, Joseph. Livesey, who had always taken the most lively interest in the work of this League. The Committee desire to offer their sincere condolences to the family of the deceased in the loss they have sustained. Mr. Livesey was a friend of humanity in its broadest aspect, who, with a deep sense of the importance of the Temperance Reformation, was unwearying in his endeavours to promote the practice of total abstinence from intoxicating drinks. His life, prolonged to an unusual extent, was devoted to the welfare of his fellows; and he must have rejoiced at the wonderful results which have followed upon the enunciation by him and his six coadjutors of the Total Abstinence Pledge in September, 1832."—ROBERT RAE, Secretary.

III.—The Scottish Temperance League.

Extract of minute adopted by the Directors of the Scottish Temperance League, 16th Sept., 1884, *inter-alia*.

" In view of the decease of Mr. Joseph Livesey which took place at Preston, on the 2nd current, in the ninety-first year of his age, the Directors agree to record their sense of the loss which the Temperance movement has sustained in the death of this eminent Temperance patriarch ; their admiration of his intellectual gifts.

his high Christian character, his dauntless courage, his enlightened zeal, his unflagging energy, his liberality, and his unwearied self-denying efforts in promoting the cause for the long period of fifty-two years. Mr. Livesey was one of the earliest and ablest pioneers of the Temperance movement, and from the time that he drew up and urged the total abstinence pledge on the 1st of September, 1832, till the time of his death, his interest in the cause suffered no abatement. During the earlier years of the movement his efforts for its advancement were very numerous and varied, and extended far beyond the town of Preston and its neighbourhood. By the delivery of his famous Malt Liquor Lecture in the principal towns and cities in the kingdom, and its immense circulation in printed form, by the publication of temperance periodicals, pamphlets, tracts, leaflets, and other means, he laid broad and deep the foundations of the movement, and did much to raise it to its present position. Few men have been honoured to take so prominent a part in the Temperance enterprise, and to witness such great results from their efforts, as Mr. Livesey was permitted to do. While mourning the loss of such a friend and co-worker, whose name has been a tower of strength from the birthday of the movement till now, the Directors are grateful to Almighty God for sparing him so long and enabling him to accomplish so great a work in his generation. They sincerely sympathise with the surviving members of his family who worthily follow in the footsteps of their honoured father in the furtherance of the movement of which he was so distinguished a pioneer, and trust that their consolations may abound."— (Signed) JAMES A. JOHNSTON, Chairman, Board of Directors; WM. JOHNSTON, Secretary.

IV.—The Western Temperance League.

At the forty-seventh Annual Conference of the Western Temperance League, held on Sept. 7th, at Salisbury, the following resolution—proposed by Mr. R. P. Edwards, seconded by Mr. W. S. Capper, and supported by Messrs. T. Hudson and John Taylor, and Revs. W. Mottram and J. Compston—was adopted:—

" That this Conference desires to place upon record their devout thankfulness to Almighty God, for the raising up and sustaining to such a ripe old age, the venerable and venerated founder of the Temperance movement, the late Joseph Livesey, of Preston. And while the Temperance and general public have sustained a great loss by his death, and are saddened thereby, they greatly rejoice that a life so unselfish, so noble, and so unique, was spared to witness so rich a harvest as the result of his arduous and untiring labours. That a copy of the above be sent to Mr. Wm. Livesey, as the representative of the family."

V.—The Irish Temperance League.

The following resolution was adopted by the Committee of this League:—

" That the Executive Committee of the Irish Temperance League, in common with all other Temperance bodies, feels deep sympathy, and hereby expresses sincere condolence with the family of the late Joseph Livesey, Esq., of Preston, who has just been called to his rest and reward, at the ripe old age of ninety. The Committee further desire to place on record a profound sense of the incalculable blessings conferred upon his country and his race by Mr. Livesey's arduous, patriotic, Christian labours in the promotion of many social reforms, but particularly of the Teetotal movement, of whose pioneer band in England he was the leading and guiding spirit, and whose advocacy with tongue and pen he perseveringly prosecuted from 1832 till the day of his lamented decease, with a devotion, ability, and success, which have earned the constant admiration and lasting gratitude of the Temperance world."

VI.—The United Kingdom Alliance.

The Annual Report of the United Kingdom Alliance, given in the *Alliance News* of October 25th, makes the following reference to Mr. Livesey's death:—
"During the year another conspicuous figure passed away. There is certainly no name in the Temperance obituary of the year more honoured or more deserving of honour than that of the veteran reformer, Joseph Livesey, who, at a good old age and full of years, a few weeks ago passed to his rest. His life, as a whole, was one of strenuous and most beneficent activity; and it is satisfactory to be able to add that during his declining years he was happy in possessing that which should accompany old age—'honour, love, obedience, troops of friends.' Your Executive have recorded their appreciation of his life and labours in the following resolution, which they passed at their meeting on Wednesday, September 3rd:—

"'That this Executive Council of the United Kingdom Alliance records an expression of its deep sympathy and condolence with the bereaved family of the late Joseph Livesey, Esq., of Preston, who died yesterday at the patriarchal age of ninety-one, and who was beloved and esteemed by all who knew him, for his nobility of character and his patriotic and philanthropic labours in behalf of temperance, education, and moral and social reform, and who was foremost amongst the pioneers and promoters of the great Temperance Reformation, based on the principle of total abstinence, which took its rise at Preston more than half a century ago.'"

VII.—Scottish Permissive Bill and Temperance Association.

"That this Executive, in common with the whole body of Temperance Reformers in the United Kingdom, records its thankful satisfaction at the blameless life, the active career, the philanthropic efforts and noble services to mankind of the late Mr. Joseph Livesey, of Preston; especially for the signal advantages which flowed to the Total Abstinence movement through his untiring and lifelong exertions in its behalf, and offers heartfelt condolence to his family on his bereavements they have sustained."

VIII.—The Independent Order of Rechabites.

The following was received from the headquarters of the above organization, which are at Manchester:—

"The Independent Order of Rechabites, representing a membership of 80,000 adults and juveniles, assure the family of the late Joseph Livesey of their great sympathy in the loss they have sustained by the death of their noble and honouring father. Regarded by all abstainers as the Father of Teetotalism, the death of Joseph Livesey comes as a bereavement to all who have adopted the principles he propounded. The fact that the Rechabite Order had from its commencement his sympathy and support is an incentive to all its members to endeavour to carry to a successful realization the glorious truths he loved so much."

From the Tent held at Preston was received the following:—

"Recognising in the life of the late Joseph Livesey the embodiment of many of the principles of our noble order, and acknowledging the value of so many years earnest work in the cause of Temperance and the general welfare of mankind so cheerfully rendered by him, we hereby record our deep sympathy and express our heartfelt condolence with the family in the bereavement caused, of so distinguished an advocate of all that is good and true."

Resolutions similar to the above were received from Tents in Manchester, Birmingham, Norwich, Exeter, Portsmouth, etc., also one from Australia.

IX.—United Kingdom Band of Hope Union.

"That the Council, delegates, members, and friends of the United Kingdom Band of Hope Union, assembled in Conference at Cardiff, desire to place on record their deep sense of the valuable service, to the cause of Temperance and all healthy and moral social reforms rendered by their recently deceased and sorely lamented coadjutor and venerable patriarch of the movement, Joseph Livesey, and sincerely and earnestly condole with his bereaved family on the great loss they have sustained."

Resolutions were received from the Band of Hope Union at Preston, also from London, Manchester, Bradford, Sheffield, Leigh, Hadfield, Skipton, etc.

X.—Good Templar Organizations.

Altogether above sixty resolutions were received from the Good Templars, some adopted at public and others at lodge meetings.

The first communication was a telegram from Mr. Joseph Malins, R. W. Grand Templar, and dispatched from Jersey on September 3rd; it was as follows: —"Grand Lodge of Channel Island, now assembled, expresses its sorrow at the death of Joseph Livesey, honours his memory, and sympathises with his family." By post the following particulars were conveyed:—"During the Session of the Grand Lodge of the Independent Order of Good Templars, of the Channel Islands, and whilst the Right Worthy Grand Templar, brother Joseph Malins, was in the chair, he, in very sorrowful words and tone, informed the Grand Lodge that he had just received a telegram informing him of the death of Mr. Joseph Livesey, the venerable and much-beloved pioneer of the Total Abstinence movement; it was immediately resolved that we suspend the business of the Grand Lodge, showing thereby our great respect for the departed hero. Upon the resumption of business, the Grand Lodge resolved that we should express to you our sincere and unfeigned regret at the irreparable loss the family has sustained."

The subjoined resolution was adopted at the Session of the Worthy Grand Lodge of the British Isles Independent Order of Good Templars, held in London, September 10th, consisting of Representatives from England, Ireland, and Scotland:—

"At an age which may be regarded as truly patriarchal, it has pleased Almighty God to terminate a life which was not only noble in itself, but also such in good works for the Social, Moral and National happiness and prosperity of his fellowmen; his removal is a national loss, and the world is the poorer for his departure from our midst. The memory of Mr. Livesey will never die, and his disinterested labours will benefit mankind to the latest generation."

A resolution was received from the Executive of the Grand Lodge of Scotland, and the resolutions passed by the various Lodges of Good Templars in England forwarded to the family of Mr. Livesey were very numerous. In a few towns more than one lodge sent communications, and some resolutions also represented districts, as East Riding (Yorkshire), South Durham, Mid-Kent, etc. We cannot, however, make the distinctions we could wish, and must content ourselves with naming the towns from which they were received, which we place in Alphabetical order:—Ardwick, Birmingham, Bedford, Blackburn, Bolton, Bury, Cambridge, Castle Cary, Chelsea, Clayton-le-Moors, Colchester, Crewe, Dalston, Driffield, Glasgow, Glossop, Gravesend, Hampstead, Hartlepool, Hindley, Hull, Hulme, Landport, Leighton Buzzard, Littleborough, Liverpool, London, Maidstone, Manchester, North Shields, Pendleton, Plaistow, Portsmouth, Prestolee, Preston, Ratcliffe, Red Hill, Salford, Shepherd's Bush, Southampton, Stoke Newington, Stone, Turton, Tutbury, Waltham Cross, Walthamstow, Widness.

XI.—Temperance Organizations in London.

Minute unanimously adopted at the Monthly Meeting of the Committee of the London Auxiliary of the United Kingdom Alliance, 15, Great George Street, London, S.W., Sept. 3rd, 1884:—

"That this Committee having heard with deep regret of the decease of the veteran Temperance Reformer, Mr. Joseph Livesey, desires to place on record its sense of the remarkable and invaluable services rendered by him to the Temperance cause, which will ever connect his name with the progress of the Temperance movement in every part of the world; and this Committee would convey to the bereaved family the expression of their heartfelt sympathy in the loss of one so universally esteemed and lamented."

The Committee of the Central Temperance Association, London, with the members and friends, assembled in public service on Sunday evening, Sept. 7th, 1884, in the Central Temperance Hall :—

"Having heard of the death of their much loved friend, Joseph Livesey, desire to express their gratitude to Almighty God for giving them the life and labours of such a man in the great cause of Temperance, by whose life and labours many thousands of homes have been made happy, and vast numbers have accepted the teaching of our Lord Jesus Christ, and through that teaching have found their way to the heavenly home."

The United Order of the Total Abstinence Sons of the Phœnix :—

"The members are not unmindful of the great service the late Joseph Livesey rendered to mankind, not only in battling with our greatest curse—the drink traffic —but in being the pioneer of the great movement which brought cheap bread to the people. We are all proud of him, knowing the courage and perseverance required in one, so many years ago, to fight against our baneful drinking customs. We shall never forget those qualities of courage, virtue, and fortitude combined in his character, and shall ever keep his name in grateful recollection."

XII.—Temperance Societies in the Provinces.

"The Committee of the Preston Temperance Society tender to the bereaved family of the late Joseph Livesey this expression of sympathy and condolence. As one of the founders of this Society and its first and only President, he was actively engaged in its work till advancing years and failing strength compelled him to rest from active labours, but in his retirement he did what he could to promote its objects. Knowing more intimately than others the services he rendered to this and other good causes, while we mourn his loss we would also express our gratitude to Almighty God for what he was enabled to do. We rejoice in the world-wide results of his labours, and pray that his departure from this life may impart a new stimulus to all Temperance Workers and hasten the final triumph of the cause with which he was so intimately associated and which he loved so well."

The MANCHESTER, Salford and District Temperance Union forwarded the following :—

"That the Executive of the Manchester, Salford and district Temperance Union desire to condole with the sorrowing family of the late Mr. Joseph Livesey, a true patriot, whose faithful and continued labours in the Temperance movement and in other great reforms, have made his name loved and revered by the nation and by all English speaking people."

"That this meeting of Temperance Advocates desires to express its sincere sympathy with the bereaved family of the late Joseph Livesey, the distinguished Temperance Pioneer, whose noble services in the Temperance cause and in other great moral movements have blessed humanity and added to the honour of the country and to the glory of God."

We cannot find space for even extracts from the numerous Resolutions sent by various Temperance Organizations in the Provinces; these included what are now known as "the Old Temperance Societies," the Gospel Temperance and Blue Ribbon Army, Gospel Temperance Mission, Gospel Temperance Union, Sons of Temperance, etc. Those from the Good Templars and Bands of Hope we have given above. We select a few extracts to indicate the general tone of the Resolutions.

The KEIGHLEY Society thus speaks of Mr. Livesey :—

"His noble and self-denying labours for the social, political, and spiritual welfare of his countrymen were of the highest and most varied character. . . . Mr. Livesey was eminently a man of action, whose well-balanced mind, sanctified by the grace of God, ever led him to the front (for which he was so well qualified) in all those important movements which during this century have been so full of blessing to our home life, and the happy effects of which will remain to this nation now the 'Labourer has gone to his reward.' 'The memory of the just is blessed.' "

From the Resolution forwarded by the ASHTON-UNDER-LYNE Society we extract as follows :—

"Leaving behind him a life full of fragrant memories and, an example to those around him, of the highest character, ever ready to help those who required assist-ance, full of kindness and teachableness, this made him beloved and esteemed by all who knew him. As a Temperance Reformer he stood out from amongst the rest as an earnest and faithful leader, giving birth to the great cause of Total Abstinence, which has already been a blessing to millions of his fellow-men, his influence and his principles having spread throughout almost all civilized nations."

The HALIFAX Society says in its Resolution that Mr. Livesey "was beloved and esteemed by all who knew him for his nobility of character and his patriotic labours in behalf of Education and Moral and Social Reform."

The ULVERSTON Society records its "deep sense of the very important services which Mr. Joseph Livesey, the veteran Temperance Reformer, rendered—as an Author, a Lecturer, and Philanthropist—to the cause of Total Abstinence and Social Reform."

Amongst other provincial societies which forwarded Resolutions were several from societies around Manchester, from Oldham, Rochdale, Bury, Blackburn, Darwen, Burnley, Sheffield, Sunderland, Wolverhampton, Lincoln, Bath, Cardiff, etc.

XIII.—South Australia.

From Adelaide came the following :—

"We, the Executive of the Grand Lodge of South Australia, under the R. W. G. L. of the World, on behalf of the Order of Good Templars, beg to tender our sympathy and condolence to the family of our late friend and brother, Mr. Joseph Livesey, who, by his Christian and consistent conduct as a thorough-going total abstainer, has during a long life endeared himself to thousands who have not seen him, and yet felt that influence which has been the result of his life-long labours; and although we are over 16,000 miles away, yet his name is widely known amongst us, and we are satisfied that while he has gone to his reward in heaven, it can be justly said of him that 'his works do follow him.'—Signed on behalf of the Order, WILLIAM BONELLA STEPHENS, G.W.C. Templar; W. W. WINWOOD, G.W.S."

XIV.—New South Wales.

The G. W. Secretary of the Grand Lodge of New South Wales of Independent Order of Good Templars, Mr. J. S. B. Price, writes from Sydney, September 18th, stating that he is requested by the Executive of Grand Lodge to forward a letter of condolence to the family of the late Joseph Livesey. Addressing them he says :—

"Let me assure you we all feel deeply the loss of one who has been identified with the cause of Total Abstinence for over half a century, and I can safely say that the name of Joseph Livesey is almost as well known here, at your antipodes, as in Great Britain; and we have here still amongst us a few veterans that worked with him in those old times when teetotallers were despised and often insulted. We feel that we owe a debt of gratitude to Mr. Livesey and his pioneers, to whom be all honour, and we are thankful to know that the present more enlightened state of public opinion is due to their early labours."

XV.—Tasmania.

Mr. W. H. Bowe, Secretary of the Tasmania Temperance Alliance, writing from their office, Macquarie St., Hobart, on September 6th, states that the news of the death of Mr. Livesey having reached Hobart on September 5th, a meeting of the Committee of the Alliance was held the same evening, at which a Resolution of deep sympathy with Mr. Livesey's family was passed. The Resolution says that the Committee "desire to acknowledge the great work which, under God, the late Joseph Livesey was instrumental in initiating more than half a century ago, and which he has so long earnestly and faithfully carried on."

INDEX.

[The old style numerals (123) refer to the FIRST, and the ordinary figures (123) to the SECOND parts of this volume.]

173

NAMES OF AUTHORS AND PERSONS

QUOTED FROM, OR REFERRED TO, IN THIS WORK.

[Persons incidentally mentioned are not all included in this list. The old style numerals refer to the FIRST, and the ordinary figures to the SECOND, parts of this volume.]

Butler & Tanner, The Selwood Printing Works, Frome, and London.

BORN MARCH 5TH 1794.—DIED SEPT 2ND 1884.

LECTURE

ON

MALT LIQUOR.

BY

JOSEPH LIVESEY.

LONDON:

NATIONAL TEMPERANCE LEAGUE PUBLICATION DEPOT,
337, STRAND.

MANCHESTER: JOHN HEYWOOD.

PRESTON: J. LIVESEY.

PRICE ONE PENNY.

*☞ Societies supplied for gratuitous circulation at
very low rates, direct from the Author,
13, Bank Parade, Preston.*

LECTURE.

LADIES AND GENTLEMEN,

My Lecture to-night will consist of a series of arguments and facts explanatory of the nature and properties of Malt Liquor.* On this subject, I regret to say, our countrymen have long laboured under two serious mistakes. They have believed, in the first place, that Malt Liquor was a highly nutritious beverage, and, next, that when pure and unadulterated, it contained no noxious substance calculated to injure the human system. I think I shall be able to convince you that both these opinions are erroneous. The drunkenness of our country, I am persuaded, has been increased by our ignorance of the properties of this liquor, and if I can assist in dispelling this ignorance, so as to serve the cause of temperance, I shall be well rewarded for my labour.

I wish it were in my power to convince the public of the great error they are labouring under as to the usefulness of beer to the labouring class or to any other class. I don't know any article of consumption about which there is a greater delusion than beer, whether it goes by this simple name or assumes the garb of ale, pale ale, porter, stout, or bitter beer; for these are all essentially the same, and are all made, if genuine, from malt and hops. No doubt many drink beer because they have acquired a liking for it; some drink it for fashion's sake; and not a few take their glass of "bitter" in the forenoon, and their glass of ale to dinner or supper because they honestly believe that it gives strength and invigorates the frame. They have heard this so often asserted, and it has been so frequently recommended by the doctor and others, that they have no doubt as to its usefulness. Besides, if you reason with them to the contrary, they tell you they "feel it does them good." They swallow the spirit which the beer contains; it stimulates the nervous system, and they mistake stimulation for strength, taking no account of the depression that follows. You may often convince a man or woman of the impropriety of drinking whiskey in its naked form, but it is not so easy to convince them that it is this same whiskey which they take when they drink their ale or porter, though if the whiskey were taken out (as it is easily done by distillation) they would pronounce all the rest worthless. I am grieved every time I meet a servant girl going to or coming out of a public-house with a pint or quart of ale for dinner. The mistress will drink a full glass, whereas if it were water she would not take more than one-third the quantity, which would be quite sufficient. She thinks it helps to assist her appetite for dinner, eating probably much more than she ought, and far beyond the waste which her body has sustained by work or exercise. And, so far from the beer promoting digestion, as some allege, it stimulates and eventually weakens the nerves of the stomach. Ultimately the constant glass to dinner so weakens the nervous system by unnatural excitement that depression supervenes, followed by a craving for a stimulant between meals. This will have to be allayed by more beer, or probably by a little wine, and after some time by ardent spirit. This is the way by which thousands of females have become tipplers, and while there is a barrel in the cellar or while the beer-jug continues to go for dinner and supper, female intemperance, with all its horrors, is sure to remain. I knew a gentleman whose wife got to drinking to such an excess that she threatened the lives both of himself and the family. He was obliged to appeal to the magistrates for protection, and she was sent to prison for some months. I asked him how she came to take the drink to such an excess. "She started," said he, "with a glass of beer to dinner,

---

* This Lecture was first delivered in 1832, and the present edition was issued many years ago. Though the Malt Tax no longer exists, the same amount is charged upon Beer, and hence the calculations founded upon the cost of malting still remain correct.

and from that she began to take another betwixt meals, and she got on till it became her master completely." I hope that every lady that hears my voice will take timely warning and never allow this deceitful article to enter her dwelling. Not only is the family jug a dangerous article to females, but it is here that children become familiar with the taste of beer and receive their first favourable impressions of its supposed good qualities. "If it is good for mamma, it is good for me," they will reason, and when they are told, as they often are, that it is not suitable for children, this exceptionable article becomes more and more an object of envy, and opportunities are often seized to take a little on the sly. And when delicate daughters cannot eat, mothers naturally think a drop would help them; but though given in kindness it is often followed by mortifying results. Even if the beer had useful properties; if it were as nutritious as milk or as nourishing as bread, still, if we duly considered its dangerous *tendency*, its awful *consequences*, in society at large, we should never allow it to come within our doors. At some boarding-schools beer is always supplied to dinner, and a taste for it once acquired is not easily eradicated; it is much more likely to grow afterwards—especially under the fostering care of indulgent mothers—into a love for wine and ardent spirits. You who are fathers and mothers should see to this when selecting schools for your children. Custom is so powerful in perpetuating pernicious practices that persons fall in with them without counting the consequences. If workmen are engaged at any kind of repairs the lady of the house feels that she must give them "'lowance," and that invariably means a glass or a pint of beer. The delivery of a message or the shaking of carpets is rewarded partly by beer. Cooks have their beer, and washerwomen generally look for it. In engaging servants, especially in London, the question of beer, or "beer money," has always to be settled. With some it would seem to be considered an absolute necessary of life. The cellars of the higher classes without the beer barrel would be considered shabbily incomplete. The servants' hall is entitled to a liberal supply, and their calling friends are made welcome to it. What is there so potent at an election as the beer barrel? In fact, the country is drenched with beer, as you know, and London more especially. The great Franklin silenced the compositors of London both by argument and example as to the non-nutritive qualities of the porter which they never ceased drinking; but London has not grown much wiser since his day.

Before proceeding further, I wish to explain the nature and composition of this favourite English beverage. Born to believe in beer, we fall in with the popular notion that it is a most useful article, notwithstanding the crying evils to which it leads in every district where it is used. A thousand denunciations are uttered against the "beer *house*," but not a word against the *beer* itself, although it is the one article, the *alcohol* it contains, that does all the mischief. This is plain, from the fact that if milk, tea, or coffee were introduced instead of beer, this simple change would put an end to all the special odiousness attaching to beer-houses. The ignorance that exists on this subject is greatly to be regretted, for a very slight investigation of the processes connected with the brewing of beer would convince the shallowest understanding that the opinion that beer is a "highly nutritious beverage" is a great delusion, and that to make it the antithesis of "*spirituous* liquour" is a dangerous error. A fuddling party of beer drinkers would be startled if you said to them, "You are enjoying your whiskey and water," and yet you would be declaring the literal truth.

The encomiums passed upon malt liquors by our public men are quite sufficient to have misled the poorer classes, who are ready enough to embrace any current opinions which chime in with their own indulgences. Gentlemen call beer "one of the necessities of life to the labouring classes," and one, I remember, went so far as to honour this beverage with the title of "liquid bread." "It will supply nourishment to the working-man," says another, "and give his family the glowing bloom of strength." And so valuable is this "national beverage" that a reverend gentleman at Ipswich went beyond his lay brotherhood, not only in stating its nourishing and healing qualities, but in fixing the precise quantity which the labouring-man ought to take. The Rev. William Potter said, "*it was necessary to support his health and strength.* He had been for nearly thirty years incumbent of a Suffolk parish, and in the habit of going among the labourers and administering to them in sickness, and he found that *what they wanted was a little home-brewed beer; it was the best medicine they could have.* The married labourer required his *three* pints of home-brewed beer daily!"

I proceed now to prove to your satisfaction, that malt liquor is *not* a "necessary of life." The fact that millions of individuals do without it, as is easily proved, and far better than with it, comprising not merely young people and non-workers, but men and women of all ages, and engaged in all kinds of labour, the hardest and hottest, and the coldest that it is possible to be employed at, is a pretty strong proof if we had no other. If it were important I might cite the testimony of masons, bricksetters, labourers, furnacemen, moulders, glass-blowers, sawyers, porters, plasterers, haymakers, shearers—in fact, all trades, and of persons both on sea and land, even those who have been exposed in the most northern latitudes to the hardest work and the severest cold. These all work, and do their work better without beer. Ask the hard working-men of Lancashire, and nine out of every ten will tell you they are never so well as when they are without beer, that "those get the best share who get the least," and tens of thousands of these who do the hardest work are healthy, robust men. The fact is, that malt liquor, having so little *feeding* or strengthening material in it, cannot give what it does not contain. You might as well ask the clouds to create sunshine, or the sun to freeze the ponds, as to hope for true muscular strength from beer drinking. But it is so important to disabuse the public mind as to the notion that beer is feeding, that I hasten to explain the processes of brewing, which will at once show that, though it is *intoxicating* it is *not a feeding* article. Good beer, as it is called, is brewed from malt and hops. The hop gives flavour and helps to preserve the liquor, but it contains no feeding properties. The malt, then, is the only substance that can make the liquor feeding. Malt is simply vegetated barley. Barley is food next in nutrition to wheat, and in this enquiry all we have to do is to ascertain *how much* of this feeding substance is found in the beer when men drink it. There are two ways of ascertaining this; the first is by analysing the beer, and the next by tracing the different processes in brewing, and noting the operations of each of these processes, viz., *ma'ting, mashing, fermenting,* and *fining,* as they bear upon the question of food. By either method we shall easily arrive at the truth.

And, first, I take a quart of strong ale, 6d. per quart, and I find it weighs 39ozs. I get a chemist to analyse it, and the following are the components of 100 parts :—

Alcohol	5·000
Extract of Barley	3·885
Acetic Acid	·030
Water	91·085
	100·000

The following presents the component parts of the quart in a more popular form :—

Quart of Ale	39	ounces.
Water	35	do.
Alcohol, or pure Spirit	1¾	do.
Remnants of Barley	2¼	do.
Total	39	do.

I now come to explain, step by step, the different processes in brewing beer, and to show how the barley—the nutritious barley—is *abstracted, wasted*, and *changed, so as to produce as much as possible* of the intoxicating ingredient, alcohol. In making a gallon of the strongest ale (nine gallons to the bushel), 6lbs. of barley are used, which, to commence with, are 6lbs. of good nutritious food, excepting the husk. I will here explain the processes of converting this into ale, and show you how, when the ale is served up, these 6lbs. are reduced to ¾lb., and in very fine ale to not more than eight or nine ounces. The barley has to undergo *four processes* before it becomes beer, in every one of which it loses part of its nutriment.

The first step is *malting*. The barley in the first instance is immersed, in cisterns of water, about two days and nights; it is then spread upon a floor, six or seven inches deep, for eight or nine days, turned over every day (the Sabbath not excepted), and occasionally sprinkled with water. The heat created by this causes the grain to germinate, that is, to produce germs and rootlets. In this state it is placed on a kiln to dry, and then being put through a machine, the sprouts are taken off and sold to farmers as "malt combs." The barley comes to the maltster about fifty-two pounds to the bushel, and returns in the shape of malt, about thirty-eight pounds, so that about one-fourth of the nutriment is lost. When I remind you of analogous cases, you will not question the truth of this. If wheat stands out and sprits in unseasonable weather, it is scarcely fit for domestic purposes; if potatoes or onions sprit in spring, they are neither so heavy nor nutritious as they were in autumn when taken from the ground; and it is just the same with barley. But why *sprit* the barley? It ought to be generally known, that the basis of all spirit is saccharine matter, and the chief reason for malting the barley is to obtain more *sweet matter*, which will yield by fermentation more spirit than unmalted barley would. The more saccharine or sugary matter, therefore, any substance contains, the more spirit can be obtained by fermentation; and that is simply the reason why ale is made from *malt* in preference to *barley*. Very few people have paid attention to what *malting* means. You have heard the lamentations of the nation when we have had unusually wet and warm weather in harvest time, and the wheat has begun to sprit. The year 1817, I remember well, when there was scarcely a sack of sound flour to be got; the people, steeped in poverty, had to bake their flour into cakes, instead of loaves, and the country was on the eve of revolution. Now, *a field of spritting wheat exactly resembles the floor of a malt kiln;* and that which we look upon as a calamity in nature, is regarded by the beer world as exquisite skill! If we heard the voice of rejoicing throughout the Kingdom that all the farmers' wheat was being sprit, and the farmers' servants employed to open out the sheaves every day, Sundays not excepted, to catch the wet, so that no grains might escape spriting, what would Colonel Barttellot and his malt tax repealing friends have to say to such an exhibition? And yet this is exactly what is being carried on throughout the malting season at 6,000 malt houses spread over the country!

The second process in ale making is called *mashing*. If the brewer were anxious to get a *feeding* liquor, he would boil the malt, and preserve the whole of the grain except the husk. He does no such thing. This he knows, would produce a thick nutritious liquor, but a very unsuitable preparation for making it intoxicating. His object is simply to extract from the grain all the sugar that was developed in malting; and to effect that, he throws it into a vessel of hot water, at the temperature of about 170 degrees. It remains in that state for some time, till the sugar is dissolved. He then draws off the liquor with great care, until it ceases to run sweet. He uses the utmost diligence to prevent the other parts of the grain, and especially the starch, from coming off. I scarcely need to tell you, for if you will examine the "grains" for yourselves, you will find that in this process there is also a great loss of nutriment. What goes to the cows and pigs in the shape of grains, is not less than one-third of the whole. You have now a sweet, palatable, and in some degree, feeding liquor. It is also perfectly innoxious; for although I would not answer for its effects upon the bowels, I assure you that whatever quantity you were to drink of the "sweet wort," it would not produce the least symptom of intoxication.

After hop water has been added, and the temperature adjusted, the liquor, by the mixture of yeast, is put to *ferment*. This I call the *third* process, and by far the most important, for it is here all the mischief is done. Up to this point it was really "*malt* liquor," unintoxicating, but by the process of fermentation it becomes *alcoholic*. Carbonic acid gas and alcohol (the intoxicating agent) are here produced. The sugar becomes decomposed, and a recomposition takes place, forming these two. Sugar being nutritious, and spirit not so, the loss of nutriment by this change and by the overflow of barm (which is part of the barley) is about 1lb.; the only gain is the *gas* and the *spirit*, the latter being the same as whiskey, for whiskey is distilled from malt liquor. I would advise you all carefully to study this chemical process of fermentation. This vinous fermentation is the first step in the *decomposing* process of the grain, and if not arrested would lead to the next—the acetous fermentation - making the liquor into vinegar, and then to the putrefactive—presenting the whole as a putrescent mass of rottenness.

The next and final process is the *fining* of the liquor. People don't like *thick* ale, and though they talk a deal about its nutritious properties, they do all they can to get rid of these. The thicker it is, the more nutritious. But modern beer-bibbers must have it *fine, transparent, frisky;* so the brewer puts the liquor to settle, and a quantity of the real food—the barley—is found at the bottom of the barrel, sometimes thrown away, and sometimes disposed of to be used in distilling illicit whiskey. Like myself, I dare say my audience is fond of cream; in milk it rises to the top, but in beer it sinks to the bottom, and so precious is it that you see it flowing down the common sewer. Now, what has become of all the barley? In order to make a gallon of strong ale,

We begin with barley	6lb.

In *malting* we have abstracted as " malt combs"	1½
In *mashing* we have disposed of as "grains"	2
In *fermenting* we have lost in producing alcohol as carbonic acid	1
In *fining* we have rejected as "barrel bottoms"	¾

Total loss	5¼lb.

So that when we come to examine the gallon of beer we find that there is not more than 12oz., often not more than 8 or 9oz., of barley left, and this chiefly gum, the worth of which, when compared with other food, is less than a penny. The "malt combs" are parts of the barley; the "grains" are parts of the barley; and the "carbonic acid gas" and "alcohol" may be said to be parts of the barley, being the production of its sugary matter, changed by fermentation; so that it is easy to see how 6lb. becomes not more than from 8 to 12 ounces. It is the alcohol or *spirit* in the ale— the whiskey in fact—which deceives people, and makes them believe they are getting strength, when they get only stimulation, which is a waste of strength. I maintain, then, that this statement demonstrates that the liquor we are contending about is *not* a "nutritious liquor," or a "necessary of life." The bit of gummy barley, drowned in the bulk, scarcely deserves the name of food. It is less than a pennyworth in a gallon, agreeing with the testimony of Baron Liebig, that "ten pints of ale would not supply as much nourishment as a pound of bread." Many persons speak of beer as the "juice of the malt." Now, it would be far more correct to call it the "juice of the pump, hopped and whiskied." There is one stage in beer-making, and one only, where the liquor—the "sweet wort"—could be called the juice of the malt, and that is at the mash-tub; after this it undergoes the changes I have named, and instead of remaining sweet and innocuous, it becomes alcoholic. When we want to do honour to our "national beverage," we speak of "Sir John Barleycorn." This is libellous. In the farmer's hands he is "barley-corn;" in the maltster's hands a portion of his vital parts are abstracted and after the malt-crusher has broken every bone in his body, the brewer by scalding water and other agencies finishes his career, and turns the poor knight's best blood into poison, casting away his last remains as "barrel bottoms!" Poor Sir John! After al this, we are told he is "the source of England's greatness;" according to one authority, the very "harbinger of civilisation!" The prevailing idea is that the excellence of beer is to be measured by the quantity of malt it contains. People who are dissatisfied are heard to say, " I don't believe there is a particle of malt *in* it." Now, it should be understood that the brewer's aim is not to keep the malt *in*, but after securing the carbonic acid gas and alcohol, as much as possible to get it *out*. People like clear, transparent ale, and the less malt there is in the liquor the more it is relished. But then they say, "It is the *spirit* of the malt." The malt itself has no spirit. We might as well talk of the spirit of wheat in bread, or the spirit of oatmeal in the poor man's porridge. The only spirit is that which I have explained, and which is the product of fermentation—whiskey. I may here state that formerly beer was much sweeter than at present, being made without hops, and when the hop was first introduced it was denounced from the pulpit; the doctors declared the people were going to be poisoned; and Parliament passed an act to interdict its use; but still the hop succeeded. The colouring of beer arises slightly from the hop, but chiefly from the same cause as the colouring of coffee, that is, the charring of the grain, which is effected on the malt-kiln. The malt for " pale ale " is the least charred, for " nut-brown " more so, and for " porter " the most of all, being roasted black.

When these facts cannot be denied, the " abominable adulteration " of the brewer is made the scape-goat. The evils of drunkenness are allowed, but they are attributed to the base practices of adulterating the beer. "Beer brewed from nothing but malt and hops," ignorance says, " will never make people drunk." There is no theme so popular as " bad beer," and the denunciation of the brewers and publicans who supply it. There is no other trade where the article is so generally condemned, and mostly by the beer drinkers themselves. I could fill a volume with quotations of this kind, beginning with the daily and weekly papers, followed by *Punch*, and backed by the speeches in Parliament and at the anti-malt tax meetings. " Beer can now, with difficulty, be had *genuine*, and too often *money cannot procure wholesome malt liquor*," so says Mr. Smee; and, after stating the high price of beer, he adds, " even at these ridiculous prices, if beer could be had *pure and good*, the Londoners, whatever might be the case in the country, would not be disposed to complain." " Beer sold at a great multitude of places is shamefully—we had almost said wickedly—adulterated." " Poisonous adulterated mixture " and " rubbish " are the epithets with which our time-honoured beverage is distinguished. Now, is it not sad that not only " thirsty souls " but moderate men should be panting after a " glass of good ale " and cannot get it? that while there is plenty of profit, no company has been formed to secure the making of *pure* malt liquor, and to rescue the nation from the fangs of these unprincipled brewers? Could no home mission be established to purify the beer barrel, and bring these rogues to repentance? " Saccharine matter, water, and salt ,' people might put up with, but when it comes to " coculus indicus, grains of paradi quassia, chiaretta, and wormwood," I confess I am almost ready to call for the resurrection of the " ale-tasters " to prevent her Majesty's lieges being poisoned outright. But all this is " bosh." It is the result of ignorance and inattention to facts. People who talk so much about beer being " doctored " assume, at the onset, that liquor made only from malt and hops *must be good* and will not intoxicate nor injure those who drink it. They are profoundly ignorant that *the purest beer is whiskey and hop water*, coloured and flavoured; and until they are disabused of these unfounded notions, they will continue to go on reiterating these silly tales about adulterations. And no greater error was ever committed by some teetotalers than to join in this cry, for it simply tends to convey the idea to the people that if they can get pure beer they will be all right. Though some brewers and publicans adulterate their drinks, yet the number of cases is much exaggerated. I believe that all respectable brewers confine themselves to malt and hops, and, of course, water, which, after all, is their best friend. The penalties for adulteration are so tremendous that, if there were no other check, few who brew on a large scale would run the risk of being convicted and exposed. Grant that some publicans do mix " water, salt, or saccharine matter," these are mixtures that can do little injury : and as for the " grains of paradise " (a species of pepper) and other drugs, I question if any of them are more injurious than the *alcohol* which the beer contains, amounting to from 9 to 18 per cent. of proof spirit, and if the beer was free from this alcohol not a man would touch it. Take it out, as they do in making whiskey, and where is the man that would wet his lips with it? The brewers have a fastidious set to deal with; for if the ale be weak they say, "It is not worth drinking," and if it be strong, and puts them out of order next morning, they are sure "it had something in it." They want it fresh and frisky, capable of touching the nerves and making them cheery; they want to be able to drink freely, and yet not to be much intoxicated; to be pretty well " up " in the evening, and yet not "down " in the morning. If it does not answer these expectations, it is "adulterated." While brewer's beer is charged with "flying into the head," making people ill and producing drunkenness, the home-brewed is always spoken of as " pure," " wholesome," and " nourishing." But the home-brewed produces the same effect when it is made equally strong with the brewer's; for instance, a man gets two horns-full at " my lord's," which was brewed for his son's majority, from nothing but malt and hops, and it makes his "head rive again next day." Now, how is this? There was no adulteration—no quassia nor grains of paradise. The simple explanation is, that the malt used contained a large quantity of saccharine; this was well washed out in mashing, and kept long enough to undergo a thorough fermentation ; a *large quantity of alcohol* was secured, which, as usual, went into the man's head. And, though this was no more feeding than penny beer, it was far more *drunkifying*, and yet was unadulterated. And this I solemnly believe, that where grains of paradise and its worst companions have killed their tens, the alcohol has killed its ten thousands. Let me entreat the teetotalers never to be led off with a false scent ; and if there be any real cause of quarrel betwixt publicans and their customers, let them settle it among themselves. The teetotalers should not lower themselves by acting as sentinels to protect the purity of the beer barrel.

But I must say a few words about home-brewing. Cobbett was a good defender of home-brewing, but he had not himself learned the nature and properties of the liquor. No more has Mr. Joshua Fielden, M.P., its present great advocate. I respect the motives of these defenders of the domestic "drink-pot;" but it is too late to bring back a practice almost obsolete, and certainly not desirable. That home-brewed beer is less injurious than public-house beer I grant, but not for the reason usually given, that public-house beer is drugged, but *because* the home-brewed *contains less spirit*—less of what Shakespeare called "devil." Drinkers now-a-days like to *feel* the effects of the liquor, and hence they go in for beer containing more alcohol, and if the publicans sold beer like the home-brewed, they would soon sell their customers. But the evil of the home-brewed is that it keeps the appetite alive and seasoned for stronger beer, and the stronger beer for something still more potent. Home-brewing, like home manufactures has long been on the decline. The people no doubt could make beer much cheaper than they can buy it, but they cannot make it equal in quality, according to the taste which now prevails. When "washing, baking, and brewing" were the ordinary weekly duties of a good wife and her daughters, the drink was of a homely character. Science had nothing to do with it, and the saccharometer was an instrument they had never heard of. The "bree" was daily on the table more as a "victual" than a stimulant, and being drunk new had scarcely time to become intoxicating. In the reign of James I "it was the custom to allow every man and boy on board the King's ships *one gallon of beer a day*"—a clear intimation of the difference in the strength of the liquor compared with what the people demand at the present time. They take it now more as a luxury, and having means to pay for it they will have it "good," let the price be what it may. Try to bring down our jolly ale drinkers, or even the common artizans, to the "home-brewed" of our ancestors, and they would turn up their noses with disdain. The style of drinking, like dressing, has made great strides, especially among the lower classes ; home-brewed has gone out of fashion, and I should doubt whether in Preston, out of 17,000 houses, seventeen can be found that brew their own. In the middle classes it is found cheaper and safer to run with the jug at meal times than to keep the barrel in the cellar. But I hope none of the ladies who hear me on this occasion will impose upon their female servants the unpleasant, not to say dangerous, task of visiting the public-house day by day for beer. It is a task, I am sure, that no respectable servant is disposed to envy.

Among the powerful causes which retard the progress of teetotalism there are none more powerful than this *ignorance* of the properties of beer. On this subject the English mind is thoroughly beclouded. Tradition and not science has been the nation's instructor. This beer—this wonderfully nutritious beverage—is nothing more or less than *adulterated water*. A pint of beer is a pint of water, coloured and flavoured, and containing sufficient of *whiskey* to excite the nerves and lead people to think it imparts strength. Notwithstanding all that has been said, and all that has been published, we find in every class—clergy, laity, rich and poor—a great want of information as to the nature and properties of our popular drinks, and as to how they act upon the human system. And while such associations as the "Society for promoting Christian Knowledge" can go out of their way to recommend beer, no wonder that this ignorance should remain. It is to this ignorance that we chiefly attribute the falling back of many of the more educated teetotallers, especially the ministers of religion. They sign the pledge for the good of others, all the while retaining a favourable opinion of the drink if taken in moderation. In doing this they exercise an act of self-denial (while thoroughly informed teetotallers deem it self-enjoyment), and the first time they feel unwell, it becomes a question whether their abstaining is not the cause, and conceiving that they are not called upon to sacrifice their health, even for the good of others, they make shipwreck of their teetotalism. In coming to this conclusion, the doctors and their old friends give them every encouragement.

It is not, however, the non-nutritive properties of beer that constitute the main ground of our opposition to it; and I have only dwelt on this so long because its nutritive properties are always urged by its votaries as their reason for using it. I oppose it because it stands in the front ranks of *intoxicants* in the minds of the people. In the whole list, I regard beer as the worst, for three reasons. First, because public opinion runs so strongly in its favour in preference to what are called "spirituous liquors." Next, because it is usually looked upon as "food," and hence it is not reserved for special occasions, but is on the table of most families with means daily, and often twice a day. And thirdly, because while wine is taken in small glasses and ardent spirits by "bottoms," "squibs," and "nips," beer is drunk in full tumblers, and I have seen a lady empty two of them at dinner without appearing at all conscious that she was going beyond moderation Notwithstanding all that has been written respecting the *identity* of the spiri in beer and wine with that in rum, gin, brandy, and whiskey, we still find the great bulk of the people ignorant upon the subject. This ignorance is daily expressed in such words as these : "I take a little beer, and I like a glass of wine, but I never taste spirits." On every licensed victualler's sign we find something to this effect: "Licensed to sell beer and wine, and *spirituous* liquors," as if beer and wine were not spirituous; and even in the last Queen's Speech we had these words:—"Her Majesty has likewise to recommend that you should undertake the amoudment of the laws which regulate the granting of licenses for the sale of fermented *and* spirituous liquors." If persons want to exhibit any offensive forms of intemperance they speak of "*gin* drinking," and "*gin* palaces;" but associate beer and wine with the "necessaries" and "enjoyments of life," and not unfrequently with the "gifts of Providence." They seem inattentive to the fact that more beer than gin is sold at these "palaces;" that in many districts five-sixths of the intemperance among the operatives is from beer, and that in England, at least, the first liking for unnatural stimulants begins with beer and wine. It is needful, therefore, that we make it quite plain that the *same* intoxicating ingredient exists in all, only in different quantities. If things were called by their right names this delusion would get exploded. If a man spoke correctly when he wants a tumbler of beer, he would say, "bring me a glass of whiskey and hop-water;" or wine, he would say, "a drop of diluted brandy." We must labour to get this point fully understood. Alcohol (pure spirit) is the same, no matter whether you get it in its rectified state at the druggists'—called "spirits of wine," or in gin or whiskey, or in Jamaica rum, or in the best or worst wines, or in malt liquors, perry, or cider. It is simply the result of fermenting any kind of liquid containing saccharine matter, the flavour and colour varying according to the article used. The broad difference made botwixt "fermented" and "distilled" liquors is also calculated to keep up this delusion. All intoxicating drinks are fermented, though all are not distilled. For instance, we take a quantity of malt, and after mashing it we ferment the produce, and *spirit* is produced. In this state it is called *beer*, yet it is from this same liquor—minus the hop—that *whiskey* is obtained. Whiskey is the soul of beer, and no one can drink beer without drinking whiskey. The distiller puts the beer into a retort, forming part of the "still," and when heat is applied, the spirit, being specifically lighter than water, ascends, and then passing through a spiral tube called the "worm," it condenses, and is then called whiskey. This is converted into gin by redistillation, with a mixture of juniper berries. Hence in making gin and whiskey we have both fermentation and distillation. When the whiskey is taken out of beer, what remains is water, and a little indigestible stuff, chiefly gum, so distasteful that no old fuddler could be induced to swallow it. So then, after all, the Scotchman that dilutes his whiskey sufficiently with pure water is not more foolish than the Londoner, who swallows all together, whiskey, hop, gum, and dirty water!

In legislation, beer has always been treated with tender feelings. Unusually large penalties have been annexed to any breach of the excise laws in relation to it. The problem of perpetual motion is not more difficult than that which our senators have all my time been endeavouring to solve, which is that men shall drink intoxicating beer and not be intoxicated. It was this ignorance that passed the Beer Bill in 1830. The Legislature, believing that beer was highly nutritious, and supposing it to be in direct antagonism to "spirits," thought they were doing the country a service in trying to bring cheap beer as near to every man's door as possible. And though the Bill has been fiercely condemned for forty years by the few better informed, yet all the evils it produced have not been sufficient to enlighten the public as to the cause being in the beer itself. When this Bill passed, supported and defended by the leading philanthropists and politicians of the day, it is affirmed that the Duke of Wellington said the passing of this Bill was a greater achievement than any of his military victories! The consequences were soon felt, and the predictions of the dissenting few fully verified. The strongest supporters of the measure were surprised by the sudden and general demoralisation produced. The Rev. Sydney Smith, who had attached great importance to the repeal of the beer tax and the establishment of beershops, writing only a fortnight after the Act came into force, says :—"The New Beer Bill has begun its operations. *Everybody is drunk.* Those who are not singing are sprawling. The sovereign people are in a beastly state." This was a glorious time for the demoralizers of the people. In Liverpool, within nineteen days from October 10th, as many as 800 licenses were taken out under the Act ; and at the end of the year the licenses applied for and granted in England and Wales rose to 24,312. Now we have to undo the work of our grandfathers, after forty years of crime, poverty, misery, and death, produced by this Bill. And I doubt whether many of the present occupiers of St. Stephen's are even yet much wiser than their predecessors. You hear the "beer shops" condemned, but when did you hear or read of the *beer* itself being ill spoken of by these gentlemen ? On the contrary, either through selfishness or ignorance, there is a clamour for the repeal of the malt tax, so that the people may drink more beer and the farmers sell more barley. To untax malt would, in fact, be a measure resembling that of 1830. It would do immense harm, and no good to any one. The seven millions of tax would have to be laid upon other articles. There would be more drunkenness than ever, and as for the farmers benefiting by an increased demand for barley, they must be stupid not to see, that while our ports are open to all the world, every increase of a shilling a quarter would be met by increased foreign importations, and prices kept down to the world's level. Barley in its natural state is as free from tax as oats, wheat, or any other grain, and it is only when it is converted into malt that the Government says—and says very properly :—"First, as a protection to morals, and next, as a source of revenue, we will tax this material, being the most convenient stage in beer-making, as we do wine and other intoxicating beverages." I feel confident that if the tax were either repealed or laid upon beer instead of malt, in a short time after the change no higher price would be obtained for the barley, with this disadvantage, that a share of the increased burden of poverty and crime would fall upon the farmers themselves.

Notwithstanding all that has been said and all that has been written, the idea of a pint of beer being good for the working man is still urged by many. 'Now, I must have a few words with you, my working men, on this point. I want to know *how* the pint is good for the working man ? In the first place : Is it calculated to *quench your thirst ?* I say, no. Just in proportion to its alcoholic strength, instead of diminishing it increases thirst. The nearer it approaches to water the more adapted it is to quench thirst. The beverage of nature—"too weak to be a sinner"—can quench thirst, and with this every animal is satisfied, excepting man. And, indeed, after all our boasted discoveries in the Temperance Cause, we have just learned to be wise as the brutes that perish. The temperance man is seldom thirsty, and requires but little drink ; the drinking man is always dry, and never has enough. Let him swallow quarts of his favourite beverage, and visit him the next morning and you will find his tongue parched with thirst, with beautiful tide marks upon his lips. The more he drinks the thirstier he is. For after all, what is your ale but spirit and coloured hop-water ? I have shown you that three gills and a half in every quart are literally water. If, therefore, you don't prefer water in its best and natural state, by the addition of a little vinegar, ginger, lemon juice, or a burnt crust, you can colour and flavour it as you please. There is nothing so good as "honest water" for quenching thirst, and as food in a liquid form there is nothing equal to milk. Look at that beautiful sparkling glass of water as it stands beside your plate; it costs you nothing, it is one of the best of God's gifts; it will do you good and no harm; it will assist digestion; it will not excite and then depress; you will drink no more of this fluid than is proper. And will you, then, instead of drinking the clear, nice, transparent element in its natural state, insist upon its being coloured with charcoal, bittered with hop, and fired with whiskey? and instead of having it for nothing, consent to purchase it at 4d., 5d., or 6d. per quart? Could folly go further than this? If, again, you plead for a pint of ale as a source of *strength*, I hope the exposition already given to-night will fully show the futility of such a plea. It is the *solids*, and not the *liquids*, upon which labouring men are to work. I have often been asked, "Can a man perform his labour on cold water?" to which I answer no, nor on cold ale either. What is it that gives strength to the miller's horse *(which drinks nothing but cold water)*, and makes its ribs wrinkle with fat? It is the *food* which it eats. And it is good food, my working friends—bread, beef, and barley pudding—from which you are to derive your strength. Again, if you drink your pint of ale for the purpose of *stimulation*, I agree that it will answer that purpose; but the effect of this stimulation, in most cases, is to injure the human system. To work by stimulation is to draw upon the constitution, and to avail yourselves of muscular power before it is due. Ale may lift you higher than yourselves, but it sure to let you fall again. You have a full development of the effect of stimulation in the Saturday night drinker. He lives twice too fast; he gets Sunday morning's life on Saturday night. And such is the excitement that, were he even to refrain from his cups on the Sunday, the rest of the Sabbath is insufficient to restore nature to her equilibrium against the hour of labour on Monday morning. Alcoholic stimulation ought to be regarded as the parent of insanity; and every one who seeks after it seems to aim a blow at that noble and heavenly gift of God --the gift of reason.

A word or two here to our kind friends, the ladies. What is so interesting as the babe hanging at its mother's breast? and what more important than to know that this same mother, by taking her beer, is transgressing the teachings of nature, and doing an injury to herself and her darling child? And yet traditional ignorance, backed by the doctor's indulgence, demands a supply of porter or beer for the nursing mother! It is taken by some to keep up their strength; a delusion in this, as in most other cases, for the beer does not, and can not, impart to the mother's milk any nutritive properties. It is often taken, as it is conceived, to secure a fuller supply for the little one, and the alcohol does this for a while as a "forcing" agent, at the same time wasting the mother's strength, endangering the future health of the child, and in many instances, creating on its part an hereditary liking for the drunkard's drink. Beer or diluted spirit is sometimes taken by mothers before bed-time to prevent restlessness on the part of the infant during the night. This is just as good as "Godfrey's Cordial" or "quietus" with which poor women are so guilty of drugging their children; only in one case the child gets it at the first, and the other at second hand. If the child is restless at night, find out the *cause* and remove it, but in any case it is far better to bear up under present inconvenience than to purchase temporary rest by undermining its future health. Numbers of medical gentlemen have given their testimony against this pernicious practice of narcotising children by beer or gin and water at second hand. "Women who act as nurses are strongly addicted to the practice of drinking porter and ale," says Dr. Macnish, "for the purpose of augmenting their milk. This common practice cannot be sufficiently deprecated. It is pernicious to both parties, and may lay the foundation of a multitude of diseases in the infant." "Alcohols are largely used by many persons in the belief that they support the system and maintain the supply of milk for the infant," says Dr. Edward Smith, "but I am convinced that it is a *serious error* and *is not an unfrequent cause of fits and emaciation in the child.*" "I have in eight years attended 137 cases of midwifery," says Mr. A. Courtney, "and have invariably found that (other things being equal) those mothers who never tasted malt liquor, wine, or spirits, *during or subsequent to the period of labour, have had the easiest cases, the earliest recoveries, and the best health afterwards.* Thousands of children are cut off annually by convulsions, &c., from the effects of those beverages, acting through the mother." The same gentleman on a public occasion remarked:—"At our last meeting eleven nursing mothers presented themselves with their children, every one of whom had nursed her child on Teetotal principles. Healthier or finer children I have never seen; and, did all mothers pursue the same system, we should, in a dozen years, see very few such puny, rickotty, diseased children as so often meet the eye at the present day." Mr. Chavasse, in his "Advice to a Wife," speaks most decidedly about the inapplicability of malt liquors to these cases.—"A nursing mother is subject to thirst: when such is the case, she ought not to fly to beer or wine to quench it; this will only add fuel to the fire. The best beverages will be—either toast and water, milk and water, barley-water and milk, or black tea. A lady who is nursing is, at times, liable to fits of depression. Let me strongly urge the importance of her abstaining from wine, and from all other stimulants, as a remedy: they would only raise her spirits for a time, and then would decrease them in an increased ratio. A drive into the country, or a short walk, or a cup of tea, or a chat with a friend, would be the best medicine." "The plain fact is," says Dr. Lees, "that if alcoholics are drunk by mothers, the alcohol goes into the milk, and so is given to the child indirectly. It never improves the quality of the milk, but makes it more watery, with less casein or nutriment, and even less oil, as analysis has often demonstrated." Let me say, then, to the ladies present who are blessed with children, or who hope to be, I could quote numerous authorities to the same effect, but I hope these will be sufficient to induce you to close your ears against any who advise Dublin Porter or Bass's Bitter for mothers and nurses.

I would now direct your attention to what is most appalling: *the amount of money spent* upon our popular drinks, the foremost of which is beer. Calculations differ, as they must do, from various causes. We know the amount of duty charged upon malt as a substitute for beer, and also the amount paid as duty upon spirits and wine. But no record is kept of the "length," as the brewers call it, that a bushel of malt is made to run in brewing. In some cases only nine gallons of water are used to the bushel of malt, whilst in others 18 gallons are used, with all the intermediate quantities. Nor have we any means, beyond probable estimates, of knowing the profits realised by brewers, "gin spinners," and the publicans. Assuming the excise standard as to the quantity of water and malt used in brewing, and calculating the retail prices of beer, wine, and ardent spirits, one statement makes the total annual amount spent in this country upon intoxicating liquors to be £101,397,310, in round numbers, say *a hundred millions*, that upon beer being £59,768,870! Another calculation, the lowest I have seen, makes the amount spent upon intoxicating drinks to be £87,317,280, that upon beer being £43,749,550. The *Economist*, some years ago, estimated the cost of beer at 60 millions. Taking any of these estimates, or taking the average of them, I need not say that we are guilty of a shocking misapplication of money; and when we add the unavoidable *cost* of the *consequences* of consuming these liquors, in the poverty, crime, and insanity of the people, their loss of time, health, and property, and all the other losses, we may indeed be surprised at the apathy of this nation in having borne with such an incumbrance so long. Need we wonder at "bad times?" Give up the drink and apply the money to the purchase of cotton and woollen cloth, furniture, and the necessaries and comforts of life, and it is impossible to say the vast impetus that would be given to the trade of this nation. I would not for the world be a participator in this waste of wealth of which the nation is guilty, and of which every glass or jug of beer that stands upon your tables is a unit. Oh, let me advise you to banish it for ever!

Passing from the enormity of this curse, as represented by the tremendous amount of *money* spent upon intoxicating liquors, I would try to arouse you still more, by placing before you, as plainly as I can, the *quantity* of drink swallowed by the "thirsty souls" of this country every year. One year's consumption of wine and distilled spirits amounts to 44,575,930 gallons; and if this were collected, three feet deep and thirty feet wide, it would extend to the length of fifteen miles. Large as this may appear, it is not till the floodgates of Messrs. Bass, Allsop, Buxton, Guinness and Co., are let open, and the "bitter beer," "pale ale," double xx," "half and half," "Dublin porter," and all the rest be added, that we have a full exhibition of the incredible quantity of "fire water" consumed by the people. The annual home consumption of beer, calculating by the excise standard of 18 gallons of water to a bushel of malt, amounts to 888,294,132 gallons; and if it were made into a canal three feet deep and thirty feet wide, it would be $299\frac{1}{4}$ miles in length, in round numbers, say 300 miles! So that mixing these three distinctive articles together, beer, wines, and spirits, we have a canal, or rather I may call it a "Dead Sea," 315 miles in length! And all this under the fostering care of a "progressing," education-loving, mission-promoting, Bible-reading, evangelizing nation! Look at it, my friends; smell at it; but don't taste it. It "bites like a serpent and stings like an adder." Apply a burning taper and, with sufficient heat below to make the spirit ascend, you have a sea of fire 315 miles in length. Imagine, if you can, ye moderate drinkers, the awful sufferings, the amount of crime and poverty, and death and murder, in all their most appalling shapes, arising from the making, selling, and drinking of this immense quantity of alcoholic liquor; and if you can still continue your friendly visits to this fiery lake, filling glasses, decanters, bottles, and barrels, and gulp their contents, all I can say is, I pity your position and hope you will soon see your error.

But this is not all. There is another phase of the brewing and distilling system that we should never cease to expose. Intoxicating drinks are bad enough if they were made from the most worthless materials; but in order to make them, many of our valuable products of the earth are destroyed, not to name those of other climes imported to us in a liquid state. I may state that in our own country, in making ale, porter, gin, and whiskey, 60 million bushels of good grain, the gift of Heaven as food for man and beast, are annually destroyed. This barley, if laid 3 feet deep and 30 feet wide, would cover a road 162 miles in length! Behold this beautiful grain turned into a dead sea of liquid poison, from the fatal effects of which scarcely a family escapes. And though generation after generation are punished—and punished daily—yet our leading men give their sanction and perform their part in this desperate game of destruction. What should we say,—what amount of frenzy would our political economists manifest,—if by some infernal mandate this quantity of barley was deliberately carted and cast into the sea? Or, if at various points of this vast spread of barley, fuel was provided, and licensed officials engaged to apply the torch and set the whole into a blaze? What a tremendous conflagration; nothing remaining except the ashes to compensate for the loss; and yet I say most deliberately that this would be child's play compared with the loss of the health, morals, happiness, and lives of millions of our people, the well-known consequences resulting from the use of these British-made intoxicating liquors. And does our enlightened country bear all this w thout a national protest, without being roused to defend its fields from pillage, and without insisting upon its grain being stored for legitimate purposes? It does; it does more; it *compels* this waste; it commissions men to do it; it says, "We like the drink, and we will have it if the people starve." Nursed in ignorance of the true properties of malt liquor; encouraged by the example and the teaching of senators, nobles, and great men, and backed by the press, in order to supply a hundred and fifty thousand whiskey-stores, gin-palaces, beer-shops, and other establishments, with the implements of demoralization and ruin, we deliberately devote the produce of 1,565,000 acres of British soil—1,500,000 for barley, and 65,000 for hops! And I may here mention that as the use of sugar is now permitted in the brewing of beer and the making of spirits, not less than 42 million pounds of this valuable article were thus used, or rather mis-used, during the last year. The sugar is wanted for no purpose but to increase the quantity of spirit, which is produced by fermentation. Nay, even this is not enough; though we complain of our limited area compared with population, and though we are obliged to get our corn and cheese and butter and bacon from the land of other countries, for which we have to pay an equivalent, yet there is a class clamouring for the repeal of the malt tax, hat *more land* may be confiscated by the farmers to the brewing and distilling interest.

Teetotalers! the corn-fields of England claim your protection; you must come forward and defend the treasures of Heaven; it is for you to rescue the people from the ignorance of ages and the slavery of appetite and fashion. Let the subject be carefully canvassed. Let the waste be carefully exposed to the gaze of the whole nation; let the political economists be invited honestly to discuss this subject as they do others affecting the wealth of the community; let our statisticians, our chemists, our men of science, be invited to investigate the question. It is a serious matter to see the fat of the land turned wholesale into a stream of liquid fire, consuming the best blessings of so many families, and our great folks either looking on with indifference or helping forward the conflagration, instead of assisting by might and main to quench the devouring element. We have a hard work to do; but loyalty to the God of Harvests, and love to His suffering children will not allow us to be silent spectators, while the produce of the broad acres of this favoured land are being carted to the stores of the brewers and the distillers. We have a great work to do. There are 6,000 malt kilns, 33,000 breweries, and 150,000 drink sellers all engaged in turning the good grain of heaven into intoxicating liquor, or tempting people in every possible shape to drink it to their own injury, not to mention the distilleries which are ever at work rendering the beer more essentially poisonous by turning it into gin and whiskey. Oh, that the time may speedily arrive when our citizens will be sufficiently enlightened and have sufficient virtue and courage to elect a legislature who will absolutely prohibit the making and selling of all beverages containing alcohol!

Now, my dear friends, by this time I think you will be convinced that the admiration in which malt liquor has been so long held is nothing less than a national delusion. To enumerate the evils drink is producing is impossible, but I may just say that flood, fire, water, slavery, potatoe rot, rinderpest, cotton famine, and our worst calamities are dwarfs beside this great monster of iniquity, which spares neither age, sex, rich nor poor, ignorant nor educated. Like as in the plagues of Egypt, there is scarcely a house unsmitten. And the worst of all is, that this is no infliction of Providence; *it is the resu't of our own ignorance, and vice, and wickedness*, and those who should be the first to rush into the breach and rescue the sufferers are the most timid and cold-hearted, the advocates of a deceitful moderation—the very path in which every drunkard made a start. Are you prepared to help us in this severe conflict with the powers of the drinking world? I hope you are. Do you ask me what I want you to do? My sincere desire, my earnest wish is, that in the first place you would never again wet your lips with any kind of alcoholic liquor. That is your *first* step, and a blessed one it will be. Your *next* is, to drain your houses of this, the worst of all nuisances. Let this deceitful enemy have no place under your roof, nor let the family table be disgraced with that which is the emblem as well as the cause of England's greatest degradation. These two steps taken, you must then brace yourselves up for duty to others. A virtuous teetotaler—enjoying the blessings of perfect sobriety—never feels happy unless he is planning and working to confer the same blessings upon others. Try to save the young before they are contaminated; and pity with all your hearts the grown-up hard drinkers, who, without brotherly help, will never be rescued. The poor drunkards, though generally despised, ought to be the object of our pity and commiseration. They are the *victims* of the ignorance, neglect, love of ease, and selfishness of which we have been guilty. Those who should have taught them better, and watched over them to prevent their first steps to ruin, are, unfortunately, drinkers themselves, rather than persons who set a safe example of abstinence. Does not our religion teach us that every man should be his brother's keeper? Cruel as we often are towards the hard drinkers, depend upon i they are great sufferers, and are ever labouring under a strong desire for deliverance Do give them all the help you can; and if you persevere in your kind attentions, you will often find their hearts overflowing with gratitude, and be well rewarded by seeing many saved from ruin. You will be greatly encouraged and be the means of strengthening others if you united yourselves with the Bands of Hope and the Temperance Societies. Should these fail to be supported and to accomplish their mission, there is no hope for this drunken country. The tipplers and moderate drinkers will continue to look on with indifference, and it is only to those who become real abstainers—to those who are out and out enemies of the drink and all the drinking usages—that I look for the success of the temperance reformation.

I invite every *lady* in this assembly to engage in this labour of love, and to give effect to those feelings of compassion and sympathy which are inherent in the female breast. Your erring sisters call for your aid; many who have fallen into habits of intoxication would give the world to be delivered. Go to them in all kindness; show a sisterly tenderness towards them, however low they may have fallen. It may be true that females are not so easily induced to abandon the liquor as the other sex; but it is equally true that some may be won over, and the reason of so many failures is that the right means have not been used. There are but few unwilling to make a trial, and if some should sign the pledge and break it, as is too common, you must not forsake them, but visit them immediately, and with words of kindness help them to start again. I often think of these words "Not seven, but seventy times seven!" Oh, that we had the feeling that dictated that heavenly expression! At the same time, I hope you will not forget how desirable it is to *prevent*, if possible, any females beginning to like the drink. Try to introduce the abstinence principle at proper times into every circle in which you move. Teach the children, teach the young girls, the young women, the young wives, and all, in fact, never to touch the drink, and you will lay the foundation for much social and domestic happiness.

In conclusion, I would say that I have had the happiness to labour in this good cause nearly fifty years, and though I have always been among the unpaid, I have been greatly rewarded. The testimonies I constantly receive from individuals and families made happy by teetotalism prove that I have not laboured in vain. And now that I have nearly finished my course, my only feeling of regret is that I have not done more. To you, my dear teetotal friends, and to the others whom I hope will soon join your ranks, I look to carry on this great work—a work based on truth, sanctioned by Divine teaching, and proved by a world-wide experience to be an unmixed blessing.

THE CHOICE OF HERCULES

A Message for To-Day.

By the Rev. Dr BLACK, Inverness.

THE choice of Hercules forms one of the most thrilling incidents in the literature of Ancient Greece. Hercules was the hero of heroes in the old classic world. In physique he was the ideal of manly strength and stature; in morals he was the embodiment of every noble virtue known to the Greek mind, and yet he very nearly made shipwreck of life. The critical moment came when as a youth he was called upon to make a supreme choice. Before him stood two angel forms. The one, with fascinating eye and siren voice, appealed for the gratification of sense—pointing to the flowery path of luxury, sensual pleasure and bodily appetite. The other—with radiant countenance, noble mien, and earnest look pled for the path of virtue —acknowledging the roughness of the road, but indicating also the grandeur of the final victory, and pointing suggestively upwards to the Unseen and the eternal world.

Hercules paused, listened, and decided—to follow the heavenly voice. The die was cast; the choice was made, and Hercules became immortalised. So it is to-day. Choice is the privilege and responsibility with which God has endowed man. "Choose ye this day" was Joshua's word to Israel, and so our Creator has ever said to us, Life or death: God or Satan: Which? And so with the forces which shall rule our life.

This is a power rendered more important from the fact that our life is, so to speak, duplex. Side by side we have the grave and the gay, each demanding control. We need not blink the fact that man cannot help being gay. God made man to be merry. Body, soul, and spirit were intended to '' rejoice," and so if we are natural we shall be merry. Man craves it. But what a poor attempt Satan and sinners make to reach it. No more mocking, empty word in the devil's vocabulary than "gay." He calls his theatres "The Gaiety," and his dancing times "The Gay Season." But alas! what sham and hollowness! I have wondered and might have wept over some of Satan's gatherings I have seen. "Poor wretches," I have said, " and is that all he can do for them?" How different with our Creator! He bids us sing with both heart and voice, and what variety He gives, "Psalms, and hymns, and spiritual songs." He wants us to be so glad that when we speak together we shall break into song. Is not the most unnatural, ungodlike creature in the world the grumbling growler—the man who never tastes the sweet nor sees the beautiful? I would not keep a songless bird—why, then, should my Lord keep me if I know not how to sing?

A SUBLIME ALTERNATIVE.

Such, then, is complex man, weighted with responsibilities, but eager to rejoice. It is in this connection Paul introduced his alternatives. Wine and the fulness of the Spirit are the two external powers man must choose between to stimulate his energies. This choice must be made. God's plan in creation seems to have been never to make anything independent. There is not a planet or fixed star in the heavens that is not kept in its place by its relation to the other bodies round it. So on earth no such thing is known as isolation. And so man cannot live unaided, as the tree must drink in sap from the soil, as the animal must take of the food provided, so man must have external aid. Cut off supplies from without and soon his energies will droop, and he becomes a limp and nerveless thing. What shall we choose, then, to stimulate our mental energy—shall we take Satan's wine cup or be filled with the Heavenly Breath of God's Holy Spirit? The " evil days " Paul speaks of intensify the need of this choice.

IF PAUL WERE BACK AGAIN !

Men talk of progress and the elevation of the people, but if Paul were back again to his ministry—need he change his text? Have we not been pained and humiliated by the manly, outspoken testimony of one of the highest authorities in mental diseases in Scotland, given in his report last year? Speaking of the large increase of rate-paid cases in his asylum Dr Clouston says "He could not himself get over the conclusion that the excessive use of alcoholic stimulants during times of brisk trade and high wages had to a large extent been the cause of the undue amount of mental disease which they had been called on to treat last year. They had, as a matter of fact, about a quarter of their whole number of admissions in whom drink was assigned as either the sole or a contributary cause of the disease attacks." As long centuries ago, then, Paul pleaded against the wine cup, so to-day he being dead yet speaketh. Twentieth century Christians, choose you this day which power ye will surrender yourselves to—Satan's alcohol or God's Spirit.

COMPARISONS ARE NOT ALWAYS ODIOUS.

It has been said that comparisons are odious, but surely sometimes they are most helpful. Let us compare these two competitors. In some things they resemble; in some they differ.

HOW THEY RESEMBLE.—To mention one thing—*they both take complete possession.* The work is within. They both go into the depths of the nature. The glory and specialty of the Spirit's work is that He possesses the whole man. The command is "Be filled with the Spirit." Just as my breath has to do with my whole being, so God's Spirit must fill me—brain, heart, and will—all are influenced when the Spirit comes. That is the need of a Spirit Saviour. The second Person is my Prophet, Priest, and King, but the Third Person, only, can be an Indweller—implanting the Life and applying the Salvation. On the side of evil, again, how Satan uses the intoxicant to seize and enslave the whole man. Other poisons have certain parts they seize and play upon, but alcohol reaches from head to feet. It makes the blood its motor, and so passes to brain, and limb, and member. The eye and tongue and walk all tell the same tale. Surely men and women do not realize what a tyrant they are taking into their being. People wonder how others live in those lands where wild beasts and vipers abound. But did all the wild beasts in the world kill as many people last year as alcohol slew in any one of our cities? Nor are the slain the only sufferers—to quote Dr Clouston again "It was certain" he says, "that for every man in whom excessive drinking caused absolute insanity, there were twenty in whom it injured the brain, blunted the moral sense, and lessened the capacity for work in lesser degrees."

STRENGTH OF CHARACTER—TRUE AND FALSE.

BUT THESE POWERS DIFFER.—For example—*one calms, the other excites.* The Christian character may be summed up in the one word "stand." The Bible goes in for firmness, stability. The Christian soldier had studded sandals for the battlefield. The enthusiasm the Fulness of the Spirit gives is seen more in deliberate standing than in hurried dash. This was the secret of the calm dignity of Peter before the Sanhedrim and Paul before Cæsar; of Luther at Worms and Knox before Mary. What a contrast to the boastful, lying, reeling drunkard, whose words are only idle noise, whose counsel is only treated with contempt. A man to be despised! Alcohol is the

4

fire that consumes : the electric spark that fires the passions. God's Spirit gives power, Satan's wine cup gives no strength, it makes no muscle, fibre, or nerve. God's Spirit puts the reins in the hands of a strengthening will—Alcohol throws them on the neck of the untamed carnality.

Results show also how they differ, for *one spiritualizes—the other brutalizes.* The trust his Creator committed to man was the formation of character. We are put into our own hands, what are we to make of ourselves? Two courses are set before us—the carnal and the spiritual. Again we are called to choose. The animal is in us and the Godlike. True, in the animal man there is intellect that may produce the beautiful—still it is only "of the earth" and may be prostituted to the vilest ends. What aid can I have then in making the most of myself, and building up a character worthy of my position? "Be filled with the Spirit," says Paul. Then every day you will die to sin and live unto righteousness, the flesh will be crucified— "Kept under," while you grow in grace, developing to the "Perfect Man." How different and downward is the work of the intoxicant, under its influence the spiritual is deadened ; the mental is maddened ; the man becomes a fool. The highest type of animal is degraded lower than the lowest. Indeed it is unfair to compare the drunken to a beast. Is there a sadder sight on earth than that of a man "made in the likeness of God" staggering on the street, or lying in the gutter? Beauty, dignity, manhood gone. And what then? Is it the asylum, or the drunkard's death-bed? And what then? Our Bible tells us no drunkard shall inherit the kingdom. How could he? And the beginning of all this lies in tampering with the intoxicating cup, fancying we need the stimulant, and is so subtle and insidious that the least likely often fall, proving that there is no safe ground, even for the strongest, save that of total abstinence. Therefore, "Unto you, O men, I call ; and my voice is to the sons of men." "I speak as unto wise men, judge ye what I say." My appeal is very specially to professing Christians—members of the Church of Christ. If these things be so—and they cannot be denied—what is the plain duty of every Christian? Can we any longer encourage by our silent acquiescence or by our example that which is working such havoc among our fellow-men? Dare we stand idly by and see our fellow-men drawn into the whirlpool of intemperance and imagine that we can remain guiltless? Surely not. Rather then let us throw off all indifference ; Let us step into the arena of life's battle, saying—I will no longer be a neutral in this Holy War with abounding intemperance. I will make my choice and follow the heavenly voice! I will join the ranks of Total Abstinence in my Church and, filled with the Spirit, do all I can for the overthrow of this giant evil.

> Once to every man and nation comes the moment to decide,
> In the strife of TRUTH WITH FALSEHOOD for the good or evil side ;
>
> .   .   .   .   .   .
>
> And the choice goes by for ever.

PRICE 1/ per 100, Post Free; 500 for 4/6, 1000 for 8/6, Carriage Unpaid, from Temperance Publication Depôts—Edinburgh: G. WALLACE ROSS, 8 North Bank Street—Glasgow: ANDREW BENNET, 232 St Vincent Street.

- *British* -

TEMPERANCE LEAGUE.

ANNUAL

CONFERENCE,

HELD AT

Huddersfield.

JUNE 30th to JULY 2nd, 1901.

The Committee tender their hearty thanks to all who contributed in any way towards the success of the Conference and Meetings.

JAMES HARTLEY, CHAIRMAN.

TOM FRANCE, TREASURER.

JOHN CALVERLEY, SECRETARY.

	£ s. d.	£ s. d
To Donations to General Fund as under :—		
Ald. G. W. Hellawell	1 1 0	
Ed. Stott, Esq.	1 1 0	
T. Walker, Esq.	1 1 0	
		3 3 0
,, Collections at Chapels and Temperance Meetings—less expenses		52 12 3
† ,, Balance owing to Treasurer....		18 1 3½

    † To be paid in equal parts by the Huddersfield Temperance Society and the Huddersfield Band of Hope Union.

£73 16 6½

Account. ☂

<table>
<tr><td></td><td></td><td colspan="3">£ s. d.</td><td colspan="3">£ s. d.</td></tr>
</table>

	£ s. d.	£ s. d.
By Cost of Hand-Book, Printing, Stationery, Advertising, Postage, &c............................	28 14 1	
Less Advertisements	6 18 0	
		21 16 1
,, Utensils Cleaning, Carriage, Gratuities, &c............		16 1 5½
,. Rent of Rooms and Lighting		1 15 6
,, Agents Expenses		3 15 11½
,, Cost of Luncheon—Tuesday & Wednesday..	32 8 8½	
Less Donations —		
W. Dawson's Exors, & J. Woodhead, Esq.	16 4 3	
W. White, Esq.	1 1 0	
H. Earnshaw, Esq.	1 0 0	
D. Hirst, Esq.	1 0 0	
Mrs. Haley	0 5 0	
Sale of Tickets, &c.	4 19 9	
	24 10 0	
		7 18 8½
,, Cost of Teas—Monday & Tuesday	14 10 2	
Less Sale of Tickets, &c.	4 15 0	
		9 15 2
,, Garden Party Expenses--Wednesday......	15 0 8	
Less Donations—		
Ald. Reuben Hirst	2 2 0	
Mr. B. T. Smith	0 5 0	
	2 7 0	
		12 13 8
		£73 16 6½

Audited and found correct, Nov. 23rd, 1901.

F. W. DEARDEN.
SAMUEL SLATER.

JOHN KING, 1795-1885.

THE FIRST MAN IN ENGLAND TO SIGN THE TOTAL ABSTINENCE PLEDGE.

JOHN KING was born at Walton-le-Dale, near Preston, on the 25th December, 1795. This village was also the birthplace of Joseph Livesey, Sir Edward Baines, and Henry Anderton, names indissolubly associated with the history of the Temperance movement. King got very little in the way of education, and as soon as he was old enough, he was apprenticed to his father to learn the business of a clogger.

In 1832 a Temperance society was at work in Preston on the "moderation" principle—abstinence from ardent spirits, gin, rum, whisky, brandy, etc., and moderation in the use of ale, beer, wines, etc., and on the 18th of June of that year John King signed that pledge, and became a worker in the society at the earnest entreaty of Mr. Joseph Livesey.

The town was systematically worked. It was divided into districts, and a member of the society, called a "captain," was appointed to each district to deliver tracts and visit his fellow members. John King was placed in charge of No. 11 district. The work was well done; and this example from 1832 of organised personal contact with the people in their own homes, and a wide distribution of literature of an educational character, is the great need of 1910.

The pledge, excluding the use of spirits only, and allowing the use of fermented liquors, soon gave occasion for eye-opening on the part of these visitors, and John King thus relates his visiting experience :—

> On August 23rd (1832) I was passing Mr. Joseph Livesey's shop in Church Street, Preston. Mr. Livesey was standing at the door, and he said to me, " John, how dost thou get on in thy district ?" I told him that some of the members got drunk, and would do so until there was a pledge to do away with the drinking of ale and porter; and I said, further, that the men of Preston were not in the habit of drinking rum, gin, or brandy, but ale and porter. Mr. Livesey then said, " If a pledge were drawn up to do away with the drinking of ale and porter, would thee sign it ?" I said I would, for I had been acting on that principle for some time, and intended never to taste intoxicating drinks again. I also said that it was my firm conviction that there would never be much good done until a law was passed to prevent both distilling and brewing.

Upon that Joseph Livesey drew up a pledge of total abstinence, which John King signed first, followed by Mr. Livesey, on this memorable August 23rd, 1832. The pledge of total abstinence to which the names of the "seven men of Preston " were attached followed, being drawn up on Saturday, September 1st, 1832, and the names attached to it are John Gratrix, Edward Dickenson, John Broadbelt, John Smith, Joseph Livesey, David Anderton, John King.

After two-and-a-half years' active work with the Preston Temperance Society, Mr. King's occupation took him to Chester. Whilst there, a Temperance meeting (anti-spirits only) was held, the Bishop presiding, and King was invited to attend. The Bishop, learning that a working man was present, connected with the Preston movement, invited him to speak. King responded, and made a sensation. He said :—

> " I canna, mi lord, spake same as t'other chaps have done; I mun spake that which comes uppermost. They tell me that ye had wine to your dinner." The Bishop smiled and bowed. " Ay," resumed King, " they towd ma so— that ye had two glasses. I tell tha what it is: Temperance Society 'll do no good wi' sich chaps as thee at its head ! "

The meeting roared, and John continued his speech. A society on the basis of total abstinence was formed in 1834, of which King was a moving spirit, and its work is still continued as the Chester Christian Temperance Society, with which the Ven. Archdeacon Barber, M.A., Mr. Beresford Adams, and the Rev. James Travis are prominently connected. King went to live in Nottinghamshire, and spread the cause at Worksop, Norton, Bassingham, and other places. At Bassingham the Rev. D. S. Wayland took the chair for King, became an adherent to the movement, and continued for many years an earnest advocate of Temperance.*

This experience we give in King's own words from an early work entitled " Temperance Reformers."

> Some time after [leaving Chester] I went into Nottinghamshire to break up clog soles. I soon began to deliver Temperance tracts in the neighbourhood where I was at work. I caused many tracts to be distributed in Worksop, and several meetings were held, and a society established there during the time I was in Nottinghamshire. The landlord of a public-house at Norton, near to the seat of the Duke of Portland, asked one of the men who worked with me if I ever intended to hold a meeting in Norton. The man told him he thought I did, if a place could be got to hold a meeting in. The landlord told him that if I would come and have a meeting, he would open his large room for the purpose. I went and spoke there. The landlord would not sell any drink that night to anyone, telling those who asked for drink that it would be wrong for him to do so, as he was the cause of the meeting being held. A little while after I went to Bassingham, a village in Lincolnshire, at the request of a landlord who kept a public-house known as " The Sportsman's Inn," Worksop. He came three miles to see if I would go to Bassingham to hold a Temperance meeting. I consented to go, and a very good meeting there was. The Vicar, the Rev. Mr. Wayland, took the chair.

In 1858, on a visit to London, King was presented with a gold medal and chain, the medal bearing the following inscription on one side :—

> John King, born December 25th, 1795; signed the teetotal pledge, August 23rd, 1832.

And on the other :—

> Presented January 4th, 1858, in St. John's Hall, Clerkenwell, by teetotal friends in London, as a token of respect to John King, of Preston, who was the first man that signed the teetotal pledge in England.

One day he met a boy in the street smoking a pipe. As he walked alongside of him, he said, " Lad, if it is necessary that such a chit as thee should smoke, then it is time the fathers left off." From that hour John King gave up smoking.

In 1840 he was appointed to a situation upon the Preston and Wyre Railway, and afterwards became station-master at Ainsdale, near Preston, from which he was discharged in 1862 through failing eyesight. An operation, however, improved his eyes, and he was then appointed a gate-keeper on the railway.

The Rev. B. Whillock, an Alliance agent, and zealous Temperance worker in this country, 1840 to 1870, now living at Baltimore, Maryland, U.S.A., and John King became acquainted in 1845, and continued close friends until the death of the latter. When Mr. Whillock was departing to America in 1870, a valedictory tea and public meeting was held at

---

* The Rev. D. S. Wayland published a sermon on Temperance in 1838 (Temperance History, by Dawson Burns, D.D., Vol. 1, p. 146). This would be after King's visit. A tombstone in Bassingham Churchyard bears the following inscription :— " To the memory of Rev. Daniel Sheppard Wayland, M.A., Perpetual Curate of Thurlby, and for upwards of 33 years Curate of this Parish, who died April 8th, 1859, aged 76 years. ' My Redeemer Liveth.' " In the chancel of the church is a white marble memorial tablet to the memory of Mrs. Wayland.

Dawley, Shropshire, in the Primitive Methodist Chapel, the Rev. Lawrence Panting, M.A. presiding. The following copy of a notice issued in relation to that meeting will be of interest to our readers :—

In order to insure the presence of several gentlemen who could not attend on Easter Monday, including Mr. John King, the tea is put off until Monday, April 25th.

Mr. J. King was the first man in England who signed the teetotal pledge, in consideration of which, some years ago, he received from London a gold medal, and silver medals from Manchester, Ireland, and India.

As a railway station-master he has been the longest in office of anyone in the kingdom, and never had anyone hurt at his station. To THE HONOUR OF TEMPERANCE.

In 1873 a penny subscription was taken up by the Good Templars through their lodges. Of the proceeds, £225 were expended on purchasing an annuity of £40 for Mr. King, and the balance (£22), after meeting expenses, presented to him. He drew this annuity for over eleven years, and died on Thursday, January 29th, 1885, in his 90th year, and was buried in the General Cemetery at Southport, the funeral being attended by a large concourse of friends. A monument was raised over his grave, bearing the following epitaph, written by the Rev. Charles Garrett :—

Sacred to the memory of John King, who was born on Dec. 25th, 1795, and who died trusting in Christ on January 29th, 1885, in his 90th year. He signed the pledge of total abstinence from all intoxicating drinks August 23rd, 1832. He was the first of the seven men of Preston who signed the pledge, and thus commenced a movement which has greatly benefited the human family, and done much to extend the Kingdom of Christ. This stone is placed here by those who have admired and followed his example. " When the enemy shall come in like a flood, the Spirit of the Lord shall lift up a standard against it."

" John King possessed a benevolent face," says a writer who knew him, " as smooth as a sea-shore pebble which had been rolled over sand, rubble, and shingle for countless ages."

" His physiognomy is remarkable for excessive power and force of character : the forehead is broad and constructive ; the downward projection of the outer corners of the eyes denotes contest and the ambition to excel ; the width of the chin shows tenacity and fidelity."

1110   C. S.

I promise to abstain from the use of all Intoxicating Liquors

as a beverage.

HE MORALS & SCIENCE OF ABSTINENCE.

By SIR ALEXANDER RUSSELL SIMPSON, M.D., D.Sc., F.R.C.P.,

Professor of Midwifery and Diseases of Women and Children ;   Dean of the Faculty of Medicine, Edinburgh University.

ROM A PAPER READ AT THE SCOTTISH NATIONAL SABBATH SCHOOLS CONVENTION.

BOUT a quarter of a century ago, some friends in Kingston took me an excursion on the St. Lawrence river.   The Speaker of the Canadian Parliament, who was of the company, made me take notice, as we sailed out from the town, that the first imposing building we were passing was a distillery. Near by was an infirmary, then a lunatic asylum, then a prison, and after these a cemetery.

I take it for granted that every Sunday school teacher has so far considered the relation of the use of alcoholic liquors to disease, derangement, degradation, and death, as to have seen the advisability of becoming a personal abstainer. I take it for granted that the love for the young that brings them every Sunday to teach the Scriptures—the only school that makes wise to salvation—makes them alive to all the dangers that beset young lives and makes them anxious to safeguard them. Supreme among the dangers that beset all our lives is the danger inherent in the common use of alcohol. Whatever be the form in which it is taken—wine, beer, spirits, or what else—it is a more common cause of loss of health, of loss of reason, of loss of character, of loss of life, than any other of the influences that tell upon our complex mechanism.

The very expression they have learned to apply to one who is overcome of wine is suggestive. Noah " drank of the wine, and was drunken." The word is never used in connection with any other drink upon our tables. We drink water, milk, tea, coffee, or what else it may be. The liquid is drunk, not we. It is taken into our system to serve its purpose, and even when we have imbibed a superfluity, remains under our control. If we fall into a barrel of water we may be drowned ; but if we could swallow a barrel we would not be drunk. But wine ! " He drank of the wine, and he was drunk." It is as if this liquid that was under our control before we swallowed it, when once we have drunk it becomes our master, as if it had drunk us and had us at its mercy. It is an intoxicant, *i.e.*, it is a poisonous thing. An intoxicated man is simply a man that is in the clutch of a poison. As he sat down at table he would say he was going to have his wine ; ere he rises, he may not know it, but the wine has him.

Alcohol and the Body.

This leads me more immediately in the direction in which I suppose you expect me, as a member of the medical profession, to offer some suggestions as to what instruction it might be desirable to impart to your young charges if much of the result of all your labour is not to be blotted out of their lives in later years through ignorance of the influence of alcohol on the body and even more on the mind of the man.

To begin with, they should be taught that wine is not a necessity of life. It is no more necessary for man than for any of the creatures around him. There are tribes and communities who live and thrive without it. The want of it is never felt by one who has not begun to use it. No household that excludes it from its dietary suffers in anything from its absence. The child reared in abstinence has missed nothing that could have helped its growth and development, or, I will add, its happiness.

We deny it a place among the necessities of life. But there is no denying it a place among life's luxuries. We must be quite honest with ourselves and with the young, and recognise that those who habitually or occasionally drink wine do so because of some gratification it affords. But we can explain to them that it is a costly luxury. The temporary gratification it yields puts a tax upon the life. It is the most dangerous luxury in which a human being can indulge, because of the risk to life and health attendant upon its use, apart altogether from its contra-moral and anti-spiritual influences.

In a graduation address eighteen years ago, I took occasion to congratulate the young doctors who during their student curriculum had had the wisdom and the courage to be members of the Total Abstinence Society, and to say to all the graduates : " You will not be long in practice before you will prove these five things—

(1) That alcohol, habitually used, can of itself produce disease from which the abstainer remains exempt.
(2) That it will aggravate disease to which all are liable.
(3) That it renders those who habitually use it more open to attacks of various forms of illness.
(4) That the alcoholist has a worse chance of recovery from a fever or an injury than an abstainer.
(5) That in the crisis of disease the alcoholist gets less benefit from stimulants than the abstainer."

[At this point the learned doctor proceeded to give a scientific account of the evil effects of alcohol upon the human body, which is shortly to be published in its entirety, and those of our readers who are specially interested in the scientific aspects of the case will be able to peruse it at their leisure.]

ALCOHOL AND LONGEVITY.

It may occur to some one to ask—But what of the people who take their daily glass of wine and live on to old age ? Well, with the splendid equipment of blood and blood-vessels with which they were endowed by nature, how much longer might they not have lived on had the deteriorating element been kept out of their system ? Metchnikoff, who first described the phagocytic action of our amoeboid cells, may exaggerate when he claims the possibility of natural longevity extending to that of Abraham and the patriarchs if we lived under more scientific conditions. But they are likeliest to come near it who all their lifetime keep their blood and tissues clear of the effect of alcohol. That by the way.

It is sometimes claimed for wine as a virtue that it stimulates the appetite. Here again experiment and observation show that if it irritates the stomach to secrete more fluid, the secretion is of lowered digestive quality. Instead of helping, it hinders digestion. Its anæsthetic effect is to prevent the stomach from recognising what it can accomplish. It tempts the drinker to take in what his stomach cannot properly digest.

Again, we begin to understand something of what it means to be immune from the attacks of certain diseases. How, for example, a person who has once had scarlatina or small-pox is usually immune against a fresh attack in the midst of an epidemic. The attendant fevers and eruptions are due to toxines—poisons developed during the multiplication in the body of specific microbes. The healthy body meets these by the production of anti-toxines, which remain for a time to immunise it. Science has found out how to produce the anti-toxines of some of the dangerous germs, and has shown how by the use of them an individual can be rendered immune in the time of an epidemic, as of plague, or if he be already the subject of an attack, may have the toxines so modified that it becomes less fatal.   Many a life has been saved in this way by Pasteur's discovery of the anti-toxine of hydrophobia.   But alcoholic persons bitten by a mad dog do not get the same good from the anti-rabic injections that is gained by people whose blood is pure of the alcoholic poison.   A Belgian physiologist was led to demonstrate on rabbits this noxious influence of alcohol from having observed that an intemperate man, bitten by a mad dog, died notwithstanding anti-rabic treatment, while a boy of thirteen, much more severely bitten on the face by the same dog on the same day, recovered under treatment.

" MEDICAL COMFORTS."

The quantity of alcoholic preparations used in our infirmary which are now, let us note, under the charge of the apothecary, and classed as " medical comforts," is thus reduced from £703 to £99, while the number of patients has gone on increasing from 4,382 to 11,140, so that whereas when I entered on my service there I, along with my colleagues, treated each patient to something like a bottle of wine apiece during their stay in hospital, they are now treated with only as much as can be got for 2⅛d. In my own ward in my last year of service the apothecary tells me the proportion for each patient during ten months' stay in the hospital was about ⅜d.   NOTA BENE.—The results to the patients, all the while, kept getting better and better.

Let me add this little word of personal testimony.   You may, if you like, say to your scholars that a retired professor of medicine set out on a tour round the world ; felt starved in Bombay, frozen in the Himalayas, and roasted in Madras; celebrated his seventy-second birthday in Shanghai with some of his old pupils and other medical missionaries who are doing splendid work for the uplift of China—abstainers every one ; passed "Antipodes day " in a tempest on the Pacific, when a fellow-passenger was thrown down the saloon stairs of the great ocean liner, and was killed ; and, after eight months of travel by sea and land, in heat and cold, in storm and calm, came back to his home in as good health as when he left, never all the time having tasted alcohol of any kind, in any clime.

I promise to abstain from the use of all intoxicating Liquors as a beverage.

NEW YEAR'S TRACT.

"CHAM-PAGNE AT NIGHT."

By JAMES GUTHRIE, Esq., J.P., Brechin.

"A verse may find him who a sermon flies."—Herbert.

EOPLE do not like a minister to have two faces, but they don't object to his having three "heads." If he has more than three heads he may find a difficulty in getting ears for them in the congregation. I might add that not only do Scotch ministers have three heads and preach three-quarters of an hour, but under each head they have three particulars. To stick, then, to the rule of three, my subject is DRUNKENNESS, and the three heads are—1st, The Curse; 2nd, The Cause; 3rd, The Cure.

My first head being THE CURSE of drunkenness, my three particulars are as follows:—Drunkenness is a *habit*, a *sin*, and a *disease*. Notice, both a sin and a

353

disease, and the sin causes the disease. Where the habit ends and the sin begins, I shall not pretend to say. "I speak as unto wise men, judge ye." Also where the sin ends and the disease begins, I am unable to tell. This much I may premise: the Habit of drinking is under our own control; the Sin is a subject for the minister to deal with; and for the Disease, we call in the doctor. This Habit is not a riding-habit, but an over-riding habit—a habit that brings many a man and many a woman to their last shift. Our strength and standpoint is this: If we never learn the habit, we shall never suffer from the sin, nor be killed off by the disease.

People say that the Curse of strong drink lies in the abuse—they "like to see a man that can either take it or want it." (These are the people who are always either taking drink or warting it.) My answer is—What is the abuse, but a continuance of the use? The evil lies in the use, because if there were no use there could be no abuse; if there were no moderate drinkers there would be no inebriates; if there were no drinking, there never could be any drunkenness.

I do not enlarge on the fact that the annual expenditure on alcoholic drink is nearly £4 per head for each of the population, nor dwell on the 120,000 deaths in our country yearly caused by drinking. The mere figures show Curse enough: men spending their money for that which is not bread; slow suicides digging their own graves—graves over which no lover or friend will ever shed a tear. Think it over: out of every six moderate drinkers, one certainly shortens his days thro' Drink. In your own circle are there no friends or relatives dying before their time—lights going out in darkness—suns setting while it should be yet noon-day?

If it be the case that Drink does more to undo the blessings of the gospel than all the other causes of sin and immorality put together, then it becomes Christian men to "look not on the wine" but with horror and dread. It behoves us all no longer to gloss over, and cover up, and make a joke of, the iniquity of drunkenness: only "Fools make a mock at sin." If Drink is the cause of one-half the disease and insanity, one-half the poverty and crime, which our Doctors and Magistrates ascribe to it, there is a call upon every philanthropist to discountenance it by every means in his power. If drinking is what keeps men from joining the Church, and causes most of the fallings and failings within the Church, it looks like the duty of every Christian man to hate it with a perfect hatred, and to put away from him altogether the evil and abominable thing.

I speak for myself. "Let every man be fully persuaded in his own mind." To me, there is but one way of doing my duty in this matter, though I allow there are many ways of avoiding it. "To him that knoweth to do good and doeth it not, to him it is sin." Just as surely is it true, that to a man who knows alcohol to be to him an evil spirit, "to him it is sin" to touch, taste, or handle it. Drink is not only the very Devil's way into some men, but many men's way into very devils. Take it literally, "wine, wherein is excess," and you won't take it at all. Bad men excuse their faults, good men forsake them.

Instead, therefore, of being heart-broken for drunkenness, we want you to take a step further and be heart-broken from drink; and instead of the churches praying—at this New Year's time—that they may be kept from drunkenness, we ask them to be more practical and pray that they might be kept from drinking. The god of the New Year world is Bacchus: "Little children, keep yourselves from idols."

Scotland is the most religious country under the sun, and one of the most drunken. What is THE CAUSE? Therein we differ. "Many men, many minds." You say the cause of drunkenness is Custom. So it is. Drinking is an old custom—as old as Noah, or even as Ann Tiquity—in fact its age is the only thing it has to recommend it. At births, baptisms, and burials we have gone on drinking each others' healths, till we have nearly drunk away our own. But if a custom is bad in itself, the being as old as sin won't make it any better. They drink who never drank before, and they who drank before now drink the more. One man drinks because he is happy, he is fond of company, and likes a social glass; another drinks because he is miserable, he prefers to drink alone, and keeps his spirits up (he says) by taking spirits down. So universal is the custom, that a man is considered very abstemious who is able to say he only takes whisky on two occasions—the one is when he has salmon to dinner, the other, when he has not.

The Americans say we have no climate in this country, we have only "samples." But many people insist that the cause of so much drinking in Scotland is The Climate. Well, the climate may be bad enough, but I don't see how drinking to it will make it any better. Men drink because they're dry, or else they will be by-and-bye, or then some other reason why. Any reason is good enough—the Dry-rot, for instance. To me, what climate we have, appears *so* moist as never, no never—well, hardly ever—to be an excuse for anybody being dry. Some drink because they're hot, and some because they're cold, some because they're young, and some because they're old.

An Irishman remarked about Scotchmen in Ceylon:—They never were at home. but when they were abroad; and he said that when they came out to Ceylon they ate and they drank, and they drank and they drank, and then they died, and after that they had the audacity to write home and blame the climate! The truth is, every man can do without his glass, except perhaps the glazier. Alcoholic drink is not necessary—either under the burning sun of the tropics, or amid the appalling cold of an Arctic winter. It is not necessary, either for Bengal in India, or for Benjamin Gall at the North Pole.

Most people drink because they are thirsty. That is a very good reason; and every animal has the same reason for drinking. Let us stick to it. A donkey eats thistles because he is an ass; but he is sensible in his drinking. If a man would drink-like-a-beast he would only drink water, and never drink more than was good for him. A toper says he drinks to cure thirst. I say he does not. His kind of drink never cured thirst, it creates it. If any young man thinks his glass of beer cures his thirst, let me tell him it is not the beer that cures his thirst, but only the water that is in it. If a glass of grog seems to quench your thirst, it is not the whisky that does it, but simply the water with which it is mixed.

Alcoholic drink is a queer thing. A man takes it down, and it goes up; it slackens his tongue, and it loosens his legs. It weakens his understanding above and his under-standing below. I call it a regular foot-and-mouth disease. Drink creates a demand rather than supplies one. As the Paisley weaver put it:—"Yae gless is plenty, twa's ower mony, three's no half eneuch." This artificial craving for alcohol makes a man seem to be actually living on the very thing which is killing him. A man with this crave in him is on a dangerous descent, like the lubricated way down which a ship is launched into the deep— once a momentum has been acquired, the course can hardly be arrested. The craving is insatiable; and the curious thing about it is, that the more the diseased desire is gratified the less is it satisfied. Every publican knows that his hardest, heaviest drinkers are always his driest, drouthiest customers. The more beer a man drinks at night, the drier he is in the morning; the more ale at night, the more ailing in the morning; the more champagne at night, the more real-pain in the morning.

To prove the value of a thing, you must show the good that it doth bring. What is whisky good for? "Cleaning silver," I am told. I might add, "Yes, especially cleaning silver out of a working-man's pocket!" Though alcohol were sold by an angel it would still produce evil, and only evil continually. It is good for killing men while they are alive, and keeping them when they are dead. If it is useful, it is only for outward application, as when the good Samaritan poured-in the oil and the wine (into the wounds, not into the mouth); or when a coachman applies whisky to his horses' knees; or when Weston, the champion walker, hardens the soles of his feet with it. That is the only form in which Weston uses alcohol,—a very good footing for drink—the *sole* use; for if other men would only keep the whisky under their feet it would never trip them. Then, it would not be (as the nigger put it) "de sin dat does mos' easily upset us."

Why then do people drink? The reason is one, though the excuses are many.

Our friends take drink simply because they like it. And why do they like it? Because of the alcohol that is in it. And why do they like the alcohol? Because of its intoxicating quality. Take the intoxicating property out of a glass of bitter beer, and oh! how bitter it is; nobody wants to drink it now. If you take the head and the headiness from a bottle of champagne, nobody would pay 5s. a bottle for *The sham*. Whosoever is deceived thereby is not wise.

THE CURE is simple, sensible, and sure. The cure of sin is the gospel, and the cure of drunkenness is Total Abstinence. As the Quaker said to his son, "John, thou canst give up drinking, as easy as thee can open thy hand." "How?" said John. "Why, when thou raisest thy glass to thy lips, just open thy hand, and thou wilt never get drunk." As Herbert remarks, "It is most just to throw that on the ground which else would throw me there." I draw the line at DRINK. The Paisley weaver drew the line at the back of one glass—we draw the line in front of one drop.

"Wine is a mocker." The only way to be sure it will not make a fool of you is never to taste it—never to let that into your mouth which Shakespeare says will steal away your brains. If it is a small sacrifice to give up drink, do it—at this glad New Year—for the sake o others; if it is a great sacrifice to give up drink, do it for your own sake. My friend, it is better to sacrifice something, than be sacrificed yourself.

"Whatsoever a man soweth that shall he also reap." Think of the children. Beware lest your habits and indulgences are repeated in your families. If you sow the seeds, you shall reap the weeds. "Our acts our angels are, or good or ill, our fatal shadows that walk by us still." There is a worm that will turn: the worm of the corkscrew. Many a reformed man has lived to see his early vices looking back at him from out the faces of his sons.

"Thou shalt not" is the key-note of every Commandment. While moderation is allowed in things good and lawful, Total-abstinence is required in things evil and hurtful. If the thing is bad, there can be no proper moderation in it. The words "Let your moderation be known unto all men" never had any reference to drink; but we must put in the stop to prevent barrel Organs in the church playing longer on that text; for, let me tell you, no such verse has any place in the revised edition of the New Testament.

Drunkenness is incurable—absolutely incurable—so long as there is drinking. This is true, alike of the individual and of society. We must work towards Local Option in the community; so that, by reducing and removing Licenses, we may check the abounding Licentiousness. Meantime, we can individually exercise our local option. In this matter, every man can be a Law unto himself; and so, if we cannot shut the public-houses, we can each shut our own mouths. We can shut our mouths against Drink, and open them in favour of Total Abstinence. So shall we have a rainy season of temperance, and an early spring-time when many new leaves shall be turned over, and many new lives begun.

"Be wise to-day"—every moderate drinker could be a Total Abstainer if he would. "'Tis madness to defer"—every inebriate would be a Total Abstainer if he could. You, if you would. He, if he could. Remember this: Drink is no respecter of persons; there is hardly a family in the land without the drink brand upon it; and every man—from the highest to the lowest—who has been lost through strong drink, became a drunkard in trying to be a moderate drinker.

New Year is the time for pledging. There are pledges of love and pledges of liquor. Some take both. Many a man dies of love—of wine. For myself, I take nothing more strengthening than sleep. But all do not think lemonade sufficient aid. And, if you feel inclined to take anything—if you feel you must take something, my parting advice to you is take THE PLEDGE.

SUBSCRIPTIONS in aid of the Distribution of the MONTHLY PICTORIAL TRACTS will be gratefully received by the Distributors.

SCOTTISH TEMPERANCE LEAGUE, 108 HOPE STREET, GLASGOW.
Price 1s. 3d. per 100. Free by Post.